Fantastic Stories Present the

Galaxy Science Fiction Super Pack #1

Positronic Publishing
PO Box 632
Floyd VA 24091

ISBN 13: 9781515421085

First Positronic Publishing Edition
10 9 8 7 6 5 4 3 2 1

FANTASTIC STORIES PRESENT THE

GALAXY SCIENCE FICTION SUPER PACK #1

THE SUPER PACK EBOOK SERIES

If you enjoyed this Super Pack you may wish to find the other books in this series. We endeavor to provide you with a quality product. But since many of these stories have been scanned typos do occasionally keep in. If you spot one please share it with us at positronicpress@yahoo.com so that we can fix it. We occasionally add additional stories to some of our Super Packs so make sure that you download fresh copies of your Super Packs from time to time to get the latest edition.

Science Fiction Super Pack #1: ISBN 978-1-63384-240-3
Science Fiction Super Pack #2: ISBN 978-1-51540-477-4
Science Fiction Super Pack #3: (Forthcoming)
Fantasy Super Pack #1: ISBN 978-1-63384-282-3
Fantasy Super Pack #2: (Forthcoming)
Conan the Barbarian Super Pack: ISBN 978-1-63384-292-2
Lord Dunsany Super Pack: ISBN 978-1-63384-725-5
Philip K. Dick Super Pack: ISBN 978-1-63384-799-6
The Pirate Super Pack # 1: ISBN 978-1-51540-193-3
The Pirate Super Pack # 2: ISBN 978-1-51540-196-4
Harry Harrison Super Pack: ISBN 978-1-51540-217-6
Andre Norton Super Pack: ISBN 978-1-51540-262-6
Marion Zimmer Bradley Super Pack: ISBN 978-1-51540-287-9
Frederik Pohl Super Pack: ISBN 978-1-51540-289-3
King Arthur Super Pack: ISBN 978-1-51540-306-7
Alan E. Nourse Super Pack: ISBN 978-1-51540-393-7
Space Science Fiction Super Pack: ISBN 978-1-51540-440-8
Wonder Stories Super Pack: ISBN 978-1-51540-454-5

ACKNOWLEDGEMENTS

"Doorstep" by Keith Laumer originally appeared in *Galaxy Magazine*, February 1961.

"The Chasers" by Daniel F. Galouye originally appeared in *Galaxy Magazine*, February 1961.

"Blueblood" by Jim Harmon originally appeared in *Galaxy Magazine*, December 1960.

"Bad Memory" by Patrick Fahy originally appeared in *Galaxy Magazine*, December 1960.

"Beach Scene" by Marshall King originally appeared in *Galaxy Magazine*, October 1960.

"The Reluctant Heroes" by Frank M. Robinson originally appeared in *Galaxy Magazine*, January 1951.

"Kreativity for Kats" by Fritz Leiber originally appeared in *Galaxy Magazine*, April 1961.

"Perfect Answer" by L. J. Stecher, Jr. originally appeared in *Galaxy Magazine*, June 1958.

Dumbwaiter" by James Stamers originally appeared in *Galaxy Magazine*, February 1960.

"The Ignoble Savages" by Evelyn E. Smith originally appeared in *Galaxy Magazine*, March 1957.

"Angel's Egg" by Edgar Pangborn originally appeared in *Galaxy Magazine*, June 1951.

"Survival Type" by J.F. Bone originally appeared in *Galaxy Magazine*, March 1957.

"Misbegotten Missionary" by Isaac Asimov originally appeared in *Galaxy Magazine*, November 1950.

"The Business, as Usual" by Jack Sharkey originally appeared in *Galaxy Magazine*, August 1960.

"No Substitutions" by Jim Harmon originally appeared in *Galaxy Magazine*, November 1958.

"Prime Difference" by Alan E. Nourse originally appeared in *Galaxy Magazine*, June 1957.

"Delay in Transit" by F. L. Wallace originally appeared in *Galaxy Magazine*, September 1952.

"My Lady Greensleeves" by Frederik Pohl originally appeared in *Galaxy Magazine*, February 1957.

"A Little Journey" by Ray Bradbury originally appeared in *Galaxy Magazine*, August 1951.

"Med Ship Man" by Murray Leinster originally appeared in *Galaxy Magazine*, October 1963.

"Spoken for" by William Morrison originally appeared in *Galaxy Magazine*, July 1955.

"A Pail of Air" by Fritz Leiber originally appeared in *Galaxy Magazine*, December 1951.

"Contagion" by Katherine MacLEAN originally appeared in *Galaxy Magazine*, October 1950.

"Pen Pal" by Milton Lesser originally appeared in *Galaxy Magazine*, July 1951.

"Delayed Action" by Charles Vincent De Vet originally appeared in *Galaxy Magazine*, September 1953.

"... and it Comes out Here" by Lester del Rey originally appeared in *Galaxy Magazine*, February 1951.

The Old Die Rich by H. L. Gold originally appeared in *Galaxy Magazine*, March 1953.

TABLE OF CONTENTS

DOORSTEP

By Keith Laumer

The general was bucking for his other star—and this miserable contraption bucked right back!

*

Steadying his elbow on the kitchen table serving as desk, Brigadier General Straut leveled his binoculars and stared out through the second-floor window of the farmhouse at the bulky object lying canted at the edge of the wood lot. He watched the figures moving over and around the gray mass, then flipped the lever on the field telephone at his elbow.

"How are your boys doing, Major?"

"General, since that box this morning—"

"I know all about the box, Bill. So does Washington by now. What have you got that's new?"

"Sir, I haven't got anything to report yet. I have four crews on it, and she still looks impervious as hell."

"Still getting the sounds from inside?"

"Intermittently, General."

"I'm giving you one more hour, Major. I want that thing cracked."

The general dropped the phone back on its cradle and peeled the cellophane from a cigar absently. He had moved fast, he reflected, after the State Police notified him at nine forty-one last night. He had his men on the spot, the area evacuated of civilians, and a preliminary report on its way to Washington by midnight. At two thirty-six, they had discovered the four-inch cube lying on the ground fifteen feet from the huge object—missile, capsule, bomb—whatever it was. But now—several hours later—nothing new.

The field phone jangled. Straut grabbed it up.

"General, we've discovered a thin spot up on the top side. All we can tell so far is that the wall thickness falls off there...."

"All right. Keep after it, Bill."

This was more like it. If Brigadier General Straut could have this thing wrapped up by the time Washington awoke to the fact that it was something big—well, he'd been waiting a long time for that second star. This was his chance, and he would damn well make the most of it.

*

He looked across the field at the thing. It was half in and half out of the woods, flat-sided, round-ended, featureless. Maybe he should go over and give it a closer look personally. He might spot something the others were missing. It might blow them all to kingdom come any second; but what the hell, he had earned his star on sheer guts in Normandy. He still had 'em.

He keyed the phone. "I'm coming down, Bill," he told the Major. On impulse, he strapped a pistol belt on. Not much use against a house-sized bomb, but the heft of it felt good.

The thing looked bigger than ever as the jeep approached it, bumping across the muck of the freshly plowed field. From here he could see a faint line running around, just below the juncture of side and top. Major Greer hadn't mentioned that. The line was quite obvious; in fact, it was more of a crack.

With a sound like a baseball smacking the catcher's glove, the crack opened, the upper half tilted, men sliding—then impossibly it stood open, vibrating, like the roof of a house suddenly lifted. The driver gunned the jeep. There were cries, and a ragged shrilling that set Straut's teeth on edge. The men were running back now, two of them dragging a third.

Major Greer emerged from behind the object, looked about, ran toward General Straut shouting. "... a man dead. It snapped; we weren't expecting it...."

Straut jumped out beside the men, who had stopped now and were looking back. The underside of the gaping lid was an iridescent black. The shrill noise sounded thinly across the field. Greer arrived, panting.

"What happened?" Straut snapped.

"I was ... checking over that thin spot, General. The first thing I knew it was ... coming up under me. I fell; Tate was at the other side. He held on and it snapped him loose, against a tree. His skull—"

"What the devil's that racket?"

"That's the sound we were getting from inside before, General. There's something in there, alive—"

"All right, pull yourself together, Major. We're not unprepared. Bring your half-tracks into position. The tanks will be here soon."

Straut glanced at the men standing about. He would show them what leadership meant.

"You men keep back," he said. He puffed his cigar calmly as he walked toward the looming object. The noise stopped suddenly; that was a relief. There was a faint and curious odor in the air, something like chlorine ... or seaweed ... or iodine.

There were no marks in the ground surrounding the thing. It had apparently dropped straight in to its present position. It was heavy, too—the soft soil was displaced in a mound a foot high all along the side.

Behind him, Straut heard a yell. He whirled. The men were pointing; the jeep started up, churned toward him, wheels spinning. He looked up. Over the edge of the gray wall, six feet above his head, a great reddish limb, like the claw of a crab, moved, groping.

Straut yanked the .45 from its holster, jacked the action and fired. Soft matter spattered, and the claw jerked back. The screeching started up again angrily, then was drowned in the engine roar as the jeep slid to a stop.

Straut stooped, grabbed up a leaf to which a quivering lump adhered, jumped into the vehicle as it leaped forward; then a shock and they were going into a spin and....

*

"Lucky it was soft ground," somebody said. And somebody else asked, "What about the driver?"

Silence. Straut opened his eyes. "What ... about...."

A stranger was looking down at him, an ordinary-looking fellow of about thirty-five.

"Easy, now, General Straut. You've had a bad spill. Everything is all right. I'm Professor Lieberman, from the University."

"The driver," Straut said with an effort.

"He was killed when the jeep went over."

"Went ... over?"

"The creature lashed out with a member resembling a scorpion's stinger. It struck the jeep and flipped it. You were thrown clear. The driver jumped and the jeep rolled on him."

Straut pushed himself up.

"Where's Greer?"

"I'm right here, sir." Major Greer stepped up, stood attentively.

"Those tanks here yet?"

"No, sir. I had a call from General Margrave; there's some sort of holdup. Something about not destroying scientific material. I did get the mortars over from the base."

Straut got to his feet. The stranger took his arm. "You ought to lie down, General—"

"Who the hell is going to make me? Greer, get those mortars in place, spaced between your tracks."

The telephone rang. Straut seized it. "General Straut."

"General Margrave here, Straut. I'm glad you're back on your feet. There'll be some scientists from the State University coming over. Cooperate with them. You're going to have to hold things together at least until I can get another man in there to—"

"Another man? General Margrave, I'm not incapacitated. The situation is under complete control—"

"It is, is it? I understand you've got still another casualty. What's happened to your defensive capabilities?"

"That was an accident, sir. The jeep—"

"We'll review that matter at a later date. What I'm calling about is more important right now. The code men have made some headway on that box of yours. It's putting out a sort of transmission."

"What kind, sir?"

"Half the message—it's only twenty seconds long, repeated—is in English. It's a fragment of a recording from a daytime radio program; one of the network men here identified it. The rest is gibberish. They're still working over it."

"What—"

"Bryant tells me he thinks there may be some sort of correspondence between the two parts of the message. I wouldn't know, myself. In my opinion, it's a threat of some sort."

"I agree, General. An ultimatum."

"Right. Keep your men back at a safe distance from now on. I want no more casualties."

*

Straut cursed his luck as he hung up the phone. Margrave was ready to relieve him, after he had exercised every precaution. He had to do something fast, before this opportunity for promotion slipped out of his hands.

He looked at Major Greer. "I'm neutralizing this thing once and for all. There'll be no more men killed."

Lieberman stood up. "General! I must protest any attack against this—"

Straut whirled. "I'm handling this, Professor. I don't know who let you in here or why—but I'll make the decisions. I'm stopping this man-killer before it comes out of its nest, maybe gets into that village beyond the woods. There are four thousand civilians there. It's my job to protect them." He jerked his head at Greer, strode out of the room.

Lieberman followed, pleading. "The creature has shown no signs of aggressiveness, General Straut—"

"With two men dead?"

"You should have kept them back—"

"Oh, it was my fault, was it?" Straut stared at Lieberman with cold fury. This civilian pushed his way in here, then had the infernal gall to accuse him, Brigadier General Straut, of causing the death of his own men. If he had the fellow in uniform for five minutes....

"You're not well, General. That fall—"

"Keep out of my way, Professor," Straut said. He turned and went on down the stairs. The present foul-up could ruin his career; and now this egghead interference....

With Greer at his side, Straut moved out to the edge of the field.

"All right, Major. Open up with your .50 calibers."

Greer called a command and a staccato rattle started up. The smell of cordite and the blue haze of gunsmoke—this was more like it. He was in command here.

Lieberman came up to Straut. "General, I appeal to you in the name of science. Hold off a little longer; at least until we learn what the message is about."

"Get back from the firing line, Professor." Straut turned his back on the civilian, raised the glasses to observe the effect of the recoilless rifle. There was a tremendous smack of displaced air, and a thunderous boom as the explosive shell struck. Straut saw the gray shape jump, the raised lid waver. Dust rose from about it. There was no other effect.

"Keep firing, Greer," Straut snapped, almost with a feeling of triumph. The thing was impervious to artillery; now who was going to say it was no threat?

"How about the mortars, sir?" Greer said. "We can drop a few rounds right inside it."

"All right, try that before the lid drops."

And what we'll try next, I don't know, he thought.

*

The mortar fired with a muffled thud. Straut watched tensely. Five seconds later, the object erupted in a gout of pale pink debris. The lid rocked, pinkish fluid running down its opalescent surface. A second burst, and a third. A great fragment of the menacing claw hung from the branch of a tree a hundred feet from the ship.

Straut grabbed up the phone. "Cease fire!"

Lieberman stared in horror at the carnage.

The telephone rang. Straut picked it up.

"General Straut," he said. His voice was firm. He had put an end to the threat.

"Straut, we've broken the message," General Margrave said excitedly. "It's the damnedest thing I ever...."

Straut wanted to interrupt, announce his victory, but Margrave was droning on.

"... strange sort of reasoning, but there was a certain analogy. In any event, I'm assured the translation is accurate. Here's how it reads in English...."

Straut listened. Then he carefully placed the receiver back on the hook.

Lieberman stared at him.

"What did it say?"

Straut cleared his throat. He turned and looked at Lieberman for a long moment before answering.

"It said, 'Please take good care of my little girl.'"

THE CHASERS

By Daniel F. Galouye

Civilizations must make sense somehow. But was this one the gaudy, impossible exception?

*

As the dust drifted clear of the ship's landing skids, at least two things became obvious:

One—although they had missed the city (if that's what it was) by miles, they had nevertheless managed to slam down near one of the numerous rural estates.

Two—the landscape would be crawling with Zaortian Fuzzy Tails for a long while to come. They were still pouring out of hatches sprung open by the crunching impact.

Kent Cassidy untangled himself from the control column and plucked one of the Fuzzy Tails from his neck. The creature scampered around until it found the ruptured hatch, then scurried through to join the squealing zoological exodus.

"There goes ten thousand credits' worth of cargo," groaned Gene Mason. His stout form was slumped in dejection before the view port.

Cassidy sniffed the refreshing air that was drifting into the ship. "Any idea where we are?"

"After the directional stabilizer blew, we made three blind jumps, all in the direction of Galactic Center. We could be *anywhere* between Zaort Seven and the Far Rim."

"Hey, look," said Cassidy.

From the hatchway, the sumptuous estate sprawled nearby, its many gabled manor closed off behind a high wire fence. Cassidy squinted, but failed to recognize the bold, flowing architectural style.

A small, bent figure clung to the wire netting of the fence. He was shouting at the ship, but his excited words were no match for the decompression hisses of the auxiliary drive.

"Humanoid?" Mason suggested.

"Human, I'd say." Cassidy gestured toward the gear locker. "Better break out the translator."

In baggy trousers and sagging blouse, the man raced back and forth behind the fence—the picture of frustrated anger. However, large, doleful eyes, complemented by a bald head and huge, pendulous ear lobes, belied his furious actions.

Presently the squeals of the Fuzzy Tails trailed off in the distance and the auxiliary drive quieted with a final sigh. And now the native's shouts rang out distinct and loud:

"Quick! From here get you! Shoo! Scram! Or out there I'll come and apart tear you!"

"It's English!" Mason exclaimed.

"Of a sort. Archaic, but understandable. And not at all friendly."

Mason scratched his blunt chin. "Guess we're not too far off the beaten star paths, eh?"

Cassidy could find no grounds for challenging this observation as they started down the ladder—not until he looked overhead and saw three suns shining in the same sky. As far as he knew, there were no settled trinary systems.

Beyond the fence the native, a wisp of a man was still fuming. "The hell away from here get! You I'm warning—no closer come!"

Mason displayed a half frown. "He's sure a sour cuss."

"You stay with the ship," said Cassidy. "I'll see what's fouling his tubes."

*

Before Cassidy reached the fence, his pet Fuzzy Tail came scampering from behind a bush. It clambered up his trousers and wrapped itself around his neck. This encouraged the speculation that perhaps the shipment of Tails could be bartered for repairs to the stabilizer—*if* there was a local space technology, and *if* they could corral the animals.

The native grew even more frenzied now as Cassidy drew up before him.

"Trespasser! Back get! My property this be! Scram! You I'll kill!"

The Fuzzy Tail uncoiled itself from around Cassidy's neck. Perching on his shoulder, it fussed back at the native in chirping, excited tones. It not only acted at times as though it owned Cassidy, but it also exercised a personal responsibility for his welfare.

"Quiet!" Cassidy snapped out.

It caught both the Fuzzy Tail and the old man by surprise. The animal bounded for cover while the native rocked back on his heels.

"Be you not just a—*little bit* afraid?" His eyebrows mounted the wrinkled expanse of his forehead.

The nearby hedge rustled and parted to let through a dark-haired girl whose tanned skin suggested accustomed exposure to the multiple sunlight. Wearing a belted tunic that lacked inches of reaching her knees, she confronted the old man calmly.

"It's all about what, Papa?" she asked, with a trace of an amused smile.

"Trespassers! On *our* property, Riva! The alarm sound! Scat! To the woods take! Or a dead duck you be!"

"Now, Papa," she chided. Then, through the fence, "Him you musn't mind. It's only his duty he's attending to."

From the distance, Cassidy had suspected the man was of Terran descent. Now, with Riva in the picture, he was certain this world was stocked either by intent or accident with true humans.

"We're from Terra," he said.

She frowned. "Ter-ra?"

"Earth. The original world—"

Incomprehension flooded her even features. But her confusion was only temporary. "Let's play."

It seemed like an altogether acceptable suggestion, Cassidy thought, eying the attractive girl. But he went on, "This is our ship and—"

"Ship?" Then she chased away her puzzlement with a sudden smile. "Some nice games I know."

There was no space technology on this planet, Cassidy decided. They'd be strictly on their own as far as repairing the directional stabilizer was concerned.

By this time Papa, his eyes focused afar, had exploded again. "Charge!" he roared. "After him! Wa-hoo! Away don't let him get!" He was gripping the fence and straining toward the field.

Cassidy turned and saw, in the distance, a skimmer vehicle floating along several feet off the ground. In full pursuit was a shouting youth who paused occasionally to seize a rock and hurl it at the craft.

The old man turned toward his daughter. "A good chase that be. Bet he wins."

"Not a chance." The girl frowned. "That be Nedal. Not so swift is he. Loses interest too quick, he does."

She surveyed Cassidy. "Be you a chaser?"

"No, but I could do with a couple of stiff shots."

This drew Papa's attention back to the matter at hand. "Trespassers! The road hit! Scat! Some dust kick up!"

"Quiet!" Cassidy shouted. "Will you listen a minute? I—"

Two loyal Fuzzy Tails came charging up to the fence and added their raucous chatter to Papa's screeching diatribe, which had continued unchecked despite Cassidy's loud, desperate plea.

In the next instant, though, it seemed that a dam had burst overhead. Materializing from nowhere, at least a ton of water poured down on the agile-tongued native, the two Fuzzy Tails, Riva and Cassidy himself, bringing an abrupt end to all the commotion.

The animals streaked for the safety of the bushes while Papa and the girl dived back through the hedge. Bedraggled, Cassidy headed for the ship, wondering what sort of meteorological quirk he had encountered.

*

"No, sir," he said some time later as he attacked the directional selector with pliers and a screwdriver, "I don't like the setup. I don't like it worth a damn."

Mason traced the power lead to the junction box beside the hatch. "Maybe they aren't *all* like that."

"In this sort of place, chances are that the first people you run into are typical. I'm afraid—"

"Say!" Mason interrupted, staring outside. "Look at this!"

Cassidy went over to the hatch and watched a dozen or so men sprinting across the field, their voices rising in excited waves. A lithe young woman was in full flight before them. But she was screaming in delight as she turned now and then to beckon them on. One overtook her and brought her down with a waist tackle. She rebounded to her feet, however, and took off again.

Two of the pursuers collided and sprawled on the ground. They sprang up and tore into each other. Unconcerned with the personal dispute, the chase struck off in a new direction, heading toward the ship as it paralleled one of the nearby fenced-in estates.

Behind the wire mesh, a burly young man came charging down the main steps of the manor and raced along with the others.

"That be the way!" he yelled encouragement. "Her go get! It's gaining you are! Hurry!"

He drew up in time to avoid crashing into the side fence, then stood there watching the chase recede in the distance.

Within a hundred feet of the ship, one of the men fell out of the group, panting. He squinted at the vessel, then crept forward, circling to the right. Within arm's reach, he walked back and forth alongside the hull, giving it a close inspection. Finally he paused and fumbled with his clothes.

Cassidy started. "Look what he's doing!"

"Against the side of the ship, too!" said Mason.

Hearing them, the native jerked his head up toward the hatch, then backed off for a better view.

"Stinkers!" he yelled, shaking his fist. "Out here come and fight! Take you both on I can!"

When they only gaped, he whirled and sped off to rejoin the chase.

"You see?" said Cassidy. "Now what do you think?"

"I think we'd better get that directional stabilizer working."

*

It took more than an hour to locate the trouble. "The rectifier circuit's shot," Cassidy said finally. "But maybe we can patch it up. Some of the amplifiers I suppose we can do without. But a hyper-oscillator we've got to have."

"Say, you're doing it too," said Mason.

"What?"

"Talking like the natives."

Cassidy looked up. "Guess it's something that grows on you. Well, what do we do now?"

"Maybe the natives can help us."

"If they don't even know where they're from, they probably left their volts and amps behind too. But that's only an assumption."

"In that case," Mason said with a sigh, "there's only one thing left to do—take Riva up on her invitation to, ah, play."

"Funny," Cassidy grunted, heading for the hatch.

"I was only joking."

"I'm not. If we can get in that house, we'll know for sure whether or not they've developed electronic devices."

Halfway across the field, they were almost run down by the laughing girl and her retinue of galloping suitors, if that's what they were. She was a well-proportioned blonde whose wind-frothed tresses suggested a nymph in flight.

At the fence, they were confronted by Riva, who smiled up at Cassidy and said, "You I was just going to come and get. Ready to play yet you are?"

He looked away and cleared his throat. "Not quite, Riva. We'd like to visit your house."

"It's some interesting games I know. Enjoying them you'd surely be." Her smile, revealing even teeth that contrasted ruddy cheeks, was as persistent as her intent on playing.

Staring at the girl, Cassidy wrestled with a pang of wistful envy over the Olympian life he had witnessed thus far on this world. Maybe they were all irresponsible and childlike. But was that bad?

*

Mason pointed in alarm toward the meadow in front of the next estate. An ominous-looking, furry thing, supported on six or eight spindly legs, was racing across their field of vision.

"Hurt you he won't," the girl assured them, noticing their apprehension. "Nothing to be afraid of there is."

"*What* is it?" Cassidy was still trying to determine whether it was an overgrown spider or a dry-land octopus.

"Look!" Mason exclaimed. "It's on a leash!"

And Cassidy noticed the thong that extended from the creature to the human who was running along behind it.

"To Wolruf he belongs," the girl explained. "One of them I can get for you too—if you want."

Her slender hand reached out through the fence and tugged at Cassidy's sleeve. "To chase me wouldn't you like?" she asked, pouting.

Glancing behind her, Cassidy spotted the girl's father bearing down on them in a sprint that was nothing short of phenomenal for his age. He began shouting with the last few strides and was in full lung when he hurled himself at the fence. "Git! Out! Away! I'll—"

Riva moved back and glanced overhead and Papa, seeing some hidden significance in her gesture, lowered his voice.

"You I'll tear into and apart I'll rip!" he went on in a menacing whisper. "Your limbs I'll scatter like—"

"Papa, it's not afraid of you they are."

"They're *not?*" He was disappointed.

"The house they want to come in and see."

He began working up a rage again, but caught himself and looked up into his daughter's face. "Mean you—*my* house they want to see?"

When she nodded Papa seized the lowest strand of wire and lifted the fence high enough for Cassidy and Mason to crawl under. "Why, arranged it can be, I think."

Its architectural prominences rendered shadowless in the tri-solar light, the manor was even more imposing close at hand. Of stone construction, it flaunted millwork and beams whose rich carvings would have been welcome on any mansion in the known Galaxy.

Mounting the steps, Mason observed, "Nice little layout they've got here."

Riva moved closer to Cassidy. "Inside is cozy," she said behind a coy smile. "Play we can *really* in there."

Papa had been at the door for some time, fumbling with the lock. In a burst of impatience, he drew off and gave it a solid kick. Then he went back and tried rattling the handle. After a while there was a click and it swung open.

Cassidy followed him into a blaze of iridescent color and unfamiliar form. The huge, circular room was like a vast diorama and it was impossible to tell exactly where the solid objects blended in with the jumbled geometric pattern of the wall.

He walked across a carpet of undulant fibers that reached well above his ankles. And he tripped across a padded, Z-shaped slab that protruded from the wall but slithered into a U and retracted as soon as it received the burden of his weight.

Laughing, Riva helped him up and he paused for a closer visual inspection of his outlandish surroundings. Objects of weird shapes and unguessable purposes hung from the ceiling, some changing form and size as he watched. Scattered about were articles of furniture (he guessed) that resembled giant starfish supported at their centers and extremities by coiled springs. Only, each arm was shaped like a trough that ran into the bowl-like central depression of the piece.

*

A gleeful scream sounded behind them and Papa went tearing by. With a running leap, he landed on an arm of one of the starfish. Its supporting spring contracted under the weight, then catapulted him ceilingward. When he came down again, it was on an arm of another starfish, then another.

The fourth collapsed, depositing him on the floor, and its spring went twanging across the room. Struggling to his feet, he staggered into something resembling a clothes tree, knocked it over and sprawled beside it.

He roared with delight as he snapped the stem of the thing across his knee and hurled the pieces at the ceiling. They scored direct hits on one of the bulky objects suspended overhead and it came crashing down with a twinkling roar amid a shower of sparks.

"Yow-ee!" he exuberated. "So much fun I never had!"

Riva helped him up. "Papa, it's control yourself you must. The last time—remember?"

But he only shook her off and went bounding through an archway. His hectic progress through the house was punctuated by sounds of crashing destruction.

"Honestly," Riva said, spreading her hands, "what to do with him I don't know."

Cassidy continued staring in the direction the old man had gone. "He's wrecking the place!"

"That he is," she admitted sighing. "And such a nice joint it be, too."

"He's just plain nuts!" said Mason.

Riva smiled. "But it's *so* much fun he has."

Cassidy moved away to get a better view of a silvery gray screen set in the wall and flanked by twin rows of dials and knobs.

"You got stereovision, Riva?" he asked.

Mason went over and twisted several of the controls until a soft light began suffusing the screen.

"Ster-eo-what?" the girl asked.

"Video, television—pictures with sound."

Her face brightened. "Pictures we got—sounds too. Right in that little window."

Just then Papa, uninhibited as ever, came storming back into the room with a lusty "Ya-hoo!" He lost his footing and crashed against the screen. Sparks shot out and the picture that was beginning to take shape faded into obscurity.

"It that settles, Papa!" Riva said, exasperated. "Outside I'm going and for what happens to you I'm not responsible!"

At the door, she paused and smiled at Cassidy. "It'll have to be out there that we play, but no less fun will we have. Put on my best cavorting clothes I'm going to."

Mason turned the knobs again, but produced nothing more than the smell of burning insulation and a few snickers from Papa.

"At least," Cassidy observed, "they evidently do know something about electronics. All we have to do now is run down one of the technicians and we might get the parts we need for the stabilizer."

*

Outside Mason dropped down on the steps and sat with his shoulders slumping. "Damnedest thing I've ever seen," he mumbled.

Cassidy paced to the edge of the porch and stared out over the field. A monstrous skimmer craft appeared in the distance, floating over toward what seemed to be a pile of trash in front of one of the estates. Twin beams of crimson light darted from the nose of the vehicle and played over the mound. In seconds, the heap had melted away and the skimmer floated on.

Wolruf was still walking his octopus-spider pet. There were now two packs of youths out chasing girls. And another skimmer car was having no difficulty surviving the stone-throwing assault of not one, but two dedicated pursuers. Outside of that, Cassidy noted, things appeared quite normal.

Mason slapped his thighs and rose. "You go see if Riva knows how we can contact the authorities. I'm going back and stay with the ship."

Cassidy watched him crawl under the fence, then went around the side of the house. When he caught sight of the girl, she was just disappearing into a smaller structure that might have been a guest house or garage.

Following, he knocked on the door and called out her name anxiously.

"To play are you ready?" There was an eager note in her voice as it came through the panel. "In come on. It's all set I'll be in a jiffy."

He turned the knob, stepped half into the room, lurched back outside and slammed the door behind him. "*Riva!*"

The door started to open, then closed again as the girl laughed. "Oh, all right. Funny you be. It's to play you want, don't you?"

He assured her that he did and added, "But there's something we have to talk about now, Riva."

"Talk, talk, talk. And it gets you where? Only wastes time, it does."

A moment later the door opened and she stood there smiling, with legs apart and hands on her hips. But he hardly had time to react to the skimpiness of her halter and skirt.

"Now," she urged as she sprang up on her toes and kissed him full on the lips, "like a chaser make! To the races we're off!"

With that, she whirled and went streaking through the next room.

*

He surveyed his surroundings. It was an ordinary bedroom with conventional furnishings—perhaps a bit crude even for a culture without any space technology. But, then, it didn't seem uncharacteristic, considering the circumstances.

Recognizing the contrast between this guest house and the manor, he frowned as he started off in search of the girl. A worrisome suspicion dogged his thoughts—there had to be sense to Riva and her father and this sumptuous estate, natives who made sport of chasing skimmer craft and voluptuous women when they weren't otherwise indiscreetly occupied. But what?

In the kitchen, he discovered Riva's shapely leg protruding from behind a cabinet. He suspected the exposure was not as accidental as she wanted him to believe. He was certain of that when, as he seized her ankle, she crawled out laughing.

Now she stood before him, unsmiling and impatient, and her slender arms reached out for his shoulders.

"Riva, this is serious!" He forced her hands down again. "I'm in trouble. I need help."

"It's to help you I've been trying all along."

"I've got to get in touch with the authorities—your government."

She looked blank.

He simplified it, "Your leaders."

"Oh, it's easy that is. There be Aline and Clio and Leah and—but that Leah! It's the cake she takes! Thirty chasers she led on the best drag-out of all. Two whole days it lasted!"

"No, Riva! Not *that* kind of leader. I mean—well, someone who gets things done. The kind who gets behind things and—"

"That be Leanc. Behind those floating cars he's getting all the time. And how he can throw so many rocks I'll never know!"

He mussed his hair in frustration, then composed himself. "How do I get to the city?"

"That crowded place with all the big houses?" When he nodded, she went on, "It's never been there I have.*Now* we play?"

He drew in a hopeless breath. "All right. Now we play. You go hide."

She radiated a warm eagerness as she initiated the game all over again with a kiss and then went sprinting toward the front of the house. He watched her disappear through the next room, then went out the nearest door, heading for the fence and his ship beyond. It had required no small degree of restraint not to go racing off after her.

At the corner of the manor he was bowled over by a shouting Papa who was in full flight as he shot out around a hedge, heading for the guest house.

"All your fault it is!" he cried, recovering his balance and plunging on. "You it be who caused this! that I'll remember!"

Cassidy sat up, arms resting on his updrawn knees, and stared after the old man.

"Ow! Riva! Ouch!" Papa clutched his rear as he neared the cottage. "Help! Oh, my aching back!"

*

Cassidy found Mason frozen in the shadow of the ship, fascinated by another girl chase that was in progress nearby.

The swirl of action swerved toward him and Mason tensed, shifting from one foot to the other. With the wind pressing her clothes in revealing tightness about her, the flaxen-haired sprite swept past and he lunged for her.

"Mason!" Cassidy shouted.

"Seemed like a good idea," Mason explained, checking himself. "Wonder what it takes to get in on that chase."

Cassidy forced a fetching thought of Riva out of his mind. "What we ought to be wondering is how soon we can blast off."

"But if we get spaceborne before the stabilizer's working, we'll only be floundering around again."

Cassidy started for the ladder. "There's one thing we *can* do—patch up the hatches and jump over to another spot on this planet. Maybe we'll find somebody who's normal, at least."

But Mason caught his arm and pointed toward Riva's estate where a skimmer car was now parked on the side of the manor opposite the guest house.

"Anybody who can drive one of those things," he suggested, "must know something about the city and how to get there. Maybe he'll even give us a lift."

*

Mason circled the skimmer craft. "It's a fine piece of workmanship," he said in admiration.

"I'll say," Cassidy agreed. "If we can find out where that was made, I'm sure we'll—"

His vision was suddenly cut off by a pair of hands that came around his head from behind and clamped themselves over his eyes. If he had any doubt as to the identity of their owner, it was soon cleared up by a soft voice next to his ear:

"Not right this is. It's chasing *me* you're supposed to be."

"Riva," he said, facing her, "we'd like to meet the person who came here in that skimmer."

"Excuses, excuses," she complained. "Always something more important than a chase it is."

"Take us to the driver of that thing," Mason prompted. "We—"

But he tensed and stared up in alarm toward the field. Cassidy followed his gaze to the skimmer vehicle that had earlier reduced a pile of trash to nothing. The craft was just now floating up to their ship.

Its two beams of sizzling red light swept over the hull from stem to stern, again and again—until there was nothing left of their ship but incandescent molten metal.

Mason displayed a sickened, then resigned expression, thrust his hands in his pockets and shuffled off toward the field.

"Getting in on one of those chases I think I'll be," he said.

But he paused outside the fence, turned to say something, then lurched back. "Cassidy! Watch out! There's one of those things!"

The spider-octopus came into view from around the rear of the manor and crawled leisurely toward the guest house. Its body, covered with a multitude of eyes and an unkempt mat of fuzz, was like a coal-black knob perched atop hairy stilts.

Evidently, Cassidy guessed as he dived behind a hedge and pulled the girl with him, the thing had gotten away from its master, for it was trailing its leash in the dust.

"It's hurt you he won't," Riva assured, quite puzzled over his apprehension. "He belongs to—"

But Cassidy clamped a hand over her mouth.

The thing reached the guest house and made a queer noise in front of the door.

Papa came outside on the double.

The spider-octopus picked up the other end of the thong and clamped its braceletlike device around the old man's wrist.

Grinning, Papa pulled toward the gate, straining at the leash.

Eventually, Cassidy was aware of Riva's smiling, inquisitive face in front of his.

"Play?" she invited.

And, glancing back at the charred remains of his ship, he didn't see why not.

BLUEBLOOD

By Jim Harmon

There were two varieties of aliens—blue and bluer—but not as blue as the Earthmen!

*

Even if I'm only a space pilot, I'm not dumb. I mean I'm not *that* dumb. I admit that Dr. Ellik and Dr. Chon outrank me, because that's the way it's got to be. A pilot is only an expendable part. But I had been the first one to see the natives on this planet, and I was the first one to point out that they came in two attractive shades of blue, light blue and dark blue.

Four Indigos were carrying an Azure. I called the others over to the screen.

"A sedan chair," identified Lee Chon. "Think the light-skinned one is a kind of a priest?"

Mike Ellik shook his head. "I doubt it. The chair isn't ornate enough. I think that's probably the standard method of travel—at least for a certain social elite."

"Do you notice anything unusual about those bully boys?"

"You tell me what you see," Ellik evaded.

"Three of them are mongoloid idiots," said Chon.

"I thought so," Ellik said, "but I wasn't quite sure—aliens and all."

"They're humanoids," Chon said, "and humanoids are my specialty. I know."

"The fourth one doesn't look much better."

"His features are slack and his jaw is loose, all right, but they aren't *made* that way. It's an expression he could change. His head isn't shaped like that."

"Um. The man in the chair is a striking specimen. No cerebral damage in him."

"I don't think the answer is brain damage. If the 'noble' trusts those four to carry him, their actions and reflexes must be pretty well coordinated. They can't have anything like palsy or epilepsy."

"They must breed a special type of slave for the job," Ellik suggested.

"They aren't slaves, Mike," I told him.

"No?" Ellik said, like talking to a kid. "And what are they, Mike?"

*

I breathed out hard, a little disgusted that big brains like Ellik and Chon couldn't see the translucent truth. "They are just four dumb slobs who can't get a better job, so they are hauling His Highness around because they have to make a living the hard way."

"That doesn't quite cover it, Johnny," Chon said. "The carriers are a completely different race."

"What's different about them?" I asked. "They've got hands to work with, eyes to see with, noses to smell with. If you kick one of them, I bet he'll hurt. It's just their bad luck to be dumb slobs."

Ellik grunted. "Unfortunately, Johnny, there are subtler differences. The darker aliens, the indigo-colored ones, seem to be definitely down further on the scale of local evolution. They must be an inferior race to the lighter, azure species."

Chon had been looking at us and listening to everything. Finally he said, "You can't be sure of that, Mike. You haven't seen all of the Indigos. Some of them may not be as far down as the common carriers."

Ellik sighed. "Explorers have to make snap decisions on insufficient data. We don't have time to see the whole damned planet before we write up a report."

"Yes, explorers have to make snap decisions," Chon repeated to himself. "Are you going to take a look at those buildings, see if it's a village?"

"I thought I'd see if our blueblood friend out there wants to show it to me," said Mike Ellik.

"He won't," I said.

They both looked at me.

"You don't have any chair and nobody to carry you," I went on. "He'll think you're just a slob."

"Jonathan," Ellik said, "you show occasional flashes of genius."

I smiled and shrugged it off. "I know I'm not nearly as smart as you boys. But that doesn't mean I can't think *at all.*"

Ellik clapped me on the shoulder. "Of course it doesn't."

But his grip was too strong.

"Johnny," Ellik said gravely, "do you think *you* could carry me?"

"Wait a minute. You want me to act like one of those slobs? That's asking a lot."

"But could you?"

"Not all the way to those buildings. What was the gravity reading, Lee?"

*

Chon closed his eyes a second. "Point nine seven three."

"There!" I said. "I couldn't tote you three or four miles piggy-back."

"Look," Chon said, "we can strip down a magnetic flyer and you can ride the seat, Mike. Johnny can pretend to carry you, like on a platter. It'll impress the yokels with the strength of our flunkies."

"*Mike* could carry *me*," I pointed out.

Chon laid a delicate hand on my back. "But, buddy, Mike outranks you."

I shook my head. "Not that way, he doesn't."

"We may be going to a lot of trouble for nothing," Mike said. "That gang may jump us as soon as we decant and try to have us for dinner."

"There's always that risk," Chon agreed solemnly, "but naturally I will remain on duty at the controls of the stun cannon."

"Securely inside," Ellik added.

"Always on duty," Chon said.

"Always inside," Ellik said.

"It's in the records, Ellik. I took the last one." Lee said it a little too sharp and it cut the kidding.

"Go soak your soft head in brine," Ellik said, disgruntled.

"Wait a minute," Chon called.

Ellik turned back. "Yeah?"

"Don't forget to take your communicator with you." Chon's voice was choked. "You may get out of line of sight if you go off with that troupe."

"I know this business," Ellik said, turning away.

"Mike, I'm sorry if I offended you. Shake, huh?"

Ellik smiled sourly. "Forget it."

"Come on, shake."

"Okay, we're buddies. Do I actually have to pump your clammy paw?"

"Please!"

"Oh, for Pete's sake!" Ellik turned around and kissed Chon on the forehead.

Ellik was just sore, of course. But the manual warns against that sort of horseplay when you've been out a long time.

"Satisfied now?" Ellik asked.

"No." Chon's voice was strained tight. "It should have been me to kiss you." Chon turned to me. "Luck out there, Johnny."

I grabbed his hand and levered it fast, before he could decide I needed kissing. "Sure thing, Lee. Thanks."

*

The buildings weren't much to see, but they were a step above primitive huts. They were adobe, or maybe plastic. The aliens understood the stress principles of the dome, Ellik said, because all the buildings had curved roofs. Unbaked pottery was what they looked like to me, and they looked as if they would be brittle as coffee-colored chalk. Actually, their ceramic surfaces were at least as hard as steel.

The Azure had welcomed Ellik with an outstretched hand. Mike wasn't one to jump to conclusions, so he just held out his own hand. The native grabbed and let it go after pulling it some.

The alien saw me apparently carrying Ellik on a seat cushion with one hand, and he kicked me in the leg. To test my muscles, I guess. I managed to keep from yelling or jumping. The Azure looked impressed and the Indigos did a bad job of hiding a lot of envy and hate.

As the Indigos toted their man along on the litter and I guided Ellik's seat cushion along the channel of magnetic feedback, the two riders began talking. Ellik's translator collar broke the language barrier, of course. It was a two-way communicator on a direct hook-up to our cybernetic calculator on the ship. The brain analyzed the phonetic structure of the alien language under various systems of logic or anti-logic and fed the translation into Ellik's ear. Then it went through its memory banks and played back the right sounds to translate Ellik's talk into the alien language. I understand things like that. I'm a pretty good mechanic.

I didn't have my translator turned on, but it seemed to me that somehow I could understand what the plug-uglies, the Indigos, were saying.

Ellik told me that it was because all their speech was based on the one universal humanoid sound, "mama." Everything good in the way of nouns and verbs (there were no other particles of speech) was some inflection of "m-m" and everything bad was "uh-m-m."

Ellik was pretty "uh-m-m."

I was *plenty* "uh-m-m." I threatened their jobs, they thought.

They were a real miserable bunch of slobs, those Indigos.

We passed through the wide places between the houses—I wouldn't call them streets—and saw a lot of Indigos crouched in doorways, watching us, and Azures being toted around.

The clothing they wore was also pretty universal for sentient bipeds—a tunic or sarong, kind of. For the Azures, it was smooth and colorful; and for the Indigos, a loincloth of some rough, dun-colored stuff.

Ellik chinned off his translator switch and leaned down toward my ear. "They are two distinct races, Johnny. Notice that *all* the Indigos are menials. There does not appear to be anything to correspond to a freedman or even a higher-ranked house servant. The Azures treat the Indigos only as animals."

"Slobs," I said. "Poor dumb slobs."

The nuclear flash washed over us, peppering us with a few excess roentgens.

We couldn't look at the spaceship going up, but we knew it was going. It was making a dawn.

The aliens were all frightened. They fell on the ground and started praying to the ship, all of them, the Azures and the Indigos.

"What's wrong with that crazy Chinaman?" Ellik yelped.

"Lee knows what he's doing," I said.

Ellik unsnapped his communicator from his belt. "Johnny says you know what you're doing, Chon. *Do you?*"

"I know." Chon's voice sounded right beside us, perfectly natural. Belt communicators work just as well as those consoles. People only buy consoles for prestige.

"Well?" Ellik demanded. "What *are* you doing, Lee?"

I thought maybe something had gone wrong with the communicator.

Chon's voice finally reached us.

"I'm leaving you and Johnny on this planet, Mike," he said.

*

An Indigo brought us in our morning supply of fruit.

Ellik kicked the Indigo. "It's overripe, blockhead. *Amum, amum.*"

The Indigo backed out, bowing, eyes very round.

Ellik felt me looking at him.

"Well, I don't *like* kicking the oaf, but that's all he's been conditioned to understand as a sign of disapproval."

"Sure," I said.

Ellik passed through the scimitar of gray shadow into the sunlight that washed lines and years out of his face. He braced a hand against the doorframe and craned his head back. It stopped and steadied.

"He's still there," Ellik said. "Sometimes I wish his orbit would decay enough to burn him up in this damned sour air." He coughed into his fist.

"He could probably correct," I suggested.

Ellik sneered. "He hasn't got the brains."

"Pretty hard for one man to manage a takeoff. He was lucky to make it into orbit."

"I just wish he would come down. Somehow, someway, I'd get to him, no matter where he went on this planet."

"I suppose that's why he stays up."

Ellik slammed his fist into his palm. "I'm going to call him again. He can't get away without us. If he fouled up a takeoff that badly, he's not going to try to solo into hyperspace."

"I don't think anyone would solo into hyperspace. I don't think he would be able to come back."

"Oh, what do you know about it?" Ellik said shortly. "He's just building up his courage to try the big jump. He's yellow, sure, but sooner or later he'll get desperate enough, or scared enough, to actually go. Then we'll be stranded for fair. This planet may not be colonized for centuries!"

"Probably never," I said. "Not after Lee's reports."

"You think he would falsify reports?" Ellik asked, blinking at me.

"I suppose he'll have to."

Ellik held his head with his hands. "Of course, of course. There's no limit to the depths to which he would plummet." He ran over to the corner and snatched a communicator off the pile of our gear. "I'm going to call him and tell him what I think of him and his wild obsession."

I didn't remind Ellik that he had been telling Chon just that at least once a day for a month. I knew his nerves got tighter and tighter and cussing out Chon helped release them and make him feel better.

"Come down, Lee!" Ellik called. "The three of us can make the jump together. You're martyring yourself for a crazy reason!"

"We've talked this over before," Chon answered. "This is the last time I'm going to respond to your call. I've made it clear to you that I think knowledge of this world will cause great suffering, a lot of death, among the majority of Earth's people."

"You're talking prejudice, Lee! *Your* prejudice. People aren't like that any more."

"We haven't gone *that* far, Mike. The bigots, the hatemongers, the pettiness and xenophobia lurking in everybody haven't been asleep that long. Just look at it from *my* side, Mike. What will the white people of Earth think about the Orientals, Negroes and Indians of Earth when they find out the dark-skinned humanoids of another planet are—measurably, unquestionably, vastly—*inferior* to the light-skinned race of the same world? I ask you, Mike!"

*

Mike Ellik said, "It's an inept analogy, Lee, and you know it."

"But most people reason by analogy," said Lee Chon. "No, Mike. I have to leave you and Johnny to prevent a recurrence of racial hatred, intolerance and all the ugly consequences on both sides. This is the last time I'll answer you, Mike. I'm getting lonesome. In a few years, I'll get hungry for human companionship. I don't want to be tempted down. Good-by, Johnny. So long, Mike."

Ellik screamed. "Wait! Answer one more call, Lee. It's the least you can do for me. I don't know when I'll make it. It may be in a few weeks or a few years. It won't be just argument, Lee. I'll have something you'll*want* to tell Earth about this place and these people."

"I'm still here. Tell it to me now," Chon's voice said.

"No. I want to get proof. Let me rig up some kind of video circuit for you. I can use parts out of our tape camera and the translators. I want to get it all across to you."

I could hear Chon breathing. "Very well. I'll answer your next call."

"Lee," I called out, "Mike and me will be expecting you to answer."

Chon laughed. "I'm not going anywhere, Johnny. Only around this world every couple of hours."

"You couldn't make the jump through hyperspace without us, Lee," Ellik said.

"That's right, Mike. I'm—I'm sorry to quarantine you two down there."

"*Quarantine!*" Ellik stormed. "*We're* not sick, Lee. *You* are the sick one!"

There wasn't any sound, not even of breathing.

"You have an idea to change Lee's mind, Mike?" I asked.

He cupped his hand on the back of my neck. "Affirmative, Jonathan. A pretty damned good one, too."

Ellik stood staring out the door, gnawing on one of his knuckles, letting the sun turn the front of him into gold, so he looked like half a statue, and half a man.

"I suppose it had to come out in him sooner or later," he said.

"What, Mike?"

"What could we expect? It's the basic quality of treachery in the Oriental mind."

*

When the shadows were at their longest and the alien sun was down the closest to the horizon without actually going under, Ellik marched up the path shoving a new Indigo. The Azures supplied Mike with all the flunkies he wanted to gather food and the like for him, as his natural right. But I thought we had enough of them hanging around our quarters. I couldn't imagine what he would want with another one.

The alien hovered at the door. Ellik kicked him in the calf to make him understand he was to go inside.

"Look at him, Johnny," Ellik said, pushing the fellow forward. "Not a mongoloid, would you say?"

"No."

The alien looked stupid—blue and stupid. His face was hanging there, but it wasn't pushed out of shape any more than the faces of the Azures. The Indigo blinked back at me. What he also looked was not friendly.

Ellik took the Indigo's cheeks in his hand and angled the face toward the light. "He's a half-breed, Johnny, or otherwise the gene was recessive. He wasn't damaged before birth, only after—when he started to breathe."

"What do you mean, Mike?"

"You ever hear of cyanosis, Johnny?"

"No."

"Well, these creatures have something like it. The Indigos don't get enough oxygen in their blood cells. It makes them sluggish; it turns them blue like the pictures of 'blue babies' in the old books."

"I never saw a picture like that in an old book," I said.

"Did you ever *see* a book? Sorry, Johnny. Just kidding." Ellik rubbed his hands together. "Well! I theorized that there is no basic difference in the

Azures and the Indigos except improper aeration of their blood. So, you see, an Indigo is only a *sick* Azure, and I am going to make this Indigo *well.*"

"How can you do that?"

"It's simple," Mike said irritably. "The Indigos must have a malformation of the heart causing an abnormal communication between the venous and arterial side of the circulation system. A little surgery and I adjust a valve in the heart. No more communication. Proper aeration. Enough oxygen. The deep blue color goes, leaving only the lighter blue of the natural pigmentation. The patient feels better, acts better, thinks better, looks better. In short, he is no longer an Indigo but an Azure."

"Is—is this what you're going to show Lee?" I ventured.

"Of course! It proves the Indigos *aren't* an inferior race. They are the same as the Azures except that they are sick. Their being sick can't reflect unfavourably on any terrestrial colored race. There is no analogy. But I have to prove it to Chon. We're going to tape the whole process and feed it to him."

"I think," I said, "that that might get to him."

"Sure it will." Ellik's jaw muscles flexed. "I should ruin Lee with this thing, but I won't. I'm not a vindictive man. Lee and I will probably be working together for years. But whenever he gets out of line—has some stubborn idea about doing something his way—don't think I won't remind him of this!"

Suddenly, he was smiling again. He turned to the gawking Indigo. He pointed two fingers at him.

"*Mmr?*" Ellik asked.

The alien tapped himself on his chest cavity twice. "*Mhaw,*" he gave his name.

"*Mhaw M'i uh M'i m M'm'-uh?*" Ellik asked him, without even using the translators.

"M-*m*-M-*m*-M," the alien went, slapping himself on the chest with his opened palms.

Ellik turned to me, grinning. "I asked him if he wanted to stop being an Indigo and become an Azure. He thinks I can do anything and he's all for it."

*

After we fed Mhaw a dose of null-shock from our packs, Doc Ellik started to slice him open with a ceramic knife he had borrowed from the Azures.

But Ellik had forgotten that the alien might get frightened seeing himself cut open, even if he couldn't feel any pain. It had never happened to him before.

The alien lumbered to his feet, his chest hanging open, showing his heart beating like some animal caught inside a blueberry pudding.

I drove a right cross into his jaw, and felt the jar all the way up to my shoulder.

He melted back down onto the pallet.

"Good work, Johnny," Ellik said, stooping and starting his work.

Right away, Mhaw started to lose that Indigo color and get real light—lighter than the Azures, in fact. None of the blue of the race was actually in the pigmentation, Mike found out. Even the Azures suffered some degree of improper aeration of the blood.

"You going to call Lee Chon now?" I asked Mike. "You going to show him the tape we had running during the operation and all?"

"Not quite yet, Johnny," he said. "First I want to educate Mhaw a bit, up to the Azure level or better. That should convince Lee."

Mhaw learned fast, probably faster than the Azures, even. Almost the first thing he wanted was for us to stop calling him Mhaw and start using an Azure name, Aedo.

Once a day, Ellik left our hut to take some exercise—a walk along the alien esplanade, he called it. I used to stay with the doctored alien, now Aedo, but we finally learned we could trust him to follow our orders—which were to stay inside, away from the others, since we didn't know how they would take him. So I got to walking along with Ellik.

As dusk lengthened, we could see the spark that was our ship in its orbit along the retreating horizon.

Ellik twisted back his head and the side of his mouth. "Look at him up there—*look!*"

The spark burned brighter and danced in another direction.

"He's gone! He left us!" Ellik said.

"It's okay. He's still there. Just corrected the orbit a little, I guess."

"No, no, no," Ellik said. "He started to make another try. But he got afraid to try to go into hyperspace alone."

"He was just correcting for orbital decay."

"You don't understand, Johnny. He's a coward. That makes him dangerous. He's getting desperate. That desperation will burst the dam of his own weakness and wash away our hope, *our lives*."

His voice hushed. He stood staring starkly ahead, his palms outstretched at his sides.

"Maybe he isn't *that* cowardly," I said hopefully.

*

"Finished," Ellik announced. He meant he had finished editing the tape showing the operation on the alien and his recovery from his blue disease, from being an Indigo to better than an Azure.

"The transmitter is finished too," I said.

Ellik had suggested a way of switching the tape camera to a video converter for one of the audio communicators, and I had been able to do it easy. It took parts from both our communicators and translators too.

Ellik fitted the coiled snake of tape into place. "This will be a great day for your people, Aedo. After our friend from heaven lands, we will be able to teach you a way to cure all of your sick, to make all the Indigos like you."

"Like me? Make like me?" Aedo said in the pidgin terrestrial that Mike Ellik had taught him.

"Yes. We'll show them how we cured you and how all can be cured."

"You make show fellow like me? Make tell make that fellow like fellow like me?"

"Everything's ready, Mike," I called.

"That's right, Aedo," Mike said. "You'll show your people the way to equality."

"Make all fellow like this fellow?" Aedo asked.

"Shall I call in Lee?" I asked Mike.

"Yes, that's right, Aedo. Just right."

"No," Aedo said.

The alien stomped the tape camera and the communicator to bits before I could get a hammerlock on him.

Ellik just stared at the complete wreck of our only means of communication with the spaceship.

"I be much man now. I much smart. Much smart than Azure hicks and

Indigo slobs. I much smart all. I much man! Not to be all same now. *No.*" The snarl hung on in Aedo's throat.

Ellik lifted his head and sort of smiled. But not quite.

"Well," he said slowly and sadly, "what could you expect in the way of gratitude from a dirty alien?"

*

The Azures did accept Aedo all right. They seem to think he must have come from some other tribe. They don't associate him with the Indigo that disappeared. No Indigo ever became an Azure before.

Of course, Azures sometimes become Indigos, we found out.

It seems there's a virus of what Ellik called pseudo-cyanosis in the air. The Azures have become a pretty resistant breed to it, while the Indigos are all easy victims. But once in a while an Azure will come down with it and turn Indigo.

Mike Ellik caught it too.

It happened pretty fast. By the time we realized what it was, he was already too stupid to finish the operation he started on himself. I had to sew him up, not very neatly.

Ellik is treated pretty much like the rest of the Indigos. So am I. He takes it all pretty calm. He can still talk a little Earth. Whenever anybody kicks him, Ellik just mutters something about, "What can fellow expect bunch lousy creeps like those fellow?"

I guess I'll get it too. I think I am getting it.

It won't be so bad for me. Just like maybe going around drunk all the time, not being able to think or coordinate very well.

It will be kind of bad being a member of an inferior race, but the thing I'll hate about it the most isn't that, or even leaving old Lee up there, circling around and waiting for our call forever.

No, the thing I hate is having it happen *now*, just when I'm beginning to *learn* something.

I'm not dead sure I know just exactly what I learned, but I think maybe I do:

You get just what you damned well expected all along from a bunch of blue-blooded mongrels!

BAD MEMORY

By Patrick Fahy

Channing wanted a planet. Had they sold him a pup?

*

Ex-vector Commander Jim Channing strode purposefully to the reception desk of Planet Enterprises, Inc.

"I want," he told the well-built blonde who was making an interested survey of his lean features, "to buy a planet."

"Yes, sir." Her interest evaporated. She took a card from a filing cabinet and handed it to him. "If you will just fill this out."

It was a simple questionnaire—type, location, size—and Channing's stylo moved rapidly over it. He hesitated only at the last, stark question, "How much are you prepared to pay?" Then he wrote neatly in the space provided "One hundred thousand credits." That was exactly the amount of his signing-off bonus. It also represented his total finances. The unimaginative minds that calculated the pay of a red-blooded space officer didn't take into account all the attractive ways of spending it that a rumbustious pioneer Vector provided.

He gave the blonde the card and she wrote a name on it. The smile she gave him was altogether impersonal. She liked the look of the big, gangling fellow with "Space" written all over his bronzed face and crinkled blue eyes, but....

She said, "Will you come this way, please?"

The name on the desk identified him as "Mr. Folan" and he was a tall, affable man.

"I think we can suit you, Commander—er—Mr. Channing," he said, "though what we have in mind mightn't be quite as large as you wish. Earth-type planets come rather high, you know. Now if you were to choose a Sirius- or a Vega-type—"

"Thank you, no," Jim said firmly. He had heard too much about the hazards of alien-type planets.

"In that case," Mr. Folan said busily, "let's see what we have available."

*

A month later the doors of the automatic shuttle slid across and admitted Jim Channing to the third planet of Phylox Beta. It also disgorged one spaceboat, a clutter of machinery, a thousand tons of strawberry plants and a fully equipped house. While he was still taking in the first glimpse of his future home, the massive doors slammed shut and the giant ship took off smoothly and silently. A moment later it winked into sub-space. He was in business.

The planet possessed only one sizable island—it could hardly be dignified by the name of continent.

The rest was covered by a vast ocean. Still, as Folan had explained, he couldn't really expect anything more—not in the line of an Earth-type, anyway—for the money.

He spent a week figuring out the remote controls that operated the planting machinery. Once it clanked into operation, it worked entirely on its own. He had only to push a few buttons to send it lumbering in new directions and the big island steadily took on a resemblance to a huge strawberry patch while Channing fished and lounged in the sun.

When the galactic trade agent came, the strawberries were waiting for him, neatly piled into a mountain of gleaming cans. He was a friendly, talkative little man, glad to exercise his tongue again after the lonely months in space.

"What are you growing here?" he asked Channing.

"Strawberries."

The friendly smile disappeared. "Every planet in the Galaxy seems to be growing strawberries this year. I can't even give them away."

"But I thought the Ursa Major colonies—"

The little man shook his head. "So does everyone else. There's a million tons of strawberries the colonies can't use headed there already. Now if it was upklin seeds—"

"Upklin seeds?"

The agent looked at him in surprise. "You mean you haven't heard about upklin seeds?"

"No. Not a thing."

"Well, of course, you are a newcomer. It's this new race that's been discovered somewhere in The Sack. They are as rich as all get-out and they have a passion for upklin seeds. Trouble is they can't grow them on local planets and they are offering fancy prices to anybody that can supply them.

I paid a thousand credits a bushel for them to your next-door neighbor on the fourth planet last week. Got a hundred bushels."

Channing did a bit of mental arithmetic. A hundred thousand credits for one crop. Whew!

"Could I grow them here?"

The agent shook his head. "You need plenty of soft marsh and a Jupiter-type atmosphere."

Then he had a sudden idea and he spoke long and seriously to Channing, explaining quite a few things that were new to him. Channing was still considering them, staring thoughtfully at the ground, after the little man left.

*

Next day Channing took off for the nearest sub-space center and a few hours later he was in Mr. Folan's office at Planet Enterprises, gingerly balancing his cap on his knee. Mr. Folan's sleek head nodded as Channing made his points and when he was finished the executive pressed a buzzer and called for the file.

"You realize, Mr. Channing," he said conversationally, as he turned over the pages, "that what you are asking will be a most expensive undertaking."

"I know that," Channing said eagerly, "but upklin seeds are such a sure-fire proposition that I thought Planet Enterprises might be willing to do the job on a percentage basis."

Mr. Folan wrote some figures on the margin of the folder and considered deeply. "Yes," he said at last, "I think it would work out on a seventy-thirty split."

"Seventy-thirty?"

Mr. Folan inclined his head graciously. "Seventy per cent for Planet Enterprises and thirty for yourself."

Channing said slowly, "That's a bit steep."

In a few brisk words, Mr. Folan showed just why he was an executive of Planet Enterprises, Inc. He gave Channing the figures for transforming the planet's characteristics to those of Jupiter; he told him what acreage of upklin seeds he could grow and the exact profit to be expected. Channing's share should be about one hundred and fifty thousand credits per crop.

Fighting a rearguard battle, Channing said, "Your three hundred and fifty thousand won't look so bad on the balance sheet, either."

Folan reeled off his figures again with practiced glibness. Channing had the sudden suspicion that his proposition wasn't entirely unexpected. But the figures sounded reasonable and he had to admit that Planet Enterprises was risking a great deal of money.

"Then there is the not inconsiderable cost of your own metamorphosis, Mr. Channing," Folan added.

"Huh?" said Channing.

There followed the most excruciating half-hour of Channing's life. Proposition followed explanation, counter-explanation followed counter-proposition. At the end of that time he emerged from the office with a stricken look and a small white card. The blonde receptionist read the look correctly and definitely and finally crossed him off her list.

*

For a jube, Ckm Dyk wasn't at all bad-looking. His four legs growing directly from the bottom of the muscular, hairy trunk were strong and sturdy—always a mark of handsomeness in a male, for the legs had to take most of the strain of a gravitational pull several times that of Earth. He had three flexible tentacles, a thin melon slice for a mouth, but nothing resembling a nose. He didn't need one, since he breathed through a set of gills at the sides of his head.

He remembered vaguely that he had once been Jim Channing, an Earthman, but the memory had nearly faded. He had been warned of that, that he would soon forget he had ever been anything except what he was now, but he had already forgotten the warning.

Phylox Beta III had changed, too, and in as great a degree. The wide ocean had become a turgid, soupy mush, covered by the trailing growths of the upklin flowers. The blue skies had turned an angry red and the sharp wind that rustled the hair on his squat body was almost pure methane.

He waddled down to the low disk-shaped skimmer and started the jets. As it pushed its way through the clinging masses of the upklin flowers, he surveyed his crop happily. This was his second crop and it promised to be even better than the first. He was going to be a very wealthy buk, he told himself. He could buy.... His mind floundered. He didn't know what Jubes longed for, what they sought wealth for. He was certain at the same time that there was a flaw in his contentment, that something was missing.

What he was missing dropped from the sky a few days later. It came in a spaceboat and was his neighbor from Phylox Beta IV. Her body hair was a rich golden brown and she wore pretty bracelets, studded with basim stones, on each of her four legs. Ckm Dyk's single eye, with its perpendicular outer eyelids and horizontal nictitating inner membranes to filter out the infra-red rays, shone with an emotion that was more than pleasure.

Her thoughts flooded his mind. There was a warm recognition of his admiration and a delicious suggestion that it wasn't unacceptable.

"The agent told me you were upklin farming. I came to see if I could be of any help," she told him.

The sentences rang like golden bells within his burgeoning consciousness. He tried to shape his answering thought coherently, but his lack of telepathic experience betrayed him. She flinched momentarily beneath the raw, undirected stream of passionate love that overwhelmed her mind.

Then an answering wave of shy, tender awareness and acquiescence laved his senses. Without the clumsy barrier of speech between them, they had scaled in a few pulsating moments the shining heights of love and devotion that human passion sometimes cannot find in a lifetime of searching.

Ckm Dyk had never been so happy. They decided to farm the two planets together so they could be with each other always. There was sound economic sense in this; with both of them helping, the output of each planet would be nearly doubled. It meant a huge increase in administrative and paper work for Ckm Dyk, but he didn't mind that. Often, as he pored over account books and production figures, a tremulous, shy devotion would envelop him in a gauzy mental cloud and he would lay down his stylo and answer Aln Muh with all the great love that surged within him.

As the months passed, his happiness increased. The perfect attunement of their minds excluded all the scalding jealousies and the offended silences of misunderstanding that can mar the most loving human relationships. They did not need to see each other; the physical presence of the beloved was unimportant; they loved more with their minds than with their bodies.

It seemed improbable that such a glorious idyll should ever be disturbed. Then, one morning, a shuttle-spacer came silently out of the red sky and landed beside the house. Ckm Dyk waddled toward it, impelled by a carefully built-in series of reflexes which he had completely forgotten about and entered its gaping maw. He never once looked at Aln Muh and the passionate entreaties that echoed through his mind only roused in him a dull irritation.

*

Jim Channing again found himself in Mr. Folan's office. The figures the tall, sleek-haired man was reading out to him made tuneful music. Even when Planet Enterprises' massive deduction was made, his share was comfortingly more than a million.

"Not bad payment, Mr. Channing, for five years of life! In any case, it's all over now—just a bad memory."

The executive smiled at him from his comfortable, familiar chair, aware of the torrents of confused thoughts hidden behind the gray eyes.

When he had come out of the stupor that succeeded the almost disintegrating effects of his re-metamorphosis, Jim Channing remembered clearly the terms of the bargain he had made. He was to become a Jube, a living nightmare, living in a nightmare world, for five years. At the end of that time, Planet Enterprises promised him, he would be given back his humanity and he would have earned enough money to keep him in luxury for the rest of his life.

They had kept their promise—to the letter. He felt it ungrateful of him that his paramount emotion was fury. He had been happy; no human attachment could ever make him as happy again. He longed for the glorious love and trust he had shared during that tremendous five years. Perhaps he had been a repulsive monster from whom any woman would run screaming. But he didn't want a woman. He wanted Aln Muh.

He said, picking his words with the greatest care, "Would a further metamorphosis be possible?"

*

Folan's jaw dropped. It was a question he'd never expected to hear from any of the men who had taken the terrible choice for the glittering reward he held out to them. Most of them had picked up their vouchers and asked the way to the nearest tavern; many of the alien races did not find alcohol compatible with their metabolisms. A few had inquired tentatively about his current receptionist. Planet Enterprises had a big turnover in pretty receptionists, but they didn't lose them to men who had been unhuman horrors for five years. One big red-haired character had wanted to start a private war against the Sirians, whose brother he had been until two days previously. But none of them had wanted to go back.

He said, "It's possible, Mr. Channing. But I must tell you that a second metamorphosis is very expensive—and it's permanent."

"You mean if I become a Jube again, I must stay one?"

The executive nodded.

Channing gestured toward the payment voucher.

"You said it was expensive. Is there enough there to cover it?"

Folan looked curiously at him. "Yes, more than enough."

He waited to hear what the big man would say next.

Channing licked dry lips. A terrible doubt assailed him. Maybe Aln Muh had been metamorphosed too. Maybe she had returned to her former self—whatever that may have been—while he sat here.

He looked down at the big, freckled hands resting on his knees. They were trembling and his palms felt moist. Without looking up, he asked, "Is the period of metamorphosis, always for a term of five years?"

"Invariably. No other term is possible in the present state of our knowledge of the technique—except permanency."

A great sigh escaped Channing. That was all right, then. Aln Muh was genuinely a Jube. The agent had told him about her—mentioned her by name, he remembered now—had said that she was upklin farming on the neighboring planet. If she had been metamorphosed, she would have been taken from him more than a year ago.

He tossed his cap on the table decisively and stood up.

"All right. I'll take the permanent treatment."

*

Ckm Dyk sucked the methane through his gills with satisfaction. It was good to be home again. He had forgotten already that he had ever been Jim Channing, that he would never be human again.

He did not know that less than five minutes after the shuttle-ship had borne him off to Galactic Enterprises, Aln Muh had sent her spaceboat hurtling toward the fiery orb of Phylox Beta, mad with the grief of having lost him. It would not have concerned him much if he had known.

Jubes make tender and devoted lovers, but they are notorious for their exceedingly bad memories.

BEACH SCENE

By Marshall King

It was a fine day at the beach for Purnie's game—but his new friends played very rough!

*

Purnie ran laughing and shouting through the forest until he could run no more. He fell headlong into a patch of blue moss and whooped with delight in having this day free for exploring. He was free to see the ocean at last.

When he had caught his breath, he looked back through the forest. No sign of the village; he had left it far behind. Safe from the scrutiny of brothers and parents, there was nothing now to stop him from going to the ocean. This was the moment to stop time.

"On your mark!" he shouted to the rippling stream and its orange whirlpools. He glanced furtively from side to side, pretending that some object might try to get a head start. "Get set!" he challenged the thin-winged bees that hovered over the abundant foliage. "Stop!" He shrieked this command upward toward the dense, low-hanging purple clouds that perennially raced across the treetops, making one wonder how tall the trees really were.

His eyes took quick inventory. It was exactly as he knew it would be: the milky-orange stream had become motionless and its minute whirlpools had stopped whirling; a nearby bee hung suspended over a paka plant, its transparent wings frozen in position for a downward stroke; and the heavy purple fluid overhead held fast in its manufacture of whorls and nimbi.

With everything around him in a state of perfect tableau, Purnie hurried toward the ocean.

If only the days weren't so short! he thought. There was so much to see and so little time. It seemed that everyone except him had seen the wonders of the beach country. The stories he had heard from his brothers and their friends had taunted him for as long as he could remember. So many times had he heard these thrilling tales that now, as he ran along, he could clearly picture the wonderland as though he were already there. There would be a rockslide of petrified logs to play on, the ocean itself with waves higher than a house, the comical three-legged tripons who never stopped munching on seaweed, and many kinds of other wonderful creatures found only at the ocean.

He bounced through the forest as though the world was reserved this day just for him. And who could say it wasn't? he thought. Wasn't this his fifth birthday? He ran along feeling sorry for four-year-olds, and even for those who were only four and a half, for they were babies and wouldn't dare try slipping away to the ocean alone. But five!

"I'll set you free, Mr. Bee—just wait and see!" As he passed one of the many motionless pollen-gathering insects he met on the way, he took care not to brush against it or disturb its interrupted task. When Purnie had stopped time, the bees—like all the other creatures he met—had been arrested in their native activities, and he knew that as soon as he resumed time, everything would pick up where it had left off.

*

When he smelled an acid sweetness that told him the ocean was not far off, his pulse quickened in anticipation. Rather than spoil what was clearly going to be a perfect day, he chose to ignore the fact that he had been forbidden to use time-stopping as a convenience for journeying far from home. He chose to ignore the oft-repeated statement that an hour of time-stopping consumed more energy than a week of foot-racing. He chose to ignore the negative maxim that "small children who stop time without an adult being present, may not live to regret it."

He chose, instead, to picture the beaming praise of family and friends when they learned of his brave journey.

The journey was long, the clock stood still. He stopped long enough to gather some fruit that grew along the path. It would serve as his lunch during this day of promise. With it under his arm he bounded along a dozen more steps, then stopped abruptly in his tracks.

He found himself atop a rocky knoll, overlooking the mighty sea!

He was so overpowered by the vista before him that his "Hurrah!" came out as a weak squeak. The ocean lay at the ready, its stilled waves awaiting his command to resume their tidal sweep. The breakers along the shoreline hung in varying stages of disarray, some having already exploded into towering white spray while others were poised in smooth orange curls waiting to start that action.

And there were new friends everywhere! Overhead, a flock of spora were frozen in a steep glide, preparatory to a beach landing. Purnie had heard of these playful creatures many times. Today, with his brothers in school, he would have the pets all to himself. Further down the beach was a pair of two-legged animals poised in mid-step, facing the spot where Purnie now stood. Some distance behind them were eight more, each of whom were motionless in a curious pose of interrupted animation. And down in the water, where the ocean ran itself into thin nothingness upon the sand, he saw standing here and there the comical tripons, those three-legged marine buffoons who made handsome careers of munching seaweed.

"Hi there!" Purnie called. When he got no reaction, he remembered that he himself was "dead" to the living world: he was still in a zone of time-stopping, on the inside looking out. For him, the world would continue to be a tableau of mannikins until he resumed time.

*

"Hi there!" he called again; but now his mental attitude was that he expected time to resume. It did! Immediately he was surrounded by activity. He heard the roar of the crashing orange breakers, he tasted the dew of acid that floated from the spray, and he saw his new friends continue the actions which he had stopped while back in the forest.

He knew, too, that at this moment, in the forest, the little brook picked up its flow where it had left off, the purple clouds resumed their leeward journey up the valley, and the bees continued their pollen-gathering without having missed a single stroke of their delicate wings. The brook, the clouds, and the insects had not been interrupted in the least; their respective tasks had been performed with continuing sureness. It was time itself that Purnie had stopped, not the world around him.

He scampered around the rockpile and down the sandy cliff to meet the tripons who, to him, had just come to life.

"I can stand on my head!" He set down his lunch and balanced himself bottoms-up while his legs pawed the air in an effort to hold him in position. He knew it was probably the worst head-stand he had ever done, for he felt weak and dizzy. Already time-stopping had left its mark on his strength. But his spirits ran on unchecked.

The tripon thought Purnie's feat was superb. It stopped munching long enough to give him a salutory wag of its rump before returning to its repast.

Purnie ran from pillar to post, trying to see and do everything at once. He looked around to greet the flock of spora, but they had glided to a spot further along the shore. Then, bouncing up to the first of the two-legged animals, he started to burst forth with his habitual "Hi there!" when he heard them making sounds of their own.

"... will be no limit to my operations now, Benson. This planet makes seventeen. Seventeen planets I can claim as my own!"

"My, my. Seventeen planets. And tell me, Forbes, just what the hell are you going to do with them—mount them on the wall of your den back in San Diego?"

"Hi there, wanna play?" Purnie's invitation got nothing more than startled glance from the animals who quickly returned to their chatter. He scampered up the beach, picked up his lunch, and ran back to them, tagging along at their heels. "I've got my lunch, want some?"

"Benson, you'd better tell your men back there to stop gawking at the scenery and get to work. Time is money. I didn't pay for this expedition just to give your flunkies a vacation."

*

The animals stopped so suddenly that Purnie nearly tangled himself in their heels.

"All right, Forbes, just hold it a minute. Listen to me. Sure, it's your money that put us here; it's your expedition all the way. But you hired me to get you here with the best crew on earth, and that's just what I've done. My job isn't over yet. I'm responsible for the safety of the men while we're here, and for the safe trip home."

"Precisely. And since you're responsible, get 'em working. Tell 'em to bring along the flag. Look at the damn fools back there, playing in the ocean with a three-legged ostrich!"

"Good God, man, aren't you human? We've only been on this planet twenty minutes! Naturally they want to look around. They half expected to find wild animals or worse, and here we are surrounded by quaint little creatures that run up to us like we're long-lost brothers. Let the men look around a minute or two before we stake out your claim."

"Bah! Bunch of damn children."

As Purnie followed along, a leg shot out at him and missed. "Benson, will you get this bug-eyed kangaroo away from me!" Purnie shrieked with joy at this new frolic and promptly stood on his head. In this position he got an upside down view of them walking away.

He gave up trying to stay with them. Why did they move so fast, anyway? What was the hurry? As he sat down and began eating his lunch, three more of the creatures came along making excited noises, apparently trying to catch up to the first two. As they passed him, he held out his lunch. "Want some?" No response.

Playing held more promise than eating. He left his lunch half eaten and went down to where they had stopped further along the beach.

"Captain Benson, sir! Miles has detected strong radiation in the vicinity. He's trying to locate it now."

"There you are, Forbes. Your new piece of real estate is going to make you so rich that you can buy your next planet. That'll make eighteen, I believe."

"Radiation, bah! We've found low-grade ore on every planet I've discovered so far, and this one'll be no different. Now how about that flag? Let's get it up, Benson. And the cornerstone, and the plaque."

"All right, lads. The sooner we get Mr. Forbes's pennant raised and his claim staked out, the sooner we can take time to look around. Lively now!"

*

When the three animals went back to join the rest of their group, the first two resumed walking. Purnie followed along.

"Well, Benson, you won't have to look far for materials to use for the base of the flag pole. Look at that rockpile up there.

"Can't use them. They're petrified logs. The ones on top are too high to carry down, and if we move those on the bottom, the whole works will slide down on top of us."

"Well—that's your problem. Just remember, I want this flag pole to be solid. It's got to stand at least—"

"Don't worry, Forbes, we'll get your monument erected. What's this with the flag? There must be more to staking a claim than just putting up a flag."

"There is, there is. Much more. I've taken care of all requirements set down by law to make my claim. But the flag? Well, you might say it represents an empire, Benson. The Forbes Empire. On each of my flags is the word FORBES, a symbol of development and progress. Call it sentiment if you will."

"Don't worry, I won't. I've seen real-estate flags before."

"Damn it all, will you stop referring to this as a real-estate deal? What I'm doing is big, man. Big! This is pioneering."

"Of course. And if I'm not mistaken, you've set up a neat little escrow system so that you not only own the planets, but you will virtually own the people who are foolish enough to buy land on them."

"I could have your hide for talking to me like this. Damn you, man! It's people like me who pay your way. It's people like me who give your space ships some place to go. It's people like me who pour good money into a chancey job like this, so that people like you can get away from thirteen-story tenement houses. Did you ever think of that?"

"I imagine you'll triple your money in six months."

When they stopped, Purnie stopped. At first he had been interested in the strange sounds they were making, but as he grew used to them, and as they in turn ignored his presence, he hopped alongside chattering to himself, content to be in their company.

He heard more of these sounds coming from behind, and he turned to see the remainder of the group running toward them.

"Captain Benson! Here's the flag, sir. And here's Miles with the scintillometer. He says the radiation's getting stronger over this way!"

"How about that, Miles?"

"This thing's going wild, Captain. It's almost off scale."

*

Purnie saw one of the animals hovering around him with a little box. Thankful for the attention, he stood on his head. "Can you do this?" He was overjoyed at the reaction. They all started making wonderful noises, and he felt most satisfied.

"Stand back, Captain! Here's the source right here! This little chuckwalla's hotter than a plutonium pile!"

"Let me see that, Miles. Well, I'll be damned! Now what do you suppose—"

By now they had formed a widening circle around him, and he was hard put to think of an encore. He gambled on trying a brand new trick: he stood on one leg.

"Benson, I must have that animal! Put him in a box."

"Now wait a minute, Forbes. Universal Law forbids—"

"This is my planet and I am the law. Put him in a box!"

"With my crew as witness, I officially protest—"

"Good God, what a specimen to take back. Radio-active animals! Why, they can reproduce themselves, of course! There must be thousands of these creatures around here someplace. And to think of those damn fools on Earth with their plutonium piles! Hah! Now I'll have investors *flocking* to me. How about it, Benson—does pioneering pay off or doesn't it?"

"Not so fast. Since this little fellow is radioactive, there may be great danger to the crew—"

"Now look here! You had planned to put *mineral* specimens in a lead box, so what's the difference? Put him in a box."

"He'll die."

"I have you under contract, Benson! You are responsible to me, and what's more, you are on my property. Put him in a box."

Purnie was tired. First the time-stopping, then this. While this day had brought more fun and excitement than he could have hoped for, the strain was beginning to tell. He lay in the center of the circle happily exhausted, hoping that his friends would show him some of their own tricks.

He didn't have to wait long. The animals forming the circle stepped back and made way for two others who came through carrying a box. Purnie sat up to watch the show.

"Hell, Captain, why don't I just pick him up? Looks like he has no intention of running away."

"Better not, Cabot. Even though you're shielded, no telling what powers the little fella has. Play it safe and use the rope."

"I swear he knows what we're saying. Look at those eyes."

"All right, careful now with that line."

"Come on, baby. Here you go. That's a boy!"

*

Purnie took in these sounds with perplexed concern. He sensed the imploring quality of the creature with the rope, but he didn't know what he was supposed to do. He cocked his head to one side as he wiggled in anticipation.

He saw the noose spinning down toward his head, and, before he knew it, he had scooted out of the circle and up the sandy beach. He was surprised at himself for running away. Why had he done it? He wondered. Never before had he felt this fleeting twinge that made him want to protect himself.

He watched the animals huddle around the box on the beach, their attention apparently diverted to something else. He wished now that he had not run away; he felt he had lost his chance to join in their fun.

"Wait!" He ran over to his half-eaten lunch, picked it up, and ran back into the little crowd. "I've got my lunch, want some?"

The party came to life once more. His friends ran this way and that, and at last Purnie knew that the idea was to get him into the box. He picked up the spirit of the tease, and deliberately ran within a few feet of the lead box, then, just as the nearest pursuer was about to push him in, he sidestepped onto safer ground. Then he heard a deafening roar and felt a warm, wet sting in one of his legs.

"Forbes, you fool! Put away that gun!"

"There you are, boys. It's all in knowing how. Just winged him, that's all. Now pick him up."

The pang in his leg was nothing: Purnie's misery lay in his confusion. What had he done wrong? When he saw the noose spinning toward him again, he involuntarily stopped time. He knew better than to use this power carelessly, but his action now was reflex. In that split second following the sharp sting in his leg, his mind had grasped in all directions to find an acceptable course of action. Finding none, it had ordered the stoppage of time.

The scene around him became a tableau once more. The noose hung motionless over his head while the rest of the rope snaked its way in transverse waves back to one of the two-legged animals. Purnie dragged himself through the congregation, whimpering from his inability to understand.

As he worked his way past one creature after another, he tried at first to not look them in the eye, for he felt sure he had done something wrong. Then he thought that by sneaking a glance at them as he passed, he might see a sign pointing to their purpose. He limped by one who had in his hand a small shiny object that had been emitting smoke from one end; the smoke now billowed in lifeless curls about the animal's head. He hobbled by another who held a small box that had previously made a hissing sound whenever Purnie was near. These things told him nothing. Before starting his climb up the knoll, he passed a tripon which, true to its reputation, was comical even in fright. Startled by the loud explosion, it had jumped four feet into the air before Purnie had stopped time. Now it hung there, its beak stuffed with seaweed and its three legs drawn up into a squatting position.

Leaving the assorted statues behind, he limped his way up the knoll, torn between leaving and staying. What an odd place, this ocean country! He wondered why he had not heard more detail about the beach animals.

Reaching the top of the bluff, he looked down upon his silent friends with a feeling of deep sorrow. How he wished he were down there playing with them. But he knew at last that theirs was a game he didn't fit into. Now there was nothing left but to resume time and start the long walk home. Even though the short day was nearly over, he knew he didn't dare use time-stopping to get himself home in nothing flat. His fatigued body and clouded mind were strong signals that he had already abused this faculty.

*

When Purnie started time again, the animal with the noose stood in open-mouthed disbelief as the rope fell harmlessly to the sand—on the spot where Purnie had been standing.

"My God, he's—he's gone."

Then another of the animals, the one with the smoking thing in his hand, ran a few steps toward the noose, stopped and gaped at the rope. "All right, you people, what's going on here? Get him in that box. What did you do with him?"

The resumption of time meant nothing at all to those on the beach, for to them time had never stopped. The only thing they could be sure of was that at one moment there had been a fuzzy creature hopping around in front of them, and the next moment he was gone.

"Is he invisible, Captain? Where is he?"

"Up there, Captain! On those rocks. Isn't that him?"

"Well, I'll be damned!"

"Benson, I'm holding you personally responsible for this! Now that you've botched it up, I'll bring him down my own way."

"Just a minute, Forbes, let me think. There's something about that fuzzy little devil that we should.... Forbes! I warned you about that gun!"

Purnie moved across the top of the rockpile for a last look at his friends. His weight on the end of the first log started the slide. Slowly at first, the giant pencils began cascading down the short distance to the sand. Purnie fell back onto solid ground, horrified at the spectacle before him. The agonizing screams of the animals below filled him with hysteria.

The boulders caught most of them as they stood ankle-deep in the surf. Others were pinned down on the sand.

"I didn't mean it!" Purnie screamed. "I'm sorry! Can't you hear?" He hopped back and forth near the edge of the rise, torn with panic and shame. "Get up! Please get up!" He was horrified by the moans reaching his ears from the beach. "You're getting all wet! Did you hear me? Please get up." He was choked with rage and sorrow. How could he have done this? He wanted his friends to get up and shake themselves off, tell him it was all right. But it was beyond his power to bring it about.

The lapping tide threatened to cover those in the orange surf.

*

Purnie worked his way down the hill, imploring them to save themselves. The sounds they made carried a new tone, a desperate foreboding of death.

"Rhodes! Cabot! Can you hear me?"

"I—I can't move, Captain. My leg, it's.... My God, we're going to drown!"

"Look around you, Cabot. Can you see anyone moving?"

"The men on the beach are nearly buried, Captain. And the rest of us here in the water—"

"Forbes. Can you see Forbes? Maybe he's—" His sounds were cut off by a wavelet gently rolling over his head.

Purnie could wait no longer. The tides were all but covering one of the animals, and soon the others would be in the same plight. Disregarding the consequences, he ordered time to stop.

Wading down into the surf, he worked a log off one victim, then he tugged the animal up to the sand. Through blinding tears, Purnie worked slowly and carefully. He knew there was no hurry—at least, not as far as his friends' safety was concerned. No matter what their condition of life or death was at this moment, it would stay the same way until he started time again. He made his way deeper into the orange liquid, where a raised hand signalled the location of a submerged body. The hand was clutching a large white banner that was tangled among the logs. Purnie worked the animal free and pulled it ashore.

It was the one who had been carrying the shiny object that spit smoke.

Scarcely noticing his own injured leg, he ferried one victim after another until there were no more in the surf. Up on the beach, he started unraveling the logs that pinned down the animals caught there. He removed a log from the lap of one, who then remained in a sitting position, his face contorted into a frozen mask of agony and shock. Another, with the weight removed, rolled over like an iron statue into a new position. Purnie whimpered in black misery as he surveyed the chaotic scene before him.

At last he could do no more; he felt consciousness slipping away from him.

He instinctively knew that if he lost his senses during a period of time-stopping, events would pick up where they had left off ... without him. For Purnie, this would be death. If he had to lose consciousness, he knew he must first resume time.

Step by step he plodded up the little hill, pausing every now and then to consider if this were the moment to start time before it was too late. With his energy fast draining away, he reached the top of the knoll, and he turned to look down once more on the group below.

Then he knew how much his mind and body had suffered: when he ordered time to resume, nothing happened.

His heart sank. He wasn't afraid of death, and he knew that if he died the oceans would roll again and his friends would move about. But he wanted to see them safe.

He tried to clear his mind for supreme effort. There was no *urging* time to start. He knew he couldn't persuade it by bits and pieces, first slowly then full ahead. Time either progressed or it didn't. He had to take one viewpoint or the other.

Then, without knowing exactly when it happened, his mind took command....

*

His friends came to life. The first one he saw stir lay on his stomach and pounded his fists on the beach. A flood of relief settled over Purnie as sounds came from the animal.

"What's the matter with me? Somebody tell me! Am I nuts? Miles! Schick! What's happening?"

"I'm coming, Rhodes! Heaven help us, man—I saw it, too. We're either crazy or those damn logs are alive!"

"It's not the logs. How about us? How'd we get out of the water? Miles, we're both cracking."

"I'm telling you, man, it's the logs, or rocks or whatever they are. I was looking right at them. First they're on top of me, then they're piled up over there!"

"Damnit, the logs didn't pick us up out of the ocean, did they? Captain Benson!"

"Are you men all right?"

"Yes sir, but—"

"Who saw exactly what happened?"

"I'm afraid we're not seeing right, Captain. Those logs—"

"I know, I know. Now get hold of yourselves. We've got to round up the others and get out of here while time is on our side."

"But what happened, Captain?"

"Hell, Rhodes, don't you think I'd like to know? Those logs are so old they're petrified. The whole bunch of us couldn't lift one. It would take super-human energy to move one of those things."

"I haven't seen anything super-human. Those ostriches down there are so busy eating seaweed—"

"All right, let's bear a hand here with the others. Some of them can't walk. Where's Forbes?"

"He's sitting down there in the water, Captain, crying like a baby. Or laughing. I can't tell which."

"We'll have to get him. Miles, Schick, come along. Forbes! You all right?"

"Ho-ho-ho! Seventeen! Seventeen! Seventeen planets, Benson, and they'll do anything I say! This one's got a mind of its own. Did you see that little trick with the rocks? Ho-ho!"

"See if you can find his gun, Schick; he'll either kill himself or one of us. Tie his hands and take him back to the ship. We'll be along shortly."

"Hah-hah-hah! Seventeen! Benson, I'm holding you personally responsible for this. Hee-hee!"

*

Purnie opened his eyes as consciousness returned. Had his friends gone?

He pulled himself along on his stomach to a position between two rocks, where he could see without being seen. By the light of the twin moons he saw that they were leaving, marching away in groups of two and three, the weak helping the weaker. As they disappeared around the curving shoreline, the voices of the last two, bringing up the rear far behind the others, fell faintly on his ears over the sound of the surf.

"Is it possible that we're all crazy, Captain?"

"It's possible, but we're not."

"I wish I could be sure."

"See Forbes up ahead there? What do you think of him?"

"I still can't believe it."

"He'll never be the same."

"Tell me something. What was the most unusual thing you noticed back there?"

"You must be kidding, sir. Why, the way those logs were off of us suddenly—"

"Yes, of course. But I mean beside that."

"Well, I guess I was kind of busy. You know, scared and mixed up."

"But didn't you notice our little pop-eyed friend?"

"Oh, him. I'm afraid not, Captain. I—I guess I was thinking mostly of myself."

"Hmmm. If I could only be sure I saw him. If only someone else saw him too."

"I'm afraid I don't follow you, sir."

"Well, damn it all, you know that Forbes took a pot shot at him. Got him in the leg. That being the case, why would the fuzzy little devil come back to his tormentors—back to us—when we were trapped under those logs?"

"Well, I guess as long as we were trapped, he figured we couldn't do him any more harm.... I'm sorry, that was a stupid answer. I guess I'm still a little shaky."

"Forget it. Look, you go ahead to the ship and make ready for take-off. I'll join you in a few minutes. I think I'll go back and look around. You know. Make sure we haven't left anyone."

"No need to do that. They're all ahead of us. I've checked."

"That's my responsibility, Cabot, not yours. Now go on."

*

As Purnie lay gathering strength for the long trek home, he saw through glazed eyes one of the animals coming back along the beach. When it was nearly directly below him, he could hear it making sounds that by now had become familiar.

"Where are you?"

Purnie paid little attention to the antics of his friend; he was beyond understanding. He wondered what they would say at home when he returned.

"We've made a terrible mistake. We—" The sounds faded in and out on Purnie's ears as the creature turned slowly and called in different directions. He watched the animal walk over to the pile of scattered logs and peer around and under them.

"If you're hurt I'd like to help!" The twin moons were high in the sky now, and where their light broke through the swirling clouds a double shadow was cast around the animal. With foggy awareness, Purnie watched the creature shake its head slowly, then walk away in the direction of the others.

Purnie's eyes stared, without seeing, at the panorama before him. The beach was deserted now, and his gaze was transfixed on a shimmering white square floating on the ocean. Across it, the last thing Purnie ever saw, was emblazoned the word FORBES.

THE RELUCTANT HEROES

By Frank M. Robinson

Pioneers have always resented their wanderlust, hated their hardships. But the future brings a new grudge—when pioneers stay put and scholars do the exploring!

*

The very young man sat on the edge of the sofa and looked nervous. He carefully studied his fingernails and ran his hands through his hair and picked imaginary lint off the upholstery.

"I have a chance to go with the first research expedition to Venus," he said.

The older man studied the very young man thoughtfully and then leaned over to his humidor and offered him a cigaret. "It's nice to have the new air units now. There was a time when we had to be very careful about things like smoking."

The very young man was annoyed.

"I don't think I want to go," he blurted. "I don't think I would care to spend two years there."

The older man blew a smoke ring and watched it drift toward the air exhaust vent.

"You mean you would miss it here, the people you've known and grown up with, the little familiar things that have made up your life here. You're afraid the glamor would wear off and you would get to hate it on Venus."

The very young man nodded miserably. "I guess that's it."

"Anything else?"

The very young man found his fingernails extremely fascinating again and finally said, in a low voice, "Yes, there is."

"A girl?"

A nod confirmed this.

It was the older man's turn to look thoughtful. "You know, I'm sure, that psychologists and research men agree that research stations should be staffed by couples. That is, of course, as soon as it's practical."

"But that might be a long time!" the very young man protested.

"It might be—but sometimes it's sooner than you think. And the goal is worth it."

"I suppose so, but—"

The older man smiled. "Still the reluctant heroes," he said, somewhat to himself.

*

Chapman stared at the radio key.

Three years on the Moon and they didn't want him to come back.

Three years on the Moon and they thought he'd be glad to stay for more. Just raise his salary or give him a bonus, the every-man-has-his-price idea. They probably thought he liked it there.

Oh, sure, he loved it. Canned coffee, canned beans, canned pills, and canned air until your insides felt as though they were plated with tin. Life in a cramped, smelly little hut where you could take only ten steps in any one direction. Their little scientific home of tomorrow with none of the modern conveniences, a charming place where you couldn't take a shower, couldn't brush your teeth, and your kidneys didn't work right.

And for double his salary they thought he'd be glad to stay for another year and a half. Or maybe three. He should probably be glad he had the opportunity.

The key started to stutter again, demanding an answer.

He tapped out his reply: "*No!*"

There was a silence and then the key stammered once more in a sudden fit of bureaucratic rage. Chapman stuffed a rag under it and ignored it. He turned to the hammocks, strung against the bulkhead on the other side of the room.

The chattering of the key hadn't awakened anybody; they were still asleep, making the animal noises that people usually make in slumber. Dowden, half in the bottom hammock and half on the floor, was snoring peacefully. Dahl, the poor kid who was due for stopover, was mumbling to himself. Julius Klein, with that look of ineffable happiness on his face, looked as if he had just squirmed under the tent to his personal idea of heaven. Donley and Bening were lying perfectly still, their covers not mussed, sleeping very lightly.

Lord, Chapman thought, I'll be happy when I can see some other faces.

"What'd they want?" Klein had one eyelid open and a questioning look on his face.

"They wanted me to stay until the next relief ship lands," Chapman whispered back.

"What did you say?"

He shrugged. "No."

"You kept it short," somebody else whispered. It was Donley, up and sitting on the side of his hammock. "If it had been me, I would have told them just what they could do about it."

*

The others were awake now, with the exception of Dahl who had his face to the bulkhead and a pillow over his head.

Dowden rubbed his eyes sleepily. "Sore, aren't you?"

"Kind of. Who wouldn't be?"

"Well, don't let it throw you. They've never been here on the Moon. They don't know what it's like. All they're trying to do is get a good man to stay on the job a while longer."

"*All* they're trying to do," Chapman said sarcastically. "They've got a fat chance."

"They think you've found a home here," Donley said.

"Why the hell don't you guys shut up until morning?" Dahl was awake, looking bitter. "Some of us still have to stay here, you know. Some of us aren't going back today."

No, Chapman thought, some of us aren't going back. You aren't. And Dixon's staying, too. Only Dixon isn't ever going back.

Klein jerked his thumb toward Dahl's bunk, held a finger to his lips, and walked noiselessly over to the small electric stove. It was his day for breakfast duty.

The others started lacing up their bunks, getting ready for their last day of work on the Moon. In a few hours they'd be relieved by members of the Third research group and they'd be on their way back to Earth.

And that includes me, Chapman thought. I'm going home. I'm finally going home.

He walked silently to the one small, quartz window in the room. It was morning—the Moon's "morning"—and he shivered slightly. The rays of the Sun were just striking the far rim of the crater and long shadows shot across the crater floor. The rest of it was still blanketed in a dark jumble of powdery pumice and jagged peaks that would make the Black Hills of Dakota look like paradise.

A hundred yards from the research bunker he could make out the small mound of stones and the forlorn homemade cross, jury-rigged out of small condensed milk tins slid over crossed iron bars. You could still see the footprints in the powdery soil where the group had gathered about the grave.

It had been more than eighteen months ago, but there was no wind to wear those tracks away. They'd be there forever.

That's what happened to guys like Dixon, Chapman thought. On the Moon, one mistake could use up your whole quota of chances.

Klein came back with the coffee. Chapman took a cup, gagged, and forced himself to swallow the rest of it. It had been in the can for so long you could almost taste the glue on the label.

*

Donley was warming himself over his cup, looking thoughtful. Dowden and Bening were struggling into their suits, getting ready to go outside. Dahl was still sitting on his hammock, trying to ignore them.

"Think we ought to radio the space station and see if they've left there yet?" Klein asked.

"I talked to them on the last call," Chapman said. "The relief ship left there twelve hours ago. They should get here"—he looked at his watch—"in about six and a half hours."

"Chap, you know, I've been thinking," Donley said quietly. "You've been here just twice as long as the rest of us. What's the first thing you're going to do once you get back?"

It hit them, then. Dowden and Bening looked blank for a minute and blindly found packing cases to sit on. The top halves of their suits were still hanging on the bulkhead. Klein lowered his coffee cup and looked grave. Even Dahl glanced up expectantly.

"I don't know," Chapman said slowly. "I guess I was trying not to think of that. I suppose none of us have. We've been like little kids who have waited so long for Christmas that they just can't believe it when it's finally Christmas Eve."

Klein nodded in agreement. "I haven't been here three years like you have, but I think I know what you mean." He warmed up to it as the idea sank in. "Just what the hell *are* you going to do?"

"Nothing very spectacular," Chapman said, smiling. "I'm going to rent a room over Times Square, get a recording of a rikky-tik piano, and drink and listen to the music and watch the people on the street below. Then I think I'll see somebody."

"Who's the somebody?" Donley asked.

Chapman grinned. "Oh, just somebody. What are you going to do, Dick?"

"Well, I'm going to do something practical. First of all, I want to turn over all my geological samples to the government. Then I'm going to sell my life story to the movies and then—why, then, I think I'll get drunk!"

Everybody laughed and Chapman turned to Klein.

"How about you, Julius?"

Klein looked solemn. "Like Dick, I'll first get rid of my obligations to the expedition. Then I think I'll go home and see my wife."

They were quiet. "I thought all members of the groups were supposed to be single," Donley said.

"They are. And I can see their reasons for it. But who could pass up the money the Commission was paying?"

"If I had to do it all over again? Me," said Donley promptly.

They laughed. Somebody said: "Go play your record, Chap. Today's the day for it."

The phonograph was a small, wind-up model that Chapman had smuggled in when he had landed with the First group. The record was old and the shellac was nearly worn off, but the music was good.

Way Back Home by Al Lewis.

*

They ran through it twice. They were beginning to feel it now, Chapman thought. They were going to go home in a little while and the idea was just starting to sink in.

"You know, Chap," Donley said, "it won't seem like the same old Moon without you on it. Why, we'll look at it when we're out spooning or something and it just won't have the same old appeal."

"Like they say in the army," Bening said, "you never had it so good. You found a home here."

The others chimed in and Chapman grinned. Yesterday or a week ago they couldn't have done it. He had been there too long and he had hated it too much.

The party quieted down after a while and Dowden and Bening finished getting into their suits. They still had a section of the sky to map before they left. Donley was right after them. There was an outcropping of rock that he wanted a sample of and some strata he wished to investigate.

And the time went faster when you kept busy.

Chapman stopped them at the lock. "Remember to check your suits for leaks," he warned. "And check the valves of your oxygen tanks."

Donley looked sour. "I've gone out at least five hundred times," he said, "and you check me each time."

"And I'd check you five hundred more," Chapman said. "It takes only one mistake. And watch out for blisters under the pumice crust. You go through one of those and that's it, brother."

Donley sighed. "Chap, you watch us like an old mother hen. You see we check our suits, you settle our arguments, you see that we're not bored and that we stay healthy and happy. I think you'd blow our noses for us if we caught cold. But some day, Chap old man, you're gonna find out that your little boys can watch out for themselves!"

But he checked his suit for leaks and tested the valve of his tank before he left.

Only Klein and Chapman were left in the bunker. Klein was at the work table, carefully labeling some lichen specimens.

"I never knew you were married," Chapman said.

Klein didn't look up. "There wasn't much sense in talking about it. You just get to thinking and wanting—and there's nothing you can do about it. You talk about it and it just makes it worse."

"She let you go without any fuss, huh?"

"No, she didn't make any fuss. But I don't think she liked to see me go, either." He laughed a little. "At least I hope she didn't."

*

They were silent for a while. "What do you miss most, Chap?" Klein asked. "Oh, I know what we said a little while ago, but I mean seriously."

Chapman thought a minute. "I think I miss the sky," he said quietly. "The blue sky and the green grass and trees with leaves on them that turn color in the Fall. I think, when I go back, that I'd like to go out in a rain storm and strip and feel the rain on my skin."

He stopped, feeling embarrassed. Klein's expression was encouraging. "And then I think I'd like to go downtown and just watch the shoppers on the sidewalks. Or maybe go to a burlesque house and smell the cheap perfume and the popcorn and the people sweating in the dark."

He studied his hands. "I think what I miss most is people—all kinds of people. Bad people and good people and fat people and thin people, and people I can't understand. People who wouldn't know an atom from an artichoke. And people who wouldn't give a damn. We're a quarter of a million miles from nowhere, Julius, and to make it literary, I think I miss my fellow man more than anything."

"Got a girl back home?" Klein asked almost casually.

"Yes."

"You're not like Dahl. You've never mentioned it."

"Same reason you didn't mention your wife. You get to thinking about it."

Klein flipped the lid on the specimen box. "Going to get married when you get back?"

Chapman was at the port again, staring out at the bleak landscape. "We hope to."

"Settle down in a small cottage and raise lots of little Chapmans, eh?"

Chapman nodded.

"That's the only future," Klein said.

He put away the box and came over to the port. Chapman moved over so they both could look out.

"Chap." Klein hesitated a moment. "What happened to Dixon?"

"He died," Chapman said. "He was a good kid, all wrapped up in science. Being on the Moon was the opportunity of a lifetime. He thought so much about it that he forgot a lot of little things—like how to stay alive. The day before the Second group came, he went out to finish some work he was interested in. He forgot to check for leaks and whether or not the valve on his tank was all the way closed. We couldn't get to him in time."

"He had his walkie-talkie with him?"

"Yes. It worked fine, too. We heard everything that went through his mind at the end."

Klein's face was blank. "What's your real job here, Chap? Why does somebody have to stay for stopover?"

"Hell, lots of reasons, Julius. You can't get a whole relief crew and let them take over cold. They have to know where you left off. They have to know where things are, how things work, what to watch out for. And then, because you've been here a year and a half and know the ropes, you have to watch them to see that they stay alive in spite of themselves. The Moon's a new environment and you have to learn how to live in it. There's a lot of things to learn—and some people just never learn."

"You're nursemaid, then."

"I suppose you could call it that."

*

Klein said, "You're not a scientist, are you?"

"No, you should know that. I came as the pilot of the first ship. We made the bunker out of parts of the ship so there wasn't anything to go back on. I'm a good mechanic and I made myself useful with the machinery. When it occurred to us that somebody was going to have to stay over, I volunteered. I thought the others were so important that it was better they should take their samples and data back to Earth when the first relief ship came."

"You wouldn't do it again, though, would you?"

"No, I wouldn't."

"Do you think Dahl will do as good a job as you've done here?"

Chapman frowned. "Frankly, I hadn't thought of that. I don't believe I care. I've put in my time; it's somebody else's turn now. He volunteered for it. I think I was fair in explaining all about the job when you talked it over among yourselves."

"You did, but I don't think Dahl's the man for it. He's too young, too much of a kid. He volunteered because he thought it made him look like a hero. He doesn't have the judgment that an older man would have. That you have."

Chapman turned slowly around and faced Klein.

"I'm not the indispensable man," he said slowly, "and even if I was, it wouldn't make any difference to me. I'm sorry if Dahl is young. So was I. I've lost three years up here. And I don't intend to lose any more."

Klein held up his hands. "Look, Chap, I didn't mean you should stay. I know how much you hate it and the time you put in up here. It's just—" His voice trailed away. "It's just that I think it's such a damn important job."

Klein had gone out in a last search for rock lichens and Chapman enjoyed one of his relatively few moments of privacy. He wandered over to his bunk and opened his barracks bag. He checked the underwear and his toothbrush and shaving kit for maybe the hundredth time and pushed the clothing down farther in the canvas. It was foolish because the bag was already packed and had been for a week. He remembered stalling it off for as long as he could and then the quiet satisfaction about a week before, when he had opened his small gear locker and transferred its meager belongings to the bag.

He hadn't actually needed to pack, of course. In less than twenty-four hours he'd be back on Earth where he could drown himself in toothpaste and buy more tee shirts than he could wear in a lifetime. He could leave behind his shorts and socks and the outsize shirts he had inherited from—who was it? Driesbach?—of the First group. Dahl could probably use them or maybe one of the boys in the Third.

*

But it wasn't like going home unless you packed. It was part of the ritual, like marking off the last three weeks in pencil on the gray steel of the bulkhead beside his hammock. Just a few hours ago, when he woke up, he had made the last check mark and signed his name and the date. His signature was right beneath Dixon's.

He frowned when he thought of Dixon and slid back the catch on the top of the bag and locked it. They should never have sent a kid like Dixon to the Moon.

He had just locked the bag when he heard the rumble of the airlock and the soft hiss of air. Somebody had come back earlier than expected. He watched the inner door swing open and the spacesuited figure clump in and unscrew its helmet.

Dahl. He had gone out to help Dowden on the Schmidt telescope. Maybe Dowden hadn't needed any help, with Bening along. Or more likely, considering the circumstances, Dahl wasn't much good at helping anybody today.

Dahl stripped off his suit. His face was covered with light beads of sweat and his eyes were frightened.

He moistened his lips slightly. "Do—do you think they'll ever have relief ships up here more often than every eighteen months, Chap? I mean, considering the advance of—"

"No," Chapman interrupted bluntly. "I don't. Not at least for ten years. The fuel's too expensive and the trip's too hazardous. On freight charges alone you're worth your weight in platinum when they send you here. Even if it becomes cheaper, Bob, it won't come about so it will shorten stopover right away." He stopped, feeling a little sorry for Dahl. "It won't be too bad. There'll be new men up here and you'll pass a lot of time getting to know them."

"Well, you see," Dahl started, "that's why I came back early. I wanted to see you about stopover. It's that—well, I'll put it this way." He seemed to be groping for an easy way to say what he wanted to. "I'm engaged back home. Really nice girl, Chap, you'd like her if you knew her." He fumbled in his pocket and found a photograph and put it on the desk. "That's a picture of Alice, taken at a picnic we were on together." Chapman didn't look. "She—we—expected to be married when I got back. I never told her about stopover, Chap. She thinks I'll be home tomorrow. I kept thinking, hoping, that maybe somehow—"

He was fumbling it badly, Chapman thought.

"You wanted to trade places with me, didn't you, Bob? You thought I might stay for stopover again, in your place?"

It hurt to look in Dahl's eyes. They were the eyes of a man who was trying desperately to stop what he was about to do, but just couldn't help himself.

"Well, yes, more or less. Oh, God, Chap, I know you want to go home! But I couldn't ask any of the others; you were the only one who could, the only one who was qualified!"

*

Dahl looked as though he was going to be sick. Chapman tried to recall all he knew about him. Dahl, Robert. Good mathematician. Graduate from one of the Ivy League schools. Father was a manufacturer of stoves or something.

It still didn't add, not quite. "You know I don't like it here any more than you do," Chapman said slowly. "I may have commitments at home, too. What made you think I would change my mind?"

Dahl took the plunge. "Well, you see," he started eagerly, too far gone to remember such a thing as pride, "you know my father's pretty well fixed. We would make it worth your while, Chap." He was feverish. "It would mean eighteen more months, Chap, but they'd be well-paid months!"

Chapman felt tired. The good feeling he had about going home was slowly evaporating.

"If you have any report to make, I think you had better get at it," he cut in, keeping all the harshness he felt out of his voice. "It'll be too late after the relief ship leaves. It'll be easier to give the captain your report than try to radio it back to Earth from here."

He felt sorrier for Dahl than he could ever remember having felt for anybody. Long after going home, Dahl would remember this.

It would eat at him like a cancer.

Cowardice is the one thing for which no man ever forgives himself.

*

Donley was eating a sandwich and looking out the port, so, naturally, he saw the ship first. "Well, whaddya know!" he shouted. "We got company!" He dashed for his suit. Dowden and Bening piled after him and all three started for the lock.

Chapman was standing in front of it. "Check your suits," he said softly. "Just be sure to check."

"Oh, what the hell, Chap!" Donley started angrily. Then he shut up and went over his suit. He got to his tank and turned white. Empty. It was only half a mile to the relief rocket, so somebody would probably have got to him in time, but.... He bit his lips and got a full tank.

Chapman and Klein watched them dash across the pumice, making the tremendous leaps they used to read about in the Sunday supplements. The port of the rocket had opened and tiny figures were climbing down the ladder. The small figures from the bunker reached them and did a short jig of welcome. Then the figures linked arms and started back. Chapman noticed one—it was probably Donley—pat the ship affectionately before he started back.

They were in the lock and the air pumped in and then they were in the bunker, taking off their suits. The newcomers were impressed and solemn, very much aware of the tremendous responsibility that rested on their shoulders. Like Donley and Klein and the members of the Second group had been when they had landed. Like Chapman had been in the First.

Donley and the others were all over them.

*

How was it back on Earth? Who had won the series? Was so-and-so still teaching at the university? What was the international situation?

Was the sky still blue, was the grass still green, did the leaves still turn color in the autumn, did people still love and cry and were there still people who didn't know what an atom was and didn't give a damn?

Chapman had gone through it all before. But was Ginny still Ginny?

Some of the men in the Third had their luggage with them. One of them—a husky, red-faced kid named Williams—was opening a box about a foot square and six inches deep. Chapman watched him curiously.

"Well, I'll be damned!" Klein said. "Hey, guys, look what we've got here!"

Chapman and the others crowded around and suddenly Donley leaned over and took a deep breath. In the box, covering a thick layer of ordinary dirt, was a plot of grass. They looked at it, awed. Klein put out his hand and laid it on top of the grass.

"I like the feel of it," he said simply.

Chapman cut off a single blade with his fingernail and put it between his lips. It had been years since he had seen grass and had the luxury of walking on it and lying on its cool thickness during those sultry summer nights when it was too hot to sleep indoors.

Williams blushed. "I thought we could spare a little water for it and maybe use the ultraviolet lamp on it some of the time. Couldn't help but bring it along; it seemed sort of like a symbol...." He looked embarrassed.

Chapman sympathized. If he had had any sense, he'd have tried to smuggle something like that up to the Moon instead of his phonograph.

"That's valuable grass," Dahl said sharply. "Do you realize that at current freight rates up here, it's worth about ten dollars a blade?"

Williams looked stricken and somebody said, "Oh, shut up, Dahl."

One of the men separated from the group and came over to Chapman. He held out his hand and said, "My name's Eberlein. Captain of the relief ship. I understand you're in charge here?"

Chapman nodded and shook hands. They hadn't had a captain on the First ship. Just a pilot and crew. Eberlein looked every inch a captain, too. Craggy face, gray hair, the firm chin of a man who was sure of himself.

"You might say I'm in charge here," Chapman said.

"Well, look, Mr. Chapman, is there any place where we can talk together privately?"

They walked over to one corner of the bunker. "This is about as private as we can get, captain," Chapman said. "What's on your mind?"

*

Eberlein found a packing crate and made himself comfortable. He looked at Chapman.

"I've always wanted to meet the man who's spent more time here than anybody else," he began.

"I'm sure you wanted to see me for more reasons than just curiosity."

Eberlein took out a pack of cigarets. "Mind if I smoke?"

Chapman jerked a thumb toward Dahl. "Ask him. He's in charge now."

The captain didn't bother. He put the pack away. "You know we have big plans for the station," he said.

"I hadn't heard of them."

"Oh, yes, *big plans*. They're working on unmanned, open-side rockets now that could carry cargo and sheet steel for more bunkers like this. Enable us to enlarge the unit, have a series of bunkers all linked together. Make good laboratories and living quarters for you people." His eyes swept the room. "Have a little privacy for a change."

Chapman nodded. "They could use a little privacy up here."

The captain noticed the pronoun. "Well, that's one of the reasons why I wanted to talk to you, Chapman. The Commission talked it over and they'd like to see you stay. They feel if they're going to enlarge it, add more bunkers and have more men up here, that a man of practical experience should be running things. They figure that you're the only man who's capable and who's had the experience."

The captain vaguely felt the approach was all wrong.

"Is that all?"

Eberlein was ill at ease. "Naturally you'd be paid well. I don't imagine any man would like being here all the time. They're prepared to double your salary—maybe even a bonus in addition—and let you have full charge. You'd be Director of the Luna Laboratories."

All this and a title too, Chapman thought.

"That's it?" Chapman asked.

Eberlein frowned. "Well, the Commission said they'd be willing to consider anything else you had in mind, if it was more money or...."

"The answer is no," Chapman said. "I'm not interested in more money for staying because I'm not interested in staying. Money can't buy it, captain. I'm sorry, but I'm afraid that you'd have to stay up here to appreciate that.

"Bob Dahl is staying for stopover. If there's something important about the project or impending changes, perhaps you'd better tell him before you go."

He walked away.

*

Chapman held the letter in both hands, but the paper still shook. The others had left the bunker, the men of the Second taking those of the Third in hand to show them the machinery and apparatus that was outside, point out the deadly blisters underneath the pumice covering, and show them how to keep out of the Sun and how to watch their air supply.

He was glad he was alone. He felt something trickle down his face and tasted salt on his lips.

The mail had been distributed and he had saved his latest letter until the others had left so he could read it in privacy. It was a short letter, very short.

It started: "Dear Joel: This isn't going to be a nice letter, but I thought it best that you should know before you came home."

There was more to it, but he hadn't even needed to read it to know what it said. It wasn't original, of course. Women who change their minds weren't exactly an innovation, either.

He crumpled the paper and held a match to it and watched it burn on the steel floor.

Three years had been a long time. It was too long a time to keep loving a man who was a quarter of a million miles away. She could look up in the night sky when she was out with somebody else now and tell him how she had once been engaged to the Man in the Moon.

It would make good conversation. It would be funny. A joke.

He got up and walked over to his phonograph and put the record on. The somewhat scratchy voice sang as if nothing had happened

Way Back Home by Al Lewis.

The record caught and started repeating the last line.

He hadn't actually wanted to play it. It had been an automatic response. He had played it lots of times before when he had thought of Earth. Of going home.

He crossed over and threw the record across the bunker and watched it shatter on the steel wall and the pieces fall to the floor.

The others came back in the bunker and the men of the Second started grabbing their bags and few belongings and getting ready to leave. Dahl sat in a corner, a peculiar expression on his face. He looked as if he wanted to cry and yet still felt that the occasion was one for rejoicing.

Chapman walked over to him. "Get your stuff and leave with the others, Dahl." His voice was quiet and hard.

Dahl looked up, opened his mouth to say something, and then shut up. Donley and Bening and Dowden were already in the airlock, ready to leave. Klein caught the conversation and came over. He gripped Chapman's arm.

"What the hell's going on, Chap? Get your bag and let's go. I know just the bistro to throw a whing-ding when we get—"

"I'm not going back," Chapman said.

Klein looked annoyed, not believing him. "Come on, what's the matter with you? You suddenly decide you don't like the blue sky and trees and stuff? Let's go!"

The men in the lock were looking at them questioningly. Some members of the Third looked embarrassed, like outsiders caught in a family argument.

"Look, Julius, I'm not going back," Chapman repeated dully. "I haven't anything to go back for."

"You're doing a much braver thing than you may think," a voice cut in. It belonged to Eberlein.

Chapman looked at him. Eberlein flushed, then turned and walked-stiffly to the lock to join the others.

Just before the inner door of the lock shut, they could hear Chapman, his hands on his hips, breaking in the Third on how to be happy and stay healthy on the Moon. His voice was ragged and strained and sounded like a top-sergeant's.

*

Dahl and Eberlein stood in the outer port of the relief ship, staring back at the research bunker. It was half hidden in the shadows of a rocky overhang that protected it from meteorites.

"They kidded him a lot this morning," Dahl said. "They said he had found a home on the Moon."

"If we had stayed an hour or so more, he might have changed his mind and left, after all," Eberlein mused, his face a thoughtful mask behind his air helmet.

"I offered him money," Dahl said painfully. "I was a coward and I offered him money to stay in my place." His face was bitter and full of disgust for himself.

Eberlein turned to him quickly and automatically told him the right thing. "We're all cowards once in a while," he said earnestly. "But your offer of money had nothing to do with his staying. He stayed because he had to stay, because we made him stay."

"I don't understand," Dahl said.

"Chapman had a lot to go home for. He was engaged to be married." Dahl winced. "We got her to write him a letter breaking it off. We knew it meant that he lost one of his main reasons for wanting to go back. I think, perhaps, that he still would have left if we had stayed and argued him into going. But we left before he could change his mind."

"That—was a lousy thing to do!"

"We had no choice. We didn't use it except as a last resort."

"I don't know of any girl who would have done such a thing, no matter what your reasons, if she was in love with a guy like Chapman," Dahl said.

"There was only one who would have," Eberlein agreed. "Ginny Dixon. She understood what we were trying to tell her. She had to; her brother had died up here."

"Why was Chapman so important?" Dahl burst out. "What could he have done that I couldn't have done—would have done if I had had any guts?"

"Perhaps you could have," Eberlein said. "But I doubt it. I don't think there were many men who could have. And we couldn't take the chance. Chapman knows how to live on the Moon. He's like a trapper who's spent all his time in the forests and knows it like the palm of his hand. He never makes mistakes, he never fails to check things. And he isn't a scientist. He would never become so preoccupied with research that he'd fail to make checks. And he can watch out for those who do make mistakes. Ginny understood that all too well."

"How did you know all this about Chapman?" Dahl asked.

"The men in the First told us some of it. And we had our own observer with you here. Bening kept us pretty well informed."

*

Eberlein stared at the bunker thoughtfully.

"It costs a lot of money to send ships up here and establish a colony. It will cost a lot to expand it. And with that kind of investment, you don't take chances. You have to have the best men for the job. You get them even if they don't want to do it."

He gestured at the small, blotchy globe of blue and green that was the Earth, riding high in the black sky.

"You remember what it was like five years ago, Dahl? Nations at each other's throats, re-arming to the teeth? It isn't that way now. We've got the one lead that nobody can duplicate or catch up on. Nobody has our technical background. I know, this isn't a military base. But it could become one."

He paused.

"But these aren't even the most important reasons, Dahl. We're at the beginnings of space travel, the first bare, feeble start. If this base on the Moon succeeds, the whole human race will be Outward Bound." He waved at the stars. "You have your choice—a frontier that lies in the stars, or a psychotic little world that tries and fails and spends its time and talents trying to find better methods of suicide.

"With a choice like that, Dahl, you can't let it fail. And personal lives and viewpoints are expendable. But it's got to be that way. There's too much at stake."

Eberlein hesitated a moment and when he started again, it was on a different track. "You're an odd bunch of guys, you and the others in the groups, Dahl. Damn few of you come up for the glamor, I know. None of you like it and none of you are really enthusiastic about it. You were all reluctant to come in the first place, for the most part. You're a bunch of pretty reluctant heroes, Dahl."

The captain nodded soberly at the bunker. "I, personally, don't feel happy about that. I don't like having to mess up other people's lives. I hope I won't have to again. Maybe somehow, someway, this one can be patched up. We'll try to."

He started the mechanism that closed the port of the rocket. His face was a study of regret and helplessness. He was thinking of a future that, despite what he had told Dahl, wasn't quite real to him.

"I feel like a cheap son of a bitch," Eberlein said.

*

The very young man said, "Do they actually care where they send us? Do they actually care what we think?"

The older man got up and walked to the window. The bunkers and towers and squat buildings of the research colony glinted in the sunlight. The colony had come a long way; it housed several thousands now.

The Sun was just rising for the long morning and farther down shadows stabbed across the crater floor. Tycho was by far the most beautiful of the craters, he thought.

It was nice to know that the very young man was going to miss it. It had taken the older man quite a long time to get to like it. But that was to be expected—he hadn't been on the Moon.

"I would say so," he said. "They were cruel, that way, at the start. But then they had to be. The goal was too important. And they made up for it as soon as they

could. It didn't take them too long to remember the men who had traded their future for the stars."

The very young man said, "Did you actually think of it that way when you first came up here?"

The older man thought for a minute. "No," he admitted. "No, we didn't. Most of us were strictly play-for-pay men. The Commission wanted men who wouldn't fall apart when the glamor wore off and there was nothing left but privation and hard work and loneliness. The men who fell for the glamor were all right for quick trips, but not for an eighteen-month stay in a research bunker. So the Commission offered high salaries and we reluctantly took the jobs. Oh, there was the idea behind the project, the vision the Commission had in mind. But it took a while for that to grow."

A woman came in the room just then, bearing a tray with glasses on it. The older man took one and said, "Your mother and I were notified yesterday that you had been chosen to go. We would like to see you go, but of course the final decision is up to you."

He sipped his drink and turned to his wife: "It has its privations, but in the long run we've never regretted it, have we, Ginny?"

KREATIVITY FOR KATS

By Fritz Leiber

They are the aliens among us—and their ways and wonders are stranger than extraterrestrials!

*

Gummitch peered thoughtfully at the molten silver image of the sun in his little bowl of water on the floor inside the kitchen window. He knew from experience that it would make dark ghost suns swim in front of his eyes for a few moments, and that was mildly interesting. Then he slowly thrust his head out over the water, careful not to ruffle its surface by rough breathing, and stared down at the mirror cat—the Gummitch Double—staring up at him.

Gummitch had early discovered that water mirrors are very different from most glass mirrors. The scentless spirit world behind glass mirrors is an upright one sharing our gravity system, its floor a continuation of the floor in the so-called real world. But the world in a water mirror has reverse gravity. One looks down into it, but the spirit-doubles in it look *up* at one. In a way water mirrors are holes or pits in the world, leading down to a spirit infinity or ghostly nadir.

Gummitch had pondered as to whether, if he plunged into such a pit, he would be sustained by the spirit gravity or fall forever. (It may well be that speculations of this sort account for the caution about swimming characteristic of most cats.)

There was at least one exception to the general rule. The looking glass on Kitty-Come-Here's dressing table also opened into a spirit world of reverse gravity, as Gummitch had discovered when he happened to look into it during one of the regular visits he made to the dressing table top, to enjoy the delightful flowery and musky odors emanating from the fragile bottles assembled there.

But exceptions to general rules, as Gummitch knew well, are only doorways to further knowledge and finer classifications. The wind could not get into the spirit world below Kitty-Come-Here's looking glass, while one of the definitive characteristics of water mirrors is that movement can very easily enter the spirit world below them, rhythmically disturbing it throughout, producing the most surreal effects, and even reducing it to chaos. Such disturbances exist only in the spirit world and are in no way a mirroring of anything in the real world: Gummitch knew that his paw did not change when it flicked the surface of the water, although the image of his paw burst into a hundred flickering fragments. (Both cats and primitive men first deduced that the world in a water mirror is a spirit world because they saw that its inhabitants were easily blown apart by the wind and must therefore be highly tenuous, though capable of regeneration.)

Gummitch mildly enjoyed creating rhythmic disturbances in the spirit worlds below water mirrors. He wished there were some way to bring their excitement and weird beauty into the real world.

*

On this sunny day when our story begins, the spirit world below the water mirror in his drinking bowl was particularly vivid and bright. Gummitch stared for a while longer at the Gummitch Double and then thrust down his tongue to quench his thirst. Curling swiftly upward, it conveyed a splash of water into his mouth and also flicked a single drop of water into the air before his nose. The sun struck the drop and it flashed like a diamond. In fact, it seemed to Gummitch that for a moment he had juggled the sun on his tongue. He shook his head amazedly and touched the side of the bowl with his paw. The bowl was brimful and a few drops fell out; they also flashed like tiny suns as they fell. Gummitch had a fleeting vision, a momentary creative impulse, that was gone from his mind before he could seize it. He shook his head once more, backed away from the bowl, and then lay down with his head pillowed on his paws to contemplate the matter. The room darkened as the sun went under a cloud and the young golden dark-barred cat looked like a pool of sunlight left behind.

Kitty-Come-Here had watched the whole performance from the door to the dining room and that evening she commented on it to Old Horsemeat.

"He backed away from the water as if it were poison," she said. "They have been putting more chlorine in it lately, you know, and maybe he can taste the fluorides they put in for dental decay."

Old Horsemeat doubted that, but his wife went on, "I can't figure out where Gummitch does his drinking these days. There never seems to be any water gone from his bowl. And we haven't had any cut flowers. And none of the faucets drip."

"He probably does his drinking somewhere outside," Old Horsemeat guessed.

"But he doesn't go outside very often these days," Kitty-Come-Here countered. "Scarface and the Mad Eunuch, you know. Besides, it hasn't rained for weeks. It's certainly a mystery to me where he gets his liquids. Boiling gets the chlorine out of water, doesn't it? I think I'll try him on some tomorrow."

"Maybe he's depressed," Old Horsemeat suggested. "That often leads to secret drinking."

This baroque witticism hit fairly close to the truth. Gummitch *was* depressed—had been depressed ever since he had lost his kittenish dreams of turning into a man, achieving spaceflight, learning and publishing all the secrets of the fourth dimension, and similar marvels. The black cloud of disillusionment at realizing he could only be a cat had lightened somewhat, but he was still feeling dull and unfulfilled.

Gummitch was at that difficult age for he-cats, between First Puberty, when the cat achieves essential maleness, and Second Puberty, when he gets broad-chested, jowly and thick-ruffed, becoming a fully armed sexual competitor. In the ordinary course of things he would have been spending much of his time exploring the outer world, detail-mapping the immediate vicinity, spying on other cats, making cautious approaches to unescorted females and in all ways comporting himself like a fledgling male. But this was prevented by the two burly toms who lived in the houses next door and who, far more interested in murder than the pursuit of mates, had entered into partnership with the sole object of bushwacking Gummitch. Gummitch's household had nicknamed them Scarface and the Mad Eunuch, the latter being one of those males whom "fixing" turns, not placid, but homicidally maniacal. Compared to these seasoned heavyweights, Gummitch was a welterweight at most. Scarface and the Mad Eunuch lay in wait for him by turns just beyond the kitchen door, so that his forays into the outside world were largely reduced to dashes for some hiding hole, followed by long, boring but perilous sieges.

He often wished that old Horsemeat's two older cats, Ashurbanipal and Cleopatra, had not gone to the country to live with Old Horsemeat's mother. They would have shown the evil bushwackers a thing or two!

*

Because of Scarface and the Mad Eunuch, Gummitch spent most of his time indoors. Since a cat is made for a half-and-half existence—half in the wild forest, half in the secure cave—he took to brooding quite morbidly. He thought over-much of ghost cats in the mirror world and of the Skeleton Cat who starved to death in a locked closet and similar grisly legends. He immersed himself in racial memories, not so much of Ancient Egypt where cats were prized as minions of the lovely cat-goddess Bast and ceremoniously mummified at the end of tranquil lives, as of the Middle Ages, when European mankind waged a genocidal war against felines as being the familiars of witches. (He thought briefly of turning Kitty-Come-Here into a witch, but his hypnotic staring and tentative ritualistic mewing only made her fidgety.) And he devoted more and more time to devising dark versions of the theory of transmigration, picturing cats as Silent Souls, Gagged People of Great Talent, and the like.

He had become too self-conscious to re-enter often the make-believe world of the kitten, yet his imagination remained as active as ever. It was a truly frustrating predicament.

More and more often and for longer periods he retired to meditate in a corrugated cardboard shoebox, open only at one end. The cramped quarters made it easier for him to think. Old Horsemeat called it the Cat Orgone Box after the famed Orgone Energy Accumulators of the late wildcat psychoanalyst Dr. Wilhelm Reich.

If only, Gummitch thought, he could devise some way of objectifying the intimations of beauty that flitted through his darkly clouded mind! Now, on the evening of the sunny day when he had backed away from his water bowl, he attacked the problem anew. He knew he had been fleetingly on the verge of a great idea, an idea involving water, light and movement. An idea he had unfortunately forgotten. He closed his eyes and twitched his nose. I must concentrate, he thought to himself, concentrate....

*

Next day Kitty-Come-Here remembered her idea about Gummitch's water. She boiled two cupfuls in a spotless enamelware saucepan, letting it cool for half an hour before using it to replace the seemingly offensive water in the young cat's bowl. It was only then she noticed that the bowl had been upset.

She casually assumed that big-footed Old Horsemeat must have been responsible for the accident, or possibly one of the two children—darting Sissy or blundering Baby. She wiped the bowl and filled it with the water she had dechlorinated.

"Come here, Kitty, come here," she called to Gummitch, who had been watching her actions attentively from the dining room door. The young cat stayed where he was. "Oh, well, if you want to be coy," she said, shrugging her shoulders.

There was a mystery about the spilled water. It had apparently disappeared entirely, though the day seemed hardly dry enough for total evaporation. Then she saw it standing in a puddle by the wall fully ten feet away from the bowl. She made a quick deduction and frowned a bit worriedly.

"I never realized the kitchen floor sloped *that* much," she told Old Horsemeat after dinner. "Maybe some beams need to be jacked up in the basement. I'd hate to think of collapsing into it while I cooked dinner."

"I'm sure this house finished all its settling thirty years ago," her husband assured her hurriedly. "That slope's always been there."

"Well, if you say so," Kitty-Come-Here allowed doubtfully.

Next day she found Gummitch's bowl upset again and the remains of the boiled water in a puddle across the room. As she mopped it up, she began to do some thinking without benefit of Concentration Box.

*

That evening, after Old Horsemeat and Sissy had vehemently denied kicking into the water bowl or stepping on its edge, she voiced her conclusions. "I think *Gummitch* upsets it," she said. "He's rejecting it. It still doesn't taste right to him and he wants to show us."

"Maybe he only likes it after it's run across the floor and got seasoned with household dust and the corpses of germs," suggested Old Horsemeat, who believed most cats were bohemian types.

"I'll have you know I *scrub* that linoleum," Kitty-Come-Here asserted.

"Well, with detergent and scouring powder, then," Old Horsemeat amended resourcefully.

Kitty-Come-Here made a scornful noise. "I still want to know where he gets his liquids," she said. "He's been off milk for weeks, you know, and he only drinks a little broth when I give him that. Yet he doesn't seem dehydrated. It's a real mystery and—"

"Maybe he's built a still in the attic," Old Horsemeat interjected.

"—and I'm going to find the answers," Kitty-Come-Here concluded, ignoring the facetious interruption. "I'm going to find out *where* he gets the water he does drink and *why* he rejects the water I give him. This time I'm going to boil it and put in a pinch of salt. Just a pinch."

"You make animals sound more delicate about food and drink than humans," Old Horsemeat observed.

"They probably are," his wife countered. "For one thing they don't smoke, or drink Martinis. It's my firm belief that animals—cats, anyway—like good food just as much as we do. And the same sort of good food. They don't enjoy canned catfood any more than we would, though they *can* eat it. Just as we could if we had to. I really don't think Gummitch would have such a passion for raw horsemeat except you started him on it so early."

"He probably thinks of it as steak tartare," Old Horsemeat said.

Next day Kitty-Come-Here found her salted offering upset just as the two previous bowls had been.

*

Such were the beginnings of the Great Spilled Water Mystery that preoccupied the human members of the Gummitch household for weeks. Not every day, but frequently, and sometimes two and three times a day, Gummitch's little bowl was upset. No one ever saw the young cat do it. But it was generally accepted that he was responsible, though for a time Old Horsemeat had theories that he did not voice involving Sissy and Baby.

Kitty-Come-Here bought Gummitch a firm-footed rubber bowl for his water, though she hesitated over the purchase for some time, certain he would be able to taste the rubber. This bowl was found upset just like his regular china one and like the tin one she briefly revived from his kitten days.

All sorts of clues and possibly related circumstances were seized upon and dissected. For instance, after about a month of the mysterious spillings, Kitty-Come-Here announced, "I've been thinking back and as far as I can remember it never happens except on sunny days."

"Oh, Good Lord!" Old Horsemeat reacted.

Meanwhile Kitty-Come-Here continued to try to concoct a kind of water that would be palatable to Gummitch. As she continued without success, her formulas became more fantastic. She quit boiling it for the most part but added a pinch of sugar, a spoonful of beer, a few flakes of oregano, a green leaf, a violet, a drop of vanilla extract, a drop of iodine....

"No wonder he rejects the stuff," Old Horsemeat was tempted to say, but didn't.

Finally Kitty-Come-Here, inspired by the sight of a greenly glittering rack of it at the supermarket, purchased a half gallon of bottled water from a famous spring. She wondered why she hadn't thought of this step earlier—it certainly ought to take care of her haunting convictions about the unpalatableness of chlorine or fluorides. (She herself could distinctly taste the fluorides in the tap water, though she never mentioned this to Old Horsemeat.)

One other development during the Great Spilled Water Mystery was that Gummitch gradually emerged from depression and became quite gay. He took to dancing cat schottisches and gigues impromptu in the living room of an evening and so forgot his dignity as to battle joyously with the vacuum-cleaner dragon when Old Horsemeat used one of the smaller attachments to curry him; the young cat clutched the hairy round brush to his stomach and madly clawed it as it *whuffled* menacingly. Even the afternoon he came home with a shoulder gashed by the Mad Eunuch he seemed strangely light-hearted and debonair.

*

The Mystery was abruptly solved one sunny Sunday afternoon. Going into the bathroom in her stocking feet, Kitty-Come-Here saw Gummitch apparently trying to drown himself in the toilet. His hindquarters were on the seat but the rest of his body went down into the bowl. Coming closer, she saw that his forelegs were braced against the opposite side of the bowl, just above the water surface, while his head thrust down sharply between his shoulders. She could distinctly hear rhythmic lapping.

To tell the truth, Kitty-Come-Here was rather shocked. She had certain rather fixed ideas about the delicacy of cats. It speaks well for her progressive grounding that she did not shout at Gummitch but softly summoned her husband.

By the time Old Horsemeat arrived the young cat had refreshed himself and was coming out of his "well" with a sudden backward undulation. He passed them in the doorway with a single mew and upward look and then made off for the kitchen.

The blue and white room was bright with sunlight. Outside the sky was blue and the leaves were rustling in a stiff breeze. Gummitch looked back once, as if to make sure his human congeners had followed, mewed again, and then advanced briskly toward his little bowl with the air of one who proposes to reveal all mysteries at once.

Kitty-Come-Here had almost outdone herself. She had for the first time poured him the bottled water, and she had floated a few rose petals on the surface.

Gummitch regarded them carefully, sniffed at them, and then proceeded to fish them out one by one and shake them off his paw. Old Horsemeat repressed the urge to say, "I told you so."

When the water surface was completely free and winking in the sunlight, Gummitch curved one paw under the side of the bowl and jerked.

Half the water spilled out, gathered itself, and then began to flow across the floor in little rushes, a silver ribbon sparkling with sunlight that divided and subdivided and reunited as it followed the slope. Gummitch crouched to one side, watching it intensely, following its progress inch by inch and foot by foot, almost pouncing on the little temporary pools that formed, but not quite touching them. Twice he mewed faintly in excitement.

*

"He's *playing* with it," Old Horsemeat said incredulously.

"No," Kitty-Come-Here countered wide-eyed, "he's *creating* something. Silver mice. Water-snakes. Twinkling vines."

"Good Lord, you're right," Old Horsemeat agreed. "It's a new art form. Would you call it water painting? Or water sculpture? Somehow I think that's best. As if a sculptor made mobiles out of molten tin."

"It's gone so quickly, though," Kitty-Come-Here objected, a little sadly. "Art ought to last. Look, it's almost all flowed over to the wall now."

"Some of the best art forms are completely fugitive," Old Horsemeat argued. "What about improvisation in music and dancing? What about jam sessions and shadow figures on the wall? Gummitch can always do it again—in fact, he must have been doing it again and again this last month. It's never exactly the same, like waves or fires. But it's beautiful."

"I suppose so," Kitty-Come-Here said. Then coming to herself, she continued, "But I don't think it can be healthy for him to go on drinking water out of the toilet. Really."

Old Horsemeat shrugged. He had an insight about the artistic temperament and the need to dig for inspiration into the smelly fundamentals of life, but it was difficult to express delicately.

Kitty-Come-Here sighed, as if bidding farewell to all her efforts with rose petals and crystalline bottled purity and vanilla extract and the soda water which had amazed Gummitch by faintly spitting and purring at him.

"Oh, well," she said, "I can scrub it out more often, I suppose."

Meanwhile, Gummitch had gone back to his bowl and, using both paws, overset it completely. Now, nose a-twitch, he once more pursued the silver streams alive with suns, refreshing his spirit with the sight of them. He was fretted by no problems about what he was doing. He had solved them all with one of his characteristically sharp distinctions: there was the *sacred* water, the sparklingly clear water to create with, and there was the water with character, the water to *drink*.

PERFECT ANSWER

By L. J. Stecher, Jr.

Getting there may be half the fun ... but it is also all of a society's chance of survival!

*

"As one god to another—let's go home," Jack Bates said.

Bill Farnum raised a space-gloved hand in negligent acknowledgment to a hastily kneeling native, and shook his head at Bates. "Let's try Deneb—it's almost in line on the way back—and then we can call it quits."

"But I want to get back and start making some profit out of this. The Galaxy is full of *Homo sapiens*. We've hit the jackpot first trip out. Let's hurry on home and cash in."

"We need more information. This is too much of a good thing—it doesn't make sense. I know there isn't much chance of finding anything out by stopping at one more solar system. But it won't delay us more than a few weeks, and it won't hurt to try."

"Yeah," said Bates. "But what's in it for us? And what if we find an inhabited planet? You know the chances are about two to one that we will. That'll make thirteen we've found on this trip. Why risk bad luck?"

"You're no more superstitious than I am," said Farnum. "You just want to get back Earthside. I'll tell you what. We'll toss a coin for it."

Bates gestured futilely toward his coverall pocket, and then remembered he was wearing a spacesuit as a precaution against possible contamination from the natives.

"And we'll use one of *my* coins this time," said Farnum, noticing the automatic motion. "I want to have a chance."

The coin dropped in Farnum's favor, and their two-man scout ship hurled itself into space.

*

Farnum operated the compact computer, aligning the ship's velocity vector precisely while the stars could still be seen. Bates controlled the engines, metering their ravenous demand for power just this side of destructive detonation, while the ship sucked energy from space—from the adjacent universe on the other side of Limbo. Finally the computer chimed, relays snicked, and the ship slid into the emptiness of Limbo as the stars winked out.

With two trained men working as a team with the computer and the elaborate engine room controls, and with a certain amount of luck, the ship would drop back into normal space a couple of weeks later, close beside their target.

"Well, that's that," said Farnum, relaxing and wiping the perspiration off his forehead. "We're back once again in the nothingness of nowhere. As I recall, it's your week for K.P. Where's the coffee?"

"Coming right up," said Bates. "But you won't like it. It's the last of the 'God-food' the Korite priests made for us."

Farnum shuddered. "Pour it out and make some fresh. With a skillet, you stink, but you're a thousand times better than Korites."

"Thanks," Bates said, getting busy. "It was the third place we stopped that they were such good cooks, wasn't it?"

"Nope. Our third stop was the Porandians. They tried to kill us—called us 'Devil spawn from the stars.' You're thinking of the fourth stop; the Balanites."

Bates shrugged. "It's kind of hard to keep them all straight. Either they fall on their knees and worship us, or they try to kill us without even asking questions. Maybe it's lucky they're all so primitive."

"It may be lucky, but it doesn't add up. More than half the stars we visit have planets that can support human life. And every one that can does. Once there must have been an interstellar empire. So why are all their civilizations so backward? They aren't primitive—they're decadent. And why do they all have such strong feelings—one way or the exact opposite—about people from the stars?"

"Isn't that why you want to try one more system?" asked Bates. "To give us another chance to get some answers? Here's your coffee. Try to drink it quietly. I'm going to get some shuteye."

*

The trip through the Limbo between adjacent universes passed uneventfully, as always. The computer chimed again on schedule, and a quick check by Farnum showed the blazing sun that suddenly appeared was Deneb, as advertised. Seventeen planets could be counted, and the fifth seemed to be Earth type. They approached it with the easy skill of long practice and swung into orbit about it.

"This is what we've been looking for!" exclaimed Farnum, examining the planet through a telescope. "They've got big cities and dams and bridges—they're civilized. Let's put the ship down."

"Wait up," said Bates. "What if they've got starman-phobia? Remember, they're people, just like us; and with people, civilization and weapons go together."

"I think you've got it backwards. If they hate us, we can probably get away before they bring up their big artillery. But what if they love us? They might want to keep us beside them forever."

Bates nodded. "I'm glad you agree with me. Let's get out of here. Nobody but us knows of the beautiful, profitable planets we've found, all ready to become part of a Terran Empire. And if we don't get back safe and sound, nobody *will* know. The information we've got is worth a fortune to us, and I want to be alive to collect it."

"Sure. But we've got the job of trying to find out why all those planets reverted to barbarism. This one hasn't; maybe the answer's here. There's no use setting up an empire if it won't last."

"It'll last long enough to keep you and me on top of the heap."

"That's not good enough. I want my kids—when I have them—to have their chances at the top of the heap too."

"Oh, all right. We'll flip a coin, then."

"We already did. You may be a sharp dealer, but you'd never welch on a bet. We're going down."

Bates shrugged. "You win. Let's put her down beside that big city over there—the biggest one, by the seashore."

As they approached the city, they noticed at its outskirts a large flat plain, dotted with gantries. "Like a spaceport," suggested Bill. "That's our target."

They landed neatly on the tarmac and then sat there quietly, waiting to see what would happen.

*

A crowd began to form. The two men sat tensely at their controls, but the throng clustering about the base of the ship showed no hostility. They also showed no reverence but, rather, a carefree interest and joyful welcome.

"Well," said Farnum at last, "looks like we might as well go outside and ask them to take us to their leader."

"I'm with you as usual," said Bates, starting to climb into his spacesuit. "Weapons?"

"I don't think so. We can't stop them if they get mad at us, and they look friendly enough. We'll start off with the 'let's be pals' routine."

Bates nodded. "After we learn the language. I always hate this part—it moves so slowly. You'd think there'd be some similarity among the tongues on different planets, wouldn't you? But each one's entirely different. I guess they've all been isolated too long."

The two men stepped out on the smooth plain, to be instantly surrounded by a laughing, chattering crowd. Farnum stared around in bewilderment at the variety of dress the crowd displayed. There were men and women in togas, in tunics, in draped dresses and kilts, in trousers and coats. Others considered a light cloak thrown over the shoulders to be adequate. There was no uniformity of style or custom.

"You pick me a boss-man out of this bunch," he muttered to Bates.

Finally a couple of young men, glowing with health and energy, came bustling through the crowd with an oblong box which they set down in front of the Earthmen. They pointed to the box and then back at Farnum and Bates, laughing and talking as they did so.

"What do you suppose they want us to do?" Farnum asked.

One of the young men clapped his hands happily and reached down to touch the box. "What do you suppose they want us to do?" asked the box distinctly.

"Oh. A recording machine. Probably to help with language lessons. Might as well help them out."

*

Farnum and Bates took turns talking at the box for half an hour. Then the young man nodded, laughed, clapped his hands again, and the two men carried it away. The crowd went with them, waving merrily as they departed.

Bates shrugged his shoulders and went back into the ship, with Farnum close behind.

A few hours after sunrise the following morning, the crowd returned, as gay and carefree as before, led by the two young men who had carried the box. Each of these two now had a small case, about the size of a camera, slung by a strap across one brawny shoulder.

As the terrestrials climbed out to meet them, the two men raised their hands and the crowd discontinued its chatter, falling silent except for an occasional tinkle of surprised laughter.

"Welcome," said the first young man clearly. "It is a great pleasure for us to have our spaceport in use again. It has been many generations since any ships have landed on it."

Farnum noticed that the voice came from the box. "Thank you for your very kind welcome," he said. "I hope that your traffic will soon increase. May we congratulate you, by the way, on the efficiency of your translators?"

"Thanks," laughed the young man. "But there was nothing to it. We just asked the Oracle and he told us what we had to do to make them."

"May we meet your—Oracle?"

"Oh, sure, if you want to. But later on. Now it's time for a party. Why don't you take off those clumsy suits and come along?"

"We don't dare remove our spacesuits. They protect us from any disease germs you may have, and you from any we may have. We probably have no resistance to each others' ailments."

"The Oracle says we have nothing that will hurt you. And we're going to spray you with this as soon as you get out of your suits. Then you won't hurt any of us." He held up a small atomizer.

Farnum glanced at Bates, who shrugged and nodded. They uneasily unfastened their spacesuits and stepped out of them, wearing only their light one-piece coveralls, and got sprayed with a pleasant-smelling mist.

The party was a great success. The food was varied and delicious. The liquors were sparkling and stimulating, without unpleasant after-effects. The women were uninhibited.

When a native got tired, he just dropped down onto the soft grass, or onto an even softer couch, and went to sleep. The Earthmen finally did the same.

*

They awoke the following morning within minutes of each other, feeling comfortable and relaxed. Bates shook his head experimentally. "No hangover," he muttered in surprise.

"No one ever feels bad after a party," said one of their guides, who had slept nearby. "The Oracle told us what to do, when we asked him."

"Quite a fellow, your Oracle," commented Bates. "Does he answer you in riddles, like most Oracles?"

The guide was shocked. "The Oracle answers any questions promptly and completely. He *never* talks in riddles."

"Can we go to see him now?" asked Farnum.

"Certainly. Come along. I'll take you to the Hall of the Oracle."

The Oracle appeared to live in a building of modest size, in the center of a tremendous courtyard. The structure that surrounded the courtyard, in contrast, was enormous and elaborate, dominating the wildly architectured city. It was, however, empty.

"Scholars used to live in this building, they tell me," said one of their guides, gesturing casually. "They used to come here to learn from the Oracle. But there's no sense in learning a lot of stuff when the Oracle has always got all the answers anyway. So now the building is empty. The big palace was built back in the days when we used to travel among the stars, as you do now."

"How long ago was that?" asked Farnum.

"Oh, I don't know. A few thousand years—a few hundred years—the Oracle can tell you if you really want to know."

Bates raised an eyebrow. "And how do you know you'll always be given the straight dope?"

The guide looked indignant. "The Oracle *always* tells the truth."

"Yes," Bates persisted, "but how do you *know?*"

"The Oracle told us so, of course. Now why don't you go in and find out for yourselves? We'll wait out here. We don't have anything to ask him."

*

Bates and Farnum went into the building and found themselves in a small, pleasant room furnished with comfortable chairs and sofas.

"Good morning," said a well-modulated voice. "I have been expecting you."

"You are the Oracle?" asked Farnum, looking around curiously.

"The name that the people of this planet have given me translates most accurately as 'Oracle'," said the voice.

"But are you actually an Oracle?"

"My principal function, insofar as human beings—that is, *Homo sapiens*—are concerned, is to give accurate answers to all questions propounded me. Therefore, insofar as humans are concerned, I am actually an Oracle."

"Then you have another function?"

"My principal function, insofar as the race that made me is concerned, is to act as a weapon."

"Oh," said Bates. "Then you are a machine?"

"I am a machine," agreed the voice.

"The people who brought us here said that you always tell them the truth. I suppose that applies when you are acting as an Oracle, instead of as a weapon?"

"On the contrary," said the voice blandly. "I function as a weapon by telling the truth."

"That doesn't make sense," protested Bates.

The machine paused for a moment before replying. "This will take a little time, gentlemen," it said, "but I am sure that I can convince you. Why don't you sit down and be comfortable? If you want refreshments, just ask for them."

"Might as well," said Bates, sitting down in an easy chair. "How about giving us some Korite God-food?"

"If you really want that bad a brew of coffee, I can make it for you, of course," said the voice, "but I am sure you would prefer some of better quality."

Farnum laughed. "Yes, please. Some good coffee, if you don't mind."

*

"Now," said the Oracle, after excellent coffee had been produced, "it is necessary for me to go back into history a few hundred thousand of your years. At that time, the people who made me entered this galaxy on one of their periodic visits of routine exploration, and contacted your ancestors. The race that constructed me populates now, as it did then, the Greater Magellanic Cloud.

"Frankly, the Magellanic race was appalled at what they found. In the time since their preceding visit, your race had risen from the slime of your mother planet and was on its way toward stars. The speed of your development was unprecedented in millions of years of history. By their standards, your race was incredibly energetic, incredibly fecund, incredibly intelligent, unbelievably warlike, and almost completely depraved.

"Extrapolation revealed that within another fifty thousand of your years, you would complete the population of this galaxy and would be totally unstoppable.

"Something had to be done, fast. There were two obvious solutions but both were unacceptable to my Makers. The first was to assume direct control over your race and to maintain that rule indefinitely, until such time as you changed your natures sufficiently to become civilizable. The expenditure of energy would be enormous and the results probably catastrophic to your race. No truly civilized people could long contemplate such a solution.

"The second obvious answer was to attempt to extirpate you from this universe as if you were a disease—as, in a sense, you are. Because your depravity was not total or necessarily permanent, this solution was also abhorrent to my Makers and was rejected.

"What was needed was a weapon that would keep operating without direct control by my People, which would not result in any greater destruction or harm to humans than was absolutely necessary; and one which would cease entirely to operate against you if you changed sufficiently to become civilizable—to become good neighbors to my Makers.

"The final solution of the Magellanic race was to construct several thousand spaceships, each containing an elaborate computer, constructed so as to give accurate answers throughout your galaxy. I am one of those ships. We have performed our function in a satisfactory manner and will continue to do so as long as we are needed."

"And that makes you a weapon?" asked Bates incredulously. "I don't get it."

*

Farnum felt a shiver go through him. "I see it. The concept is completely diabolical."

"It's not diabolical at all," answered the Oracle. "When you become capable of civilization, we can do you no further harm at all. We will cease to be a weapon at that time."

"You mean you'll stop telling the truth at that time?" asked Bates.

"We will continue to function in accordance with our design," answered the voice, "but it will no longer do you harm. Incidentally, your phrase 'telling the truth' is almost meaningless. We answer all questions in the manner most completely understandable to you, within the framework of your language and your understanding, and of the understanding and knowledge of our Makers. In the objective sense, what we answer is not necessarily the Truth; it is merely the truest form of the answer that we can state in a manner that you can understand."

"And you'll answer any question at all?" asked Bates in some excitement.

"With one or two exceptions. We will not, for example, tell you how we may be destroyed."

Bates stood up and began pacing the floor. "Then whoever possesses you can be the most powerful man in the Universe!"

"No. Only in this galaxy."

"That's good enough for me!"

"Jack," said Farnum urgently, "let's get out of here. I want to talk to you."

"In a minute, in a minute," said Bates impatiently. "I've got one more question." He turned to face the wall from which the disembodied voice appeared to emanate. "Is it possible to arrange it so that you would answer only one man's questions—mine, for example?"

"I can tell you how to arrange it so that I will respond to only your questions—for so long as you are alive."

"Come on," pleaded Farnum. "I've got to talk to you right now."

"Okay," said Bates, smiling. "Let's go."

*

When they were back in their ship, Farnum turned desperately to Bates. "Can't you see what a deadly danger that machine is to us all? We've got to warn Earth as fast as we can and get them to quarantine this planet—and any other planets we find that have Oracles."

"Oh, no, you don't," said Bates. "You aren't getting the chance to have the Oracle all to yourself. With that machine, we can rule the whole galaxy. We'll be the most powerful people who ever lived! It's sure lucky for us that you won the toss of the coin and we stopped here."

"But don't you see that the Oracle will destroy Earth?"

"Bushwah. You heard it say it can only destroy people who aren't civilized. It said that it's a spaceship, so I'll bet we can get it to come back to Earth with us, and tell us how we can be the only ones who can use it."

"We've got to leave here right away—without asking it any more questions."

Bates shook his head. "Quit clowning."

"I never meant anything more in my life. Once we start using that machine—if we ask it even one question to gain advantage for ourselves—Earth's civilization is doomed. Can't you see that's what happened to those other planets we visited? Can't you see what is happening to this planet we're on now?"

"No, I can't," answered Bates stubbornly. "The Oracle said there are only a few thousand like him. You could travel through space for hundreds of years and never be lucky enough to find one. There can't be an Oracle on every planet we visited."

"There wouldn't have to be," said Farnum. "There must be hundreds of possible patterns—all of them destructive in the presence of greed and laziness and lust for power. For example, a planet—maybe this one—gets space travel. It sets up colonies on several worlds. It's expanding and dynamic. Then it finds an Oracle and takes it back to its own world. With all questions answered for it, the civilization stops being dynamic and starts to stagnate. It stops visiting its colonies and they drift toward barbarism.

"Later," Farnum went on urgently, "somebody else reaches the stars, finds the planet with the Oracle—and takes the thing back home. Can you imagine what will happen to these people on this world if they lose their Oracle? Their own learning and traditions and way of life have been destroyed—just take a look at their anarchic clothing and architecture. The Oracle is the only thing that keeps them going—downhill—and makes sure they don't start back again."

"It won't happen that way to us," Bates argued. "We won't let the Oracle get into general use, so Earth won't ever learn to depend on it. I'm going to find out from it how to make it work for the two of us alone. You can come along and share the gravy or not, as you choose. I don't care. But you aren't going to stop me."

Bates turned and strode out of the ship.

*

Farnum pounded his fist into his palm in despair, and then ran to a locker. Taking out a high-power express rifle, he loaded it carefully and stepped out through the airlock. Bates showed clearly in his telescopic sights, still walking toward the Hall of the Oracle. Farnum fired at the legs, but he wasn't that good a shot; the bullet went through the back.

Farnum jittered between bringing Bates back and taking off as fast as the ship could go. The body still lay there, motionless; there was nothing he could do for the Oracle's first Earth victim—the first and the last, he swore grimly. He had to speed home and make them understand the danger before they found another planet with an Oracle, so that they could keep clear of its deadly temptations. The Magellanic race could be outwitted yet, in spite of their lethal cleverness.

Then he felt a sudden icy chill along his spine. Alone, he could never operate the spaceship—and Bates was dead. He was trapped on the planet.

For hours, he tried to think of some way of warning Earth. It was imperative that he get back. There had to be a way.

He realized finally that there was only one solution to his problem. He sighed shudderingly and walked slowly from the spaceship toward the Hall of the Oracle, past Bates' body.

"One question, though," he muttered to himself. "Only one."

DUMBWRITER

By James Stamers

Antimony IX divers can't be seen, of course ... but don't have anything in mind when one of them is around you!

*

The man ahead of me had a dragon in his baggage. So the Lamavic boys confiscated it. Lamavic—Livestock, Animal, Mineral and Vegetable, International Customs—does not like to find dragons curled up in a thermos. And since this antipathy was a two-way exchange, the Lamavic inspectors at Philadelphia International were singed and heated all ways by the time they got to me. I knew them well.

"Mr. Sol Jones?"

"That's right," I said, watching the would-be dragon smuggler being marched away. A very amateur job. I could have told him. There are only two ways to smuggle a dragon nowadays.

"Any livestock to declare, Mr. Jones?"

"I have no livestock on my person or in my baggage, nor am I accompanied by any material prohibited article," I said carefully, for I saw they were recording.

The little pink, bald inspector with a charred collar looked at his colleague. "Anything known?"

His colleague looked down at me from six feet of splendid physique, smiled unpleasantly, and flipped the big black record book.

"'Sol Jones,'" he read, "'Lamavic four-star offender. Galactic registration: six to tenth power: 763918. Five foot ten inches, Earth scale. Blue eyes, hair variable and usually nondescript brown, ear lobes and cranial....' You're not disputing identity, Mr. Jones?"

"Oh, no. That's me."

"I see. 'Irrevocable Galactic citizenship for services to family of Supreme President Xgol in matter of asteroid fungus, subsequent Senatorial amnesty confirmed, previous sentences therefore omitted. Lamavic offenses thereafter include no indictable evidence but total twenty-four minor fines for introducing prohibited livestock onto various planets. Suspected complicity in Lamavic cases One through Seventy-six as follows: mobile sands, crystal thinkers, recording turtle, operatic fish, giant mastodon.' Mr. Jones, you seem to have given us trouble before."

"Before what?"

"Before this—er—"

"That," I said, "is an Unconstitutional remark. I am giving no trouble. I have made a full declaration. I demand the rights of a Galactic citizen."

He apologized, as he had to. This merely made both inspectors angry, but they were going to search me anyway. I knew that. Certainly I am a smuggler, and I had in fact a little present for my girl Florence—a wedding present, I hoped—but they would never find it. This time I really had them fooled, and I intended to extract maximum pleasure from watching their labors.

*

I saw the Lamavic records once. The next leading offender has only two stars and he's out on Ceres in the penal colony. My four stars denote that I disapprove of all these rules prohibiting the carrying of livestock from one planet to another. Other people extend the Galactic Empire; I extend my Galactic credit. You want an amusing extraterrestrial pet to while away the two-hour work week, I can provide one. Of course, this pet business was overdone in the early days when any space-hopper could bring little foreign monsters back to the wife and kiddies. Any weird thing could come in and did.

"You are aware, Mr. Jones, that you have declared that you are not trying to bring in any prohibited life-form, whether animal, mineral, vegetable, or any or all of these?"

"I am," I said.

"You are further aware of the penalties for a false declaration?"

"In my case, I believe I could count on thirty years' invigorating work on a penal planet."

"You could, Mr. Jones. You certainly could."

"Well, I've made my declaration."

"Will you step this way?"

Very polite in Philadelphia Spaceport. I followed the inspectors into the screening cubicles. There was a nasty looking device in the corner.

"I thought those things were illegal," I said.

"Unfortunately, Mr. Jones, you are, as you know, quite right. We may not employ a telepath instrument on any unconvicted person."

They looked sorry, but I wasn't. A telepath would have told them immediately where I had Florence's pet, and all about it. I smiled at them. They paid no attention, took my passport and began turning up the Lamavic manual on Antimony IX, Livestock of, Prohibited Forms. I had just come from there and so had Florence's little diver, which I had brought as a happy surprise. I sat down. The two inspectors looked as if they were going to say something, then continued flipping pages of their manual.

"Here it is—Antimony IX."

One of them read out the prohibitions and the other tried to watch me and the reflex counter behind me at the same time—a crude instrument which should be used, in my professional view, only to determine a person's capacities for playing poker with success.

"Ants-water, babblers, bunces, candelabra plants, catchem-fellers, Cythia Majoris, divers, dunces, dimple-images, drakes, dunking dogs, dogs-savage, dogs-water, dogs-not-otherwise-provided-for, unspec., elephants-miniature, fish-any...."

They went on. Antimony IX is teeming with life and almost every specimen is prohibited on other planets. We had passed the divers, anyway. I smiled and gave the reflex counter a strong jerk just as the smaller inspector was saying "Mammoths." They looked at me in silence.

"Funny man," one said, and they went on reading.

"Okay," the large inspector said at last. "We'll examine him for everything."

*

For the next three hours, they took blood specimens to see if I had microscopic livestock hidden there, they X-rayed me and my baggage, fluoroscoped everything again, put the baggage through an irritator life-indexer, investigated my orifices in detail with a variety of instruments, took skin scrapings in case I was wearing a false layer, and the only thing they found was my dark glasses.

"Why don't you wear modern contact lenses?"

"It's none of your business," I said, "but these old-style spectacles have liquid lenses."

There was a flurry and they sent away for analysis a small drop from one of the lenses. There were no signs of prohibited life in the liquid.

"I could have told you that," I said. "It's dicyanin, a vegetable extract. Diminishes the glare."

I put the glasses on my nose and hooked on the earpieces. The effect was medieval, but I could see the little diver now. I could also see disturbing evidence of the inspectors' mental condition. A useful little device invented by Dr. W. J. Kilner (1847-1920) for the study of the human aura in sickness and health. After a little practice, which I was not going to allow the Lamavic inspectors, the retina became sufficiently sensitive to see the micro-wave aura when you looked through the dicyanin screen. As was true of most of these psi pioneers at that time, nothing was done to further Kilner's work when he died. I noticed, without surprise, that the inspectors had a mental field of very limited extent and that the little diver had survived the journey nicely.

"Can I go now?" I asked.

"This time, Mr. Jones."

When I left, the repair staff was building a new inspection barrier to replace the parts the dragon had got. Such an amateur performance! Leave smuggling to professionals and we'd have Lamavic disbanded from boredom in ten years. I nearly slipped on the fine silica dioxide which had fused in the air when the dragon got annoyed. Nasty, dangerous pets.

The one for Florence was the only contraband I was carrying this trip, which was purely pleasure. She was waiting for me in her apartment, tall, golden, luscious, and all mine. She thought I was in import-export, which in a sense was true.

"I've missed you so much, Sol," she said, twining herself on me and the couch like a Venusian water-nymph. "Did you bring me a present?"

I lay back and let her kiss me.

"Of course I did. A small but very valuable present."

I let her kiss me again.

"Not—a Jupiter diamond, Sol?"

"Much rarer than that, and more useful."

"Oh. Useful."

"Something to help you in the house when we're married, honey. Now, don't pout so prettily, or I'll never get around to showing you."

My homecoming was not developing quite as I planned, but I put this down to womanly, if not exactly maidenly, quirks. When she found out what

I had brought her, I was sure she would be all over me again. I put on my dark glasses so that I could see where the diver was.

"Would you like a drink, honey?" I asked.

"I don't mind," she said sulkily.

*

I looked at the diver, concentrated hard on the thought of a bottle from the cabinet, two glasses and a pitcher of ice from the kitchen. He went revolving through the air obediently and the items came floating out neatly. Florence nearly shattered the windows with her screams.

"Now calm down, honey," I said, catching her. "Calm down. It's just a little present I brought you."

The bottle, glasses and pitcher dropped gently onto the table beside us.

"See?" I said. "Service at a thought. Remote control. The end of housework. Kiss me."

She didn't.

"You mean you did that, Sol?"

"Not me, exactly. I've brought you a little baby diver, honey, all the way from Antimony IX, just for you. There isn't another one on Earth. In fact, I doubt if there's another one outside Antimony IX. I had a lot of trouble securing this rare and valuable present for you."

"I don't like it. It gives me the creeps."

"Honey," I said carefully, "this is a little baby. It couldn't hurt a mouse. It's about six inches in diameter, and all it is doing is to teleport what you want it to teleport."

"Then why can't I see it?"

"If you could see it, I wouldn't have been allowed to bring it for you, honey, because a whole row of nasty-minded Solar Civil Servants would have seen it too, and they would have taken it from your own sweet Sol."

"They can have it."

"Honey, this is a *rare* and *valuable* pet! It will *do* things for you."

"So you think I need something done for me. Well! I'm glad you came right out and said this before we were married!"

The following series of "but—but—" from me and irrelevance from Florence occupied an hour, but hardly mentioned the diver. Eventually I got her back into my arms.

My urges for Florence were strictly biological, though intense. There were little chances for intellectual exchanges between us, but I was more interested in the broad probabilities of her as a woman. I could go commune with wild and exotic intelligences on foreign planets any time I had the fare. As a woman, Florence was what I wanted.

"Back on Antimony IX," I explained carefully, "life is fierce and rugged. So, to keep from being eaten, these little divers evolved themselves into little minds with no bodies at all, and they feed off solar radiation. Now, honey, minds are not made of the same stuff brains are made of, good solid tissue and gray matter and neural cortex—"

"Don't be dirty, Sol."

"There is nothing dirty about the body, honey. Minds are invisible but detectable in the micro-wavelengths on any sensitive counter, and look like little glass eggs when you can see them—as I can, by using these glasses. In fact, your diver is over by the window now. But, having evolved this far, they came across a little difficulty and couldn't evolve any further. So there they are, handy little minds for teleporting whatever you want moved, and reading other people's thoughts."

*

She gasped. "Did you say reading other people's thoughts?

"Certainly," I said. "As a matter of fact, that's what stopped the divers from evolving further. If they brush against any thinking creature, they pick up whatever thought is in the creature's conscious mind. But they also pick up the subliminal activity, if you follow me—and down at that level of a mind such as man's, his thoughts are not only the present unconscious thoughts but also a good slice of what is to him still the future. It's one of those space-time differences. The divers are not really on the same space-time reference as the physical world, but that makes them all the more useful, because our minds aren't either."

"Did you say reading other people's thoughts, like a telepath?" she persisted.

"Exactly like a telepath, or any other class of psi. We're really living on a much wider scale than we're conscious of, but our mind only tracks down one point in time-space in a straight line, which happens to fit our bodies. Our subliminal mind is way out in every direction, including time—and when you pick up fragments of this consciously, you're a psi, that's all. So the divers got thoroughly confused—that's what it amounts to—and never evolved any further. So you see, honey, it's all perfectly natural."

"I think you're just dirty."

"Eh?"

"Everyone *hates* telepaths. You know that."

"I don't."

"Oh, you go wandering all over the Galaxy—but my friends—what could I say to my friends if they learned I had something like a telepath in the apartment?"

"It's only a baby diver, I keep telling you, honey. And anyway, you'll be able to tell what they're really thinking about you."

Florence looked thoughtful. "And what they've been doing?"

"Sometimes they will do what they think they'll do. And sometimes they don't make it. But it's what their subliminal plans to have happen, yes."

She kissed me. "I think it's a lovely present, Sol."

She snuggled up to me and I concentrated on bringing the diver over to her. I thought I'd read her, just for a joke, and see what she had in mind. I took a close look.

"What's the matter, Sol?"

"Oh, honey! You beautiful creature!"

"This is nice—but what made you say that?"

"I just got the diver to show me your mind, and bits of the next two weeks you have in mind. It's going to be a lovely, lovely vacation."

She blushed very violently and got angry. "You had no right to look at what I was thinking, Sol!"

"It wasn't what you were thinking so much as what you will be thinking, honey. I figure in it quite well."

"I won't have it, Sol! Do you hear me? I think spying on people is detestable!"

"I thought you liked the idea of tagging your friends?"

"That's different. Either we go somewhere without that whatever-it-is, or you can marry someone else. I don't mind having it around after we're married, but not before, Sol. Do you understand?"

I was already reaching for the video yellow pages.

*

I turned on the television-wall in the apartment before we left and instructed the diver to stay around and watch it. They are very curious creatures, inquisitive, always chasing new ideas, and I thought that should hold the diver happily for several days. Meanwhile, I had booked adjoining rooms at the Asteroid-Central.

The Asteroid-Central advertised in the video yellow pages that it practiced the Most Rigid Discrimination—meaning no telepaths, clairvoyants, clairaudients or psychometrists. Life was hard on a psi outside Government circles. But life was much harder on the rest of the world seeking secluded privacy and discretion. The Asteroid-Central was so discreet, you could hardly see where you were going. Dim lights, elegant figures passing in the gloom, singing perfumes of the gentlest kind, and "Guaranteed Psi-Free" on every bedroom door.

I was humming idly in my room, with one eye on the communicating door through which, were she but true to her own mind, Florence would shortly come, and I turned on the television-wall only to see how less fortunate people were spending their leisure. An idle and most regrettable gesture.

There was a quiz-game on International Channel 462, dull and just finishing. All the contestants seemed to know all the answers. In fact, the man who won the trip around the Rings of Saturn, did so by answering the question before the Martian quiz-master had really finished reading it out. When the winner turned sharply on the other contestants and knocked them down, yelling, "So that's what you think of my mother, is it?" the wall was blacked out and we were taken straight to the Solar Party Convention.

The nominee this decade was human. He seemed to be speaking on his aims, his pure record and altruistic intentions. The stereo cameras looked over the heads of the delegates. Starting in the row by the main aisle, each delegate shot to his feet and started booing and jeering. It rippled down the rows like a falling pack of cards, each delegate in turn after the man in front of him, and each row picking up where the back of the previous row left off. It was as if someone were passing a galvanizing brush along the heads of the delegates, row by row.

Or as if a diver were refreshing the delegates with a clear picture of their nominee's mind.

I groaned and called Florence.

"Look," I said when she came. "That damned pet has followed the program back to the cameras from your apartment, and there he is lousing up the Convention."

"I vote Earth," she told me indifferently.

"That isn't the point, honey. I'll have to bring the diver here, and quickly."

"You do that, Sol. I'll be at home when you get rid of it."

By the time the diver picked up my thoughts and came flickering into the room through the walls, Florence had left.

I felt the diver off the back of my head, made my thoughts as kindly as possible, and went downstairs to the largest, longest bar.

*

The evening passed profitably because I was invited to join a threesome of crooks at cards. With the aid of the little diver, I was able to shorten the odds to a pleasant margin in my favor. But this was doing nothing about Florence. A not altogether funny remark about teleporting the cards did, however, suggest the answer.

After the transaction was over, I sent the diver off to a friend on the faculty of Luke University, where they had a long history of psi investigation and where the diver could be guaranteed to be kept busy rolling dice and such. This was easy to fix by a video call. There had been times in the past when certain services to the Extra-terrestrial Zoology and Botanical Tanks had made me discreetly popular with the faculty, and anyway they thought I was doing them a favor. They promised to keep the little diver busy for an indefinite period.

I reported to Florence, and after a certain amount of feminine shall-I-shan't-I, she came back to the Asteroid-Central.

This time I did not turn on the television-wall. I lay still. I said nothing. I hardly thought at all. And after several years compressed themselves into every minute, my own true honey, Florence, slid open the communicating door and came into the room.

She walked shyly toward me, hiding modestly within a floating nightgown as opaque as a very clear soap bubble.

I stood up, held out my arms and she came toward me, smiling—and stopped to pick up something on the carpet.

"Ooo, Sol! Look! A Jupiter diamond!"

She held up the largest and most expensive diamond I have ever seen.

I was just going to claim credit for this little gift when another appeared, and another, and a long line marching over the carpet like an ant trail. They came floating in under the door.

Now love is for vacations, and between my own sweet Florence and a diamond mine there is no comparison. I put on my dicyanin glasses and saw the baby diver was back and at work teleporting. I said so, but this time there were no hysterics from Florence.

"I was just thinking of him," she said, "and wishing you had brought me a Jupiter diamond instead."

"Well, honey, it looks as if you've got both."

I watched her scrambling on the carpet, gathering handfuls of diamonds and not in the least interested in me.

On Antimony IX, the little divers switched from one space-time point to another simultaneously, and the baby diver had come back from the Solar Party Convention the same way. I thought of it and it came; Florence had just thought of it and here it was. But now it seemed to be flitting lightly from Earth to Jupiter and back with diamonds, so perhaps there was no interplanetary distance to a mind.

This had a future. I could see myself with a winter and a summer planet of my own, even happily paying Earth, Solar and Galactic taxes.

"Well, honey, don't you worry," I said. "You don't like divers, so I'll take it back and give you something else. Just leave it to Sol."

"Take your foot off that diamond, Sol Jones! You gave me this dear little diver and he's mine!"

*

She sat back on her heels and thought. The evidence of her thinking immediately came trickling through the door—Venusian opals set in a gold bracelet half a pound heavy, Martian sleeze furs, spider-web stockings, platinum belts. The room was beginning to look like a video fashion center, a Galactic merchandise mart. And after Florence put on a coat and opened the door, her ideas began to get bigger.

"This is fun!" she cried, teleporting like mad. "Why, I can have anything in the Galaxy just by thinking about it!"

"Now, honey, think of the benefits to humanity! This is too big to be used for personal gain. This should be dedicated—"

"This is dedicated to me, Sol Jones, so just you keep your fingers off it. Why, the cute little thing—look, he's been out to Saturn for me!"

I made a decision. Think wide and grand, Sol Jones, I said. Sacrifice yourself for the greater good.

"Florence, honey, you know I love you. Will you marry me?"

That stopped her. "You mean it, Sol?"

"Of course."

"It's not just because of this diver?"

"Why, honey, how could you think such a thing? If I'd never brought it in for you, I'd still want to marry you."

"You never said so before," she said. "But okay. If you do it now. Right now, Sol Jones."

So the merchandise stopped coming in while we plugged into the video and participated in a moving and legal ceremony. The marriage service was expensive, but after all we could teleport in a few thousand credit blanks from the Solar Treasury. Immediately after we had switched off, we did so.

"Are you sure you married me for myself, Sol?"

"I swear it, honey. No other thought entered my head. Just you."

I made a few notes while Florence planned the house we would have, furnished with rare materials from anywhere. I thought one of the medium asteroids would do for a base for Sol Jones Intragalactic Transport. I could see it all, vast warehouses and immediate delivery of anything from anywhere. I wondered if there was a limit to the diver's capacity, so Florence desired an encyclopedia and in it came, floating through the doorway.

"It says," she read, "not much is known about Antimony IX divers because none have ever been known to leave their planet."

"They probably need the stimulus of an educated mind," I said. "Anyway, this one can get diamonds from Jupiter and so on, and that's what matters."

*

I kissed the wife of the President of Sol Jones Intragalactic and was interrupted by discreet tapping on the door. The manager of the Asteroid-Central beamed at us.

"Excuse," he said. "But we understand you have just been married, Mr. and Mrs. Jones."

"Irrevocably," I said.

"Felicitations. The Asteroid-Central will be sending up complimentary euphorics. There is just a small point, Mr. Jones. We notice you have a large selection of valuable gifts for the bride."

He looked round the room and smiled at the piles of stuff Florence had thought of.

"Of course," he went on, "we trust your stay will be pleasant and perhaps you will let us know if you will be wanting anything else."

"I expect we will, but we'll let you know," I said.

"Thank you, Mr. Jones. It is merely that we noticed you had emptied every showcase on the ground floor and, a few moments ago, teleported the credit contents of the bar up here. Not of importance, really; it is all charged on your bill."

"You saw it and didn't stop it?" I yelled.

"Oh, no, Mr. Jones. We always make an exception for Antimony IX divers. Limited creatures, really, but good for our business. We get about one a month—smuggled in, you know. But the upkeep proves too expensive. Some women do shop without more than a passing thought, don't they?"

I saw what he meant, but Mrs. Sol Jones took it very philosophically.

"Never mind, Sol—you have me."

"Or vice versa, honey," I said.

THE IGNOBLE SAVAGES

By Evelyn E. Smith

Snaddra had but one choice in its fight to afford to live belowground—underhandedly pretend theirs was an aboveboard society!

*

"Go Away from me, Skkiru," Larhgan said, pushing his hand off her arm. "A beggar does not associate with the high priestess of Snaddra."

"But the Earthmen aren't due for another fifteen minutes," Skkiru protested.

"Of what importance are fifteen minutes compared to eternity!" she exclaimed. Her lovely eyes fuzzed softly with emotion. "You don't seem to realize, Skkiru, that this isn't just a matter of minutes or hours. It's forever."

"Forever!" He looked at her incredulously. "You mean we're going to keep this up as a permanent thing? You're joking!"

Bbulas groaned, but Skkiru didn't care about that. The sad, sweet way Larhgan shook her beautiful head disturbed him much more, and when she said, "No, Skkiru, I am not joking," a tiny pang of doubt and apprehension began to quiver in his second smallest left toe.

"This is, in effect, good-by," she continued. "We shall see each other again, of course, but only from a distance. On feast days, perhaps you may be permitted to kiss the hem of my robe ... but that will be all."

Skkiru turned to the third person present in the council chamber. "Bbulas, this is your fault! It was all your idea!"

There was regret on the Dilettante's thin face—an obviously insincere regret, the younger man knew, since he was well aware how Bbulas had always felt about the girl.

"I am sorry, Skkiru," Bbulas intoned. "I had fancied you understood. This is not a game we are playing, but a new way of life we are adopting. A necessary way of life, if we of Snaddra are to keep on living at all."

"It's not that I don't love you, Skkiru," Larhgan put in gently, "but the welfare of our planet comes first."

*

She had been seeing too many of the Terrestrial fictapes from the library, Skkiru thought resentfully. There was too damn much Terran influence on this planet. And this new project was the last straw.

No longer able to control his rage and grief, he turned a triple somersault in the air with rage. "Then why was I made a beggar and she the high priestess? You arranged that purposely, Bbulas. You—"

"Now, Skkiru," Bbulas said wearily, for they had been through all this before, "you know that all the ranks and positions were distributed by impartial lot, except for mine, and, of course, such jobs as could carry over from the civilized into the primitive."

Bbulas breathed on the spectacles he was wearing, as contact lenses were not considered backward enough for the kind of planet Snaddra was now supposed to be, and attempted to wipe them dry on his robe. However, the thick, jewel-studded embroidery got in his way and so he was forced to lift the robe and wipe all three of the lenses on the smooth, soft, spun metal of his top underskirt.

"After all," he went on speaking as he wiped, "I have to be high priest, since I organized this culture and am the only one here qualified to administer it. And, as the president himself concurred in these arrangements, I hardly think you—a mere private citizen—have the right to question them."

"Just because you went to school in another solar system," Skkiru said, whirling with anger, "you think you're so smart!"

"I won't deny that I do have educational and cultural advantages which were, unfortunately, not available to the general populace of this planet. However, even under the old system, I was always glad to utilize my superior attainments as Official Dilettante for the good of all and now—"

"Sure, glad to have a chance to rig this whole setup so you could break up things between Larhgan and me. You've had your eye on her for some time."

Skkiru coiled his antennae at Bbulas, hoping the insult would provoke him into an unbecoming whirl, but the Dilettante remained calm. One of the chief outward signs of Terran-type training was self-control and Bbulas had been thoroughly terranized.

I hate Terrestrials, Skkiru said to himself. *I hate Terra.* The quiver of anxiety had risen up his leg and was coiling and uncoiling in his stomach. He hoped it wouldn't reach his antennae—if he were to break down and psonk in front of Larhgan, it would be the final humiliation.

"Skkiru!" the girl exclaimed, rotating gently, for she, like her fiance—her erstwhile fiance, that was, for the new regime had caused all such ties to be severed—and every other literate person on the planet, had received her education at the local university. Although sound, the school was admittedly provincial in outlook and very poor in the emotional department. "One would almost think that the lots had some sort of divine intelligence behind them, because you certainly are behaving in a beggarly manner!"

"And I have already explained to you, Skkiru," Bbulas said, with a patience much more infuriating than the girl's anger, "that I had no idea of who was to become my high priestess. The lots chose Larhgan. It is, as the Earthmen say, kismet."

*

He adjusted the fall of his glittering robe before the great polished four-dimensional reflector that formed one wall of the chamber.

Kismet, Skkiru muttered to himself, *and a little sleight of hand.* But he didn't dare offer this conclusion aloud; the libel laws of Snaddra were very severe. So he had to fall back on a weak, "And I suppose it is kismet that makes us all have to go live out on the ground during the day, like—like savages."

"It is necessary," Bbulas replied without turning.

"Pooh," Skkiru said. "Pooh, *pooh*, POOH!"

Larhgan's dainty earflaps closed. "Skkiru! Such language!"

"As you said," Bbulas murmured, contemptuously coiling one antenna at Skkiru, "the lots chose well and if you touch me, Skkiru, we shall have another drawing for beggar and you will be made a metal-worker."

"But I can't work metal!"

"Then that will make it much worse for you than for the other outcasts," Bbulas said smugly, "because you will be a pariah without a trade."

"Speaking of pariahs, that reminds me, Skkiru, before I forget, I'd better give you back your grimpatch—" Larhgan handed the glittering bauble to him—"and you give me mine. Since we can't be betrothed any longer, you might want to give yours to some nice beggar girl."

"I don't want to give my grimpatch to some nice beggar girl!" Skkiru yelled, twirling madly in the air.

"As for me," she sighed, standing soulfully on her head, "I do not think I shall ever marry. I shall make the religious life my career. Are there going to be any saints in your mythos, Bbulas?"

"Even if there will be," Bbulas said, "you certainly won't qualify if you keep putting yourself into a position which not only represents a trait wholly out of keeping with the new culture, but is most unseemly with the high priestess's robes."

Larhgan ignored his unfeeling observations. "I shall set myself apart from mundane affairs," she vowed, "and I shall pretend to be happy, even though my heart will be breaking."

It was only at that moment that Skkiru realized just how outrageous the whole thing really was. There must be another solution to the planet's problem. "Listen—" he began, but just then excited noises filtered down from overhead. It was too late.

"Earth ship in view!" a squeaky voice called through the intercom. "Everybody topside and don't forget your shoes."

Except the beggar. Beggars went barefoot. Beggars suffered. Bbulas had made him beggar purposely, and the lots were a lot of slibwash.

"Hurry up, Skkiru."

*

Bbulas slid the ornate headdress over his antennae, which, already gilded and jeweled, at once seemed to become a part of it. He looked pretty damn silly, Skkiru thought, at the same time conscious of his own appearance—which was, although picturesque enough to delight romantic Terrestrial hearts, sufficiently wretched to charm the most hardened sadist.

"Hurry up, Skkiru," Bbulas said. "They mustn't suspect the existence of the city underground or we're finished before we've started."

"For my part, I wish we'd never started," Skkiru grumbled. "What was wrong with our old culture, anyway?"

That was intended as a rhetorical question, but Bbulas answered it anyway. He always answered questions; it had never seemed to penetrate his mind that school-days were long since over.

"I've told you a thousand times that our old culture was too much like the Terrans' own to be of interest to them," he said, with affected weariness. "After all, most civilized societies are basically similar; it is only primitive societies that differ sharply, one from the other—and we have to be different to attract Earthmen. They're pretty choosy. You've got to give them what they want, and that's what they want. Now take up your post on the edge of the field, try to look hungry, and remember this isn't for you or for me, but for Snaddra."

"For Snaddra," Larhgan said, placing her hand over her anterior heart in a gesture which, though devout on Earth—or so the fictapes seemed to indicate—was obscene on Snaddra, owing to the fact that certain essential organs were located in different areas in the Snaddrath than in the corresponding Terrestrial life-form. Already the Terrestrial influence was corrupting her, Skkiru thought mournfully. She had been such a nice girl, too.

"We may never meet on equal terms again, Skkiru," she told him, with a long, soulful glance that made his hearts sink down to his quivering toes, "but I promise you there will never be anyone else for me—and I hope that knowledge will inspire you to complete cooperation with Bbulas."

"If that doesn't," Bbulas said, "I have other methods of inspiration."

"All right," Skkiru answered sulkily. "I'll go to the edge of the field, and I'll speak broken Inter-galactic, and I'll forsake my normal habits and customs, and I'll even *beg*. But I don't have to like doing it, and I don't intend to like doing it."

All three of Larhgan's eyes fuzzed with emotion. "I'm proud of you, Skkiru," she said brokenly.

Bbulas sniffed. The three of them floated up to ground level in a triple silence.

*

"Alms, for the love of Ipsnadd," Skkiru chanted, as the two Terrans descended from the ship and plowed their way through the mud to meet a procession of young Snaddrath dressed in elaborate ceremonial costumes, and singing a popular ballad—to which less ribald, as well as less inspiring, words than the originals had been fitted by Bbulas, just in case, by some extremely remote chance, the Terrans had acquired a smattering of Snadd somewhere. Since neither party was accustomed to navigating mud, their progress was almost imperceptible.

"Alms, for the love of Ipsnadd," chanted Skkiru the beggar. His teeth chattered as he spoke, for the rags he wore had been custom-weatherbeaten for him by the planet's best tailor—now a pariah, of course, because Snadd tailors were, naturally, metal-workers—and the wind and the rain were joyously making their way through the demolished wires. Never before had Skkiru been on the surface of the planet, except to pass over, and he had actually touched it only when taking off and landing. The Snaddrath had no means of land transport, having previously found it unnecessary—but now both air-cars and self-levitation were on the prohibited list as being insufficiently primitive.

The outside was no place for a civilized human being, particularly in the wet season or—more properly speaking on Snaddra—the wetter season. Skkiru's feet were soaked with mud; not that the light sandals worn by the members of the procession appeared to be doing them much good, either. It gave him a kind of melancholy pleasure to see that the privileged ones were likewise trying to repress shivers. Though their costumes were rich, they were also scanty, particularly in the case of the females, for Earthmen had been reported by tape and tale to be humanoid.

As the mud clutched his toes, Skkiru remembered an idea he had once gotten from an old sporting fictape of Terrestrial origin and had always planned to experiment with, but had never gotten around to—the weather had always been so weathery, there were so many other more comfortable sports, Larhgan had wanted him to spend more of his leisure hours with her, and so on. However, he still had the equipment, which he'd salvaged from a wrecked air-car, in his apartment—and it was the matter of a moment to run down, while Bbulas was looking the other way, and get it.

Bbulas couldn't really object, Skkiru stilled the nagging quiver in his toe, because what could be more primitive than any form of land transport? And even though it took time to get the things, they worked so well that, in spite of the procession's head start, he was at the Earth ship long before the official greeters had reached it.

*

The newcomers were indeed humanoid, he saw. Only the peculiarly pasty color of their skins and their embarrassing lack of antennae distinguished them visibly from the Snaddrath. They were dressed much as the Snaddrath had been before they had adopted primitive garb.

In fact, the Terrestrials were quite decent-looking life-forms, entirely different from the foppish monsters Skkiru had somehow expected to represent the cultural ruling race. Of course, he had frequently seen pictures of them, but everyone knew how easily those could be retouched. Why, it was the Terrestrials themselves, he had always understood, who had invented the art of retouching—thus proving beyond a doubt that they had something to hide.

"Look, Raoul," the older of the two Earthmen said in Terran—which the Snaddrath were not, according to the master plan, supposed to understand, but which most of them did, for it was the fashionable third language on most of the outer planets. "A beggar. Haven't seen one since some other chaps and I were doing a spot of field work on that little planet in the Arcturus system—what was its name? Glotch, that's it. Very short study, it turned out to be. Couldn't get more than a pamphlet out of it, as we were unable to stay long enough to amass enough material for a really definitive work. The natives tried to eat us, so we had to leave in somewhat of a hurry."

"Oh, they were cannibals?" the other Earthman asked, so respectfully that it was easy to deduce he was the subordinate of the two. "How horrible!"

"No, not at all," the other assured him. "They weren't human—another species entirely—so you could hardly call it cannibalism. In fact, it was quite all right from the ethical standpoint, but abstract moral considerations seemed less important to us than self-preservation just then. Decided that, in this case, it would be best to let the missionaries get first crack at them. Soften them up, you know."

"And the missionaries—did they soften them up, Cyril?"

"They softened up the missionaries, I believe." Cyril laughed. "Ah, well, it's all in the day's work."

"I hope these creatures are not man-eaters," Raoul commented, with a polite smile at Cyril and an apprehensive glance at the oncoming procession—*creatures indeed*! Skkiru thought, with a mental sniff. "We have come such a long and expensive way to study them that it would be indeed a pity if we also were forced to depart in haste. Especially since this is my first field trip and I would like to make good at it."

"Oh, you will, my boy, you will." Cyril clapped the younger man on the shoulder. "I have every confidence in your ability."

Either he was stupid, Skkiru thought, or he was lying, in spite of Bbulas' asseverations that untruth was unknown to Terrestrials—which had always seemed highly improbable, anyway. How could any intelligent life-form possibly stick to the truth all the time? It wasn't human; it wasn't even humanoid; it wasn't even polite.

"The natives certainly appear to be human enough," Raoul added, with an appreciative glance at the females, who had been selected for the processional honor with a view to reported Terrestrial tastes. "Some slight differences, of course—but, if two eyes are beautiful, three eyes can be fifty per cent lovelier, and chartreuse has always been my favorite color."

If they stand out here in the cold much longer, they are going to turn bright yellow. His own skin, Skkiru knew, had faded from its normal healthy emerald to a sickly celadon.

*

Cyril frowned and his companion's smile vanished, as if the contortion of his superior's face had activated a circuit somewhere. *Maybe the little one's a robot!* However, it couldn't be—a robot would be better constructed and less interested in females than Raoul.

"Remember," Cyril said sternly, "we must not establish undue rapport with the native females. It tends to detract from true objectivity."

"Yes, Cyril," Raoul said meekly.

Cyril assumed a more cheerful aspect "I should like to give this chap something for old times' sake. What do you suppose is the medium of exchange here?"

Money, Skkiru said to himself, but he didn't dare contribute this piece of information, helpful though it would be.

"How should I know?" Raoul shrugged.

"Empathize. Get in there, old chap, and start batting."

"Why not give him a bar of chocolate, then?" Raoul suggested grumpily. "The language of the stomach, like the language of love, is said to be a universal one."

"Splendid idea! I always knew you had it in you, Raoul!"

Skkiru accepted the candy with suitable—and entirely genuine—murmurs of gratitude. Chocolate was found only in the most expensive of the planet's delicacy shops—and now neither delicacy shops nor chocolate were to be found, so, if Bbulas thought he was going to save the gift to contribute it later to the Treasury, the "high priest" was off his rocker.

To make sure there would be no subsequent dispute about possession, Skkiru ate the candy then and there. Chocolate increased the body's resistance to weather, and never before had he had to endure so much weather all at once.

On Earth, he had heard, where people lived exposed to weather, they often sickened of it and passed on—which helped to solve the problem of birth control on so vulgarly fecund a planet. Snaddra, alas, needed no such measures, for its population—like its natural resources—was dwindling rapidly. Still, Skkiru thought, as he moodily munched on the chocolate, it would have been better to flicker out on their own than to descend to a subterfuge like this for nothing more than survival.

*

Being a beggar, Skkiru discovered, did give him certain small, momentary advantages over those who had been alloted higher ranks. For one thing, it was quite in character for him to tread curiously upon the strangers' heels all the way to the temple—a ramshackle affair, but then it had been run up in only three days—where the official reception was to be held. The principal difficulty was that, because of his equipment, he had a little trouble keeping himself from overshooting the strangers. And though Bbulas might frown menacingly at him—and not only for his forwardness—that was in character on both sides, too.

Nonetheless, Skkiru could not reconcile himself to his beggarhood, no matter how much he tried to comfort himself by thinking at least he wasn't a pariah like the unfortunate metal-workers who had to stand segregated from the rest by a chain of their own devising—a poetic thought, that was, but well in keeping with his beggarhood. Beggars were often poets, he believed, and poets almost always beggars. Since metal-working was the chief industry of Snaddra, this had provided the planet automatically with a large lowest caste. Bbulas had taken the easy way out.

Skkiru swallowed the last of the chocolate and regarded the "high priest" with a simple-minded mendicant's grin. However, there were volcanic passions within him that surged up from his toes when, as the wind and rain whipped through his scanty coverings, he remembered the snug underskirts Bbulas was wearing beneath his warm gown. They were metal, but they were solid. All the garments visible or potentially visible were of woven metal, because, although there was cloth on the planet, it was not politic for the Earthmen to discover how heavily the Snaddrath depended upon imports.

As the Earthmen reached the temple, Larhgan now appeared to join Bbulas at the head of the long flight of stairs that led to it. Although Skkiru had seen her in her priestly apparel before, it had not made the emotional impression upon him then that it did now, when, standing there, clad in beauty, dignity and warm clothes, she bade the newcomers welcome in several thousand words not too well chosen for her by Bbulas—who fancied himself a speech-writer as well as a speech-maker, for there was no end to the man's conceit.

The difference between her magnificent garments and his own miserable rags had their full impact upon Skkiru at this moment. He saw the gulf that had been dug between them and, for the first time in his short life, he felt the tormenting pangs of caste distinction. She looked so lovely and so remote.

"... and so you are most welcome to Snaddra, men of Earth," she was saying in her melodious voice. "Our resources may be small but our hearts are large, and what little we have, we offer with humility and with love. We hope that you will enjoy as long and as happy a stay here as you did on Nemeth...."

Cyril looked at Raoul, who, however, seemed too absorbed in contemplating Larhgan's apparently universal charms to pay much attention to the expression on his companion's face.

"... and that you will carry our affection back to all the peoples of the Galaxy."

*

She had finished. And now Cyril cleared his throat. "Dear friends, we were honored by your gracious invitation to visit this fair planet, and we are honored now by the cordial reception you have given to us."

The crowd yoomped politely. After a slight start, Cyril went on, apparently deciding that applause was all that had been intended.

"We feel quite sure that we are going to derive both pleasure and profit from our stay here, and we promise to make our intensive analysis of your culture as painless as possible. We wish only to study your society, not to tamper with it in any way."

Ha, ha, Skkiru said to himself. *Ha, ha, ha!*

"But why is it," Raoul whispered in Terran as he glanced around out of the corners of his eyes, "that only the beggar wears mudshoes?"

"Shhh," Cyril hissed back. "We'll find out later, when we've established rapport. Don't be so impatient!"

Bbulas gave a sickly smile. Skkiru could almost find it in his hearts to feel sorry for the man.

"We have prepared our best hut for you, noble sirs," Bbulas said with great self-control, "and, by happy chance, this very evening a small but unusually interesting ceremony will be held outside the temple. We hope you will be able to attend. It is to be a rain dance."

"Rain dance!" Raoul pulled his macintosh together more tightly at the throat. "But why do you want rain? My faith, not only does it rain now, but the planet seems to be a veritable sea of mud. Not, of course," he added hurriedly as Cyril's reproachful eye caught his, "that it is not attractive mud. Finest mud I have ever seen. Such texture, such color, such aroma!"

Cyril nodded three times and gave an appreciative sniff.

"But," Raoul went on, "one can have too much of even such a good thing as mud...."

The smile did not leave Bbulas' smooth face. "Yes, of course, honorable Terrestrials. That is why we are holding this ceremony. It is not a dance to bring on rain. It is a dance to *stop* rain."

He was pretty quick on the uptake, Skkiru had to concede. However, that was not enough. The man had no genuine organizational ability. In the time he'd had in which to plan and carry out a scheme for the improvement of Snaddra, surely he could have done better than this high-school theocracy. For one thing, he could have apportioned the various roles so that each person would be making a definite contribution to the society, instead of creating some positions plums, like the priesthood, and others prunes, like the beggarship.

What kind of life was that for an active, ambitious young man, standing around begging? And, moreover, from whom was Skkiru going to beg? Only the Earthmen, for the Snaddrath, no matter how much they threw themselves into the spirit of their roles, could not be so carried away that they would give handouts to a young man whom they had been accustomed to see basking in the bosom of luxury.

*

Unfortunately, the fees that he'd received in the past had not enabled him both to live well and to save, and now that his fortunes had been so drastically reduced, he seemed in a fair way of starving to death. It gave him a gentle, moody pleasure to envisage his own funeral, although, at the same time, he realized that Bbulas would probably have to arrange some sort of pension for him; he could not expect Skkiru's patriotism to extend to abnormal limits. A man might be willing to die for his planet in many ways—but wantonly starving to death as the result of a primitive affectation was hardly one of them.

All the same, Skkiru reflected as he watched the visitors being led off to the native hut prepared for them, how ignominious it would be for one of the brightest young architects on the planet to have to subsist miserably on the dole just because the world had gone aboveground. The capital had risen to the surface and the other cities would soon follow suit. Meanwhile, a careful system of tabus had been designed to keep the Earthmen from discovering the existence of those other cities.

He could, of course, emigrate to another part of the planet, to one of them, and stave off his doom for a while—but that would not be playing the game. Besides, in such a case, he wouldn't be able to see Larhgan.

As if all this weren't bad enough, he had been done an injury which struck directly at his professional pride. He hadn't even been allowed to help in planning the huts. Bbulas and some workmen had done all that themselves with the aid of some antique blueprints that had been put out centuries before by a Terrestrial magazine and had been acquired from a rare tape-and-book dealer on Gambrell, for, Skkiru thought, far too high a price. He could have designed them himself just as badly and much more cheaply.

It wasn't that Skkiru didn't understand well enough that Snaddra had been forced into making such a drastic change in its way of life. What resources it once possessed had been depleted and—aside from minerals—they had never been very extensive to begin with. All life-forms on the planet were on the point of extinction, save fish and rice—the only vegetable that would grow on Snaddra, and originally a Terran import at that. So food and fiber had to be brought from the other planets, at fabulous expense, for Snaddra was not on any of the direct trade routes and was too unattractive to lure the tourist business.

Something definitely had to be done, if it were not to decay altogether. And that was where the Planetary Dilettante came in.

*

The traditional office of Planetary Dilettante was a civil-service job, awarded by competitive examination whenever it fell vacant to the person who scored highest in intelligence, character and general gloonatz. However, the tests were inadequate when it came to measuring sense of proportion, adaptiveness and charm—and there, Skkiru felt, was where the essential flaw lay. After all, no really effective test would have let a person like Bbulas come out on top.

The winner was sent to Gambrell, the nearest planet with a Terran League University, to be given a thorough Terran-type education. No individual on Snaddra could afford such schooling, no matter how great his personal fortune, because the transportation costs were so immense that only a government could afford them. That was the reason why only one person in each generation could be chosen to go abroad at the planet's expense and acquire enough finish to cover the rest of the population.

The Dilettante's official function had always been, in theory, to serve the planet when an emergency came—and this, old Luccar, the former President, had decided, when he and the Parliament had awakened to the fact that Snaddra was falling into ruin, was an emergency. So he had, after considerable soul-searching, called upon Bbulas to plan a method of saving Snaddra—and Bbulas, happy to be in the limelight at last, had come up with this program.

It was not one Skkiru himself would have chosen. It was not one, he felt, that any reasonable person would have chosen. Nevertheless, the Bbulas Plan had been adopted by a majority vote of the Snaddrath, largely because no one had come up with a feasible alternative and, as a patriotic citizen, Skkiru would abide by it. He would accept the status of beggar; it was his duty to do so. Moreover, as in the case of the planet, there was no choice.

But all was not necessarily lost, he told himself. Had he not, in his anthropological viewings—though Bbulas might have been the only one privileged to go on ethnological field trips to other planets, he was not the only one who could use a library—seen accounts of societies where beggarhood could be a rewarding and even responsible station in life? There was no reason why, within the framework of the primitive society Bbulas had created to allure Terran anthropologists, Skkiru should not make something of himself and show that a beggar was worthy of the high priestess's hand—which would be entirely in the Terran primitive tradition of romance.

"Skkiru!" Bbulas was screaming, as he spun, now that the Terrans were out of ear- and eye-shot "Skkiru, you idiot, listen to me! What are those ridiculous things you are wearing on your silly feet?"

Skkiru protruded all of his eyes in innocent surprise. "Just some old pontoons I took from a wrecked air-car once. I have a habit of collecting junk and I thought—"

Bbulas twirled madly in the air. "You are not supposed to think. Leave all the thinking to me!"

"Yes, Bbulas," Skkiru said meekly.

*

He would have put up an argument, but he had bigger plans in mind and he didn't want them impeded in any way.

"But they seem like an excellent idea," Luccar suggested. "Primitive and yet convenient."

Bbulas slowed down and gulped. After all, in spite of the fact that he was now only chief yam-stealer—being prevented from practicing his profession simply because there were no yams on the planet and no one was quite certain what they were—Luccar had once been elected President by a large popular majority. And a large popular majority is decidedly a force to be reckoned with anywhere in the Galaxy.

"Any deviations arouse comment," Bbulas explained tightly.

"But if we all—"

"There would not be enough pontoons to go around, even if we stripped all the air-cars."

"I see," Luccar said thoughtfully. "We couldn't make—?"

"No time!" Bbulas snapped. "All right, Skkiru—get those things off your feet!"

"Will do," Skkiru agreed. It would be decidedly unwise to put up an argument now. So he'd get his feet muddy; it was all part of the higher good.

Later, as soon as the rain-dance rehearsals were under way, he slipped away. No part had been assigned to him anyhow, except that of onlooker, and he thought he could manage that without practice. He went down to the library, where, since all the attendants were aboveground, he could browse in the stacks to his hearts' content, without having to fill out numerous forms and be shoved about like a plagiarist or something.

If the Earthmen were interested in really primitive institutions, he thought, they should have a look at the city library. The filing system was really medieval. However, the library would, of course, be tabu for them, along with the rest of the city, which was not supposed to exist.

As far as the Terrans were to know, the group of lumpy stone huts (they should, properly speaking, have been wood, but wood was too rare and expensive) was the capital of Snaddra. It would be the capital of Snaddra for the Snaddrath, too, except during the hours of rest, when they would be permitted to retire unobtrusively to their cozy well-drained quarters beneath the mud. Life was going to be hard from now on—unless the Bbulas Plan moved faster than Bbulas himself had anticipated. And that would never happen without implementation from without. From without Bbulas, that was.

Skkiru got to work on the tex-tapes and soon decided upon his area of operations. Bbulas had concentrated so much effort on the ethos of the planet that he had devoted insufficient detail to the mythos. That, therefore, was the field in which Skkiru felt he must concentrate. And concentrate he did.

*

The rain dance, which had been elaborately staged by the planet's finest choreographers, came to a smashing climax, after which there was a handsome display of fireworks.

"But it is still raining," Raoul protested.

"Did you expect the rain to stop?" Bbulas asked, his eyes bulging with involuntary surprise. "I mean—" he said, hastily retracting them—"well, it doesn't always stop right away. The gods may not have been feeling sufficiently propitious."

"Thought you had only one god, old boy," Cyril observed, after giving his associate a searching glance. "Chap by the name of Whipsnade or some such."

"Ipsnadd. He is our chief deity. But we have a whole pantheon. Major gods and minor gods. Heroes and demigods and nature spirits—"

"And do not forget the prophets," Larhgan put in helpfully. As former Chief Beauty of the planet (an elective civil-service office), she was not accustomed to being left out of things. "We have many prophets. And saints. I myself am studying to be a "

Bbulas glared at her. Though her antennae quivered sulkily, she stopped and said no more—for the moment, anyway.

"Sounds like quite a complex civilization," Cyril commented.

"No, no!" Bbulas protested in alarm. "We are a simple primitive people without technological pretensions."

"You don't need any," Cyril assured him. "Not when you have fireworks that function in the rain."

Inside himself, Skkiru guffawed.

"We are a simple people," Bbulas repeated helplessly. "A very simple and very primitive people."

"Somehow," Raoul said, "I feel you may have a quality that civilization may have lost." The light in his eyes was recognizable to any even remotely humanoid species as a mystic glow.

But Cyril seemed well in command of the situation. "Come now, Raoul," he laughed, clapping his young colleague on the shoulder, "don't fall into the Rousseau trap—noble savage and all that sort of rot!"

"But that beggar!" Raoul insisted. "Trite, certainly, but incredible nonetheless! Before, one only read of such things—"

A glazed look came into two of Bbulas' eyes, while the third closed despairingly. "What beggar? What beggar? Tell me—I must know ... as if I didn't really," he muttered in Snaddrath.

"The only beggar we've seen on this planet so far. That one."

*

With a wave of his hand, Cyril indicated the modest form of Skkiru, attempting to conceal himself behind Luccar's portly person.

"I realize it was only illusion, but, as my associate says, a remarkably good one. And," Cyril added, "an even more remarkable example of cultural diffusion."

"What do you mean? Please, gracious and lovable Terrans, deign to tell me what you mean. What did that insufferable beggar do?"

In spite of himself, Skkiru's knees flickered. *Fool*, he told himself, *you knew it was bound to come out sooner or later. Take courage in your own convictions; be convinced by your own courage. All he really can do is yell.*

"He did the Indian rope trick for us," Raoul explained. "And very well, too. Very well indeed."

"The—Indian rope trick!" Bbulas spluttered. "Why, the—" And then he recollected his religious vocation, as well as his supposed ignorance. "Would you be so kind as to tell me what the Indian rope trick is, good sirs?"

"Well, he did it with a chain, actually."

"We have no ropes on this planet," Larhgan contributed. "We are backward."

"And a small boy went up and disappeared," Raoul finished.

Suddenly forgetting the stiff-upper-lip training for which the planet had gone to such great expense, Bbulas spun around and around in a fit of bad temper, to Skkiru's great glee. Fortunately, the Dilettante retained enough self-control to keep his feet on the ground—perhaps remembering that to fail to do so would compound Skkiru's crime.

"Dervishism!" Raoul exclaimed, his eyes incandescent with interest. He pulled out his notebook. After biting his lip thoughtfully, Cyril did the same.

"Just like Skkiru!" Bbulas gasped as he spun slowly to a stop. "He is a disruptive cultural mechanism. Leading children astray!"

"But not at all," Raoul pointed out politely. "The boy came back unharmed and in the best of spirits."

"So far as we could see," Cyril amended. "Of course there may have been psychic damage."

"Which boy was it?" Bbulas demanded.

*

Cyril pointed to the urchin in question—a rather well-known juvenile delinquent, though the Terrestrials, of course, couldn't know that.

"He is a member of my own clan," Bbulas said. "He will be thrashed soundly."

"But why punish him?" Raoul asked. "What harm has he done?"

"Shhh," Cyril warned him. "You may be touching on a tabu. What's the matter with you, anyway? One would think you had forgotten every lesson you ever learned."

"Oh, I am truly sorry!" Raoul's face became a pleasing shade of pink, which made him look much more human. Maybe it was the wrong color, but at least it was a color. "Please to accept my apologies, reverend sir."

"It's quite all right." Bbulas reverted to graciousness. "The boy should not have associated with a beggar—especially that one. If he did not hold his post by time-hallowed tradition, we would—dispose of him. He has always been a trouble-maker."

"But I do not understand," Raoul persisted. Skkiru could not understand why Cyril did not stop him again. "The beggar did the trick very effectively. I know it was all illusion, but I should like to know just how he created such an illusion, and, moreover, how the Indian rope trick got all the way to—"

"It was all done by magic," Bbulas said firmly. "Magic outside the temple is not encouraged, because it is black magic, and so it is wrong. The magic of the priests is white magic, and so it is right. Put that down in your little book."

Raoul obediently wrote it down. "Still, I should like to know—"

"Let us speak of pleasanter things," Bbulas interrupted again. "Tomorrow night, we are holding a potlatch and we should be honored to have the pleasure of your company."

"Delighted," Raoul bowed.

"I was wrong," Cyril said. "This is not a remarkable example of cultural diffusion. It is a remarkable example of a diffuse culture."

*

"But I cannot understand," Raoul said to Cyril later, in the imagined privacy of their hut. "Why are you suspicious of this charming, friendly people, so like the natives that the textbooks lead one to expect?"

Naturally, Skkiru—having made his way in through a secret passage known only to the entire population of the city and explicitly designed for espionage, and was spying outside the door—thought, *we are textbook natives. Not only because we were patterned on literary prototypes, but because Bbulas never really left school—in spirit, anyway. He is the perpetual undergraduate and his whole scheme is nothing more than a grandiose Class Night.*

"Precisely what I've been thinking," Cyril said. "So like the textbooks—all the textbooks put together."

"What do you mean? Surely it is possible for analogous cultural features to develop independently in different cultures?"

"Oh, it's possible, all right. Probability—particularly when it comes to such a great number of features packed into one small culture—is another matter entirely."

"I cannot understand you," Raoul objected. "What do you want of these poor natives? To me, it seems everything has been of the most idyllic. Rapport was established almost immediately."

"A little too immediately, perhaps, don't you think? You haven't had much experience, Raoul, so you might not be aware it usually isn't as easy as this."

Cyril flung himself down on one of the cots that had been especially hardened for Terrestrial use and blew smoke rings at the ceiling. Skkiru was dying for a cigarette himself, but that was another cultural feature the Snaddrath had to dispense with now—not that smoking was insufficiently primitive, but that tobacco was not indigenous to the planet.

"That is because they are not a hostile people," Raoul insisted. "Apparently they have no enemies. Nonetheless, they are of the utmost interest. I hardly expected to land a society like this on my very first field trip," he added joyfully. "Never have I heard of so dynamic a culture! Never!"

"Nor I," Cyril agreed, "and this is far from being my very first field trip. It has a terribly large number of strange elements in it—strange, that is, when considered in relationship to the society as a whole. Environmental pressures seem to have had no effect upon their culture. For instance, don't you think it rather remarkable that a people with such an enormously complex social structure as theirs should wear clothing so ill adapted to protect them from the weather?"

*

"Well," Raoul pointed out enthusiastically—another undergraduate type, Skkiru observed, happiest with matters that either resembled those in books or came directly from them, so that they could be explicitly pigeonholed—"the Indians of Tierra del Fuego wore nothing but waist-length sealskin capes even in the bitterest cold. Of course, this civilization is somewhat more advanced than theirs in certain ways, but one finds such anomalies in all primitive civilizations, does one not?"

"That's true to a certain extent. But one would think they'd at least have developed boots to cope with the mud. And why was the beggar the only one to wear mudshoes? Why, moreover—" Cyril narrowed his eyes and pointed his cigarette at Raoul—"did he wear them only the first time and subsequently appear barefooted?"

"That *was* odd," Raoul admitted, "but—"

"And the high priest spoke of thrashing that boy. You should know, old chap, that cruelty to children is in inverse ratio to the degree of civilization."

Raoul stared at his colleague. "My faith, are you suggesting that we go see how hard they hit him, then?"

Cyril laughed. "All I suggest is that we keep a very open mind about this society until we can discover what fundamental attitudes are controlling such curious individual as well as group behavior."

"But assuredly. That is what we are here for, is it not? So why are you disturbing yourself so much?"

But it was Raoul, Skkiru thought, who appeared much more disturbed than Cyril. It was understandable—the younger man was interested only in straightforward ethnologizing and undoubtedly found the developing complications upsetting.

"Look," Cyril continued. "They call this place a hut. It's almost a palace."

My God, Skkiru thought, *what kind of primitive conditions are they used to?*

"That is largely a question of semantics," Raoul protested. "But regard—the roof leaks. Is that not backward enough for you, eh?" And Raoul moved to another part of the room to avoid receiving indisputable proof of the leakage on his person. "What is more, the sanitary arrangements are undeniably primitive."

"The roofs of many palaces leak, and there is no plumbing to speak of, and still they are not called huts. And tell me this—why should the metal-workers be the pariahs? Why *metal-workers?*"

Raoul's eyes opened wide. "You know there is often an outcast class with no apparent rationale behind its establishment. All the tapes—"

"True enough, but you will remember that the reason the smiths of Masai were pariahs was that they manufactured weapons which might tempt people to commit bloodshed. I keep remembering them, somehow. I keep remembering so many things here...."

"But we have seen no weapons on this planet," Raoul argued. "In fact, the people seem completely peaceful."

"Right you are." Cyril blew another smoke ring. "Since this is a planet dependent chiefly upon minerals, why make the members of its most important industry the out-group?"

"You think it is that they may be secretly hostile?"

Cyril smiled. "I think they may be secretly something, but hardly hostile."

Aha, Skkiru thought. *Bbulas, my splendidly scaled friend, I will have something interesting to tell you.*

*

"You idiot!" Bbulas snarled later that night, as most of the Snaddrath met informally in the council chamber belowground, the new caste distinctions being, if not forgotten, at least in abeyance—for everyone except Bbulas. "You imbecile!" He whirled, unable to repress his Snadd emotions after a long behaviorally Terran day. "I have half a mind to get rid of you by calling down divine judgment."

"How would you do that?" Skkiru demanded, emboldened by the little cry of dismay, accompanied by a semi-somersault, which Larhgan gave. In spite of everything, she still loved him; she would never belong to Bbulas, though he might plan until he was ochre in the face.

"Same way you did the rope trick. Only you wouldn't come back, my boy. Nice little cultural trait for the ethnologists to put in their peace pipes and smoke. Never saw such people for asking awkward questions." Bbulas sighed and straightened his antennae with his fingers, since their ornaments made them too heavy to allow reflective verticalization. "Reminds me of final exams back on Gambrell."

"Anthropologists *always* ask awkward questions—everybody knows that," Larhgan put in. "It's their function. And I don't think you should speak that way to Skkiru, Bbulas. Like all of us, he's only trying to do his best. No man—or woman—can do more."

She smiled at Skkiru and his hearts whirled madly inside him. Only a dolt, he thought, would give way to despair; there was no need for this intolerable situation to endure for a lifetime. If only he could solve the problem more quickly than Bbulas expected or—Skkiru began to understand—wanted, Larhgan could be his again.

"With everybody trying to run this planet," Bbulas snarled, taking off his headdress, "no wonder things are going wrong."

Luccar intervened. Although it was obvious that he had been enjoying to a certain extent the happy anonymity of functionless yam-stealer, old elective responsibilities could not but hang heavy over a public servant of such unimpeachable integrity.

"After all," the old man said, "secretly we're still a democracy, and secretly I am still President, and secretly I'm beginning to wonder if perhaps we weren't a little rash in—"

"Look here, all of you," Bbulas interrupted querulously. "I'm not doing this for my own amusement."

*

But that's just what you are doing, Skkiru thought, *even though you wouldn't admit it to yourself, nor would you think of it as amusement.*

"You know what happened to Nemeth," Bbulas continued, using an argument that had convinced them before, but that was beginning to wear a little thin now. "Poorest, most backward planet in the whole Galaxy. A couple of ethnologists from Earth stumbled on it a little over a century ago and what happened? More kept on coming; the trade ships followed. Now it's the richest, most advanced planet in that whole sector. There's no reason why the same thing can't happen to us in this sector, if we play our cards carefully."

"But maybe these two won't tell other anthropologists about us," Luccar said. "Something the older one remarked certainly seemed to imply as much. Maybe they don't want the same thing to happen again—in which case, all this is a waste of time. Furthermore," he concluded rather petulantly, "at my age, I don't like running about in the open; it's not healthful."

"If they don't tell other anthropologists about us," Bbulas said, his face paling to lime-green with anxiety, "we can spread the news unobtrusively ourselves. Just let one study be published, even under false coordinates, and we can always hire a good public relations man to let our whereabouts leak out. Please, everybody, stick to your appointed tasks and let me do the worrying. You haven't even given this culture a chance! It's hardly more than a day old and all I hear are complaints, complaints, complaints."

"You'd better worry," Skkiru said smugly, "because already those Terrans think there's something fishy about this culture. Ha, ha! Did you get that—fishy?"

Only Larhgan laughed. She loved him.

"How do you know they're suspicious?" Bbulas demanded. "Are you in their confidence? Skkiru, if you've been talking—"

"All I did was spy outside their door," Skkiru said hastily. "I knew *you* couldn't eavesdrop; it wouldn't look dignified if you were caught. But beggars do that kind of thing all the time. And I wanted to show you I could be of real use."

He beamed at Larhgan, who beamed back.

"I could have kept my findings to myself," he went on, "but I came to tell you. In fact—" he dug in his robe—"I even jotted down a few notes."

"It wasn't at all necessary, Skkiru," Bbulas said in a tired voice. "We took the elementary precaution of wiring their hut for sound and a recorder is constantly taking down their every word."

"Hut!" Skkiru kept his antennae under control with an effort, but his retort was feeble. "They think it's a palace. You did them too well, Bbulas."

"I may have overdone the exterior architecture a bit," the high priest admitted. "Not that it seems relevant to the discussion. Although I've been trying to arrange our primitivism according to Terrestrial ideas of cultural backwardness, I'm afraid many of the physical arrangements are primitive according to our conceptions rather than theirs."

*

"Why *must* we be primitive according to Terran ideas?" Luccar wanted to know. "Why must we be slaves even to fashions in backwardness?"

"Hear, hear!" cried an anonymous voice.

"And thank you, Skkiru," the former President continued, "for telling me they were suspicious. I doubt that Bbulas would have taken the trouble to inform me of so trivial a matter."

"As high priest," Bbulas said stiffly, "I believe the matter, trivial or not, now falls within my province."

"Shame!" cried an anonymous voice—or it might have been the same one.

Bbulas turned forest-green and his antennae twitched. "After all, you yourself, Luccar, agreed to accept the role of elder statesman—"

"Yam-stealer," Luccar corrected him bitterly, "which is not the same thing."

"On Earth, it is. And," Bbulas went on quickly, "as for our assuming primitive Earth attitudes, where else are we going to get our attitudes from? We can't borrow any primitive attitudes from Nemeth, because they're too well known. And since there are no other planets we know of with intelligent life-forms that have social structures markedly different from the major Terran ones—except for some completely non-humanoid cultures, which, for physiological reasons, we are incapable of imitating—we have to rely upon records of primitive Terran sources for information. Besides, a certain familiarity with the traits manifested will make the culture more understandable to the Terrans, and, hence, more attractive to them psychologically." He stopped and straightened out his antennae.

"In other words," Skkiru commented, emboldened by a certain aura of sympathy he felt emanating from Larhgan, at least, and probably from Luccar, too, "he doesn't have the imagination to think up any cultural traits for himself, so he has to steal them—and that's the easiest place to steal them from."

"This is none of your business, Skkiru," Bbulas snapped. "You just beg."

"It's the business of all of us, Bbulas," Luccar corrected softly. "Please to remember that, no matter what our alloted roles, we are all concerned equally in this."

"Of course, of course, but please let me handle the situation in my own way, since I made the plans. And, Skkiru," the Dilettante added with strained grace, "you may have a warm cloak to wear as soon as we can get patches welded on."

Then Bbulas took a deep breath and reverted to his old cheer-leader manner. "Now we must all get organized for the potlatch. We can give the Terrans those things the Ladies' Aid has been working on all year for the charity bazaar and, in exchange, perhaps they will give us more chocolate bars—" he glanced reproachfully at Skkiru—"and other food."

"And perhaps some yams," Luccar suggested, "so that—God save us—I can steal them."

"I'll definitely work on that," Bbulas promised.

*

Skkiru was glad that, as beggar, he held no prominent position at the feast—in reality, no position at all—for he hated fish. And fish, naturally, would be the chief refreshment offered, since the Snaddrath did not want the Terrans to know that they had already achieved that degrading dependency upon the tin can that marks one of the primary differences between savagery and civilization.

There were fish pâté on rice crackers, fish soup with rice, boiled fish, baked fish, fried fish and a pilau of rice with fish. There were fish chitlins, fish chips, fish cakes, fish candy and guslat—a potent distillation of fermented fish livers—to wash it all down. And even in the library, where Skkiru sought refuge from the festivities, fishy fumes kept filtering down through the ventilating system to assail his nostrils.

Bbulas had been right in a way, Skkiru had to admit to himself upon reflection. In trying to improve his lot, Skkiru had taken advantage of the Snaddrath's special kinetic talents, which had been banned for the duration—and so he had, in effect, committed a crime.

This time, however, he would seek to uplift himself in terms acceptable to the Terrans on a wholly indigenous level, and in terms which would also hasten the desired corruptive process—in a nice way, of course—so that the Snaddrath civilization could be profitably undermined as fast as possible and Larhgan be his once again. It was a hard problem to solve, but he felt sure he could do it. Anything Bbulas could do, he could do better.

Then he had it! And the idea was so wonderful that he was a little sorry at the limited range it would necessarily cover. His part really should be played out before a large, yoomping audience, but he was realistic enough to see that it would be most expedient for him to give a private performance for the Earthmen alone.

On the other hand, he now knew it should be offered outside the hut, because the recorder would pick up his cries and Bbulas would be in a spin—as he would be about any evidence of independent thinking on the planet. Bbulas was less interested in the planet's prospering, it was now clear to Skkiru, than in its continuing in a state where he would remain top fish.

*

Fortunately, the guslat had done its work, and by the time the Earthmen arrived at the door to their hut, they were alone. The rest of the company either had fallen into a stupor or could not trust themselves to navigate the mud.

The Earthmen—with an ingeniousness which would have augured well for the future development of their race, had it not already been the (allegedly) most advanced species in the Galaxy—had adapted some spare parts from their ship into replicas of Skkiru's mudshoes. They did, in truth, seem none too steady on their feet, but he was unable to determine to what degree this was a question of intoxication and what degree a question of navigation.

"Alms, for the love of Ipsnadd." He thrust forward his begging bowl.

"Regard, it is the beggar! Why were you not at the festivities, worthy mendicant?" Raoul hiccuped. "Lovely party. Beautiful women. Delicious fish."

Skkiru started to stand on his head, then remembered this was no longer a socially acceptable expression of grief and cast his eyes down. "I was not invited," he said sadly.

"Like the little match girl," Raoul sympathized. "My heart bleeds for you, good match gi—good beggar. Does your heart not bleed for him, Cyril?"

"Bad show," the older ethnologist agreed, with a faint smile. "But that's what you've got to expect, if you're going to be a primitive."

He was very drunk, Skkiru decided; he must be, to phrase his sentiments so poorly. Unless he—but no, Skkiru refused to believe that. He didn't mind Cyril's being vaguely suspicious, but that was as far as he wanted him to go. Skkiru's toes apprehensively started to quiver.

"How can you say a thing like that to a primitive?" Raoul demanded. "If he were not a primitive, it would be all right to call him a primitive, but one does not accuse primitives of being primitives. It's—it's downright primitive; that's what it is!"

"You need some coffee, my boy." Cyril grinned. "Black coffee. That guslat of theirs is highly potent stuff."

They were about to go inside. Skkiru had to act quickly. He slumped over. Although he had meant to land on the doorstep, he lacked the agility to balance himself with the precision required and so he fell smack into the mud. The feel of the slime on his bare feet had been bad enough; oozing over his skin through the interstices of his clothing, it was pure hell. What sacrifices he was making for his planet! And for Larhgan. The thought of her would have to sustain him through this viscous ordeal, for there was nothing else solid within his grasp.

"Ubbl," he said, lifting his head from the ooze, so that they could see the froth coming out of his mouth. "Glubbl."

*

Raoul clutched Cyril. "What is he doing?"

"Having an epileptic fit, I rather fancy. Go on, old man," Cyril said to Skkiru. "You're doing splendidly. Splendidly!"

"I see the sky!" Skkiru howled, anxious to get his prophecies over with before he sank any deeper in the mud. "It is great magic. I see many ships in the sky. They are all coming to Snaddra...."

"Bearing anthropologists and chocolate bars, I suppose," murmured Cyril.

"Shhh," Raoul said indignantly. "You must not interrupt. He is having personal contact with the supernatural, a very important element of the primitive ethos."

"Thank you," Cyril said. "I'll try to remember that."

So will I, thought Skkiru. "They carry learned men and food for the spiritually and physically hungry people of Snaddra," he interrupted impatiently. "They carry warm clothing for the poor and miserable people of

Snaddra. They carry yams for the larcenous and frustrated people of Snaddra."

"Yams!" Raoul echoed. "*Yams!*"

"Shhh, this is fascinating. Go on, beggar."

But the mud sogging over Skkiru's body was too much. The fit could be continued at a later date—and in a drier location.

"Where am I?" he asked, struggling to a sitting position.

"You are on Snaddra, fifth planet of the sun Weebl," Raoul began, "in—"

"Weeeeebl," Skkiru corrected, getting to his feet with the older ethnologist's assistance. "What happened?" He beat futilely at the mud caught in the meshes of his metal rags. "I feel faint."

"Come in and have some coffee with us," Cyril invited. This also was part of Skkiru's plan, for he had no intention of going back across that mud, if he could possibly help it. He had nothing further to say that the recorders should not hear. Bbulas might object to his associating with the Earthmen, but he couldn't do much if the association seemed entirely innocent. At the moment, Snaddra might be a theocracy, but the democratic hangover was still strong.

"I would rather have some hot chocolate," Skkiru said. "That is, if you have no objection to drinking with a beggar."

"My dear fellow—" Cyril put an arm around Skkiru's muddy shoulders—"we ethnologists do not hold with caste distinctions. Come in and have chocolate—with a spot of rum, eh? That'll make you right as a trivet in a matter of seconds."

*

It wasn't until much later, after several cups of the finest chocolate he had ever tasted, that Skkiru announced himself to feel quite recovered.

"Please do not bother to accompany me to the door," he said. "I can find my own way. You do me too much honor. I would feel shamefaced."

"But—" Cyril began.

"No," Skkiru said. "It is—it is bad form here. I insist. I must go my way alone."

"All right," Cyril agreed.

Raoul looked at him in some surprise.

"All right," Cyril repeated in a louder tone. "Go by yourself, if an escort would bother you. But please give the door a good bang, so the lock will catch."

Skkiru slammed the door lustily to simulate the effect of departure and then he descended via the secret passage inside the hut itself, scrabbling a little because the hot chocolate seemed strangely to have affected his sense of balance.

The rest of the Snaddrath were in the council chamber gloating over the loot from the potlatch. It was, as a matter of fact, a good take.

"Where were you, Skkiru?" Bbulas asked, examining a jar of preserved kumquats suspiciously. "Up to no good, I'll be bound."

"Oh, my poor Skkiru!" Larhgan exclaimed, before Skkiru could say anything. "How muddy and wretched-looking you are! I don't like this whole thing," she told Bbulas. "It's cruel. Being high priestess isn't nearly as much fun as I thought it would be."

"This is not supposed to be fun," the Dilettante informed her coldly. "It is in dead earnest. Since the question has been brought up, however, what did happen to you, Skkiru?"

"I—er—fell down and, being a beggar, I had no other garments to change into."

"You'll survive," Bbulas said unfeelingly. "On Earth, I understand, people fall into mud all the time. Supposed to have a beneficial effect—and any effect on you, Skkiru, would have to be beneficial."

Larhgan was opening her mouth to say something—probably, Skkiru thought fondly, in his defense—when there came a thud and a yell from the passage outside. Two yells, in fact. And two thuds.

"My faith," exclaimed a Terrestrial voice, "but how did the beggar descend! I am sure every bone in my body is broken."

"I think you'll find him possessed of means of locomotion not known to us. But you're not hurt, old chap—only bruised."

And Cyril came into the council chamber, followed by a limping Raoul. "Good evening, ladies and gentlemen. I trust this is not an intrusion, although I'm quite sure you'll tell us we've broken a whole slue of tabus."

"You!" Bbulas screamed at Skkiru. "You must have used the passage in the hut! You let them follow you!"

Losing control of his own reflexes, he began to whirl madly.

*

"But regard this!" Raoul exclaimed, staring around him. "To build a place like this beneath the mud—name of a name, these people must have hydraulic engineering far superior to anything on Earth!"

"You are too kind," the former hydraulic engineer said deprecatingly. "Actually, it's quite simple—"

"This is not a primitive civilization at all, Raoul," Cyril explained. "They've been faking it from tapes. Probably have a culture very much like ours, with allowances for climatic differences, of course. Oh, undoubtedly it would be provincial, but—"

"We are not provincial," Larhgan said coldly. "Primitive, yes. Provincial, no! We are—"

"But why should they do a thing like this to us?" Raoul wailed.

"I imagine they did it to get on the trade routes, as Nemeth did. They've been trying not to talk about Nemeth all the while. Must have been rather a strain. You ought to be ashamed of yourselves!" Cyril told the assembled Snaddrath. "Very bad form!"

Bbulas was turning paler and paler as he whirled. "All your fault," he gasped hoarsely to Skkiru. "All your fault!"

And that was true, Skkiru realized. His antennae quivered, but he didn't even try to restrain them. He had meant well, yet he had messed up the planet's affairs far more seriously than Bbulas had. He had ruined their hopes, killed all their chances by his carelessness. He, Skkiru, instead of being his planet's savior, was its spoiler. He psonked violently.

But Larhgan moved nearer to him. "It's all over, anyhow," she whispered, "and you know what? I'm glad. I'm glad we failed. I'd rather starve as myself than succeed as a sham."

Skkiru controlled himself. Silently, he took the grimpatch out of his carrier and, as silently, she took it back.

"My faith, they must have had plumbing all the time!" Raoul complained.

"Very likely," said Cyril sternly. "Looks as if we've suffered for nothing."

"Such people!" Raoul said. "True primitives, I am sure, would never have behaved so unfeelingly!"

Cyril smiled, but his face was hard as he turned back to the Snaddrath. "We'll radio Gambrell in the morning to have a ship dispatched to pick us up. I'm not sure but that we have a good case for fraud against you."

"We're destroyed!" Bbulas shrieked as the full emotional impact of the situation hit him. "An interplanetary lawsuit would ruin Snaddra entirely."

His cries were echoed in the howls of the other Snaddrath, their antennae psonking, their eyes bulging.

*

Agonized by his sorrow, Bbulas lost all emotional restraint, forgot about his Terrestrial training, and turned upside down in a spasm of grief. Since there was no longer any reason to repress their natural manifestation of feeling, all the Snaddrath followed suit, their antennae twisting in frenzy as they ululated.

And then, to Skkiru's surprise and the surprise of all the rest, Cyril stopped and took out his notebook. "Wait a minute," he said as Raoul did likewise. All four Earthly eyes were shining with a glow that was recognizable to any even remotely humanoid species as the glow of intellectual fervor. "Wait just a minute! Our plans are altered. We may stay, after all!"

One by one, the Snaddrath reversed to upright positions, but did not retract their eyes, for they were still staring at the Earthmen. Skkiru knew now what had been bothering him about the Terrestrials all along. They were crazy—that was what it was. Who but maniacs would want to leave their warm, dry planets and go searching the stars for strange cultures, when they could stay quietly at home in peace and comfort with their families?

Skkiru's hand reached out for Larhgan's and found it.

ANGEL'S EGG

By Edgar Pangborn

When adopting a pet, choose the species that is most intelligent, obedient, loyal, fun to play with, yet a shrewd, fearless protector. For the best in pets—choose a human being!

*

Mr. Cleveland McCarran
Federal Bureau of Investigation
Washington, D. C.

Dear Sir:

In compliance with your request, I enclose herewith a transcript of the pertinent sections of the journal of Dr. David Bannerman, deceased. The original document is being held at this office until proper disposition can be determined.

Our investigation has shown no connection between Dr. Bannerman and any organization, subversive or otherwise. So far as we can learn he was exactly what he seemed, an inoffensive summer resident, retired, with a small independent income—a recluse to some extent, but well spoken of by local tradesmen and other neighbors. A connection between Dr. Bannerman and the type of activity that concerns your Department would seem most unlikely.

The following information is summarized from the earlier parts of Dr. Bannerman's journal, and tallies with the results of our own limited inquiry.

He was born in 1898 at Springfield, Massachusetts, attended public school there, and was graduated from Harvard College in 1922, his studies having been interrupted by two years' military service. He was wounded in action in the Argonne, receiving a spinal injury. He earned a doctorate in Biology, 1926. Delayed after-effects of his war injury necessitated hospitalization, 1927-'28. From 1929 to 1948 he taught elementary sciences in a private school in Boston. He published two textbooks in introductory biology, 1929 and 1937. In 1948 he retired from teaching: a pension and a modest income from textbook royalties evidently made this possible.

Aside from the spinal injury, which caused him to walk with a stoop, his health is said to have been fair. Autopsy findings suggested that the spinal condition must have given him considerable pain; he is not known to have mentioned this to anyone, not even his physician, Dr. Lester Morse. There is no evidence whatever of drug addiction or alcoholism.

At one point early in his journal, Dr. Bannerman describes himself as "a naturalist of the puttering type. I would rather sit on a log than write monographs; it pays off better." Dr. Morse, and others who knew Dr. Bannerman personally, tell me that this conveys a hint of his personality.

*

I am not qualified to comment on the material of this journal, except to say that I have no evidence to support (or to contradict) Dr. Bannerman's statements. The journal has been studied only by my immediate superiors, by Dr. Morse, and by myself. I take it for granted you will hold the matter in strictest confidence.

With the journal I am also enclosing a statement by Dr. Morse, written at my request for our records and for your information. You will note that he says, with some qualifications, that "death was not inconsistent with an embolism." He has signed a death certificate on that basis. You will recall from my letter of August 5 that it was Dr. Morse who discovered Dr. Bannerman's body. Because he was a close personal friend of the deceased, Dr. Morse did not feel able to perform the autopsy himself. It was done by a Dr. Stephen Clyde of this city, and was virtually negative as regards cause of death, neither confirming nor contradicting Dr. Morse's original tentative diagnosis. If you wish to read the autopsy report in full, I shall be glad to forward a copy.

Dr. Morse tells me that so far as he knows, Dr. Bannerman had no near relatives. He never married. For the last twelve summers he occupied a small cottage on a back road about twenty-five miles from this city, and had few visitors. The neighbor Steele mentioned in the journal is a farmer, age 68, of good character, who tells me he "never got really acquainted with Dr. Bannerman."

At this office we feel that unless new information comes to light, further active investigation is hardly justified.

Respectfully yours,

Garrison Blaine
Capt., State Police
Augusta, Me.

Encl: Extract from Journal of David Bannerman, dec'd. Statement by Lester Morse, M.D.

*

LIBRARIAN'S NOTE: The following document, originally attached as an unofficial "rider" to the foregoing letter, was donated to this institution in 1994 through the courtesy of Mrs. Helen McCarran, widow of the martyred first President of the World Federation. Other personal and state papers of President McCarran, many of them dating from the early period when he was employed by the FBI, are accessible to public view at the Institute of World History, Copenhagen.

*

EXTRACT FROM JOURNAL OF DAVID BANNERMAN JUNE 1-JULY 29, 1951

It must have been at least three weeks ago when we had that flying saucer flurry. Observers the other side of Katahdin saw it come down this side; observers this side saw it come down the other. Size anywhere from six inches to sixty feet in diameter (or was it cigar-shaped?) and speed whatever you please. Seem to recall that witnesses agreed on a rosy-pink light. There was the inevitable gobbledegookery of official explanation designed to leave everyone impressed, soothed and disappointed.

I paid scant attention to the excitement and less to the explanations—naturally, I thought it was just a flying saucer. But now Camilla has hatched out an angel.

I have eight hens, all yearlings except Camilla; this is her third spring. I boarded her two winters at my neighbor Steele's farm when I closed this shack and shuffled my chilly bones off to Florida, because even as a pullet she had a manner which overbore me. I could never have eaten Camilla. If she had looked at the ax with that same expression of rancid disapproval (and she would) I should have felt I was beheading a favorite aunt. Her only concession to sentiment is the annual rush of maternity to the brain—normal, for a case-hardened White Plymouth Rock.

This year she stole a nest successfully, in a tangle of blackberry. By the time I located it, I estimated I was about two weeks too late. I had to outwit her by watching from a window; she is far too acute to be openly trailed from feeding ground to nest. When I had bled and pruned my way to her hideout, she was sitting on nine eggs and hating my guts. They could not be fertile, since I keep no rooster, and I was about to rob her when I saw the ninth egg was not hers, nor any other chicken's.

*

It was a deep blue, transparent, with flecks of inner light that made me think of the first stars in a clear evening. It was the same size as Camilla's eggs. There was an embryo, but nothing I could recognize.

I returned the egg to Camilla's bare and fevered breastbone, and went back to the house for a long cool drink.

That was ten days ago. I know I ought to have kept a record; I examined the blue egg every day, watching how some nameless life grew within it, until finally the angel chipped the shell deftly in two parts. This was evidently done with the aid of small horny out-growths on her elbows; these growths were sloughed off on the second day.

I wish I had seen her break the shell, but when I visited the blackberry tangle three days ago she was already out. She poked her exquisite head through Camilla's neck feather, smiled sleepily, and snuggled back into darkness to finish drying off. So what could I do, more than save the broken shell and wriggle my clumsy self out of there?

I had removed Camilla's own eggs the day before—Camilla was only moderately annoyed. I was nervous about disposing of them even though they were obviously Camilla's, but no harm was done. I cracked each one to be sure. Very frankly rotten eggs and nothing more.

In the evening of that day I thought of rats and weasels, as I should have earlier. I hastily prepared a box in the kitchen and brought the two in, the angel quiet in my closed hand. They are there now. I think they are comfortable.

Three days after hatching, the angel is the length of my fore-finger, say three inches tall, with about the relative proportions of a six-year-old girl. Except for head, hands, and probably the soles of her feet, she is clothed in feathery down the color of ivory. What can be seen of her skin is a glowing pink—I do mean glowing, like the inside of certain seashells. Just above the small of her back are two stubs which I take to be infantile wings. They do not suggest an extra pair of specialized forelimbs. I think they are wholly differentiated organs; perhaps they will be like the wings of an insect. Somehow I never thought of angels buzzing. Maybe she won't. I know very little about angels.

*

At present the stubs are covered with some dull tissue, no doubt a protective sheath to be discarded when the membranes (if they are membranes) are ready to grow. Between the stubs is a not very prominent ridge—special musculature, I suppose. Otherwise her shape is quite human, even to a pair of minuscule mammalian pin-heads just visible under the down.

How that can make sense in an egg-laying organism is beyond my comprehension. Just for the record, so is a Corot landscape; so is Schubert's Unfinished; so is the flight of a hummingbird, or the other-world of frost on a windowpane.

The down on her head has grown visibly in three days and is of different quality from the body down. Later it may resemble human hair, probably as a diamond resembles a chunk of granite....

A curious thing has happened. I went to Camilla's box after writing that. Judy[1] was already lying in front of it, unexcited. The angel's head was out from under the feathers, and I thought, with more verbal distinctness than such thoughts commonly take, *So here I am, a naturalist of middle years and cold sober, observing a three-inch oviparous mammal with down and wings.*

The thing is—she giggled!

Now it might have been only amusement at my appearance, which to her must be enormously gross and comic. But another thought formed unspoken: *I am no longer lonely.* And her face, hardly bigger than a dime, immediately changed from laughter to a brooding and friendly thoughtfulness.

Judy and Camilla are old friends. Judy seems untroubled by the angel. I have no worries about leaving them alone together.

*

June 3

I made no entry last night. The angel was talking to me, and when that was finished I drowsed off immediately on a cot which I have moved into the kitchen to be near them.

I had never been strongly impressed by the evidence for extrasensory perception. It is fortunate that my mind was able to accept the novelty, since to the angel it is clearly a matter of course. Her tiny mouth is most expressive, but moves only for that reason and for eating—not for speech. Probably she could speak to her own kind if she wished, but I dare say the sound would be above the range of my hearing as well as my understanding.

Last night after I brought the cot in and was about to finish my puttering bachelor supper, she climbed to the edge of the box and pointed, first at herself and then at the top of the kitchen table. Afraid to let my vast hand take hold of her, I held it out flat and she sat in my palm. Camilla was inclined to fuss, but the angel looked over her shoulder and Camilla subsided, watchful but no longer alarmed.

The table-top is porcelain, and the angel shivered. I folded a towel and spread a silk handkerchief on top of that; the angel sat on this arrangement with apparent comfort, near my face. I was not even bewildered, without realizing why. That doesn't seem possible, does it? But there was a good reason.

She reached me first with visual imagery. How can I make it plain that this had nothing in common with my sleeping dreams? There was no weight of symbolism from my littered past, no discoverable connection with any of yesterday's commonplaces, indeed no actual involvement of my personality at all. I saw. I was moving vision, though without eyes or other flesh. And while my mind saw, it also knew where my flesh was, seated at the kitchen table. If anyone had entered the kitchen, if there had been a noise of alarm out in the henhouse, I should have known it.

*

There was a valley such as I have not seen, and never will, on Earth. I have seen many beautiful places on this planet—some of them were even tranquil. Once I took a slow steamer to New Zealand and had the Pacific as a play-thing for many days. I can hardly say how I knew this was not Earth. The grass of the valley was a familiar green. A river below me was a blue and silver thread under sunlight. There were trees much like pine and maple, and maybe that is what they were. But it was not Earth. I was aware of mountains heaped to strange heights on either side of the valley—snow, rose, amber, gold. The amber tint was unlike any mountain color I have noticed in this world at mid-day.

Or I may have known it was not Earth, simply because her mind—dwelling within some unimaginable brain smaller than the tip of my little finger—told me so.

I watched two inhabitants of that world come flying, to rest in the field of sunny grass where my bodiless vision had brought me. Adult forms, such as my angel would surely be when she had her growth, except that both of these were male and one of them was dark-skinned. The latter was also old, with a thousand-wrinkled face, knowing and full of tranquillity; the other was flushed and lively with youth. Both were beautiful. The down of the brown-skinned old one was reddish-tawny; the other's was ivory with hints of orange. Their wings were true membranes, with more variety of subtle iridescence than I have seen even in the wings of a dragonfly; I could not say that any color was dominant, for each motion brought a ripple of change.

These two sat at their ease on the grass. I realized that they were talking to each other, though their lips did not move in speech more than once or twice. They would nod, smile, now and then illustrate something with twinkling hands.

A huge rabbit lolloped past them. I knew—thanks to my own angel's efforts, I supposed—that this animal was of the same size as our common wild ones. Later a blue-green snake three times the size of the angels came flowing through the grass. The old one reached out to stroke its head carelessly, and I think he did it without interrupting whatever he was saying.

Another creature came in leisured leaps. He was monstrous, yet I felt no alarm in the angels or myself. Imagine a being built somewhat like a kangaroo up to the head, about eight feet tall, and katydid-green. Really the thick balancing tail and enormous legs were the only kangaroolike features about him. The body above the massive thighs was not dwarfed, but thick and square. The arms and hands were quite humanoid, and the head was round, manlike except for its face—there was only a single nostril and his mouth was set in the vertical. The eyes were large and mild.

I received an impression of high intelligence and natural gentleness.

In one of his manlike hands he carried two tools, so familiar and ordinary that I knew my body by the kitchen table had laughed in startled recognition. But after all, a garden spade and rake are basic. Once invented—I expect we did it ourselves in the Neolithic—there is little reason why they should change much down the millennia.

This farmer halted by the angels, and the three conversed a while. The big head nodded agreeably. I believe the young angel made a joke; certainly the convulsions in the huge green face made me think of laughter. Then this amiable monster turned up the grass in a patch a few yards square, broke the sod and raked the surface smooth, just as any competent gardener might do, except that he moved with the relaxed smoothness of a being whose strength far exceeds the requirements of his task....

*

I was back in my kitchen with everyday eyes. My angel was exploring the table. I had a loaf of bread there, and a dish of strawberries in cream. She was trying a breadcrumb, seemed to like it fairly well. I offered the strawberries. She broke off one of the seeds and nibbled it, but didn't care so much for the pulp. I held up the great spoon with sugary cream. She steadied it with both hands to try some. I think she liked it.

It had been stupid of me not to realize that she would be hungry. I brought wine from the cupboard; she watched inquiringly, so I put a couple of drops on the handle of a spoon. The taste really pleased her. She chuckled and patted her tiny stomach, though I'm afraid it wasn't very good sherry. I brought some crumbs of cake, but she indicated that she was full, came close to my face and motioned me to lower my head.

She reached up until she could press both hands against my forehead—I felt it only enough to know her hands were there—and she stood so a long time, trying to tell me something.

It was difficult. Pictures come through with relative ease, but now she was transmitting an abstraction of a complex kind. My clumsy brain suffered in the effort to receive. Something did come across, but I have only the crudest way of passing it on. Imagine an equilateral triangle; place the following words one at each corner—"recruiting," "collecting," "saving." The meaning she wanted to convey ought to be near the center of the triangle.

I had also the sense that her message provided a partial explanation of her errand in this lovable and damnable world.

She looked weary when she stood away from me. I put out my palm and she climbed into it, to be carried back to the nest.

She did not talk to me tonight, nor eat, but she gave a reason, coming out from Camilla's feathers long enough to turn her back and show me the wing-stubs. The protective sheaths have dropped off; the wings are rapidly growing. They are probably damp and weak. She was quite tired and went back into the warm darkness almost at once.

Camilla must be exhausted, too. I don't think she has been off the nest more than twice since I brought them into the house.

*

June 4

Today she can fly.

I learned it in the afternoon, when I was fiddling about in the garden and Judy was loafing in the sunshine she loves. Something apart from sight and sound called me to hurry back to the house. I saw my angel through the screen door before I opened it. One of her feet had caught in a hideous loop of loose wire at a break in the mesh. Her first tug of alarm must have tightened the loop so that her hands were not strong enough to force it open.

Fortunately I was able to cut the wire with a pair of shears before I lost my head; then she could free her foot without injury. Camilla had been frantic, rushing around fluffed up, but—here's an odd thing—perfectly silent. None of the recognized chicken-noises of dismay. If an ordinary chick had been in trouble, she would have raised the roof.

*

The angel flew to me and hovered, pressing her hands on my forehead. The message was clear at once: "No harm done." She flew down to tell Camilla the same thing.

Yes, in the same way. I saw Camilla standing near my feet with her neck out and head low, and the angel put a hand on either side of her scraggy comb. Camilla relaxed, clucked in the normal way, and spread her wings for a shelter. The angel went under it, but only to oblige Camilla, I think—at least, she stuck her head through the wing feathers and winked.

She must have seen something else then, for she came out and flew back to me and touched a finger to my cheek, looked at the finger, saw it was wet, put it in her mouth, made a face, and laughed at me.

We went outdoors into the sun (Camilla, too) and the angel gave me an exhibition of what flying ought to be. Not even Wagner can speak of joy as her first free flying did. At one moment she would be hanging in front of my eyes, radiant and delighted; the next instant she would be a dot of color against a cloud. Try to imagine something that would make a hummingbird seem dull and sluggish!

They do hum. Softer than a hummingbird; louder than a dragonfly. Something like the sound of hawk-moths—*Hemaris thisbe*, for instance, the one I used to call Hummingbird Moth when I was a child.

I was frightened, naturally. Frightened first at what might happen to her, but that was unnecessary; I don't think she would be in danger from any savage animal except possibly Man. I saw a Cooper's hawk slant down the invisible toward the swirl of color where she was dancing by herself. Presently she was drawing iridescent rings around him. Then, while he soared in smaller circles, I could not see her, but (maybe she felt my fright) she was again in front of me, pressing my forehead in the now familiar way.

I knew she was amused, and caught the idea that the hawk was a "lazy character." Not quite the way I'd describe *Accipiter Cooperi*, but it's all in the point of view. I believe she had been riding his back, no doubt with her telepathic hands on his predatory head.

Later I was frightened by the thought that she might not want to return to me. Could I compete with sunlight and open sky? The passage of that terror through me brought her swiftly back, and her hands said with great clarity: "Don't ever be afraid of anything. It isn't necessary for you."

Once this afternoon I was saddened by the realization that old Judy can take little part in what goes on now. I can well remember Judy running like the wind. The angel must have heard this thought in me, for she stood a long time beside Judy's drowsy head, while Judy's tail thumped cheerfully on the warm grass....

*

In the evening the angel made a heavy meal on two or three cake crumbs and another drop of sherry, and we had what was almost a sustained conversation. I will write it in that form this time, rather than grope for anything more exact.

I asked her: "How far away is your home?"

"My home is here."

"I meant the place your people came from."

"Ten light years."

"The images you showed me—that quiet valley—that is ten light years away?"

"Yes. But that was my father talking to you, through me. He was grown when the journey began. He is two hundred and forty years old—our years, thirty-two days longer than each of yours."

Mainly I was conscious of a flood of relief. I had feared, on the basis of terrestrial biology that her explosively rapid growth after hatching must foretell a brief life. But it's all right—she can outlive me, and by a few hundred years at that.

"Your father is here now, on this planet? Shall I see him?"

She took her hands away—listening, I believe. The answer was: "No. He is sorry. He is ill and cannot live long. I am to see him in a few days, when I fly a little better. He taught me for twenty years after I was born."

"I don't understand. I thought that—"

"Later, friend. My father is grateful for your kindness to me."

I don't know what I thought about that. I felt no faintest trace of condescension in the message.

"And he was showing me things he had seen with his own eyes, ten light years away?"

"Yes." Then she wanted me to rest a while; I am sure she knows what a huge effort it is for my primitive brain to function in this way. But before she ended the conversation by humming down to her nest she gave me this, and I received it with such clarity that I cannot be mistaken: "He says that only fifty million years ago it was a jungle there, just as Terra is now."

*

June 8

When I woke four days ago, the angel was having breakfast, and little Camilla was dead. The angel watched me rub sleep out of my eyes, watched me discover Camilla, and then flew to me.

I received this: "Does it make you unhappy?"

"I don't know exactly." You can get fond of a hen, especially a cantankerous and homely old one whose personality has a lot in common with your own.

"She was old. She wanted a flock of chicks, and I couldn't stay with her. So I—" something obscure here; probably my mind was trying too hard to grasp it—"so I saved her life." I could make nothing else out of it. She said "saved."

Camilla's death looked natural, except that I should have expected the death contractions to muss the straw and that hadn't happened. Maybe the angel had arranged the old lady's body for decorum, though I don't see how her muscular strength would have been equal to it, Camilla weighed at least seven pounds.

As I was burying her at the edge of the garden and the angel was humming over my head, I recalled a thing which, when it happened, I had dismissed as a dream. Merely a moonlight image of the angel standing in the nest box with her hands on Camilla's head, then pressing her mouth gently on Camilla's throat, just before the hen's head sank down out of my line of vision. Probably I actually awoke and saw it happen. I am somehow unconcerned—even, as I think more about it, pleased.

After the burial the angel's hands said: "Sit on the grass and we'll talk. Question me; I'll tell you what I can. My father asks you to write it down."

So that is what we have been doing for the last four days. I have been going to school, a slow but willing pupil. Rather than enter anything in this journal, for in the evenings I was exhausted, I made notes as best I could. The angel has gone now to see her father and will not return until morning. I shall try to make a readable version of my notes.

Since she had invited questions, I began with something which had been bothering me, as a would-be naturalist, exceedingly. I couldn't see how creatures no larger than the adults I had observed could lay eggs, as large as Camilla's. Nor could I understand why, if they were hatched in an almost adult condition and able to eat a varied diet, she had any use for that ridiculous, lovely and apparently functional pair of breasts.

*

When the angel grasped my difficulty, she exploded with laughter—her kind, which buzzed her all over the garden and caused her to fluff my hair on the wing and pinch my earlobe. She lit on a rhubarb leaf and gave a delectably naughty representation of herself as a hen laying an egg, including the cackle. She got me to bumbling helplessly—my kind of laughter—and it was some time before we could quiet down. Then she did her best to explain.

They are true mammals, and the young—not more than two or at most three in a lifetime averaging two hundred and fifty years—are delivered in very much the human way. The baby is nursed, human fashion, until his brain begins to respond a little to their unspoken language. That takes three to four weeks. Then he is placed in an altogether different medium.

She could not describe that clearly, because there was very little in my educational storehouse to help me grasp it. It is some gaseous medium which arrests bodily growth for an almost indefinite period, while mental growth continues. It took them, she says, about seven thousand years to perfect this technique after they first hit on the idea; they are never in a hurry.

The infant remains under this delicate and precise control for anywhere from fifteen to thirty years, the period depending not only on his mental vigor, but also on the type of lifework he tentatively elects as soon as his brain is knowing enough to make a choice. During this period his mind is guided with patience by teachers who—

*

It seems those teachers know their business. This was peculiarly difficult for me to assimilate, although the facts came through clearly enough. In their world, the profession of teacher is more highly honored than any other—can such a thing be possible?—and so difficult to enter that only the strongest minds dare to attempt it.

I had to rest a while after absorbing that.

An aspirant must spend fifty years, not including the period of infantile education, merely getting ready to begin, and the acquisition of factual knowledge, while not understressed, takes only a small proportion of those fifty years. Then, if he's good enough, he can take a small part in the elementary instruction of a few babies, and if he does well on that basis for another thirty or forty years, he is considered a fair beginner....

Once upon a time I myself lurched around stuffy classrooms, trying to insert a few predigested facts—I wonder how many of them *were* facts—into the minds of bored and preoccupied adolescents, some of whom may have liked me moderately well. I was even able to shake hands and be nice while their terribly well-meaning parents explained to me how they ought to be educated. So much of our human effort goes down the drain of futility, I sometimes wonder how we ever got as far as the Bronze Age. Somehow we did, though, and a short way beyond.

After that preliminary stage of an angel's education is finished, the baby is transferred to more ordinary surroundings, and his bodily growth completes itself in a very short time. Wings grow abruptly, as I have seen, and he reaches a maximum height of six inches by our measure. Only then does he enter on that lifetime of two hundred and fifty years, for not until then does his body begin to age. My angel has been a living personality for many years, but will not celebrate her first birthday for almost a year. I like to think of that.

At about the same time that they learned the principles of interplanetary travel, approximately twelve million years ago, these people also learned how growth could be rearrested at any point short of full maturity. At first the knowledge served no purpose except in the control of illnesses which still occasionally struck them at that time. But when the long periods of time required for space travel were considered, the advantages became obvious.

*

So it happens that my angel was born ten light years away. She was trained by her father and many others in the wisdom of seventy million years—that, she tells me, is the approximate sum of their *recorded* history—and then she was safely sealed and cherished in what my superamebic brain regarded as a blue egg. Education did not proceed at that time; her mind went to sleep with the rest of her. When Camilla's warmth made her wake and grow again, she remembered what to do with the little horny bumps provided for her elbows. And came out into this planet, God help her.

I wondered why her father should have chosen any combination so unreliable as an old hen and a human being. Surely he must have had plenty of excellent ways to bring the shell to the right temperature. Her answer should have satisfied me immensely, but I am still compelled to wonder about it.

"Camilla was a nice hen, and my father studied your mind while you were asleep. It was a bad landing, and much was broken—no such landing was ever made before after so long a journey. Only four other grown-ups could come with my father. Three of them died en route and he is very ill. And there were nine other children to care for."

Yes, I knew she'd said that an angel thought I was good enough to be trusted with his daughter. If it upsets me, all I need do is look at her and then in the mirror. As for the explanation, I can only conclude there must be more which I am not ready to understand. I was worried about those nine others, but she assured me they were all well, and I sensed that I ought not to ask more about them at present.

*

Their planet, she says, is closely similar to this, a trifle larger, moving in a somewhat longer orbit around a sun like ours. Two gleaming moons, smaller than ours—their orbits are such that two-moon nights come rarely; they are "magic," and she will ask her father to show me one, if he can. Because of a slower rotation, their day has twenty-six of our hours. Their atmosphere is mainly nitrogen and oxygen in the proportion familiar to us; slightly richer in some of the rare gases. The climate is now what we should call tropical and subtropical, but they have known glacial rigors like those in our world's past. There are only two great continental land masses, and many thousands of large islands.

Their total population is only five billion.

It seems my angel wants to become a student of animal life here on Earth. I, her teacher! But bless her for the notion anyhow. We sat and traded animals for a couple of hours last night; I found it restful, after the mental struggle to grasp more difficult matters. Judy was something new to her. They have several luscious monsters on that planet, but, in her view, so have we.

She told me of a blue sea-snake fifty feet long, relatively harmless, that bellows cowlike and comes into the tidal marshes to lay black eggs; so I gave her a whale. She offered a bat-winged, day-flying ball of mammalian fluff as big as my head and weighing under an ounce; I matched her with a marmoset. She tried me with a small-size pink brontosaur, very rare, but I was ready with the duck-billed platypus, and that caused us to exchange some pretty funny remarks about mammalian eggs. All trivial in a way; also the happiest evening in my fifty-three tangled years of life.

She was a trifle hesitant to explain those kangaroolike people, until she was sure I really wanted to know. It seems they are about the nearest parallel to human life on that planet; not a near parallel, of course, as she was careful to explain. Agreeable and always friendly souls, though they weren't always so, I'm sure, and of a somewhat more alert intelligence than we possess. Manual workers mainly, because they prefer it nowadays, but some of them are excellent mathematicians. The first practical spaceship was built by a group of them, with assistance, of course.

Names offer a difficulty. Because of the nature of the angelic language, they have scant use for them except for the purpose of written record, and writing naturally plays little part in their daily life—no occasion to write a letter when distance is no obstacle to the speech of your mind. An angel's formal name is about as important to him, as, say, my Social Security number is to me.

*

She has not told me hers, because my mind can't grasp the phonetics on which their written language is based. As we would speak a friend's name, an angel will project the friend's image to his friend's receiving mind. More pleasant and more intimate, I think, although it was a shock to me at first to glimpse my own ugly mug in my mind's eye.

Stories are occasionally written, if there is something in them that should be preserved precisely as it was in the first telling. But in their world the true story-teller has a more important place than the printer. He offers one of the best of their quieter pleasures; a good one can hold his audience for a week and never tire them.

"What is this 'angel' in your mind when you think of me?" she asked once.

"A being men have imagined for centuries, when they thought of themselves as they might like to be, and not as they are."

I did not try too painfully hard to learn much about the principles of space travel. The most my brain could take in of her explanation was something like: "Rocket, then phototropism." Now that makes scant sense. So far as I know, phototropism—movement toward light—is an *organic* phenomenon. One thinks of it as a response of protoplasm, in some plants and animal organisms, most of them simple, to the stimulus of light; certainly not as a force capable of moving inorganic matter.

I think that whatever may be the principle she was describing, this word phototropism was merely the nearest thing to it in my reservoir of language. If I did know the physical principles which brought them here, and could write them in terms accessible to technicians, I would not do it.

Here is a thing I am afraid no hypothetical reader of this journal would believe:

These people, as I have written, learned their method of space travel some twelve million years ago, yet this is the first time they have ever used it to convey them to another planet. The heavens are rich in worlds, she tells me; on many of them there is life, often on very primitive levels. No external force prevented her people from going forth, colonizing, conquering, as far as they pleased. They could have populated a whole Galaxy. They did not, because they believed they were not ready. More precisely—

Not good enough!

*

Only fifty million years ago, by her account, did they learn, as we may learn eventually, that intelligence without goodness is worse than high explosive in the hands of a baboon. For beings advanced beyond the level of Pithecanthropus, intelligence is a cheap commodity—not too hard to develop, hellishly easy to use for unconsidered ends. Whereas goodness is not to be achieved without unending effort of the hardest kind, within the self, whether the self be man or angel.

It is clear even to me that the conquest of evil is only one step, not the most important. Goodness, she tried to tell me, is an altogether positive quality; the part of living nature that swarms with such monstrosities as cruelty, meanness, bitterness, greed is not to be filled by a vacuum when these horrors are eliminated.

Kindness, for only one example. Anybody who defines kindness only as the absence of cruelty doesn't understand the nature of either.

*

They do not aim at perfection, these angels, only at the attainable. They passed through many millenia while advances in technology merely worsened their condition and increased the peril of self-annihilation. They came through that, in time. War was at length so far outgrown that its recurrence was impossible, and the development of wholly rational beings could begin. Then they were ready to start growing up, through more millenia of self-searching, self-discipline, seeking to earn the simple out of the complex, discovering how to use knowledge and not be used by it. Even then, of course, they slipped back often enough. There were what she refers to as eras of fatigue. In their dimmer past, they had had many dark ages, lost civilizations, hopeful beginnings ending in dust. Earlier still they had come out of the slime, as we did.

But their period of deepest uncertainty and sternest self-appraisal did not come until twelve million years ago, when they knew a Universe could be theirs for the taking, and knew they were not yet good enough.

They are in no more hurry than the stars. She tried to convey something, tentatively, at this point, which was really beyond both of us. It had to do with time (not as I understand time) being perhaps the most essential attribute of God (not as I was ever able to understand that word). Seeing my mental exhaustion, she gave up the effort, and later told me that the conception was extremely difficult for her, too—not only, I gathered, because of her youth and relative ignorance. There was also a hint that her father might not have wished her to bring my brain up to a hurdle like that one....

Of course they explored. Their little spaceships were roaming the ether before there was anything like man on Earth—roaming and listening, observing, recording; never entering nor taking part in the life of any home but their own. For five million years they even forbade themselves to go beyond their own solar system, though it would have been easy to do so. And in the following seven million years, although they traveled to incredible distances, the same stern restraint was held in force.

It was altogether unrelated to what we should call fear. That, I think, is as extinct in them as hate. There was so much to do at home! I wish I could imagine it. They mapped the heavens, and played in their own sunlight.

Naturally I cannot tell you what goodness is. I know only, moderately well, what it seems to mean to us human beings. It appears that the best of us can, often with enormous difficulty, however, achieve a manner of life in which goodness somewhat overbalances our aggressive, hostile tendencies for the greater part of the time. We are, in other words, a fraction alive; the rest is in the dark. Dante was a bitter masochist; Beethoven a frantic and miserable snob, Shakespeare wrote potboilers. And Christ said: "My Father, if it be possible, let this cup pass from me."

But give us fifty million years—I am no pessimist. After all, I've watched one-celled organisms on the slide, and listened to Brahms' Fourth. Night before last I said to the angel: "In spite of everything, you and I are kindred."

She granted me agreement.

*

June 9

She was lying on my pillow this morning so that I could see her when I awoke.

Her father has died, and she was with him when it happened. There was again that thought-impression which I could interpret only to mean that his life had been "saved." I was still sleep-bound when my mind asked: "What will you do?"

"Stay with you, if you wish it, for the rest of your life." The last part of the message was clouded, but I am familiar with that now. It seems to mean there is some further element which eludes me. I could not be mistaken about the part I did receive. It gives me amazing speculations. Being only fifty-three, I might live another thirty or forty years.

She was preoccupied this morning, but whatever she felt about her father's death that might be paralleled by sadness in a human being was hidden from me. She did say her father was sorry he had not been able to show me a two-moon night.

One adult, then, remains in this world. Except to say that he is two hundred years old and full of knowledge, and that he endured the long journey without serious ill effects, she has told me little about him. And there are ten children including herself.

Something was sparkling at her throat. When she was aware of my interest in it, she took it off and I fetched a magnifying glass. A necklace; under the glass, much like our finest human workmanship, if your imagination can reduce it to the proper scale. The stones appeared similar to the jewels we know; diamonds, sapphires, rubies, emeralds, the diamonds snapping out every color under heaven; but there were two or three very dark purple stones unlike anything I know—not amethysts, I am sure. The necklace was strung on something more slender than cobweb, and the design of the joining clasp was too delicate for my glass to help me. The necklace had been her mother's, she told me. As she put it back around her throat, I thought I saw the same shy pride that any human girl might feel in displaying a new pretty.

She wanted to show me other things she had brought, and flew to the table where she had left a sort of satchel an inch and a half long—quite a load for her to fly with, but the translucent substance is so light that when she rested the satchel on my finger I scarcely felt it. She arranged a few articles eagerly for my inspection, and I put the glass to work again.

One was a jeweled comb; she ran it through the down on her chest and legs to show me its use. There was a set of tools too small for the glass to interpret them; I learned later they were a sewing kit. A book, and some writing instrument much like a metal pencil. The book, I understand, is a blank record for her to use as needed.

And finally, when I was fully awake and dressed and we had finished breakfast, she reached in the bottom of the satchel for a parcel that was heavy for her and made me understand it was a gift for me. "My father made it for you, but I put in the stone myself, last night." She unwrapped it. A ring, precisely the size for my little finger.

*

I broke down somewhat. She understood that, and sat on my shoulder patting my earlobe till I had command of myself.

I have no idea what the jewel is. It shifts with the light from purple to jade green to amber. The metal resembles platinum in appearance, except for a tinge of rose at certain angles of light. When I stare into the stone, I think

I see—never mind that now. I am not ready to write it down, and perhaps never will be, unless I am sure.

We improved our housekeeping, later in the morning. I showed her over the house. It isn't much—Cape Codder, two rooms up and two down. Every corner interested her, and when she found a shoebox in the bedroom closet, she asked for it. At her direction, I have arranged it on a chest near my bed and the window which shall be always open. She says the mosquitoes will not bother me, and I don't doubt her.

I unearthed a white silk scarf for the bottom of the box. After asking my permission—as if I could want to refuse her anything!—she got her sewing kit and snipped off a piece of the scarf several inches square, folded it on itself several times, and sewed it into a narrow pillow an inch long. So now she has a proper bed and a room of her own. I wish I had something less coarse than silk, but she insists she's pleased with it.

We have not talked very much today. In the afternoon she flew out for an hour's play in the cloud-country. When she returned, she let me know that she needed a long sleep. She is still sleeping, I think. I am writing this downstairs, fearing the light might disturb her.

Is it possible I can have thirty or forty years in her company? I wonder how teachable my mind still is. I seem to be able to assimilate new facts as well as I ever could; this ungainly carcass should be durable, with reasonable care. Of course, facts without a synthesizing imagination are no better than scattered bricks, but perhaps my imagination—

I don't know.

Judy wants out. I shall turn in when she comes back. I wonder if poor Judy's life could be—the word is certainly "saved." I must ask.

*

June 10

Last night when I stopped writing I did go to bed, but I was restless, refusing sleep. At some time in the small hours—there was light from a single moon—she flew over to me. The tensions dissolved away like an illness and my mind was able to respond with a certain calm.

I made plain that I would never willingly part company with her, which I am sure she already knew, and she gave me to understand that there are two alternatives for the remainder of my life. The choice, she says, is altogether mine, and I must take time to be sure of my decision.

I can live out my natural span, whatever it proves to be, and she will not leave me for long at any time. She will be there to advise, teach, help me in anything good I care to undertake. She says she would enjoy this; for some reason she is, as we'd say in our language, fond of me.

Lord, the books I could write! I fumble for words now, in the usual human way. Whatever I put on paper is a miserable fraction, of the potential; the words themselves are rarely the right ones. But under her guidance—

I could take a fair part in shaking the world. With words alone. I could preach to my own people. Before long, I would be heard.

I could study and explore. What small nibblings we have made at the sum of available knowledge! Suppose I brought in one leaf from outdoors, or one common little bug—in a few hours of studying it with her, I'd know more of my own specialty than a flood of the best textbooks could tell me.

She has also let me know that when she and those who came with her have learned a little more about humanity, it should be possible to improve my health greatly, and probably my life expectancy. I don't imagine my back could ever straighten, but she thinks the pain might be cleared away, entirely without drugs. I could have a clearer mind, in a body that would neither fail nor torment me.

Then there is the other alternative.

It seems they have developed a technique by means of which any unresisting living subject, whose brain is capable of memory at all, can experience *total recall*. It is a by-product, I understand, of their silent speech, and a very recent one. They have practiced it for only a few thousand years, and since their own understanding of the phenomenon is very incomplete, they classify it among their experimental techniques.

In a general way, it may somewhat resemble that reliving of the past which psychoanalysis can sometimes bring about in a limited way for therapeutic purposes. But you must imagine that sort of thing tremendously magnified and clarified, capable of including every detail which has ever registered on the subject's brain.

*

The purpose is not therapeutic, as we would understand it; quite the opposite. The end result is—death.

Whatever is recalled, by this process is transmitted to the receiving mind, which can retain it, and record any or all of it, if such a record is desired; but to the subject who recalls, it is a flowing away, without return. Thus it is not a true "remembering," but a giving. The mind is swept clear, naked of all its past, and, along with memory, life withdraws also. Very quietly.

At the end, I suppose it must be like standing without resistance in the engulfment of a flood tide, until finally the waters close over.

That, it seems, is how Camilla's life was "saved." When I finally grasped that, I laughed, and the angel of course caught the reason. I was thinking about my neighbor Steele, who boarded Camilla for me in his henhouse for a couple of winters.

Somewhere safe in the angelic records there must be a hen's-eye image of the patch in the seat of Steele's pants. And naturally Camilla's view of me too; not too unkind, I hope. She couldn't help the expression on her rigid little face, and I don't believe it ever meant anything.

At the other end of the scale is the saved life of my angel's father. Recall can be a long process, she says, depending on the intricacy and richness of the mind recalling; and in all but the last stages it can be halted at will. Her father's recall was begun when they were still far out in space and he knew that he could not long survive the journey.

When that journey ended, the recall had progressed so far that very little actual memory remained to him of his life on that other planet. He had what must be called a deductive memory—from the material of the years not yet given away, he could reconstruct what must have been, and I assume the other adult who survived the passage must have been able to shelter him from errors that loss of memory might involve. This, I infer, is why he could not show me a two-moon night.

I forgot to ask her whether the images he did send me were from actual or deductive memory. Deductive, I think, for there was a certain dimness about them not present when my angel gives me a picture of something seen with her own eyes.

Jade-green eyes, by the way. Were you wondering?

In the same fashion, my own life could be saved. Every aspect of existence that I ever touched, that ever touched me, could be transmitted to some perfect record—the nature of the written record is beyond me, but I have no doubt of its relative perfection. Nothing important, good or bad, would be lost. And they need a knowledge of humanity, if they are to carry out whatever it is they have in mind.

It would be difficult, she tells me, and sometimes painful. Most of the effort would be hers, but some of it would have to be mine. In her period of infantile education, she elected what we should call zoology as her life work; for that reason she was given intensive theoretical training in this technique. Right now I guess she knows more than anyone else on this planet not only about what makes a hen tick, but how it feels to be a hen.

Though a beginner, she is in all essentials already an expert. She can help me, she thinks, if I choose this alternative. At any rate, she could ease me over the toughest spots, keep my courage from flagging.

For it seems that this process of recall is painful to an advanced intellect—without condescension, she calls us very advanced—because, while all pretense and self-delusion are stripped away, there remains conscience, still functioning by whatever standards of good and bad the individual has developed in his lifetime. Our present knowledge of our own motives is such a pathetically small beginning! Hardly stronger than an infant's first effort to focus his eyes.

*

I am merely wondering how much of my life, if I choose this way, will seem to me altogether hideous. Certainly plenty of the "good deeds" which I still cherish in memory like so many well-behaved cherubs will turn up with the leering aspect of greed or petty vanity or worse.

Not that I am a bad man, in any reasonable sense of the term. I respect myself; no occasion to grovel and beat my chest. I'm not ashamed to stand comparison with any other fair sample of the species. But there you are: I *am* human, and under the aspect of eternity so far, plus this afternoon's newspaper, that is a rather serious thing.

Without real knowledge, I think of this total recall as something like a passage down a corridor of a myriad images, now dark, now brilliant, now pleasant, now horrible—guided by no certainty except an awareness of the open blind door at the end of it. It could have its pleasing moments and its consolations. I don't see how it could ever approximate the delight and satisfaction of living a few more years in this world with the angel lighting on my shoulder when she wishes, and talking to me.

I had to ask her how great a value such a record would be to them. Obvious enough—they can be of little use to us, by their standards, until they understand us, and they came here to be of use to us as well as to themselves.

And understanding us, to them, means knowing us inside out with a completeness such as our most dedicated and laborious scholars could never imagine. I remember, about those twelve million years: they will not touch us until they are certain no harm will come of it.

On our tortured planet, however, there is a time factor. They know that well enough, of course....

Recall cannot begin unless the subject is willing or unresisting; to them, that has to mean willing, for any being with intellect enough to make a considered choice. Now, I wonder how many they could find who would be honestly willing to make that uneasy journey into death, for no reward except an assurance that they were serving their own kind and the angels.

More to the point, I wonder if I would be able to achieve such willingness myself, even with her help.

When this had been explained to me, she urged me again to make no hasty decision. And she pointed out to me what my thoughts were already groping at—why not both alternatives, within a reasonable limit of time? Why couldn't I have ten or fifteen years or more with her, and then undertake the total recall, perhaps not until my physical powers had started toward senility? I thought that over.

This morning I had almost decided to choose that most welcome and comfortable solution. Then my daily paper was delivered. Not that I needed any such reminder.

*

In the afternoon I asked her if she knew whether, in the present state of human technology, it would be possible for our folly to actually destroy this planet. She did not know, for certain. Three of the other children have gone away to different parts of the world, to learn what they can about that. But she had to tell me that such a thing has happened before, elsewhere in the Universe. I guess I won't write a letter to the papers advancing an explanation for the occasional appearance of a nova among the stars. Doubtless others have hit on the same hypothesis without the aid of angels.

And that is not all I must consider. I could die by accident or sudden disease before I had begun to give my life.

Only now, at this very late moment, rubbing my sweaty forehead and gazing into the lights of that wonderful ring, have I been able to put together some obvious facts in the required synthesis.

I don't know, of course, what forms their assistance to us will take. I suspect human beings won't see or hear much of the angels for a long time to come. Now and then disastrous decisions may be altered, and those who believe themselves wholly responsible won't realize why their minds worked that way. Here and there, maybe an influential mind will be rather strangely nudged into a better course. Something like that. There may be new discoveries and inventions of kinds that will tend to neutralize the menace of our nastiest playthings.

But whatever the angels decide to do, the record and analysis of my fairly typical life will be an aid. It could even be the small weight deciding the balance between triumph and failure. That is Fact One.

Two: my angel and her brothers and sisters, for all their amazing level of advancement, are also of perishable protoplasm. Therefore, if this ball of mud becomes a ball of flame, they also will be destroyed. Even if they have the means to use their spaceship again or to build another, it might easily happen that they would not learn their danger in time to escape. And for all I know, this could be tomorrow. Or tonight.

So there can no longer be any doubt as to my choice, and I will tell her when she wakes.

*

July 9

Tonight[2] there is no recall; I am to rest a while. I see it is almost a month since I last wrote in this journal. My total recall began three weeks ago, and already the first twenty-eight years of my life have been saved.

It was a week after I told the angel my decision before she was prepared to start the recall. During that week she searched my present mind more closely than I should have imagined was possible: she had to be sure.

During that week, of hard questions, I dare say she learned more about my kind than has ever gone on record even in a physician's office; I hope she did. To any psychiatrist who might question that, I offer a naturalist's suggestion. It is easy to imagine, after some laborious time, that we have noticed everything a given patch of ground can show us. But alter the view-point only a little—dig down a foot with a spade, say, or climb a tree-branch and look downward—it's a whole new world.

When the angel was not exploring me in this fashion, she took pains to make me glimpse the satisfactions and million rewarding experiences I might have if I chose the other way. I see how necessary that was; at the time it seemed almost cruel. She had to do it, for my own sake, and I am glad that I was somehow able to stand fast to my original choice. So was she, in the end; she has even said she loves me for it. What that troubling word means to her is not within my mind. I am satisfied to take it in the human sense.

Since I no longer require normal sleep, the recall begins at night, as soon as the lights begin to go out in the village and there is little danger of interruption. Daytimes, I putter about in my usual fashion. I have sold Steele my hens, and Judy's life was saved a week ago. That practically winds up my affairs, except that I went to write a codicil to my will. I might as well do that now, right here in this journal, instead of bothering my lawyer. It should be legal.

To Whom It May Concern: I hereby bequeath to my friend Lester Morse, M.D., of Augusta, Maine, the ring which will be found at my death on the fifth finger of my left hand. I would urge Dr. Morse to retain this ring in his private possession at all times, and to make provision for its disposal, in the event of his own death, to some person in whose character he places the utmost faith.

(Signed) David Bannerman[3]

Tonight she has gone away for a while, and I am to rest and do as I please till she returns. I shall spend the time filling in some blanks in this record, but I am afraid it will be a spotty job, because there is so much I no longer care about.

*

Except for the lack of desire for sleep, and a bodily weariness which is not at all unpleasant, I notice no physical effects thus far. I have no faintest recollection of anything that happened earlier than my twenty-eighth birthday. My deductive memory seems rather efficient, and I am sure I could reconstruct most of the story if it were worth the bother. This afternoon I grubbed around among some old letters of that period, but they weren't very interesting.

My knowledge of English is unaffected; I can still read scientific German and some French, because I had occasion to use those languages fairly often after I was twenty-eight. The scraps of Latin dating from high school are gone. So are algebra and all but the simplest proposition of high school geometry: I never needed them.

*

I can remember thinking of my mother after twenty-eight, but I do not know whether the image this provides really resembles her. My father died when I was thirty-one, so I remember him as a sick old man. I believe I had a younger brother, but he must have died in childhood.[4]

Judy's passing was tranquil—pleasant for her, I think. It took the better part of a day. We went out to an abandoned field I know, and she lay blinking in the sunshine with the angel sitting by her, while I dug a grave and then rambled off after wild raspberries. Toward evening the angel came and told me I could bury Judy—it was finished. And most interesting, she said. I don't see how there can have been anything distressing about it for Judy. After all, what hurts us worst is to have our favorite self-deceptions stripped away, and I don't think Judy had any.

I have not found the recall painful, at least not in retrospect. There must have been sharp moments, mercifully forgotten along with their causes, as if the process had gone on under anesthesia. Certainly there were plenty of incidents in my first twenty-eight years which I should not care to offer to the understanding of any but the angels. Quite often I must have been mean, selfish, base in any number of ways, if only to judge by the record since twenty-eight. Those old letters touch on a few of these things. To me, they now matter only as material for a record which is safely out of my hands.

However, to any person I may have harmed, I wish to say this: you were hurt by aspects of my humanity which may not, in a few million years, be quite so common among us. Against these darker elements I struggled, in my human fashion, as you do yourselves. The effort is not wasted.

One evening—I think it was June 12—Lester dropped around for sherry and chess. Hadn't seen him in quite a while, and haven't since. There is a moderate polio scare this summer and it keeps him on the jump.

The angel retired behind some books on an upper shelf—I'm afraid it was dusty—and had fun with our chess. She had a fair view of your bald spot, Lester. Later she remarked that she liked your looks, but can't you do something about that weight? She suggested an odd expedient, which I believe has occurred to your medical self from time to time—eating less.

Maybe she shouldn't have done what she did with those chess games. Nothing more than my usual blundering happened until after my first ten moves; by that time I suppose she had absorbed the principles, and she took over. I was not fully aware of it until I saw you looking like a boiled duck. I had imagined my astonishing moves were the result of my own damn cleverness.

*

Seriously, Lester, think back to that evening. You've played in stiff amateur tournaments; you know your own abilities and you know mine. Ask yourself whether I could have done anything like that without help. I tell you again I didn't study the game in the interval when you weren't here. I've never even had a chess book in the library, and if I had, no amount of study would take me into your class. I haven't that sort of mentality; just your humble sparring partner, and I've enjoyed it on that basis, as you might enjoy watching a prima donna surgeon pull off some miracle you wouldn't dream of attempting yourself. Even if your game had been away below par that evening, and I don't think it was, I could never have pinned your ears back three times running, without help. That evening you were a long way out of *your* class, that's all.

I couldn't tell you anything about it at the time—she was clear on that point—so I could only bumble and preen myself and leave you mystified. But she wants me to write anything I choose in this journal, and somehow, Lester, I think you may find the next few decades pretty interesting. You're still young, some ten years younger than I. I think you'll see many things that I wish I might see come to pass—or I would so wish if I were not convinced that my choice was the right one.

Most of those new events will not be spectacular, I'd guess. Many of the turns to a better way will hardly be recognized at the time for what they are, by you or anyone else. Obviously, our nature being what it is, we shall not change overnight. To hope for that would be as absurd as it is to imagine that any formula, ideology, theory of social pattern can bring us into Utopia. As I see it, Lester—and I think your consulting room would have told you the same even if your own intuition were not enough—there is only one battle of importance: Armageddon. And Armageddon field is within each individual.

At the moment I believe I am the happiest man who ever lived.

*

July 20

All but the last ten years are now given away. The physical fatigue, though still pleasant, is quite overwhelming. I am not troubled by the weeds in my garden patch—merely a different sort of flowers where I had planned something else. An hour ago she brought me the seed of a blown dandelion, to show me how lovely it was. I don't suppose I had ever noticed. I hope whoever takes over this place will bring it back to farming; they say the ten acres below the house used to be good potato land, nice early ground.

It is delightful to sit in the sun, as if I were old.

After thumbing over earlier entries in this journal, I see I have often felt quite bitter toward my own kind. I deduce that I must have been a lonely man, with much of the loneliness self-imposed. A great part of my bitterness must have been no more than one ugly by-product of a life spent too much apart. Some of it doubtless came from objective causes, yet I don't believe I ever had more cause than any moderately intelligent man who would like to see his world a pleasanter place than it has been. My angel tells me that the scar on my back is due to an injury received in some early stage of the war that still goes on. That could have soured me, perhaps. It's all right; it's in the record.

She is racing with a hummingbird—holding back, I think, to give the swift little green fluff a break.

*

Another note for you, Lester. I have already indicated my ring is to be yours. I don't want to tell you what I have discovered of its properties, for fear it might not give you the same pleasure and interest that it has given me. Of course, like any spot of shifting light and color, it is an aid to self-hypnosis. It is more, much more than that, but—find out for yourself, at some time when you are a little protected from everyday distractions.

I know it can't harm you, because I know its source.

By the way, I wish you would convey to my publishers my request that they either discontinue printing my *Introductory Biology* or else bring out a new edition revised in accordance with some notes you will find in the top left drawer of my library desk. I glanced through that book after my angel assured me that I wrote it, and I was amazed. However, I'm afraid my notes are messy—I call them mine by a poetic license—and they may be too advanced for the present day, though the revision is mainly a matter of leaving out certain generalities that aren't so. Use your best judgment. It's a very minor textbook, and the thing isn't too important.

A last wriggle of my vanishing personal vanity.

*

July 27

I have seen a two-moon night. It was given to me by that remaining grown-up, at the end of a wonderful visit, when he and six of those nine other children came to see me. It was last night, I think—yes, must have been. First there was a murmur of wings above the house; my angel flew in laughing. Then they were here, all about me, full of gaiety and colored fire, showing off in every way they knew would please me. Each one had something graceful and friendly to say to me. One brought me a moving image of the St. Lawrence seen at morning from half a mile up—clouds, eagles—now how could he know that would delight me so much?

And each one thanked me for what I had done.

But it's been so easy!

And at the end the old one—his skin is quite black, and his down is white and gray—gave the remembered image of a two-moon night. He saw it some sixty years ago.

I have not even considered making an effort to describe it. My fingers will not hold this pencil much longer tonight. Oh, soaring buildings of white and amber, untroubled countryside, silver on curling rivers, a glimpse of open sea. A moon rising in clarity, another setting in a wreath of cloud, between them a wide wandering of unfamiliar stars. Here and there the angels, worthy after fifty million years to live in such night.

No, I cannot describe anything like that. But you human kindred of mine, I can do something better. I can tell you that this two-moon night, glorious as it was, was no more beautiful than a night under a single moon on this ancient and familiar Earth might be—if you will imagine that human evil has been cleared away, and that our own people have started at last on the greatest of all explorations, themselves.

*

July 29

Nothing now remains to give away but the memory of the time that has passed since the angel came. I am to rest as long as I wish, write whatever I want. Then I shall get myself over to the bed and lie down as if for sleep. She tells me that I can keep my eyes open; she will close them for me when I no longer see her.

I remain convinced that our human case is hopeful. I feel sure that in only a few thousand years we may be able to perform some of the simpler preparatory tasks, such as casting out evil and loving our neighbors. And if that should prove to be so, who can doubt that in another few million years, or even less, we might be only a little lower than the angels?

*

LIBRARIAN'S NOTE: As is generally known, the original of the *Bannerman Journal* is said to have been in the possession of Dr. Lester Morse at the time of the latter's disappearance in 1964, and that disappearance has remained an unsolved mystery to the present day. McCarran is known to have visited Capt. Garrison Blaine in October, 1951, but no record remains of that visit. Capt. Blaine appears to have been a bachelor who lived alone. He was killed in line of duty, December, 1951. McCarran is believed not to have written about nor discussed the Bannerman affair with anyone else. It is almost certain that he himself removed the extract and related papers from the files—unofficially, it would seem—when he severed his connection with the FBI in 1957. At any rate, they were found among his effects after his assassination, and were released to the public, considerably later, by Mrs. McCarran.

The following memorandum was originally attached to the extract from the *Bannerman Journal.* It carries the McCarran initialing.

*

Aug. 11, 1951

The original letter of complaint written by Stephen Clyde, M.D., and mentioned in the accompanying letter of Captain Blaine, has unfortunately been lost, owing perhaps to an error in filing.

Personnel presumed responsible have been instructed not to allow such error to be repeated except if, as and/or when necessary.

C.McC.

On the margin of this memorandum there was a penciled notation, later erased. Iodine vapor has been used to bring out the unmistakable McCarran script. The notation read in part as follows: *Far be it from a* McC. *to lose his job except if, as and or*—the rest is undecipherable, except for a terminal word which is regrettably unparliamentary.

*

STATEMENT BY LESTER MORSE, M.D. DATED AUGUST 9, 1951

On the afternoon of July 30, 1951, acting on what I am obliged to describe as an unexpected impulse, I drove out to the country for the purpose of calling on my friend Dr. David Bannerman. I had not seen him nor had word from him since the evening of June 12 of this year, 1951.

*

After knocking, calling to him and hearing no response, I went upstairs to his bedroom and found him dead. From superficial indications I judged that death must have taken place during the previous night. He was lying on his bed on his left side, comfortably disposed as if for sleep, but fully dressed, with a fresh shirt and clean summer slacks. His eyes and mouth were closed, and there was no trace of the disorder to be expected at even the easiest death.

*

Because of these signs I assumed, soon as I had determined the absence of breath and heartbeat and noted the chill of the body, that some neighbor must have already found him, performed these simple rites of respect for him, and probably notified a local physician or other responsible person. I therefore waited, Dr. Bannerman had no telephone, expecting that someone would soon call.

Dr. Bannerman's journal was on a table near his bed, open to that page on which he had written a codicil to his will. I read that part. Later, while I was waiting for others to come, I read the remainder of the journal, as he apparently wished me to do. The ring he mentions was on the fifth finger of his left hand, and it is now in my possession.

When writing that codicil, Dr. Bannerman must have overlooked or forgotten the fact that in his formal will, written some months earlier, he had appointed me executor. If there are legal technicalities involved, I shall be pleased to co-operate fully with the proper authorities.

The ring, however, will remain in my keeping, since that was Dr. Bannerman's expressed wish, and I am not prepared to offer it for examination or discussion under any circumstances.

The notes for a revision of one of his textbooks were in his desk, as indicated in the journal. They are by no means "messy," nor are they particularly revolutionary except in so far as he wished to re-phrase, as theory or hypothesis, certain statements which I would have regarded as axiomatic. This is not my field, and I am not competent to judge. I shall take up the matter with his publishers at the earliest opportunity.[5]

So far as I can determine, and bearing in mind the results of the autopsy performed by Stephen Clyde, M.D., the death of Dr. David Bannerman was not inconsistent with the presence of an embolism of some type not distinguishable on post mortem. I have so stated on the certificate of death. I am compelled to add one other item of medical opinion for what it may be worth:

I am not a psychiatrist, but, owing to the demands of general practise, I have found it advisable to keep as up to date as possible with current findings and opinion in this branch of medicine. Dr. Bannerman possessed, in my opinion, emotional and intellectual stability to a higher degree than anyone else of comparable intelligence in the entire field of my acquaintance, personal and professional.

*

If it is suggested that he was suffering from a hallucinatory psychosis, I can only say that it must have been of a type quite outside my experience and not described, so far as I know, anywhere in the literature of psychopathology.

Dr. Bannerman's house, on the afternoon of July 30, was in good order. Near the open, unscreened window of his bedroom there was a coverless shoebox with a folded silk scarf in the bottom. I found no pillow such as Dr. Bannerman describes in the journal, but observed that a small section had been cut from the scarf. In this box, and near it, there was a peculiar fragrance, faint, aromatic, very sweet, such as I have never encountered before and therefore cannot describe.

It may or may not have any bearing on the case that, while I remained in his house that afternoon, I felt no sense of grief or personal loss, although Dr. Bannerman had been a loved and honored friend for a number of years. I merely had, and have, a conviction that after the completion of some very great undertaking, he had found peace.

The ring he bequeathed to me has confirmed that.

*

[1]Dr. Bannerman's dog, mentioned often earlier in the journal, a nine-year-old English setter. According to an entry of May 15, 1951, she was then beginning to go blind—BLAINE

[2]At this point Dr. Bannerman's handwriting alters curiously. From here on he used a soft pencil instead of a pen, and the script shows signs of haste. In spite of this, however, it is actually much clearer, steadier and easier to read than the earlier entries in his normal hand.—BLAINE

[3]In spite of superficial changes in the handwriting, this signature has been certified genuine by an expert graphologist.—BLAINE

[4]Dr. Bannerman's mother died in 1918 of influenza. His brother (three years older, not younger) died of pneumonia, 1906.—BLAINE

[5]LIBRARIAN'S NOTE: But it seems he never did. No new edition of "Introductory Biology" was ever brought out, and the textbook has been out of print since 1952.

SURVIVAL TYPE

By J. F. Bone

Score one or one million was not enough for the human race. It had to be all or nothing ... with one man doing every bit of scoring!

*

Arthur Lanceford slapped futilely at the sith buzzing hungrily around his head. The outsized eight-legged parody of a mosquito did a neat half roll and zoomed out of range, hanging motionless on vibrating wings a few feet away.

A raindrop staggered it momentarily, and for a fleeting second, Lanceford had the insane hope that the arthropod would fall out of control into the mud. If it did, that would be the end of it, for Niobian mud was as sticky as flypaper. But the sith righted itself inches short of disaster, buzzed angrily and retreated to the shelter of a nearby broadleaf, where it executed another half roll and hung upside down, watching its intended meal with avid anticipation.

Lanceford eyed the insect distastefully as he explored his jacket for repellent and applied the smelly stuff liberally to his face and neck. It wouldn't do much good. In an hour, his sweat would remove whatever the rain missed—but for that time, it should discourage the sith. As far as permanent discouraging went, the repellent was useless. Once one of those eight-legged horrors checked you off, there were only two possible endings to the affair—either you were bitten or you killed the critter.

It was as simple as that.

He had hoped that he would be fast enough to get the sith before it got him. He had been bitten once already and the memory of those paralyzed three minutes while the bloodsucker fed was enough to last him for a lifetime. He readjusted his helmet, tucking its fringe of netting beneath his collar. The netting, he reflected gloomily, was like its owner—much the worse for wear. However, this trek would be over in another week and he would be able to spend the next six months at a comfortable desk job at the Base, while some other poor devil did the chores of field work.

*

He looked down the rain-swept trail winding through the jungle. Niobe—a perfect name for this wet little world. The Bureau of Extraterrestrial

Exploration couldn't have picked a better, but the funny thing about it was that they hadn't picked it in the first place. Niobe was the native word for Earth, or perhaps "the world" would be a more accurate definition. It was a coincidence, of course, but the planet and its mythological Greek namesake had much in common.

Niobe, like Niobe, was all tears—a world of rain falling endlessly from an impenetrable overcast, fat wet drops that formed a grieving background sound that never ceased, sobbing with soft mournful noises on the rubbery broadleaves, crying with obese splashes into forest pools, blubbering with loud, dismal persistence on the sounding board of his helmet. And on the ground, the raindrops mixed with the loesslike soil of the trail to form a gluey mud that clung in huge pasty balls to his boots.

Everywhere there was water, running in rivulets of tear-streaks down the round cheeks of the gently sloping land—rivulets that merged and blended into broad shallow rivers that wound their mourners' courses to the sea. Trekking on Niobe was an amphibious operation unless one stayed in the highlands—a perpetual series of fords and river crossings.

And it was hot, a seasonless, unchanging, humid heat that made a protection suit an instrument of torture that slowly boiled its wearer in his own sweat. But the suit was necessary, for exposed human flesh was irresistible temptation to Niobe's bloodsucking insects. Many of these were no worse than those of Earth, but a half dozen species were deadly. The first bite sensitized. The second killed—anaphylactic shock, the medics called it. And the sith was one of the deadly species.

Lanceford shrugged fatalistically. Uncomfortable as a protection suit was, it was better to boil in it than die without it.

He looked at Kron squatting beside the trail and envied him. It was too bad that Earthmen weren't as naturally repellent to insects as the dominant native life. Like all Niobians, the native guide wore no clothing—ideal garb for a climate like this. His white, hairless hide, with its faint sheen of oil, was beautifully water-repellent.

Kron, Lanceford reflected, was a good example of the manner in which Nature adapts the humanoid form for survival on different worlds. Like the dominant species on every intelligent planet in the explored galaxy, he was an erect, bipedal, mammalian being with hands that possessed an opposable thumb. Insofar as that general description went, Kron resembled humanity—but there were differences.

*

Squatting, the peculiar shape of Kron's torso and the odd flexibility of his limbs were not apparent. One had the tendency to overlook the narrow-shouldered, cylindrical body and the elongated tarsal and carpal bones that gave his limbs four major articulations rather than the human three, and to concentrate upon the utterly alien head.

It jutted forward from his short, thick neck, a long-snouted, vaguely doglike head with tiny ears lying close against the hairless, dome-shaped cranium. Slitlike nostrils, equipped with sphincter muscles like those of a terrestrial seal, argued an originally aquatic environment, and the large intelligent eyes set forward in the skull to give binocular vision, together with the sharp white carnassial teeth and pointed canines, indicated a carnivorous ancestry. But the modern Niobians, although excellent swimmers, were land dwellers and ate anything.

Lanceford couldn't repress an involuntary shudder at some of the things they apparently enjoyed. Tastes differed—enormously so between Earthmen and Niobians.

There was no doubt that the native was intelligent, yet he, like the rest of his race, was a technological moron. It was strange that a race which had a well-developed philosophy and an amazing comprehension of semantics could be so backward in mechanics. Even the simpler of the BEE's mechanisms left the natives confused. It was possible that they could learn about machinery, but Lanceford was certain that it would take a good many years before the first native mechanic would set up a machine shop on this planet.

Lanceford finished tucking the last fold of face net under his collar, and as he did so, Kron stood up, rising to his five-foot height with a curious flexible grace. Standing, he looked something like a double-jointed alabaster Anubis—wearing swim fins. His broad, webbed feet rested easily on the surface of the mud, their large area giving him flotation that Lanceford envied. As a result, his head was nearly level with that of the human, although there was better than a foot difference in their heights.

Lanceford looked at Kron inquiringly. "You have a place in mind where we can sleep tonight?"

"Sure, Boss. We'll be coming to hunthouse soon. We go now?"

"Lead on," Lanceford said, groaning silently to himself—another hunthouse with its darkness and its smells. He shrugged. He could hardly expect anything else up here in the highlands. Oh, well, he'd managed to last through the others and this one could be no worse. At that, even an airless room full of natives was preferable to spending a night outside. And the sith wouldn't follow them. It didn't like airless rooms filled with natives.

He sighed wearily as he followed Kron along the dim path through the broadleaf jungle. Night was coming, and with darkness, someone upstairs turned on every faucet and the sheets of rain that fell during the day changed abruptly into a deluge. Even the semi-aquatic natives didn't like to get caught away from shelter during the night.

The three moved onward, immersed in a drumming wilderness of rain—the Niobian sliding easily over the surface of the mud, the Earthman plowing painfully through it, and the sith flitting from the shelter of one broadleaf to the next, waiting for a chance to feed.

*

The trail widened abruptly, opening upon one of the small clearings that dotted the rain-forest jungle. In the center of the clearing, dimly visible through the rain and thickening darkness, loomed the squat thatch-roofed bulk of a hunthouse, a place of shelter for the members of the hunters' guild who provided fresh meat for the Niobian villages. Lanceford sighed a mingled breath of relief and unpleasant anticipation.

As he stepped out into the clearing, the sith darted from cover, heading like a winged bullet for Lanceford's neck. But the man was not taken by surprise. Pivoting quickly, he caught the iridescent blur of the bloodsucker's wings. He swung his arm in a mighty slap. The high-pitched buzz and Lanceford's gloved hand met simultaneously at his right ear. The buzz stopped abruptly. Lanceford shook his head and the sith fell to the ground, satisfactorily swatted. Lanceford grinned—score one for the human race.

He was still grinning as he pushed aside the fiber screen closing the low doorway of the hunthouse and crawled inside. It took a moment for his eyes to become accustomed to the gloom within, but his nose told him even before his eyes that the house was occupied. The natives, he thought wryly, must be born with no sense of smell, otherwise they'd perish from sheer propinquity. One could never honestly say that familiarity with the odor of a Niobian bred contempt—nausea was the right word.

The interior was typical, a dark rectangle of windowless limestone walls enclosing a packed-dirt floor and lined with a single deck of wooden sleeping platforms. Steeply angled rafters of peeled logs intersected at a knife-sharp ridge pierced with a circular smokehole above the firepit in the center of the room. Transverse rows of smaller poles lashed to the rafters supported the thick broadleaf thatch that furnished protection from the rain and sanctuary for uncounted thousands of insects.

A fire flickered ruddily in the pit, hissing as occasional drops of rain fell into its heart from the smokehole, giving forth a dim light together with clouds of smoke and steam that rose upward through the tangled mass of greasy cobwebs filling the upper reaches of the rafters. Some of the smoke found its way through the smokehole, but most of it hung in an acrid undulating layer some six feet above the floor.

The glow outlined the squatting figures of a dozen or so natives clustered around the pit, watching the slowly rotating carcass of a small deerlike rodent called a sorat, which was broiling on a spit above the flames. Kron was already in the ring, talking earnestly to one of the hunters—a fellow-tribesman, judging from the tattoo on his chest.

To a Niobian, the scene was ordinary, but to Lanceford it could have been lifted bodily from the inferno. He had seen it before, but the effect lost nothing by repetition. There was a distinctly hellish quality to it—to the reds and blacks of the flickering fire and the shadows. He wouldn't have been particularly surprised if Satan himself appeared in the center of the firepit complete with horns, hoofs and tail. A hunthouse, despite its innocuousness, looked like the southeast corner of Hades.

*

Clustered around the fire, the hunters turned to look at him curiously and, after a single eye-filling stare, turned back again. Niobians were almost painfully polite. Although Earthmen were still enough of a curiosity to draw attention, one searching look was all their customs allowed. Thereafter, they minded their own business. In some ways, Lanceford reflected, native customs had undeniable merit.

Presently Kron rose from his place beside the fire and pointed out two empty sleeping platforms where they would spend the night. Lanceford chose one and sank wearily to its resilient surface. Despite its crude construction, a Niobian sleeping platform was comfortable. He removed his pack, pulled off his mud-encrusted boots and lay back with a grunt of relaxation. After a day like this, it was good to get off his feet. Weariness flowed over him.

He awoke to the gentle pressure of Kron's hand squeezing his own. "The food is cooked," the Niobian said, "and you are welcomed to share it."

Lanceford nodded, his stomach crawling with unpleasant anticipation. A native meal was something he would prefer to avoid. His digestive system could handle the unsavory mess, but his taste buds shrank from the forthcoming assault. What the natives classed as a delicate and elusive flavor was sheer torture to an Earthman.

Possibly there was some connection between their inefficient olfactory apparatus and their odd ideas of flavor, but whatever the physical explanation might be, it didn't affect the fact that eating native food was an ordeal. Yet he couldn't refuse. That would be discourteous and offensive, and one simply didn't offend the natives. The BEE was explicit about that. Courtesy was a watchword on Niobe.

He took a place by the fire, watching with concealed distaste as one of the hunters reached into the boiling vat beside the firepit with a pair of wooden tongs and drew forth the native conception of a hors d'oeuvre. They called it vorkum—a boiled sorat paunch stuffed with a number of odorous ingredients. It looked almost as bad as it smelled.

The hunter laid the paunch on a wooden trencher, scraped the greenish scum from its surface and sliced it open. The odor poured out, a gagging essence of decaying vegetables, rotten eggs and overripe cheese.

Lanceford's eyes watered, his stomach tautened convulsively, but the Niobians eyed the reeking semi-solid eagerly. No meal on Niobe was considered worthy of the name unless a generous helping of vorkum started it off.

*

An entree like that could ruin the most rugged human appetite, but when it was the forerunner of a main dish of highly spiced barbecue, vorkum assumed the general properties of an emetic. Lanceford grimly controlled the nausea and tactfully declined the greasy handful which Kron offered. The Niobian never seemed to learn. At every meal they had eaten during their past month of travel on Niobe, Kron had persistently offered him samples of the mess. With equal persistence, he had refused. After all, there were limits.

But polite convention required that he eat something, so he took a small portion of the barbecued meat and dutifully finished it. The hunters eyed him curiously, apparently wondering how an entity who could assimilate relatively untasty sorat should refuse the far greater delicacy of vorkum. But it was a known fact that the ways of Earthmen were strange and unaccountable.

The hunters didn't protest when he retired to his sleeping platform and the more acceptable concentrates from his pack. His hunger satisfied, he lay back on the resilient vines and fell into a sleep of exhaustion. It had been a hard day.

Lanceford's dreams were unpleasant. Nightmare was the usual penalty of sitting in on a Niobian meal and this one was worse than usual. Huge siths, reeking of vorkum, pursued him as he ran naked and defenseless across a swampy landscape that stretched interminably ahead. The clinging mud reduced his speed to a painful crawl as he frantically beat off the attacks of the blood-suckers.

The climax was horror. One of the siths slipped through his frantically beating hands and bit him on the face. The shocking pain of the bite wakened him, a cry of terror and anguish still on his lips.

He looked around wildly. He was still in the hunthouse. It was just a dream.

He chuckled shakily. These nightmares sometimes were too real for comfort. He was drenched with sweat, which was not unusual, but there was a dull ache in his head and the hot tense pain that encompassed the right side of his face had not been there when he had fallen asleep.

He touched his face with a tentative finger, exploring the hot puffiness and the enormously swollen ear with a gentle touch. It was where he had struck the sith, but surely he couldn't have hit that hard.

He gasped, a soft breath of dismay, as realization dawned. He had smashed the sith hard enough to squeeze some of the insect's corrosive body juices through his face net—and they had touched his skin! That wouldn't normally have been bad, but the sith bite he had suffered a week ago had sensitized him. He was developing an anaphylactic reaction—a severe one, judging from the swelling.

That was the trouble with exploration; one occasionally forgot that a world was alien. Occasionally danger tended to recede into a background of familiarity—he had smashed the sith before it had bitten him, so therefore it couldn't hurt him. He grimaced painfully, the movement bringing another twinge to his swollen face. He should have known better.

He swore mildly as he opened his Aid Kit and extracted a sterile hypo. The super-antihistamine developed by the Bureau was an unpredictable sort of thing. Sometimes it worked and sometimes it didn't. He removed the screw cap that sealed the needle and injected the contents of the syringe into his arm. He hoped that this was one of the times the drug worked. If it wasn't, he reflected grimly, he wouldn't be long for this world.

He sighed and lay back. There wasn't anything more to do now. All he could do was wait and see if the anti-allergen worked.

*

The Bureau of Extraterrestrial Exploration had discovered Niobe barely three years ago, yet already the planet was famous not only for its peculiar climate, but also for the number of men who had died upon its watery surface. Knowledge of this planet was bought with life, grim payment to decrease the lag between discovery and the day men could live and work on Niobe without having to hide beneath domes or behind protection suits. Lanceford never questioned the necessity or the inevitable price that must be paid. Like every other BEE agent, he knew that Niobe was crash priority—a world that*had* to be understood in minimum time.

For Niobe was a made to order herbarium for a swampland plant called viscaya. The plant was originally native to Algon IV, but had been spread to practically every suitable growth center in the Galaxy. It was the source of a complex of alkaloids known as gerontin, and gerontin had the property of tripling or quadrupling the normal life span of mammals.

It was obvious that viscayaculture should have a tremendous distribution throughout the Confederation worlds. But unfortunately the right conditions existed in very few places in the explored galaxy. Despite the fact that most life is based on carbon, oxygen and water, there is still very little free water in the Galaxy. Most planets of the Confederation are semi-arid, with the outstanding exceptions of Terra and Lyrane. But these two worlds were the seats of human and humanoid power for so long that all of their swampland had been drained and reclaimed centuries ago.

And it was doubly unfortunate that gerontin so far defied synthesis. According to some eminent chemists, the alkaloid would probably continue to do so until some facet of the Confederation reached a Class VIII culture level. Considering that Terra and Lyrane, the two highest cultures, were only

Class VII, and that Class level steps took several thousands of years to make, a policy of waiting for synthesis was not worth considering.

The result was that nobody was happy until Niobe was discovered. The price of illicit gerontin was astronomical and most of the Confederation's supply of the drug was strictly rationed to those whom the government thought most valuable to the Confederation as a whole. Of course, the Confederation officialdom was included, which caused considerable grumbling. In the nick of time, Niobe appeared upon the scene, and Niobe had environment in abundance!

The wheels of the Confederation began to turn. The BEE was given a blank check and spurred on by a government which, in turn, was being spurred on by the people who composed it. The exploration of Niobe proceeded at all possible speed. With so many considerations weighed against them, what did a few lives matter? For the sake of the billions of humanoids in the Confederation, their sacrifice was worthwhile even if only a few days or hours were saved between discovery and exploitation.

*

Lanceford groaned as a violent pain shot through his head. The anti-allergin apparently wasn't going to work, for it should have had some effect by now. He shrugged mentally—it was the chance one took in this business. But he couldn't say that he hadn't been warned. Even old Sims had told him, called him a unit in the BEE's shortcut trial and error scheme—an error, it looked like now.

Seemed rather silly—a Class VII civilization using techniques that were old during the Dark Ages before the Atomic Revolution, sending foot parties to explore a world in the chance that they might discover something that the search mechs missed—anything that would shorten the lag time. It was incomprehensible, but neither Sims nor the BEE would do a thing like this without reason. And whatever it was, he wasn't going to worry about it. In fact, there wasn't much time left to worry. The reaction was observably and painfully worse.

It was important that the news of his death and the specimens he had collected get back to Base Alpha. They might have value in this complex game Alvord Sims was playing with men, machines and Niobe. But Base Alpha was a good hundred miles away and, in his present condition, he couldn't walk a hundred feet.

For a moment, he considered setting up the powerful little transmitter he carried in his pack, but his first abortive motion convinced him it was useless. The blinding agony that swept through him at the slightest movement left no doubt that he would never finish the business of setting up the antenna, let alone send a message.

It was a crime that handie-talkies couldn't be used here on Niobe, but their range, limited at best, was practically nonexistent on a planet that literally seemed to be one entire "dead spot." A fixed-frequency job broadcasting on a directional beam was about the only thing that could cover distance, and that required a little technical know-how to set up the antenna and focus it on Base Alpha. There would be no help from Kron. Despite his intelligence, the native could no more assemble a directional antenna than spread pink wings and fly.

There was only one thing to do—get a note off to Sims, if he could still write, and ask Kron to deliver the note and his pack to the Base.

He fumbled with his jacket, and with some pain produced a stylus and a pad. But it was difficult to write. Painful, too. Better get Kron over here while he could still talk and tell him what he wanted.

The stylus slipped from numb fingers as Lanceford called hoarsely, "Kron! Come here! I need you!"

*

Kron looked down compassionately at the swollen features of the Earthman. He had seen the kef effect before, among the young of his people who were incautious or inexperienced, but he had never seen it among the aliens. Surprisingly, the effects were the same—the livid swellings, the gasping breath, the pain. Strange how these foreigners reacted like his own people.

He scratched his head and pulled thoughtfully at one of his short ears. It was his duty to help Lanceford, but how could he? The Earthman had denied his help for weeks, and Niobians simply didn't disregard another's wishes. Kron scowled, the action lending a ferocious cast to his doglike face. Tolerance was a custom hallowed by ages of practice. It went to extremes—even with life at stake, a person's wishes and beliefs must be respected.

Kron buried his long-snouted head in his hands, a gesture that held in it all the frustration which filled him.

The human was apparently resolved to die. He had told Kron his last wishes, which didn't include a request for help, but merely to get his pack back to the others in their glass dome. It was astonishing that such an obviously intelligent species should have so little flexibility. They didn't understand the first principles of adaptation. Always and forever, they held to their own ways, trying with insensate stubbornness to mold nature to their will—and when nature overcome their artificial defenses, they died, stubborn, unregenerate, inflexible to the end. They were odd, these humans—odd and a little frightening.

Lanceford breathed wheezily. The swelling had invaded the inner tissues of his throat and was beginning to compress his windpipe. It was uncomfortable, like inhaling liquid fire, and then there was the constant desire to cough and the physical inability to do so.

"Dirty luck," he whispered. "Only a week more and I'd have had it made—the longest trek a man's made on this benighted planet."

Kron nodded, but then belatedly realized that the human was muttering to himself. He listened. There might be something important in these dying murmurings, something that might explain their reasons for being here and their strange driving haste that cared nothing for life.

"It's hard to die so far from one's people, but I guess that can't be helped. Old Sims gave me the score. Like he said, a man doesn't have much choice of where he dies in the BEE."

"You don't want to die!" Kron exploded.

"Of course not," Lanceford said with weak surprise. He hadn't dreamed that Kron was nearby. This might well destroy the Imperturbable Earthman myth that the BEE had fostered.

"Not even if it is in accord with your customs and rituals?"

"What customs?"

"Your clothing, your eating habits, your ointments—are these not part of your living plan?"

Despite the pain that tore at his throat, Lanceford managed a chuckle. This was ridiculous. "Hell, no! Our only design for living is to stay alive, particularly on jobs like this one. We don't wear these suits and repellent because we *like* to. We do it to stay alive. If we could, we'd go around nearly as naked as you do."

"Do you mind if I help you?" Kron asked diffidently. "I think I can cure you." He leaned forward anxiously to get the man's reply.

"I'd take a helping hand from the devil himself, if it would do any good."

Kron's eyes were brilliant. He hummed softly under his breath, the Niobian equivalent of laughter. "And all the time we thought—" he began, and then broke off abruptly. Already too much time was wasted without losing any more in meditating upon the ironies of life.

He turned toward the firepit, searched for a moment among the stones, nodded with satisfaction and returned to where Lanceford lay. The hunthouse was deserted save for himself and the Earthman. With characteristic Niobian delicacy, the hunters had left, preferring to endure the night rain than be present when the alien died. Kron was thankful that they were gone, for what he was about to do would shock their conservative souls.

*

Lanceford was dimly conscious of Kron prying his swollen jaws apart and forcing something wet and slippery down his throat. He swallowed, the act a tearing pain to the edematous membranes of his gullet, but the stuff slid down, leaving a trail of fire in its wake. The act triggered another wave of pain that left him weak and gasping. He couldn't take much more of this. It wouldn't be long now before the swelling invaded his lungs to such a degree that he would strangle. It wasn't a pleasant way to die.

And then, quite suddenly, the pain eased. A creeping numbness spread like a warm black blanket over his outraged nervous system. The stuff Kron had given him apparently had some anesthetic properties. He felt dimly grateful, even though the primitive native nostrum would probably do no good other than to ease the pain.

The blackness went just far enough to paralyze the superficial areas of his nervous system. It stopped the pain and left him unable to move, but the deeper pathways of thought and reason remained untouched. He was conscious, although no external sensation intruded on his thoughts. He couldn't see Kron—the muscles that moved his eyes were as paralyzed as the other muscles of his body and the native was outside his field of vision—but somehow he knew exactly what the Niobian was doing. He was washing mucus from his hands in a bowl of water standing beside the fire pit *and he was wondering wryly whether forced feeding was on the list of human tabus*!

Lanceford's mind froze, locked in a peculiar contact that was more than awareness. The sensation was indescribable. It was like looking through an open door into the living room of a stranger's house.

He was aware of the incredible complexity and richness of Kron's thoughts, of oddly sardonic laughter, of pity and regret that such a little thing as understanding should cause death and suffering through its lack, of bewildered admiration for the grim persistence of the alien Earthmen, mixed with a wondering curiosity about what kept them here—what the true reasons were for their death-defying persistence and stubbornness—of an ironic native paraphrase for the Terran saying, "Every man to his own taste," and a profound speculation upon what fruits might occur from true understanding between his own race and the aliens.

It was a strangely jumbled kaleidoscopic flash that burned across the explorer's isolated mind, a flash that passed almost as soon as it had come, as though an invisible door had closed upon it.

But one thing in that briefly shocking contact stood out with great clarity. The Niobians were as eager as the BEE to establish a true contact, a true understanding, for the message was there, plain in Kron's mind that he was thinking not only for himself but for a consensus of his people, a decision arrived at as a result of discussion and thought—a decision of which every Niobian was aware and with which most Niobians agreed.

*

The magnitude of that thought and its implications staggered Lanceford's imagination.

After two years of exploration and contact with the dominant race of this planet, the BEE still knew literally nothing about the sort of people with whom they were dealing. This instantaneous, neural contact proved that. Equated against the information dished out in Basic Training, it merely emphasized the fact that the BEE was grossly ignorant.

Anthropological Intelligence had a lot to account for—the job they'd done so far could have been performed by low-grade morons. In wishing to avoid the possibility of giving offense, in hiding behind a wall of courtesy and convention, there had been no contact worthy of the name. Yet here was the possibility of a rapport that could be closer than any which existed between any races in the Galaxy.

Lanceford groaned with silent frustration. To learn this when he was dying was the bitterest of ironies. In any other circumstances, the flash of insight could be parlayed into a key which might unlock the entire problem of

Niobian relationships.

Bitterly he fought against the curtain of unconsciousness that closed down on him, trying by sheer will to stay awake, to make some move that could be interpreted, to leave some clue to what he had learned.

It was useless. The darkness closed in, inexorable and irresistible.

*

Arthur Lanceford opened his eyes, surprised that he was still alive. The pain was gone from his face and the swelling had subsided. He grinned with relief—his luck had held out.

And then the relief vanished in a wave of elation. He held the key. He knew the basics for mutual understanding. And he would be alive to deliver them to the specialists who could make them operate.

He chuckled. Whatever the cure was—the BEE drug, Kron's treatment, whatever it was, it didn't matter. The important thing was that he was going to live.

He wondered whether that flash of insight just before unconsciousness had been real or a figment of delirium. It could have been either, but Lanceford clung to the belief that the contact was genuine. There was far too much revealed in that sudden flash that was entirely alien to his normal patterns of thought.

He wondered what had triggered that burst of awareness. The BEE drug, the stuff Kron had given him, the poison of the sith and the histamines floating around in his system—it could have been any one of a number of things, or maybe a complex of various factors that had interacted to make him super-receptive for an instant of time.

It was something that would have to be reported and studied with the meticulous care which the BEE gave to any facet of experience that was out of the ordinary. A solution might possibly be found, or the whole thing might wind up as one of those dead ends that were so numerous in Exploration work. But that was out of his field and, in consequence, out of his hands. His specialty wasn't parapsychological research.

Kron was standing beside his bed, long doglike face impassive, looking at him with pleased satisfaction. Behind him, a group of natives were clustered around the cooking fire. It was as if no time had passed since the allergy struck—but Lanceford knew differently. Still, the lost time didn't matter. The bright joy that he was going to live transcended such unimportant things.

"Looks like you won't have to bury me after all," Lanceford said happily.

He stretched his arms over his head. He felt wonderful. His body was cool and comfortably free of the hot confinement of the protection suit. He did a slow horrified doubletake as he realized that he was lying on the sleeping platform practically naked—a tempting hors d'oeuvre for the thousand and one species of Niobe's biting insects.

"Where's my suit?" he half shouted.

*

Kron smiled. "You don't need it, friend Lanceford. If you will notice, you are not bitten. Nor will you be."

"Why not?"

Kron didn't answer. It wasn't the proper time, and the euphoria that he and the Earthman were enjoying was too pleasant to shatter.

Lanceford didn't press the matter. Apparently Kron knew what he was talking about. Lanceford had been watching one particularly vicious species of biting fly hover above his body. The insect would approach, ready to enjoy a mandible full of human epidermis, but, about six inches from his body, would slow down and come to a stop, hanging frustrated in midair. Finally the fly gave up and flew off into the darkness of the rafters. Lanceford hoped that one of the spiders would get it—but he was convinced. Whatever happened to him while he was unconscious had made him as insect-repellent as the Niobians.

The smell of cooking came from the firepit and, incredibly, it smelled good.

Lanceford looked startledly at Kron. "I'm hungry."

"An excellent sign," Kron replied. "You are nearly cured. Soon you will be able to finish this trek."

"Incidentally," Lanceford said, "for the first time since I have been out on this showerbath world of yours, you're cooking something that smells fit to eat. I think I'd like to try it."

Kron's eyebrows rose and he hummed softly under his breath. This was something entirely unexpected—an added delight, like the flavor of komal in a sorat stew. He savored it slowly, enjoying its implications.

"What is it?" Lanceford persisted.

"A dish called akef," Kron said. The name was as good as any and certainly described the effect well enough.

*

The last hundred miles had been a breeze. Lanceford stood at the edge of the clearing, looking across the planed-off landscape to the shimmering hemispherical bulk of Base Alpha, glistening like a giant cabochon jewel under Niobe's dark sky. Without the protection suit to slow him down and hamper his movements, what would have been a week's trip had been shortened to four days.

In a few minutes, he would be back among his own kind—and he wasn't sure whether he was glad or sorry. Of course, there was a certain satisfaction in bringing back a first-class discovery—perhaps the greatest in the short history of Niobian exploration—but there was a stigma attached to the way it had been found. It wouldn't be easy to confess that it had practically been forced upon him, but it would have to be done. It would have been much nicer to have found the answer by using his head. There would have been some really deserved prestige in that.

*

He sighed and turned to Kron. "Farewell, friend," he said soberly, "and thanks."

"We are even," Kron replied. "You saved my life from a roka and I saved yours from the sith. The scales are balanced."

Lanceford blinked. He had forgotten that incident where he had shot the big catlike animal shortly after the 'copter had dropped them for the start of their journey back to Base. Apparently it was after Kron—or at least the native had thought so. Lanceford grinned ruefully. Score another point for blind luck.

"But, Kron, it's not that easy. You have given me a secret of your people and I shall have to tell it to mine."

"I expected that you would. Besides, it is no secret. Even our children know its composition and how to make it. We have never held it from you. You simply wouldn't accept it. But it is about time, friend Lanceford, that your race began learning something of Niobe if they wish to remain here—and it is about time that we began learning something about you. I think that there will be some rather marked changes in the future. And in that regard, I leave you with the question of whether a civilization should be judged entirely upon its apparent technological achievements."

"I—" Lanceford began.

"You have learned how we avoid the insects," Kron continued, maneuvering past the abortive interruption, "and perhaps someday you will know the full answer to my question. But in the meantime, you and your kind will be free to move through our world, to learn our ways, and to teach us yours. It should be a fair exchange."

"Thanks to akef," Lanceford said fervently, "we should be able to do just that."

*

Kron smiled. "You have used the drug enough to have overcome the mental block that prevented you from naming it before. The word I coined from your own language of science is no longer necessary."

"I suppose not, but it's pleasanter to think of it that way."

"You Earthmen! Sometimes I wonder how you ever managed to achieve a civilization with your strange attitudes toward unpleasant facts." Kron smiled broadly, relishing the memory of his deception and Lanceford's shocked awakening to the truth. "I hope," he continued, "that you have forgiven my little deceit and the destruction of your protective clothing."

"Of course. How could I do otherwise? It's so nice to be rid of that sweatbox that I'd forgive anything." Lanceford frowned. "But there's one thing that puzzles me. How did you disguise the stuff?"

"I didn't," Kron replied cryptically. "You did." He turned away and, with characteristic Niobian abruptness, walked off into the jungle. His job was done and natives were never ones to dally with leavetaking, although their greetings were invariably ceremonious.

Lanceford watched until the native was out of sight and then walked slowly across the clearing toward the dome. He had learned a lot these past few days, enough to make him realize that his basic training had been so inadequate as to be almost criminal. It was lacking in many of the essentials for survival and, moreover, was slanted entirely wrong from a psychological point of view.

Sure, it was good enough to enable a man to get along, but it seemed to be particularly designed to deny the fact that the natives obviously possessed a first-rate culture of their own. It didn't say so directly, but the implications were there. And that was wrong. The natives possessed a civilization that was probably quite as high as the one Terra possessed. It was simply oriented differently. One thing was certain—the Confederation wasn't going to expropriate or exploit *this* planet without the natives' consent. It would be suicide if they tried.

He grinned. Actually there would be no reason for such action. It was always easier to deal with advanced races than to try to conquer or educate primitive ones. Kron had the right idea—understanding, exchange, appreciation—Confederation culture for Niobian. It would make a good and productive synthesis.

Still grinning, Lanceford opened the airlock and stepped inside, ignoring the pop-eyed guard who eyed his shorts and sandals with an expression of incredulous disbelief.

*

Alvord Sims, Regional Director, Niobe Division BEE, looked up from his desk and smiled. The smile became a nose-wrinkling grimace as Lanceford swung the pack from his shoulders and set it carefully on the floor.

"Glad to see that you made it, Lanceford," Sims said. "But what's that awful smell? You should have done something about it. You stink like a native."

"All the baths in the world won't help, sir," Lanceford said woodenly.

He was tired of the stares and the sniffs he had encountered since he had entered the base. In his present condition, a fellow-human smelled as bad to him as he did to them, but he didn't complain about it and he saw no reason why they should. Humanity should apply more courtesy and consideration to members of their own species.

"It's inside me," he explained. "My metabolism's changed. And incidentally, sir, you don't smell so sweet yourself."

Sims sputtered for a moment and then shrugged. "Perhaps not," he admitted. "One can't help sweating in this climate even with air-conditioning."

"It's the change inside me," Lanceford said. "I suppose it'll wear off in time, once I've been on a normal diet. But I didn't think that was too important in view of the information I have. I've learned something vital, something that you should know at once. That's why I'm here."

"That's decent of you," Sims replied, "but an interoffice memo would have served just as well as a personal visit. My stomach isn't as good as it once was. Ulcers, you know."

"The executive's disease," Lanceford commented.

Sims nodded. "Well, Arthur, what did you find that was so important?"

"That we've been fools."

Sims sighed. "That's nothing new. We've been fools since the day we left Earth to try and conquer the stars."

"That's not what I mean, sir. I mean that we've been going at this Niobe business the wrong way. What we need is to understand the natives, instead of trying to understand the planet."

"Out of the mouths of babes and probationers—" Sims said with gentle irony.

"It pays off," Lanceford replied doggedly. "Take my case. I've found out why the natives are insect-proof!"

"That's a new wrinkle. Can you prove it?"

"Certainly. I came the last hundred miles in shorts."

"What happened to your suit?"

"Kron destroyed it accidentally."

"Accidentally—hah!" Sims snorted. "Niobians never do things accidentally."

*

Lanceford looked sharply at the director. The observation carried a wealth of implications that his sharpened senses were quick to grasp. "Then you know the natives aren't simple savages, the way we were taught in Basic Training?"

"Of course! They're a non-technical Class V at the very least—maybe higher. Somehow they've never oriented their civilization along mechanical lines, or maybe they tried it once and found it wanting. But no one in the upper echelons has ever thought they were stupid or uncivilized."

"Then why—"

"Later," Sims said. "You're entitled to an explanation, but right now I'd appreciate it if you'd finish your statement. What makes the natives insect-proof?"

"Vorkum."

"That gunk?"

"That's the repellent."

"In more ways than one," Sims said.

"It's not so bad after you get used to it. It just smells awful at first."

"That's an understatement, if I ever heard one."

*

"Perhaps the lab can analyze it and find the active principle," Lanceford said hopefully.

"If they do, I'll bet it is distilled quintessence of skunk," Sims replied gloomily. "I'll be willing to bet that our native friends tried that trick ages ago and gave it up for a bad job. They're pretty fair biochemists as well as being philosophers."

"Could be," Lanceford said thoughtfully. "I never thought of that."

"You'd better start thinking all the time. These lads are *smart*. Why do you think we have this complicated rigmarole about native relations and respect? Man, we're running scared. We don't want to lose this planet, and anything less than the kid-glove treatment would be sheer suicide until we learn how far we can go. These natives have an organization that'd knock your eye out. I didn't believe it myself until I got the proof. As you learn more about it, you'll understand what I mean. We're dealing with an ecological *unit* on this planet!"

"But I thought—"

"That you were here to explore a primitive world?"

"Wasn't that what I was trained for?"

"No. We can do that sort of thing with a couple of geodetic cruisers. We don't need men trekking through the jungles to assay a world's physical resources. That business went out of date during the Dark Ages. There's a better reason than that for these treks."

"Like what?"

"You asked the question. Now answer it," Sims said. "You have enough data."

Lanceford thought for a moment "I can see one reason," he said slowly.

"Yes?"

"The trek could be a test. It could be used to determine whether or not the probationer was a survival type—a sort of final examination before he's turned loose in a responsible job here in the BEE."

*

Sims smiled. "Bull's-eye! It's part of the speedup—a pretty brutal part, but one that can't be helped if we want to get this planet in line quickly enough to stop the riot that's brewing in the Confederation. It's as much for Niobe's good as ours, because the Confederation wants that gerontin like an alcoholic wants another drink—and they're not going to wait for normal exploration and development. That's why the treks. It's a tough course. Failure can and often does mean death. Usually we can pull a misfit out in time, but not always. If you live through the trek and we don't have to pull you out, though, you've proved yourself a survival type—and you're over the first hurdle.

"Then we check with your guide and anyone you happen to meet en route. The natives are very cooperative about such things. If you pass their evaluation, you're ready to join the club. It's been forming ever since we landed here two years ago, but it's still pretty exclusive. It's the nucleus of the BEE's mission here, the one that'll get things rolling with the gerontin plantations. We'll know about you in a few more minutes after the Cyb Unit gets through processing your data." Sims grinned at the thunderstruck youngster.

Lanceford nodded glumly. "I'll probably fail. I sure didn't use my head. I never caught the significance of the trek, I failed to deduce the reason for the insect-repellent qualities of the natives, and I missed the implications of their culture until I had almost reached Base. Those things are obvious. Any analytical brain would have figured them out."

"They're only obvious when you know what you're looking for," Sims said gently. "Personally, I think you did an excellent job, considering the handicaps you have faced. And the discovery of the vorkum was masterly."

Lanceford blushed. "I hate to admit it, but Kron literally shoved the stuff down my throat."

"I didn't mean the *method* by which you learned that vorkum was the stuff we've been searching for," Sims said. "I meant the *results* you obtained. Results are what count in this business. Call it luck if you wish, but there is more to it than that. Some people are just naturally lucky and those are the sort we need here. They're survival types. A lot is going to depend on having those so-called lucky people in the right places when we settle Niobe's status in the Confederation."

He paused as the message tube beside his desk burped a faint hiss of compressed air and a carrier dropped out into the receiving basket.

"Somehow I think that this is your membership card to the club," he said. He read it, smiled, and passed the sheet to Lanceford. "And now, Arthur, before I appoint you as a Niobe Staff member, I'd like to know one thing."

"What is that, sir?"

"Just why in the name of hell did you bring that pack in here with you? I've just realized where that smell is coming from!"

"I didn't dare leave it anywhere," Lanceford said. "Someone might have thrown it down a disposal chute."

"I wouldn't blame them. That's vorkum you have in there, isn't it?"

Lanceford nodded. "Yes, sir. I didn't want to lose it."

"Why not? We can always get more from the natives if we need it."

"I know that, sir. *We* can, but this is all *I'll* get for the next six months, and if I ration myself carefully, it might last that long. You see, sir, it's mildly habit-forming—like cigarettes—and one gets accustomed to it. And besides, you really don't know what flavor is until you've tried vorkum on chocolate."

MISBEGOTTEN MISSIONARY

By Isaac Asimov

It was a lovable little creature, anxious to help solve the troubles of the world. Moreover, it had the answer! But what man ever takes free advice?

He had slipped aboard the ship! There had been dozens waiting outside the energy barrier when it had seemed that waiting would do no good. Then the barrier had faltered for a matter of two minutes (which showed the superior-ity of unified organisms over life fragments) and he was across.

None of the others had been able to move quickly enough to take advantage of the break, but that didn't matter. All alone, he was enough. No others were necessary.

And the thought faded out of satisfaction and into loneliness. It was a terribly unhappy and unnatural thing to be parted from all the rest of the unified organism, to be a life fragment oneself. How could these aliens stand being fragments?

It increased his sympathy for the aliens. Now that he experienced fragmentation himself, he could feel, as though from a distance, the terrible isolation that made them so afraid. It was fear born of that isolation that dictated their actions. What but the insane fear of their condition could have caused them to blast an area, one mile in diameter, into dull-red heat before landing their ship? Even the organized life ten feet deep in the soil had been destroyed in the blast.

He engaged reception, listening eagerly, letting the alien thought saturate him. He enjoyed the touch of life upon his consciousness. He would have to ration that enjoyment. He must not forget himself.

But it could do no harm to listen to thoughts. Some of the fragments of life on the ship thought quite clearly, considering that they were such primitive, incomplete creatures. Their thoughts were like tiny bells.

Roger Oldenn said, "I feel contaminated. You know what I mean? I keep washing my hands and it doesn't help."

Jerry Thorn hated dramatics and didn't look up. They were still maneuvering in the stratosphere of Saybrook's Planet and he preferred to watch the panel dials. He said, "No reason to feel contaminated. Nothing happened."

"I hope not," said Oldenn. "At least they had all the field men discard their spacesuits in the air lock for complete disinfection. They had a radiation bath for all men entering from outside. I suppose nothing happened."

"Why be nervous, then?"

"I don't know. I wish the barrier hadn't broken down."

"Who doesn't? It was an accident."

"I wonder." Oldenn was vehement. "I was here when it happened. My shift, you know. There was no reason to overload the power line. There was equipment plugged into it that had no damn business near it. None whatsoever."

"All right. People are stupid."

"Not that stupid. I hung around when the Old Man was checking into the matter. None of them had reasonable excuses. The armor-baking circuits, which were draining off two thousand watts, had been put into the barrier line. They'd been using the second subsidiaries for a week. Why not this time? They couldn't give any reason."

"Can you?"

Oldenn flushed. "No, I was just wondering if the men had been"—he searched for a word—"hypnotized into it. By those things outside."

Thorn's eyes lifted and met those of the other levelly. "I wouldn't repeat that to anyone else. The barrier was down only two minutes. If anything had happened, if even a spear of grass had drifted across it would have shown up in our bacteria cultures within half an hour, in the fruit-fly colonies in a matter of days. Before we got back it would show up in the hamsters, the rabbits, maybe the goats. Just get it through your head, Oldenn, that nothing happened. Nothing."

Oldenn turned on his heel and left. In leaving, his foot came within two feet of the object in the comer of the room. He did not see it.

He disengaged his reception centers and let the thoughts flow past him unperceived. These life fragments were not important, in any case, since they were not fitted for the continuation of life. Even as fragments, they were incomplete.

The other types of fragments now—they were different. He had to be careful of them. The temptation would be great, and he must give no indication, none at all, of his existence on board ship till they landed on their home planet.

He focused on the other parts of the ship, marveling at the diversity of life. Each item, no matter how small, was sufficient to itself. He forced himself to contemplate this, until the unpleasantness of the thought grated on him and he longed for the normality of home.

Most of the thoughts he received from the smaller fragments were vague and fleeting, as you would expect. There wasn't much to be had from them, but that meant their need for completeness was all the greater. It was that which touched him so keenly.

There was the life fragment which squatted on its haunches and fingered the wire netting that enclosed it. Its thoughts were clear, but limited. Chiefly, they concerned the yellow fruit a companion fragment was eating. It wanted the fruit very deeply. Only the wire netting that separated the fragments prevented its seizing the fruit by force.

He disengaged reception in a moment of complete revulsion. These fragments competed for food!

He tried to reach far outward for the peace and harmony of home, but it was already an immense distance away. He could reach only into the nothingness that separated him from sanity.

He longed at the moment even for the feel of the dead soil between the barrier and the ship. He had crawled over it last night. There had been no life upon it, but it had been the soil of home, and on the other side of the barrier there had still been the comforting feel of the rest of organized life.

He could remember the moment he had located himself on the surface of the ship, maintaining a desperate suction grip until the air lock opened. He had entered, moving cautiously between the outgoing feet. There had been an inner lock and that had been passed later. Now he lay here, a life fragment himself, inert and unnoticed.

Cautiously, he engaged reception again at the previous focus. The squatting fragment of life was tugging furiously at the wire netting. It still wanted the other's food, though it was the less hungry of the two.

*

Larsen said, "Don't feed the damn thing. She isn't hungry; she's just sore because Tillie had the nerve to eat before she herself was crammed full. The greedy ape! I wish we were back home and I never had to look another animal in the face again."

He scowled at the older female chimpanzee frowningly and the chimp mouthed and chattered back to him in full reciprocation.

Rizzo said, "Okay, okay. Why hang around here, then? Feeding time is over. Let's get out."

They went past the goat pens, the rabbit hutches, the hamster cages.

Larsen said bitterly, "You volunteer for an exploration voyage. You're a hero. They send you off with speeches—and make a zoo keeper out of you."

"They give you double pay."

"All right, so what? I didn't sign up just for the money. They said at the original briefing that it was even odds we wouldn't come back, that we'd end up like Saybrook. I signed up because I wanted to do something important."

"Just a bloomin' bloody hero," said Rizzo.

"I'm not an animal nurse."

Rizzo paused to lift a hamster out of the cage and stroke it. "Hey," he said, "did you ever think that maybe one of these hamsters has some cute little baby hamsters inside, just getting started?"

"Wise guy! They're tested every day."

"Sure, sure." He muzzled the little creature, which vibrated its nose at him. "But just suppose you came down one morning and found them there. New little hamsters looking up at you with soft, green patches of fur where the eyes ought to be."

"Shut up, for the love of Mike," yelled Larsen.

"Little soft, green patches of shining fur," said Rizzo, and put the hamster down with a sudden loathing sensation.

He engaged reception again and varied the focus. There wasn't a specialized life fragment at home that didn't have a rough counterpart on ship-board.

There were the moving runners in various shapes, the moving swimmers, and the moving fliers. Some of the fliers were quite large, with perceptible thoughts; others were small, gauzy-winged creatures. These last transmitted only patterns of sense perception, imperfect patterns at that, and added nothing intelligent of their own.

There were the non-movers, which, like the non-movers at home, were green and lived on the air, water, and soil. These were a mental blank. They knew only the dim, dim consciousness of light, moisture, and gravity.

And each fragment, moving and non-moving, had its mockery of life.

Not yet. Not yet. . . .

He clamped down hard upon his feelings. Once before, these life fragments had come, and the rest at home had tried to help them—too quickly. It had not worked. This time they must wait.

If only these fragments did not discover him.

They had not, so far. They had not noticed him lying in the corner of the pilot room. No one had bent down to pick up and discard him. Earlier, it had meant he could not move. Someone might have turned and stared at the stiff wormlike thing, not quite six inches long. First stare, then shout, and then it would all be over.

But now, perhaps, he had waited long enough. The takeoff was long past. The controls were locked; the pilot room was empty.

It did not take him long to find the chink in the armor leading to the recess where some of the wiring was. They were dead wires.

The front end of his body was a rasp that cut in two a wire of just the right diameter. Then, six inches away, he cut it in two again. He pushed the snipped-off section of the wire ahead of him packing it away neatly and invisibly into a corner of recess. Its outer covering was a brown elastic material and its core was gleaming, ruddy metal. He himself could not reproduce the core, of course, but that was not necessary. It was enough that the pellicle that covered him had been carefully bred to resemble a wire's surface.

He returned and grasped the cut sections of the wire before and behind. He tightened against them as his little suction disks came into play. Not even a seam showed.

They could not find him now. They could look right at him and see only a continuous stretch of wire.

Unless they looked very closely indeed and noted that, in a certain spot on this wire, there were two tiny patches of soft and shining green fur.

"It is remarkable," said Dr. Weiss, "that little green hairs can do so much."

Captain Loring poured the brandy carefully. In a sense, this was a celebration. They would be ready for the jump through hyperspace in two hours, and after that, two days would see them back on Earth.

"You are convinced, then, the green fur is the sense organ?" he asked.

"It is," said Weiss. Brandy made him come out in splotches, but he was aware of the need of celebration—quite aware. "The experiments were conducted under difficulties, but they were quite significant."

The captain smiled stiffly. " 'Under difficulties' is one way of phrasing it. I would never have taken the chances you did to run them."

"Nonsense. We're all heroes aboard this ship, all volunteers, all great men with trumpet, fife, and fanfare. You took the chance of coming here."

"You were the first to go outside the barrier."

"No particular risk involved," Weiss said. "I burned the ground before me as I went, to say nothing of the portable barrier that surrounded me. Nonsense, Captain. Let's all take our medals when we come back; let's take them without attempt at gradation. Besides, I'm a male."

"But you're filled with bacteria to here." The captain's hand made a quick, cutting gesture three inches above his head. "Which makes you as vulnerable as a female would be."

They paused for drinking purposes. "Refill?" asked the captain.

"No, thanks. I've exceeded my quota already."

"Then one last for the spaceroad." He lifted his glass in the general direction of Saybrook's Planet, no longer visible, its sun only a bright star in the visiplate. "To the little green hairs that gave Saybrook his first lead."

Weiss nodded. "A lucky thing. We'll quarantine the planet, of course."

The captain said, "That doesn't seem drastic enough. Someone might always land by accident someday and not have Saybrook's insight, or his guts. Suppose he did not blow up his ship, as Saybrook did. Suppose he got back to some inhabited place."

The captain was somber. "Do you suppose they might ever develop interstellar travel on their own?"

"I doubt it. No proof, of course. It's just that they have such a completely different orientation. Their entire organization of life has made tools unnecessary. As far as we know, even a stone ax doesn't exist on the planet."

"I hope you're right. Oh, and, Weiss, would you spend some time with Drake?"

"The Galactic Press fellow?"

"Yes. Once we get back, the story of Saybrook's Planet will be released for the public and I don't think it would be wise to oversensationalize it. I've asked Drake to let you consult with him on the story. You're a biologist and enough of an authority to carry weight with him. Would you oblige?"

"A pleasure."

The captain closed his eyes wearily and shook his head.

"Headache, Captain?"

"No. Just thinking of poor Saybrook."

He was weary of the ship. Awhile back there had been a queer, momentary sensation, as though he had been turned inside out. It was alarming and he had searched the minds of the keen-thinkers for an explanation. Apparently the ship had leaped across vast stretches of empty space by cutting across something they knew as "hyperspace." The keen-thinkers were ingenious.

But—he was weary of the ship. It was such a futile phenomenon. These life fragments were skillful in their constructions, yet it was only a measure of their unhappiness, after all. They strove to find in the control of inanimate matter what they could not find in themselves. In their unconscious yearning for completeness, they built machines and scoured space, seeking, seeking . . .

These creatures, he knew, could never, in the very nature of things, find that for which they were seeking. At least not until such time as he gave it to them. He quivered a little at the thought.

Completeness!

These fragments had no concept of it, even. "Completeness" was a poor word.

In their ignorance they would even fight it. There had been the ship that had come before. The first ship had contained many of the keen-thinking fragments. There had been two varieties, life producers and the sterile ones. (How different this second ship was. The keen-thinkers were all sterile, while the other fragments, the fuzzy-thinkers and the no-thinkers, were all producers of life. It was strange.)

How gladly that first ship had been welcomed by all the planet! He could remember the first intense shock at the realization that the visitors were fragments and not complete. The shock had give way to pity, and the pity to action. It was not certain how they would fit into the community, but there had been no hesitation. All life was sacred and somehow room would have been made for them—for all of them, from the large keen-thinkers to the little multipliers in the darkness.

But there had been a miscalculation. They had not correctly analyzed the course of the fragments' ways of thinking. The keen-thinkers became aware of what had been done and resented it. They were frightened, of course; they did not understand.

They had developed the barrier first, and then, later, had destroyed themselves, exploding their ships to atoms.

Poor, foolish fragments.

This time, at least, it would be different. They would be saved, despite themselves.

*

John Drake would not have admitted it in so many words, but he was very proud of his skill on the photo-typer. He had a travel-kit model, which was a six-by-eight, featureless dark plastic slab, with cylindrical bulges on either end to hold the roll of thin paper. It fitted into a brown leather case, equipped with a beltlike contraption that held it closely about the waist and at one hip. The whole thing weighed less than a pound.

Drake could operate it with either hand. His fingers would flick quickly and easily, placing their light pressure at exact spots on the blank surface, and, soundlessly, words would be written.

He looked thoughtfully at the beginning of his story, then up at Dr. Weiss. "What do you think, Doc?"

"It starts well."

Drake nodded. "I thought I might as well start with Saybrook himself. They haven't released his story back home yet. I wish I could have seen Saybrook's original report. How did he ever get it through, by the way?"

"As near as I could tell, he spent one last night sending it through the sub-ether. When he was finished, he shorted the motors, and converted the entire ship into a thin cloud of vapor a millionth of a second later. The crew and himself along with it."

"What a man! You were in this from the beginning, Doc?"

"Not from the beginning," corrected Weiss gently. "Only since the receipt of Saybrook's report."

He could not help thinking back. He had read that report, realizing even then how wonderful the planet must have seemed when Saybrook's colonizing expedition first reached it. It was practically a duplicate of Earth, with an abounding plant life and a purely vegetarian animal life.

There had been only the little patches of green fur (how often had he used that phrase in his speaking and thinking!) which seemed strange. No living individual on the planet had eyes. Instead, there was this fur. Even the plants, each blade or leaf or blossom, possessed the two patches of richer green.

Then Saybrook had noticed, startled and bewildered, that there was no conflict for food on the planet. All plants grew pulpy appendages which were eaten by the animals. These were regrown in a matter of hours. No other parts of the plants were touched. It was as though the plants fed the animals as part of the order of nature. And the plants themselves did not grow in overpowering profusion. They might almost have been cultivated, they were spread across the available soil so discriminately.

How much time, Weiss wondered, had Saybrook had to observe the strange law and order on the planet?—the fact that insects kept their numbers reasonable, though no birds ate them; that the rodentlike things did not swarm, though no carnivores existed to keep them in check.

*

And then there had come the incident of the white rats.

That prodded Weiss. He said, "Oh, one correction, Drake. Hamsters were not the first animals involved. It was the white rats."

"White rats," said Drake, making the correction in his notes.

"Every colonizing ship," said Weiss, "takes a group of white rats for the purpose of testing any alien foods. Rats, of course, are very similar to human beings from a nutritional viewpoint. Naturally, only female white rats are taken."

Naturally. If only one sex was present, there was no danger of unchecked multiplication in case the planet proved favorable. Remember the rabbits in Australia.

"Incidentally, why not use males?" asked Drake.

"Females are hardier," said Weiss, "which is lucky, since that gave the situation away. It turned out suddenly that all the rats were bearing young."

"Right. Now that's where I'm up to, so here's my chance to get some things straight. For my own information, Doc, how did Saybrook find out they were in a family way?"

"Accidentally, of course. In the course of nutritional investigations, rats are dissected for evidence of internal damage. Their condition was bound to be discovered. A few more were dissected; same results. Eventually, all that lived gave birth to young—with no male rats aboard!"

"And the point is that all the young were born with little green patches of fur instead of eyes."

"That is correct. Saybrook said so and we corroborate him. After the rats, the pet cat of one of the children was obviously affected. When it finally kittened, the kittens were not born with closed eyes but with little patches of green fur. There was no tomcat aboard.

"Eventually Saybrook had the women tested. He didn't tell them what for. He didn't want to frighten them. Every single one of them was in the early stages of pregnancy, leaving out of consideration those few who had been pregnant at the time of embarkation. Saybrook never waited for any child to be born, of course. He knew they would have no eyes, only shining patches of green fur.

"He even prepared bacterial cultures (Saybrook was a thorough man) and found each bacillus to show microscopic green spots."

Drake was eager. "That goes way beyond our briefing—or, at least, the briefing I got. But granted that life on Saybrook's Planet is organized into a unified whole, how is it done?"

"How? How are your cells organized into a unified whole? Take an individual cell out of your body, even a brain cell, and what is it by itself? Nothing. A little blob of protoplasm with no more capacity for anything human than an amoeba. Less capacity, in fact, since it couldn't live by itself. But put the cells together and you have something that could invent a spaceship or write a symphony."

"I get the idea," said Drake.

Weiss went on, "All life on Saybrook's Planet is a single organism. In a sense, all life on Earth is too, but it's a fighting dependence, a dog-eat-dog dependence. The bacteria fix nitrogen; the plants fix carbon; animals eat plants and each other; bacterial decay hits everything. It comes full circle. Each grabs as much as it can, and is, in turn, grabbed.

"On Saybrook's Planet, each organism has its place, as each cell in our body does. Bacteria and plants produce food, on the excess of which animals feed, providing in turn carbon dioxide and nitrogenous wastes. Nothing is produced more or less than is needed. The scheme of life is intelligently altered to suit the local environment. No group of life forms multiplies more or less than is needed, just as the cells in our body stop multiplying when there are enough of them for a given purpose. When they don't stop multiplying, we call it cancer. And that's what life on Earth really is, the kind of organic organization we have, compared to that on Saybrook's Planet. One big cancer. Every species, every individual doing its best to thrive at the expense of every other species and individual."

"You sound as if you approve of Saybrook's Planet, Doc."

"I do, in a way. It makes sense out of the business of living. I can see their viewpoint toward us. Suppose one of the cells of your body could be conscious of the efficiency of the human body as compared with that of the cell itself, and could realize that this was only the result of the union of many cells into a higher whole. And then suppose it became conscious of the existence of free-living cells, with bare life and nothing more. It might feel a very strong desire to drag the poor thing into an organization. It might feel sorry for it, feel perhaps a sort of missionary spirit. The things on Saybrook's Planet—or the thing; one should use the singular—feels just that, perhaps."

"And went ahead by bringing about virgin births, eh, Doc? I've got to go easy on that angle of it. Post-office regulations, you know."

"There's nothing ribald about it, Drake. For centuries we've been able to make the eggs of sea urchins, bees, frogs, et cetera develop without the intervention of male fertilization. The touch of a needle was sometimes enough, or just immersion in the proper salt solution. The thing on Saybrook's Planet can cause fertilization by the controlled use of radiant energy. That's why an appropriate energy barrier stops it; interference, you see, or static.

"They can do more than stimulate the division and development of an unfertilized egg. They can impress their own characteristics upon its nucleoproteins, so that the young are born with the little patches of green fur, which serve as the planet's sense organ and means of communication. The young, in other words, are not individuals, but become part of the thing on Saybrook's Planet. The thing on the planet, not at all incidentally, can impregnate any species—plant, animal, or microscopic."

"Potent stuff," muttered Drake.

"Totipotent," Dr. Weiss said sharply. "Universally potent. Any fragment of it is totipotent. Given time, a single bacterium from Saybrook's Planet can convert all of Earth into a single organism! We've got the experimental proof of that."

Drake said unexpectedly, "You know, I think I'm a millionaire, Doc. Can you keep a secret?"

Weiss nodded, puzzled.

"I've got a souvenir from Saybrook's Planet," Drake told him, grinning. "It's only a pebble, but after the publicity the planet will get, combined with the fact that it's quarantined from here on in, the pebble will be all any human being will ever see of it. How much do you suppose I could sell the thing for?"

Weiss stared. "A pebble?" He snatched at the object shown him, a hard, gray ovoid. "You shouldn't have done that, Drake. It was strictly against regulations."

"I know. That's why I asked if you could keep a secret. If you could give me a signed note of authentication—What's the matter, Doc?"

Instead of answering, Weiss could only chatter and point. Drake ran over and stared down at the pebble. It was the same as before—

Except that the light was catching it at an angle, and it showed up two little green spots. Look very closely; they were patches of green hairs.

He was disturbed. There was a definite air of danger within the ship. There was the suspicion of his presence aboard. How could that be? He had done nothing yet. Had another fragment of home come aboard and been less cautious? That would be impossible without his knowledge, and though he probed the ship intensely, he found nothing.

And then the suspicion diminished, but it was not quite dead. One of the keen-thinkers still wondered, and was treading close to the truth.

How long before the landing? Would an entire world of life fragments be deprived of completeness? He clung closer to the severed ends of the wire he had been specially bred to imitate, afraid of detection, fearful for his altruistic mission.

*

Dr. Weiss had locked himself in his own room. They were already within the solar system, and in three hours they would be landing. He had to think. He had three hours in which to decide.

Drake's devilish "pebble" had been part of the organized life on Saybrook's Planet, of course, but it was dead. It was dead when he had first seen it, and if it hadn't been, it was certainly dead after they fed it into the hyper-atomic motor and converted it into a blast of pure heat. And the bacterial cultures still showed normal when Weiss anxiously checked.

That was not what bothered Weiss now.

Drake had picked up the "pebble" during the last hours of the stay on Saybrook's Planet—after the barrier breakdown. What if the breakdown had been the result of a slow, relentless mental pressure on the part of the thing on the planet? What if parts of its being waited to invade as the barrier dropped? If the "pebble" had not been fast enough and had moved only after the barrier was reestablished, it would have been killed. It would have lain there for Drake to see and pick up.

It was a "pebble," not a natural life form. But did that mean it was not some kind of life form? It might have been a deliberate production of the planet's single organism—a creature deliberately designed to look like a pebble, harmless-seeming, unsuspicious. Camouflage, in other words—a shrewd and frighteningly successful camouflage.

Had any other camouflaged creature succeeded in crossing the barrier before it was reestablished—with a suitable shape filched from the minds of the humans aboard ship by the mind-reading organism of the planet? Would it have the casual appearance of a paperweight? Of an ornamental brass-head nail in the captain's old-fashioned chair? And how would they locate it? Could they search every part of the ship for the telltale green patches— even down to individual microbes?

And why camouflage? Did it intend to remain undetected for a time? Why? So that it might wait for the landing on Earth?

An infection after landing could not be cured by blowing up a ship. The bacteria of Earth, the molds, yeasts, and protozoa, would go first. Within a year the non-human young would be arriving by the uncountable billions.

Weiss closed his eyes and told himself it might not be such a bad thing. There would be no more disease, since no bacterium would multiply at the expense of its host, but instead would be satisfied with its fair share of what was available. There would be no more overpopulation; the hordes of man-kind would decline to adjust themselves to the food supply. There would be no more wars, no crime, no greed.

But there would be no more individuality, either.

Humanity would find security by becoming a cog in a biological machine. A man would be brother to a germ, or to a liver cell.

He stood up. He would have a talk with Captain Loring. They would send their report and blow up the ship, just as Saybrook had done.

He sat down again. Saybrook had had proof, while he had only the conjectures of a terrorized mind, rattled by the sight of two green spots on a pebble. Could he kill the two hundred men on board ship because of a feeble suspicion?

He had to think!

He was straining. Why did he have to wait? If he could only welcome those who were aboard now. Now!

Yet a cooler, more reasoning part of himself told him that he could not. The little multipliers in the darkness would betray their new status in fifteen minutes, and the keen-thinkers had them under continual observation. Even one mile from the surface of their planet would be too soon, since they might still destroy themselves and their ship out in space.

Better to wait for the main air locks to open, for the planetary air to swirl in with millions of the little multipliers. Better to greet each one of them into the brotherhood of unified life and let them swirl out again to spread the message.

Then it would be done! Another world organized, complete!

He waited. There was the dull throbbing of the engines working mightily to control the slow dropping of the ship; the shudder of contact with planetary surface, then—

He let the jubilation of the keen-thinkers sweep into reception, and his own jubilant thoughts answered them. Soon they would be able to receive as well as himself. Perhaps not these particular fragments, but the fragments that would grow out of those which were fitted for the continuation of life.

The main air locks were about to be opened—

And all thought ceased.

*

Jerry Thorn thought, Damn it, something's wrong now.

He said to Captain Loring, "Sorry. There seems to be a power break-down. The locks won't open."

"Are you sure, Thorn? The lights are on."

"Yes, sir. We're investigating it now."

He tore away and joined Roger Oldenn at the air-lock wiring box. "What's wrong?"

"Give me a chance, will you?" Oldenn's hands were busy. Then he said, "For the love of Pete, there's a six-inch break in the twenty-amp lead."

"What? That can't be!"

Oldenn held up the broken wires with their clean, sharp, sawn-through ends.

Dr. Weiss joined them. He looked haggard and there was the smell of brandy on his breath.

He said shakily, "What's the matter?"

They told him. At the bottom of the compartment, in one corner, was the missing section.

Weiss bent over. There was a black fragment on the floor of the compartment. He touched it with his finger and it smeared, leaving a sooty smudge on his finger tip. He rubbed it off absently.

There might have been something taking the place of the missing section of wire. Something that had been alive and only looked like wire, yet something that would heat, die, and carbonize in a tiny fraction of a second once the electrical circuit which controlled the air lock had been closed.

He said, "How are the bacteria?"

A crew member went to check, returned and said, "All normal, Doc."

The wires had meanwhile been spliced, the locks opened, and Dr. Weiss stepped out into the anarchic world of life that was Earth.

"Anarchy," he said, laughing a little wildly. "And it will stay that way."

THE BUSINESS, AS USUAL

By Jack Sharkey

Giving Certain Powers the business for a change would be a joy—but it must not backfire—and here at last was the perfect recoilless diddle!

*

In 1962, the United States Air Force found itself possessed of a formidable tool of battle, a radar resistant airplane. While this was the occasion for much rejoicing among the Defense Department members who were cleared for Top Secret, this national-defense solution merely posed a greater problem: What should we do with it?

"There must," said the Secretary of Defense, "be some utilization of this new device to demonstrate to 'Certain Powers' that the world can be made safe for Freedom and Democracy!"

"'Certain Powers,' my foot," said the President. "Why don't we ever come out and just say it?"

"Policy," the Secretary said. "We've always walked softly in our Foreign Policy; especially softly in cases where we didn't have the 'big stick' to carry."

"Well," grumbled the President, "we've got the big stick now. What do we do with it?"

"We just want to shake it a bit," said the Secretary. "No contusions intended, of course. We just have to let them know we *have* it, but are too kind-hearted to use it. Unless provoked, naturally."

"I can see," said the President, "that this new plane is burning a hole in your pocket. Suppose we do send it flying over Rus—"

"*Mister* President!" said the Secretary of Defense.

The President sighed. "All right, all right. Flying over 'Certain Areas,' then. Let's say we get it there. Fine. What do we do with it? Drop leaflets?"

"No. That comes under the proselytizing clause in the Geneva Conference of '59."

"I don't suppose a small—well, you know."

"Aggression," said the Secretary. "We'd lose face in the Middle East."

"So?" demanded the President, spreading his hands. "They don't like us anyhow, do they? Or the competition—or each other, for that matter."

"That's not the point. We have to *feel* as though our dollars are buying friends, whether or not it's true."

"Well, then, what *can* we do?" said the President. "No leaflets, no aggression. We couldn't maybe seed their clouds and make it rain on them?"

"And get sued by other countries for artificially creating low-pressure conditions that, they could claim, robbed them of their rightful rainfall? We've had it happen right here between our own states."

"Maybe we should just forget about it, then?"

"Never! It must be demonstrated to the world that—"

"We could take a full-page ad in the New York *Times*."

"It just isn't done that way," the Secretary protested.

"Why not? It'd save money, wouldn't it? A simple ad like, '*Hey, there, Certain Powers! Lookie what we got!*' What'd be wrong with that?"

"They'd accuse us of Capitalistic Propaganda, that's what! And to get the egg off our face, we'd have to demonstrate the plane and—"

"And be right back where we are now," the President realized aloud, nodding gloomily. "Okay, so what do we do?"

The Secretary looked to left and right, although they were alone together in a soundproofed, heavily guarded room, before replying.

"We drop an agent!" he whispered.

*

The President blinked twice before responding. "Have you gone mad? What man in his right mind would volunteer for such a thing? 'Drop an agent,' indeed! Ten minutes after landing, he'd be up against a wall and shot. Wouldn't *that* be lovely for Freedom and Democracy? We'd have the R—the Certain Powers gloating over the air waves for weeks about nipping a Capitalist Assassination Plot in the bud, not to mention the Mothers of America beating down the White House door because one of Our Boys was sacrificed. You know how our country reacts: If an entire division is wiped out, we bite the bullet and erect statues and make speeches and then forget it. But let a single man get in dutch and the whole populace goes crazy until something is 'done' about it. No, it won't work."

"May I finish?" said the Secretary patiently.

The President shrugged. "Why not?"

"This agent would be something special, sir. One that would not only demonstrate our new aircraft, but which would positively leave the R—damn, you've got *me* doing it!—Certain Powers tied in knots. In point of fact, our military psychologists think that this agent might be the wedge to split Communism apart in hopeless panic!"

"Really?" the President said, with more enthusiasm than he had shown throughout the entire meeting. "I'd like to meet this agent."

The Secretary pressed a black button upon the conference table. An instant later, the door opened and the Secretary's personal aide stepped in. "Yes, sir?"

"Jenkins, have the corridor cleared and Secret Service men posted at all entrances and exits. When it's safe, bring in Agent X-45." He paused. "And Professor Blake, too."

"At once, sir." Jenkins hurried out.

"X-45?" said the President. "Has he no name?"

The Secretary smiled inscrutably. "Teddy, sir."

"Why that smirk?"

"You'll see, sir."

They sat in fidgety silence for another minute, and then a buzzer sounded, twice.

"Ah, that's Jenkins," said the Secretary, and pressed the button once more.

Jenkins came in, followed by a tall gray-haired man who carried a large black suitcase. The President arose, and, as Jenkins left the room again, shook hands with the man. "Agent X-45?" he asked.

"Professor Charles Blake," the man corrected him calmly. "Agent X-45 is in here."

The President stared. "In the *suitcase*? What are we sending? A *dwarf*?"

"Hardly," said the Secretary, snapping up the hasps on the suitcase and opening it upon the table. "This," he said, lifting something from under tissue-paper padding, "is Agent X-45."

The President's gaze was returned by two shiny black eyes, set on either side of a little brown muzzle with a gentle, stitched-on smile. Agent X-45 was clad in flight helmet, miniature jacket and tiny boots, with a baggy pair of brown canvas trousers belted at the waist with a bandolier holding a dozen small wooden bullets, and dangling a patent-leather holster containing a plastic water pistol. And he wore a small parachute and harness.

"But that's a teddy bear!" cried the President.

"Precisely," Professor Blake said.

*

"I think I'll sit down," said the President, and did so, visibly looking like a man who believes he is surrounded by lunatics.

"And look here!" said the Secretary, slipping his hand within Teddy's jacket and withdrawing a small oilskin pouch. "It's rather rudimentary, but the Cyrillic lettering is genuine, and our ambassador assures us the layout is correct."

The President took the pouch, unfolded it and drew out a small sheet of paper, covered with the inscrutable letterings, and numerous rectangles and curving red lines.

"I give up," he said. "What is it?"

"A map of the Kremlin," said the Secretary, his eyes dancing. "That big red 'X' is the location of the Politburo Council Chamber."

"Perhaps," the President said weakly, "you could explain...?"

"Mister President," said Professor Blake, "I am the new Chief of Propaganda for the government."

The President nodded, poured himself a glass of water from a pitcher and drained it. "Yes, yes?" he said.

"Naturally, I have spent my career studying the psychology of a Certain Power...."

The President groaned. "Please, gentlemen, let's name names! It need never go outside this room. My lips are sealed!"

The professor and the Secretary exchanged a look, a raising of eyebrows, then a shrug of surrender.

"Very well," said Blake. "Russia—"

"There," said the President. "That's more like it."

Blake cleared his throat and went on.

"We know the weak spot in the Russian armor is the mentality of the average Communist official," he explained, while the Secretary, who had heard this all before, fiddled with the straps of Teddy's parachute and hummed softly to himself. "They have a distrust complex. Everything and everybody is under 24-hour-a-day suspicion."

"Yes, so I hear," said the President.

"What do you suppose would happen to an agent that was caught by the Russians?" asked Blake.

"I'd rather not even think about that."

"Not the sadistic details, sir. I mean the general train of events, from the time of capture onward."

The President pondered this. "After his capture," he said thoughtfully, "he would be questioned. Through various methods—hopelessly at variance with the regulations of the Geneva Convention—they would discover his mission, and then he would be shot, I guess, or imprisoned."

Blake nodded grimly. "And what if an agent landed there that could *not* divulge his mission?"

*

The Secretary stopped fiddling with the harness and watched the President's face. On the worn features he read first puzzlement, then incredulity, then a flash of sheer amazement.

"Good heavens!" said the President. "They'd—they'd have to admit a defeat, I suppose...."

"But can they?" Blake leaned forward and slammed his fist upon the tabletop. "Can the Communist mentality ever admit that it's been bested?"

"I—I guess not. At least, they never do," said the President. "But this—" he wagged a forefinger at the stuffed thing on the table—"this certainly won't upset them. I mean, after all...." He looked from one to the other for agreement and found none. "But, gentlemen, it's nothing but a stuffed bear!"

"It won't upset them?" queried Blake slowly. "Are you sure?"

"Of course I'm sure. They'll find the bear, wherever it lands, and they'll—well, they'll *know* it's a gag and just laugh at us."

"*How* will they know?" Blake persisted.

"Well, they'll be *pretty* well certain!" the President said scathingly: "I mean a stuffed toy—"

"Would they give up on something of which they were 'pretty well' certain?"

"They'd have to. Teddy, here, certainly couldn't tell them anything. They'd say it was a joke and forget it...." His voice barely sounded the last few words. He no longer believed them. A smile flickered upon his face. "Gentlemen, you don't think they'd—"

"The Russians," said Blake, without emotion, "would go off their rockers, sir. To be unable to explain a thing like this would devastate their morale. The Communist is a man who must hold all the aces. He'll shuffle and reshuffle until he gets them, too. Well, we're giving him a cold deck, sir.

There are no aces for him to find."

"Hmmm," said the President. "As long as there's any doubt in their minds, they'll have to keep plugging at it, won't they! And since there's no solution—" His smile grew calculating. "Yes, yes I begin to see. It's a small thing, to be sure, but I find I must leap at the opportunity to stick a few ants in *their* pants for a change."

"It won't wipe them out," began the Secretary.

"But it'll wear them down a little," Blake finished.

"Done!" said the President. "How soon can we get Operation Frustration under way?"

"The plane is ready to leave right now," said the Secretary, with a small blush. "I—I rather thought you'd see this thing our way."

The President frowned at this, then shrugged. "Good enough. Let's get this bear into the air."

*

"You sure this plane will work?" asked the President, averting his face from the spray of leaves caught up in the shrieking jet stream of the waiting plane.

"It's too simple not to," said Blake, clutching the suitcase—on whose side a large red "Top Secret" had been stenciled—to his chest, and shouting over the scream of the plane. "The radar-resistant device is nothing more than a radio-receiver that blankets the structure, making the entire plane a receiver. If it receives the radar impulses, they can't bounce back and make a blip on the enemy radar screens."

The President sighed. "You make it sound almost too easy. Very well." He shook the man's hand. "Good luck."

"Thank you, sir," said Blake, patting the suitcase. "I'll take good care of Teddy."

The President nodded and moved away. Blake boarded the jet, and, minutes later, the President was watching a last fading streamer of the twin exhausts dwindling upon the eastern horizon.

"I shan't sleep till he's back," said the Secretary.

"Nor I," said the President. "I have the weirdest damned apprehension...."

"About what, sir?" asked the Secretary, as they made their way from the field.

"About the—" the President looked around, then lowered his voice to a whisper—"the Russians. There's something in their makeup we may have overlooked."

"Impossible, sir," said the Secretary of Defense. "Blake is our top psychologist."

"I hope you're right. If this fails, I'd hate for it to be traced to us."

"It can't be. The jacket was made in Japan, the boots in Mexico, the parachute in—"

"I know, I know," said the President. "But if they *should* trace it to us, we'll be a laughing-stock."

"They won't," the Secretary assured him.

*

Two days later, Blake was back, his manner jovial when he met in secret session once more with the two executives.

"Couldn't have gone more perfectly, gentlemen," he said, rubbing his hands together and bouncing on his toes. "We passed directly over Moscow, at a height of ten miles, on the stroke of midnight. The night was overcast and starless. Teddy was dropped through the bomb bay. I saw his parachute open myself. He's down there now, and we're sure to see signs any day now of the little cracks in the Iron Curtain."

"You had no trouble with the enemy?" the President asked, though the answer—since Blake was back alive—was obvious.

"None," Blake said. "The radar shield performed exactly as specified, sir. Not a blink of a searchlight nor a single ground-to-air rocket did we see. Perhaps, on hearing us pass by, they sent up an investigating plane or two, but we were long gone by then. That's the advantage of moving faster than the sound you make," he added pontifically.

"I still feel we've overlooked something," said the President. "In the back of my mind, a small voice keeps trying to remind me of something about the Russians, something that should have made me veto this whole scheme at the start."

Blake looked puzzled. "What about them, sir? If it's in regard to their psychology, I can assure you—"

"I don't mean their psychology at *all*," said the President. "No, wait—yes, I do, in a minor way. They must pursue this thing, no matter what, but—"

A light glimmered, then burned brightly in the President's eyes, and he stood up and smacked his fist into his open palm. "Of course!" he said. "Their methods!"

"Methods?" asked Blake, a little nervously.

The President's reply was interrupted by a knock at the door. The three men exchanged a look; then the Secretary jabbed the button, and Jenkins came in.

"This just came for you, sir," he said, handing the Secretary a small envelope, and making his exit silently.

The President waited impatiently as the envelope was torn open and its contents read. Then the Secretary's hands opened limply and the message fell upon the table.

"Diplomatic note—Russian—Teddy," he whispered.

"What!" yelped the President. He snatched the paper from the table and read it, then sank into his chair once more, his face grim and eyes suspiciously moist. "The dirty, lowdown, rotten...."

Blake, hovering at tableside, hesitated a moment, then asked, "What about Teddy? What's happened?"

"What we might have expected," said the Secretary dolefully.

"You don't mean—" Blake mumbled, horrified. He couldn't continue, just waited for the worst.

The President nodded miserably.

"He's confessed."

No Substitutions

By Jim Harmon

If it was happening to him, all right, he could take that ... but what if he was happening to it?

*

Putting people painlessly to sleep is really a depressing job. It keeps me awake at night thinking of all those bodies I have sent to the vaults, and it interferes to a marked extent with my digestion. I thought before Councilman Coleman came to see me that there wasn't much that could bother me worse.

Coleman came in the morning before I was really ready to face the day. My nerves were fairly well shot from the kind of work I did as superintendent of Dreamland. I chewed up my pill to calm me down, the one to pep me up, the capsule to strengthen my qualities as a relentless perfectionist. I washed them down with gin and orange juice and sat back, building up my fortitude to do business over the polished deck of my desk.

But instead of the usual morning run of hysterical relatives and masochistic mystics, I had to face one of my superiors from the Committee itself.

Councilman Coleman was an impressive figure in a tailored black tunic. His olive features were set off by bristling black eyes and a mobile mustache. He probably scared most people, but not me. Authority doesn't frighten me any more. I've put to sleep too many megalomaniacs, dictators, and civil servants.

"Warden Walker, I've been following your career with considerable interest," Coleman said.

"My career hasn't been very long, sir," I said modestly. I didn't mention that *nobody* could last that long in my job. At least, none had yet.

"I've followed it from the first. I know every step you've made."

I didn't know whether to be flattered or apprehensive. "That's fine," I said. It didn't sound right.

"Tell me," Coleman said, crossing his legs, "what do you think of Dreamland in principle?"

"Why, it's the logical step forward in penal servitude. Man has been heading toward this since he first started civilizing himself. After all, some criminals *can't* be helped psychiatrically. We can't execute them or turn them free; we have to imprison them."

I waited for Coleman's reaction. He merely nodded.

"Of course, it's barbaric to think of a prison as a place of punishment," I continued. "A prison is a place to keep a criminal away from society for a specific time so he can't harm that society for that time. Punishment, rehabilitation, all of it is secondary to that. The purpose of confinement is confinement."

*

The councilman edged forward an inch. "And you really think Dreamland is the most humane confinement possible?"

"Well," I hedged, "it's the most humane we've found yet. I suppose living through a—uh—movie with full sensory participation for year after year can get boring."

"I should think so," Coleman said emphatically. "Warden, don't you sometimes feel the old system where the prisoners had the diversions of riots, solitary confinement, television, and jailbreaks may have made time easier to serve? Do these men ever think they are *actually* living these vicarious adventures?"

That was a question that made all of us in the Dreamland service uneasy. "No, Councilman, they don't. They know they aren't really Alexander of Macedonia, Tarzan, Casanova, or Buffalo Bill. They are conscious of all the time that is being spent out of their real lives; they know they have relatives and friends outside the dream. They know, unless—"

Coleman lifted a dark eyebrow above a black iris. "Unless?"

I cleared my throat. "Unless they go mad and really believe the dream they are living. But as you know, sir, the rate of madness among Dreamland inmates is only slightly above the norm for the population as a whole."

"How do prisoners like that adjust to reality?"

Was he deliberately trying to ask tough questions? "They don't. They think they are having some kind of delusion. Many of them become schizoid and pretend to go along with reality while secretly 'knowing' it to be a lie."

Coleman removed a pocket secretary and broke it open. "About these new free-choice models—do you think they genuinely are an improvement over the old fixed-image machines?"

"Yes, sir," I replied. "By letting the prisoner project his own imagination onto the sense tapes and giving him a limited amount of alternatives to a situation, we can observe whether he is conforming to society to a larger extent."

"I'm glad you said that, Walker," Councilman Coleman told me warmly. "As I said, I've been following your career closely, and if you get through the next twenty-four-hour period as you have through the foregoing part of your Dream, you will be awakened at this time tomorrow. Congratulations!"

I sat there and took it.

He was telling *me*, the superintendent of Dreamland, that my own life here was only a Dream such as I fed to my own prisoners. It was unbelievably absurd, a queasy little joke of some kind. But I didn't deny it.

*

If it *were* true, if I had forgotten that everything that happened was only a Dream, and if I admitted it, the councilman would know I was mad. *It couldn't be true.* Yet—

Hadn't I thought about it ever since I had been appointed warden and transferred from my personnel job at the plant?

Whenever I had come upon two people talking, and it seemed as if I had come upon those same two people talking the same talk before, hadn't I wondered for an instant if it couldn't be a Dream, not reality at all?

Once I had experienced a Dream for five or ten minutes. I was driving a ground car down a spidery road made into a dismal tunnel by weeping trees, a dank, lavender maze. I had known at the time it was a Dream, but still, as the moments passed, I became more intent on the difficult road before me, my blocky hands on the steering wheel, thick fingers typing out the pattern of motion on the drive buttons.

I could remember that. Maybe I couldn't remember being shoved into the prison vault for so many years for such and such a crime.

I didn't really believe this, not then, but I couldn't afford to make a mistake, even if it were only some sort of intemperate test—as I was confident it was, with a sweet, throbbing fury against the man who would employ such a jagged broadsword for prying in his bureaucratic majesty.

"I've always thought," I said, "that it would be a good idea to show a prisoner what the modern penal system was all about by giving him a Dream in which he dreamed about Dreamland itself."

"Yes, indeed," Coleman concurred. Just that and no more.

I leaned intimately across my beautiful oak desk. "I've thought that projecting officials into the Dream and letting them talk with the prisoners might be a more effective form of investigation than mere observation."

"I should say so," Coleman remarked, and got up.

I *had* to get more out of him, some proof, some clue beyond the preposterous announcement he had made.

"I'll see you tomorrow at this time then, Walker." The councilman nodded curtly and turned to leave my office.

I held onto the sides of my desk to keep from diving over and teaching him to change his concept of humor.

The day was starting. If I got through it, giving a good show, I would be released from my Dream, he had said smugly.

But if this was a dream, did I want probation to reality?

*

Horbit was a twitchy little man whose business tunic was the same rodent color as his hair. He had a pronounced tic in his left cheek. "I have to get back," he told me with compelling earnestness.

"Mr. Horbit—Eddie—" I said, glancing at his file projected on my desk pad, "I can't put you back into a Dream. You served your full time for your crime. The maximum."

"But I haven't adjusted to society!"

"Eddie, I can shorten sentences, but I can't expand them beyond the limit set by the courts."

A tear of frustration spilled out of his left eye with the next twitch. "But Warden, sir, my psychiatrist said that I was unable to cope with reality. Come on now, Warden, you don't want a guy who can't cope with reality running around loose." He paused, puzzled. "Hell, I don't know why I can't express myself like I used to."

He could express himself much better in his Dream. He had been Abraham Lincoln in his Dream, I saw. He had lived the life right up to the night when he was taking in *An American Cousin* at the Ford Theater. Horbit couldn't accept history that he had no more life to live. He only knew that if in his delirium he could gain Dreamland once more, he could get back to the hard realities of dealing with the problems of Reconstruction.

"*Please*," he begged.

I looked up from the file. "I'm sorry, Eddie."

His eyes narrowed, both of them, on the next twitch. "Warden, I can always go out and commit another anti-social act."

"I'm afraid not, Eddie. The file shows you are capable of only one crime. And you don't have a wife any more, and she doesn't have a lover."

Horbit laughed. "Your files aren't infallible, Warden."

With one gesture, he ripped open his tunic and tore into his own flesh. No, not his own flesh. Pseudo-flesh. He took out the gun that was underneath.

"The beamer is made of X-ray-transparent plastic, Warden, but it works as well as one made of steel and lead."

"Now that you've got it in here," I said in time with the pulse in my throat, "what are you going to do with it?"

"I'm going to make you go down to the vaults and put me back to sleep, Warden."

I nodded. "I suppose you can do that. But what's to prevent me from waking you up as soon as I've taken away your gun?"

"This!" He tossed a sheet of paper onto my desk.

"What's this?" I asked unnecessarily. I could read it.

"A confession that you accepted a bribe to put me back to sleep," Horbit said, his tic beating out a feverish tempo. "As soon as you've signed it, I'll use your phone to have it telefaxed to the Registrar of Private Documents."

I had to admire the thought behind the idea. Horbit was convinced that I was only a figment of his unfocused imagination, but he was playing the game with uncompromising logic, trusting that even madness had hard and tight rules behind it.

There was also something else I admired about the plan.

It could work.

Once he fed that document to the archives, I would be obligated to help him even without the gun. My word would probably be taken that I had been forced to do it at gunpoint, but there would always be doubts, enough to wreck my career when it came time for promotion.

Nothing like this had ever happened in my years as warden.

*

Suddenly, Coleman's words hit me in the back of the neck. *If I got through the next twenty-four hours.* This had to be some kind of test.

But a test for what?

Had I been deliberately told that I was living only a Dream to see if my ethics would hold up even when I thought I wasn't dealing with reality?

Or if this *was* only a Dream, was it a test to see if I was morally ready to return to the real, the earnest world?

But if it was a test to see if I was ready for reality, did I want to pass it? My life was nerve-racking and mind-wrecking, but I liked the challenge—it was the only life I knew or could believe in.

What was I going to do?

The only thing I knew was that I couldn't tune in tomorrow and find out.

The time was *now.*

Horbit motioned the gun to my desk set. "Sign that paper."

I reached out and took hold of his wrist. I squeezed.

Horbit's screams brought in the guards.

I picked up the gun from where he had dropped it and handed it to Captain Keller, my head guard, a tough old bird who wore his uniform like armor.

"Trying to force his way back to the sleep tanks," I told Keller.

He nodded. "Happened before. Back when old man Preston lost his grip."

Preston had been my predecessor. He had lost his hold on reality like all the others before him who had served long as warden of Dreamland. A few had quit while they were still ahead and spent the rest of their lives recuperating. Our society didn't produce individuals tough enough to stand the strain of putting their fellow human beings to sleep for long.

One of Keller's men had stabbed Horbit's arm with a hypospray to blanket the pain from his broken wrist, and the man was quieter.

"I couldn't have done it, Warden," Horbit mumbled drowsily. "I couldn't kill anybody. Unless it was like that other time."

"Of course, Eddie," I said.

I had banked on that, hadn't I, when I made my move?

Or did I?

Wasn't it perhaps a matter of knowing that all of it wasn't real and that the safety cutoffs in even a free-choice model of a Dream Machine couldn't let me come to any real harm? I had been suspiciously brave, disarming a dedicated maniac. With only an hour to spare for gym a day, I could barely press 350 pounds. I was hardly in shape for personal combat.

On the other hand, maybe I actually wanted something to go wrong so my sleep sentence would be extended. Or was it that, in some sane part of my mind, I wanted release from unreality badly enough to take any risk to prove that I was morally capable of returning to the real world?

It was a carrousel and I couldn't catch the brass ring no matter how many turns I went spinning through.

I hardly heard Horbit when he half-shouted at me as my men led him from the room. Glancing up sharply, I saw him straining purposefully against the bonds of muscle and narcotic that held him.

"You have to send me back now, Warden," he was shrilling. "You have to! I tried to coerce you with a gun. That's a crime, Warden—you *know* that's a crime! I have to be put to sleep!"

Keller flicked his mustache with a thick thumbnail. "How about that? You won't let a guy back into the sleepy-bye pads, so he pulls a gun on you to make you, and *that* makes him eligible. He couldn't lose, Warden. No, sir, he had it made."

My answer to Keller was forming, building up in my jaw muscles, but I took a pill and it went away.

"Hold him in the detention quarters," I said finally. "I'm going to make a study of this."

Keller winked knowingly and sauntered out of the office, his left hand swinging the blackjack the Committee had taken away from him a decade before.

The problem of what to do with Keller wasn't particularly atypical of the ones I had to solve daily and I wasn't going to let that worry me. Much.

I pressed my button to let Mrs. Engle know I was ready for the next interview.

*

They came. There were the hysterical relatives, the wives and mothers and brothers who demanded that their kin be Awakened because they were special cases, not really guilty, or needed at home, or possessed of such awesome talents and qualities as to be exempt from the laws of lesser men.

Once in a while I granted a parole for a prisoner to see a dying mother or if some important project was falling apart without his help, but most of the time I just sat with my eyes propped open, letting a sea of vindictive screeching and beseeching wailings wash around me.

The relatives and legal talent were spaced with hungry-eyed mystics who were convinced they could contemplate God and their navels both conscientiously as an incarnation of Gautama. To risk sounding religiously intolerant, I usually kicked these out pretty swiftly.

The onetime inmate who wanted back in after a reprieve was fairly rare. Few of them ever got *that* crazy.

But it was my luck to get another the same day, *the* day for me, as Horbit.

Paulson was a tall, lean man with sad eyes. The clock above his sharp shoulder bone said five till noon. I didn't expect him to take much out of my lunch hour.

"Warden," Paulson said, "I've decided to give myself up. I murdered a blind beggar the other night."

"For his pencils?" I asked.

Paulson shifted uneasily. "No, sir. For his money. I needed some extra cash and I was stronger than he was, so why shouldn't I take it?"

I examined the projection of his file. He was an embezzler, not a violent man. He had served his time and been released. Conceivably he might embezzle again, but the Committee saw to it that temptation was never again placed in his path. He would not commit a crime of violence.

"Look, Paulson," I said, a trifle testily, "if you have so little conscience as to kill a blind old man for a few dollars, where do you suddenly get enough guilt feelings to cause you to give yourself up?"

Paulson tried his insufficient best to smile evilly. "It wasn't conscience, Warden. I never lie awake a minute whenever I kill anybody. It's just—well, Dreaming isn't so bad. Last time I was Allen Pinkerton, the detective. It was exciting. A lot more exciting than the kind of life I lead."

I nodded solemnly. "Yes, no doubt strangling old men in the streets can be pretty dull for a red-blooded man of action."

"Yes," Paulson said earnestly, "it does get to be a humdrum routine. I've been experimenting with all sorts of murders, but I just don't seem to get much of a kick out of them now. I'd like to try it from the other end as Pinkerton again. Of course, if you can't arrange it, I guess I'll have to go out and see what I can do with, say, an ax." His eye glittered almost convincingly.

"Paulson, you know I could have you watched night and day if I thought you really were a murderer. But I can't send you back to the sleep vaults without proof and conviction for a crime."

"That doesn't sound very reasonable," Paulson objected. "Turning loose a homicidal maniac who is offering to go back to the vaults of his own free will just because you lack a little trifling proof of his guilt."

"Sure," I told him, "but I don't want to share the same noose with you. My job is to keep the innocent out and the convicted in. And I do my job, Paulson."

"But you have to! If you don't, I'll have to go out and establish my guilt with another crime. Do you want a crime on your hands, Warden?"

I studied his record. There was a chance, just a chance....

"Do you want to wait voluntarily in the detention quarters?" I asked him.

He agreed readily enough.

I watched him out of the office and rang for lunch.

The news on the wall video was dull as usual. A man got tired of hearing peace, safety, prosperity and brotherly love all the time. I dug into my strained spinach, raw hamburger, and chewed up my white pill, my red pill, my ebony pill, and my second white pill. The gin and tomato juice took the taste away.

I was ready for the afternoon session.

*

Matrons were finishing the messy job of dragging a hysterical woman out of the office when Keller came back. He had a stubborn look on his flattened, red face.

"New prisoner asking to see you personal," Keller reported. "Told him no. Okay?"

"No," I said. "He can see me. That's the law and you know it. He isn't violent, is he?" I asked in some concern. The room was still in disarray.

"Naw, he ain't violent, Warden. He just thinks he's somebody important."

"Sounds like a case for therapy, not Dreamland. Who does he think he is?"

"One of the Committee—Councilman Coleman."

"Mm-hmm. And who is he really, Captain?"

"Councilman Coleman."

I whistled. "What did they nail him on?"

"Misuse of authority."

"And he didn't get a suspended for that?"

"Wasn't his first offense. Still want to see him?"

I gave a lateral wave of my hand. "Of course."

My pattern of living—call it my office routine—had been re-established through the day. I hadn't had a chance to brood much over the bombshell Coleman had tossed in my lap in the morning, but now I could think.

Coleman entered wearing the same black tunic, the same superior attitude. His black eyes fastened on me.

"Sit down, Councilman," I directed.

He deigned to comply.

I studied the files flashed before me. Several times before, Coleman had been guilty of slight misuses of his authority: helping his friends, harming his enemies. Not enough to make him be impeached from the Committee. His job was so hypersensitive that if every transgression earned dismissal, no one could hold the position more than a day. Even with the best intentions, mistakes can be taken for deliberate errors. Not to mention the converse. For his earlier errors, Coleman had first received a suspended sentence, then two terminal sentences to be fixed by the warden. My predecessors had given him first a few weeks, then a few months of sleep in Dreamland.

*

Coleman's eyes didn't frighten me; I focused right on the pupils. "That was a pretty foul trick, Councilman. Did you hope to somehow frighten me out of executing this sentence by what you told me this morning?"

I couldn't follow his reasoning. Just how making me think my life was only a Dream such as I imposed on my own prisoners could help him, I couldn't see.

"Warden Walker," Coleman intoned in his magnificent voice, "I'm shocked. *I* am not personally monitoring your Dream. The Committee as a whole will decide whether you are capable of returning to the real world. Moreover, please don't get carried away. I'm not concerned with what you do to this sensory projection of myself, beyond how it helps to establish your moral capabilities."

"I suppose," I said heavily, "that I could best establish my high moral character by excusing you from this penal sentence?"

"Not at all," Councilman Coleman asserted. "According to the facts as you know them, I am 'guilty' and must be confined."

I was stymied for an instant. I had expected him to say that I must know that he was incapable of committing such an error and I must pardon him despite the misguided rulings of the courts. Then I thought of something else.

"You show symptoms of being a habitual criminal, Coleman. I think you deserve *life*."

Coleman cocked his head thoughtfully, concerned. "That seems rather extreme, Warden."

"You would suggest a shorter sentence?"

"If it were my place to choose, yes. A few years, perhaps. But life—no, I think not."

I threw up my hands. You don't often see somebody do that, but I did. I couldn't figure him. Coleman had wealth and power as a councilman in the real world, but I had thought somehow he wanted to escape to a Dream world. Yet he didn't want to be in for life, the way Paulson and Horbit did.

There seemed to be no point or profit in what he had told me that morning, nothing in it for him.

Unless—

Unless what he said was literally true.

I stood up. My knees wanted to quit halfway up, but I made it. "This," I said, "is a difficult decision for me, sir. Would you make yourself comfortable here for a time, Councilman?"

Coleman smiled benignly. "Certainly, Warden."

I walked out of my office, slowly and carefully.

*

Horbit was sitting in his detention quarters idly flicking through a book tape on the Civil War when I found him. The tic in his cheek marked time with every new page.

"President Lincoln," I said reverently.

Horbit looked up, his eyes set in a clever new way. "*You* call me that. Does it mean I am recovering? You don't mean now that I'm getting back my right senses?"

"Mr. President, the situation you find yourself in now is something stranger and more evil than any madness. I am not a phantom of your mind—I am a *real* man. This wild, distorted place is a *real* place."

"Do you think you can pull the wool over my eyes, you scamp? Mine eyes have seen the glory."

"Yes, sir." I sat down beside him and looked earnestly into his twitching face. "But I know you have always believed in the occult."

He nodded slowly. "I *have* often suspected this was hell."

"Not quite, sir. The occult has its own rigid laws. It is perfectly scientific. This world is in another dimension—one that is not length, breadth or thickness—but a real one nevertheless."

"An interesting theory. Go ahead."

"This world is more scientifically advanced than the one you come from—and this advanced science has fallen into the hands of a well-meaning despot."

Horbit nodded again. "The Jefferson Davis type."

He didn't understand Lincoln's beliefs very well, but I pretended to go along with him. "Yes, sir. He—our leader—doubts your abilities as President. He is not above meddling in the affairs of an alien world if he believes he is doing good. He has convicted you to this world in that belief."

He chuckled. "Many of my countrymen share his convictions."

"Maybe," I said. "But many here do not. I don't. I know you must return to guide the Reconstruction. But first you must convince our leader of your worth."

"How am I going to accomplish that?" Horbit asked worriedly.

"You are going to have a companion from now on, an agent of the leader, who will pretend to be something he isn't. You must pretend to believe in what he claims to be, and convince him of your high intelligence, moral responsibilities, and qualities of leadership."

"Yes," Horbit said thoughtfully, "yes. I must try to curb my tendency for telling off-color jokes. My wife is always nagging me about that."

*

Paulson was only a few doors away from Horbit. I found him with his long, thin legs stretched out in front of him, staring dismally into the gloom of the room. No wonder he found reality so boring and depressing with so downbeat a mood cycle. I wondered why they hadn't been able to do something about adjusting his metabolism.

"Paulson," I said gently, "I want to speak with you."

He bolted upright in his chair. "You're going to put me back to sleep."

"I came to talk to you about that," I admitted.

I pulled up a seat and adjusted the lighting so only his face and mine seemed to float bodiless in a sea of night, two moons of flesh.

"Paulson—or should I call you Pinkerton?—this will come as a shock, a shock I know only a fine analytical mind like yours could stand. You think your life as the great detective was only a Dream induced by some miraculous machine. But, sir, believe me: that life was *real*."

Paulson's eyes rolled slightly back into his head and changed their luster. "Then *this* is the Dream. I've thought—"

"No!" I snapped. "This world is also real."

I went through the same Fourth Dimension waltz as I had auditioned for Horbit. At the end of it, Paulson was nodding just as eagerly.

"I could be destroyed for telling you this, but our leader is planning the most gigantic conquest known to any intelligent race in the Universe. He is going to conquer Earth in all its possible futures and all its possible pasts. After that, there are other planets."

"He must be stopped!" Paulson shouted.

I laid my palm on his arm. "Armies can't stop him, nor can fantastic secret weapons. Only one thing can stop him: the greatest detective who ever lived. Pinkerton!"

"Yes," Paulson said. "I suppose I could."

"He knows that. But he's a fiend. He wants a battle of wits with you, his only possible foe, for the satisfaction of making a fool of you."

"Easier said than done, my friend," Paulson said crisply.

"True," I agreed, "but he is devious, the devil! He plans to convince you that he also has been removed to this world from his own, even as you have. He will claim to be Abraham Lincoln."

"No!"

"Yes, and he will pretend to find you accidentally and get you to help him find a way back to his own world, glorying in making a fool of you. But you can use every moment to learn his every weakness."

"But wait. I know President Lincoln well. I guarded him on his first inauguration trip. How could this leader of yours fool me? Does he look like the President?"

"Not at all. But remember, the dimensional shift changes physical appearance. You've noticed that in yourself."

"Yes, of course," Paulson muttered. "But he couldn't hoax me. My keen powers of deduction would have seen through him in an instant!"

*

I saw Horbit and Paulson happily off in each other's company. Paulson was no longer bored by a reality in which he was matching wits with the first master criminal of the paratime universe, and Horbit was no longer hopeless in his quest to gain another reality because he knew he was not merely insane now.

It was a pair of fantastic stories that no man in his right mind would believe—but that didn't make them invalid to a brace of ex-Sleepers. They *wanted* to believe them. The stories gave them what they were after—without me having to break the law and put them to sleep for crimes they hadn't committed.

They would find out some day that I had lied to them, but maybe by that time they would have realized this world wasn't so bad.

Fortunately, I was confident from their psych records that they were both incapable of ending their little game by homicide, no matter how justified they might think it was.

"Hey, Warden," Captain Keller bellowed as I approached my office door, "when are you going to let me throw that stiff Coleman into the sleepy-bye vaults? He's still sitting in there on your furniture as smug as you please."

"You don't sound as if you like our distinguished visitor very well," I remarked.

"It's not that. I just don't think he deserves any special privileges. Besides, it was guys like him that took away our nightsticks. My boys didn't like that. Look at me—I'm defenseless!"

I looked at his square figure. "Not quite, Captain, not quite."

Now was the time.

I stretched out my wet palm toward the door.

Was or was not Coleman telling the truth when he said this life of mine was itself only a Dream? If it was, did I want to finish my last day with the right decision so I could return to some alien reality? Or did I deliberately want to make a mistake so I could continue living the opiate of my Dream?

Then, as I touched the door, I knew the only decision that could have any meaning for me.

Councilman Coleman didn't look as if he had moved since I had left him. He was unwrinkled, unperspiring, his eyes and mustache crisp as ever. He smiled at me briefly in supreme confidence.

I changed my decision then, in that moment. And, in the next, changed it back to my original choice.

"Coleman," I said, "you can get out of here. As warden, I'm granting you a five-year probation."

The councilman stood up swiftly, his eyes catching little sparks of yellow light. "I don't approve of your decision, Warden. Not at all. Unless you alter it, I'll be forced to convince the rest of the Committee that your decisions are becoming faulty, that you are losing your grip just as all your predecessors did."

My muscles relaxed in a spasm and it took the fresh flow of adrenalin to get me to the chair behind my desk. I took a pill. I took two pills.

"Tell me, Councilman, what happened to the offer to release me from this phony Dream? Now you are talking as if *this*world was the *real* one."

Coleman parted his lips, but then the planes of his face shifted into another pattern. "You never believed me."

"Almost, but not quite. You knew I was on the narrow edge in this kind of job, but I'm not as far out as you seemed to have thought."

"I can still wreck your career, you know."

"I don't think so. That would constitute a misuse of authority, and the next time you turn up before me, I'm going to give you *life* in Dreamland."

Coleman sat back down suddenly.

"You don't want life as a Sleeper, do you?" I pursued. "You did want a relatively *short* sentence of a few months or a few years. I can think of two reasons why. The answer is probably a combination of both. In the first place, you are a joy-popper with Dreams—you don't want to live out your life in one, but you like a brief Dream every few years like an occasional dose of a narcotic. In the second place, you probably have political reasons for wanting to hide out somewhere in safety for the next few years. The world isn't as placid as the newscasts sometimes make it seem."

*

He didn't say anything. I didn't think he had to.

"You wanted to make sure I made a painfully scrupulous decision in your case," I went on. "You didn't want me to pardon you completely because of your high position, but at the same time you didn't want too long a sentence. But I'm doing you no favors. You get no time from me, Coleman."

"How did you decide to do this?" he asked. "Don't tell me you never doubted. We've all doubted since we found out about the machines: which was real and which was the Dream? How did you decide to risk this?"

"I acted the only way I could act," I said. "I decided I had to act as if my life was real and that you were lying. I decided that because, if all this were false, if I could have no more confidence in my own mind and my own senses than that, I didn't give a damn if it *were* all a Dream."

Coleman stood up and walked out of my office.

The clock told me it was after five. I began clearing my desk.

Captain Keller stuck his head in, unannounced. "Hey, Warden, there's an active one out here. He claims that Dreamland compromises His plan for the Free Will of the Universe."

"Well, escort him inside, Captain," I said.

I put away my pills. Solving simple problems such as the new visitor presented always helped me to relax.

PRIME DIFFERENCE

By Alan E. Nourse

Being two men rolled out of one would solve my problems—but which one would I be?

*

I suppose that every guy reaches a point once in his lifetime when he gets one hundred and forty per cent fed up with his wife.

Understand now—I've got nothing against marriage or any thing like that. Marriage is great. It's a good old red-blooded American Institution. Except that it's got one defect in it big enough to throw a cat through, especially when you happen to be married to a woman like Marge—

It's so *permanent.*

Oh, I'd have divorced Marge in a minute if we'd been living in the Blissful 'Fifties—but with the Family Solidarity Amendment of 1968, and all the divorce taxes we have these days since the women got their teeth into politics, to say nothing of the Aggrieved Spouse Compensation Act, I'd have been a pauper for the rest of my life if I'd tried it. That's aside from the social repercussions involved.

You can't really blame me for looking for another way out. But a man has to be desperate to try to buy himself an Ego Prime.

So, all right, I was desperate. I'd spent eight years trying to keep Marge happy, which was exactly seven and a half years too long.

Marge was a dream to look at, with her tawny hair and her sulky eyes and a shape that could set your teeth chattering—but that was where the dream stopped.

She had a tongue like a #10 wood rasp and a list of grievances long enough to paper the bedroom wall. When she wasn't complaining, she was crying, and when she wasn't crying, she was pointing out in chilling detail exactly where George Faircloth fell short as a model husband, which happened to be everywhere. Half of the time she had a "beastly headache" (for which I was personally responsible) and the other half she was sore about something, so ninety-nine per cent of the time we got along like a couple of tomcats in a packing case.

*

Maybe we just weren't meant for each other. I don't know. I used to envy guys like Harry Folsom at the office. His wife is no joy to live with either, but at least he could take a spin down to Rio once in a while with one of the stenographers and get away with it.

I knew better than to try. Marge was already so jealous that I couldn't even smile at the company receptionist without a twinge of guilt. Give Marge something real to howl about, and I'd be ready for the Rehab Center in a week.

But I'd underestimated Marge. She didn't need anything real, as I found out when Jeree came along.

Business was booming and the secretaries at the office got shuffled around from time to time. Since I had an executive-type job, I got an executive-type secretary. Her name was Jeree and she was gorgeous. As a matter of fact, she was better than gorgeous. She was the sort of secretary every businessman ought to have in his office. Not to do any work—just to sit there.

Jeree was tall and dark, and she could convey more without saying anything than I ever dreamed was possible. The first day she was there, she conveyed to me very clearly that if I cared to supply the opportunity, she'd be glad to supply the motive.

That night, I could tell that Marge had been thinking something over during the day. She let me get the first bite of dinner halfway to my mouth, and then she said, "I hear you got a new secretary today."

I muttered something into my coffee cup and pretended not to hear.

Marge turned on her Accusing Look #7. "I also hear that she's five-foot-eight and tapes out at 38-25-36 and thinks you're handsome."

Marge had quite a spy system.

"She couldn't be much of a secretary," she added.

"She's a perfectly good secretary," I blurted, and kicked myself mentally. I should have known Marge's traps by then.

Marge exploded. I didn't get any supper, and she was still going strong at midnight. I tried to argue, but when Marge got going, there was no stopping her. I had my ultimatum, as far as Jeree was concerned.

Harry Folsom administered the *coup de grace* at coffee next morning. "What you need is an Ego Prime," he said with a grin. "Solve all your problems. I hear they work like a charm."

I set my coffee cup down. Bells were ringing in my ears. "Don't be ridiculous. It's against the law. Anyway, I wouldn't think of such a thing. It's—it's indecent."

Harry shrugged. "Just joking, old man, just joking. Still, it's fun to think about, eh? Freedom from wife. Absolutely safe and harmless. Not even too expensive, if you've got the right contacts. And I've got a friend who knows a guy—"

Just then, Jeree walked past us and flashed me a big smile. I gripped my cup for dear life and still spilled coffee on my tie.

As I said, a guy gets fed up.

And maybe opportunity would only knock once.

And an Ego Prime would solve all my problems, as Harry had told me.

*

It was completely illegal, of course. The wonder was that Ego Prime, Inc., ever got to put their product on the market at all, once the nation's housewives got wind of just what their product was.

From the first, there was rigid Federal control and laws regulating the use of Primes right down to the local level. You could get a license for a Utility model Prime if you were a big business executive, or a high public official, or a movie star, or something like that; but even then his circuits had to be inspected every two months, and he had to have a thousand built-in Paralyzers, and you had to specify in advance exactly what you wanted your Prime to be able to do when, where, how, why, and under what circumstances.

The law didn't leave a man much leeway.

But everybody knew that if you *really* wanted a personal Prime with all his circuits open and no questions asked, you could get one. Black market prices were steep and you ran your own risk, but it could be done.

Harry Folsom told his friend who knew a guy, and a few greenbacks got lost somewhere, and I found myself looking at a greasy little man with a black mustache and a bald spot, up in a dingy fourth-story warehouse off lower Broadway.

"Ah, yes," the little man said. "Mr. Faircloth. We've been expecting you."

*

I didn't like the looks of the guy any more than the looks of the place. "I've been told you can supply me with a—"

He coughed. "Yes, yes. I understand. It might be possible." He fingered his mustache and regarded me from pouchy eyes. "Busy executives often come to us to avoid the—ah—unpleasantness of formal arrangements. Naturally, we only act as agents, you might say. We never see the merchandise ourselves—" He wiped his hands on his trousers. "Now were you interested in the ordinary Utility model, Mr. Faircloth?"

I assumed he was just being polite. You didn't come to the back door for Utility models.

"Or perhaps you'd require one of our Deluxe models. Very careful workmanship. Only a few key Paralyzers in operation and practically complete circuit duplication. Very useful for—ah—close contact work, you know. Social engagements, conferences—"

I was shaking my head. "I want a *Super* Deluxe model," I told him.

He grinned and winked. "Ah, indeed! You want perfect duplication. Yes, indeed. Domestic situations can be—awkward, shall we say. Very awkward—"

I gave him a cold stare. I couldn't see where my domestic problems were any affairs of his. He got the idea and hurried me back to a storeroom.

"We keep a few blanks here for the basic measurement. You'll go to our laboratory on 14th Street to have the minute impressions taken. But I can assure you you'll be delighted, simply delighted."

The blanks weren't very impressive—clay and putty and steel, faceless, brainless. He went over me like a tailor, checking measurements of all sorts. He was thorough—embarrassingly thorough, in fact—but finally he was finished. I went on to the laboratory.

And that was all there was to it.

*

Practical androids had been a pipe dream until Hunyadi invented the Neuro-pantograph. Hunyadi had no idea in the world what to do with it once he'd invented it, but a couple of enterprising engineers bought him body and soul, sub-contracted the problems of anatomy, design, artistry, audio and visio circuitry, and so forth, and ended up with the modern Ego Primes we have today.

I spent a busy two hours under the NP microprobes; the artists worked outside while the NP technicians worked inside. I came out of it pretty woozy, but a shot of Happy-O set that straight. Then I waited in the recovery room for another two hours, dreaming up ways to use my Prime when I got him. Finally the door opened and the head technician walked in, followed by a tall, sandy-haired man with worried blue eyes and a tired look on his face.

*

"Meet George Faircloth Prime," the technician said, grinning at me like a nursing mother.

I shook hands with myself. Good firm handshake, I thought admiringly. Nothing flabby about it.

I slapped George Prime on the shoulder happily. "Come on, Brother," I said. "You've got a job to do."

But, secretly, I was wondering what Jeree was doing that night.

George Prime had remote controls, as well as a completely recorded neurological analogue of his boss, who was me. George Prime thought what I thought about the same things I did in the same way I did. The only difference was that what I told George Prime to do, George Prime did.

If I told him to go to a business conference in San Francisco and make the smallest possible concessions for the largest possible orders, he would go there and do precisely that. His signature would be my signature. It would hold up in court.

And if I told him that my wife Marge was really a sweet, good-hearted girl and that he was to stay home and keep her quiet and happy any time I chose, he'd do that, too.

George Prime was a duplicate of me right down to the sandy hairs on the back of my hands. Our fingerprints were the same. We had the same mannerisms and used the same figures of speech. The only physical difference apparent even to an expert was the tiny finger-depression buried in the hair above his ear. A little pressure there would stop George Prime dead in his tracks.

He was so lifelike, even I kept forgetting that he was basically just a pile of gears.

I'd planned very carefully how I meant to use him, of course.

Every man who's been married eight years has a sanctuary. He builds it up and maintains it against assault in the very teeth of his wife's natural instinct to clean, poke, pry and rearrange things. Sometimes it takes him years of diligent work to establish his hideout and be confident that it will stay inviolate, but if he starts early enough, and sticks with it long enough, and is fierce enough and persistent enough and crafty enough, he'll probably win in the end. The girls hate him for it, but he'll win.

With some men, it's just a box on their dressers, or a desk, or a corner of an unused back room. But I had set my sights high early in the game. With me, it was the whole workshop in the garage.

*

At first, Marge tried open warfare. She had to clean the place up, she said. I told her I didn't *want* her to clean it up. She could clean the whole house as often as she chose, but *I*would clean up the workshop.

After a couple of sharp engagements on that field, Marge staged a strategic withdrawal and reorganized her attack. A little pile of wood shavings would be on the workshop floor one night and be gone the next. A wrench would be back on the rack—upside down, of course. An open paint can would have a cover on it.

I always knew. I screamed loudly and bitterly. I ranted and raved. I swore I'd rig up a booby-trap with a shotgun.

So she quit trying to clean in there and just went in once in a while to take a look around. I fixed that with the old toothpick-in-the-door routine. Every time she so much as set foot in that workshop, she had a battle on her hands for the next week or so. She could count on it. It was that predictable.

She never found out how I knew, and after seven years or so, it wore her down. She didn't go into the workshop any more.

As I said, you've got to be persistent, but you'll win.

Eventually.

If you're *really* persistent.

Now all my effort paid off. I got Marge out of the house for an hour or two that day and had George Prime delivered and stored in the big closet in the workshop. They hooked his controls up and left me a manual of instructions for running him. When I got home that night, there he was, just waiting to be put to work.

After supper, I went out to the workshop—to get the pipe I'd left there, I said. I pushed George Prime's button, winked at him and switched on the free-behavior circuits.

"Go to it, Brother," I said.

George Prime put my pipe in his mouth, lit it and walked back into the house.

Five minutes later, I heard them fighting.

It sounded so familiar that I laughed out loud. Then I caught a cab on the corner and headed uptown.

We had quite a night, Jeree and I. I got home just about time to start for work, and sure enough, there was George Prime starting my car, business suit on, briefcase under his arm.

I pushed the recall and George Prime got out of the car and walked into the workshop. He stepped into his cradle in the closet. I turned him off and then drove away in the car.

Bless his metallic soul, he'd even kissed Marge good-by for me!

*

Needless to say, the affairs of George Faircloth took on a new sparkle with George Prime on hand to cover the home front.

For the first week, I was hardly home at all. I must say I felt a little guilty, leaving poor old George Prime to cope with Marge all the time—he looked and acted so human, it was easy to forget that he literally couldn't care less. But I felt apologetic all the same whenever I took him out of his closet.

"She's really a sweet girl underneath it all," I'd say. "You'll learn to like her after a bit."

"Of course I like her," George Prime said. "You told me to, didn't you? Stop worrying. She's really a sweet girl underneath it all."

He sounded convincing enough, but still it bothered me. "You're sure you understand the exchange mechanism?" I asked. I didn't want any foul-ups there, as you can imagine.

"Perfectly," said George Prime. "When you buzz the recall, I wait for the first logical opportunity I can find to come out to the workshop, and you take over."

"But you might get nervous. You might inadvertently tip her off."

George Prime looked pained. "Really, old man! I'm a Super Deluxe model, remember? I don't have fourteen activated Hunyadi tubes up in this cranial vault of mine just for nothing. You're the one that's nervous. I'll take care of everything. Relax."

So I did.

Jeree made good all her tacit promises and then some. She had a very cozy little apartment on 34th Street where we went to relax after a hard day at the office. When we weren't doing the town, that is. As long as Jeree didn't try too much conversation, everything was wonderful.

And then, when Jeree got a little boring, there was Sybil in the accounting department. Or Dorothy in promotion. Or Jane. Or Ingrid.

I could go on at some length, but I won't. I was building quite a reputation for myself around the office.

Of course, it was like buying your first 3-V set. In a week or so, the novelty wears off a little and you start eating on schedule again. It took a little while, but I finally had things down to a reasonable program.

Tuesday and Thursday nights, I was informally "out" while formally "in." Sometimes I took Sunday nights "out" if things got too sticky around the house over the weekend. The rest of the time, George Prime cooled his heels in his closet. Locked up, of course. Can't completely trust a wife to observe a taboo, no matter how well trained she is.

There, was an irreconcilable amount of risk. George Prime had to quick-step some questions about my work at the office—there was no way to supply him with current data until the time for his regular two-month refill and pattern-accommodation at the laboratory. In the meantime, George Prime had to make do with what he had.

But as he himself pointed out he was a Super Deluxe model.

*

Marge didn't suspect a thing. In fact, George Prime seemed to be having a remarkable effect on her. I didn't notice anything at first—I was hardly ever home. But one night I found my pipe and slippers laid out for me, and the evening paper neatly folded on my chair, and it brought me up short. Marge had been extremely docile lately. We hadn't had a good fight in days. Weeks, come to think of it.

I thought it over and shrugged. Old age, I figured. She was bound to mellow sometime.

But pretty soon I began to wonder if she wasn't mellowing a little too much.

One night when I got home, she kissed me almost as though she really meant it. There wasn't an unpleasant word all through dinner, which happened to be steak with mushrooms, served in the dining room (!) by candlelight (!!) with dinner music that Marge could never bear, chiefly because I liked it.

We sat over coffee and cigarettes, and it seemed almost like old times. *Very* old times, in fact I even caught myself looking at Marge again—really *looking* at her, watching the light catch in her hair, almost admiring the sparkle in her brown eyes. Sparkle, I said, not glint.

As I mentioned before, Marge was always easy to look at. That night, she was practically ravishing.

"What are you doing to her?" I asked George Prime later, out in the workshop.

"Why, nothing," said George Prime, looking innocent. He couldn't fool me with his look, though, because it was exactly the look I use when I'm guilty and pretending to be innocent.

"There must be *something.*"

George Prime shrugged. "Any woman will warm up if you spend enough time telling her all the things she wants to hear and pay all the attention to her that she wants paid to her. That's elemental psychology. I can give you page references."

I ought to mention that George Prime had a complete set of basic texts run into his circuits, at a slightly additional charge. Never can tell when an odd bit of information will come in useful.

"Well, you must be doing quite a job," I said. *I'd* never managed to warm Marge up much.

"I try," said George Prime.

"Oh, I'm not complaining," I hastened to add, forgetting that a Prime's feelings can't be hurt and that he was only acting like me because it was in character. "I was just curious."

"Of course, George."

"I'm really delighted that you're doing so well."

"Thank you, George."

But the next night when I was with Dawn, who happens to be a gorgeous redhead who could put Marge to shame on practically any field of battle except maybe brains, I kept thinking about Marge all evening long, and wondering if things weren't getting just a little out of hand.

*

The next evening I almost tripped over George Prime coming out of a liquor store. I ducked quickly into an alley and flagged him. "*What are you doing out on the street?*"

He gave me my martyred look. "Just buying some bourbon. You were out."

"But you're not supposed to be off the premises—"

"Marge asked me to come. I couldn't tell her I was sorry, but her husband wouldn't let me, could I?"

"Well, certainly not—"

"You want me to keep her happy, don't you? You don't want her to get suspicious."

"No, but suppose somebody saw us together! If she ever got a hint—"

"I'm sorry," George Prime said contritely. "It seemed the right thing to do. *You* would have done it. At least that's what my judgment center maintained. We had quite an argument."

"Well, tell your judgment center to use a little sense," I snapped. "I don't want it to happen again."

The next night, I stayed home, even though it was Tuesday night. I was beginning to get worried. Of course, I did have complete control—I could snap George Prime off any time I wanted, or even take him in for a complete recircuiting—but it seemed a pity. He was doing such a nice job.

Marge was docile as a kitten, even more so than before. She sympathized with my hard day at the office and agreed heartily that the boss, despite all appearances, was in reality a jabbering idiot. After dinner, I suggested a movie, but Marge gave me an odd sort of look and said she thought it would be much nicer to spend the evening at home by the fire.

I'd just gotten settled with the paper when she came into the living room and sat down beside me. She was wearing some sort of filmy affair I'd never laid eyes on before, and I caught a whiff of my favorite perfume.

"Georgie?" she said.

"Uh?"

"Do you still love me?"

I set the paper down and stared at her. "How's that? Of course I still—"

"Well, sometimes you don't act much like it."

"Mm. I guess I've—uh—got an awful headache tonight." Damn that perfume!

"Oh," said Marge.

"In fact, I thought I'd turn in early and get some sleep—"

"Sleep," said Marge. There was no mistaking the disappointment in her voice. Now I knew that things were out of hand.

The next evening, I activated George Prime and caught the taxi at the corner, but I called Ruby and broke my date with her. I took in an early movie alone and was back by ten o'clock. I left the cab at the corner and walked quietly up the path toward the garage.

Then I stopped. I could see Marge and George Prime through the living room windows.

George Prime was kissing my wife the way I hadn't kissed her in eight long years. It made my hair stand on end. And Marge wasn't exactly fighting him off, either. She was coming back for more. After a little, the lights went off.

George Prime was a Super Deluxe model, all right.

*

I dashed into the workshop and punched the recall button as hard as I could, swearing under my breath. How long had this been going on? I punched the button again, viciously, and waited.

George Prime didn't come out.

It was plenty cold out in the workshop that night and I didn't sleep a wink. About dawn, out came George Prime, looking like a man with a four-day hangover.

Our conversation got down to fundamentals. George Prime kept insisting blandly that, according to my own directions, he was to pick the first logical opportunity to come out when I buzzed, and that was exactly what he'd done.

I was furious all the way to work. I'd take care of this nonsense, all right. I'd have George Prime rewired from top to bottom as soon as the laboratory could take him.

But I never phoned the laboratory. The bank was calling me when I got to the office. They wanted to know what I planned to do about that check of mine that had just bounced.

"What check?" I asked.

"The one you wrote to cash yesterday—five hundred dollars—against your regular account, Mr. Faircloth."

The last I'd looked, I'd had about three thousand dollars in that account. I told the man so rather bluntly.

"Oh, no, sir. That is, you *did* until last week. But all these checks you've been cashing have emptied the account."

He flashed the checks on the desk screen. My signature was on every one of them.

"What about my special account?" I'd learned long before that an account

Marge didn't know about was sound rear-guard strategy.

"That's been closed out for two weeks."

I hadn't written a check against that account for over a year! I glared at the ceiling and tried to think things through.

I came up with a horrible thought.

Marge had always had her heart set on a trip to Bermuda. Just to get away from it all, she'd say. A second honeymoon.

I got a list of travel agencies from the business directory and started down them. The third one I tried had a pleasant tenor voice. "No, sir, not *Mrs.* Faircloth. *You* bought two tickets. One way. Champagne flight to Bermuda."

"When?" I choked out.

"Why, today, as a matter of fact. It leaves Idlewild at eleven o'clock—"

I let him worry about my amnesia and started home fast. I didn't know what they'd given that Prime for circuits, but there was no question now that he was out of control—*way*out of control. And poor Marge, all worked up for a second honeymoon—

Then it struck me. Poor Marge? Poor sucker George! No Prime in his right circuits would behave this way without some human guidance and that meant only one thing: Marge had spotted him. It had happened before. Couple of nasty court battles I'd read about. And she'd known all about George Prime.

For how long?

*

When I got home, the house was empty. George Prime wasn't in his closet. And Marge wasn't in the house.

They were gone.

I started to call the police, but caught myself just in time. I couldn't very well complain to the cops that my wife had run off with an android.

Worse yet, I could get twenty years for having an illegal Prime wandering around.

I sat down and poured myself a stiff drink.

My own wife deserting me for a pile of bearings.

It was indecent.

Then I heard the front door open and there was Marge, her arms full of grocery bundles. "Why, darling! You're home early!"

I just blinked for a moment. Then I said, "You're still here!"

"Of course. Where did you think I'd be?"

"But I thought—I mean the ticket office—"

She set down the bundles and kissed me and looked up into my eyes, almost smiling, half reproachful. "You didn't really think I'd go running off with something out of a lab, did you?"

"Then—you knew?"

"Certainly I knew, silly. You didn't do a very good job of instructing him, either. You gave him far too much latitude. Let him have ideas of his own and all that. And next thing I knew, he was trying to get me to run off with him to Hawaii or someplace."

"Bermuda," I said.

And then Marge was in my arms, kissing me and snuggling her cheek against my chest.

"Even though he looked like you, I knew he couldn't be," she said. "He was like you, but he wasn't *you*, darling. And all I ever want is you. I just never appreciated you before...."

I held her close and tried to keep my hands from shaking. George Faircloth, Idiot, I thought. She'd never been more beautiful. "But what did you do with him?"

"I sent him back to the factory, naturally. They said they could blot him out and use him over again. But let's not talk about that any more. We've got more interesting things to discuss."

Maybe we had, but we didn't waste a lot of time talking. It was the Marge I'd once known and I was beginning to wonder how I could have been so wrong about her. In fact unless my memory was getting awfully porous, the old Marge was *never* like this—

I kissed her tenderly and ran my hands through her hair, and felt the depression with my fore-finger, and then I knew what had really happened.

That Marge always had been a sly one.

I wondered how she was liking things in Bermuda.

*

Marge probably thought she'd really put me where I belonged, but the laugh was on her, after all.

As I said, the old Marge was never like the new one. Marge Prime makes Jeree and Sybil and Dorothy and Dawn and Jane and Ruby all look pretty sad by comparison.

She cooks like a dream and she always brings me my pipe and slippers. As they say, there's nothing a man likes more than to be appreciated.

A hundred per cent appreciated, with a factory guarantee to correct any slippage, which would only be temporary, anyhow.

One of these days, we'll take that second honeymoon. But I think we'll go to Hawaii.

DELAY IN TRANSIT

By F. L. Wallace

An unprovoked, meaningless night attack is terrifying enough on your own home planet, worse on a world across the Galaxy. But the horror is the offer of help that cannot be accepted!

*"Muscles tense," said Dimanche. "Neural index 1.76, unusually high. Adrenalin squirting through his system. In effect, he's stalking you. Intent: probably assault with a deadly weapon."

"Not interested," said Cassal firmly, his subvocalization inaudible to anyone but Dimanche. "I'm not the victim type. He was standing on the walkway near the brink of the thoroughfare. I'm going back to the habitat hotel and sit tight."

"First you have to get there," Dimanche pointed out. "I mean, is it safe for a stranger to walk through the city?"

"Now that you mention it, no," answered Cassal. He looked around apprehensively. "Where is he?"

"Behind you. At the moment he's pretending interest in a merchandise display."

A native stamped by, eyes brown and incurious. Apparently he was accustomed to the sight of an Earthman standing alone, Adam's apple bobbing up and down silently. It was a Godolphian axiom that all travelers were crazy.

Cassal looked up. Not an air taxi in sight; Godolph shut down at dusk. It would be pure luck if he found a taxi before morning. Of course he *could*walk back to the hotel, but was that such a good idea?

A Godolphian city was peculiar. And, though not intended, it was peculiarly suited to certain kinds of violence. A human pedestrian was at a definite disadvantage.

"Correction," said Dimanche. "Not simple assault. He has murder in mind."

"It still doesn't appeal to me," said Cassal. Striving to look unconcerned, he strolled toward the building side of the walkway and stared into the interior of a small cafe. Warm, bright and dry. Inside, he might find safety for a time.

Damn the man who was following him! It would be easy enough to elude him in a normal city. On Godolph, nothing was normal. In an hour the streets would be brightly lighted—for native eyes. A human would consider it dim.

"Why did he choose me?" asked Cassal plaintively. "There must be something he hopes to gain."

"I'm working on it," said Dimanche. "But remember, I have limitations. At short distances I can scan nervous systems, collect and interpret physiological data. I can't read minds. The best I can do is report what a person says or subvocalizes. If you're really interested in finding out why he wants to kill you, I suggest you turn the problem over to the godawful police."

"Godolph, not godawful," corrected Cassal absently.

That was advice he couldn't follow, good as it seemed. He could give the police no evidence save through Dimanche. There were various reasons, many of them involving the law, for leaving the device called Dimanche out of it. The police would act if they found a body. His own, say, floating face-down on some quiet street. That didn't seem the proper approach, either.

"Weapons?"

"The first thing I searched him for. Nothing very dangerous. A long knife, a hard striking object. Both concealed on his person."

Cassal strangled slightly. Dimanche needed a good stiff course in semantics. A knife was still the most silent of weapons. A man could die from it. His hand strayed toward his pocket. He had a measure of protection himself.

"Report," said Dimanche. "Not necessarily final. Based, perhaps, on tenuous evidence."

"Let's have it anyway."

"His motivation is connected somehow with your being marooned here. For some reason you can't get off this planet."

That was startling information, though not strictly true. A thousand star systems were waiting for him, and a ship to take him to each one.

Of course, the one ship he wanted hadn't come in. Godolph was a transfer point for stars nearer the center of the Galaxy. When he had left Earth, he had known he would have to wait a few days here. He hadn't expected a delay of nearly three weeks. Still, it wasn't unusual. Interstellar schedules over great distances were not as reliable as they might be.

Was this man, whoever and whatever he might be, connected with that delay? According to Dimanche, the man thought he was. He was self-deluded or did he have access to information that Cassal didn't?

*

Denton Cassal, sales engineer, paused for a mental survey of himself. He was a good engineer and, because he was exceptionally well matched to his instrument, the best salesman that Neuronics, Inc., had. On the basis of these qualifications, he had been selected to make a long journey, the first part of which already lay behind him. He had to go to Tunney 21 to see a man. That man wasn't important to anyone save the company that employed him, and possibly not even to them.

The thug trailing him wouldn't be interested in Cassal himself, his mission, which was a commercial one, nor the man on Tunney. And money wasn't the objective, if Dimanche's analysis was right. What *did* the thug want?

Secrets? Cassal had none, except, in a sense, Dimanche. And that was too well kept on Earth, where the instrument was invented and made, for anyone this far away to have learned about it.

And yet the thug wanted to kill him. Wanted to? Regarded him as good as dead. It might pay him to investigate the matter further, if it didn't involve too much risk.

"Better start moving." That was Dimanche. "He's getting suspicious."

Cassal went slowly along the narrow walkway that bordered each side of that boulevard, the transport tide. It was raining again. It usually was on Godolph, which was a weather-controlled planet where the natives like rain.

He adjusted the controls of the weak force field that repelled the rain. He widened the angle of the field until water slanted through it unhindered. He narrowed it around him until it approached visibility and the drops bounced away. He swore at the miserable climate and the near amphibians who created it.

A few hundred feet away, a Godolphian girl waded out of the transport tide and climbed to the walkway. It was this sort of thing that made life dangerous for a human—Venice revised, brought up to date in a faster-than-light age.

Water. It was a perfect engineering material. Simple, cheap, infinitely flexible. With a minimum of mechanism and at break-neck speed, the ribbon of the transport tide flowed at different levels throughout the city. The Godolphian merely plunged in and was carried swiftly and noiselessly to his destination. Whereas a human—Cassal shivered. If he were found drowned, it would be considered an accident. No investigation would be made. The thug who was trailing him had certainly picked the right place.

The Godolphian girl passed. She wore a sleek brown fur, her own. Cassal was almost positive she muttered a polite "Arf?" as she sloshed by. What she meant by that, he didn't know and didn't intend to find out.

"Follow her," instructed Dimanche. "We've got to investigate our man at closer range."

*

Obediently, Cassal turned and began walking after the girl. Attractive in an anthropomorphic, seal-like way, even from behind. Not graceful out of her element, though.

The would-be assassin was still looking at merchandise as Cassal retraced his steps. A man, or at least man type. A big fellow, physically quite capable of violence, if size had anything to do with it. The face, though, was out of character. Mild, almost meek. A scientist or scholar. It didn't fit with murder.

"Nothing," said Dimanche disgustedly. "His mind froze when we got close. I could feel his shoulderblades twitching as we passed. Anticipated guilt, of course. Projecting to you the action he plans. That makes the knife definite."

Well beyond the window at which the thug watched and waited, Cassal stopped. Shakily he produced a cigarette and fumbled for a lighter.

"Excellent thinking," commended Dimanche. "He won't attempt anything on this street. Too dangerous. Turn aside at the next deserted intersection and let him follow the glow of your cigarette."

The lighter flared in his hand. "That's one way of finding out," said Cassal. "But wouldn't I be a lot safer if I just concentrated on getting back to the hotel?"

"I'm curious. Turn here."

"Go to hell," said Cassal nervously. Nevertheless, when he came to that intersection, he turned there.

It was a Godolphian equivalent of an alley, narrow and dark, oily slow-moving water gurgling at one side, high cavernous walls looming on the other.

He would have to adjust the curiosity factor of Dimanche. It was all very well to be interested in the man who trailed him, but there was also the problem of coming out of this adventure alive. Dimanche, an electronic instrument, naturally wouldn't consider that.

"Easy," warned Dimanche. "He's at the entrance to the alley, walking fast. He's surprised and pleased that you took this route."

"I'm surprised, too," remarked Cassal. "But I wouldn't say I'm pleased. Not just now."

"Careful. Even subvocalized conversation is distracting." The mechanism concealed within his body was silent for an instant and then continued: "His blood pressure is rising, breathing is faster. At a time like this, he may be ready to verbalize why he wants to murder you. This is critical."

"That's no lie," agreed Cassal bitterly. The lighter was in his hand. He clutched it grimly. It was difficult not to look back. The darkness assumed an even more sinister quality.

"Quiet," said Dimanche. "He's verbalizing about you."

"He's decided I'm a nice fellow after all. He's going to stop and ask me for a light."

"I don't think so," answered Dimanche. "He's whispering: 'Poor devil. I hate to do it. But it's really his life or mine'."

"He's more right than he knows. Why all this violence, though? Isn't there any clue?"

"None at all," admitted Dimanche. "He's very close. You'd better turn around."

*

Cassal turned, pressed the stud on the lighter. It should have made him feel more secure, but it didn't. He could see very little.

A dim shadow rushed at him. He jumped away from the water side of the alley, barely in time. He could feel the rush of air as the assailant shot by.

"Hey!" shouted Cassal.

Echoes answered; nothing else did. He had the uncomfortable feeling that no one was going to come to his assistance.

"He wasn't expecting that reaction," explained Dimanche. "That's why he missed. He's turned around and is coming back."

"I'm armed!" shouted Cassal.

"That won't stop him. He doesn't believe you."

Cassal grasped the lighter. That is, it had been a lighter a few seconds before. Now a needle-thin blade had snapped out and projected stiffly. Originally it had been designed as an emergency surgical instrument. A little imagination and a few changes had altered its function, converting it into a compact, efficient stiletto.

"Twenty feet away," advised Dimanche. "He knows you can't see him, but he can see your silhouette by the light from the main thoroughfare. What he doesn't know is that I can detect every move he makes and keep you posted below the level of his hearing."

"Stay on him," growled Cassal nervously. He flattened himself against the wall.

"To the right," whispered Dimanche. "Lunge forward. About five feet. Low."

Sickly, he did so. He didn't care to consider the possible effects of a miscalculation. In the darkness, how far was five feet? Fortunately, his estimate was correct. The rapier encountered yielding resistance, the soggy kind: flesh. The tough blade bent, but did not break. His opponent gasped and broke away.

"Attack!" howled Dimanche against the bone behind his ear. "You've got him. He can't imagine how you know where he is in the darkness. He's afraid."

Attack he did, slicing about wildly. Some of the thrusts landed; some didn't. The percentage was low, the total amount high. His opponent fell to the ground, gasped and was silent.

Cassal fumbled in his pockets and flipped on a light. The man lay near the water side of the alley. One leg was crumpled under him. He didn't move.

"Heartbeat slow," said Dimanche solemnly. "Breathing barely perceptible."

"Then he's not dead," said Cassal in relief.

Foam flecked from the still lips and ran down the chin. Blood oozed from cuts on the face.

"Respiration none, heartbeat absent," stated Dimanche.

*

Horrified, Cassal gazed at the body. Self-defense, of course, but would the police believe it? Assuming they did, they'd still have to investigate. The rapier was an illegal concealed weapon. And they would question him until they discovered Dimanche. Regrettable, but what could he do about it?

Suppose he were detained long enough to miss the ship bound for Tunney 21?

Grimly, he laid down the rapier. He might as well get to the bottom of this. Why had the man attacked? What did he want?

"I don't know," replied Dimanche irritably. "I can interpret body data—a live body. I can't work on a piece of meat."

Cassal searched the body thoroughly. Miscellaneous personal articles of no value in identifying the man. A clip with a startling amount of money in it. A small white card with something scribbled on it. A picture of a woman and a small child posed against a background which resembled no world Cassal had ever seen. That was all.

Cassal stood up in bewilderment. Dimanche to the contrary, there seemed to be no connection between this dead man and his own problem of getting to Tunney 21.

Right now, though, he had to dispose of the body. He glanced toward the boulevard. So far no one had been attracted by the violence.

He bent down to retrieve the lighter-rapier. Dimanche shouted at him. Before he could react, someone landed on him. He fell forward, vainly trying to grasp the weapon. Strong fingers felt for his throat as he was forced to the ground.

He threw the attacker off and staggered to his feet. He heard footsteps rushing away. A slight splash followed. Whoever it was, he was escaping by way of water.

Whoever it was. The man he had thought he had slain was no longer in sight.

"Interpret body data, do you?" muttered Cassal. "Liveliest dead man I've ever been strangled by."

"It's just possible there are some breeds of men who can control the basic functions of their body," said Dimanche defensively. "When I checked him, he had no heartbeat."

"Remind me not to accept your next evaluation so completely," grunted Cassal. Nevertheless, he was relieved, in a fashion. He hadn't *wanted* to kill the man. And now there was nothing he'd have to explain to the police.

He needed the cigarette he stuck between his lips. For the second time he attempted to pick up the rapier-lighter. This time he was successful. Smoke swirled into his lungs and quieted his nerves. He squeezed the weapon into the shape of a lighter and put it away.

Something, however, was missing—his wallet.

The thug had relieved him of it in the second round of the scuffle. Persistent fellow. Damned persistent.

It really didn't matter. He fingered the clip he had taken from the supposedly dead body. He had intended to turn it over to the police. Now he might as well keep it to reimburse him for his loss. It contained more money than his wallet had.

Except for the identification tab he always carried in his wallet, it was more than a fair exchange. The identification, a rectangular piece of plastic, was useful in establishing credit, but with the money he now had, he wouldn't need credit. If he did, he could always send for another tab.

A white card fluttered from the clip. He caught it as it fell. Curiously he examined it. Blank except for one crudely printed word, STAB. His unknown assailant certainly had tried.

*

The old man stared at the door, an obsolete visual projector wobbling precariously on his head. He closed his eyes and the lettering on the door disappeared. Cassal was too far away to see what it had been. The technician opened his eyes and concentrated. Slowly a new sign formed on the door.

TRAVELERS AID BUREAU

Murra Foray, First Counselor

It was a drab sign, but, then, it was a dismal, backward planet. The old technician passed on to the next door and closed his eyes again.

With a sinking feeling, Cassal walked toward the entrance. He needed help and he had to find it in this dingy rathole.

Inside, though, it wasn't dingy and it wasn't a rathole. More like a maze, an approved scientific one. Efficient, though not comfortable. Travelers Aid was busier than he thought it would be. Eventually he managed to squeeze into one of the many small counseling rooms.

A woman appeared on the screen, crisp and cool. "Please answer everything the machine asks. When the tape is complete, I'll be available for consultation."

Cassal wasn't sure he was going to like her. "Is this necessary?" he asked. "It's merely a matter of information."

"We have certain regulations we abide by." The woman smiled frostily. "I can't give you any information until you comply with them."

"Sometimes regulations are silly," said Cassal firmly. "Let me speak to the first counselor."

"You are speaking to her," she said. Her face disappeared from the screen.

Cassal sighed. So far he hadn't made a good impression.

Travelers Aid Bureau, in addition to regulations, was abundantly supplied with official curiosity. When the machine finished with him, Cassal had the feeling he could be recreated from the record it had of him. His individuality had been capsuled into a series of questions and answers. One thing he drew the line at—why he wanted to go to Tunney 21 was his own business.

The first counselor reappeared. Age, indeterminate. Not, he supposed, that anyone would be curious about it. Slightly taller than average, rather on the slender side. Face was broad at the brow, narrow at the chin and her eyes were enigmatic. A dangerous woman.

*

She glanced down at the data. "Denton Cassal, native of Earth. Destination, Tunney 21." She looked up at him. "Occupation, sales engineer. Isn't that an odd combination?" Her smile was quite superior.

"Not at all. Scientific training as an engineer. Special knowledge of customer relations."

"Special knowledge of a thousand races? How convenient." Her eyebrows arched.

"I think so," he agreed blandly. "Anything else you'd like to know?"

"Sorry. I didn't mean to offend you."

He could believe that or not as he wished. He didn't.

"You refused to answer why you were going to Tunney 21. Perhaps I can guess. They're the best scientists in the Galaxy. You wish to study under them."

Close—but wrong on two counts. They were good scientists, though not necessarily the best. For instance, it was doubtful that they could build Dimanche, even if they had ever thought of it, which was even less likely.

There was, however, one relatively obscure research worker on Tunney 21 that Neuronics wanted on their staff. If the fragments of his studies that had reached Earth across the vast distance meant anything, he could help Neuronics perfect instantaneous radio. The company that could build a radio to span the reaches of the Galaxy with no time lag could set its own price, which could be control of all communications, transport, trade—a galactic monopoly. Cassal's share would be a cut of all that.

His part was simple, on the surface. He was to persuade that researcher to come to Earth, *if he could*. Literally, he had to guess the Tunnesian's price before the Tunnesian himself knew it. In addition, the reputation of Tunnesian scientists being exceeded only by their arrogance, Cassal had to convince him that he wouldn't be working for ignorant Earth savages. The existence of such an instrument as Dimanche was a key factor.

Her voice broke through his thoughts. "Now, then, what's your problem?"

"I was told on Earth I might have to wait a few days on Godolph. I've been here three weeks. I want information on the ship bound for Tunney 21."

"Just a moment." She glanced at something below the angle of the screen. She looked up and her eyes were grave. "*Rickrock* C arrived yesterday. Departed for Tunney early this morning."

"Departed?" He got up and sat down again, swallowing hard. "When will the next ship arrive?"

"Do you know how many stars there are in the Galaxy?" she asked.

He didn't answer.

*

"That's right," she said. "Billions. Tunney, according to the notation, is near the center of the Galaxy, inside the third ring. You've covered about a third of the distance to it. Local traffic, anything within a thousand light-years, is relatively easy to manage. At longer distances, you take a chance. You've had yours and missed it. Frankly, Cassal, I don't know when another ship bound for Tunney will show up on or near Godolph. Within the next five years—maybe."

*

He blanched. "How long would it take to get there using local transportation, star-hopping?"

"Take my advice: don't try it. Five years, if you're lucky."

"I don't need that kind of luck."

"I suppose not." She hesitated. "You're determined to go on?" At the emphatic nod, she sighed. "If that's your decision, we'll try to help you. To start things moving, we'll need a print of your identification tab."

"There's something funny about her," Dimanche decided. It was the usual speaking voice of the instrument, no louder than the noise the blood made in coursing through arteries and veins. Cassal could hear it plainly, because it was virtually inside his ear.

Cassal ignored his private voice. “Identification tab? I don’t have it with me. In fact, I may have lost it.”

She smiled in instant disbelief. “We’re not trying to pry into any part of your past you may wish concealed. However, it’s much easier for us to help you if you have your identification. Now if you can’t *remember* your real name and where you put your identification—” She arose and left the screen. “Just a moment.”

He glared uneasily at the spot where the first counselor wasn’t. His *real* name!

“Relax,” Dimanche suggested. “She didn’t mean it as a personal insult.”

Presently she returned.

“I have news for you, whoever you are.”

“Cassal,” he said firmly. “Denton Cassal, sales engineer, Earth. If you don’t believe it, send back to—” He stopped. It had taken him four months to get to Godolph, non-stop, plus a six-month wait on Earth for a ship to show up that was bound in the right direction. Over distances such as these, it just wasn’t practical to send back to Earth for anything.

“I see you understand.” She glanced at the card in her hand. “The spaceport records indicate that when *Rickrock* C took off this morning, there was a Denton Cassal on board, bound for Tunney 21.”

“It wasn’t I,” he said dazedly. He knew who it was, though. The man who had tried to kill him last night. The reason for the attack now became clear. The thug had wanted his identification tab. Worse, he had gotten it.

“No doubt it wasn’t,” she said wearily. “Outsiders don’t seem to understand what galactic travel entails.”

Outsiders? Evidently what she called those who lived beyond the second transfer ring. Were those who lived at the edge of the Galaxy, beyond the first ring, called Rimmers? Probably.

*

She was still speaking: “Ten years to cross the Galaxy, without stopping. At present, no ship is capable of that. Real scheduling is impossible. Populations shift and have to be supplied. A ship is taken off a run for repairs and is never put back on. It’s more urgently needed elsewhere. The man who depended on it is left waiting; years pass before he learns it’s never coming.

"If we had instantaneous radio, that would help. Confusion wouldn't vanish overnight, but it would diminish. We wouldn't have to depend on ships for all the news. Reservations could be made ahead of time, credit established, lost identification replaced—"

"I've traveled before," he interrupted stiffly. "I've never had any trouble."

She seemed to be exaggerating the difficulties. True, the center was more congested. Taking each star as the starting point for a limited number of ships and using statistical probability as a guide—why, no man would arrive at his predetermined destination.

But that wasn't the way it worked. Manifestly, you couldn't compare galactic transportation to the erratic paths of air molecules in a giant room. Or could you?

For the average man, anyone who didn't have his own inter-stellar ship, was the comparison too apt? It might be.

"You've traveled outside, where there are still free planets waiting to be settled. Where a man is welcome, if he's able to work." She paused. "The center is different. Populations are excessive. Inside the third ring, no man is allowed off a ship without an identification tab. They don't encourage immigration."

In effect, that meant no ship bound for the center would take a passenger without identification. No ship owner would run the risk of having a permanent guest on board, someone who couldn't be rid of when his money was gone.

Cassal held his head in his hands. Tunney 21 was inside the third ring.

"Next time," she said, "don't let anyone take your identification."

"I won't," he promised grimly.

*

The woman looked directly at him. Her eyes were bright. He revised his estimate of her age drastically downward. She couldn't be as old as he. Nothing outward had happened, but she no longer seemed dowdy. Not that he was interested. Still, it might pay him to be friendly to the first counselor.

"We're a philanthropic agency," said Murra Foray. "Your case is special, though—"

"I understand," he said gruffly. "You accept contributions."

She nodded. "If the donor is able to give. We don't ask so much that you'll have to compromise your standard of living." But she named a sum that would force him to do just that if getting to Tunney 21 took any appreciable time.

He stared at her unhappily. "I suppose it's worth it. I can always work, if I have to."

"As a salesman?" she asked. "I'm afraid you'll find it difficult to do business with Godolphians."

Irony wasn't called for at a time like this, he thought reproachfully.

"Not just another salesman," he answered definitely. "I have special knowledge of customer reactions. I can tell exactly—"

He stopped abruptly. Was she baiting him? For what reason? The instrument he called Dimanche was not known to the Galaxy at large. From the business angle, it would be poor policy to hand out that information at random. Aside from that, he needed every advantage he could get. Dimanche was his special advantage.

"Anyway," he finished lamely, "I'm a first class engineer. I can always find something in that line."

"A scientist, maybe," murmured Murra Foray. "But in this part of the Milky Way, an engineer is regarded as merely a technician who hasn't yet gained practical experience." She shook her head. "You'll do better as a salesman."

He got up, glowering. "If that's all—"

"It is. We'll keep you informed. Drop your contribution in the slot provided for that purpose as you leave."

A door, which he hadn't noticed in entering the counselling cubicle, swung open. The agency was efficient.

"Remember," the counselor called out as he left, "identification is hard to work with. Don't accept a crude forgery."

He didn't answer, but it was an idea worth considering. The agency was also eminently practical.

The exit path guided him firmly to an inconspicuous and yet inescapable contribution station. He began to doubt the philanthropic aspect of the bureau.

*

"I've got it," said Dimanche as Cassal gloomily counted out the sum the first counselor had named.

"Got what?" asked Cassal. He rolled the currency into a neat bundle, attached his name, and dropped it into the chute.

"The woman, Murra Foray, the first counselor. She's a Huntner."

"What's a Huntner?"

"A sub-race of men on the other side of the Galaxy. She was vocalizing about her home planet when I managed to locate her."

"Any other information?"

"None. Electronic guards were sliding into place as soon as I reached her. I got out as fast as I could."

"I see." The significance of that, if any, escaped him. Nevertheless, it sounded depressing.

"What I want to know is," said Dimanche, "why such precautions as electronic guards? What does Travelers Aid have that's so secret?"

Cassal grunted and didn't answer. Dimanche could be annoyingly inquisitive at times.

Cassal had entered one side of a block-square building. He came out on the other side. The agency was larger than he had thought. The old man was staring at a door as Cassal came out. He had apparently changed every sign in the building. His work finished, the technician was removing the visual projector from his head as Cassal came up to him. He turned and peered.

"You stuck here, too?" he asked in the uneven voice of the aged.

"Stuck?" repeated Cassal. "I suppose you can call it that. I'm waiting for my ship." He frowned. He was the one who wanted to ask questions. "Why all the redecoration? I thought Travelers Aid was an old agency. Why did you change so many signs? I could understand it if the agency were new."

The old man chuckled. "Re-organization. The previous first counselor resigned suddenly, in the middle of the night, they say. The new one didn't like the name of the agency, so she ordered it changed."

She would do just that, thought Cassal. "What about this Murra Foray?"

The old man winked mysteriously. He opened his mouth and then seemed overcome with senile fright. Hurriedly he shuffled away.

Cassal gazed after him, baffled. The old man was afraid for his job, afraid of the first counselor. Why he should be, Cassal didn't know. He shrugged and went on. The agency was now in motion in his behalf, but he didn't intend to depend on that alone.

*

"The girl ahead of you is making unnecessary wriggling motions as she walks," observed Dimanche. "Several men are looking on with approval. I don't understand."

Cassal glanced up. They walked that way back in good old L.A. A pang of homesickness swept through him.

"Shut up," he growled plaintively. "Attend to the business at hand."

"Business? Very well," said Dimanche. "Watch out for the transport tide."

Cassal swerved back from the edge of the water. Murra Foray had been right. Godolphians didn't want or need his skills, at least not on terms that were acceptable to him. The natives didn't have to exert themselves. They lived off the income provided by travelers, with which the planet was abundantly supplied by ship after ship.

Still, that didn't alter his need for money. He walked the streets at random while Dimanche probed.

"Ah!"

"What is it?"

"That man. He crinkles something in his hands. Not enough, he is subvocalizing."

"I know how he feels," commented Cassal.

"Now his throat tightens. He bunches his muscles. 'I know where I can get more,' he tells himself. He is going there."

"A sensible man," declared Cassal. "Follow him."

Boldly the man headed toward a section of the city which Cassal had not previously entered. He believed opportunity lay there. Not for everyone. The shrewd, observant, and the courageous could succeed if—The word that the quarry used was a slang term, unfamiliar to either Cassal or Dimanche. It didn't matter as long as it led to money.

Cassal stretched his stride and managed to keep the man in sight. He skipped nimbly over the narrow walkways that curved through the great buildings. The section grew dingier as they proceeded. Not slums; not the show-place city frequented by travelers, either.

Abruptly the man turned into a building. He was out of sight when Cassal reached the structure.

He stood at the entrance and stared in disappointment. "Opportunities Inc.," Dimanche quoted softly in his ear. "Science, thrills, chance. What does that mean?"

"It means that we followed a gravity ghost!"

"What's a gravity ghost?"

"An unexplained phenomena," said Cassal nastily. "It affects the instruments of spaceships, giving the illusion of a massive dark body that isn't there."

"But you're not a pilot. I don't understand."

"You're not a very good pilot yourself. We followed the man to a gambling joint."

"Gambling," mused Dimanche. "Well, isn't it an opportunity of a sort? Someone inside is thinking of the money he's winning."

"The owner, no doubt."

Dimanche was silent, investigating. "It is the owner," he confirmed finally. "Why not go in, anyway. It's raining. And they serve drinks." Left unstated was the admission that Dimanche was curious, as usual.

*

Cassal went in and ordered a drink. It was a variable place, depending on the spectator—bright, cheerful, and harmonious if he were winning, garish and depressingly vulgar if he were not. At the moment Cassal belonged to neither group. He reserved judgment.

An assortment of gaming devices were in operation. One in particular seemed interesting. It involved the counting of electrons passing through an aperture, based on probability.

"Not that," whispered Dimanche. "It's rigged."

"But it's not necessary," Cassal murmured. "Pure chance alone is good enough."

"They don't take chances, pure or adulterated. Look around. How many Godolphians do you see?"

Cassal looked. Natives were not even there as servants. Strictly a clip joint, working travelers.

Unconsciously, he nodded. "That does it. It's not the kind of opportunity I had in mind."

"Don't be hasty," objected Dimanche. "Certain devices I can't control. There may be others in which my knowledge will help you. Stroll around and sample some games."

Cassal equipped himself with a supply of coins and sauntered through the establishment, disbursing them so as to give himself the widest possible acquaintance with the layout.

"That one," instructed Dimanche.

It received a coin. In return, it rewarded him with a large shower of change. The money spilled to the floor with a satisfying clatter. An audience gathered rapidly, ostensibly to help him pick up the coins.

"There was a circuit in it," explained Dimanche. "I gave it a shot of electrons and it paid out."

"Let's try it again," suggested Cassal.

"Let's not," Dimanche said regretfully. "Look at the man on your right."

Cassal did so. He jammed the money back in his pocket and stood up. Hastily, he began thrusting the money back into the machine. A large and very unconcerned man watched him.

"You get the idea," said Dimanche. "It paid off two months ago. It wasn't scheduled for another this year." Dimanche scrutinized the man in a multitude of ways while Cassal continued play. "He's satisfied," was the report at last. "He doesn't detect any sign of crookedness."

"*Crookedness?*"

"On your part, that is. In the ethics of a gambling house, what's done to insure profit is merely prudence."

*

They moved on to other games, though Cassal lost his briefly acquired enthusiasm. The possibility of winning seemed to grow more remote.

"Hold it," said Dimanche. "Let's look into this."

"Let me give *you* some advice," said Cassal. "This is one thing we can't win at. Every race in the Galaxy has a game like this. Pieces of plastic with values printed on them are distributed. The trick is to get certain arbitrarily selected sets of values in the plastics dealt to you. It seems simple, but against a skilled player a beginner can't win."

"Every race in the Galaxy," mused Dimanche. "What do men call it?"

"Cards," said Cassal, "though there are many varieties within that general classification." He launched into a detailed exposition of the subject. If it were something he was familiar with, all right, but a foreign deck and strange rules—

Nevertheless, Dimanche was interested. They stayed and observed.

The dealer was clumsy. His great hands enfolded the cards. Not a Godolphian nor quite human, he was an odd type, difficult to place.

Physically burly, he wore a garment chiefly remarkable for its ill-fitting appearance. A hard round hat jammed closely over his skull completed the outfit. He was dressed in a manner that, somewhere in the Universe, was evidently considered the height of fashion.

"It doesn't seem bad," commented Cassal. "There might be a chance."

"Look around," said Dimanche. "Everyone thinks that. It's the classic struggle, person against person and everyone against the house. Naturally, the house doesn't lose."

"Then why are we wasting our time?"

"Because I've got an idea," said Dimanche. "Sit down and take a hand."

"Make up your mind. You said the house doesn't lose."

"The house hasn't played against us. Sit down. You get eight cards, with the option of two more. I'll tell you what to do."

Cassal waited until a disconsolate player relinquished his seat and stalked moodily away. He played a few hands and bet small sums in accordance with Dimanche's instructions. He held his own and won insignificant amounts while learning.

It was simple. Nine orders, or suits, of twenty-seven cards each. Each suit would build a different equation. The lowest hand was a quadratic. A cubic would beat it. All he had to do was remember his math, guess at what he didn't remember, and draw the right cards.

"What's the highest possible hand?" asked Dimanche. There was a note of abstraction in his voice, as if he were paying more attention to something else.

Cassal peeked at the cards that were face-down on the table. He shoved some money into the betting square in front of him and didn't answer.

"You had it last time," said Dimanche. "A three dimensional encephalocurve. A time modulated brainwave. If you had bet right, you could have owned the house by now."

"I did? Why didn't you tell me?"

"Because you had it three successive times. The probabilities against that are astronomical. I've got to find out what's happening before you start betting recklessly."

"It's not the dealer," declared Cassal. "Look at those hands."

They were huge hands, more suitable, seemingly, for crushing the life from some alien beast than the delicate manipulation of cards. Cassal continued to play, betting brilliantly by the only standard that mattered: he won.

*

One player dropped out and was replaced by a recruit from the surrounding crowd. Cassal ordered a drink. The waiter was placing it in his hand when Dimanche made a discovery.

"I've got it!"

A shout from Dimanche was roughly equivalent to a noiseless kick in the head. Cassal dropped the drink. The player next to him scowled but said nothing. The dealer blinked and went on dealing.

"What have you got?" asked Cassal, wiping up the mess and trying to keep track of the cards.

"How he fixes the deck," explained Dimanche in a lower and less painful tone. "Clever."

Muttering, Cassal shoved a bet in front of him.

"Look at that hat," said Dimanche.

"Ridiculous, isn't it? But I see no reason to gloat because I have better taste."

"That's not what I meant. It's pulled down low over his knobby ears and touches his jacket. His jacket rubs against his trousers, which in turn come in contact with the stool on which he sits."

"True," agreed Cassal, increasing his wager. "But except for his physique, I don't see anything unusual."

"It's a circuit, a visual projector broken down into components. The hat is a command circuit which makes contact, via his clothing, with the broadcasting unit built into the chair. The existence of a visual projector is completely concealed."

Cassal bit his lip and squinted at his cards. "Interesting. What does it have to do with anything?"

"The deck," exclaimed Dimanche excitedly. "The backs are regular, printed with an intricate design. The front is a special plastic, susceptible to the influence of the visual projector. He doesn't need manual dexterity. He can make any value appear on any card he wants. It will stay there until he changes it."

Cassal picked up the cards. "I've got a Loreenaroo equation. Can he change that to anything else?"

"He can, but he doesn't work that way. He decides before he deals who's going to get what. He concentrates on each card as he deals it. He can change a hand after a player gets it, but it wouldn't look good."

"It wouldn't." Cassal wistfully watched the dealer rake in his wager. His winnings were gone, plus. The newcomer to the game won.

He started to get up. "Sit down," whispered Dimanche. "We're just beginning. Now that we know what he does and how he does it, we're going to take him."

*

The next hand started in the familiar pattern, two cards of fairly good possibilities, a bet, and then another card. Cassal watched the dealer closely. His clumsiness was only superficial. At no time were the faces of the cards visible. The real skill was unobservable, of course—the swift bookkeeping that went on in his mind. A duplication in the hands of the players, for instance, would be ruinous.

Cassal received the last card. "Bet high," said Dimanche. With trepidation, Cassal shoved the money into the betting area.

The dealer glanced at his hand and started to sit down. Abruptly he stood up again. He scratched his cheek and stared puzzledly at the players around him. Gently he lowered himself onto the stool. The contact was even briefer. He stood up in indecision. An impatient murmur arose. He dealt himself a card, looked at it, and paid off all the way around. The players buzzed with curiosity.

"What happened?" asked Cassal as the next hand started.

"I induced a short in the circuit," said Dimanche. "He couldn't sit down to change the last card he got. He took a chance, as he had to, and dealt himself a card, anyway."

"But he paid off without asking to see what we had."

"It was the only thing he could do," explained Dimanche. "He had duplicate cards."

The dealer was scowling. He didn't seem quite so much at ease. The cards were dealt and the betting proceeded almost as usual. True, the dealer was nervous. He couldn't sit down and stay down. He was sweating. Again he paid off. Cassal won heavily and he was not the only one.

The crowd around them grew almost in a rush. There is an indefinable sense that tells one gambler when another is winning.

This time the dealer stood up. His leg contacted the stool occasionally. He jerked it away each time he dealt to himself. At the last card he hesitated. It was amazing how much he could sweat. He lifted a corner of the cards. Without indicating what he had drawn, determinedly and deliberately he sat down. The chair broke. The dealer grinned weakly as a waiter brought him another stool.

"They still think it may be a defective circuit," whispered Dimanche.

The dealer sat down and sprang up from the new chair in one motion. He gazed bitterly at the players and paid them.

"He had a blank hand," explained Dimanche. "He made contact with the broadcasting circuit long enough to erase, but not long enough to put anything in it's place."

The dealer adjusted his coat. "I have a nervous disability," he declared thickly. "If you'll pardon me for a few minutes while I take a treatment—"

"Probably going to consult with the manager," observed Cassal.

"He is the manager. He's talking with the owner."

"Keep track of him."

*

A blonde, pretty, perhaps even Earth-type human, smiled and wriggled closer to Cassal. He smiled back.

"Don't fall for it," warned Dimanche. "She's an undercover agent for the house."

Cassal looked her over carefully. "Not much under cover."

"But if she should discover—"

"Don't be stupid. She'll never guess you exist. There's a small lump behind my ear and a small round tube cleverly concealed elsewhere."

"All right," sighed Dimanche resignedly. "I suppose people will always be a mystery to me."

The dealer reappeared, followed by an unobtrusive man who carried a new stool. The dealer looked subtly different, though he was the same person. It took a close inspection to determine what the difference was. His clothing was new, unrumpled, unmarked by perspiration. During his brief absence, he had been furnished with new visual projector equipment, and it had been thoroughly checked out. The house intended to locate the source of the disturbance.

Mentally, Cassal counted his assets. He was solvent again, but in other ways his position was not so good.

"Maybe," he suggested, "we should leave. With no further interference from us, they might believe defective equipment is the cause of their losses."

"Maybe," replied Dimanche, "you think the crowd around us is composed solely of patrons?"

"I see," said Cassal soberly.

He stretched his legs. The crowd pressed closer, uncommonly aggressive and ill-tempered for mere spectators. He decided against leaving.

"Let's resume play." The dealer-manager smiled blandly at each player. He didn't suspect any one person—yet.

"He might be using an honest deck," said Cassal hopefully.

"They don't have that kind," answered Dimanche. He added absently: "During his conference with the owner, he was given authority to handle the situation in any way he sees fit."

Bad, but not too bad. At least Cassal was opposing someone who had authority to let him keep his winnings, *if he could be convinced.*

The dealer deliberately sat down on the stool. Testing. He could endure the charge that trickled through him. The bland smile spread into a triumphant one.

"While he was gone, he took a sedative," analyzed Dimanche. "He also had the strength of the broadcasting circuit reduced. He thinks that will do it."

"Sedatives wear off," said Cassal. "By the time he knows it's me, see that it has worn off. Mess him up."

*

The game went on. The situation was too much for the others. They played poorly and bet atrociously, on purpose. One by one they lost and dropped out. They wanted badly to win, but they wanted to live even more.

The joint was jumping, and so was the dealer again. Sweat rolled down his face and there were tears in his eyes. So much liquid began to erode his fixed smile. He kept replenishing it from some inner source of determination.

Cassal looked up. The crowd had drawn back, or had been forced back by hirelings who mingled with them. He was alone with the dealer at the table. Money was piled high around him. It was more than he needed, more than he wanted.

"I suggest one last hand," said the dealer-manager, grimacing. It sounded a little stronger than a suggestion.

Cassal nodded.

"For a substantial sum," said the dealer, naming it.

Miraculously, it was an amount that equaled everything Cassal had. Again Cassal nodded.

"Pressure," muttered Cassal to Dimanche. "The sedative has worn off. He's back at the level at which he started. Fry him if you have to."

The cards came out slowly. The dealer was jittering as he dealt. Soft music was lacking, but not the motions that normally accompanied it. Cassal couldn't believe that cards could be so bad. Somehow the dealer was rising to the occasion. Rising and sitting.

"There's a nerve in your body," Cassal began conversationally, "which, if it were overloaded, would cause you to drop dead."

The dealer didn't examine his cards. He didn't have to. "In that event, someone would be arrested for murder," he said. "You."

That was the wrong tack; the humanoid had too much courage. Cassal passed his hand over his eyes. "You can't do this to men, but, strictly speaking, the dealer's not human. Try suggestion on him. Make him change the cards. Play him like a piano. Pizzicato on the nerve strings."

Dimanche didn't answer; presumably he was busy scrambling the circuits.

The dealer stretched out his hand. It never reached the cards. Danger: Dimanche at work. The smile dropped from his face. What remained was pure anguish. He was too dry for tears. Smoke curled up faintly from his jacket.

"Hot, isn't it?" asked Cassal. "It might be cooler if you took off your cap."

The cap tinkled to the floor. The mechanism in it was destroyed. What the cards were, they were. Now they couldn't be changed.

"That's better," said Cassal.

*

He glanced at his hand. In the interim, it had changed slightly. Dimanche had got there.

The dealer examined his cards one by one. His face changed color. He sat utterly still on a cool stool.

"You win," he said hopelessly.

"Let's see what you have."

The dealer-manager roused himself. "You won. That's good enough for you, isn't it?"

Cassal shrugged. "You have Bank of the Galaxy service here. I'll deposit my money with them *before* you pick up your cards."

The dealer nodded unhappily and summoned an assistant. The crowd, which had anticipated violence, slowly began to drift away.

"What did you do?" asked Cassal silently.

"Men have no shame," sighed Dimanche. "Some humanoids do. The dealer was one who did. I forced him to project onto his cards something that wasn't a suit at all."

"Embarrassing if that got out," agreed Cassal. "What did you project?"

Dimanche told him. Cassal blushed, which was unusual for a man.

The dealer-manager returned and the transaction was completed. His money was safe in the Bank of the Galaxy.

"Hereafter, you're not welcome," said the dealer morosely. "Don't come back."

Cassal picked up the cards without looking at them. "And no accidents after I leave," he said, extending the cards face-down. The manager took them and trembled.

"He's an honorable humanoid, in his own way," whispered Dimanche. "I think you're safe."

It was time to leave. "One question," Cassal called back. "What do you call this game?"

Automatically the dealer started to answer. "Why, everyone knows...." He sat down, his mouth open.

It was more than time to leave.

Outside, he hailed an air taxi. No point in tempting the management.

"Look," said Dimanche as the cab rose from the surface of the transport tide.

A technician with a visual projector was at work on the sign in front of the gaming house. Huge words took shape: WARNING—NO TELEPATHS ALLOWED.

There were no such things anywhere, but now there were rumors of them.

*

Arriving at the habitat wing of the hotel, Cassal went directly to his room. He awaited the delivery of the equipment he had ordered and checked through it thoroughly. Satisfied that everything was there, he estimated the size of the room. Too small for his purpose.

He picked up the intercom and dialed Services. "Put a Life Stage Cordon around my suite," he said briskly.

The face opposite his went blank. "But you're an Earthman. I thought—"

"I know more about my own requirements than your Life Stage Bureau. Earthmen do have life stages. You know the penalty if you refuse that service."

There were some races who went without sleep for five months and then had to make up for it. Others grew vestigial wings for brief periods and had to fly with them or die; reduced gravity would suffice for that. Still others—

But the one common feature was always a critical time in which certain conditions were necessary. Insofar as there was a universal law, from one end of the Galaxy to the other, this was it: The habitat hotel had to furnish appropriate conditions for the maintenance of any life-form that requested it.

The Godolphian disappeared from the screen. When he came back, he seemed disturbed.

"You spoke of a suite. I find that you're listed as occupying one room."

"I am. It's too small. Convert the rooms around me into a suite."

"That's very expensive."

"I'm aware of that. Check the Bank of the Galaxy for my credit rating."

He watched the process take place. Service would be amazingly good from now on.

"Your suite will be converted in about two hours. The Life Stage Cordon will begin as soon after that as you want. If you tell me how long you'll need it, I can make arrangements now."

"About ten hours is all I'll need." Cassal rubbed his jaw reflectively. "One more thing. Put a perpetual service at the spaceport. If a ship comes in bound for Tunney 21 or the vicinity of it, get accommodations on it for me. And hold it until I get ready, no matter what it costs."

He flipped off the intercom and promptly went to sleep. Hours later, he was awakened by a faint hum. The Life Stage Cordon had just been snapped safely around his newly created suite.

"Now what?" asked Dimanche.

"I need an identification tab."

"You do. And forgeries are expensive and generally crude, as that Huntner woman, Murra Foray, observed."

*

Cassal glanced at the equipment. “Expensive, yes. Not crude when we do it.”

“*We* forge it?” Dimanche was incredulous.

“That’s what I said. Consider it this way. I’ve seen my tab a countless number of times. If I tried to draw it as I remember it, it would be inept and wouldn’t pass. Nevertheless, that memory is in my mind, recorded in neuronic chains, exact and accurate.” He paused significantly. “You have access to that memory.”

“At least partially. But what good does that do?”

“Visual projector and plastic which will take the imprint. I think hard about the identification as I remember it. You record and feed it back to me while I concentrate on projecting it on the plastic. After we get it down, we change the chemical composition of the plastic. It will then pass everything except destructive analysis, and they don’t often do that.”

Dimanche was silent. “Ingenious,” was its comment. “Part of that we can manage, the official engraving, even the electron stamp. That, however, is gross detail. The print of the brain area is beyond our capacity. We can put down what you remember, and you remember what you saw. You didn’t see fine enough, though. The general area will be recognizable, but not the fine structure, nor the charges stored there nor their interrelationship.”

“But we’ve got to do it,” Cassal insisted, pacing about nervously.

“With more equipment to probe—”

“Not a chance. I got one Life Stage Cordon on a bluff. If I ask for another, they’ll look it up and refuse.”

“All right,” said Dimanche, humming. The mechanical attempt at music made Cassal’s head ache. “I’ve got an idea. Think about the identification tab.”

Cassal thought.

“Enough,” said Dimanche. “Now poke yourself.”

“Where?”

“Everywhere,” replied Dimanche irritably. “One place at a time.”

Cassal did so, though it soon became monotonous.

Dimanche stopped him. “Just above your right knee.”

“What above my right knee?”

“The principal access to that part of your brain we’re concerned with,” said

Dimanche. "We can't photomeasure your brain the way it was originally done, but we can investigate it remotely. The results will be simplified, naturally. Something like a scale model as compared to the original. A more apt comparison might be that of a relief map to an actual locality."

"Investigate it remotely?" muttered Cassal. A horrible suspicion touched his consciousness. He jerked away from that touch. "What does that mean?"

"What it sounds like. Stimulus and response. From that I can construct an accurate chart of the proper portion of your brain. Our probing instruments will be crude out of necessity, but effective."

"I've already visualized those probing instruments," said Cassal worriedly. "Maybe we'd better work first on the official engraving and the electron stamp, while I'm still fresh. I have a feeling...."

"Excellent suggestion," said Dimanche.

Cassal gathered the articles slowly. His lighter would burn and it would also cut. He needed a heavy object to pound with. A violent irritant for the nerve endings. Something to freeze his flesh....

Dimanche interrupted: "There are also a few glands we've got to pick up. See if there's a stimi in the room."

"Stimi? Oh yes, a stimulator. Never use the damned things." But he was going to. The next few hours weren't going to be pleasant. Nor dull, either.

Life could be difficult on Godolph.

*

As soon as the Life Stage Cordon came down, Cassal called for a doctor. The native looked at him professionally.

"Is this a part of the Earth life process?" he asked incredulously. Gingerly, he touched the swollen and lacerated leg.

Cassal nodded wearily. "A matter of life and death," he croaked.

"If it is, then it is," said the doctor, shaking his head. "I, for one, am glad to be a Godolphian."

"To each his own habitat," Cassal quoted the motto of the hotel.

Godolphians were clumsy, good-natured caricatures of seals. There was nothing wrong with their medicine, however. In a matter of minutes he was feeling better. By the time the doctor left, the swelling had subsided and the open wounds were fast closing.

Eagerly, he examined the identification tab. As far as he could tell, it was perfect. What the scanner would reveal was, of course, another matter. He had to check that as best he could without exposing himself.

Services came up to the suite right after he laid the intercom down. A machine was placed over his head and the identification slipped into the slot. The code on the tab was noted; the machine hunted and found the corresponding brain area. Structure was mapped, impulses recorded, scrambled, converted into a ray of light which danced over a film.

The identification tab was similarly recorded. There was now a means of comparison.

Fingerprints could be duplicated—that is, if the race in question had fingers. Every intelligence, however much it differed from its neighbors, had a brain, and tampering with that brain was easily detected. Each identification tab carried a psychometric number which corresponded to the total personality. Alteration of any part of the brain could only subtract from personality index.

The technician removed the identification and gave it to Cassal. "Where shall I send the strips?"

"You don't," said Cassal. "I have a private message to go with them."

"But that will invalidate the process."

"I know. This isn't a formal contract."

Removing the two strips and handing them to Cassal, the technician wheeled the machine away. After due thought, Cassal composed the message.

Travelers Aid Bureau Murra Foray, first counselor:

If you were considering another identification tab for me, don't. As you can see, I've located the missing item.

He attached the message to the strips and dropped them into the communication chute.

*

He was wiping his whiskers away when the answer came. Hastily he finished and wrapped himself, noting but not approving the amused glint in her eyes as she watched. His morals were his own, wherever he went.

"Denton Cassal," she said. "A wonderful job. The two strips were in register within one per cent. The best previous forgery I've seen was six per cent, and that was merely a lucky accident. It couldn't be duplicated. Let me congratulate you."

His dignity was professional. "I wish you weren't so fond of that word 'forgery.' I told you I mislaid the tab. As soon as I found it, I sent you proof. I want to get to Tunney 21. I'm willing to do anything I can to speed up the process."

Her laughter tinkled. "You don't *have* to tell me how you did it or where you got it. I'm inclined to think you made it. You understand that I'm not concerned with legality as such. From time to time the agency has to furnish missing documents. If there's a better way than we have, I'd like to know it."

He sighed and shook his head. For some reason, his heart was beating fast. He wanted to say more, but there was nothing to say.

When he failed to respond, she leaned toward him. "Perhaps you'll discuss this with me. At greater length."

"At the agency?"

She looked at him in surprise. "Have you been sleeping? The agency is closed for the day. The first counselor can't work all the time, you know."

Sleeping? He grimaced at the remembrance of the self-administered beating. No, he hadn't been sleeping. He brushed the thought aside and boldly named a place. Dinner was acceptable.

Dimanche waited until the screen was dark. The words were carefully chosen.

"Did you notice," he asked, "that there was no apparent change in clothing and makeup, yet she seemed younger, more attractive?"

"I didn't think you could trace her that far."

"I can't. I looked at her through your eyes."

"Don't trust my reaction," advised Cassal. "It's likely to be subjective."

"I don't," answered Dimanche. "It is."

*

Cassal hummed thoughtfully. Dimanche was a business neurological instrument. It didn't follow that it was an expert in human psychology.

*

Cassal stared at the woman coming toward him. Center-of-the-Galaxy fashion. Decadent, of course, or maybe ultra-civilized. As an Outsider, he wasn't sure which. Whatever it was, it did to the human body what should have been done long ago.

And this body wasn't exactly human. The subtle skirt of proportions betrayed it as an offshoot or deviation from the human race. Some of the new sub-races stacked up against the original stock much in the same way

Cro-Magnons did against Neanderthals, in beauty, at least.

Dimanche spoke a single syllable and subsided, an event Cassal didn't notice. His consciousness was focused on another discovery: the woman was Murra Foray.

He knew vaguely that the first counselor was not necessarily what she had seemed that first time at the agency. That she was capable of such a metamorphosis was hard to believe, though pleasant to accept. His attitude must have shown on his face.

"Please," said Murra Foray. "I'm a Huntner. We're adept at camouflage."

"Huntner," he repeated blankly. "I knew that. But what's a Huntner?"

She wrinkled her lovely nose at the question. "I didn't expect you to ask that. I won't answer it now." She came closer. "I thought you'd ask which was the camouflage—the person you see here, or the one at the Bureau?"

He never remembered the reply he made. It must have been satisfactory, for she smiled and drew her fragile wrap closer. The reservations were waiting.

Dimanche seized the opportunity to speak. "There's something phony about her. I don't understand it and I don't like it."

"You," said Cassal, "are a machine. You don't have to like it."

"That's what I mean. You *have* to like it. You have no choice."

Murra Foray looked back questioningly. Cassal hurried to her side.

The evening passed swiftly. Food that he ate and didn't taste. Music he heard and didn't listen to. Geometric light fugues that were seen and not observed. Liquor that he drank—and here the sequence ended, in the complicated chemistry of Godolphian stimulants.

Cassal reacted to that smooth liquid, though his physical reactions were not slowed. Certain mental centers were depressed, others left wide open, subject to acceleration at whatever speed he demanded.

Murra Foray, in his eyes at least, might look like a dream, the kind men have and never talk about. She was, however, interested solely in her work, or so it seemed.

*

"Godolph is a nice place," she said, toying with a drink, "if you like rain. The natives seem happy enough. But the Galaxy is big and there are lots of strange planets in it, each of which seems ideal to those who are adapted to it. I don't have to tell you what happens when people travel. They get stranded. It's not the time spent in actual flight that's important; it's waiting for the right ship to show up and then having all the necessary documents. Believe me, that can be important, as you found out."

He nodded. He had.

"That's the origin of Travelers Aid Bureau," she continued. "A loose organization, propagated mainly by example. Sometimes it's called Star Travelers Aid. It may have other names. The aim, however, is always the same: to see that stranded persons get where they want to go."

She looked at him wistfully, appealingly. "That's why I'm interested in your method of creating identification tabs. It's the thing most commonly lost. Stolen, if you prefer the truth."

She seemed to anticipate his question. "How can anyone use another's identification? It can be done under certain circumstances. By neural lobotomy, a portion of one brain may be made to match, more or less exactly, the code area of another brain. The person operated on suffers a certain loss of function, of course. How great that loss is depends on the degree of similarity between the two brain areas before the operation took place."

She ought to know, and he was inclined to believe her. Still, it didn't sound feasible.

"You haven't accounted for the psychometric index," he said.

"I thought you'd see it. That's diminished, too."

Logical enough, though not a pretty picture. A genius could always be made into an average man or lowered to the level of an idiot. There was no operation, however, that could raise an idiot to the level of a genius.

The scramble for the precious identification tabs went on, from the higher to the lower, a game of musical chairs with grim over-tones.

She smiled gravely. "You haven't answered my implied question."

The company that employed him wasn't anxious to let the secret of Dimanche get out. They didn't sell the instrument; they made it for their own use. It was an advantage over their competitors they intended to keep. Even on his recommendation, they wouldn't sell to the agency.

Moreover, it wouldn't help Travelers Aid Bureau if they did. Since she was first counselor, it was probable that she'd be the one to use it. She couldn't make identification for anyone except herself, and then only if she developed exceptional skill.

The alternative was to surgery it in and out of whoever needed it. When that happened, secrecy was gone. Travelers couldn't be trusted.

*

He shook his head. "It's an appealing idea, but I'm afraid I can't help you."

"Meaning you won't."

This was intriguing. Now it was the agency, not he, who wanted help.

"Don't overplay it," cautioned Dimanche, who had been consistently silent.

She leaned forward attentively. He experienced an uneasy moment. Was it possible she had noticed his private conversation? Of course not. Yet—

"Please," she said, and the tone allayed his fears. "There's an emergency situation and I've got to attend to it. Will you go with me?" She smiled understandingly at his quizzical expression. "Travelers Aid is always having emergencies."

She was rising. "It's too late to go to the Bureau. My place has a number of machines with which I keep in touch with the spaceport."

"I wonder," said Dimanche puzzledly. "She doesn't subvocalize at all. I haven't been able to get a line on her. I'm certain she didn't receive any sort of call. Be careful. This might be a trick."

"Interesting," said Cassal. He wasn't in the mood to discuss it.

Her habitation was luxurious, though Cassal wasn't impressed. Luxury was found everywhere in the Universe. Huntner women weren't. He watched as she adjusted the machines grouped at one side of the room. She spoke in a low voice; he couldn't distinguish words. She actuated levers, pressed buttons: impedimenta of communication.

At last she finished. "I'm tired. Will you wait till I change?"

Inarticulately, he nodded.

"I think her 'emergency' was a fake," said Dimanche flatly as soon as she left. "I'm positive she wasn't operating the communicator. She merely went through the motions."

"Motions," murmured Cassal dreamily, leaning back. "And what motions."

"I've been watching her," said Dimanche. "She frightens me."

"I've been watching her, too. Maybe in a different way."

"Get out of here while you can," warned Dimanche. "She's dangerous."

*

Momentarily, Cassal considered it. Dimanche had never failed him. He ought to follow that advice. And yet there was another explanation.

"Look," said Cassal. "A machine is a machine. But among humans there are men and women. What seems dangerous to you may be merely a pattern of normal behavior...." He broke off. Murra Foray had entered.

Strictly from the other side of the Galaxy, which she was. A woman can be slender and still be womanly beautiful, without being obvious about it. Not that Murra disdained the obvious, technically. But he could see through technicalities.

The tendons in his hands ached and his mouth was dry, though not with fear. An urgent ringing pounded in his ears. He shook it out of his head and got up.

She came to him.

The ringing was still in his ears. It wasn't a figment of imagination; it was a real voice—that of Dimanche, howling:

"Huntner! It's a word variant. In their language it means Hunter. *She can hear me!*"

"Hear you?" repeated Cassal vacantly.

She was kissing him.

"A descendant of carnivores. An audio-sensitive. She's been listening to you and me all the time."

"Of course I have, ever since the first interview at the bureau," said Murra. "In the beginning I couldn't see what value it was, but you convinced me." She laid her hand gently over his eyes. "I hate to do this to you, dear, but I've got to have Dimanche."

She had been smothering him with caresses. Now, deliberately, she began smothering him in actuality.

Cassal had thought he was an athlete. For an Earthman, he was. Murra Foray, however, was a Huntner, which meant hunter—a descendant of incredibly strong carnivores.

He didn't have a chance. He knew that when he couldn't budge her hands and he fell into the airless blackness of space.

*

Alone and naked, Cassal awakened. He wished he hadn't. He turned over and, though he tried hard not to, promptly woke up again. His body was willing to sleep, but his mind was panicked and disturbed. About what, he wasn't sure.

He sat up shakily and held his roaring head in his hands. He ran aching fingers through his hair. He stopped. The lump behind his ear was gone.

"Dimanche!" he called, and looked at his abdomen.

There was a thin scar, healing visibly before his eyes.

"Dimanche!" he cried again. "Dimanche!"

There was no answer. Dimanche was no longer with him.

He staggered to his feet and stared at the wall. She'd been kind enough to return him to his own rooms. At length he gathered enough strength to rummage through his belongings. Nothing was missing. Money, identification—all were there.

He could go to the police. He grimaced as he thought of it. The neighborly Godolphian police were hardly a match for the Huntner; she'd fake them out of their skins.

He couldn't prove she'd taken Dimanche. Nothing else normally considered valuable was missing. Besides, there might even be a local prohibition against Dimanche. Not by name, of course; but they could dig up an ancient ordinance—invasion of privacy or something like that. Anything would do if it gave them an opportunity to confiscate the device for intensive study.

For the police to believe his story was the worst that could happen. They might locate Dimanche, but he'd never get it.

He smiled bitterly and the effort hurt. "Dear," she had called him as she had strangled and beaten him into unconsciousness. Afterward singing, very likely, as she had sliced the little instrument out of him.

He could picture her not very remote ancestors springing from cover and overtaking a fleeing herd—

No use pursuing that line of thought.

Why did she want Dimanche? She had hinted that the agency wasn't always concerned with legality as such. He could believe her. If she wanted it for making identification tabs, she'd soon find that it was useless. Not that that was much comfort—she wasn't likely to return Dimanche after she'd made that discovery.

*

For that matter, what was the purpose of Travelers Aid Bureau? It was a front for another kind of activity. Philanthropy had nothing to do with it.

If he still had possession of Dimanche, he'd be able to find out. Everything seemed to hinge on that. With it, he was nearly a superman, able to hold his own in practically all situations—anything that didn't involve a Huntner woman, that is.

Without it—well, Tunney 21 was still far away. Even if he should manage to get there without it, his mission on the planet was certain to fail.

He dismissed the idea of trying to recover it immediately from Murra Foray. She was an audio-sensitive. At twenty feet, unaided, she could hear a heartbeat, the internal noise muscles made in sliding over each other. With Dimanche, she could hear electrons rustling. As an antagonist she was altogether too formidable.

*

He began pulling on his clothing, wincing as he did so. The alternative was to make another Dimanche. *If* he could. It would be a tough job even for a neuronic expert familiar with the process. He wasn't that expert, but it still had to be done.

The new instrument would have to be better than the original. Maybe not such a slick machine, but more comprehensive. More wallop. He grinned as he thought hopefully about giving Murra Foray a surprise.

Ignoring his aches and pains, he went right to work. With money not a factor, it was an easy matter to line up the best electronic and neuron concerns on Godolph. Two were put on a standby basis. When he gave them plans, they were to rush construction at all possible speed.

Each concern was to build a part of the new instrument. Neither part was of value without the other. The slow-thinking Godolphians weren't likely to make the necessary mental connection between the seemingly unrelated projects.

He retired to his suite and began to draw diagrams. It was harder than he thought. He knew the principles, but the actual details were far more complicated than he remembered.

Functionally, the Dimanche instrument was divided into three main phases. There was a brain and memory unit that operated much as the human counterpart did. Unlike the human brain, however, it had no body to control, hence more of it was available for thought processes. Entirely neuronic in construction, it was far smaller than an electronic brain of the same capacity.

The second function was electronic, akin to radar. Instead of material objects, it traced and recorded distant nerve impulses. It could count the heartbeat, measure the rate of respiration, was even capable of approximate analysis of the contents of the bloodstream. Properly focused on the nerves of tongue, lips or larynx, it transmitted that data back to the neuronic brain, which then reconstructed it into speech. Lip reading, after a fashion, carried to the ultimate.

Finally, there was the voice of Dimanche, a speaker under the control of the neuronic brain.

For convenience of installation in the body, Dimanche was packaged in two units. The larger package was usually surgeried into the abdomen. The small one, containing the speaker, was attached to the skull just behind the ear. It worked by bone conduction, allowing silent communication between operator and instrument. A real convenience.

It wasn't enough to know this, as Cassal did. He'd talked to the company experts, had seen the symbolical drawings, the plans for an improved version. He needed something better than the best though, that had been planned.

The drawback was this: *Dimanche was powered directly by the nervous system of the body in which it was housed.* Against Murra Foray, he'd be over-matched. She was stronger than he physically, probably also in the production of nervous energy.

One solution was to make available to the new instrument a larger fraction of the neural currents of the body. That was dangerous—a slight miscalculation and the user was dead. Yet he had to have an instrument that would overpower her.

Cassal rubbed his eyes wearily. How could he find some way of supplying additional power?

Abruptly, Cassal sat up. That was the way, of course—an auxiliary power pack that need not be surgeried into his body, extra power that he would use only in emergencies.

Neuronics, Inc., had never done this, had never thought that such an instrument would ever be necessary. They didn't need to overpower their customers. They merely wanted advance information via subvocalized thoughts.

It was easier for Cassal to conceive this idea than to engineer it. At the end of the first day, he knew it would be a slow process.

Twice he postponed deadlines to the manufacturing concerns he'd engaged. He locked himself in his rooms and took Anti-Sleep against the doctor's vigorous protests. In one week he had the necessary drawings, crude but legible. An expert would have to make innumerable corrections, but the intent was plain.

One week. During that time Murra Foray would be growing hourly more proficient in the use of Dimanche.

*

Cassal followed the neuronics expert groggily, seventy-two hours sleep still clogging his reactions. Not that he hadn't needed sleep after that week. The Godolphian showed him proudly through the shops, though he wasn't at all interested in their achievements. The only noteworthy aspect was the grand scale of their architecture.

"We did it, though I don't think we'd have taken the job if we'd known how hard it was going to be," the neuronics expert chattered. "It works exactly as you specified. We had to make substitutions, of course, but you understand that was inevitable."

He glanced anxiously at Cassal, who nodded. That was to be expected. Components that were common on Earth wouldn't necessarily be available here. Still, any expert worth his pay could always make the proper combinations and achieve the same results.

Inside the lab, Cassal frowned. "I thought you were keeping my work separate. What is this planetary drive doing here?"

The Godolphian spread his broad hands and looked hurt. "Planetary drive?" He tried to laugh. "This is the instrument you ordered!"

Cassal started. It was supposed to fit under a flap of skin behind his ear. A Three World saurian couldn't carry it.

He turned savagely on the expert. "I told you it had to be small."

"But it is. I quote your orders exactly: 'I'm not familiar with your system of measurement, but make it tiny, very tiny. Figure the size you think it will have to be and cut it in half. And then cut *that* in half.' This is the fraction remaining."

It certainly was. Cassal glanced at the Godolphian's hands. Excellent for swimming. No wonder they built on a grand scale. Broad, blunt, webbed hands weren't exactly suited for precision work.

Valueless. Completely valueless. He knew now what he would find at the other lab. He shook his head in dismay, personally saw to it that the instrument was destroyed. He paid for the work and retrieved the plans.

Back in his rooms again, he sat and thought. It was still the only solution. If the Godolphians couldn't do it, he'd have to find some race that could. He grabbed the intercom and jangled it savagely. In half an hour he had a dozen leads.

The best seemed to be the Spirella. A small, insectlike race, about three feet tall, they were supposed to have excellent manual dexterity, and were technically advanced. They sounded as if they were acquainted with the necessary fields. Three light-years away, they could be reached by readily available local transportation within the day. Their idea of what was small was likely to coincide with his.

He didn't bother to pack. The suite would remain his headquarters. Home was where his enemies were.

He made a mental correction—enemy.

*

He rubbed his sensitive ear, grateful for the discomfort. His stomach was sore, but it wouldn't be for long. The Spirella had made the new instrument just as he had wanted it. They had built an even better auxiliary power unit than he had specified. He fingered the flat cases in his pocket. In an emergency, he could draw on these, whereas Murra Foray would be limited to the energy in her nervous system.

What he had now was hardly the same instrument. A Military version of it, perhaps. It didn't seem right to use the same name. Call it something staunch and crisp, suggestive of raw power. Manche. As good a name as any. Manche against Dimanche. Cassal against a queen.

He swung confidently along the walkway beside the transport tide. It was raining. He decided to test the new instrument. The Godolphian across the way bent double and wondered why his knees wouldn't work. They had suddenly become swollen and painful to move. Maybe it was the climate.

And maybe it wasn't, thought Cassal. Eventually the pain would leave, but he hadn't meant to be so rough on the native. He'd have to watch how he used Manche.

He scouted the vicinity of Travelers Aid Bureau, keeping at least one building between him and possible detection. Purely precautionary. There was no indication that Murra Foray had spotted him. For a Huntner, she wasn't very alert, apparently.

He sent Manche out on exploration at minimum strength. The electronic guards which Dimanche had spoken of were still in place. Manche went through easily and didn't disturb an electron. Behind the guards there was no trace of the first counselor.

He went closer. Still no warning of danger. The same old technician shuffled in front of the entrance. A horrible thought hit him. It was easy enough to verify. Another "reorganization" *had* taken place. The new sign read:

STAR TRAVELERS AID BUREAU

STAB *Your Hour*

of Need

Delly Mortinbras, first counselor

Cassal leaned against the building, unable to understand what it was that frightened and bewildered him. Then it gradually became, if not clear, at least not quite so muddy.

STAB was the word that had been printed on the card in the money clip that his assailant in the alley had left behind. Cassal had naturally interpreted it as an order to the thug. It wasn't, of course.

The first time Cassal had visited the Travelers Aid Bureau, it had been in the process of reorganization. The only purpose of the reorganization, he realized now, had been to change the name so he wouldn't translate the word on the slip into the original initials of the Bureau.

Now it probably didn't matter any more whether or not he knew, so the name had been changed back to Star Travelers Aid Bureau—STAB.

That, he saw bitterly, was why Murra Foray had been so positive that the identification tab he'd made with the aid of Dimanche had been a forgery.

She had known the man who robbed Cassal of the original one, perhaps had even helped him plan the theft.

*

That didn't make sense to Cassal. Yet it had to. He'd suspected the organization of being a racket, but it obviously wasn't. By whatever name it was called, it actually was dedicated to helping the stranded traveler. The question was—which travelers?

There must be agency operatives at the spaceport, checking every likely prospect who arrived, finding out where they were going, whether their papers were in order. Then, just as had happened to Cassal, the prospect was robbed of his papers so somebody stranded here could go on to that destination!

The shabby, aging technician finished changing the last door sign and hobbled over to Cassal. He peered through the rain and darkness.

"You stuck here, too?" he quavered.

"No," said Cassal with dignity, shaky dignity. "I'm not stuck. I'm here because I want to be."

"You're crazy," declared the old man. "I remember—"

Cassal didn't wait to find out what it was he remembered. An impossible land, perhaps, a planet which swings in perfect orbit around an ideal sun. A continent which reared a purple mountain range to hold up a honey sky. People with whom anyone could relax easily and without worry or anxiety. In short, his own native world from which, at night, all the constellations were familiar.

Somehow, Cassal managed to get back to his suite, tumbled wearily onto his bed. The show-down wasn't going to take place.

Everyone connected with the agency—including Murra Foray—had been "stuck here" for one reason or another: no identification tab, no money, whatever it was. That was the staff of the Bureau, a pack of desperate castaways. The "philanthropy" extended to them and nobody else. They grabbed their tabs and money from the likeliest travelers, leaving them marooned here—and they in turn had to join the Bureau and use the same methods to continue their journeys through the Galaxy.

It was an endless belt of stranded travelers robbing and stranding other travelers, who then had to rob and strand still others, and so on and on....

*

Cassal didn't have a chance of catching up with Murra Foray. She had used the time—and Dimanche—to create her own identification tab and escape. She was going back to Kettikat, home of the Huntners, must already be light-years away.

Or was she? The signs on the Bureau had just been changed. Perhaps the ship was still in the spaceport, or cruising along below the speed of light. He shrugged defeatedly. It would do him no good; he could never get on board.

He got up suddenly on one elbow. He couldn't, but Manche could! Unlike his old instrument, it could operate at tremendous distances, its power no longer dependent only on his limited nervous energy.

With calculated fury, he let Manche strike out into space.

"There you are!" exclaimed Murra Foray. "I thought you could do it."

"Did you?" he asked coldly. "Where are you now?"

"Leaving the atmosphere, if you can call the stuff around this planet an atmosphere."

"It's not the atmosphere that's bad," he said as nastily as he could. "It's the philanthropy."

"Please don't feel that way," she appealed. "Huntners are rather unusual people, I admit, but sometimes even we need help. I had to have Dimanche and I took it."

"At the risk of killing me."

Her amusement was strange; it held a sort of sadness. "I didn't hurt you. I couldn't. You were too cute, like a—well, the animal native to Kettikat that would be called a teddy bear on Earth. A cute, lovable teddy bear."

"Teddy bear," he repeated, really stung now. "Careful. This one may have claws."

"Long claws? Long enough to reach from here to Kettikat?" She was laughing, but it sounded thin and wistful.

Manche struck out at Cassal's unspoken command. The laughter was canceled.

"Now you've done it," said Dimanche. "She's out cold."

There was no reason for remorse; it was strange that he felt it. His throat was dry.

"So you, too, can communicate with me. Through Manche, of course. I built a wonderful instrument, didn't I?"

"A fearful one," said Dimanche sternly. "She's unconscious."

"I heard you the first time." Cassal hesitated. "Is she dead?"

Dimanche investigated. "Of course not. A little thing like that wouldn't hurt her. Her nerve system is marvelous. I think it could carry current for a city. Beautiful!"

"I'm aware of the beauty," said Cassal.

*

An awkward silence followed. Dimanche broke it. "Now that I know the facts, I'm proud to be her chosen instrument. Her need was greater than yours."

Cassal growled, "As first counselor, she had access to every—"

"Don't interrupt with your half truths," said Dimanche. "Huntners *are* special; their brain structure, too. Not necessarily better, just different. Only the auditory and visual centers of their brains resemble that of man. You can guess the results of even superficial tampering with those parts of her mind. And stolen identification would involve lobotomy."

He could imagine? Cassal shook his head. No, he couldn't. A blinded and deaf Murra Foray would not go back to the home of the Huntners. According to her racial conditioning, a sightless young tiger should creep away and die.

Again there was silence. "No, she's not pretending unconsciousness," announced Dimanche. "For a moment I thought—but never mind."

The conversation was lasting longer than he expected. The ship must be obsolete and slow. There were still a few things he wanted to find out, if there was time.

"When are you going on Drive?" he asked.

"We've been on it for some time," answered Dimanche.

"Repeat that!" said Cassal, stunned.

"I said that we've been on faster-than-light drive for some time. Is there anything wrong with that?"

Nothing wrong with that at all. Theoretically, there was only one means of communicating with a ship hurtling along faster than light, and that way hadn't been invented.

Hadn't been until he had put together the instrument he called Manche.

Unwittingly, he had created far more than he intended. He ought to have felt elated.

Dimanche interrupted his thoughts. "I suppose you know what she thinks of you."

"She made it plain enough," said Cassal wearily. "A teddy bear. A brainless, childish toy."

"Among the Huntners, women are vigorous and aggressive," said Dimanche. The voice grew weaker as the ship, already light-years away, slid into unfathomable distances. "Where words are concerned, morals are very strict. For instance, 'dear' is never used unless the person means it. Huntner men are weak and not over-burdened with intelligence."

The voice was barely audible, but it continued: "The principal romantic figure in the dreams of women...." Dimanche failed altogether.

"Manche!" cried Cassal.

Manche responded with everything it had. "... is the teddy bear."

The elation that had been missing, and the triumph, came now. It was no time for hesitation, and Cassal didn't hesitate. Their actions had been directed against each other, but their emotions, which each had tried to ignore, were real and strong.

The gravitor dropped him to the ground floor. In a few minutes, Cassal was at the Travelers Aid Bureau.

Correction. Now it was Star Travelers Aid Bureau.

And, though no one but himself knew it, even that was wrong. Quickly he found the old technician.

"There's been a reorganization," said Cassal bluntly. "I want the signs changed."

The old man drew himself up. "Who are you?"

"I've just elected myself," said Cassal. "I'm the new first counselor."

He hoped no one would be foolish enough to challenge him. He wanted an organization that could function immediately, not a hospital full of cripples.

The old man thought about it. He was merely a menial, but he had been with the bureau for a long time. He was nobody, nothing, but he could recognize power when it was near him. He wiped his eyes and shambled out into the fine cold rain. Swiftly the new signs went up.

TRAVELERS AID BUREAU

S. T. A. *with us*

Denton Cassal, first counselor

*

Cassal sat at the control center. Every question cubicle was visible at a glance. In addition there was a special panel, direct from the spaceport, which recorded essential data about every newly arrived traveler. He could think of a few minor improvements, but he wouldn't have time to put them into effect. He'd mention them to his assistant, a man with a fine, logical mind. Not really first-rate, of course, but well suited to his secondary position. Every member quickly rose or sank to his proper level in this organization, and this one had, without a struggle.

Business was dull. The last few ships had brought travelers who were bound for unimaginably dreary destinations, nothing he need be concerned with.

He thought about the instrument. It was the addition of power that made the difference. Dimanche plus power equaled Manche, and Manche raised the user far above the level of other men. There was little to fear.

But essentially the real value of Manche lay in this—it was a beginning. Through it, he had communicated with a ship traveling far faster than light. The only one instrument capable of that was instantaneous radio. Actually it wasn't radio, but the old name had stuck to it.

Manche was really a very primitive model of instantaneous radio. It was crude; all first steps were. Limited in range, it was practically valueless for that purpose now. Eventually the range would be extended. Hitch a neuronic manufactured brain to human one, add the power of a tiny atomic battery, and Manche was created.

The last step was his share of the invention. Or maybe the credit belonged to Murra Foray. If she hadn't stolen Dimanche, it never would have been necessary to put together the new instrument.

The stern lines on his face relaxed. Murra Foray. He wondered about the marriage customs of the Huntners. He hoped marriage was a custom on Kettikat.

Cassal leaned back; officially, his mission was complete. There was no longer any need to go to Tunney 21. The scientist he was sent to bring back might as well remain there in obscure arrogance. Cassal knew he should return to Earth immediately. But the Galaxy was wide and there were lots of places to go.

Only one he was interested in, though—Kettikat, as far from the center of the Galaxy as Earth, but in the opposite direction, incredibly far away in terms of trouble and transportation. It would be difficult even for a man who had the services of Manche.

Cassal glanced at the board. Someone wanted to go to Zombo.

"Delly," he called to his assistant. "Try 13. This may be what you want to get back to your own planet."

Delly Mortinbras nodded gratefully and cut in.

Cassal continued scanning. There was more to it than he imagined, though he was learning fast. It wasn't enough to have identification, money, and a destination. The right ship might come in with standing room only. Someone had to be "persuaded" that Godolph was a cozy little place, as good as any for an unscheduled stopover.

It wouldn't change appreciably during his lifetime. There were too many billions of stars. First he had to perfect it, isolate from dependence on the human element, and then there would come the installation. A slow process, even with Murra to help him.

Someday he would go back to Earth. He should be welcome. The information he was sending back to his former employers, Neuronics, Inc., would more than compensate them for the loss of Dimanche.

Suddenly he was alert. A report had just come in.

Once upon a time, he thought tenderly, scanning the report, there was a teddy bear that could reach to Kettikat. With claws—but he didn't think they would be needed.

MY LADY GREENSLEEVES

by Frederik Pohl

This guard smelled trouble and it could be counted on to come—for a nose for trouble was one of the many talents bred here!

I

His name was Liam O'Leary and there was something stinking in his nostrils. It was the smell of trouble. He hadn't found what the trouble was yet, but he would. That was his business. He was a captain of guards in Estates-General Correctional Institution—better known to its inmates as the Jug—and if he hadn't been able to detect the scent of trouble brewing a cell-block away, he would never have survived to reach his captaincy.

And her name, he saw, was Sue-Ann Bradley, Detainee No. WFA-656R.

He frowned at the rap sheet, trying to figure out what got a girl like her into a place like this. And, what was more important, why she couldn't adjust herself to it, now that she was in.

He demanded: "Why wouldn't you mop out your cell?"

The girl lifted her head angrily and took a step forward. The block guard, Sodaro, growled warningly: "Watch it, auntie!"

O'Leary shook his head. "Let her talk, Sodaro." It said in the *Civil Service Guide to Prison Administration*: "Detainees will be permitted to speak in their own behalf in disciplinary proceedings." And O'Leary was a man who lived by the book.

She burst out: "I never got a chance! That old witch Mathias never told me I was supposed to mop up. She banged on the door and said, 'Slush up, sister!' And then, ten minutes later, she called the guards and told them I refused to mop."

The block guard guffawed. "Wipe talk—that's what she was telling you to do. Cap'n, you know what's funny about this? This Bradley is—"

"Shut up, Sodaro."

*

Captain O'leary put down his pencil and looked at the girl. She was attractive and young—not beyond hope, surely. Maybe she had got off to a wrong start, but the question was, would putting her in the disciplinary block help straighten her out? He rubbed his ear and looked past her at the line of prisoners on the rap detail, waiting for him to judge their cases.

He said patiently: "Bradley, the rules are you have to mop out your cell. If you didn't understand what Mathias was talking about, you should have asked her. Now I'm warning you, the next time—"

"Hey, Cap'n, wait!" Sodaro was looking alarmed. "This isn't a first offense. Look at the rap sheet. Yesterday she pulled the same thing in the mess hall." He shook his head reprovingly at the prisoner. "The block guard had to break up a fight between her and another wench, and she claimed the same business—said she didn't understand when the other one asked her to move along." He added virtuously: "The guard warned her then that next time she'd get the Greensleeves for sure."

Inmate Bradley seemed to be on the verge of tears. She said tautly: "I don't care. I don't care!"

O'Leary stopped her. "That's enough! Three days in Block O!"

It was the only thing to do—for her own sake as much as for his. He had managed, by strength of will, not to hear that she had omitted to say "sir" every time she spoke to him, but he couldn't keep it up forever and he certainly couldn't overlook hysteria. And hysteria was clearly the next step for her.

All the same, he stared after her as she left. He handed the rap sheet to Sodaro and said absently: "Too bad a kid like her has to be here. What's she in for?"

"You didn't know, Cap'n?" Sodaro leered. "She's in for conspiracy to violate the Categoried Class laws. Don't waste your time with her, Cap'n. She's a figger-lover!"

Captain O'Leary took a long drink of water from the fountain marked "Civil Service." But it didn't wash the taste out of his mouth, the smell from his nose.

What got into a girl to get her mixed up with that kind of dirty business? He checked out of the cell blocks and walked across the yard, wondering about her. She'd had every advantage—decent Civil Service parents, a good education, everything a girl could wish for. If anything, she had had a better environment than O'Leary himself, and look what she had made of it.

The direction of evolution is toward specialization and Man is no exception, but with the difference that his is the one species that creates its own environment in which to specialize. From the moment that clans formed, specialization began—the hunters using the weapons made by the flint-chippers, the food cooked in clay pots made by the ceramists, over fire made by the shaman who guarded the sacred flame.

Civilization merely increased the extent of specialization. From the born mechanic and the man with the gift of gab, society evolved to the point of smaller contact and less communication between the specializations, until now they could understand each other on only the most basic physical necessities—and not even always then.

But this was desirable, for the more specialists, the higher the degree of civilization. The ultimate should be the complete segregation of each specialization—social and genetic measures to make them breed true, because the unspecialized man is an uncivilized man, or at any rate he does not advance civilization. And letting the specializations mix would produce genetic undesirables: clerk-laborer or Professional-GI misfits, for example, being only half specialized, would be good at no specialization.

And the basis of this specialization society was: "The aptitude groups are the true races of mankind." Putting it into law was only the legal enforcement of a demonstrable fact.

"Evening, Cap'n." A bleary old inmate orderly stood up straight and touched his cap as O'Leary passed by.

"Evening."

*

O'Leary noted, with the part of his mind that always noted those things, that the orderly had been leaning on his broom until he'd noticed the captain coming by. Of course, there wasn't much to sweep—the spray machines and sweeperdozers had been over the cobblestones of the yard twice already that day. But it was an inmate's job to keep busy. And it was a guard captain's job to notice when they didn't.

There wasn't anything wrong with that job, he told himself. It was a perfectly good civil-service position—better than post-office clerk, not as good as Congressman, but a job you could be proud to hold. He *was* proud of it. It was *right* that he should be proud of it. He was civil-service born and bred, and naturally he was proud and content to do a good, clean civil-service job.

If he had happened to be born a fig—a *clerk*, he corrected himself—if he had happened to be born a clerk, why, he would have been proud of that, too. There wasn't anything wrong with being a clerk—or a mechanic or a soldier, or even a laborer, for that matter.

Good laborers were the salt of the Earth! They weren't smart, maybe, but they had a—well, a sort of natural, relaxed joy of living. O'Leary was a broad-minded man and many times he had thought almost with a touch of envy how *comfortable* it must be to be a wipe—a *laborer*. No responsibilities. No worries. Just an easy, slow routine of work and loaf, work and loaf.

Of course, he wouldn't *really* want that kind of life, because he was Civil Service and not the kind to try to cross over class barriers that weren't *meant* to be—

"Evening, Cap'n."

He nodded to the mechanic inmate who was, theoretically, in charge of maintaining the prison's car pool, just inside the gate.

"Evening, Conan," he said.

Conan, now—he was a big buck greaser and he would be there for the next hour, languidly poking a piece of fluff out of the air filter on the prison jeep. Lazy, sure. Undependable, certainly. But he kept the cars going—and, O'Leary thought approvingly, when his sentence was up in another year or so, he would go back to his life with his status restored, a mechanic on the outside as he had been inside, and he certainly would never risk coming back to the Jug by trying to pass as Civil Service or anything else. He knew his place.

So why didn't this girl, this Sue-Ann Bradley, know hers?

II

Every prison has its Greensleeves—sometimes they are called by different names. Old Marquette called it "the canary;" Louisiana State called it "the red hats;" elsewhere it was called "the hole," "the snake pit," "the Klondike." When you're in it, you don't much care what it is called; it is a place for punishment.

And punishment is what you get.

Block O in Estates-General Correctional Institution was the disciplinary block, and because of the green straitjackets its inhabitants wore, it was called the Greensleeves. It was a community of its own, an enclave within the larger city-state that was the Jug. And like any other community, it had its leading citizens ... two of them. Their names were Sauer and Flock.

Sue-Ann Bradley heard them before she reached the Greensleeves. She was in a detachment of three unfortunates like herself, convoyed by an irritable guard, climbing the steel steps toward Block O from the floor below, when she heard the yelling.

"Owoo-o-o," screamed Sauer from one end of the cell block and "Yow-w-w!" shrieked Flock at the other.

The inside deck guard of Block O looked nervously at the outside deck guard. The outside guard looked impassively back—after all, he was on the outside.

The inside guard muttered: "Wipe rats! They're getting on my nerves."

The outside guard shrugged.

"Detail, *halt*!" The two guards turned to see what was coming in as the three new candidates for the Greensleeves slumped to a stop at the head of the stairs. "Here they are," Sodaro told them. "Take good care of 'em, will you? Especially the lady—she's going to like it here, because there's plenty of wipes and greasers and figgers to keep her company." He laughed coarsely and abandoned his charges to the Block O guards.

The outside guard said sourly: "A woman, for God's sake. Now O'Leary knows I hate it when there's a woman in here. It gets the others all riled up."

"Let them in," the inside guard told him. "The others are riled up already."

Sue-Ann Bradley looked carefully at the floor and paid them no attention. The outside guard pulled the switch that turned on the tanglefoot electronic fields that swamped the floor of the block corridor and of each individual cell. While the fields were on, you could ignore the prisoners—they simply could not move fast enough, against the electronic drag of the field, to do any harm. But it was a rule that, even in Block O, you didn't leave the tangler fields on all the time—only when the cell doors had to be opened or a prisoner's restraining garment removed.

Sue-Ann walked bravely forward through the opened gate—and fell flat on her face. It was her first experience of a tanglefoot field. It was like walking through molasses.

The guard guffawed and lifted her up by one shoulder. "Take it easy, auntie. Come on, get in your cell." He steered her in the right direction and pointed to a greensleeved straitjacket on the cell cot. "Put that on. Being as you're a lady, we won't tie it up, but the rules say you got to wear it and the rules—Hey. She's crying!" He shook his head, marveling. It was the first time he had ever seen a prisoner cry in the Greensleeves.

However, he was wrong. Sue-Ann's shoulders were shaking, but not from tears. Sue-Ann Bradley had got a good look at Sauer and at Flock as she passed them by and she was fighting off an almost uncontrollable urge to retch.

*

Sauer and Flock were what are called prison wolves. They were laborers—"wipes," for short—or, at any rate, they had been once. They had spent so much time in prisons that it was sometimes hard even for them to remember what they really were, outside. Sauer was a big, grinning redhead with eyes like a water moccasin. Flock was a lithe five-footer with the build of a water moccasin—and the sad, stupid eyes of a calf.

Sauer stopped yelling for a moment. "Hey, Flock!"

"What do you want, Sauer?" called Flock from his own cell.

"We got a lady with us! Maybe we ought to cut out this yelling so as not to disturb the lady!" He screeched with howling, maniacal laughter. "Anyway, if we don't cut this out, they'll get us in trouble, Flock!"

"Oh, you think so?" shrieked Flock. "Jeez, I wish you hadn't said that, Sauer. You got me scared! I'm so scared, I'm gonna have to yell!"

The howling started all over again.

The inside guard finished putting the new prisoners away and turned off the tangler field once more. He licked his lips. "Say, you want to take a turn in here for a while?"

"Uh-uh." The outside guard shook his head.

"You're yellow," the inside guard said moodily. "Ah, I don't know why I don't quit this lousy job. Hey, you! Pipe down or I'll come in and beat your head off!"

"Ee-ee-ee!" screamed Sauer in a shrill falsetto. "I'm scared!" Then he grinned at the guard, all but his water-moccasin eyes. "Don't you know you can't hurt a wipe by hitting him on the head, Boss?"

"Shut *up*!" yelled the inside guard.

Sue-Ann Bradley's weeping now was genuine. She simply could not help it. The crazy yowling of the hard-timers, Sauer and Flock, was getting under her skin. They weren't even—even *human*, she told herself miserably, trying to weep silently so as not to give the guards the satisfaction of hearing her—they were animals!

Resentment and anger, she could understand. She told herself doggedly that resentment and anger were natural and right. They were perfectly normal expressions of the freedom-loving citizen's rebellion against the vile and stifling system of Categoried Classes. It was *good* that Sauer and Flock still had enough spirit to struggle against the vicious system—

But did they have to scream so?

The senseless yelling was driving her crazy. She abandoned herself to weeping and she didn't even care who heard her any more. Senseless!

It never occurred to Sue-Ann Bradley that it might not be senseless, because noise hides noise. But then she hadn't been a prisoner very long.

III

"I smell trouble," said O'Leary to the warden.

"Trouble? Trouble?" Warden Schluckebier clutched his throat and his little round eyes looked terrified—as perhaps they should have. Warden Godfrey Schluckebier was the almighty Caesar of ten thousand inmates in the Jug, but privately he was a fussy old man trying to hold onto the last decent job he would have in his life.

"Trouble? *What* trouble?"

O'Leary shrugged. "Different things. You know Lafon, from Block A? This afternoon, he was playing ball with the laundry orderlies in the yard."

The warden, faintly relieved, faintly annoyed, scolded: "O'Leary, what did you want to worry me for? There's nothing wrong with playing ball in the yard. That's what recreation periods are for."

"You don't see what I mean, Warden. Lafon was a professional on the outside—an architect. Those laundry cons were laborers. Pros and wipes don't mix; it isn't natural. And there are other things."

O'Leary hesitated, frowning. How could you explain to the warden that it didn't *smell*right?

"For instance—Well, there's Aunt Mathias in the women's block. She's a pretty good old girl—that's why she's the block orderly. She's a lifer, she's got no place to go, she gets along with the other women. But today she put a woman named Bradley on report. Why? Because she told Bradley to mop up in wipe talk and Bradley didn't understand. Now Mathias wouldn't—"

The warden raised his hand. "Please, O'Leary, don't bother me about that kind of stuff." He sighed heavily and rubbed his eyes. He poured himself a cup of steaming black coffee from a brewpot, reached in a desk drawer for something, hesitated, glanced at O'Leary, then dropped a pale blue tablet into the cup. He drank it down eagerly, ignoring the scalding heat.

He leaned back, looking suddenly happier and much more assured.

"O'Leary, you're a guard captain, right? And I'm your warden. You have your job, keeping the inmates in line, and I have mine. Now your job is just as important as my job," he said piously. "*Everybody's* job is just as important as everybody else's, right? But we have to stick to our own jobs. We don't want to try to *pass*."

O'Leary snapped erect, abruptly angry. Pass! What the devil way was that for the warden to talk to him?

"Excuse the expression, O'Leary," the warden said anxiously. "I mean, after all, 'Specialization is the goal of civilization,' right?" He was a great man for platitudes, was Warden Schluckebier. "*You* know you don't want to worry about *my* end of running the prison. And *I* don't want to worry about *yours*. You see?" And he folded his hands and smiled like a civil-service Buddha.

*

O'Leary choked back his temper. "Warden, I'm telling you that there's trouble coming up. I smell the signs."

"Handle it, then!" snapped the warden, irritated at last.

"But suppose it's too big to handle. Suppose—"

"It isn't," the warden said positively. "Don't borrow trouble with all your supposing, O'Leary." He sipped the remains of his coffee, made a wry face, poured a fresh cup and, with an elaborate show of not noticing what he was doing, dropped three of the pale blue tablets into it this time.

He sat beaming into space, waiting for the jolt to take effect.

"Well, then," he said at last. "You just remember what I've told you tonight, O'Leary, and we'll get along fine. 'Specialization is the—' Oh, curse the thing."

His phone was ringing. The warden picked it up irritably.

That was the trouble with those pale blue tablets, thought O'Leary; they gave you a lift, but they put you on edge.

"Hello," barked the warden, not even glancing at the viewscreen. "What the devil do you want? Don't you know I'm—What? You did *what*? You're going to WHAT?"

He looked at the viewscreen at last with a look of pure horror. Whatever he saw on it, it did not reassure him. His eyes opened like clamshells in a steamer.

"O'Leary," he said faintly, "my mistake."

And he hung up—more or less by accident; the handset dropped from his fingers.

The person on the other end of the phone was calling from Cell Block O.

Five minutes before, he hadn't been anywhere near the phone and it didn't look as if his chances of ever getting near it were very good. Because five minutes before, he was in his cell, with the rest of the hard-timers of the Greensleeves.

His name was Flock.

He was still yelling. Sue-Ann Bradley, in the cell across from him, thought that maybe, after all, the man was really in pain. Maybe the crazy screams were screams of agony, because certainly his face was the face of an agonized man.

The outside guard bellowed: "Okay, okay. Take ten!"

Sue-Ann froze, waiting to see what would happen. What actually did happen was that the guard reached up and closed the switch that actuated the tangler fields on the floors of the cells. The prison rules were humanitarian, even for the dregs that inhabited the Greensleeves. Ten minutes out of every two hours, even the worst case had to be allowed to take his hands out of the restraining garment.

"Rest period" it was called—in the rule book. The inmates had a less lovely term for it.

*

At the guard's yell, the inmates jumped to their feet.

Bradley was a little slow getting off the edge of the steel-slat bed—nobody had warned her that the eddy currents in the tangler fields had a way of making metal smoke-hot. She gasped but didn't cry out. Score one more painful lesson in her new language course. She rubbed the backs of her thighs gingerly—and slowly, slowly, for the eddy currents did not permit you to move fast. It was like pushing against rubber; the faster you tried to move, the greater the resistance.

The guard peered genially into her cell. "You're okay, auntie." She proudly ignored him as he slogged deliberately away on his rounds. He didn't have to untie her and practically stand over her while she attended to various personal matters, as he did with the male prisoners. It was not much to be grateful for, but Sue-Ann Bradley was grateful. At least she didn't have to live *quite* like a fig—like an underprivileged clerk, she told herself, conscience-stricken.

Across the hall, the guard was saying irritably: "What the hell's the matter with you?" He opened the door of the cell with an asbestos-handled key held in a canvas glove.

Flock was in that cell and he was doubled over.

The guard looked at him doubtfully. It could be a trick, maybe. Couldn't it? But he could see Flock's face and the agony in it was real enough. And Flock was gasping, through real tears: "Cramps. I—I—"

"Ah, you wipes always got a pain in the gut." The guard lumbered around Flock to the draw-strings at the back of the jacket. Funny smell in here, he told himself—not for the first time. And imagine, some people didn't believe that wipes had a smell of their own! But this time, he realized cloudily, it was a rather unusual smell. Something burning. Almost like meat scorching.

It wasn't pleasant. He finished untying Flock and turned away; let the stinking wipe take care of his own troubles. He only had ten minutes to get all the way around Block O and the inmates complained like crazy if he didn't make sure they all got the most possible free time. He was pretty good at snowshoeing through the tangler field. He was a little vain about it, even; at times he had been known to boast of his ability to make the rounds in two minutes, every time.

Every time but this.

For Flock moaned behind him, oddly close.

The guard turned, but not quickly enough. There was Flock—astonishingly, he was half out of his jacket; his arms hadn't been in the sleeves at all! And in one of the hands, incredibly, there was something that glinted and smoked.

"All right," croaked Flock, tears trickling out of eyes nearly shut with pain.

But it wasn't the tears that held the guard; it was the shining, smoking thing, now poised at his throat. A shiv! It looked as though it had been made out of a bed-spring, ripped loose from its frame God knows how, hidden inside the greensleeved jacket God knows how—filed, filed to sharpness over endless hours.

No wonder Flock moaned—the eddy currents in the shiv were slowly cooking his hand; and the blister against his abdomen, where the shiv had been hidden during other rest periods, felt like raw acid.

*

"All right," whispered Flock, "just walk out the door and you won't get hurt. Unless the other screw makes trouble, you won't get hurt, so tell him not to, you hear?"

He was nearly fainting with the pain.

But he hadn't let go.

He didn't let go. And he didn't stop.

IV

It was Flock on the phone to the warden—Flock with his eyes still streaming tears, Flock with Sauer standing right behind him, menacing the two bound deck guards.

Sauer shoved Flock out of the way. "Hey, Warden!" he said, and the voice was a cheerful bray, though the serpent eyes were cold and hating. "Warden, you got to get a medic in here. My boy Flock, he hurt himself real bad and he needs a doctor." He gestured playfully at the guards with the shiv. "I tell you, Warden. I got this knife and I got your guards here. Enough said? So get a medic in here quick, you hear?"

And he snapped the connection.

O'Leary said: "Warden, I told you I smelled trouble!"

The warden lifted his head, glared, started feebly to speak, hesitated, and picked up the long-distance phone. He said sadly to the prison operator: "Get me the governor—fast."

Riot!

The word spread out from the prison on seven-league boots.

It snatched the city governor out of a friendly game of Seniority with his manager and their wives—and just when he was holding the Porkbarrel Joker concealed in the hole.

It broke up the Base Championship Scramble Finals at Hap Arnold Field to the south, as half the contestants had to scramble in earnest to a Red Alert that was real.

It reached to police precinct houses and TV newsrooms and highway checkpoints, and from there it filtered into the homes and lives of the nineteen million persons that lived within a few dozen miles of the Jug.

Riot. And yet fewer than half a dozen men were involved.

A handful of men, and the enormous bulk of the city-state quivered in every limb and class. In its ten million homes, in its hundreds of thousands of public places, the city-state's people shook under the impact of the news from the prison.

For the news touched them where their fears lay. Riot! And not merely a street brawl among roistering wipes, or a bar-room fight of greasers relaxing from a hard day at the plant. The riot was down among the corrupt sludge that underlay the state itself. Wipes brawled with wipes and no one cared; but in the Jug, all classes were cast together.

*

Forty miles to the south, Hap Arnold Field was a blaze of light. The airmen tumbled out of their quarters and dayrooms at the screech of the alert siren, and behind them their wives and children stretched and yawned and worried. An alert! The older kids fussed and complained and their mothers shut them up. No, there wasn't any alert scheduled for tonight; no, they didn't know where Daddy was going; no, the kids couldn't get up yet—it was the middle of the night.

And as soon as they had the kids back in bed, most of the mothers struggled into their own airwac uniforms and headed for the briefing area to hear.

They caught the words from a distance—not quite correctly. "Riot!" gasped an aircraftswoman first-class, mother of three. "The wipes! I *told* Charlie they'd get out of hand and—Alys, we aren't safe. You know how they are about GI women! I'm going right home and get a club and stand right by the door and—"

"Club!" snapped Alys, radarscope-sergeant, with two children querulously awake in her nursery at home. "What in God's name is the use of a club? You can't hurt a wipe by hitting him on the head. You'd better come along to Supply with me and draw a gun—you'll need it before this night is over."

But the airmen themselves heard the briefing loud and clear over the scramble-call speakers, and they knew it was not merely a matter of trouble in the wipe quarters. The Jug! The governor himself had called them out;

they were to fly interdicting missions at such-and-such levels on such-and-such flight circuits around the prison.

The rockets took off on fountains of fire; and the jets took off with a whistling roar; and last of all, the helicopters took off ... and they were the ones who might actually accomplish something. They took up their picket posts on the prison perimeter, a pilot and two bombardiers in each 'copter, stone-faced, staring grimly alert at the prison below.

They were ready for the breakout.

But there wasn't any breakout.

The rockets went home for fuel. The jets went home for fuel. The helicopters hung on—still ready, still waiting.

The rockets came back and roared harmlessly about, and went away again. They stayed away. The helicopter men never faltered and never relaxed. The prison below them was washed with light—from the guard posts on the walls, from the cell blocks themselves, from the mobile lights of the guard squadrons surrounding the walls.

North of the prison, on the long, flat, damp developments of reclaimed land, the matchbox row houses of the clerical neighborhoods showed lights in every window as the figgers stood ready to repel invasion from their undesired neighbors to the east, the wipes. In the crowded tenements of the laborers' quarters, the wipes shouted from window to window; and there were crowds in the bright streets.

"The whole bloody thing's going to blow up!" a helicopter bombardier yelled bitterly to his pilot, above the flutter and roar of the whirling blades. "Look at the mobs in Greaserville! The first breakout from the Jug's going to start a fight like you never saw and we'll be right in the middle of it!"

He was partly right. He would be right in the middle of it—for every man, woman and child in the city-state would be right in the middle of it. There was no place anywhere that would be spared. *No mixing.* That was the prescription that kept the city-state alive. There's no harm in a family fight—and aren't all mechanics a family, aren't all laborers a clan, aren't all clerks and office workers related by closer ties than blood or skin?

But the declassed cons of the Jug were the dregs of every class; and once they spread, the neat compartmentation of society was pierced. The breakout would mean riot on a bigger scale than any prison had ever known.

But he was also partly wrong. Because the breakout wasn't seeming to come.

*

The Jug itself was coming to a boil.

Honor Block A, relaxed and easy at the end of another day, found itself shaken alert by strange goings-on. First there was the whir and roar of the Air Force overhead. *Trouble.*Then there was the sudden arrival of extra guards, doubling the normal complement—day-shift guards, summoned away from their comfortable civil-service homes at some urgent call. *Trouble for sure.*

Honor Block A wasn't used to trouble. A Block was as far from the Greensleeves of O Block as you could get and still be in the Jug. Honor Block A belonged to the prison's halfbreeds—the honor prisoners, the trusties who did guards' work because there weren't enough guards to go around. They weren't Apaches or Piutes; they were camp-following Injuns who had sold out for the white man's firewater. The price of their service was privilege—many privileges.

Item: TV sets in every cell. Item: Hobby tools, to make gadgets for the visitor trade—the only way an inmate could earn an honest dollar. Item: In consequence, an exact knowledge of everything the outside world knew and put on its TV screens (including the grim, alarming reports of "trouble at Estates-General"), and the capacity to convert their "hobby tools" to—other uses.

An honor prisoner named Wilmer Lafon was watching the TV screen with an expression of rage and despair.

Lafon was a credit to the Jug—he was a showpiece for visitors. Prison rules provided for prisoner training—it was a matter of "rehabilitation." Prisoner rehabilitation is a joke and a centuries-old one at that; but it had its serious uses, and one of them was to keep the prisoners busy. It didn't much matter at what.

Lafon, for instance, was being "rehabilitated" by studying architecture. The guards made a point of bringing inspection delegations to his cell to show him off. There were his walls, covered with pin-ups—but not of women. The pictures were sketches Lafon had drawn himself; they were of buildings, highways, dams and bridges; they were splendidly conceived and immaculately executed.

*

"Looka that!" the guards would rumble to their guests. "There isn't an architect on the outside as good as this boy! What do you say, Wilmer? Tell the gentlemen—how long you been taking these correspondence courses in architecture? Six years! Ever since he came to the Jug."

And Lafon would grin and bob his head, and the delegation would go, with the guards saying something like: "Believe me, that Wilmer could design a whole skyscraper—and it wouldn't fall down, either!"

And they were perfectly, provably right. Not only could Inmate Lafon design a skyscraper, but he had already done so. More than a dozen of them. And none had fallen down.

Of course, that was more than six years back, before he was convicted and sent to the Jug. He would never design another. Or if he did, it would never be built. For the plain fact of the matter was that the Jug's rehabilitation courses were like rehabilitation in every prison since crime and punishment began. They kept the inmates busy. They made a show of purpose for an institution that had never had a purpose beyond punishment.

And that was all.

For punishment for a crime is not satisfied by a jail sentence. How does it hurt a man to feed and clothe and house him, with the bills paid by the state? Lafon's punishment was that he, as an architect, was *through.*

Savage tribes used to lop off a finger or an ear to punish a criminal. Civilized societies confine their amputations to bits and pieces of the personality. Chop-chop, and a man's reputation comes off; chop-chop again, and his professional standing is gone; chop-chop, and he has lost the respect and trust of his fellows.

The jail itself isn't the punishment. The jail is only the shaman's hatchet that performs the amputation. If rehabilitation in a jail worked—if it were *meant* to work—it would be the end of jails.

Rehabilitation? Rehabilitation for what?

*

Wilmer Lafon switched off the television set and silently pounded his fist into the wall.

Never again to return to the Professional class! For, naturally, the conviction had cost him his membership in the Architectural Society and *that* had cost him his Professional standing.

But still—just to be out of the Jug, that would be something! And his whole hope of ever getting out lay not here in Honor Block A, but in the turmoil of the Greensleeves, a hundred meters and more than fifty armed guards away.

He was a furious man. He looked into the cell next door, where a con named Garcia was trying to concentrate on a game of Solitaire Splitfee. Once Garcia had been a Professional, too; he was the closest thing to a friend Wilmer Lafon had. Maybe he could now help to get Lafon where he wanted—*needed!*—to be.

Lafon swore silently and shook his head. Garcia was a spineless milksop, as bad as any clerk—Lafon was nearly sure there was a touch of the inkwell somewhere in his family. Shrewd and slippery enough, like all figgers. But you couldn't rely on him in a pinch.

Lafon would have to do it all himself.

He thought for a second, ignoring the rustle and mumble of the other honor prisoners of Block A. There was no help for it; he would have to dirty his hands with physical activity.

Outside on the deck, the guards were grumbling to each other. Lafon wiped the scowl off his black face, put on a smile, rehearsed what he was going to say, and politely rattled the door of his cell.

"Shut up down there!" one of the screws bawled. Lafon recognized the voice; it was the guard named Sodaro. That was all to the good. He knew Sodaro and he had some plans for him.

He rattled the cell door again and called: "Chief, can you come here a minute, please?"

Sodaro yelled: "Didn't you hear me? Shut up!" But he came wandering by and looked into Lafon's tidy little cell.

"What the devil do you want?" he growled.

Lafon said ingratiatingly: "What's going on, Chief?"

"Shut your mouth," Sodaro said absently and yawned. He hefted his shoulder holster comfortably. That O'Leary, what a production he had made of getting the guards back! And here he was, stuck in Block A on the night he had set aside for getting better acquainted with that little blue-eyed statistician from the Census office.

"Aw, Chief. The television says there's something going on in the Greensleeves. What's the score?"

Sodaro had no reason not to answer him, but it was his unvarying practice to make a con wait before doing anything the con wanted. He gave Lafon a ten-second stare before he relented.

"The score? Sauer and Flock took over Block O. What about it?"

Much, much about it! But Lafon looked away to hide the eagerness in his eyes. Perhaps, after all, it was not too late....

He suggested humbly: "You look a little sleepy. Do you want some coffee?"

"Coffee?" Sodaro scratched. "You got a cup for me?"

"Certainly! I've got one put aside—swiped it from the messhall—not the one I use myself."

"Um." Sodaro leaned on the cell door. "You know I could toss you in the Greensleeves for stealing from the messhall."

*

"Aw, chief!" Lafon grinned.

"You been looking for trouble. O'Leary says you were messing around with the bucks from the laundry detail," Sodaro said halfheartedly. But he didn't really like picking on Lafon, who was, after all, an agreeable inmate to have on occasion. "All right. Where's the coffee?"

They didn't bother with tanglefoot fields in Honor Block A. Sodaro just unlocked the door and walked in, hardly bothering to look at Lafon. He took three steps toward the neat little desk at the back of the cell, where Lafon had rigged up a drawing board and a table, where Lafon kept his little store of luxury goods.

Three steps.

And then, suddenly aware that Lafon was very close to him, he turned, astonished—a little too late. He saw that Lafon had snatched up a metal chair; he saw Lafon swinging it, his black face maniacal; he saw the chair coming down.

He reached for his shoulder holster, but it was very much too late for that.

V

Captain O'Leary dragged the scared little wretch into the warden's office. He shook the con angrily. "Listen to this, Warden! The boys just brought this one in from the Shops Building. Do you know what he's been up to?"

The warden wheezed sadly and looked away. He had stopped even answering O'Leary by now. He had stopped talking to Sauer on the interphone when the big convict called, every few minutes, to rave and threaten and demand a doctor. He had almost stopped doing everything except worry and weep. But—still and all, he was the warden. He was the one who gave the orders.

O'Leary barked: "Warden, this little greaser has bollixed up the whole tangler circuit for the prison. If the cons get out into the yard now, you won't be able to tangle them. You know what that means? They'll have the freedom of the yard, and who knows what comes next?"

The warden frowned sympathetically. "Tsk, tsk."

O'Leary shook the con again. "Come on, Hiroko! Tell the warden what you told the guards."

The con shrank away from him. Sweat was glistening on his furrowed yellow forehead. "I—I had to do it, Cap'n! I shorted the wormcan in the tangler subgrid, but I had to! I got a signal—'Bollix the grid tonight or some day you'll be in the yard and we'll static you!' What could I do, Cap'n? I didn't want to—"

O'Leary pressed: "Who did the signal come from?"

The con only shook his head, perspiring still more.

The warden asked faintly: "What's he saying?"

O'Leary rolled his eyes to heaven. And this was the warden—couldn't even understand shoptalk from the mouths of his own inmates!

He translated: "He got orders from the prison underground to short-circuit the electronic units in the tangler circuit. They threatened to kill him if he didn't."

The warden drummed with his fingers on the desk.

"The tangler field, eh? My, yes. That is important. You'd better get it fixed, O'Leary. Right away."

"Fixed? Warden, who's going to fix it? You know as well as I do that every mechanic in the prison is a con. Even if one of the guards would do a thing like that—and I'd bust him myself if he did!—he wouldn't know where to start. That's mechanic work."

The warden swallowed. He had to admit that O'Leary was right. Naturally nobody but a mechanic—and a specialist electrician from a particular subgroup of the greaser class at that—could fix something like the tangler field generators.

He said absently: "Well, that's true enough. After all, 'Specialization is the goal of civilization,' you know."

O'Leary took a deep breath. He needed it.

He beckoned to the guard at the door. "Take this greaser out of here!"

The con shambled out, his head hanging.

*

O'Leary turned to the warden and spread his hands.

"Warden," he said, "don't you see how this thing is building up? Let's not just wait for the place to explode in our faces! Let me take a squad into Block O before it's too late."

The warden pursed his lips thoughtfully and cocked his head, as though he were trying to find some trace of merit in an unreasonable request.

He said at last: "No."

O'Leary made a passionate sound that was trying to be bad language, but he was too raging mad to articulate it. He walked stiffly away from the limp, silent warden and stared out the window.

At least, he told himself, *he* hadn't gone to pieces. It was his doing, not the warden's, that all the off-duty guards had been dragged double-time back to the prison, his doing that they were now ringed around the outer walls or scattered on extra-man patrols throughout the prison.

It was something, but O'Leary couldn't believe that it was enough. He'd been in touch with half a dozen of the details inside the prison on the intercom and each of them had reported the same thing. In all of E-G, not a single prisoner was asleep. They were talking back and forth between the cells and the guards couldn't shut them up. They were listening to concealed radios and the guards didn't dare make a shakedown to find them. They were working themselves up to something. To what?

O'Leary didn't want ever to find out what. He wanted to go in there with a couple of the best guards he could get his hands on—shoot his way into the Greensleeves if he had to—and clean out the infection.

But the warden said no.

O'Leary stared balefully at the hovering helicopters.

The warden was the warden. He was placed in that position through the meticulously careful operations of the Civil Service machinery, maintained in that position year after year through the penetrating annual inquiries of the Reclassification Board. It was*subversive* to think that the Board could have made a mistake!

But O'Leary was absolutely sure that the warden was a scared, ineffectual jerk.

*

The interphone was ringing again. The warden picked up the handpiece and held it bonelessly at arm's length, his eyes fixed glassily on the wall. It was Sauer from the Greensleeves again. O'Leary could hear his maddened bray.

"I warned you, Warden!" O'Leary could see the big con's contorted face in miniature, in the view screen of the interphone. The grin was broad and jolly, the snake's eyes poisonously cold. "I'm going to give you five minutes, Warden, you hear? Five minutes! And if there isn't a medic in here in five minutes to take care of my boy Flock—your guards have had it! I'm going to slice off an ear and throw it out the window, you hear me? And five minutes later, another ear. And five minutes later—"

The warden groaned weakly. "I've called for the prison medic, Sauer. Honestly I have! I'm sure he's coming as rapidly as he—"

"Five minutes!" And the ferociously grinning face disappeared.

O'Leary leaned forward. "Warden, let me take a squad in there!"

The warden gazed at him for a blank moment "Squad? No, O'Leary. What's the use of a squad? It's a medic I have to get in there. I have a responsibility to those guards and if I don't get a medic—"

A cold, calm voice from the door: "I am here, Warden."

O'Leary and the warden both jumped up.

The medic nodded slightly. "You may sit down."

"Oh, Doctor! Thank heaven you're here!" The warden was falling all over himself, getting a chair for his guest, flustering about.

O'Leary said sharply: "Wait a minute, Warden. You can't let the doctor go in alone!"

"He isn't alone!" The doctor's intern came from behind him, scowling belligerently at O'Leary. Youngish, his beard pale and silky, he was a long way from his first practice. "I'm here to assist him!"

O'Leary put a strain on his patience. "They'll eat you up in there, Doc! Those are the worst cons in the prison. They've got two hostages already. What's the use of giving them two more?"

The medic fixed him with his eyes. He was a tall man and he wore his beard proudly. "Guard, do you think you can prevent me from healing a sufferer?" He folded his hands over his abdomen and turned to leave.

The intern stepped aside and bowed his head.

O'Leary surrendered. "All right, you can go. But I'm coming with you—with a squad!"

*

Inmate Sue-Ann Bradley cowered in her cell. The Greensleeves was jumping. She had never—no, *never*, she told herself wretchedly—thought that it would be anything like this. She listened unbelievingly to the noise the released prisoners were making, smashing the chairs and commodes in their cells, screaming threats at the bound guards.

She faced the thought with fear, and with the sorrow of a murdered belief that was worse than fear. It was bad that she was in danger of dying right here and now, but what was even worse was that the principles that had brought her to the Jug were dying, too.

Wipes were *not* the same as Civil-Service people!

A bull's roar from the corridor and a shocking crash of glass—that was Flock, and apparently he had smashed the TV interphone.

"What in the world are they *doing*?" Inmate Bradley sobbed to herself. It was beyond comprehension. They were yelling words that made no sense to her, threatening punishments on the guards that she could barely imagine. Sauer and Flock were laborers; some of the other rioting cons were clerks, mechanics—even Civil-Service or Professionals, for all she could tell. But she could hardly understand any of them. Why was the quiet little Chinese clerk in Cell Six setting fire to his bed?

There did seem to be a pattern, of sorts. The laborers were rocketing about, breaking things at random. The mechanics were pleasurably sabotaging the electronic and plumbing installations. The white-collar categories were finding their dubious joys in less direct ways—liking setting fire to a bed. But what a mad pattern!

The more Sue-Ann saw of them, the less she understood.

It wasn't just that they *talked* differently. She had spent endless hours studying the various patois of shoptalk and it had defeated her; but it wasn't just that.

It was bad enough when she couldn't understand the words—as when that trusty Mathias had ordered her in wipe shoptalk to mop out her cell. But what was even worse was not understanding the thought behind the words.

Sue-Ann Bradley had consecrated her young life to the belief that all men were created free and equal—and alike. Or alike in all the things that mattered, anyhow. Alike in hopes, alike in motives, alike in virtues. She had turned her back on a decent Civil-Service family and a promising Civil-Service career to join the banned and despised Association for the Advancement of the Categoried Classes—

Screams from the corridor outside.

Sue-Ann leaped to the door of her cell to see Sauer clutching at one of the guards. The guard's hands were tied, but his feet were free; he broke loose from the clumsy clown with the serpent's eyes, almost fell, ran toward Sue-Ann.

There was nowhere else to run. The guard, moaning and gasping, tripped, slid, caught himself and stumbled into her cell. "Please!" he begged. "That crazy Sauer—he's going to cut my ear off! For heaven's sake, ma'am—stop him!"

*

Sue-Ann stared at him, between terror and tears. Stop Sauer! If only she could. The big redhead was lurching stiffly toward them—raging, but not so angry that the water-moccasin eyes showed heat.

"Come here, you figger scum!" he roared.

The epithet wasn't even close—the guard was Civil Service through and through—but it was like a reviving whip-sting to Sue-Ann Bradley.

"Watch your language, Mr. Sauer!" she snapped incongruously.

Sauer stopped dead and blinked.

"Don't you dare hurt him!" she warned. "Don't you see, Mr. Sauer, you're playing into their hands? They're trying to divide us. They pit mechanic against clerk, laborer against armed forces. And you're helping them! Brother Sauer, I beg—"

The redhead spat deliberately on the floor.

He licked his lips, and grinned an amiable clown's grin, and said in his cheerful, buffoon bray: "Auntie, go verb your adjective adjective noun."

Sue-Ann Bradley gasped and turned white. She had known such words existed—but only theoretically. She had never expected to *hear* them. And certainly she would never have believed she would hear them, applied to her, from the lips of a—a *laborer*.

At her knees, the guard shrieked and fell to the floor.

"Sauer! Sauer!" A panicky bellow from the corridor; the red-haired giant hesitated. "Sauer, come on out here! There's a million guards coming up the stairs. Looks like trouble!"

Sauer said hoarsely to the unconscious guard: "I'll take care of *you*." And he looked blankly at the girl, and shook his head, and hurried back outside to the corridor.

Guards were coming, all right—not a million of them, but half a dozen or more. And leading them all was the medic, calm, bearded face looking straight ahead, hands clasped before him, ready to heal the sick, comfort the aged or bring new life into the world.

"Hold it!" shrieked little Flock, crouched over the agonizing blister on his abdomen, gun in hand, peering insanely down the steps. "Hold it or—"

"Shut up." Sauer called softly to the approaching group: "Let only the doc come up. Nobody else!"

The intern faltered; the guards stopped dead; the medic said calmly: "I must have my intern with me." He glanced at the barred gate wonderingly.

Sauer hesitated. "Well—all right. But no guards!"

A few yards away, Sue-Ann Bradley was stuffing the syncoped form of the guard into her small washroom.

It was time to take a stand. No more cowering, she told herself desperately. No more waiting. She closed the door on the guard, still unconscious, and stood grimly before it. Him, at least, she would save if she could. They could get him, but only over her dead body.

Or anyway, she thought with a sudden throbbing in her throat, over her body.

VI

After O'Leary and the medic left, the warden tottered to a chair—but not for long. His secretary appeared, eyes bulging. "The governor!" he gasped.

Warden Schluckebier managed to say: "Why, Governor! How good of you to come—"

The governor shook him off and held the door open for the men who had come with him. There were reporters from all the news services, officials from the township governments within the city-state. There was an Air GI with major's leaves on his collar—"Liaison, sir," he explained crisply to the warden, "just in case you have any orders for our men up there." There were nearly a dozen others.

The warden was quite overcome.

The governor rapped out: "Warden, no criticism of you, of course, but I've come to take personal charge. I'm superseding you under Rule Twelve, Paragraph A, of the Uniform Civil Service Code. Right?"

"Oh, *right!*" cried the warden, incredulous with joy.

"The situation is bad—perhaps worse than you think. I'm seriously concerned about the hostages those men have in there. And I had a call from Senator Bradley a short time ago—"

"Senator Bradley?" echoed the warden.

"Senator *Sebastian* Bradley. One of our foremost civil servants," the governor said firmly. "It so happens that his daughter is in Block O as an inmate."

The warden closed his eyes. He tried to swallow, but the throat muscles were paralyzed.

"There is no question," the governor went on briskly, "about the propriety of her being there. She was duly convicted of a felonious act, namely conspiracy and incitement to riot. But you see the position."

The warden saw all too well.

"Therefore," said the governor. "I intend to go in to Block O myself. Sebastian Bradley is an old and personal friend—as well," he emphasized, "as being a senior member of the Reclassification Board. I understand a medic is going to Block O. I shall go with him."

The warden managed to sit up straight. "He's gone. I mean they already left, Governor. But I assure you Miss Brad—Inmate Bradley—that is, the young lady is in no danger. I have already taken precautions," he said, gaining confidence as he listened to himself talk. "I—uh—I was deciding on a course of action as you came in. See, Governor, the guards on the walls are all armed. All they have to do is fire a couple of rounds into the yard and then the 'copters could start dropping tear gas and light fragmentation bombs and—"

The governor was already at the door. "You will *not*," he said; and: "Now which way did they go?"

*

O'Leary was in the yard and he was smelling trouble, loud and strong. The first he knew that the rest of the prison had caught the riot fever was when the lights flared on in Cell Block A.

"That Sodaro!" he snarled, but there wasn't time to worry about that Sodaro. He grabbed the rest of his guard detail and double-timed it toward the New Building, leaving the medic and a couple of guards walking sedately toward the Old. Block A, on the New Building's lowest tier, was already coming to life; a dozen yards, and Blocks B and C lighted up.

And a dozen yards more and they could hear the yelling; and it wasn't more than a minute before the building doors opened.

The cons had taken over three more blocks. How? O'Leary didn't take time even to guess. The inmates were piling out into the yard. He took one look at the rushing mob. Crazy! It was Wilmer Lafon leading the rioters, with a guard's gun and a voice screaming threats! But O'Leary didn't take time to worry about an honor prisoner gone bad, either.

"Let's get out of here!" he bellowed to the detachment, and they ran.

Just plain ran. Cut and ran, scattering as they went.

"Wait!" screamed O'Leary, but they weren't waiting. Cursing himself for letting them get out of hand, O'Leary salvaged two guards and headed on the run for the Old Building, huge and dark, all but the topmost lights of Block O.

They saw the medic and his escort disappearing into the bulk of the Old Building and they saw something else. There were inmates between them and the Old Building! The Shops Building lay between—with a dozen more cell blocks over the workshops that gave it its name—and there was a milling rush of activity around its entrance, next to the laundry shed—

The laundry shed.

O'Leary stood stock still. Lafon leading the breakout from Block A. The little greaser who was a trusty in the Shops Building sabotaging the yard's tangler circuit. Sauer and Flock taking over the Greensleeves with a manufactured knife and a lot of guts.

Did it fit together? Was it all part of a plan?

That was something to find out—but not just then. "Come on," O'Leary cried to the two guards, and they raced for the temporary safety of the main gates.

The whole prison was up and yelling now.

O'Leary could hear scattered shots from the beat guards on the wall—*Over their heads, over their heads!* he prayed silently. And there were other shots that seemed to come from inside the walls—guards shooting, or convicts with guards' guns, he couldn't tell which. The yard was full of convicts now, in bunches and clumps; but none near the gate. And they seemed to have lost some of their drive. They were milling around, lit by the searchlights from the wall, yelling and making a lot of noise ... but going nowhere in particular. Waiting for a leader, O'Leary thought, and wondered briefly what had become of Lafon.

"You Captain O'Leary?" somebody demanded.

*

He turned and blinked. Good Lord, the governor! He was coming through the gate, waving aside the gate guards, alone. "You him?" the governor repeated. "All right, glad I found you. I'm going into Block O with you."

O'Leary swallowed and waved inarticulately at the teeming cons. True, there were none immediately near by—but there were plenty in the yard! Riots meant breaking things up; already the inmates had started to break up the machines in the laundry shed and the athletic equipment in the yard lockers. When they found a couple of choice breakables like O'Leary and the governor, they'd have a ball!

"But, Governor—"

"But my foot! Can you get me in there or can't you?"

O'Leary gauged their chances. It wasn't more than fifty feet to the main entrance to the Old Building—not at the moment guarded, since all the guards were in hiding or on the walls, and not as yet being invaded by the inmates at large.

He said: "You're the boss. Hold on a minute—" The searchlights were on the bare yard cobblestones in front of them; in a moment, the searchlights danced away.

"Come on!" cried O'Leary, and jumped for the entrance. The governor was with him and a pair of the guards came stumbling after.

They made it to the Old Building.

Inside the entrance, they could hear the noise from outside and the yelling of the inmates who were still in their cells. But around them was nothing but gray steel walls and the stairs going all the way up to Block O.

"Up!" panted O'Leary, and they clattered up the steel steps.

They would have made it—if it hadn't been for the honor inmate, Wilmer Lafon, who knew what he was after and had headed for the Greensleeves through the back way. In fact, they did make it—but not the way they planned. "Get out of the way!" yelled O'Leary at Lafon and the half-dozen inmates with him; and "Go to hell!" screamed Lafon, charging; and it was a rough-and-tumble fight, and O'Leary's party lost it, fair and square.

So when they got to Block O, it was with the governor marching before a convict-held gun, and with O'Leary cold unconscious, a lump from a gun-butt on the side of his head.

*

As they came up the stairs, Sauer was howling at the medic: "You got to fix up my boy! He's dying and all you do is sit there!"

The medic said patiently: "My son, I've dressed his wound. He is under sedation and I must rest. There will be other casualties."

Sauer raged, but that was as far as it went. Even Sauer wouldn't attack a medic. He would as soon strike an Attorney, or even a Director of Funerals. It wasn't merely that they were Professionals. Even among the Professional class, they were special; not superior, exactly, but *apart*. They certainly were not for the likes of Sauer to fool with and Sauer knew it.

"Somebody's coming!" bawled one of the other freed inmates.

*

Sauer jumped to the head of the steps, saw that Lafon was leading the group, stepped back, saw whom Lafon's helpers were carrying and leaped forward again.

"Cap'n O'Leary!" he roared. "Gimme!"

"Shut up," said Wilmer Lafon, and pushed the big redhead out of the way. Sauer's jaw dropped and the snake eyes opened wide.

"Wilmer," he protested feebly. But that was all the protest he made, because the snake's eyes had seen that Lafon held a gun. He stood back, the big hands half outstretched toward the unconscious guard captain, O'Leary, and the cold eyes became thoughtful.

And then he saw who else was with the party. "Wilmer! You got the governor there!"

Lafon nodded. "Throw them in a cell," he ordered, and sat down on a guard's stool, breathing hard. It had been a fine fight on the steps, before he and his boys had subdued the governor and the guards, but Wilmer Lafon wasn't used to fighting. Even six years in the Jug hadn't turned an architect into a laborer; physical exertion simply was not his metier.

Sauer said coaxingly: "Wilmer, won't you leave me have O'Leary for a while? If it wasn't for me and Flock, you'd still be in A Block and—"

"Shut up," Lafon said again, gently enough, but he waved the gun muzzle. He drew a deep breath, glanced around him and grinned. "If it wasn't for you and Flock," he mimicked. "If it wasn't for you and Flock! Sauer, you wipe clown, do you think it took*brains* to file down a shiv and start things rolling? If it wasn't for *me*, you and Flock would have beaten up a few guards, and had your kicks for half an hour, and then the whole prison would fall in on you! It was me, Wilmer Lafon, who set things up and you know it!"

He was yelling and suddenly he realized he was yelling. And what was the use, he demanded of himself contemptuously, of trying to argue with a bunch of lousy wipes and greasers? They'd never understand the long, soul-killing hours of planning and sweat. They wouldn't realize the importance of the careful timing—of arranging that the laundry cons would start a disturbance in the yard right after the Greensleeves hard-timers kicked off the riot, of getting the little greaser Hiroko to short-circuit the yard field so the laundry cons could start their disturbances.

It took a *Professional* to organize and plan—yes, and to make sure that he himself was out of it until everything was ripe, so that if anything went wrong, *he* was all right. It took somebody like Wilmer Lafon—a *Professional*, who had spent six years too long in the Jug—

And who would shortly be getting out.

VII

Any prison is a ticking bomb. Estates-General was in process of going off.

From the Greensleeves, where the trouble had started, clear out to the trusty farms that ringed the walls, every inmate was up and jumping. Some were still in their cells—the scared ones, the decrepit oldsters, the short-termers who didn't dare risk their early discharge. But for every man in his cell, a dozen were out and yelling.

A torch, licking as high as the hanging helicopters, blazing up from the yard—that was the laundry shed. Why burn the laundry? The cons couldn't have said. It was burnable and it was there—burn it!

The yard lay open to the wrath of the helicopters, but the helicopters made no move. The cobblestones were solidly covered with milling men. The guards were on the walls, sighting down their guns; the helicopter bombardiers had their fingers on the bomb trips. There had been a few rounds fired over the heads of the rioters, at first.

Nothing since.

In the milling mob, the figures clustered in groups. The inmates from Honor Block A huddled under the guards' guns at the angle of the wall. They had clubs—all the inmates had clubs—but they weren't using them.

Honor Block A: On the outside, Civil Service and Professionals. On the inside, the trusties, the "good" cons.

They weren't the type for clubs.

With all of the inmates, you looked at them and you wondered what twisted devil had got into their heads to land them in the Jug. Oh, perhaps you could understand it—a little bit, at least—in the case of the figgers in Blocks B and C, the greasers in the Shop Building—that sort. It was easy enough for some of the Categoried Classes to commit a crime and thereby land in jail.

Who could blame a wipe for trying to "pass" if he thought he could get away with it? But when he didn't get away with it, he wound up in the Jug and that was logical enough. And greasers liked Civil-Service women—everyone knew that.

There was almost a sort of logic to it, even if it was a sort of inevitable logic that made decent Civil-Service people see red. You *had* to enforce the laws against rape if, for instance, a greaser should ask an innocent young female postal clerk for a date. But you could understand what drove him to it. The Jug was full of criminals of that sort. And the Jug was the place for them.

But what about Honor Block A?

Why would a Wilmer Lafon—a certified public architect, a Professional by category—do his own car repairs and get himself jugged for malpractice? Why would a dental nurse sneak back into the laboratory at night and cast an upper plate for her mother? She must have realized she would be caught.

But she had done it. And she had been caught; and there she was, this wild night, huddled under the helicopters, uncertainly waving the handle of a floor mop. It was a club.

She shivered and turned to the stocky convict next to her. "Why don't they break down the gate?" she demanded. "How long are we going to hang around here, waiting for the guards to get organized and pick us all off one at a time?"

The convict next to her sighed and wiped his glasses with a beefy hand. Once he had been an Income-Tax Accountant, disbarred and convicted on three counts of impersonating an attorney when he took the liberty of making changes in a client's lease. He snorted: "They expect us to do *their* dirty work."

The two of them glared angrily and fearfully at the other convicts in the yard.

And the other convicts, huddled greaser with greaser, wipe with wipe, glared ragingly back. It wasn't *their* place to plan the strategy of a prison break.

*

Captain Liam O'Leary muttered groggily: "They don't want to escape. All they want is to make trouble. I know cons!"

He came fully awake and sat up and focused his eyes. His head was hammering.

That girl, that Bradley, was leaning over him. She looked scared and sick. "Sit still! Sauer is just plain crazy—listen to them yelling out there!"

O'Leary sat up and looked around, one hand holding his drumming skull.

"They *do* want to escape," said Sue-Ann Bradley. "Listen to what they're saying!"

*

O'Leary discovered that he was in a cell. There was a battle going on outside. Men were yelling, but he couldn't see them.

He jumped up, remembering. "The governor!"

Sue-Ann Bradley said: "He's all right. I *think* he is, anyway. He's in the cell right next to us, with a couple guards. I guess they came up with you." She shivered as the yells in the corridor rose. "Sauer is angry at the medic," she explained. "He wants him to fix Flock up so they can—'crush out,' I think he said. The medic says he can't do it. You see, Flock got burned pretty badly with a knife he made. Something about the tanglefoot field—"

"Eddy currents," said O'Leary dizzily.

"Anyway, the medic—"

"Never mind the medic. What's Lafon doing?"

"Lafon? The Negro?" Sue-Ann Bradley frowned. "I didn't know his name. He started the whole thing, the way it sounds. They're waiting for the mob down in the yard to break out and then they're going to make a break—"

"Wait a minute," growled O'Leary. His head was beginning to clear. "What about you? Are you in on this?"

She hung between laughter and tears. Finally: "Do I *look* as if I am?"

O'Leary took stock. Somehow, somewhere, the girl had got a length of metal pipe—from the plumbing, maybe. She was holding it in one hand, supporting him with the other. There were two other guards in the cell, both out cold—one from O'Leary's squad, the other, O'Leary guessed, a desk guard who had been on duty when the trouble started.

"I wouldn't let them in," she said wildly. "I told them they'd have to kill me before they could touch that guard."

O'Leary said suspiciously: "You belonged to that Double-A-C, didn't you? You were pretty anxious to get in the Greensleeves, disobeying Auntie Mathias's orders. Are you sure you didn't know this was going to—"

It was too much. She dropped the pipe, buried her head in her hands. He couldn't tell if she laughed or wept, but he could tell that it hadn't been like that at all.

"I'm sorry," he said awkwardly, and touched her helplessly on the shoulder.

*

He turned and looked out the little barred window, because he couldn't think of any additional way to apologize. He heard the wavering beat in the air and saw them—bobbing a hundred yards up, their wide metal vanes fluttering and hissing from the jets at the tips. The GI 'copters. Waiting—as everyone seemed to be waiting.

Sue-Ann Bradley asked shakily: "Is anything the matter?"

O'Leary turned away. It was astonishing, he thought, what a different perspective he had on those helicopter bombers from inside Block O. Once he had cursed the warden for not ordering at least tear gas to be dropped.

He said harshly: "Nothing. Just that the 'copters have the place surrounded."

"Does it make any difference?"

He shrugged. Does it make a difference? The difference between trouble and tragedy, or so it now seemed to Captain O'Leary. The riot was trouble. They could handle it, one way or another. It was his job, any guard's job, to handle *prison* trouble.

But to bring the GIs into it was to invite race riot. Not prison riot—race riot. Even the declassed scum in the Jug would fight back against the GIs.

They were used to having the Civil-Service guards over them—that was what guards were for. Civil-Service guards guarded. What else? It was their job—as clerking was a rigger's job, and machines were a greaser's, and pick-and-shovel strong-arm work was a wipe's.

But the Armed Services—their job was to defend the country against forces outside—in a world that had only inside forces. The cons wouldn't hold still under attack from the GIs.*Race riot!*

But how could you tell that to a girl like this Bradley? O'Leary glanced at her covertly. She *looked* all right. Rather nice-looking, if anything. But he hadn't forgotten why she was in E-G. Joining a terrorist organization, the Association for the Advancement of the Categoried Classes.

Actually getting up on street corners and proposing that greasers' children be allowed to go to school with GIs, that wipes inter-marry with Civil Service. Good Lord, they'd be suggesting that doctors eat with laymen next!

The girl said evenly: "Don't look at me that way. I'm not a monster."

O'Leary coughed. "Sorry. I didn't know I was staring." She looked at him with cold eyes. "I mean," he said, "you don't *look* like anybody who'd get mixed up in—well, miscegenation."

"Miscegenation!" she blazed. "You're all alike! You talk about the mission of the Categoried Classes and the rightness of segregation, but it's always just the one thing that's in your minds—sex! I'll tell you this, Captain O'Leary—I'd rather many a decent, hard-working clerk any day than the sort of Civil-Service trash I've seen around here!"

O'Leary cringed. He couldn't help it. Funny, he told himself, I thought I was shockproof—but this goes too far!

A bull-roar from the corridor. Sauer.

O'Leary spun. The big redhead was yelling: "Bring the governor out here. Lafon wants to talk to him!"

*

O'Leary went to the door of the cell, fast.

A slim, pale con from Block A was pushing the governor down the hall, toward Sauer and Lafon. The governor was a strong man, but he didn't struggle. His face was as composed and remote as the medic's; if he was afraid, he concealed it extremely well.

Sue-Ann Bradley stood beside O'Leary. "What's happening?"

He kept his eyes on what was going on. "Lafon is going to try to use the governor as a shield, I think." The voice of Lafon was loud, but the noises outside made it hard to understand. But O'Leary could make out what the dark ex-Professional was saying: "—know damn well you did something. But what? *Why don't they crush out?*"

Mumble-mumble from the Governor. O'Leary couldn't hear the words.

But he could see the effect of them in Lafon's face, hear the rage in Lafon's voice. "Don't call me a liar, you civvy punk! You did something. I had it all planned, do you hear me? The laundry boys were going to rush the gate, the Block A bunch would follow—and then I was going to breeze right through. But you loused it up somehow. You must've!"

His voice was rising to a scream. O'Leary, watching tautly from the cell, thought: He's going to break. He can't hold it in much longer.

"All *right*!" shouted Lafon, and even Sauer, looming behind him, looked alarmed. "It doesn't matter what you did. I've got you now and *you* are going to get me out of here. You hear? I've got this gun and the two of us are going to walk right out, through the gate, and if anybody tries to stop us—"

"Hey," said Sauer, waking up.

"—if anybody tries to stop us, you'll get a bullet right in—"

"*Hey!*" Sauer was roaring loud as Lafon himself now. "What's this talk about the *two* of you? You aren't going to leave me and Flock!"

"Shut up," Lafon said conversationally, without taking his eyes off the governor.

But Sauer, just then, was not the man to say "shut up" to, and especially he was not a man to take your eyes away from.

"That's torn it," O'Leary said aloud. The girl started to say something.

But he was no longer there to hear.

It looked very much as though Sauer and Lafon were going to tangle. And when they did, it was the end of the line for the governor.

*

Captain O'Leary hurtled out of the sheltering cell and skidded down the corridor. Lafon's face was a hawk's face, gleaming with triumph. As he saw O'Leary coming toward him, the hawk sneer froze. He brought the gun up, but O'Leary was a fast man.

O'Leary leaped on the lithe black honor prisoner. Lafon screamed and clutched; and O'Leary's lunging weight drove him back against the wall. Lafon's arm smacked against the steel grating and the gun went flying. The two of them clinched and fell, gouging, to the floor.

Grabbing the advantage, O'Leary hammered the con's head against the deck, hard enough to split a skull. And perhaps it split Lafon's, because the dark face twitched and froth appeared at the lips; and the body slacked.

One down!

Now Sauer was charging. O'Leary wriggled sidewise and the big redhead blundered crashing into the steel grate. Sauer fell and O'Leary caught at him. He tried hammering the head as he swarmed on top of the huge clown. But Sauer only roared the louder. The bull body surged under O'Leary and then Sauer was on top and O'Leary wasn't breathing. Not at all.

Good-by, Sue-Ann, O'Leary said silently, without meaning to say anything of the kind; and even then he wondered why he was saying it.

O'Leary heard a gun explode beside his head.

Amazing, he thought, I'm breathing again! The choking hands were gone from his throat.

It took him a moment to realize that it was Sauer who had taken the bullet, not him. Sauer who now lay dead, not O'Leary. But he realized it when he rolled over, and looked up, and saw the girl with the gun still in her hand, staring at him and weeping.

He sat up. The two guards still able to walk were backing Sue-Ann Bradley up. The governor was looking proud as an eagle, pleased as a mother hen.

The Greensleeves was back in the hands of law and order.

The medic came toward O'Leary, hands folded. "My son," he said, "if your throat needs—"

O'Leary interrupted him. "I don't need a thing, Doc! I've got everything I want right now."

VIII

Inmate Sue-Ann Bradley cried: "They're coming! O'Leary, they're coming!"

The guards who had once been hostages clattered down the steps to meet the party. The cons from the Greensleeves were back in their cells. The medic, after finishing his chores on O'Leary himself, paced meditatively out into the wake of the riot, where there was plenty to keep him busy. A faintly guilty expression tinctured his carven face. Contrary to his oath to care for all humanity in anguish, he had not liked Lafon or Sauer.

The party of fresh guards appeared and efficiently began re-locking the cells of the Greensleeves.

"Excuse me, Cap'n," said one, taking Sue-Ann Bradley by the arm. "I'll just put this one back—"

"I'll take care of her," said Liam O'Leary. He looked at her sideways as he rubbed the bruises on his face.

The governor tapped him on the shoulder. "Come along," he said, looking so proud of himself, so pleased. "Let's go out in the yard for a breath of fresh air." He smiled contentedly at Sue-Ann Bradley. "You, too."

O'Leary protested instinctively: "But she's an inmate!"

"And I'm a governor. Come along."

They walked out into the yard. The air was fresh, all right. A handful of cons, double-guarded by sleepy and irritable men from the day shift, were hosing down the rubble on the cobblestones. The yard was a mess, but it was quiet now. The helicopters were still riding their picket line, glowing softly in the early light that promised sunrise.

"My car," the governor said quietly to a state policeman who appeared from nowhere. The trooper snapped a salute and trotted away.

"I killed a man," said Sue-Ann Bradley, looking a little ill.

"You saved a man," corrected the governor. "Don't weep for that Lafon. He was willing to kill a thousand men if he had to, to break out of here."

"But he never did break out," said Sue-Ann.

The governor stretched contentedly. "He never had a chance. Laborers and clerks join together in a breakout? It would never happen. They don't even speak the same language—as you have discovered, my dear."

*

Sue-Ann blazed: "I still believe in the equality of Man!"

"Oh, please do," the governor said, straight-faced. "There's nothing wrong with that. Your father and I are perfectly willing to admit that men are equal—but we can't admit that all men are the *same*. Use your eyes! What you believe in is your business, but," he added, "when your beliefs extend to setting fire to segregated public lavatories as a protest move, which is what got you arrested, you apparently need to be taught a lesson. Well, perhaps you've learned it. You were a help here tonight and that counts for a lot."

Captain O'Leary said, face furrowed: "What about the warden, Governor? They say the category system is what makes the world go round; it fits the right man to the right job and keeps him there. But look at Warden Schluckebier! He fell completely apart at the seams. He—"

"Turn that statement around, O'Leary."

"Turn—?"

The governor nodded. "You've got it reversed. Not the right man for the job—the right job for the man! We've got Schluckebier on our hands, see? He's been born; it's too late to do anything about that. He will go to pieces in an emergency. So where do we put him?"

O'Leary stubbornly clamped his jaw, frowning.

"We put him," the governor went on gently, "where the best thing to *do* in a crisis is to go to pieces! Why, O'Leary, you get some hot-headed man of action in here, and every time an inmate sneezes, you'll have bloodshed! And there's no harm in a prison riot. Let the poor devils work off steam. I wouldn't have bothered to get out of bed for it—except I was worried about the hostages. So I came down to make sure they were protected in the best possible way."

O'Leary's jaw dropped. "But you were—"

The governor nodded. "I was a hostage myself. That's one way to protect them, isn't it? By giving the cons a hostage that's worth more to them."

He yawned and looked around for his car. "So the world keeps going around," he said. "Everybody is somebody else's outgroup and maybe it's a bad thing, but did you ever stop to realize that we don't have wars any more? The categories stick tightly together. Who is to say that that's a bad thing?"

He grinned. "Reminds me of a story, if you two will pay attention to me long enough to listen. There was a meeting—this is an old, *old* story—a neighborhood meeting of the leaders of the two biggest women's groups on the block. There were eighteen Irish ladies from the Church Auxiliary and three Jewish ladies from B'nai B'rith. The first thing they did was have an election for a temporary chairwoman. Twenty-one votes were cast. Mrs. Grossinger from B'nai B'rith got three and Mrs. O'Flaherty from the Auxiliary got eighteen. So when Mrs. Murphy came up to congratulate Mrs. O'Flaherty after the election, she whispered: 'Good for you! But isn't it terrible, the way these Jews stick together?'"

He stood up and waved a signal as his long official car came poking hesitantly through the gate.

"Well," he declared professionally, "that's that. As we politicians say, any questions?"

Sue-Ann hesitated. "Yes, I guess I do have a question," she said. "What's a Jew?"

*

It was full dawn at last. The recall signal had come and the helicopters were swooping home to Hap Arnold Field.

A bombardier named Novak, red-eyed and grumpy, was amusing himself on the homeward flight by taking practice sights on the stream of work-bound mechanics as they fluttered over Greaserville.

"Could pick 'em off like pigeons," he said sourly to his pilot, as he dropped an imaginary bomb on a cluster of a dozen men. "For two cents, I'd do it, too. The only good greaser is a dead greaser."

His pilot, just as weary, said loftily: "Leave them alone. The best way to handle them is to leave them alone."

And the pilot was perfectly right; and that was the way the world went round, spinning slowly and unstoppably toward the dawn.

A LITTLE JOURNEY

By Ray Bradbury

She'd paid good money to see the inevitable ...and then had to work to make it happen!

*

There were two important things—one, that she was very old; two, that Mr. Thirkell was taking her to God. For hadn't he patted her hand and said: "Mrs. Bellowes, we'll take off into space in my rocket, and go to find Him together."

And that was how it was going to be. Oh, this wasn't like any other group Mrs. Bellowes had ever joined. In her fervor to light a path for her delicate, tottering feet, she had struck matches down dark alleys, and found her way to Hindu mystics who floated their flickering, starry eyelashes over crystal balls. She had walked on the meadow paths with ascetic Indian philosophers imported by daughters-in-spirit of Madame Blavatsky. She had made pilgrimages to California's stucco jungles to hunt the astrological seer in his natural habitat. She had even consented to signing away the rights to one of her homes in order to be taken into the shouting order of a temple of amazing evangelists who had promised her golden smoke, crystal fire, and the great soft hand of God coming to bear her home.

None of these people had ever shaken Mrs. Bellowes' faith, even when she saw them sirened away in a black wagon in the night, or discovered their pictures, bleak and unromantic, in the morning tabloids. The world had roughed them up and locked them away because they knew too much, that was all.

And then, two weeks ago, she had seen Mr. Thirkell's advertisement in New York City:

COME TO MARS!

Stay at the Thirkell Restorium for one week. And then,
on into space on the greatest adventure life can offer!
Send for Free Pamphlet: "Nearer My God To Thee."
Excursion rates. Round trip slightly lower.

"Round trip," Mrs. Bellowes had thought. "But who would come back after seeing Him?"

And so she had bought a ticket and flown off to Mars and spent seven mild days at Mr. Thirkell's Restorium, the building with the sign on it which flashed: THIRKELL'S ROCKET TO HEAVEN! She had spent the week bathing in limpid waters and erasing the care from her tiny bones, and now she was fidgeting, ready to be loaded into Mr. Thirkell's own special private rocket, like a bullet, to be fired on out into space beyond Jupiter and Saturn and Pluto. And thus—who could deny it?—you would be getting nearer and nearer to the Lord. How wonderful! Couldn't you just feel Him drawing near? Couldn't you just sense His breath, His scrutiny, His Presence?

"Here I am," said Mrs. Bellowes, "an ancient rickety elevator, ready to go up the shaft. God need only press the button."

Now, on the seventh day, as she minced up the steps of the Restorium, a number of small doubts assailed her.

"For one thing," she said aloud to no one, "it isn't quite the land of milk and honey here on Mars that they said it would be. My room is like a cell, the swimming pool is really quite inadequate, and, besides, how many widows who look like mushrooms or skeletons want to swim? And, finally, the whole Restorium smells of boiled cabbage and tennis shoes!"

She opened the front door and let it slam, somewhat irritably.

She was amazed at the other women in the auditorium. It was like wandering in a carnival mirror-maze, coming again and again upon yourself—the same floury face, the same chicken hands, and jingling bracelets. One after another of the images of herself floated before her. She put out her hand, but it wasn't a mirror; it was another lady shaking her fingers and saying:

"We're waiting for Mr. Thirkell. Sh!"

"Ah," whispered everyone.

The velvet curtains parted.

Mr. Thirkell appeared, fantastically serene, his Egyptian eyes upon everyone. But there was something, nevertheless, in his appearance which made one expect him to call "Hi!" while fuzzy dogs jumped over his legs, through his hooped arms, and over his back. Then, dogs and all, he should dance with a dazzling piano-keyboard smile off into the wings.

Mrs. Bellowes, with a secret part of her mind which she constantly had to grip tightly, expected to hear a cheap Chinese gong sound when Mr. Thirkell entered. His large liquid dark eyes were so improbable that one of the old ladies had facetiously claimed she saw a mosquito cloud hovering over them as they did around summer rain-barrels. And Mrs. Bellowes sometimes caught the scent of the theatrical mothball and the smell of calliope steam on his sharply pressed suit.

But with the same savage rationalization that had greeted all other disappointments in her rickety life, she bit at the suspicion and whispered, "This time it's real. This time it'll work. Haven't we got a rocket?"

Mr. Thirkell bowed. He smiled a sudden Comedy Mask smile. The old ladies looked in at his epiglottis and sensed chaos there.

Before he even began to speak, Mrs. Bellowes saw him picking up each of his words, oiling it, making sure it ran smooth on its rails. Her heart squeezed in like a tiny fist, and she gritted her porcelain teeth.

"Friends," said Mr. Thirkell, and you could hear the frost snap in the hearts of the entire assemblage.

"No!" said Mrs. Bellowes ahead of time. She could hear the bad news rushing at her, and herself tied to the track while the immense black wheels threatened and the whistle screamed, helpless.

"There will be a slight delay," said Mr. Thirkell.

In the next instant, Mr. Thirkell might have cried, or been tempted to cry, "Ladies, be seated!" in minstrel-fashion, for the ladies had come up at him from their chairs, protesting and trembling.

"Not a very long delay." Mr. Thirkell put up his hands to pat the air.

"How long?"

"Only a week."

"A week!"

"Yes. You can stay here at the Restorium for seven more days, can't you? A little delay won't matter, will it, in the end? You've waited a lifetime. Only a few more days."

At twenty dollars a day, thought Mrs. Bellowes, coldly.

"What's the trouble?" a woman cried.

"A legal difficulty," said Mr. Thirkell.

"We've a rocket, haven't we?"

"Well, ye-ess."

"But I've been here a whole month, waiting," said one old lady. "Delays, delays!"

"That's right," said everyone.

"Ladies, ladies," murmured Mr. Thirkell, smiling serenely.

"We want to see the rocket!" It was Mrs. Bellowes forging ahead, alone, brandishing her fist like a toy hammer.

Mr. Thirkell looked into the old ladies' eyes, a missionary among albino cannibals.

"Well, now," he said.

"Yes, now!" cried Mrs. Bellowes.

"I'm afraid—" he began.

"So am I!" she said. "That's why we want to see the ship!"

"No, no, now, Mrs.—" He snapped his fingers for her name.

"Bellowes!" she cried. She was a small container, but now all the seething pressures that had been built up over long years came steaming through the delicate vents of her body. Her cheeks became incandescent. With a wail that was like a melancholy factory whistle, Mrs. Bellowes ran forward and hung to him, almost by her teeth, like a summer-maddened Spitz. She would not and never could let go, until he died, and the other women followed, jumping and yapping like a pound let loose on its trainer, the same one who had petted them and to whom they had squirmed and whined joyfully an hour before, now milling about him, creasing his sleeves and frightening the Egyptian serenity from his gaze.

"This way!" cried Mrs. Bellowes, feeling like Madame Lafarge. "Through the back! We've waited long enough to see the ship. Every day he's put us off, every day we've waited, now let's see."

"No, no, ladies!" cried Mr. Thirkell, leaping about.

They burst through the back of the stage and out a door, like a flood, bearing the poor man with them into a shed, and then out, quite suddenly, into an abandoned gymnasium.

"There it is!" said someone. "The rocket."

And then a silence fell that was terrible to entertain.

There was the rocket.

Mrs. Bellowes looked at it and her hands sagged away from Mr. Thirkell's collar.

The rocket was something like a battered copper pot. There were a thousand bulges and rents and rusty pipes and dirty vents on and in it. The ports were clouded over with dust, resembling the eyes of a blind hog.

Everyone wailed a little sighing wail.

"Is that the rocket ship Glory Be to the Highest?" cried Mrs. Bellowes, appalled.

Mr. Thirkell nodded and looked at his feet.

"For which we paid out our one thousand dollars apiece and came all the way to Mars to get on board with you and go off to find Him?" asked Mrs. Bellowes.

"Why, that isn't worth a sack of dried peas," said Mrs. Bellowes.

"It's nothing but junk!"

Junk, whispered everyone, getting hysterical.

"Don't let him get away!"

Mr. Thirkell tried to break and run, but a thousand possum traps closed on him from every side. He withered.

Everybody walked around in circles like blind mice. There was a confusion and a weeping that lasted for five minutes as they went over and touched the Rocket, the Dented Kettle, the Rusty Container for God's Children.

"Well," said Mrs. Bellowes. She stepped up into the askew doorway of the rocket and faced everyone. "It looks as if a terrible thing has been done to us," she said. "I haven't any money to go back home to Earth and I've too much pride to go to the Government and tell them a common man like this has fooled us out of our life's savings. I don't know how you feel about it, all of you, but the reason all of us came is because I'm eighty-five, and you're eighty-nine, and you're seventy-eight, and all of us are nudging on toward a hundred, and there's nothing on Earth for us, and it doesn't appear there's anything on Mars either. We all expected not to breathe much more air or crochet many more doilies or we'd never have come here. So what I have to propose is a simple thing—to take a chance."

She reached out and touched the rusted hulk of the rocket.

"This is our rocket. We paid for our trip. And we're going to take our trip!"

Everyone rustled and stood on tiptoes and opened an astonished mouth.

Mr. Thirkell began to cry. He did it quite easily and very effectively.

"We're going to get in this ship," said Mrs. Bellowes, ignoring him. "And we're going to take off to where we were going."

Mr. Thirkell stopped crying long enough to say, "But it was all a fake. I don't know anything about space. He's not out there, anyway. I lied. I don't know where He is, and I couldn't find Him if I wanted to. And you were fools to ever take my word on it."

"Yes," said Mrs. Bellowes, "we were fools. I'll go along on that. But you can't blame us, for we're old, and it was a lovely, good and fine idea, one of the loveliest ideas in the world. Oh, we didn't really fool ourselves that we could get nearer to Him physically. It was the gentle, mad dream of old people, the kind of thing you hold onto for a few minutes a day, even though you know it's not true. So, all of you who want to go, you follow me in the ship."

"But you can't go!" said Mr. Thirkell. "You haven't got a navigator. And that ship's a ruin!"

"You," said Mrs. Bellowes, "will be the navigator."

She stepped into the ship, and after a moment, the other old ladies pressed forward. Mr. Thirkell, windmilling his arms frantically, was nevertheless pressed through the port, and in a minute the door slammed shut. Mr. Thirkell was strapped into the navigator's seat, with everyone talking at once and holding him down. The special helmets were issued to be fitted over every gray or white head to supply extra oxygen in case of a leakage in the ship's hull, and at long last the hour had come and Mrs. Bellowes stood behind Mr. Thirkell and said, "We're ready, sir."

He said nothing. He pleaded with them silently, using his great, dark, wet eyes, but Mrs. Bellowes shook her head and pointed to the control.

"Takeoff," agreed Mr. Thirkell morosely, and pulled a switch.

Everybody fell. The rocket went up from the planet Mars in a great fiery glide, with the noise of an entire kitchen thrown down an elevator shaft, with a sound of pots and pans and kettles and fires boiling and stews bubbling, with a smell of burned incense and rubber and sulphur, with a color of yellow fire, and a ribbon of red stretching below them, and all the old women singing and holding to each other, and Mrs. Bellowes crawling upright in the sighing, straining, trembling ship.

"Head for space, Mr. Thirkell."

"It can't last," said Mr. Thirkell, sadly. "This ship can't last. It will—"

It did.

The rocket exploded.

Mrs. Bellowes felt herself lifted and thrown about dizzily, like a doll. She heard the great screamings and saw the flashes of bodies sailing by her in fragments of metal and powdery light.

"Help, help!" cried Mr. Thirkell, far away, on a small radio beam.

The ship disintegrated into a million parts, and the old ladies, all one hundred of them, were flung straight on ahead with the same velocity as the ship.

As for Mr. Thirkell, for some reason of trajectory, perhaps, he had been blown out the other side of the ship. Mrs. Bellowes saw him falling separate and away from them, screaming, screaming.

There goes Mr. Thirkell, thought Mrs. Bellowes.

And she knew where he was going. He was going to be burned and roasted and broiled good, but very good.

Mr. Thirkell was falling down into the Sun.

And here we are, thought Mrs. Bellowes. Here we are, going on out, and out, and out.

There was hardly a sense of motion at all, but she knew that she was traveling at fifty thousand miles an hour and would continue to travel at that speed for an eternity, until....

She saw the other women swinging all about her in their own trajectories, a few minutes of oxygen left to each of them in their helmets, and each was looking up to where they were going.

Of course, thought Mrs. Bellowes. Out into space. Out and out, and the darkness like a great church, and the stars like candles, and in spite of everything, Mr. Thirkell, the rocket, and the dishonesty, we are going toward the Lord.

And there, yes, there, as she fell on and on, coming toward her, she could almost discern the outline now, coming toward her was His mighty golden hand, reaching down to hold her and comfort her like a frightened sparrow....

"I'm Mrs. Amelia Bellowes," she said quietly, in her best company voice. "I'm from the planet Earth."

MED SHIP MAN

by Murray Leinster

I

Calhoun regarded the communicator with something like exasperation as his taped voice repeated a standard approach-call for the twentieth time. But no answer came, which had become irritating a long time ago. This was a new Med Service sector for Calhoun. He'd been assigned to another man's tour of duty because the other man had been taken down with romance. He'd gotten married, which ruled him out for Med Ship duty. So now Calhoun listened to his own voice endlessly repeating a call that should have been answered immediately.

Murgatroyd the *tormal* watched with beady, interested eyes. The planet Maya lay off to port of the Med Ship *Esclipus Twenty*. Its almost circular disk showed full size on a vision screen beside the ship's control board. The image was absolutely clear and vividly colored. There was an ice cap in view. There were continents. There were seas. The cloud system of a considerable cyclonic disturbance could be noted off at one side, and the continents looked reasonably as they should, and the seas were of that muddy, indescribable tint which indicates deep water.

Calhoun's own voice, taped an hour earlier, sounded in a speaker as it went again to the communicator and then to the extremely visible world a hundred thousand miles away.

"*Calling ground*," said Calhoun's recorded voice. "*Med Ship* Esclipus Twenty *calling ground to report arrival and ask coordinates for landing. Our mass is fifty standard tons. Repeat, five-oh tons. Purpose of landing, planetary health inspection.*"

*

The recorded voice stopped. There was silence except for the taped random noises which kept the inside of the ship from feeling like the inside of a tomb.

Murgatroyd said: "*Chee?*"

Calhoun said ironically, "Undoubtedly, Murgatroyd. Undoubtedly! Whoever's on duty at the spaceport stepped out for a moment, or dropped dead, or did something equally inconvenient. We have to wait until he gets back or somebody else takes over."

Murgatroyd said "*Chee!*" again and began to lick his whiskers. He knew that when Calhoun called on the communicator, another human voice should reply. Then there should be conversation, and shortly the force-fields of a landing-grid should take hold of the Med Ship and draw it planet-ward. In time it ought to touch ground in a spaceport with a gigantic, silvery landing-grid rising skyward all about it. Then there should be people greeting Calhoun cordially and welcoming Murgatroyd with smiles and petting.

"*Calling ground*," said the recorded voice yet again. "*Med Ship* Esclipus Twenty—"

It went on through the formal notice of arrival. Murgatroyd waited in pleasurable anticipation. When the Med Ship arrived at a port of call humans gave him sweets and cakes, and they thought it charming that he drank coffee just like a human, only with more gusto. Aground, Murgatroyd moved zestfully in society while Calhoun worked. Calhoun's work was conferences with planetary health officials, politely receiving such information as they thought important, and tactfully telling them about the most recent developments in medical science as known to the Interstellar Medical Service.

"Somebody," said Calhoun darkly, "is going to catch the devil for this!"

The communicator loudspeaker spoke abruptly.

"Calling Med Ship," said a voice. "Calling Med Ship *Esclipus Twenty*! Liner *Candida* calling. Have you had an answer from ground?"

Calhoun blinked. Then he said curtly:

"Not yet. I've been calling all of half an hour, and never a word out of them!"

"We've been in orbit twelve hours," said the voice from emptiness. "Calling all the while. No answer. We don't like it."

Calhoun flipped a switch that threw a vision screen into circuit with the ship's electron telescope. A starfield appeared and shifted wildly. Then a bright dot centered itself. He raised the magnification. The bright dot swelled and became a chubby commercial ship, with the false ports that passengers like to believe they looked through when in space. Two relatively large cargo ports on each side showed that it carried heavy freight in addition to passengers. It was one of those workhorse intra-cluster ships that distributed the freight and passengers the long-haul liners dumped off only at established transshipping ports.

Murgatroyd padded across the Med Ship's cabin and examined the image with a fine air of wisdom. It did not mean anything to him, but *tormals* imitate human actions as parrots and parrakeets imitate human speech. He said, "*Chee!*" as if making an observation of profound significance, then went back to the cushion and again curled up.

"We don't see anything wrong aground," the liner's voice complained, "but they don't answer calls! We don't get any scatter-signals either. We went down to two diameters and couldn't pick up a thing. And we have a passenger to land. He insists on it!"

*

By ordinary, communications between different places on a planet's surface use frequencies the ion-layers of the atmosphere either reflect or refract down past the horizon. But there is usually some small leakage to space, and line-of-sight frequencies are generally abundant. It is one of the annoyances of a ship coming in to port that space near most planets is usually full of local signals.

"I'll check," said Calhoun curtly. "Stand by."

The *Candida* would have arrived off Maya as the Med Ship had done, and called down as Calhoun had been doing. It was very probably a ship on schedule and the grid operator at the spaceport should have expected it. Space commerce was important to any planet, comparing more or less with the export-import business of an industrial nation in ancient times on Earth. Planets had elaborate traffic-aid systems for the cargo-carriers which moved between solar systems as they'd once moved between continents on Earth. Such traffic aids were very carefully maintained. Certainly for a spaceport landing-grid not to respond to calls for twelve hours running seemed ominous.

"We've been wondering," said the *Candida* querulously, "if there could be something radically wrong below. Sickness, for example."

The word "sickness" was a substitute for a more alarming word. But a plague had nearly wiped out the population of Dorset, once upon a time, and the first ships to arrive after it had broken out most incautiously went down to ground, and so carried the plague to their next two ports of call. Nowadays quarantine regulations were enforced very strictly indeed.

"I'll try to find out what's the matter," said Calhoun.

"We've got a passenger," repeated the *Candida* aggrievedly, "who insists that we land him by space-boat if we don't make a ship landing. He says he has important business aground."

Calhoun did not answer. The rights of passengers were extravagantly protected, these days. To fail to deliver a passenger to his destination entitled him to punitive damages which no spaceline could afford. So the Med Ship would seem heaven-sent to the *Candida*'s skipper. Calhoun could relieve him of responsibility.

The telescope screen winked and showed the surface of the planet a hundred thousand miles away. Calhoun glared at the image on the port screen and guided the telescope to the spaceport city—Maya City. He saw highways and blocks of buildings. He saw the spaceport and its landing-grid. He could see no motion, of course.

He raised the magnification. He raised it again. Still no motion. He upped the magnification until the lattice-pattern of the telescope's amplifying crystal began to show. But at the ship's distance from the planet, a ground-car would represent only the fortieth of a second of arc. There was atmosphere, too, with thermals; anything the size of a ground-car simply couldn't be seen.

But the city showed quite clearly. Nothing massive had happened to it. No large-scale physical disaster had occurred. It simply did not answer calls from space.

*

Calhoun flipped off the screen.

"I think," he said irritably into the communicator microphone, "I suspect I'll have to make an emergency landing. It could be something as trivial as a power failure—" but he knew that was wildly improbable—"or it could be—anything. I'll land on rockets and tell you what I find."

The voice from the *Candida* said hopefully:

"Can you authorize us to refuse to land our passenger for his own protection? He's raising the devil! He insists that his business demands that he be landed."

A word from Calhoun as a Med Service man would protect the spaceliner from a claim for damages. But Calhoun didn't like the look of things. He realized, distastefully, that he might find practically anything down below. He might find that he had to quarantine the planet and himself with it. In such a case he'd need the *Candida* to carry word of the quarantine to other planets and thus to Med Service sector headquarters.

"We've lost a lot of time," insisted the *Candida*. "Can you authorize us—"

"Not yet," said Calhoun. "I'll tell you when I land."

"But—"

"I'm signing off for the moment," said Calhoun. "Stand by."

He headed the little ship downward, and as it gathered velocity he went over the briefing sheets covering this particular world. He'd never touched ground here before. His occupation, of course, was seeing to the dissemination of medical science as it developed under the Med Service. The Service itself was neither political nor administrative. But it was important. Every human-occupied world was supposed to have a Med Ship visit at least once in four years to verify the state of public health.

Med Ship men like Calhoun offered advice on public-health problems. When something out of the ordinary turned up, the Med Service had a staff of researchers who hadn't been wholly baffled yet. There were great ships which could carry the ultimate in laboratory equipment and specialized personnel to any place where they were needed. Not less than a dozen inhabited worlds in this sector alone owed the survival of their populations to the Med Service, and the number of those which couldn't have been colonized without Med Service help was legion.

Calhoun reread the briefing. Maya was one of four planets in this general area whose life systems seemed to have had a common origin, suggesting that the Arrhenius theory of space-traveling spores was true in some limited sense. A genus of ground-cover plants with motile stems and leaves and cannibalistic tendencies was considered strong evidence of common origin.

The planet had been colonized for two centuries now, and produced organic compounds of great value from indigenous plants, most of which were used in textile manufacture. There were no local endemic infections to which men were susceptible. A number of human-use crops were grown. Cereals, grasses and grains, however, could not be grown because of the native ground-cover motile-stem plants. All wheat and cereal food had to be imported, which fact severely limited Maya's population. There were about two million people on the planet, settled on a peninsula in the Yucatan Sea and a small area of mainland. Public-health surveys had shown a great many things about a great many subjects ... but there was no mention of anything to account for the failure of the spaceport to respond to arrival calls from space. Naturally!

The Med Ship drove on down, and the planet revolved beneath it.

As Maya's sunlit hemisphere enlarged, Calhoun kept the telescope's field wide. He saw cities, and vast areas of cleared land where native plants were grown as raw materials for the organics' manufacturies. He saw very little true chlorophyll green, though. Mayan foliage tended to a dark olive color.

*

At fifty miles he was sure that the city streets were empty even of ground-car traffic. There was no spaceship aground in the landing-grid. There were no ground-cars in motion on the splendid, multiple-lane highways.

At thirty miles altitude there were still no signals in the atmosphere, though when he tried amplitude-modulation reception he picked up static. But there was no normally modulated signal on the air at any frequency. At twenty miles—no. At fifteen miles, broadcast power was available, which proved that the landing-grid was working as usual, tapping the upper atmosphere for electric charges to furnish power for all the planet's needs.

From ten miles down to ground-touch, Calhoun was busy.

It is not too difficult to land a ship on rockets, with reasonably level ground to land on. But landing at a specific spot is something else. Calhoun juggled the ship to descend inside the grid itself. His rockets burned out pencil-thin holes through the clay and stone beneath the tarmac. He cut them off.

Silence. Stillness. The Med Ship's outside microphones picked up small noises of wind blowing over the city. There was no other sound at all.

—No. There was a singularly deliberate clicking sound, not loud and not fast. Perhaps a click—a double click—every two seconds. That was all.

Calhoun went into the airlock, with Murgatroyd frisking a little in the expectation of great social success among the people of this world. When Calhoun cracked the outer airlock door he smelled something. It was a faintly sour, astringent odor that had the quality of decay in it. But it was no kind of decay he recognized. Again stillness and silence. No traffic-noise; not even the almost inaudible murmur that every city has in all its ways at all hours. The buildings looked as buildings should look at daybreak, except that the doors and windows were open. It was somehow shocking.

A ruined city is dramatic. An abandoned city is pathetic. This was neither.

It was something new. It felt as if everybody had walked away, out of sight, within the past few minutes.

Calhoun headed for the spaceport building with Murgatroyd ambling puzzledly at his side. Murgatroyd was disturbed. There should be people here! They should welcome Calhoun and admire him—Murgatroyd—and he should be a social lion with all the sweets he could eat and all the coffee he could put into his expandable belly. But nothing happened! Nothing at all.

"*Chee?*" he asked anxiously.

"They've gone away," growled Calhoun. "They probably left in ground-cars. There's not one in sight."

There wasn't. Calhoun could look out through the grid foundations and see long, sunlit and absolutely empty streets. He arrived at the spaceport building. There was—there had been—a green area about the base of the structure. There was not a living plant left. Leaves were wilted and limp. The remains had become almost a jelly of collapsed stems and blossoms of dark olive-green. The plants were dead; but not long enough to have dried up. They might have wilted two or three days before.

Calhoun went in the building. The spaceport log lay open on a desk. It recorded the arrival of freight to be shipped away—undoubtedly—on the *Candida* now uneasily in orbit somewhere aloft. There was no sign of disorder. It was exactly as if the people here had walked out to look at something interesting, and hadn't come back.

Calhoun trudged out of the spaceport and to the streets and buildings of the city proper. It was incredible! Doors were opened or unlocked. Merchandise in the shops lay on display, exactly as it had been spread out to interest customers. There was no sign of confusion anywhere. Even in a restaurant there were dishes and flatware on the tables. The food in the plates was stale, as if three days old, but it hadn't yet begun to spoil. The appearance of everything was as if people at their meals had simply, at some signal, gotten up and walked out without any panic or disturbance.

Calhoun made a wry face. He'd remembered something. Among the tales that had been carried from Earth to the other worlds of the galaxy there was a completely unimportant mystery story which people still sometimes tried to write an ending to. It was the story of an ancient sailing ship called the *Marie Celeste*, which was found drifting aimlessly in the middle of the ocean. There was food on the cabin table, and the galley stove was still warm. There was no sign of any trouble, or terror, or disturbance which might cause the ship to be abandoned. But there was not a living soul on board. Nobody had ever been able to contrive a believable explanation.

"Only," said Calhoun to Murgatroyd, "this is on a larger scale. The people of this city walked out about three days ago, and didn't come back. Maybe all the people on the planet did the same, since there's not a communicator in operation anywhere. To make the understatement of the century, Murgatroyd, I don't like this. I don't like it a bit!"

II

On the way back to the Med Ship, Calhoun stopped at another place where, on a grass-growing planet, there would have been green sward. There were Earth-type trees, and some native ones, and between them there should have been a lawn. The trees were thriving, but the ground-cover plants were collapsed and rotting.

Calhoun picked up a bit of the semi-slime and smelled it. It was faintly sour, astringent, the same smell he'd noticed when he opened the airlock door. He threw the stuff away and brushed off his hands. Something had killed the ground-cover plants which had the habit of killing Earth-type grass when planted here.

He listened. Everywhere that humans live, there are insects and birds and other tiny creatures which are essential parts of the ecological system to which the human race is adjusted. They have to be carried to and established upon every new world that mankind hopes to occupy. But there was no sound of such living creatures here.

It was probable that the bellowing roar of the Med Ship's emergency rockets was the only real noise the city had heard since its people went away.

The stillness bothered Murgatroyd. He said, "*Chee!*" in a subdued tone and stayed close to Calhoun. Calhoun shook his head. Then he said abruptly:

"Come along, Murgatroyd!"

He went back to the building housing the grid controls. He didn't look at the spaceport log this time. He went to the instruments recording the second function of a landing-grid. In addition to lifting up and letting down ships of space, a landing-grid drew down power from the ions of the upper atmosphere and broadcast it. It provided all the energy that humans on a world could need. It was solar power, in a way, absorbed and stored by a layer of ions miles high, which then could be drawn on and distributed by the grid. During his descent Calhoun had noted that broadcast power was still available. Now he looked at what the instruments said.

The needle on the dial showing power-drain moved slowly back and forth. It was a rhythmic movement, going from maximum to minimum power-use, and then back again. Approximately six million kilowatts was being taken out of the broadcast every two seconds for half of one second. Then the drain cut off for a second and a half, and went on again for half a second.

Frowning, Calhoun raised his eyes to a very fine color photograph on the wall above the power dials. It was a picture of the human-occupied part of Maya, taken four thousand miles out in space. It had been enlarged to four feet by six, and Maya City could be seen as an irregular group of squares and triangles measuring a little more than half an inch by three-quarters. The detail was perfect. It was possible to see perfectly straight, infinitely thin lines moving out from the city. They were multiple-lane highways, mathematically straight from one city to another, and then mathematically straight—though at a new angle—until the next. Calhoun stared thoughtfully at them.

"The people left the city in a hurry," he told Murgatroyd, "and there was little confusion, if any. So they knew in advance that they might have to go. They were ready for it. If they took anything, they had it ready packed in their cars. But they hadn't been sure they'd have to go because they were going about their businesses as usual. All the shops were open and people were eating in restaurants, and so on."

Murgatroyd said, "*Chee!*" as if in full agreement.

"Now," demanded Calhoun, "where did they go? The question's really where could they go! There were about eight hundred thousand people in this city. There'd be cars for everyone, of course, and two hundred thousand cars would take everybody. But that's a lot of ground-cars! Put 'em two hundred feet apart on a highway, and that's twenty-six cars to the mile on each lane. Run them at a hundred miles an hour on a twelve-lane road—using all lanes one way—and that's twenty-six hundred cars per lane per hour, and that's thirty-one thousand ... two highways make sixty-two ... three highways.... With two highways they could empty the city in under three hours, and with three highways close to two. Since there's no sign of panic, that's what they must have done. Must have worked it out in advance, too. Maybe they'd done it before it happened ... whatever it was that happened."

*

He searched the photograph which was so much more detailed than a map. There were mountains to the north of Maya City, but only one highway led north. There were more mountains to the west. One highway went into them, but not through. To the south there was sea, which curved around some three hundred miles from Maya City and put the human colony on Maya on a peninsula.

"They went east," said Calhoun presently. He traced lines with his finger. "Three highways go east; that's the only way they could go quickly. They hadn't been sure they'd have to go but they knew where to go when they did. So when they got their warning, they left. On three highways, to the east. And we'll follow them and ask what the hell they ran away from. Nothing's visible here!"

He went back to the Med Ship, Murgatroyd skipping with him.

As the airlock door closed behind them, he heard a click from the outside-microphone speakers. He listened. It was a doubled clicking, as of something turned on and almost at once turned off again. There was a two-second cycle, the same as that of the power drain. Something drawing six million kilowatts went on and immediately off again every two seconds. It made a sound in speakers linked to outside microphones, but it didn't make a noise in the air. The microphone clicks were induction; pick-up; like cross-talk on defective telephone cables.

Calhoun shrugged his shoulders almost up to his ears. He went to the communicator.

"Calling *Candida*—" he began, and the answer almost leaped down his throat.

"*Candida* to Med Ship. Come in! Come in! What's happened down there?"

"The city's deserted without any sign of panic," said Calhoun, "and there's power and nothing seems to be broken down. But it's as if somebody had said, 'Everybody clear out' and they did. That doesn't happen on a whim! What's your next port of call?"

The *Candida*'s voice told him, hopefully.

"Take a report," commanded Calhoun. "Deliver it to the public health office immediately you land. They'll get it to Med Service sector headquarters. I'm going to stay here and find out what's been going on."

He dictated, growing irritated as he did so because he couldn't explain what he reported. Something serious had taken place, but there was no clue as to what it was. Strictly speaking, it wasn't certainly a public health affair. But any emergency the size of this one involved public health factors.

"I'm remaining aground to investigate," finished Calhoun. "I will report further when or if it is possible. Message ends."

"What about our passenger?"

"To the devil with your passenger!" said Calhoun peevishly. "Do as you please!"

*

He cut off the communicator and prepared for activity outside the ship. Presently he and Murgatroyd went to look for transportation. The Med Ship couldn't be used for a search operation; it didn't carry enough rocket fuel. They'd have to use a ground vehicle.

It was again shocking to note that nothing had moved but sun shadows. Again it seemed that everybody had simply walked out of some door or other and failed to come back. Calhoun saw the windows of jewelers' shops. Treasures lay unguarded in plain view. He saw a florist's shop. Here there were Earth-type flowers apparently thriving, and some strange beautiful flowers with olive-green foliage which throve as well as the Earth-plants. There was a cage in which a plant had grown, and that plant was wilting and about to rot. But a plant that had to be grown in a cage....

He found a ground-car agency, perhaps for imported cars, perhaps for those built on Maya. He went in and from the cars on display he chose one, an elaborate sports car. He turned its key and it hummed. He drove it carefully out into the empty street, Murgatroyd sitting interestedly beside him.

"This is luxury, Murgatroyd," said Calhoun. "Also it's grand theft. We medical characters can't usually afford such things. Or have an excuse to steal them. But these are parlous times, so we take a chance."

"*Chee!*" said Murgatroyd.

"We want to find a fugitive population and ask what they ran away from. As of the moment, it seems that they ran away from nothing. They may be pleased to know they can come back."

Murgatroyd again said, "*Chee!*"

Calhoun drove through vacant ways. It was somehow nerve-racking. He felt as if someone should pop out and say "Boo!" at any instant. He discovered an elevated highway and a ramp leading up to it. At a cloverleaf he drove eastward, watching sharply for any sign of life. There was none.

He was nearly out of the city when he felt the chest impact of a sonic boom, and then heard a trailing away growling sound which seemed to come from farther away as it died out. It was the result of something traveling faster than sound, so that the noise it made far away had to catch up with the sound it emitted nearby.

He stared up. He saw a parachute blossom as a bare speck against the blue. Then he heard the even deeper-toned roaring of a supersonic craft climbing skyward. It could be a spaceliner's lifeboat, descended into atmosphere and going out again.

It was. It had left a parachute behind, and now went back to space to rendezvous with its parent ship.

"That," said Calhoun impatiently, "will be the *Candida*'s passenger. He was insistent enough."

He scowled. The *Candida*'s voice had said its passenger demanded to be landed for business reasons. And Calhoun had a prejudice against some kinds of business men who would think their own affairs more important than anything else. Two standard years before, he'd made a planetary health inspection on Texia II, in another galactic sector. It was a llano planet and a single giant business enterprise. Illimitable prairies had been sown with an Earth-type grass which destroyed the native ground-cover—the reverse of the ground-cover situation here—and the entire planet was a monstrous range for beef cattle. Dotted about were gigantic slaughterhouses, and cattle in masses of tens of thousands were shifted here and there by ground-induction fields which acted as fences. Ultimately the cattle were driven by these same induction fences to the slaughter houses and actually into the chutes where their throats were slit. Every imaginable fraction of a credit of profit was extracted from their carcasses, and Calhoun had found it appalling.

He was not sentimental about cattle, but the complete cold-bloodedness of the entire operation sickened him. The same cold-bloodedness was practised toward the human employees who ran the place. Their living quarters were sub-marginal. The air stank of cattle murder. Men worked for the Texia Company or they did not work. If they did not work they did not eat. If they worked and ate,—Calhoun could see nothing satisfying in being alive on a world like that! His report to Med Service had been biting. He'd been prejudiced against businessmen ever since.

*

But a parachute descended, blowing away from the city. It would land not too far from the highway he followed. And it didn't occur to Calhoun not to help the unknown chutist. He saw a small figure dangling below the chute. He slowed the ground-car as he estimated where the parachute would land.

He was off the twelve-lane highway and on a feeder road when the chute was a hundred feet high. He was racing across a field of olive-green plants that went all the way to the horizon when the parachute actually touched ground. There was a considerable wind. The man in the harness bounced. He didn't know how to spill the air. The chute dragged him.

Calhoun sped ahead, swerved and ran into the chute. He stopped the car and the chute stopped with it. He got out.

The man lay in a hopeless tangle of cordage. He thrust unskilfully at it. When Calhoun came up he said suspiciously:

"Have you a knife?"

Calhoun offered a knife, politely opening its blade. The man slashed at the cords and freed himself. There was an attache case lashed to his chute harness. He cut at those cords. The attache case not only came clear, but opened. It dumped out an incredible mass of brand new, tightly packed interstellar credit certificates. Calhoun could see that the denominations were one thousand and ten thousand credits. The man from the chute reached under his armpit and drew out a blaster.

It was not a service weapon. It was elaborate, practically a toy. With a dour glance at Calhoun he put it in a side pocket and gathered up the scattered money. It was an enormous sum, but he packed it back. He stood up.

"My name is Allison," he said in an authoritative voice. "Arthur Allison. I'm much obliged. Now I'll ask you to take me to Maya City."

"No," said Calhoun politely. "I just left there. It's deserted. I'm not going back. There's nobody there."

"But I've important bus—" The other man stared. "It's deserted? But that's impossible!"

"Quite," agreed Calhoun, "but it's true. It's abandoned. Uninhabited. Everybody's left it. There's no one there at all."

The man who called himself Allison blinked unbelievingly. He swore. Then he raged profanely.

But he was not bewildered by the news. Which, upon consideration, was itself almost bewildering. But then his eyes grew shrewd. He looked about him.

"My name is Allison," he repeated, as if there were some sort of magic in the word. "Arthur Allison. No matter what's happened, I've some business to do here. Where have the people gone? I need to find them."

"I need to find them too," said Calhoun. "I'll take you with me, if you like."

"You've heard of me." It was a statement, confidently made.

"Never," said Calhoun politely. "If you're not hurt, suppose you get in the car? I'm as anxious as you are to find out what's happened. I'm Med Service."

*

Allison moved toward the car.

"Med Service, eh? I don't think much of the Med Service! You people try to meddle in things that are none of your business!"

Calhoun did not answer. The muddy man, clutching the attache case tightly, waded through the olive-green plants to the car and climbed in. Murgatroyd said cordially, "*Chee-chee!*" but Allison viewed him with distaste.

"What's this?"

"He's Murgatroyd," said Calhoun. "He's a *tormal.* He's Med service personnel."

"I don't like beasts," said Allison coldly.

"He's much more important to me than you are," said Calhoun, "if the matter should come to a test."

Allison stared at him as if expecting him to cringe. Calhoun did not. Allison showed every sign of being an important man who expected his importance to be recognized and catered to. When Calhoun stirred impatiently he got into the car and growled a little. Calhoun took his place. The ground-car hummed. It rose on the six columns of air which took the place of wheels and slid across the field of dark-green plants, leaving the parachute deflated across a number of rows, and a trail of crushed-down plants where it had moved.

It reached the highway again. Calhoun ran the car up on the highway's shoulder, and then suddenly checked. He'd noticed something.

He stopped the car and got out. Where the ploughed field ended, and before the coated surface of the highway began, there was a space where on another world one would expect to see green grass.

On this planet grass did not grow; but there would normally be some sort of self-planted vegetation where there was soil and sunshine and moisture. There had been such vegetation here, but now there was only a thin, repellent mass of slimy and decaying foliage. Calhoun bent down to it.

It had a sour, faintly astringent smell of decay. These were the ground-cover plants of Maya of which Calhoun had read. They had motile stems, leaves and flowers, and they had cannibalistic tendencies. They were the local weeds which made it impossible to grow grain for human use upon this world.

And they were dead.

Calhoun straightened up and returned to the car. Plants like this were wilted at the base of the spaceport building, and on another place where there should have been sward. Calhoun had seen a large dead member of the genus in a florist's, that had been growing in a cage before it died. There was a singular coincidence here: humans ran away from something, and something caused the death of a particular genus of cannibal weeds.

It did not exactly add up to anything in particular, and certainly wasn't evidence for anything at all. But Calhoun drove on in a vaguely puzzled mood. The germ of a guess was forming in his mind. He couldn't pretend to himself that it was likely, but it was surely no more unlikely than most of a million human beings abandoning their homes at a moment's notice.

III

They came to the turnoff for a town called Tenochitlan, some forty miles from Maya City. Calhoun swung off the highway to go through it.

Whoever had chosen the name Maya for this planet had been interested in the legends of Yucatan, back on Earth. There were many instances of such hobbies in a Med Ship's list of ports of call. Calhoun touched ground regularly on planets that had been named for countries and towns when men first roamed the stars, and nostalgically christened their discoveries with names suggested by homesickness. There was a Tralee, and a Dorset, and an Eire. Colonists not infrequently took their world's given name as a pattern and chose related names for seas and peninsulas and mountain chains. On Texia the landing-grid rose near a town called Corral and the principal meat-packing settlement was named Roundup.

Whatever the name Tenochitlan would have suggested, though, was denied by the town itself. It was small, with a pleasing local type of architecture. There were shops and some factories, and many strictly private homes, some clustered close together and others in the middles of considerable gardens. In those gardens also there was wilt and decay among the cannibal plants. There was no grass, because the plants prevented it, but now the motile plants themselves were dead. Except for the one class of killed growing things, however, vegetation was luxuriant.

But the little city was deserted. Its streets were empty, its houses untenanted. Some houses were apparently locked up here, though, and Calhoun saw three or four shops whose stock in trade had been covered over before the owners departed. He guessed that either this town had been warned earlier than the spaceport city, or else they knew they had time to get in motion before the highways were filled with the cars from the west.

Allison looked at the houses with keen, evaluating eyes. He did not seem to notice the absence of people. When Calhoun swung back on the great road beyond the little city, Allison regarded the endless fields of dark-green plants with much the same sort of interest.

"Interesting," he said abruptly when Tenochitlan fell behind and dwindled to a speck. "Very interesting! I'm interested in land. Real property, that's my business. I've a land-owning corporation on Thanet Three. I've some holdings on Dorset, too, and elsewhere. It just occurred to me: what's all this land and the cities worth, with the people all run away?"

"What," asked Calhoun, "are the people worth who've run?"

Allison paid no attention. He looked shrewd. Thoughtful.

"I came here to buy land," he said. "I'd arranged to buy some hundreds of square miles. I'd buy more if the price were right. But—as things are, it looks like the price of land ought to go down quite a bit. Quite a bit!"

"It depends," said Calhoun, "on whether there's anybody left alive to sell it to you, and what sort of thing has happened."

Allison looked at him sharply.

"Ridiculous!" he said authoritatively. "There's no question of their being alive!"

"They thought there might be," observed Calhoun. "That's why they ran away. They hoped they'd be safe where they ran to. I hope they are."

Allison ignored the comment. His eyes remained intent and shrewd. He was not bewildered by the flight of the people of Maya. His mind was busy with contemplation of that flight from the standpoint of a man of business.

*

The car went racing onward. The endless fields of dark green rushed past to the rear. The highway was deserted, just three strips of surfaced road, mathematically straight, going on to the horizon. They went on by tens and scores of miles, each strip wide enough to allow four ground-cars to run side by side. The highway was intended to allow all the produce of all these fields to be taken to market or a processing plant at the highest possible speed and in any imaginable quantity. The same roads had allowed the cities to be deserted instantly the warning—whatever the warning was—arrived.

Fifty miles beyond Tenochitlan there was a mile-long strip of sheds containing agricultural machinery for crop culture and trucks to carry the crops to market. There was no sign of life about the machinery, nor in a further hour's run to westward.

Then there was a city visible to the left. But it was not served by this particular highway, but another. There was no sign of any movement in its streets. It moved along the horizon to the left and rear. Presently it disappeared.

Half an hour later still, Murgatroyd said:

"*Chee!*"

He stirred uneasily. A moment later he said "*Chee!*" again.

Calhoun turned his eyes from the road. Murgatroyd looked unhappy. Calhoun ran his hand over the *tormal*'s furry body. Murgatroyd pressed against him. The car raced on. Murgatroyd whimpered a little. Calhoun's hand felt the little animal's muscles tense sharply, and then relax, and after a little tense again. Murgatroyd said almost hysterically:

"*Chee-chee-chee-chee!*"

Calhoun stopped the car, but Murgatroyd did not seem to be relieved. Allison said impatiently, "What's the matter?"

"That's what I'm trying to find out," said Calhoun.

He felt Murgatroyd's pulse. The role of Murgatroyd in the Med Ship *Esclipus Twenty* was not only that of charming companion in the long, isolated runs in overdrive. Murgatroyd was a part of the Med Service. His tribe had been discovered on a planet in the Deneb sector, and men had made pets of them, to the high satisfaction of the *tormals*. Presently it was discovered that veterinarians never had *tormals* for patients. They were invariably in robustuous good health. They contracted no infections from other animals; they shared no infections with anybody else. The Med Service discovered that *tormals* possessed a dynamic immunity to germ and bacteria-caused diseases. Even viruses injected into their bloodstreams only provoked an immediate, overwhelming development of antibodies, so that *tormals* couldn't be given any known disease. Which was of infinite value to the Med Service.

Now every Med Ship that could be supplied with a *tormal* carried a small, affectionate, whiskered member of the tribe. Men liked them, and they adored men. And when, as sometimes happened, by mutation or the simple enmity of nature, a new kind of infection appeared in human society—why—*tormals* defeated it. They produced specific antibodies to destroy it. Men analyzed the antibodies and synthesized them, and they were available to all the humans who needed them. So a great many millions of humans stayed alive, because *tormals* were pleasant little animals with a precious genetic gift of good health.

*

Calhoun looked at his sweep-second watch, timing the muscular spasms that Murgatroyd displayed. They coincided with irregularities in Murgatroyd's heartbeat, coming at approximately two-second intervals. The tautening of the muscles lasted just about half a second.

"But I don't feel it!" said Calhoun.

Murgatroyd whimpered again and said, "*Chee-chee!*"

"What's going on?" demanded Allison with the impatience of a very important man indeed. "If the beast's sick, he's sick! I've got to find—"

Calhoun opened his med kit and went carefully through it until he found what he needed. He put a pill into Murgatroyd's mouth.

"Swallow it!" he commanded.

Murgatroyd resisted, but the pill went down. Calhoun watched him sharply. Murgatroyd's digestive system was delicate, but it was dependable. Anything that might be poisonous, Murgatroyd's stomach rejected instantly and emphatically.

The pill stayed down.

"Look!" said Allison indignantly. "I've got business to do! In this attache case I have millions of interstellar credits, in cash, to pay down on purchases of land and factories. I ought to make some damned good deals! And I figure that that's as important as anything else you can think of! It's a damned sight more important than a beast with a belly-ache!"

Calhoun looked at him coldly.

"Do you own land on Texia?" he asked.

Allison's mouth dropped open. Extreme suspicion and unease appeared on his face. As a sign of the unease, his hand went to the side coat pocket in which he'd put a blaster. He didn't pluck it out. Calhoun's left fist swung around and landed. He took Allison's elaborate pocket blaster and threw it away among the monotonous rows of olive-green plants. He returned to absorbed observation of Murgatroyd.

In five minutes the muscular spasms diminished. In ten, Murgatroyd frisked. But he seemed to think that Calhoun had done something remarkable. In the warmest of tones he said:

"*Chee!*"

"Very good," said Calhoun. "We'll go ahead. I suspect you'll do as well as we do—for a while."

The car lifted the few inches the air columns sustained it above the ground. It went on, still to the eastward. But Calhoun drove more slowly now.

"Something was giving Murgatroyd rhythmic muscular spasms," he said coldly. "I gave him medication to stop them. He's more sensitive than we are, so he reacted to a stimulus we haven't noticed yet. But I think we'll notice it presently."

Allison seemed to be dazed at the affront given him. It appeared to be unthinkable that anybody might lay hands on him.

"What the devil has that to do with me?" he demanded angrily. "And what did you hit me for? You're going to pay for this!"

"Until I do," Calhoun told him, "you'll be quiet. And it does have the devil to do with you. There was a Med Service gadget once—a tricky little device to produce contraction of chosen muscles. It was useful for re-starting stopped hearts without the need of an operation. It regulated the beat of hearts that were too slow or dangerously irregular. But some businessman had a bright idea and got a tame researcher to link that gadget to ground induction currents. I suspect you know that businessman!"

"I don't know what you're talking about," snapped Allison. But he was singularly tense.

"I do," said Calhoun unpleasantly. "I made a public health inspection on Texia a couple of years ago. The whole planet is a single, gigantic, cattle-raising enterprise. They don't use metal fences—the herds are too big to be stopped by such things. They don't use cowboys—they cost money. On Texia they use ground-induction and the Med Service gadget linked together to serve as cattle fences. They act like fences, though they're projected through the ground. Cattle become uncomfortable when they try to cross them. So they draw back. So men control them. They move them from place to place by changing the cattle fences, which are currents induced in the ground. The cattle have to keep moving or be punished by the moving fence. They're even driven into the slaughterhouse chutes by ground-induction fields! That's the trick on Texia, where induction fields herd cattle. I think it's the trick on Maya, where people are herded like cattle and driven out of their cities so the value of their fields and factories will drop,—so a land buyer can find bargains!"

"You're insane!" snapped Allison. "I just landed on this planet! You saw me land! I don't know what happened before I got here! How could I?"

"You might have arranged it," said Calhoun.

*

Allison assumed an air of offended and superior dignity. Calhoun drove the car onward at very much less than the head-long pace he'd been keeping to. Presently he looked down at his hands on the steering wheel. Now and then the tendons to his fingers seemed to twitch. At rhythmic intervals, the skin crawled on the back of his hands. He glanced at Allison. Allison's hands were tightly clenched.

"There's a ground-induction fence in action, all right," said Calhoun calmly. "You notice? It's a cattle fence and we're running into it. If we were cattle, now, we'd turn around and move away."

"I don't know what you're talking about!" said Allison.

But his hands stayed clenched. Calhoun slowed the car still more. He began to feel, all over his body, that every muscle tended to twitch at the same time. It was a horrible sensation. His heart muscles tended to contract too, simultaneously with the rest, but one's heart has its own beat rate. Sometimes the normal beat coincided with the twitch. Then his heart pounded violently—so violently that it was painful. But equally often the imposed contraction of the heart muscles came just after a normal contraction, and then it stayed tightly knotted for half a second. It missed a beat, and the feeling was agony.

No animal would have pressed forward in the face of such sensations. It would have turned back long ago. No animal. Not even Man.

Calhoun stopped the car. He looked at Murgatroyd. Murgatroyd was completely himself. He looked inquiringly at Calhoun. Calhoun nodded to him, but he spoke—with some difficulty—to Allison.

"We'll see—if this thing—builds up. You know that it's the Texia—trick. A ground-induction unit set up—here. It drove people—like cattle. Now we've—run into it.—It's holding people—like cattle."

He panted. His chest muscles contracted with the rest, so that his breathing was interfered with. But Murgatroyd, who'd been made uneasy and uncomfortable before Calhoun noticed anything wrong, was now bright and frisky. Medication had desensitized his muscles to outside stimuli. He would be able to take a considerable electric shock without responding to it.

But he could be killed by one that was strong enough.

A savage anger filled Calhoun. Everything fitted together. Allison had put his hand convenient to his blaster when Calhoun mentioned Texia. It meant that Calhoun suspected what Allison knew to be true. A cattle-fence unit had been set up on Maya, and it was holding—like cattle—the people it had previously driven—like cattle. Calhoun could deduce with some precision exactly what had been done. The first experience of Maya with the cattle fence would have been very mild. It would have been low-power, causing just enough uneasiness to be noticed. It would have moved from west to east, slowly, and it would have reached a certain spot and there faded out. And it would have been a mystery and an uncomfortable thing, and nobody would understand it on Maya. In a week it would almost be forgotten. But then there'd come a stronger disturbance. And it would travel like the first one; down the length of the peninsula on which the colony lay, but stopping at the same spot as before, and then fading away to nothingness. And this also would have seemed mysterious. But nobody would suspect humans of causing it. There would be theorizing and much questioning, but it would be considered an unfamiliar natural event.

Probably the third use of the cattle fence would be most disturbing. This time it would be acutely painful. But it would move into the cities and through them and past them, and it would go down the peninsula to where it had stopped and faded on two previous occasions.

The people of Maya would be disturbed and scared. But they considered that they knew it began to the westward of Maya City, and moved toward the east at such-and-such a speed, and it went so far and no farther. And they would organize themselves to apply this carefully worked out information.

It would not occur to any of them that they had learned how to be driven like cattle.

*

Calhoun, of course, could only reason that this must have happened. But nothing else could have taken place. Perhaps there were more than three uses of the moving cattle fence to get the people prepared to move past the known place at which it always faded to nothingness. They might have been days apart, or weeks apart, or months. There might have been stronger manifestations followed by weaker ones and then stronger ones again.

But there was an inductive cattle fence across the highway here. Calhoun had driven into it. Every two seconds the muscles of his body tensed. Sometimes his heart missed a beat at the time that his breathing stopped, and sometimes it pounded violently. It seemed that the symptoms became more and more unbearable.

He got out his med kit, with hands that spasmodically jerked uncontrollably. He fumbled out the same medication he'd given Murgatroyd. He took two of the pellets.

"In reason," he said coldly, "I ought to let you take what this damned thing would give you. But—here!"

Allison had panicked. The *idea* of a cattle fence suggested discomfort, of course, but it did not imply danger. The *experience* of a cattle fence, designed for huge hoofed beasts instead of men, was terrifying. Allison gasped. He made convulsive movements. Calhoun himself moved erratically. For one and a half seconds out of two, he could control his muscles. For half a second at a time, he could not. But he poked a pill into Allison's mouth.

"Swallow it!" he commanded. "Swallow!"

The ground-car rested tranquilly on the highway, which here went on for a mile and then dipped in a gentle incline and then rose once more. The totally level fields to right and left came to an end here. Native trees grew, trailing preposterously with long fronds. Brushwood hid much of the ground. That looked normal. But the lower, ground-covering vegetation was wilted and rotting.

Allison choked upon the pellet. Calhoun forced a second upon him. Murgatroyd looked inquisitively at first one and then the other of the two men. He said:

"*Chee? Chee?*"

Calhoun lay back in his seat, breathing carefully to keep alive. But he couldn't do anything about his heartbeat. The sun shone brightly, though now it was low, toward the horizon. There were clouds in the reddened sky. A gentle breeze blew. Everything, to outward appearance, was peaceful and tranquil and commonplace upon this small world.

But in the area that human beings had taken over there were cities which were still and silent and deserted, and somewhere—somewhere!—the population of the planet waited uneasily for the latest of a series of increasingly terrifying phenomena to come to an end. Up to this time the strange, creeping, universal affliction had begun at one place, and moved slowly to another, and then diminished and ceased to be. But this was the greatest and worst of the torments. And it hadn't ended. It hadn't diminished. After three days it continued at full strength at the place where previously it had stopped and died away.

The people of Maya were frightened. They couldn't return to their homes. They couldn't go anywhere. They hadn't prepared for an emergency to last for days. They hadn't brought supplies of food.

It began to look as if they were going to starve.

IV

Calhoun was in very bad shape when the sports car came to the end of the highway.

First, all the multiple roadways of the route that had brought him here were joined by triple ribbons of road-surface from the north. For a space there were twenty-four lanes available to traffic. They flowed together, and then there were twelve. Here there was evidence of an enormous traffic concentration at some time now past. Brush and small trees were crushed and broken where cars had been forced to travel off the hard-surface roadways and through undergrowth. The twelve lanes dwindled to six, and the unpaved area on either side showed that innumerable cars had been forced to travel off the highway altogether. Then there were three lanes, and then two, and finally only a single ribbon of pavement where no more than two cars could run side by side. The devastation on either hand was astounding. All visible vegetation for half a mile to right and left was crushed and tangled. And then the narrow surfaced road ceased to be completely straight. It curved around a hillock—and here the ground was no longer perfectly flat—and came to an end.

And Calhoun saw all the ground-cars of the planet gathered and parked together.

There were no buildings. There were no streets. There was nothing of civilization but tens and scores of thousands of ground-cars. They were extraordinary to look at, stopped at random, their fronts pointed in all directions, their air-column tubes thrusting into the ground so that there might be trouble getting them clear again.

Parked bumper to bumper in closely placed lines, in theory twenty-five thousand cars could be parked on a square mile of ground. But there were very many times that number of cars here, and some places were unsuitable for parking, and there were lanes placed at random and there'd been no special effort to put the maximum number of cars in the smallest place. So the surface transportation system of the planet Maya spread out over some fifty sprawling square miles. Here, cars were crowded closely. There, there was much room between them. But it seemed that as far as one could see in the twilight there were glistening vehicles gathered confusedly, so there was nothing else to be seen but an occasional large tree rising from among them.

Calhoun came to the end of the surfaced road. He'd waited for the pellets he'd taken and given to Allison to have the effect they'd had on Murgatroyd. That had come about. He'd driven on. But the strength of the inductor field had increased to the intolerable. When he stopped the sports car he showed the effects of what he'd been through.

Figures on foot converged upon him instantly. There were eager calls.

"It's stopped? You got through? We can go back?"

Calhoun shook his head. It was just past sunset and many brilliant colorings showed in the western sky, but they couldn't put color into Calhoun's face. His cheeks were grayish and his eyes were deep-sunk, and he looked like someone in the last stages of exhaustion. He said heavily:

"It's still there. We came through. I'm Med Service. Have you got a government here? I need to talk to somebody who can give orders."

*

If he'd asked two days earlier there would have been no answer, because the fugitives were only waiting for a disaster to come to an end. One day earlier, he might have found men with authority busily trying to arrange for drinking water for something like two millions of people, in the entire absence of wells or pumps or ways of making either. And if he'd been a day later, it is rather likely that he'd have found savage disorder. But he arrived at sundown three days after the flight from the cities. There was no food to speak of, and water was drastically short, and the fugitives were only beginning to suspect that they would never be able to leave this place—and that they might die here.

Men left the growing crowd about the sports car to find individuals who could give orders. Calhoun stayed in the car, resting from the unbearable strain he'd undergone. The ground-inductor cattle fence had been ten miles deep. One mile was not bad. Only Murgatroyd had noticed it. After two miles Calhoun and Allison suffered; but the medication strengthened them to take it. But there'd been a long, long way in the center of the induction-field in which existence was pure torment. Calhoun's muscles defied him for part of every two-second cycle, and his heart and lungs seemed constantly about to give up even the pretense of working. In that part of the cattle-fence field, he'd hardly dared drive faster than a crawl, in order to keep control of the car when his own body was uncontrollable. But presently the field strength lessened and ultimately ended.

Now Murgatroyd looked cordially at the figures who clustered about the car. He'd hardly suffered at all. He'd had half as much of the medication as Calhoun himself, and his body weight was only a tenth of Calhoun's. He'd made out all right. Now he looked expectantly at what became a jammed mass of crowding men about the vehicle that had come through the invisible barrier across the highway. They hoped desperately for news to produce hope. But Murgatroyd waited zestfully for somebody to welcome him and offer him cakes and sweets, and undoubtedly presently a cup of coffee.

But nobody did.

It was a long time before there was a stirring at the edge of the crowd. Night had fully fallen then, and for miles and miles in all directions lights in the ground cars of Maya's inhabitants glowed brightly. They drew upon broadcast power, naturally, for their motors and their lights. Off to one side someone shouted. Calhoun turned on his headlights for a guide. More shoutings. A knot of men struggled to get through the crowd. With difficulty, presently, they reached the car.

"They say you got through," panted a tall man, "but you can't get back. They say—"

Calhoun roused himself. Allison, beside him, stirred. The tall man panted again:

"I'm the planetary president. What can we do?"

"First, listen," said Calhoun tiredly.

He'd had a little rest. Not much, but some. The actual work he'd done in driving three hundred-odd miles from Maya City was trivial. But the continuous, and lately violent, spasms of his heart and breathing muscles had been exhausting. He heard Murgatroyd say ingratiatingly, "*Chee-chee-chee-chee*," and put his hand on the little animal to quiet him.

"The thing you ran away from," said Calhoun with effort, "is a type of ground-induction field using broadcast power from the grid. It's used on Texia to confine cattle to their pastures and to move them where they're wanted to be. But it was designed for cattle. It's a cattle fence. It could kill humans."

*

He went on, his voice gaining strength and steadiness as he spoke. He explained, precisely, how a ground-induction field was projected in a line at a right angle to its source. It could be moved by adjustments of the apparatus by which it was projected.

"But—but if it uses broadcast power," the planetary president said urgently, "then if the power broadcast is cut off it has to stop! If you got through it coming here, tell us how to get through going back and we'll cut off the power broadcast ourselves! We've got to do something immediately. The whole planet's here. There's no food! There's no water! Something has to be done before we begin to die!"

"But," said Calhoun, "if you cut off the power you'll die anyway! You've got a couple of million people here, and you're a hundred miles from food. Without power you couldn't get to food or bring it here. Cut the power and you're still stranded here. Without power you'll die as soon as with it."

There was a sound from the listening men around. It was partly a growl and partly a groan.

"I've just found this out," said Calhoun. "I didn't know until the last ten miles exactly what the situation was, and I had to come here to be sure. Now I need some people to help me. It won't be pleasant. I may have enough medication to get a dozen people back through. It'll be safer if I take only six. Get a doctor to pick me six men. Good heart action. Sound lungs. Two should be electronics engineers. The others should be good shots. If you get them ready, I'll give them the same stuff that got us through. It's desensitizing medication, but it will do only so much. And try and find some weapons for them."

Voices murmured all around. Men hastily explained to other men what Calhoun had said. The creeping disaster before which they'd all fled,—it was not a natural catastrophe, but an artificial one! Men had made it! They'd been herded here and their wives and children were hungry because of something men had done!

A low-pitched, buzzing, humming sound came from the crowd about the sports car. For the moment, nobody asked what could be the motive for men to do what had been done. Pure fury filled the mob. Calhoun leaned closer to Allison.

"I wouldn't get out of the car if I were you," he said in a low tone. "I certainly wouldn't try to buy any real property at a low price!"

Allison shivered. There was a vast, vast stirring as the explanation passed from man to man. Figures moved away in the darkness. Lighted car windows winked as they moved through the obscurity. The population of Maya was spread out over very many square miles of what had been wilderness, and there was no elaborate communication system by which information could be spread quickly. But long before dawn there'd be nobody who didn't know that they'd fled from a man-made danger and were held here like cattle, behind a cattle fence, apparently abandoned to die.

*

Allison's teeth chattered. He was a business man and up to now he'd thought as one. He'd made decisions in offices, with attorneys and secretaries and clerks to make the decisions practical and safe, without any concern for any consequences other than financial ones.

He saw possible consequences to himself, here and now. He'd landed on

Maya because he considered the matter too important to trust to anybody else. Even riding with Calhoun on the way here, he'd only been elated and astonished at the success of the intended coup. He'd raised his aim. For a while he'd believed that he'd end as the sole proprietor of the colony on Maya, with every plant growing for his profit, and every factory earning money for him, and every inhabitant his employee. It had been the most grandiose possible dream. The details and the maneuvers needed to complete it flowed into his mind.

But now his teeth chattered. At ten words from Calhoun he would literally be torn to pieces by the raging men about him. His attache case with millions of credits in cash—it would be proof of whatever Calhoun chose to say. Allison knew terror down to the bottom of his soul. But he dared not move from Calhoun's side, even though a single sentence in the calmest of voices would destroy him, and he'd never faced actual, understood, physical danger before.

Presently men came, one by one, to take orders from Calhoun. They were able-bodied and grim-faced men. Two were electronics engineers, as he'd specified. One was a policeman. There were two mechanics and a doctor who was also amateur tennis champion of the planet. Calhoun doled out to them the pellets that reduced the sensitiveness of muscles to externally applied stimuli. He gave instructions. They'd go as far into the cattle fence as they could reasonably endure. Then they'd swallow the pellets and let them act. Then they'd go on. His stock of pellets was limited. He could give three to each man.

Murgatroyd squirmed disappointedly as this briefing went on. Obviously, he wasn't to make a social success here. He was annoyed, and he needed more space. Calhoun tossed Allison's attache case behind the seats. Allison was too terrified to protest. It still did not increase the space left on the front seat between Calhoun and Allison.

Four humming ground cars lifted eight inches off the ground and hovered there on columns of rushing air. Calhoun took the lead. His headlights moved down the single-lane road to which two joining twelve-lane highways had shrunk. Behind him, other headlights moved into line. Calhoun's car moved away into the darkness. The others followed.

Brilliant stars shone overhead. A cluster of thousands of suns, a hundred light-years away, made a center of illumination that gave Maya's night the quality of a vivid if diffused moonlight. The cars went on. Presently Calhoun felt the twitchings of minor muscular spasms. He was riding into the field which had been first devised for purposes remote from the herding of cattle or humans, but applied to the first use on the planet Texia, and now applied to the second here.

The road became two, and then four, and then eight lanes wide. Then four lanes swirled off to one side, and the remaining four presently doubled, and then widened again, and it was the twelve-lane turnpike that had brought Calhoun here from Maya City.

*

But the rhythmic interference with his body grew stronger. Allison had spoken not one single word while Calhoun conferred with the people of Maya beyond the highway. His teeth chattered as they started back. He didn't attempt to speak during the beginning of the ride through the cattle-fence field. His teeth chattered, and stopped, and chattered again, and at long last he panted despairingly:

"Are you going to let the thing kill me?"

Calhoun stopped. The cars behind him stopped. He gave Allison two pellets and took two himself. With Murgatroyd insistently accompanying him, he went along the cars which trailed him. He made sure the six men he'd asked for took their pellets and that they had an adequate effect. He went back to the sports car.

Allison whimpered a little when he and Murgatroyd got back in.

"I thought," said Calhoun conversationally, "that you might try to take off by yourself, just now. It would solve a problem for me. Of course it wouldn't solve any for you. But I don't think your problems have any solution, now."

He started the car up again. It moved forward. The other cars trailed dutifully. They went on through the starlit night. Calhoun noted that the effect of the cattle fence was less than it had been before. The first desensitizing pellets had not wholly lost their effect when he added to it. But he kept his speed low until he was certain the other drivers had endured the anguish of passing through the cattle-fence field.

Presently he was confident that the cattle field was past. He sent his car up to eighty miles an hour. The other cars followed faithfully. To a hundred. They did not drop behind. The car hummed through the night at top speed—a hundred and twenty, a hundred and thirty miles an hour. The three other cars' headlights faithfully kept pace with him.

Allison, said desperately, "Look! I—don't understand what's happened. You talk as if I'd planned all this. I—did have advance notice of a—a research project here. But it shouldn't have held the people there for days! Something went wrong! I only believed that people would want to leave Maya. I'd only planned to buy as much acreage as I could, and control of as many factories as possible. That's all! It was business! Only business!"

Calhoun did not answer. Allison might be telling the truth. Some businessmen would think it only intelligent to frighten people into selling their holdings below true value. Something of the sort happened every day in stock exchanges. But the people of Maya could have died!

For that matter, they still might. They couldn't return to their homes and food so long as broadcast power kept the cattle-fence in existence. But they could not return to their homes and food supplies if the power broadcast was cut off, either.

Over all the night surface of the world of Maya there was light only on one highway at one spot, and a multitude of smaller, lesser lights where the people of Maya waited to find out whether they would live or die.

V

Calhoun considered coldly. They were beyond what had been the farthest small city on the multiple highway. They would go on past now-starlit fields of plants native to Maya, passing many places where trucks loaded with the plants climbed up to the roadway and headed for the factories which made use of them. The fields ran for scores of miles along the highway's length. They reached out beyond the horizon,—perhaps scores of miles in that direction, too. There were thousands upon thousands of square miles devoted to the growing of the dark-green vegetation which supplied the raw materials for Maya's space exports. Some hundred-odd miles ahead, the small town of Tenochitlan lay huddled in the light of the distant star-cluster. Beyond that, more highway and Maya City. Beyond that—

Calhoun reasoned that the projector to make the induction cattle fence would be beyond Maya City, somewhere in the mountains the photograph in the spaceport building showed. A large highway went into those mountains for a limited distance only.

A ground-inductor projector field always formed at a right angle to the projector which was its source. It could be adjusted—the process was analogous to focusing—to come into actual being at any distance desired, and the distance could be changed. To drive the people of Maya City eastward, the projector of a cattle fence—about which they would know nothing; it would be totally strange and completely mysterious—the projector of the cattle fence would need to be west of the people to be driven. Logically, it would belong in the mountains. Practically, it would be concealed. Drawing on broadcast power to do its work, there would be no large power source needed to give it the six million kilowatts it required. It should be quite easy to hide beyond any quick or easy discovery. Hunting it out might require weeks of searching.

But the people beyond the end of the highway couldn't wait. They had no food, and holes scrabbled down to ground-water by men digging with their bare hands simply would not be adequate. The cattle fence had to be cut off immediately—while the broadcast of power had to be continued.

Calhoun made an abrupt grunting noise. Phrasing the thing that needed to be done was practically a blueprint of how to do it. Simple! He'd need the two electronics engineers, of course. But that would be the trick....

He drove on at a hundred thirty miles an hour with his lips set wrily. The three other cars came behind him. Murgatroyd watched the way ahead. Mile after mile, half-minute after half-minute, the headlights cast brilliantly blinding beams before the cars. Murgatroyd grew bored. He said, "*Chee!*" in a discontented fashion and tried to curl up between Allison and Calhoun. There wasn't room. He crawled over the seat-back. He moved about, back there. There were rustling sounds. He settled down. Presently there was silence. Undoubtedly he had draped his furry tail across his nose and gone soundly off to sleep.

Allison spoke suddenly. He'd had time to think, but he had no practice in various ways of thinking.

"How much money have you got?" he asked.

"Not much," said Calhoun. "Why?"

"I—haven't done anything illegal," said Allison, with an unconvincing air of confidence, "but I could be put to some inconvenience if you were to accuse me before others of what you've accused me personally. You seem to think that I planned a criminal act. That the action I know of—the research project I'd heard of—that it became—that it got out of hand is likely. But I am entirely in the clear. I did nothing in which I did not have the advice of counsel. I am legally unassailable. My lawyers—"

*

"That's none of my business," Calhoun told him. "I'm a medical man. I landed here in the middle of what seemed to be a serious public health situation. I went to see what had happened. I've found out. I still haven't the answer,—not the whole answer anyway. But the human population of Maya is in a state of some privation, not to say danger. I hope to end it. But I've nothing to do with anybody's guilt or innocence of crime or criminal intent or anything else."

Allison swallowed. Then he said with smooth confidence:

"But you could cause me inconvenience. I would appreciate it if you would—would—"

"Cover up what you've done?" asked Calhoun.

"No! I've done nothing wrong. But you could simply use discretion. I landed by parachute to complete some business deals I'd arranged months ago. I will go through with them. I will leave on the next ship. That's perfectly open and above board. Strictly business. But you could make a—an unpleasing public image of me. Yet I have done nothing any other business man wouldn't do! I did happen to know of a research project—"

"I think," said Calhoun without heat, "that you sent men here with a cattle-fence device from Texia to frighten the people on Maya. They wouldn't know what was going on. They'd be scared; they'd want to get away. So you'd be able to buy up practically all the colony for the equivalent of peanuts. I can't prove that," he conceded, "but that's my opinion. But you want me not to state it. Is that right?"

"Exactly!" said Allison. He'd been shaken to the core, but he managed the tone and the air of a dignified man of business discussing an unpleasant subject with fine candor. "I assure you you are mistaken. You agree that you can't prove your suspicions. If you can't prove them, you shouldn't state them. That is simple ethics. You agree to that!"

Calhoun looked at him curiously.

"Are you waiting for me to tell you my price?"

"I'm waiting," said Allison reprovingly, "for you to agree not to cause me embarrassment. I won't be ungrateful. After all, I'm a person of some influence. I could do a great deal to your benefit. I'd be glad—"

"Are you working around to guess at a price I'll take?" asked Calhoun with the same air of curiosity.

He seemed much more curious than indignant, and much more amused than curious. Allison sweated suddenly. Calhoun didn't appear to be bribable. But Allison knew desperation.

"If you want to put it that way—yes," he said harshly. "You can name your own figure. I mean it!"

"I won't say a word about you," said Calhoun. "I won't need to. The characters who're operating your cattle fence will do all the talking that's necessary. Things all fit together,—except for one item. They've been dropping into place all the while we've been driving down this road."

"I said you can name your own figure!" Allison's voice was shrill. "I mean it! Any figure! Any!"

Calhoun shrugged.

"What would a Med Ship man do with money? Forget it!"

He drove on. The highway turnoff to Tenochitlan appeared. Calhoun went steadily past it. The other connection with the road through the town appeared. He left it behind.

Allison's teeth chattered again.

The buildings of Maya City began to appear, some twenty minutes later. Calhoun slowed and the other cars closed up. He opened a window and called:

"We want to go to the landing-grid first. Somebody lead the way!"

A car went past and guided the rest assuredly to a ramp down from the now-elevated road, and through utterly dark streets, of which some were narrow and winding, and came out abruptly where the landing-grid rose skyward. At the bottom its massive girders looked huge and cyclopean in the starlight, but the higher courses looked like silver lace against the stars.

*

They went to the control building. Calhoun got out. Murgatroyd hopped out after him, dust clinging to his fur. He shook himself, and a ten-thousand-credit interstellar credit certificate fell to the ground. Murgatroyd had made a soft place for sleeping out of the contents of Allison's attache case. It was assuredly the most expensive if not the most comfortable sleeping cushion a *tormal* ever had. Allison sat still as if numbed. He did not even pick up the certificate.

"I need you two electronics men," said Calhoun. Then he said apologetically to the others, "I only figured out something on the way here. I'd believed we might have to take some drastic action, come daybreak. But now I doubt it. I do suggest, though, that you turn off the car headlights and get set to do some shooting if anybody turns up. I don't know whether they will or not."

He led the way inside. He turned on lights. He went to the place where dials showed the amount of power actually being used of the enormous amount available. Those dials now showed an extremely small power drain, considering that the cities of a planet depended on the grid. But the cities were dark and empty of people. The demand needle wavered back and forth, rhythmically. Every two seconds the demand for power went up by six million kilowatts, approximately. The demand lasted for half a second, and stopped. For a second and a half the power in use was reduced by six million kilowatts. During this period only automatic pumps and ventilators and freezing equipment drew on the broadcast power for energy. Then the six-million-kilowatt demand came again for half a second.

"The cattle fence," said Calhoun, "works for half a second out of every two seconds. It's intermittent or it would simply paralyze animals that wandered into it. Or people. Being intermittent, it drives them out instead. There'll be tools and parts for equipment here, in case something needs repair. I want you to make something new."

The two electronics technicians asked questions.

"We need," said Calhoun, "an interruptor that will cut off the power broadcast for the half-second the ground-induction field is supposed to be on. Then it should turn on the broadcast power for the second and a half the cattle fence is supposed to be off. That will stop the cattle-fence effect, and I think a ground car should be able to work with power that's available for three half-seconds out of four."

The electronics men blinked at him. Then they grinned and set to work. Calhoun went exploring. He found a lunch box in a desk with three very stale sandwiches in it. He offered them around.

It appeared that nobody wanted to eat while their families—at the end of the highway—were still hungry.

The electronics men called on the two mechanics to help build something. They explained absorbedly to Calhoun that they were making a cutoff which would adjust to any sudden six-million-kilowatt demand, no matter what time interval was involved. A change in the tempo of the cattle-fence cycle wouldn't bring it back on.

"That's fine!" said Calhoun. "I wouldn't have thought of that!"

He bit into a stale sandwich and went outside. Allison sat limply, despairingly, in his seat in the car.

"The cattle fence is going off," said Calhoun without triumph. "The people of the city will probably begin to get here around sunrise."

"I—I did nothing legally wrong!" said Allison, dry-throated. "Nothing! They'd have to prove that I knew what the—consequences of the research project would be. That couldn't be proved! It couldn't! So I've done nothing legally wrong...."

Calhoun went inside, observing that the doctor who was also tennis champion, and the policeman who'd come to help him, were keeping keen eyes on the city and the foundations of the grid and all other places from which trouble might come.

There was a fine atmosphere of achievement in the power-control room. The power itself did not pass through these instruments, but relays here controlled buried massive conductors which supplied the world with power. And one of the relays had been modified. When the cattle-fence projector closed its circuit, the power went off. When the ground-inductor went off, the power went on. There was no longer a barrier across the highways leading to the east. It was more than probable that ground cars could run on current supplied for one and a half seconds out of every two. They might run jerkily, but they would run.

*

Half an hour later, the amount of power drawn from the broadcast began to rise smoothly and gradually. It could mean only that cars were beginning to move.

Forty-five minutes later still, Calhoun heard stirrings outside. He went out. The two men on guard gazed off into the city. Something moved there. It was a ground-car, running slowly and without lights. Calhoun said undisturbedly:

"Whoever was running the cattle fence found out their gadget wasn't working. Their lights flickered, too. They came to see what was the matter at the landing-grid. But they've seen the lighted windows. Got your blasters handy?"

But the unlighted car turned and raced away. Calhoun only shrugged.

"They haven't a prayer," he said. "We'll take over their apparatus as soon as it's light. It'll be too big to destroy, and there'll be fingerprints and such to identify them as the men who ran it. And they're not natives. When the police start to look for the strangers who were living where the cattle-fence projector was set up.... They can go into the jungles where there's nothing to eat, or they can give themselves up."

He moved toward the door of the control building once more. Allison said desperately:

"They'll have hidden their equipment. You'll never be able to find it!"

Calhoun shook his head in the starlight.

"Anything that can fly can spot it in minutes. Even on the ground one can walk almost straight to it. You see, something happened they didn't count on. That's why they've left it turned on at full power. The earlier, teasing uses of the cattle fence were low-power. Annoying, to start with, and uncomfortable the second time, and maybe somewhat painful the third. But the last time it was full power."

He shrugged. He didn't feel like a long oration. But it was obvious. Something had killed the plants of a certain genus of which small species were weeds that destroyed Earth-type grasses. The ground-cover plants—and the larger ones, like the one Calhoun had seen decaying in a florist's shop which had had to be grown in a cage—the ground-cover plants had motile stems and leaves and blossoms. They were cannibals. They could move their stems to reach, and their leaves to enclose, and their flowers to devour other plants, even perhaps small animals. The point, though, was that they had some limited power of motion. Earth-style sensitive vines and flycatcher plants had primitive muscular tissues. The local ground-cover plants had them too. And the cattle-fence field made those tissues contract spasmodically. Powerfully. Violently. Repeatedly. Until they died of exhaustion. The full-power cattle-fence field had exterminated Mayan ground-cover plants all the way to the end of the east-bound highway. And inevitably—and very conveniently—also up to the exact spot where the cattle-fence field had begun to be projected. There would be an arrow-shaped narrowing of the wiped-out ground-cover plants where the cattle-field had been projected. It would narrow to a point which pointed precisely to the cattle-fence projector.

"Your friends," said Calhoun, "will probably give themselves up and ask for mercy. There's not much else they can do."

Then he said:

"They might even get it. D'you know, there's an interesting side effect of the cattle fence. It kills the plants that have kept Earth-type grasses from growing here. Wheat can be grown here now, whenever and as much as the people please. It should make this a pretty prosperous planet, not having to import all its bread."

*

The ground cars of the inhabitants of Maya City did begin to arrive at sunrise. Within an hour after daybreak, very savagely intent persons found the projector and turned it off.

By noon there was still some anger on the faces of the people of Maya, but there'd been little or no damage, and life took up its normal course again. Murgatroyd appreciated the fact that things went back to normal. For him it was normal to be welcomed and petted when the Med Ship *Esclipus Twenty* touched ground. It was normal for him to move zestfully in admiring human society, and to drink coffee with great gusto.

And while Murgatroyd moved in human society, enjoying himself hugely, Calhoun went about his business. Which, of course, was conferences with planetary health officials, politely receiving such information as they thought important, and tactfully telling them about the most recent developments in medical science.

What else was a Med Ship man for?

SPOKEN FOR

By William Morrison

He was lost—anyone could see that—but she had no idea how entirely lost he was nor why!

*

Half of Jupiter's great disk and most of the other moons were below the horizon when the man stepped out of the plane and changed her life. As far as Carol Marsh was concerned, he was ordinary enough in appearance. And she wasn't ordinarily attracted to ordinary men.

He was slightly over medium height, his features were not quite regular, and he had a deep tan over what had started out as a sunburn, so that she decided he had misjudged the strength of the sun on some planet with a thin atmosphere.

She frowned as she watched him look around. She was annoyed by the fact that it took him almost a minute to get his bearings and realize that she was first, a human being and second, a girl well worth a man's attention.

Even the troubled expression in his eyes was something she held against him. A man shouldn't look troubled. A man should be confident, self-assured in a manner that also assured the girl he spoke to. She remembered that back on Earth John Burr had been completely self-assured.

It was startling to realize that it was with this newcomer, whose appearance she had every reason to dislike, that she had fallen suddenly and completely in love, as suddenly and completely as if she had fallen off a cliff.

"I'm looking for some people," he said. "But I suppose—" His very voice was ill at ease, and that was something else she should have held against him. And against herself. She had always resented men whose voices betrayed their lack of confidence. "I suppose it's no use," he went on. "I'd recognize the house."

"Who are the people you're looking for?"

He took out a wallet, and from it drew a stereo picture. Two children, a boy and a girl, were standing with a smiling young woman in front of a sturdy, old-fashioned plastic house. Their clothes were out of fashion by a year or so, but that depended on where you were. Mars, for instance, was always three years behind Earth. Here on Ganymede, on the other hand, you might even be ahead of Earth in some respects.

*

As Carol's eyes lifted to his, she saw him staring at the picture with such longing that she at once knew herself for a fool. *They're his wife and children,* she thought. *He's trying to find them. And I had to fall in love with him at first sight.*

His eyes were on her now, and she said, "I'm sorry, I've never seen them."

"Have you lived around here long?"

"Five years."

"Then this can't be the place." He stood there irresolutely and started to turn slowly away without even a word of thanks to her.

"My father may have heard about them," said Carol, knowing herself for a fool again.

Past experience, she told herself ruefully, had taught her nothing. The thing to do was to let him go and forget him as quickly as possible, before she learned anything about him, before her feeling for him could become anything more than an irrational, momentary impulse. The stronger the bonds of knowledge and interest between them, the more painful they would be to break. And the breaking was inevitable.

The house where she and her father lived was a simple dome-shaped building, its walls and furniture both made of a silicon plastic whose raw materials had come from the ground on which it stood. There were rugs and draperies of a slightly different composition, woven on the all-purpose Household Helper that her father had bought before leaving Earth. They lived comfortably enough, she thought, as she led the man in.

But he hardly noticed the house or anything in it. When they reached the library and her father looked up from the book he was reading, only then did the man display interest. The book was a favorite of her father's and it made him unhappy to cut his reading short.

Nevertheless, he turned off the projector, stood up, and said, "Yes, Carol?"

"This man is looking for some—some friends of his, Dad. I thought you might be able to help him."

She held out the picture and, to her relief, her father stared at that instead of at her. Sometimes he was a little too shrewd; if she was making a fool of herself, there was no need for him to know it. He could be a sardonic man and he did not suffer fools gladly, even in his own family. He was of the opinion that she had used up her quota of foolishness with John Burr.

He was shaking his head. "Sorry, I've never seen them. Are you sure they live around here?"

"No," said the man. "I'm not sure. I'm not sure of anything, except that they're my wife and kids. And I've got to find them."

"Have you checked at the District Office?"

"I did that first. They couldn't help me, but they said their records weren't complete yet."

"They're complete enough, I should think. Maybe they don't list every prospector who wanders around without settling down, but they wouldn't be likely to miss a woman and two children. I'm afraid that you're wasting your time looking on Ganymede."

The man's face clouded. "It isn't a waste of my time," he said. "I've got nothing else to do with it. And I have to find them. They need me."

*

Mr. Marsh looked away from the man to his daughter, and Carol was a little slow in avoiding his eyes. "I see," he said, and she had an idea of what he meant by that. He saw too much.

If he knew, there was nothing she could do about it. She said, "Perhaps Mr.—"

She paused, and the man said dully, "Callendar."

"Perhaps if Mr. Callendar would have dinner with us and tell us a little more, we'd be better able to help."

"Not a bad idea, Carol. We should know a little more."

Carol selected a dinner and pressed the button that would start its preparation.

Her father said casually, "You are a stranger to Ganymede, aren't you, Mr. Callendar?"

"I'm not sure of that," said the man.

Her father's eyebrows went up.

Carol said, "But you do come from one of Jupiter's moons?"

"I can't remember which one. There are a lot of things that my memory's hazy about. I can't even recall the name of the company I worked for as an engineer."

"That may not be so strange. I find difficulty remembering the school where I taught on Earth. P.S. 654, wasn't it, Dad?"

"P.S. 634," Mr. Marsh corrected briefly.

"You see?" she said. "Do you remember your wife's name? And the names of your children?"

"I wouldn't forget *them*," he said. "My wife's name was Mona." He stared at the wall for a moment, his face without expression. "I can still see the way she looked when I left to undergo treatment. Paul was—let's see, he must be about nine, maybe ten, by this time. And Wilma must be six or seven. I remember how scared she was that time she found a harmless little phytopod. She thought it was going to bite her."

"Phytopod?" said Carol. "We don't have them around here. What do they look like?"

"They're small and furry, and have two feet that look like roots. When they stand still you're likely to mistake them for plants."

"You *do* recall some things," said Carol.

"The little things that don't tell me where to look. I remember the time we went on a picnic—I don't recall how many moons there were in the sky—and the ground began to shake. It didn't do any damage, but Wilma was terrified. Paul took it in his stride, though."

"There aren't any earthquakes on Ganymede," said her father. "If your memory of that incident is correct, you're looking in the wrong place."

"I suppose so," he said. "But what's the right place?"

"Perhaps if you thought of a few more incidents, we might figure it out. It's the little things you don't forget that can be most helpful."

*

What nonsense, thought Carol, although she kept the thought to herself. The little things can be most *harmful*. They keep the pain, and the memory of pain, alive and vivid. She remembered little things about John all too well—the careless way he wore his clothes, and the way he combed his hair, the cigarettes he smoked, and the foods he liked to eat. And the stupid way she had let herself fall in love with him.

She hadn't even had the excuse of its happening suddenly, as it had happened now. She had begun to love John as she had come to know him, disregarding all the evidence of his selfishness, of his genuine inability to care for any one else than John Burr.

Unaware of what was going on in her mind, Callendar was saying, with somewhat more animation than he had previously shown, "I think you're right, Mr. Marsh. I've kept my troubles too much to myself. Maybe you can't actually do anything for me, but it wouldn't hurt me to talk. I should have done my talking long ago. When they found me."

"Where did they find you?" asked her father. "And what did you mean before, when you said you're not sure of anything?"

"They picked me up in a lifeboat, drifting some place between Mars and Jupiter. The motor was off, but the power pile was working, and the air-purifying equipment was on. I was apparently hibernating. I might have been that way for six months or a year."

"And you don't remember—" said Carol.

"There's plenty I don't remember, but as I've said, my memory isn't a complete blank. My wife and I and the kids had settled down in a new colony—exactly where it was is one of the things I forget. I believe now that it wasn't Ganymede. Maybe it was some other moon of Jupiter's.

"Anyway, I seem to recall having some trouble with my health, and being taken onto an inter-planetary hospital ship for treatment—L-treatment, they called it. That's where they put me to sleep. What happened after that, I can only guess. The ship must have been involved in some accident. I must have been transferred to the lifeboat."

"Alone?" asked Carol's father.

"No. There were two other patients with me. They were found dead. I was the only one left alive. The bodies of the crew members who transferred us weren't found at all. They might have gone back for more patients and then been unable to get away again."

"Who found your lifeboat?"

"The crew of a freighter, who spotted it drifting across a space lane. They took me on board and revived me. But they were in a hurry and didn't have much time to stay and investigate."

*

Mr. Marsh was thoughtful and silent.

Carol asked, "Weren't there any records in the lifeboat?"

"Nobody thought of that, at least not in the beginning. At first, when I regained consciousness, my mind was almost a complete blank. Then I began to remember things, but not enough. I couldn't recall where the colony had been, and after I had recovered enough to be able to get around, I began looking for my wife and children. I haven't come across a trace of them, although I've been on many worlds."

The food had long been ready and waiting. Until now, no one had thought of getting it. He stared as if through the wall and Carol, after she had set the dishes before him, had to remind him of their presence. When he did eat, it was automatically, without enjoyment.

Afterward, her father surprised Carol by saying, "Why not stay with us overnight, Mr. Callendar? We have an extra room, and tomorrow I may be able to give you a little helpful information."

The man's eyes came alive. "You're serious? You think that from what I told you, you'll be able to guess where I came from?"

"I used the word 'might.' Don't get your hopes up too much."

His face fell again. "Thanks for warning me," he said in a flat tone.

When, later on, he had gone to his room, Carol said, "Dad, do you really think you can help him?"

"That depends on your idea of help. Why are you so interested in him? Perhaps you're falling in love with him, Carol?"

"I think so."

"Under the circumstances, that's completely idiotic. Would there be any sense in asking *why* you fell in love with him?"

"Well, he looked so *lost*! I guess it's maternal—"

"As genuine a case of the grand passion as I've ever encountered," he said drily. "Almost as genuine as your previous experience."

Carol flushed. "He isn't like John."

*

"Fortunately, you are right. Burr was essentially a selfish baby. I can't imagine him spending *his* life looking for a wife and children he had lost. In future, Carol, if you must fall in love at all, do it suddenly. You choose much better that way."

"Yes, I know," she said. "Except for the fact that the wife and children may interfere. But don't worry, Dad. This time I'm not quitting my job and moving several million miles away to try to forget."

"There'll be no need for that." His face took on a troubled expression. "You'll have to face your problem right here."

*

"You haven't answered *my* question," said Carol. "Do you really think you can help him?"

"That isn't an easy one to answer. We'll have to prepare him for a shock, Carol. A first-class shock. That's why I wanted to be sure you were in love with him. It may make things easier for him to stand."

"What things?"

Her father hesitated. "Have you ever heard of this L-treatment he mentioned?"

She shook her head.

"I thought not. Carol," he said, and his voice was unexpectedly full of compassion, "you're going to have a very sick man on your hands. It won't be pleasant for either you or me, and it's going to be horrible for him. But it must be gone through. He must be told."

"For heaven's sake, what is it?"

"The L in L-treatment," he said slowly, "stands for longevity. That was what he was treated for. But you see now why it was found to be dangerous and discontinued. The reason you never heard of it is that it was developed and discarded two hundred years ago. Callendar wasn't adrift in space for a year or two, as he thinks. He was adrift for two centuries."

"No! Oh, *no*!"

"That's why the clothes in those pictures seemed odd. They've been in style and out again half a dozen times, with slight changes each time. That is why, furthermore, he can't find his wife and children on any of Jupiter's moons. The moons were first colonized ninety years ago."

"But he says—"

"He'll never see his wife and children again. They've lived their lives and died and been buried in the past. He should have died with them in his own time and not lived into ours."

"No," said Carol, "or I'd never have known him."

She was white and trembling, and her father pulled her to him and let her head rest on his shoulder.

Mr. Marsh said, "Perhaps you're right. I don't know. Anyway, he'll have to be told. And for your sake, I'd better do the telling."

Carol was silent, and they both thought of the sleeping man who didn't know that his old life had ended and that a new life was to begin so painfully in the morning.

A PAIL OF AIR

By Fritz Leiber

The dark star passed, bringing with it eternal night and turning history into incredible myth in a single generation!

*

Pa had sent me out to get an extra pail of air. I'd just about scooped it full and most of the warmth had leaked from my fingers when I saw the thing.

You know, at first I thought it was a young lady. Yes, a beautiful young lady's face all glowing in the dark and looking at me from the fifth floor of the opposite apartment, which hereabouts is the floor just above the white blanket of frozen air. I'd never seen a live young lady before, except in the old magazines—Sis is just a kid and Ma is pretty sick and miserable—and it gave me such a start that I dropped the pail. Who wouldn't, knowing everyone on Earth was dead except Pa and Ma and Sis and you?

Even at that, I don't suppose I should have been surprised. We all see things now and then. Ma has some pretty bad ones, to judge from the way she bugs her eyes at nothing and just screams and screams and huddles back against the blankets hanging around the Nest. Pa says it is natural we should react like that sometimes.

When I'd recovered the pail and could look again at the opposite apartment, I got an idea of what Ma might be feeling at those times, for I saw it wasn't a young lady at all but simply a light—a tiny light that moved stealthily from window to window, just as if one of the cruel little stars had come down out of the airless sky to investigate why the Earth had gone away from the Sun, and maybe to hunt down something to torment or terrify, now that the Earth didn't have the Sun's protection.

I tell you, the thought of it gave me the creeps. I just stood there shaking, and almost froze my feet and did frost my helmet so solid on the inside that I couldn't have seen the light even if it had come out of one of the windows to get me. Then I had the wit to go back inside.

Pretty soon I was feeling my familiar way through the thirty or so blankets and rugs Pa has got hung around to slow down the escape of air from the Nest, and I wasn't quite so scared. I began to hear the tick-ticking of the clocks in the Nest and knew I was getting back into air, because there's no sound outside in the vacuum, of course. But my mind was still crawly and uneasy as I pushed through the last blankets—Pa's got them faced with aluminum foil to hold in the heat—and came into the Nest.

*

Let me tell you about the Nest. It's low and snug, just room for the four of us and our things. The floor is covered with thick woolly rugs. Three of the sides are blankets, and the blankets roofing it touch Pa's head. He tells me it's inside a much bigger room, but I've never seen the real walls or ceiling.

Against one of the blanket-walls is a big set of shelves, with tools and books and other stuff, and on top of it a whole row of clocks. Pa's very fussy about keeping them wound. He says we must never forget time, and without a sun or moon, that would be easy to do.

The fourth wall has blankets all over except around the fireplace, in which there is a fire that must never go out. It keeps us from freezing and does a lot more besides. One of us must always watch it. Some of the clocks are alarm and we can use them to remind us. In the early days there was only Ma to take turns with Pa—I think of that when she gets difficult—but now there's me to help, and Sis too.

It's Pa who is the chief guardian of the fire, though. I always think of him that way: a tall man sitting cross-legged, frowning anxiously at the fire, his lined face golden in its light, and every so often carefully placing on it a piece of coal from the big heap beside it. Pa tells me there used to be guardians of the fire sometimes in the very old days—vestal virgins, he calls them—although there was unfrozen air all around then and you didn't really need one.

He was sitting just that way now, though he got up quick to take the pail from me and bawl me out for loitering—he'd spotted my frozen helmet right off. That roused Ma and she joined in picking on me. She's always trying to get the load off her feelings, Pa explains. He shut her up pretty fast. Sis let off a couple of silly squeals too.

Pa handled the pail of air in a twist of cloth. Now that it was inside the Nest, you could really feel its coldness. It just seemed to suck the heat out of everything. Even the flames cringed away from it as Pa put it down close by the fire.

Yet it's that glimmery white stuff in the pail that keeps us alive. It slowly melts and vanishes and refreshes the Nest and feeds the fire. The blankets keep it from escaping too fast. Pa'd like to seal the whole place, but he can't—building's too earthquake-twisted, and besides he has to leave the chimney open for smoke.

Pa says air is tiny molecules that fly away like a flash if there isn't something to stop them. We have to watch sharp not to let the air run low. Pa always keeps a big reserve supply of it in buckets behind the first blankets, along with extra coal and cans of food and other things, such as pails of snow to melt for water. We have to go way down to the bottom floor for that stuff, which is a mean trip, and get it through a door to outside.

You see, when the Earth got cold, all the water in the air froze first and made a blanket ten feet thick or so everywhere, and then down on top of that dropped the crystals of frozen air, making another white blanket sixty or seventy feet thick maybe.

Of course, all the parts of the air didn't freeze and snow down at the same time.

First to drop out was the carbon dioxide—when you're shoveling for water, you have to make sure you don't go too high and get any of that stuff mixed in, for it would put you to sleep, maybe for good, and make the fire go out. Next there's the nitrogen, which doesn't count one way or the other, though it's the biggest part of the blanket. On top of that and easy to get at, which is lucky for us, there's the oxygen that keeps us alive. Pa says we live better than kings ever did, breathing pure oxygen, but we're used to it and don't notice. Finally, at the very top, there's a slick of liquid helium, which is funny stuff. All of these gases in neat separate layers. Like a pussy caffay, Pa laughingly says, whatever that is.

*

I was busting to tell them all about what I'd seen, and so as soon as I'd ducked out of my helmet and while I was still climbing out of my suit, I cut loose. Right away Ma got nervous and began making eyes at the entry-slit in the blankets and wringing her hands together—the hand where she'd lost three fingers from frostbite inside the good one, as usual. I could tell that Pa was annoyed at me scaring her and wanted to explain it all away quickly, yet could see I wasn't fooling.

"And you watched this light for some time, son?" he asked when I finished.

I hadn't said anything about first thinking it was a young lady's face.

Somehow that part embarrassed me.

"Long enough for it to pass five windows and go to the next floor."

"And it didn't look like stray electricity or crawling liquid or starlight focused by a growing crystal, or anything like that?"

He wasn't just making up those ideas. Odd things happen in a world that's about as cold as can be, and just when you think matter would be frozen dead, it takes on a strange new life. A slimy stuff comes crawling toward the Nest, just like an animal snuffing for heat—that's the liquid helium. And once, when I was little, a bolt of lightning—not even Pa could figure where it came from—hit the nearby steeple and crawled up and down it for weeks, until the glow finally died.

"Not like anything I ever saw," I told him.

He stood for a moment frowning. Then, "I'll go out with you, and you show it to me," he said.

Ma raised a howl at the idea of being left alone, and Sis joined in, too, but Pa quieted them. We started climbing into our outside clothes—mine had been warming by the fire. Pa made them. They have plastic headpieces that were once big double-duty transparent food cans, but they keep heat and air in and can replace the air for a little while, long enough for our trips for water and coal and food and so on.

Ma started moaning again, "I've always known there was something outside there, waiting to get us. I've felt it for years—something that's part of the cold and hates all warmth and wants to destroy the Nest. It's been watching us all this time, and now it's coming after us. It'll get you and then come for me. Don't go, Harry!"

Pa had everything on but his helmet. He knelt by the fireplace and reached in and shook the long metal rod that goes up the chimney and knocks off the ice that keeps trying to clog it. Once a week he goes up on the roof to check if it's working all right. That's our worst trip and Pa won't let me make it alone.

"Sis," Pa said quietly, "come watch the fire. Keep an eye on the air, too. If it gets low or doesn't seem to be boiling fast enough, fetch another bucket from behind the blanket. But mind your hands. Use the cloth to pick up the bucket."

Sis quit helping Ma be frightened and came over and did as she was told. Ma quieted down pretty suddenly, though her eyes were still kind of wild as she watched Pa fix on his helmet tight and pick up a pail and the two of us go out.

*

Pa led the way and I took hold of his belt. It's a funny thing, I'm not afraid to go by myself, but when Pa's along I always want to hold on to him. Habit, I guess, and then there's no denying that this time I was a bit scared.

You see, it's this way. We know that everything is dead out there. Pa heard the last radio voices fade away years ago, and had seen some of the last folks die who weren't as lucky or well-protected as us. So we knew that if there was something groping around out there, it couldn't be anything human or friendly.

Besides that, there's a feeling that comes with it always being night, *cold* night. Pa says there used to be some of that feeling even in the old days, but then every morning the Sun would come and chase it away. I have to take his word for that, not ever remembering the Sun as being anything more than a big star. You see, I hadn't been born when the dark star snatched us away from the Sun, and by now it's dragged us out beyond the orbit of the planet Pluto, Pa says, and taking us farther out all the time.

I found myself wondering whether there mightn't be something on the dark star that wanted us, and if that was why it had captured the Earth. Just then we came to the end of the corridor and I followed Pa out on the balcony.

I don't know what the city looked like in the old days, but now it's beautiful. The starlight lets you see it pretty well—there's quite a bit of light in those steady points speckling the blackness above. (Pa says the stars used to twinkle once, but that was because there was air.) We are on a hill and the shimmery plain drops away from us and then flattens out, cut up into neat squares by the troughs that used to be streets. I sometimes make my mashed potatoes look like it, before I pour on the gravy.

Some taller buildings push up out of the feathery plain, topped by rounded caps of air crystals, like the fur hood Ma wears, only whiter. On those buildings you can see the darker squares of windows, underlined by white dashes of air crystals. Some of them are on a slant, for many of the buildings are pretty badly twisted by the quakes and all the rest that happened when the dark star captured the Earth.

Here and there a few icicles hang, water icicles from the first days of the cold, other icicles of frozen air that melted on the roofs and dripped and froze again. Sometimes one of those icicles will catch the light of a star and send it to you so brightly you think the star has swooped into the city. That was one of the things Pa had been thinking of when I told him about the light, but I had thought of it myself first and known it wasn't so.

He touched his helmet to mine so we could talk easier and he asked me to point out the windows to him. But there wasn't any light moving around inside them now, or anywhere else. To my surprise, Pa didn't bawl me out and tell me I'd been seeing things. He looked all around quite a while after filling his pail, and just as we were going inside he whipped around without warning, as if to take some peeping thing off guard.

I could feel it, too. The old peace was gone. There was something lurking out there, watching, waiting, getting ready.

Inside, he said to me, touching helmets, "If you see something like that again, son, don't tell the others. Your Ma's sort of nervous these days and we owe her all the feeling of safety we can give her. Once—it was when your sister was born—I was ready to give up and die, but your Mother kept me trying. Another time she kept the fire going a whole week all by herself when I was sick. Nursed me and took care of the two of you, too."

*

"You know that game we sometimes play, sitting in a square in the Nest, tossing a ball around? Courage is like a ball, son. A person can hold it only so long, and then he's got to toss it to someone else. When it's tossed your way, you've got to catch it and hold it tight—and hope there'll be someone else to toss it to when you get tired of being brave."

His talking to me that way made me feel grown-up and good. But it didn't wipe away the thing outside from the back of my mind—or the fact that Pa took it seriously.

*

It's hard to hide your feelings about such a thing. When we got back in the Nest and took off our outside clothes, Pa laughed about it all and told them it was nothing and kidded me for having such an imagination, but his words fell flat. He didn't convince Ma and Sis any more than he did me. It looked for a minute like we were all fumbling the courage-ball. Something had to be done, and almost before I knew what I was going to say, I heard myself asking Pa to tell us about the old days, and how it all happened.

He sometimes doesn't mind telling that story, and Sis and I sure like to listen to it, and he got my idea. So we were all settled around the fire in a wink, and Ma pushed up some cans to thaw for supper, and Pa began. Before he did, though, I noticed him casually get a hammer from the shelf and lay it down beside him.

It was the same old story as always—I think I could recite the main thread of it in my sleep—though Pa always puts in a new detail or two and keeps improving it in spots.

He told us how the Earth had been swinging around the Sun ever so steady and warm, and the people on it fixing to make money and wars and have a good time and get power and treat each other right or wrong, when without warning there comes charging out of space this dead star, this burned out sun, and upsets everything.

You know, I find it hard to believe in the way those people felt, any more than I can believe in the swarming number of them. Imagine people getting ready for the horrible sort of war they were cooking up. Wanting it even, or at least wishing it were over so as to end their nervousness. As if all folks didn't have to hang together and pool every bit of warmth just to keep alive. And how can they have hoped to end danger, any more than we can hope to end the cold?

Sometimes I think Pa exaggerates and makes things out too black. He's cross with us once in a while and was probably cross with all those folks. Still, some of the things I read in the old magazines sound pretty wild. He may be right.

*

The dark star, as Pa went on telling it, rushed in pretty fast and there wasn't much time to get ready. At the beginning they tried to keep it a secret from most people, but then the truth came out, what with the earthquakes and floods—imagine, oceans of *unfrozen* water!—and people seeing stars blotted out by something on a clear night. First off they thought it would hit the Sun, and then they thought it would hit the Earth. There was even the start of a rush to get to a place called China, because people thought the star would hit on the other side. But then they found it wasn't going to hit either side, but was going to come very close to the Earth.

Most of the other planets were on the other side of the Sun and didn't get involved. The Sun and the newcomer fought over the Earth for a little while—pulling it this way and that, like two dogs growling over a bone, Pa described it this time—and then the newcomer won and carried us off. The Sun got a consolation prize, though. At the last minute he managed to hold on to the Moon.

That was the time of the monster earthquakes and floods, twenty times worse than anything before. It was also the time of the Big Jerk, as Pa calls it, when all Earth got yanked suddenly, just as Pa has done to me once or twice, grabbing me by the collar to do it, when I've been sitting too far from the fire.

You see, the dark star was going through space faster than the Sun, and in the opposite direction, and it had to wrench the world considerably in order to take it away.

The Big Jerk didn't last long. It was over as soon as the Earth was settled down in its new orbit around the dark star. But it was pretty terrible while it lasted. Pa says that all sorts of cliffs and buildings toppled, oceans slopped over, swamps and sandy deserts gave great sliding surges that buried nearby lands. Earth was almost jerked out of its atmosphere blanket and the air got so thin in spots that people keeled over and fainted—though of course, at the same time, they were getting knocked down by the Big Jerk and maybe their bones broke or skulls cracked.

We've often asked Pa how people acted during that time, whether they were scared or brave or crazy or stunned, or all four, but he's sort of leery of the subject, and he was again tonight. He says he was mostly too busy to notice.

You see, Pa and some scientist friends of his had figured out part of what was going to happen—they'd known we'd get captured and our air would freeze—and they'd been working like mad to fix up a place with airtight walls and doors, and insulation against the cold, and big supplies of food and fuel and water and bottled air. But the place got smashed in the last earthquakes and all Pa's friends were killed then and in the Big Jerk. So he had to start over and throw the Nest together quick without any advantages, just using any stuff he could lay his hands on.

I guess he's telling pretty much the truth when he says he didn't have any time to keep an eye on how other folks behaved, either then or in the Big Freeze that followed—followed very quick, you know, both because the dark star was pulling us away very fast and because Earth's rotation had been slowed in the tug-of-war, so that the nights were ten old nights long.

Still, I've got an idea of some of the things that happened from the frozen folk I've seen, a few of them in other rooms in our building, others clustered around the furnaces in the basements where we go for coal.

In one of the rooms, an old man sits stiff in a chair, with an arm and a leg in splints. In another, a man and woman are huddled together in a bed with heaps of covers over them. You can just see their heads peeking out, close together. And in another a beautiful young lady is sitting with a pile of wraps huddled around her, looking hopefully toward the door, as if waiting for someone who never came back with warmth and food. They're all still and stiff as statues, of course, but just like life.

Pa showed them to me once in quick winks of his flashlight, when he still had a fair supply of batteries and could afford to waste a little light. They scared me pretty bad and made my heart pound, especially the young lady.

*

Now, with Pa telling his story for the umpteenth time to take our minds off another scare, I got to thinking of the frozen folk again. All of a sudden I got an idea that scared me worse than anything yet. You see, I'd just remembered the face I'd thought I'd seen in the window. I'd forgotten about that on account of trying to hide it from the others.

What, I asked myself, if the frozen folk were coming to life? What if they were like the liquid helium that got a new lease on life and started crawling toward the heat just when you thought its molecules ought to freeze solid forever? Or like the electricity that moves endlessly when it's just about as cold as that? What if the ever-growing cold, with the temperature creeping down the last few degrees to the last zero, had mysteriously wakened the frozen folk to life—not warm-blooded life, but something icy and horrible?

That was a worse idea than the one about something coming down from the dark star to get us.

Or maybe, I thought, both ideas might be true. Something coming down from the dark star and making the frozen folk move, using them to do its work. That would fit with both things I'd seen—the beautiful young lady and the moving, starlike light.

The frozen folk with minds from the dark star behind their unwinking eyes, creeping, crawling, snuffing their way, following the heat to the Nest.

I tell you, that thought gave me a very bad turn and I wanted very badly to tell the others my fears, but I remembered what Pa had said and clenched my teeth and didn't speak.

We were all sitting very still. Even the fire was burning silently. There was just the sound of Pa's voice and the clocks.

And then, from beyond the blankets, I thought I heard a tiny noise. My skin tightened all over me.

Pa was telling about the early years in the Nest and had come to the place where he philosophizes.

"So I asked myself then," he said, "what's the use of going on? What's the use of dragging it out for a few years? Why prolong a doomed existence of hard work and cold and loneliness? The human race is done. The Earth is done. Why not give up, I asked myself—and all of a sudden I got the answer."

Again I heard the noise, louder this time, a kind of uncertain, shuffling tread, coming closer. I couldn't breathe.

"Life's always been a business of working hard and fighting the cold," Pa was saying. "The earth's always been a lonely place, millions of miles from the next planet. And no matter how long the human race might have lived, the end would have come some night. Those things don't matter. What matters is that life is good. It has a lovely texture, like some rich cloth or fur, or the petals of flowers—you've seen pictures of those, but I can't describe how they feel—or the fire's glow. It makes everything else worth while. And that's as true for the last man as the first."

And still the steps kept shuffling closer. It seemed to me that the inmost blanket trembled and bulged a little. Just as if they were burned into my imagination, I kept seeing those peering, frozen eyes.

"So right then and there," Pa went on, and now I could tell that he heard the steps, too, and was talking loud so we maybe wouldn't hear them, "right then and there I told myself that I was going on as if we had all eternity ahead of us. I'd have children and teach them all I could. I'd get them to read books. I'd plan for the future, try to enlarge and seal the Nest. I'd do what I could to keep everything beautiful and growing. I'd keep alive my feeling of wonder even at the cold and the dark and the distant stars."

But then the blanket actually did move and lift. And there was a bright light somewhere behind it. Pa's voice stopped and his eyes turned to the widening slit and his hand went out until it touched and gripped the handle of the hammer beside him.

*

In through the blanket stepped the beautiful young lady. She stood there looking at us the strangest way, and she carried something bright and unwinking in her hand. And two other faces peered over her shoulders—men's faces, white and staring.

Well, my heart couldn't have been stopped for more than four or five beats before I realized she was wearing a suit and helmet like Pa's homemade ones, only fancier, and that the men were, too—and that the frozen folk certainly wouldn't be wearing those. Also, I noticed that the bright thing in her hand was just a kind of flashlight.

The silence kept on while I swallowed hard a couple of times, and after that there was all sorts of jabbering and commotion.

They were simply people, you see. We hadn't been the only ones to survive; we'd just thought so, for natural enough reasons. These three people had survived, and quite a few others with them. And when we found out *how* they'd survived, Pa let out the biggest whoop of joy.

They were from Los Alamos and they were getting their heat and power from atomic energy. Just using the uranium and plutonium intended for bombs, they had enough to go on for thousands of years. They had a regular little airtight city, with air-locks and all. They even generated electric light and grew plants and animals by it. (At this Pa let out a second whoop, waking Ma from her faint.)

But if we were flabbergasted at them, they were double-flabbergasted at us.

One of the men kept saying, "But it's impossible, I tell you. You can't maintain an air supply without hermetic sealing. It's simply impossible."

That was after he had got his helmet off and was using our air. Meanwhile, the young lady kept looking around at us as if we were saints, and telling us we'd done something amazing, and suddenly she broke down and cried.

They'd been scouting around for survivors, but they never expected to find any in a place like this. They had rocket ships at Los Alamos and plenty of chemical fuel. As for liquid oxygen, all you had to do was go out and shovel the air blanket at the top *level*. So after they'd got things going smoothly at Los Alamos, which had taken years, they'd decided to make some trips to likely places where there might be other survivors. No good trying long-distance radio signals, of course, since there was no atmosphere to carry them around the curve of the Earth.

Well, they'd found other colonies at Argonne and Brookhaven and way around the world at Harwell and Tanna Tuva. And now they'd been giving our city a look, not really expecting to find anything. But they had an instrument that noticed the faintest heat waves and it had told them there was something warm down here, so they'd landed to investigate. Of course we hadn't heard them land, since there was no air to carry the sound, and they'd had to investigate around quite a while before finding us. Their instruments had given them a wrong steer and they'd wasted some time in the building across the street.

*

By now, all five adults were talking like sixty. Pa was demonstrating to the men how he worked the fire and got rid of the ice in the chimney and all that. Ma had perked up wonderfully and was showing the young lady her cooking and sewing stuff, and even asking about how the women dressed at Los Alamos. The strangers marveled at everything and praised it to the skies. I could tell from the way they wrinkled their noses that they found the Nest a bit smelly, but they never mentioned that at all and just asked bushels of questions.

In fact, there was so much talking and excitement that Pa forgot about things, and it wasn't until they were all getting groggy that he looked and found the air had all boiled away in the pail. He got another bucket of air quick from behind the blankets. Of course that started them all laughing and jabbering again. The newcomers even got a little drunk. They weren't used to so much oxygen.

Funny thing, though—I didn't do much talking at all and Sis hung on to Ma all the time and hid her face when anybody looked at her. I felt pretty uncomfortable and disturbed myself, even about the young lady. Glimpsing her outside there, I'd had all sorts of mushy thoughts, but now I was just embarrassed and scared of her, even though she tried to be nice as anything to me.

I sort of wished they'd all quit crowding the Nest and let us be alone and get our feelings straightened out.

And when the newcomers began to talk about our all going to Los Alamos, as if that were taken for granted, I could see that something of the same feeling struck Pa and Ma, too. Pa got very silent all of a sudden and Ma kept telling the young lady, "But I wouldn't know how to act there and I haven't any clothes."

The strangers were puzzled like anything at first, but then they got the idea. As Pa kept saying, "It just doesn't seem right to let this fire go out."

*

Well, the strangers are gone, but they're coming back. It hasn't been decided yet just what will happen. Maybe the Nest will be kept up as what one of the strangers called a "survival school." Or maybe we will join the pioneers who are going to try to establish a new colony at the uranium mines at Great Slave Lake or in the Congo.

Of course, now that the strangers are gone, I've been thinking a lot about Los Alamos and those other tremendous colonies. I have a hankering to see them for myself.

You ask me, Pa wants to see them, too. He's been getting pretty thoughtful, watching Ma and Sis perk up.

"It's different, now that we know others are alive," he explains to me. "Your mother doesn't feel so hopeless any more. Neither do I, for that matter, not having to carry the whole responsibility for keeping the human race going, so to speak. It scares a person."

I looked around at the blanket walls and the fire and the pails of air boiling away and Ma and Sis sleeping in the warmth and the flickering light.

"It's not going to be easy to leave the Nest," I said, wanting to cry, kind of. "It's so small and there's just the four of us. I get scared at the idea of big places and a lot of strangers."

He nodded and put another piece of coal on the fire. Then he looked at the little pile and grinned suddenly and put a couple of handfuls on, just as if it was one of our birthdays or Christmas.

"You'll quickly get over that feeling son," he said. "The trouble with the world was that it kept getting smaller and smaller, till it ended with just the Nest. Now it'll be good to have a real huge world again, the way it was in the beginning."

I guess he's right. You think the beautiful young lady will wait for me till I grow up? I'll be twenty in only ten years.

CONTAGION

by Katherine MacLEAN

Minos was such a lovely planet. Not athing seemed wrong with it. Excepting the food,perhaps. And a disease that wasn't really.

It was like an Earth forest in the fall, but it was not fall. The forest leaves were green and copper and purple and fiery red, and a wind sent patches of bright greenish sunlight dancing among the leaf shadows.

The hunt party of the *Explorer* filed along the narrow trail, guns ready, walking carefully, listening to the distant, half familiar cries of strange birds.

A faint crackle of static in their earphones indicated that a gun had been fired.

"Got anything?" asked June Walton. The helmet intercom carried her voice to the ears of the others without breaking the stillness of the forest.

"Took a shot at something," explained George Barton's cheerful voice in her earphones. She rounded a bend of the trail and came upon Barton standing peering up into the trees, his gun still raised. "It looked like a duck."

"This isn't Central Park," said Hal Barton, his brother, coming into sight. His green spacesuit struck an incongruous note against the bronze and red forest. "They won't all look like ducks," he said soberly.

"Maybe some will look like dragons. Don't get eaten by a dragon, June," came Max's voice quietly into her earphones. "Not while I still love you." He came out of the trees carrying the blood sample kit, and touched her glove with his, the grin on his ugly beloved face barely visible in the mingled light and shade. A patch of sunlight struck a greenish glint from his fishbowl helmet.

*

They walked on. A quarter of a mile back, the space ship *Explorer* towered over the forest like a tapering skyscraper, and the people of the ship looked out of the viewplates at fresh winds and sunlight and clouds, and they longed to be outside.

But the likeness to Earth was danger, and the cool wind might be death, for if the animals were like Earth animals, their diseases might be like Earth diseases, alike enough to be contagious, different enough to be impossible to treat. There was warning enough in the past. Colonies had vanished, and traveled spaceways drifted with the corpses of ships which had touched on some plague planet.

The people of the ship waited while their doctors, in airtight spacesuits, hunted animals to test them for contagion.

The four medicos, for June Walton was also a doctor, filed through the alien homelike forest, walking softly, watching for motion among the copper and purple shadows.

They saw it suddenly, a lighter moving copper patch among the darker browns. Reflex action swung June's gun into line, and behind her someone's gun went off with a faint crackle of static, and made a hole in the leaves beside the specimen. Then for a while no one moved.

This one looked like a man, a magnificently muscled, leanly graceful, humanlike animal. Even in its callused bare feet, it was a head taller than any of them. Red-haired, hawk-faced and darkly tanned, it stood breathing heavily, looking at them without expression. At its side hung a sheath knife, and a crossbow was slung across one wide shoulder.

They lowered their guns.

"It needs a shave," Max said reasonably in their earphones, and he reached up to his helmet and flipped the switch that let his voice be heard. "Something we could do for you, Mac?"

The friendly drawl was the first voice that had broken the forest sounds. June smiled suddenly. He was right. The strict logic of evolution did not demand beards; therefore a non-human would not be wearing a three day growth of red stubble.

Still panting, the tall figure licked dry lips and spoke. "Welcome to Minos. The Mayor sends greetings from Alexandria."

"English?" gasped June.

"We were afraid you would take off again before I could bring word to you.... It's three hundred miles.... We saw your scout plane pass twice, but we couldn't attract its attention."

*

June looked in stunned silence at the stranger leaning against the tree. Thirty-six light years—thirty-six times six trillion miles of monotonous space travel—to be told that the planet was already settled! "We didn't know there was a colony here," she said. "It is not on the map."

"We were afraid of that," the tall bronze man answered soberly. "We have been here three generations and yet no traders have come."

Max shifted the kit strap on his shoulder and offered a hand. "My name is Max Stark, M.D. This is June Walton, M.D., Hal Barton, M.D., and George Barton, Hal's brother, also M.D."

"Patrick Mead is the name," smiled the man, shaking hands casually. "Just a hunter and bridge carpenter myself. Never met any medicos before."

The grip was effortless but even through her airproofed glove June could feel that the fingers that touched hers were as hard as padded steel.

"What—what is the population of Minos?" she asked.

He looked down at her curiously for a moment before answering. "Only one hundred and fifty." He smiled. "Don't worry, this isn't a city planet yet. There's room for a few more people." He shook hands with the Bartons quickly. "That is—you are people, aren't you?" he asked startlingly.

"Why not?" said Max with a poise that June admired.

"Well, you are all so—so—" Patrick Mead's eyes roamed across the faces of the group. "So varied."

They could find no meaning in that, and stood puzzled.

"I mean," Patrick Mead said into the silence, "all these—interesting different hair colors and face shapes and so forth—" He made a vague wave with one hand as if he had run out of words or was anxious not to insult them.

"Joke?" Max asked, bewildered.

June laid a hand on his arm. "No harm meant," she said to him over the intercom. "We're just as much of a shock to him as he is to us."

She addressed a question to the tall colonist on outside sound. "What should a person look like, Mr. Mead?"

He indicated her with a smile. "Like you."

June stepped closer and stood looking up at him, considering her own description. She was tall and tanned, like him; had a few freckles, like him; and wavy red hair, like his. She ignored the brightly humorous blue eyes.

"In other words," she said, "everyone on the planet looks like you and me?"

Patrick Mead took another look at their four faces and began to grin. "Like me, I guess. But I hadn't thought of it before. I did not think that people could have different colored hair or that noses could fit so many ways onto faces. I was judging by my own appearance, but I suppose any fool can walk on his hands and say the world is upside down!" He laughed and sobered. "But then why wear spacesuits? The air is breathable."

"For safety," June told him. "We can't take any chances on plague."

Pat Mead was wearing nothing but a loin cloth and his weapons, and the wind ruffled his hair. He looked comfortable, and they longed to take off the stuffy spacesuits and feel the wind against their own skins. Minos was like home, like Earth.... But they were strangers.

"Plague," Pat Mead said thoughtfully. "We had one here. It came two years after the colony arrived and killed everyone except the Mead families. They were immune. I guess we look alike because we're all related, and that's why I grew up thinking that it is the only way people can look."

Plague. "What was the disease?" Hal Barton asked.

"Pretty gruesome, according to my father. They called it the melting sickness. The doctors died too soon to find out what it was or what to do about it."

"You should have trained for more doctors, or sent to civilization for some." A trace of impatience was in George Barton's voice.

Pat Mead explained patiently, "Our ship, with the power plant and all the books we needed, went off into the sky to avoid the contagion, and never came back. The crew must have died." Long years of hardship were indicated by that statement, a colony with electric power gone and machinery stilled, with key technicians dead and no way to replace them. June realized then the full meaning of the primitive sheath knife and bow.

"Any recurrence of melting sickness?" asked Hal Barton.

"No."

"Any other diseases?"

"Not a one."

Max was eyeing the bronze red-headed figure with something approaching awe. "Do you think all the Meads look like that?" he said to June on the intercom. "I wouldn't mind being a Mead myself!"

*

Their job had been made easy by the coming of Pat. They went back to the ship laughing, exchanging anecdotes with him. There was nothing now to keep Minos from being the home they wanted, except the melting sickness, and, forewarned against it, they could take precautions.

The polished silver and black column of the *Explorer* seemed to rise higher and higher over the trees as they neared it. Then its symmetry blurred all sense of specific size as they stepped out from among the trees and stood on the edge of the meadow, looking up.

"Nice!" said Pat. "Beautiful!" The admiration in his voice was warming.

"It was a yacht," Max said, still looking up, "second hand, an old-time beauty without a sign of wear. Synthetic diamond-studded control board and murals on the walls. It doesn't have the new speed drives, but it brought us thirty-six light years in one and a half subjective years. Plenty good enough."

The tall tanned man looked faintly wistful, and June realized that he had never had access to a full library, never seen a movie, never experienced luxury. He had been born and raised on Minos.

*

"May I go aboard?" Pat asked hopefully.

Max unslung the specimen kit from his shoulder, laid it on the carpet of plants that covered the ground and began to open it.

"Tests first," Hal Barton said. "We have to find out if you people still carry this so-called melting sickness. We'll have to de-microbe you and take specimens before we let you on board. Once on, you'll be no good as a check for what the other Meads might have."

Max was taking out a rack and a stand of preservative bottles and hypodermics.

"Are you going to jab me with those?" Pat asked with interest.

"You're just a specimen animal to me, bud!" Max grinned at Pat Mead, and Pat grinned back. June saw that they were friends already, the tall pantherish colonist, and the wry, black-haired doctor. She felt a stab of guilt because she loved Max and yet could pity him for being smaller and frailer than Pat Mead.

"Lie down," Max told him, "and hold still. We need two spinal fluid samples from the back, a body cavity one in front, and another from the arm."

Pat lay down obediently. Max knelt, and, as he spoke, expertly swabbed and inserted needles with the smooth speed that had made him a fine nerve surgeon on Earth.

High above them the scout helioplane came out of an opening in the ship and angled off toward the west, its buzz diminishing. Then, suddenly, it veered and headed back, and Reno Unrich's voice came tinnily from their earphones:

"What's that you've got? Hey, what are you docs doing down there?" He banked again and came to a stop, hovering fifty feet away. June could see his startled face looking through the glass at Pat.

Hal Barton switched to a narrow radio beam, explained rapidly and pointed in the direction of Alexandria. Reno's plane lifted and flew away over the odd-colored forest.

"The plane will drop a note on your town, telling them you got through to us," Hal Barton told Pat, who was sitting up watching Max dexterously put the blood and spinal fluids into the right bottles without exposing them to air.

"We won't be free to contact your people until we know if they still carry melting sickness," Max added. "You might be immune so it doesn't show on you, but still carry enough germs—if that's what caused it—to wipe out a planet."

"If you do carry melting sickness," said Hal Barton, "we won't be able to mingle with your people until we've cleared them of the disease."

"Starting with me?" Pat asked.

"Starting with you," Max told him ruefully, "as soon as you step on board."

"More needles?"

"Yes, and a few little extras thrown in."

"Rough?"

"It isn't easy."

A few minutes later, standing in the stalls for spacesuit decontamination, being buffeted by jets of hot disinfectant, bathed in glares of sterilizing ultraviolet radiation, June remembered that and compared Pat Mead's treatment to theirs.

In the *Explorer*, stored carefully in sealed tanks and containers, was the ultimate, multi-purpose cureall. It was a solution of enzymes so like the key catalysts of the human cell nucleus that it caused chemical derangement and disintegration in any non-human cell. Nothing could live in contact with it but human cells; any alien intruder to the body would die. Nucleocat Cureall was its trade name.

But the cureall alone was not enough for complete safety. Plagues had been known to slay too rapidly and universally to be checked by human treatment. Doctors are not reliable; they die. Therefore spaceways and interplanetary health law demanded that ship equipment for guarding against disease be totally mechanical in operation, rapid and efficient.

Somewhere near them, in a series of stalls which led around and around like a rabbit maze, Pat was being herded from stall to stall by peremptory mechanical voices, directed to soap and shower, ordered to insert his arm into a slot which took a sample of his blood, given solutions to drink, bathed in germicidal ultraviolet, shaken by sonic blasts, breathing air thick with sprays of germicidal mists, being directed to put his arms into other slots where they were anesthesized and injected with various immunizing solutions.

Finally, he would be put in a room of high temperature and extreme dryness, and instructed to sit for half an hour while more fluids were dripped into his veins through long thin tubes.

All legal spaceships were built for safety. No chance was taken of allowing a suspected carrier to bring an infection on board with him.

*

June stepped from the last shower stall into the locker room, zipped off her spacesuit with a sigh of relief, and contemplated herself in a wall mirror. Red hair, dark blue eyes, tall....

"I've got a good figure," she said thoughtfully.

Max turned at the door. "Why this sudden interest in your looks?" he asked suspiciously. "Do we stand here and admire you, or do we finally get something to eat?"

"Wait a minute." She went to a wall phone and dialed it carefully, using a combination from the ship's directory. "How're you doing, Pat?"

The phone picked up a hissing of water or spray. There was a startled chuckle. "Voices, too! Hello, June. How do you tell a machine to go jump in the lake?"

"Are you hungry?"

"No food since yesterday."

"We'll have a banquet ready for you when you get out," she told Pat and hung up, smiling. Pat Mead's voice had a vitality and enjoyment which made shipboard talk sound like sad artificial gaiety in contrast.

They looked into the nearby small laboratory where twelve squealing hamsters were protestingly submitting to a small injection each of Pat's blood. In most of them the injection was followed by one of antihistaminics and adaptives. Otherwise the hamster defense system would treat all non-hamster cells as enemies, even the harmless human blood cells, and fight back against them violently.

One hamster, the twelfth, was given an extra large dose of adaptive, so that if there were a disease, he would not fight it or the human cells, and thus succumb more rapidly.

"How ya doing, George?" Max asked.

"Routine," George Barton grunted absently.

On the way up the long spiral ramps to the dining hall, they passed a viewplate. It showed a long scene of mountains in the distance on the horizon, and between them, rising step by step as they grew farther away, the low rolling hills, bronze and red with patches of clear green where there were fields.

Someone was looking out, standing very still, as if she had been there a long time—Bess St. Clair, a Canadian woman. "It looks like Winnipeg," she told them as they paused. "When are you doctors going to let us out of this blithering barberpole? Look," she pointed. "See that patch of field on the south hillside, with the brook winding through it? I've staked that hillside for our house. When do we get out?"

*

Reno Ulrich's tiny scout plane buzzed slowly in from the distance and began circling lazily.

"Sooner than you think," Max told her. "We've discovered a castaway colony on the planet. They've done our tests for us by just living here. If there's anything here to catch, they've caught it."

"People on Minos?" Bess's handsome ruddy face grew alive with excitement.

"One of them is down in the medical department," June said. "He'll be out in twenty minutes."

"May I go see him?"

"Sure," said Max. "Show him the way to the dining hall when he gets out. Tell him we sent you."

"Right!" She turned and ran down the ramp like a small girl going to a fire. Max grinned at June and she grinned back. After a year and a half of isolation in space, everyone was hungry for the sight of new faces, the sound of unfamiliar voices.

*

They climbed the last two turns to the cafeteria, and entered to a rich subdued blend of soft music and quiet conversations. The cafeteria was a section of the old dining room, left when the rest of the ship had been converted to living and working quarters, and it still had the original finely grained wood of the ceiling and walls, the sound absorbency, the soft music spools and the intimate small light at each table where people leisurely ate and talked.

They stood in line at the hot foods counter, and behind her June could hear a girl's voice talking excitedly through the murmur of conversation.

"—new man, honest! I saw him through the viewplate when they came in. He's down in the medical department. A real frontiersman."

The line drew abreast of the counters, and she and Max chose three heaping trays, starting with hydroponic mushroom steak, raised in the growing trays of water and chemicals; sharp salad bowl with rose tomatoes and aromatic peppers; tank-grown fish with special sauce; four different desserts, and assorted beverages.

Presently they had three tottering trays successfully maneuvered to a table. Brant St. Clair came over. "I beg your pardon, Max, but they are saying something about Reno carrying messages to a colony of savages, for the medical department. Will he be back soon, do you know?"

Max smiled up at him, his square face affectionate. Everyone liked the shy Canadian. "He's back already. We just saw him come in."

"Oh, fine." St. Clair beamed. "I had an appointment with him to go out and confirm what looks like a nice vein of iron to the northeast. Have you seen Bess? Oh—there she is." He turned swiftly and hurried away.

A very tall man with fiery red hair came in surrounded by an eagerly talking crowd of ship people. It was Pat Mead. He stood in the doorway, alertly scanning the dining room. Sheer vitality made him seem even larger than he was. Sighting June, he smiled and began to thread toward their table.

"Look!" said someone. "There's the colonist!" Shelia, a pretty, jeweled woman, followed and caught his arm. "Did you *really* swim across a river to come here?"

Overflowing with good-will and curiosity, people approached from all directions. "Did you actually walk three hundred miles? Come, eat with us. Let me help choose your tray."

Everyone wanted him to eat at their table, everyone was a specialist and wanted data about Minos. They all wanted anecdotes about hunting wild animals with a bow and arrow.

"He needs to be rescued," Max said. "He won't have a chance to eat."

June and Max got up firmly, edged through the crowd, captured Pat and escorted him back to their table. June found herself pleased to be claiming the hero of the hour.

*

Pat sat in the simple, subtly designed chair and leaned back almost voluptuously, testing the way it gave and fitted itself to him. He ran his eyes over the bright tableware and heaped plates. He looked around at the rich grained walls and soft lights at each table. He said nothing, just looking and feeling and experiencing.

"When we build our town and leave the ship," June explained, "we will turn all the staterooms back into the lounges and ballrooms and cocktail bars that used to be inside."

"Oh, I'm not complaining," Pat said negligently. He cocked his head to the music, and tried to locate its source.

"That's big of you," said Max with gentle irony.

They fell to, Pat beginning the first meal he had had in more than a day.

Most of the other diners finished when they were halfway through, and began walking over, diffidently at first, then in another wave of smiling faces, handshakes, and introductions. Pat was asked about crops, about farming methods, about rainfall and floods, about farm animals and plant breeding, about the compatibility of imported Earth seeds with local ground, about mines and strata.

There was no need to protect him. He leaned back in his chair and drawled answers with the lazy ease of a panther; where he could think of no statistic, he would fill the gap with an anecdote. It developed that he enjoyed spinning campfire yarns and especially being the center of interest.

Between bouts of questions, he ate with undiminished and glowing relish.

June noticed that the female specialists were prolonging the questions more than they needed, clustering around the table laughing at his jokes, until presently Pat was almost surrounded by pretty faces, eager questions, and chiming laughs. Shelia the beautiful laughed most chimingly of all.

June nudged Max, and Max shrugged indifferently. It wasn't anything a man would pay attention to, perhaps. But June watched Pat for a moment more, then glanced uneasily back to Max. He was eating and listening to Pat's answers and did not feel her gaze. For some reason Max looked almost shrunken to her. He was shorter than she had realized; she had forgotten that he was only the same height as herself. She was dimly aware of the clear lilting chatter of female voices increasing at Pat's end of the table.

"That guy's a menace," Max said, and laughed to himself, cutting another slice of hydroponic mushroom steak. "What's eating you?" he added, glancing aside at her when he noticed her sudden stillness.

"Nothing," she said hastily, but she did not turn back to watching Pat Mead. She felt disloyal. Pat was only a superb animal. Max was the man she loved. Or—was he? Of course he was, she told herself angrily. They had gone colonizing together because they wanted to spend their lives together; she had never thought of marrying any other man. Yet the sense of dissatisfaction persisted, and along with it a feeling of guilt.

Len Marlow, the protein tank-culture technician responsible for the mushroom steaks, had wormed his way into the group and asked Pat a question. Now he was saying, "I don't dig you, Pat. It sounds like you're putting the people into the tanks instead of the vegetables!" He glanced at them, looking puzzled. "See if you two can make anything of this. It sounds medical to me."

Pat leaned back and smiled, sipping a glass of hydroponic burgundy. "Wonderful stuff. You'll have to show us how to make it."

Len turned back to him. "You people live off the country, right? You hunt and bring in steaks and eat them, right? Well, say I have one of those steaks right here and I want to eat it, what happens?"

*

"Go ahead and eat it. It just wouldn't digest. You'd stay hungry."

"Why?" Len was aggrieved.

"Chemical differences in the basic protoplasm of Minos. Different amino linkages, left-handed instead of right-handed molecules in the carbohydrates, things like that. Nothing will be digestible here until you are adapted chemically by a little test-tube evolution. Till then you'd starve to death on a full stomach."

Pat's side of the table had been loaded with the dishes from two trays, but it was almost clear now and the dishes were stacked neatly to one side. He started on three desserts, thoughtfully tasting each in turn.

"Test-tube evolution?" Max repeated. "What's that? I thought you people had no doctors."

"It's a story." Pat leaned back again. "Alexander P. Mead, the head of the Mead clan, was a plant geneticist, a very determined personality and no man to argue with. He didn't want us to go through the struggle of killing off all Minos plants and putting in our own, spoiling the face of the planet and upsetting the balance of its ecology. He decided that he would adapt our genes to this planet or kill us trying. He did it all right.'"

"Did which?" asked June, suddenly feeling a sourceless prickle of fear.

"Adapted us to Minos. He took human cells—"

*

She listened intently, trying to find a reason for fear in the explanation. It would have taken many human generations to adapt to Minos by ordinary evolution, and that only at a heavy toll of death and hunger which evolution exacts. There was a shorter way: Human cells have the ability to return to their primeval condition of independence, hunting, eating and reproducing alone.

Alexander P. Mead took human cells and made them into phagocytes. He put them through the hard savage school of evolution—a thousand generations of multiplication, hardship and hunger, with the alien indigestible food always present, offering its reward of plenty to the cell that reluctantly learned to absorb it.

"Leucocytes can run through several thousand generations of evolution in six months," Pat Mead finished. "When they reached to a point where they would absorb Minos food, he planted them back in the people he had taken them from."

"What was supposed to happen then?" Max asked, leaning forward.

"I don't know exactly how it worked. He never told anybody much about it, and when I was a little boy he had gone loco and was wandering ha-ha-ing around waving a test tube. Fell down a ravine and broke his neck at the age of eighty."

"A character," Max said.

Why was she afraid? "It worked then?"

"Yes. He tried it on all the Meads the first year. The other settlers didn't want to be experimented on until they saw how it worked out. It worked. The Meads could hunt, and plant while the other settlers were still eating out of hydroponics tanks."

"It worked," said Max to Len. "You're a plant geneticist and a tank culture expert. There's a job for you."

"Uh-*uh*!" Len backed away. "It sounds like a medical problem to me. Human cell control—right up your alley."

"It is a one-way street," Pat warned. "Once it is done, you won't be able to digest ship food. I'll get no good from this protein. I ate it just for the taste."

Hal Barton appeared quietly beside the table. "Three of the twelve test hamsters have died," he reported, and turned to Pat. "Your people carry the germs of melting sickness, as you call it. The dead hamsters were injected with blood taken from you before you were de-infected. We can't settle here unless we de-infect everybody on Minos. Would they object?"

"We wouldn't want to give you folks germs," Pat smiled. "Anything for safety. But there'll have to be a vote on it first."

The doctors went to Reno Ulrich's table and walked with him to the hangar, explaining. He was to carry the proposal to Alexandria, mingle with the people, be persuasive and wait for them to vote before returning. He was to give himself shots of cureall every two hours on the hour or run the risk of disease.

*

Reno was pleased. He had dabbled in sociology before retraining as a mechanic for the expedition. "This gives me a chance to study their mores." He winked wickedly. "I may not be back for several nights." They watched through the viewplate as he took off, and then went over to the laboratory for a look at the hamsters.

Three were alive and healthy, munching lettuce. One was the control; the other two had been given shots of Pat's blood from before he entered the ship, but with no additional treatment. Apparently a hamster could fight off melting sickness easily if left alone. Three were still feverish and ruffled, with a low red blood count, but recovering. The three dead ones had been given strong shots of adaptive and counter histamine, so their bodies had not fought back against the attack.

June glanced at the dead animals hastily and looked away again. They lay twisted with a strange semi-fluid limpness, as if ready to dissolve. The last hamster, which had been given the heaviest dose of adaptive, had apparently lost all its hair before death. It was hairless and pink, like a still-born baby.

"We can find no micro-organisms," George Barton said. "None at all. Nothing in the body that should not be there. Leucosis and anemia. Fever only for the ones that fought it off." He handed Max some temperature charts and graphs of blood counts.

June wandered out into the hall. Pediatrics and obstetrics were her field; she left the cellular research to Max, and just helped him with laboratory routine. The strange mood followed her out into the hall, then abruptly lightened.

Coming toward her, busily telling a tale of adventure to the gorgeous Shelia Davenport, was a tall, red-headed, magnificently handsome man. It was his handsomeness which made Pat such a pleasure to look upon and talk with, she guiltily told herself, and it was his tremendous vitality.... It was like meeting a movie hero in the flesh, or a hero out of the pages of a book—Deer-slayer, John Clayton, Lord Greystoke.

She waited in the doorway to the laboratory and made no move to join them, merely acknowledged the two with a nod and a smile and a casual lift of the hand. They nodded and smiled back.

"Hello, June," said Pat and continued telling his tale, but as they passed he lightly touched her arm.

"Oh, pioneer!" she said mockingly and softly to his passing profile, and knew that he had heard.

*

That night she had a nightmare. She was running down a long corridor looking for Max, but every man she came to was a big bronze man with red hair and bright blue eyes who grinned at her.

The pink hamster! She woke suddenly, feeling as if alarm bells had been ringing, and listened carefully, but there was no sound. She had had a nightmare, she told herself, but alarm bells were still ringing in her unconscious. Something was wrong.

Lying still and trying to preserve the images, she groped for a meaning, but the mood faded under the cold touch of reason. Damn intuitive thinking! A pink hamster! Why did the unconscious have to be so vague? She fell asleep again and forgot.

They had lunch with Pat Mead that day, and after it was over Pat delayed June with a hand on her shoulder and looked down at her for a moment. "I want you, June," he said and then turned away, answering the hails of a party at another table as if he had not spoken. She stood shaken, and then walked to the door where Max waited.

She was particularly affectionate with Max the rest of the day, and it pleased him. He would not have been if he had known why. She tried to forget Pat's blunt statement.

June was in the laboratory with Max, watching the growth of a small tank culture of the alien protoplasm from a Minos weed, and listening to Len Marlow pour out his troubles.

"And Elsie tags around after that big goof all day, listening to his stories. And then she tells me I'm just jealous, I'm imagining things!" He passed his hand across his eyes. "I came away from Earth to be with Elsie.... I'm getting a headache. Look, can't you persuade Pat to cut it out, June? You and Max are his friends."

"Here, have an aspirin," June said. "We'll see what we can do."

"Thanks." Len picked up his tank culture and went out, not at all cheered.

*

Max sat brooding over the dials and meters at his end of the laboratory, apparently sunk in thought. When Len had gone, he spoke almost harshly.

"Why encourage the guy? Why let him hope?"

"Found out anything about the differences in protoplasm?" she evaded.

"Why let him kid himself? What chance has he got against that hunk of muscle and smooth talk?"

"But Pat isn't after Elsie," she protested.

"Every scatter-brained woman on this ship is trailing after Pat with her tongue hanging out. Brant St. Clair is in the bar right now. He doesn't say what he is drinking about, but do you think Pat is resisting all these women crowding down on him?"

"There are other things besides looks and charm," she said, grimly trying to concentrate on a slide under her binocular microscope.

"Yeah, and whatever they are, Pat has them, too. Who's more competent to support a woman and a family on a frontier planet than a handsome bruiser who was born here?"

"I meant," June spun around on her stool with unexpected passion, "there is old friendship, and there's fondness, and memories, and loyalty!" She was half shouting.

"They're not worth much on the second-hand market," Max said. He was sitting slumped on his lab stool, looking dully at his dials. "Now *I'm* getting a headache!" He smiled ruefully. "No kidding, a real headache. And over other people's troubles yet!"

Other people's troubles.... She got up and wandered out into the long curving halls. "I want you June," Pat's voice repeated in her mind. Why did the man have to be so overpoweringly attractive, so glaring a contrast to Max? Why couldn't the universe manage to run on without generating troublesome love triangles?

*

She walked up the curving ramps to the dining hall where they had eaten and drunk and talked yesterday. It was empty except for one couple talking forehead to forehead over cold coffee.

She turned and wandered down the long easy spiral of corridor to the pharmacy and dispensary. It was empty. George was probably in the test lab next door, where he could hear if he was wanted. The automatic vendor of harmless euphorics, stimulants and opiates stood in the corner, brightly decorated in pastel abstract designs, with its automatic tabulator graph glowing above it.

Max had a headache, she remembered. She recorded her thumbprint in the machine and pushed the plunger for a box of aspirins, trying to focus her attention on the problem of adapting the people of the ship to the planet Minos. An aquarium tank with a faint solution of histamine would be enough to convert a piece of human skin into a community of voracious active phagocytes individually seeking something to devour, but could they eat enough to live away from the rich sustaining plasma of human blood?

After the aspirins, she pushed another plunger for something for herself. Then she stood looking at it, a small box with three pills in her hand—Theobromine, a heart strengthener and a confidence-giving euphoric all in one, something to steady shaky nerves. She had used it before only in emergency. She extended a hand and looked at it. It was trembling. Damn triangles!

While she was looking at her hand there was a click from the automatic drug vendor. It summed the morning use of each drug in the vendors throughout the ship, and recorded it in a neat addition to the end of each graph line. For a moment she could not find the green line for anodynes and the red line for stimulants, and then she saw that they went almost straight up.

There were too many being used—far too many to be explained by jealousy or psychosomatic peevishness. This was an epidemic, and only one disease was possible!

The disinfecting of Pat had not succeeded. Nucleocat Cureall, killer of all infections, had not cured! Pat had brought melting sickness into the ship with him!

Who had it?

The drugs vendor glowed cheerfully, uncommunicative. She opened a panel in its side and looked in on restless interlacing cogs, and on the inside of the door saw printed some directions.... "To remove or examine records before reaching end of the reel—"

After a few fumbling minutes she had the answer. In the cafeteria at breakfast and lunch, thirty-eight men out of the forty-eight aboard ship had taken more than his norm of stimulant. Twenty-one had taken aspirin as well. The only woman who had made an unusual purchase was herself!

She remembered the hamsters that had thrown off the infection with a short sharp fever, and checked back in the records to the day before. There was a short rise in aspirin sales to women at late afternoon. The women were safe.

It was the men who had melting sickness!

Melting sickness killed in hours, according to Pat Mead. How long had the men been sick?

*

As she was leaving, Jerry came into the pharmacy, recorded his thumbprint and took a box of aspirin from the machine.

She felt all right. Self-control was working well and it was pleasant still to walk down the corridor smiling at the people who passed. She took the emergency elevator to the control room and showed her credentials to the technician on watch.

"Medical Emergency." At a small control panel in the corner was a large red button, precisely labeled. She considered it and picked up the control room phone. This was the hard part, telling someone, especially someone who had it—Max.

She dialed, and when the click on the end of the line showed he had picked the phone up, she told Max what she had seen.

"No women, just the men," he repeated. "That right?"

"Yes."

"Probably it's chemically alien, inhibited by one of the female sex hormones. We'll try sex hormone shots, if we have to. Where are you calling from?"

She told him.

"That's right. Give Nucleocat Cureall another chance. It might work this time. Push that button."

She went to the panel and pushed the large red button. Through the long height of the *Explorer*, bells woke to life and began to ring in frightened clangor, emergency doors thumped shut, mechanical apparatus hummed into life and canned voices began to give rapid urgent directions.

A plague had come.

*

She obeyed the mechanical orders, went out into the hall and walked in line with the others. The captain walked ahead of her and the gorgeous Shelia Davenport fell into step beside her. "I look like a positive hag this morning. Does that mean I'm sick? Are we all sick?"

June shrugged, unwilling to say what she knew.

Others came out of all rooms into the corridor, thickening the line. They could hear each room lock as the last person left it, and then, faintly, the hiss of disinfectant spray. Behind them, on the heels of the last person in line, segments of the ship slammed off and began to hiss.

They wound down the spiral corridor until they reached the medical treatment section again, and there they waited in line.

"It won't scar my arms, will it?" asked Shelia apprehensively, glancing at her smooth, lovely arms.

The mechanical voice said, "Next. Step inside, please, and stand clear of the door."

"Not a bit," June reassured Shelia, and stepped into the cubicle.

Inside, she was directed from cubicle to cubicle and given the usual buffeting by sprays and radiation, had blood samples taken and was injected with Nucleocat and a series of other protectives. At last she was directed through another door into a tiny cubicle with a chair.

"You are to wait here," commanded the recorded voice metallically. "In twenty minutes the door will unlock and you may then leave. All people now treated may visit all parts of the ship which have been protected. It is forbidden to visit any quarantined or unsterile part of the ship without permission from the medical officers."

Presently the door unlocked and she emerged into bright lights again, feeling slightly battered.

She was in the clinic. A few men sat on the edge of beds and looked sick. One was lying down. Brant and Bess St. Clair sat near each other, not speaking.

Approaching her was George Barton, reading a thermometer with a puzzled expression.

"What is it, George?" she asked anxiously.

"Some of the women have slight fever, but it's going down. None of the fellows have any—but their white count is way up, their red count is way down, and they look sick to me."

She approached St. Clair. His usually ruddy cheeks were pale, his pulse was light and too fast, and his skin felt clammy. "How's the headache? Did the Nucleocat treatment help?"

"I feel worse, if anything."

"Better set up beds," she told George. "Get everyone back into the clinic."

"We're doing that," George assured her. "That's what Hal is doing."

She went back to the laboratory. Max was pacing up and down, absently running his hands through his black hair until it stood straight up. He stopped when he saw her face, and scowled thoughtfully. "They are still sick?" It was more a statement than a question.

She nodded.

"The Cureall didn't cure this time," he muttered. "That leaves it up to us. We have melting sickness and according to Pat and the hamsters, that leaves us less than a day to find out what it is and learn how to stop it."

Suddenly an idea for another test struck him and he moved to the work table to set it up. He worked rapidly, with an occasional uncoordinated movement betraying his usual efficiency.

It was strange to see Max troubled and afraid.

She put on a laboratory smock and began to work. She worked in silence. The mechanicals had failed. Hal and George Barton were busy staving off death from the weaker cases and trying to gain time for Max and her to work. The problem of the plague had to be solved by the two of them alone. It was in their hands.

Another test, no results. Another test, no results. Max's hands were shaking and he stopped a moment to take stimulants.

She went into the ward for a moment, found Bess and warned her quietly to tell the other women to be ready to take over if the men became too sick to go on. "But tell them calmly. We don't want to frighten the men." She lingered in the ward long enough to see the word spread among the women in a widening wave of paler faces and compressed lips; then she went back to the laboratory.

Another test. There was no sign of a micro-organism in anyone's blood, merely a growing horde of leucocytes and phagocytes, prowling as if mobilized to repel invasion.

*

Len Marlow was wheeled in unconscious, with Hal Barton's written comments and conclusions pinned to the blanket.

"I don't feel so well myself," the assistant complained. "The air feels thick. I can't breathe."

June saw that his lips were blue. "Oxygen short," she told Max.

"Low red corpuscle count," Max answered. "Look into a drop and see what's going on. Use mine; I feel the same way he does." She took two drops of Max's blood. The count was low, falling too fast.

Breathing is useless without the proper minimum of red corpuscles in the blood. People below that minimum die of asphyxiation although their lungs are full of pure air. The red corpuscle count was falling too fast. The time she and Max had to work in was too short.

"Pump some more CO_2 into the air system," Max said urgently over the phone. "Get some into the men's end of the ward."

*

She looked through the microscope at the live sample of blood. It was a dark clear field and bright moving things spun and swirled through it, but she could see nothing that did not belong there.

"Hal," Max called over the general speaker system, "cut the other treatments, check for accelerating anemia. Treat it like monoxide poisoning—CO_2 and oxygen."

She reached into a cupboard under the work table, located two cylinders of oxygen, cracked the valves and handed one to Max and one to the assistant. Some of the bluish tint left the assistant's face as he breathed and he went over to the patient with reawakened concern.

"Not breathing, Doc!"

Max was working at the desk, muttering equations of hemoglobin catalysis.

"Len's gone, Doc," the assistant said more loudly.

"Artificial respiration and get him into a regeneration tank," said June, not moving from the microscope. "Hurry! Hal will show you how. The oxidation and mechanical heart action in the tank will keep him going. Put anyone in a tank who seems to be dying. Get some women to help you. Give them Hal's instructions."

The tanks were ordinarily used to suspend animation in a nutrient bath during the regrowth of any diseased organ. It could preserve life in an almost totally destroyed body during the usual disintegration and regrowth treatments for cancer and old age, and it could encourage healing as destruction continued ... but they could not prevent ultimate death as long as the disease was not conquered.

The drop of blood in June's microscope was a great, dark field, and in the foreground, brought to gargantuan solidity by the stereo effect, drifted neat saucer shapes of red blood cells. They turned end for end, floating by the humped misty mass of a leucocyte which was crawling on the cover glass. There were not enough red corpuscles, and she felt that they grew fewer as she watched.

She fixed her eye on one, not blinking in fear that she would miss what might happen. It was a tidy red button, and it spun as it drifted, the current moving it aside in a curve as it passed by the leucocyte.

Then, abruptly, the cell vanished.

June stared numbly at the place where it had been.

Behind her, Max was calling over the speaker system again: "Dr. Stark speaking. Any technician who knows anything about the life tanks, start bringing more out of storage and set them up. Emergency."

"We may need forty-seven," June said quietly.

"We may need forty-seven," Max repeated to the ship in general. His voice did not falter. "Set them up along the corridor. Hook them in on extension lines."

His voice filtered back from the empty floors above in a series of dim echoes. What he had said meant that every man on board might be on the point of heart stoppage.

*

June looked blindly through the binocular microscope, trying to think. Out of the corner of her eyes she could see that Max was wavering and breathing more and more frequently of the pure, cold, burning oxygen of the cylinders. In the microscope she could see that there were fewer red cells left alive in the drop of his blood. The rate of fall was accelerating.

She didn't have to glance at Max to know how he would look—skin pale, black eyebrows and keen brown eyes slightly squinted in thought, a faint ironical grin twisting the bluing lips. Intelligent, thin, sensitive, his face was part of her mind. It was inconceivable that Max could die. He couldn't die. He couldn't leave her alone.

She forced her mind back to the problem. All the men of the *Explorer* were at the same point, wherever they were.

Moving to Max's desk, she spoke into the intercom system: "Bess, send a couple of women to look through the ship, room by room, with a stretcher. Make sure all the men are down here." She remembered Reno. "Sparks, heard anything from Reno? Is he back?"

Sparks replied weakly after a lag. "The last I heard from Reno was a call this morning. He was raving about mirrors, and Pat Mead's folks not being real people, just carbon copies, and claiming he was crazy; and I should send him the psychiatrist. I thought he was kidding. He didn't call back."

"Thanks, Sparks." Reno was lost.

Max dialed and spoke to the bridge over the phone. "Are you okay up there? Forget about engineering controls. Drop everything and head for the tanks while you can still walk."

June went back to the work table and whispered into her own phone. "Bess, send up a stretcher for Max. He looks pretty bad."

There had to be a solution. The life tanks could sustain life in a damaged body, encouraging it to regrow more rapidly, but they merely slowed death as long as the disease was not checked. The postponement could not last long, for destruction could go on steadily in the tanks until the nutritive solution would hold no life except the triumphant microscopic killers that caused melting sickness.

There were very few red blood corpuscles in the microscope field now, incredibly few. She tipped the microscope and they began to drift, spinning slowly. A lone corpuscle floated through the center. She watched it as the current swept it in an arc past the dim off-focus bulk of the leucocyte. There was a sweep of motion and it vanished.

For a moment it meant nothing to her; then she lifted her head from the microscope and looked around. Max sat at his desk, head in hand, his rumpled short black hair sticking out between his fingers at odd angles. A pencil and a pad scrawled with formulas lay on the desk before him. She could see his concentration in the rigid set of his shoulders. He was still thinking; he had not given up.

*

"Max, I just saw a leucocyte grab a red blood corpuscle. It was unbelievably fast."

"Leukemia," muttered Max without moving. "Galloping leukemia yet! That comes under the heading of cancer. Well, that's part of the answer. It might be all we need." He grinned feebly and reached for the speaker set. "Anybody still on his feet in there?" he muttered into it, and the question was amplified to a booming voice throughout the ship. "Hal, are you still going? Look, Hal, change all the dials, change the dials, set them to deep melt and regeneration. One week. This is like leukemia. Got it? This is like leukemia."

June rose. It was time for her to take over the job. She leaned across his desk and spoke into the speaker system. "Doctor Walton talking," she said. "This is to the women. Don't let any of the men work any more; they'll kill themselves. See that they all go into the tanks right away. Set the tank dials for deep regeneration. You can see how from the ones that are set."

Two exhausted and frightened women clattered in the doorway with a stretcher. Their hands were scratched and oily from helping to set up tanks.

"That order includes you," she told Max sternly and caught him as he swayed.

Max saw the stretcher bearers and struggled upright. "Ten more minutes," he said clearly. "Might think of an idea. Something not right in this setup.

I have to figure how to prevent a relapse, how the thing started."

He knew more bacteriology than she did; she had to help him think. She motioned the bearers to wait, fixed a breathing mask for Max from a cylinder of CO_2 and the opened one of oxygen. Max went back to his desk.

She walked up and down, trying to think, remembering the hamsters. The melting sickness, it was called. Melting. She struggled with an impulse to open a tank which held one of the men. She wanted to look in, see if that would explain the name.

Melting Sickness....

Footsteps came and Pat Mead stood uncertainly in the doorway. Tall, handsome, rugged, a pioneer. "Anything I can do?" he asked.

She barely looked at him. "You can stay out of our way. We're busy."

"I'd like to help," he said.

"Very funny." She was vicious, enjoying the whip of her words. "Every man is dying because you're a carrier, and you want to help."

*

He stood nervously clenching and unclenching his hands. "A guinea pig, maybe. I'm immune. All the Meads are."

"Go away." God, why couldn't she think? What makes a Mead immune?

"Aw, let 'im alone," Max muttered. "Pat hasn't done anything." He went waveringly to the microscope, took a tiny sliver from his finger, suspended it in a slide and slipped it under the lens with detached habitual dexterity. "Something funny going on," he said to June. "Symptoms don't feel right."

After a moment he straightened and motioned for her to look. "Leucocytes, phagocytes—" He was bewildered. "My own—"

She looked in, and then looked back at Pat in a growing wave of horror. "They're not your own, Max!" she whispered.

Max rested a hand on the table to brace himself, put his eye to the microscope, and looked again. June knew what he saw. Phagocytes, leucocytes, attacking and devouring his tissues in a growing incredible horde, multiplying insanely.

Not his phagocytes! Pat Mead's! The Meads' evolved cells had learned too much. They were contagious. And not Pat Mead's.... How much alike *were* the Meads?... Mead cells contagious from one to another, not a disease attacking or being fought, but acting as normal leucocytes in whatever body they were in! The leucocytes of tall, red-headed people, finding no strangeness in the bloodstream of any of the tall, red-headed people. No strangeness.... A toti-potent leucocyte finding its way into cellular wombs.

The womblike life tanks. For the men of the *Explorer*, a week's cure with deep melting to de-differentiate the leucocytes and turn them back to normal tissue, then regrowth and reforming from the cells that were there. From the cells that *were* there. *From the cells that were there....*

"Pat—"

"I know." Pat began to laugh, his face twisted with sudden understanding. "I understand. I get it. I'm a contagious personality. That's funny, isn't it?"

Max rose suddenly from the microscope and lurched toward him, fists clenched. Pat caught him as he fell, and the bewildered stretcher bearers carried him out to the tanks.

*

For a week June tended the tanks. The other women volunteered to help, but she refused. She said nothing, hoping her guess would not be true.

"Is everything all right?" Elsie asked her anxiously. "How is Jerry coming along?" Elsie looked haggard and worn, like all the women, from doing the work that the men had always done.

"He's fine," June said tonelessly, shutting tight the door of the tank room. "They're all fine."

"That's good," Elsie said, but she looked more frightened than before.

June firmly locked the tank room door and the girl went away.

The other women had been listening, and now they wandered back to their jobs, unsatisfied by June's answer, but not daring to ask for the actual truth. They were there whenever June went into the tank room, and they were still there—or relieved by others; June was not sure—when she came out. And always some one of them asked the unvarying question for all the others, and June gave the unvarying answer. But she kept the key. No woman but herself knew what was going on in the life tanks.

Then the day of completion came. June told no one of the hour. She went into the room as on the other days, locked the door behind her, and there was the nightmare again. This time it was reality and she wandered down a path between long rows of coffinlike tanks, calling, "Max! Max!" silently and looking into each one as it opened.

But each face she looked at was the same. Watching them dissolve and regrow in the nutrient solution, she had only been able to guess at the horror of what was happening. Now she knew.

They were all the same lean-boned, blond-skinned face, with a pin-feather growth of reddish down on cheeks and scalp. All horribly—and handsomely—the same.

A medical kit lay carelessly on the floor beside Max's tank. She stood near the bag. "Max," she said, and found her throat closing. The canned voice of the mechanical mocked her, speaking glibly about waking and sitting up. "I'm sorry, Max...."

The tall man with rugged features and bright blue eyes sat up sleepily and lifted an eyebrow at her, and ran his hand over his red-fuzzed head in a gesture of bewilderment.

"What's the matter, June?" he asked drowsily.

She gripped his arm. "Max—"

He compared the relative size of his arm with her hand and said wonderingly, "You shrank."

"I know, Max. I know."

He turned his head and looked at his arms and legs, pale blond arms and legs with a down of red hair. He touched the thick left arm, squeezed a pinch of hard flesh. "It isn't mine," he said, surprised. "But I can feel it."

Watching his face was like watching a stranger mimicking and distorting Max's expressions. Max in fear. Max trying to understand what had happened to him, looking around at the other men sitting up in their tanks. Max feeling the terror that was in herself and all the men as they stared at themselves and their friends and saw what they had become.

"We're all Pat Mead," he said harshly. "All the Meads are Pat Mead. That's why he was surprised to see people who didn't look like himself."

"Yes, Max."

"Max," he repeated. "It's me, all right. The nervous system didn't change." His new blue eyes held hers. "My love didn't, either. Did yours? Did it, June?"

"No, Max." But she couldn't know yet. She had loved Max with the thin, ironic face, the rumpled black hair and the twisted smile that never really hid his quick sympathy. Now he was Pat Mead. Could he also be Max? "Of course I still love you, darling."

He grinned. It was still the wry smile of Max, though fitting strangely on the handsome new blond face. "Then it isn't so bad. It might even be pretty good. I envied him this big, muscular body. If Pat or any of these Meads so much as looks at you, I'm going to knock his block off. Understand?"

*

She laughed and couldn't stop. It wasn't that funny. But it was still Max, trying to be unafraid, drawing on humor. Maybe the rest of the men would also be their old selves, enough so the women would not feel that their men were strangers.

Behind her, male voices spoke characteristically. She did not have to turn to know which was which: "This is one way to keep a guy from stealing your girl," that was Len Marlow; "I've got to write down all my reactions," Hal Barton; "Now I can really work that hillside vein of metal," St. Clair. Then others complaining, swearing, laughing bitterly at the trick that had been played on them and their flirting, tempted women. She knew who they were. Their women would know them apart, too.

"We'll go outside," Max said. "You and I. Maybe the shock won't be so bad to the women after they see me." He paused. "You didn't tell them, did you?"

"I couldn't. I wasn't sure. I—was hoping I was wrong."

She opened the door and closed it quickly. There was a small crowd on the other side.

"Hello, Pat," Elsie said uncertainly, trying to look past them into the tank room before the door shut.

"I'm not Pat, I'm Max," said the tall man with the blue eyes and the fuzz-reddened skull. "Listen—"

"Good heavens, Pat, what happened to your hair?" Shelia asked.

"I'm Max," insisted the man with the handsome face and the sharp blue eyes. "Don't you get it? I'm Max Stark. The melting sickness is Mead cells. We caught them from Pat. They adapted us to Minos. They also changed us all into Pat Mead."

The women stared at him, at each other. They shook their heads.

"They don't understand," June said. "I couldn't have if I hadn't seen it happening, Max."

"It's Pat," said Shelia, dazedly stubborn. "He shaved off his hair. It's some kind of joke."

Max shook her shoulders, glaring down at her face. "I'm Max. Max Stark. They all look like me. Do you hear? It's funny, but it's not a joke. Laugh for us, for God's sake!"

"It's too much," said June. "They'll have to see."

She opened the door and let them in. They hurried past her to the tanks, looking at forty-six identical blond faces, beginning to call in frightened voices:

"Jerry!"

"Harry!"

"Lee, where are you, sweetheart—"

June shut the door on the voices that were growing hysterical, the women terrified and helpless, the men shouting to let the women know who they were.

"It isn't easy," said Max, looking down at his own thick muscles. "But you aren't changed and the other girls aren't. That helps."

Through the muffled noise and hysteria, a bell was ringing.

"It's the airlock," June said.

Peering in the viewplate were nine Meads from Alexandria. To all appearances, eight of them were Pat Mead at various ages, from fifteen to fifty, and the other was a handsome, leggy, red-headed girl who could have been his sister.

Regretfully, they explained through the voice tube that they had walked over from Alexandria to bring news that the plane pilot had contracted melting sickness there and had died.

They wanted to come in.

*

June and Max told them to wait and returned to the tank room. The men were enjoying their new height and strength, and the women were bewilderedly learning that they could tell one Pat Mead from another, by voice, by gesture of face or hand. The panic was gone. In its place was a dull acceptance of the fantastic situation.

Max called for attention. "There are nine Meads outside who want to come in. They have different names, but they're all Pat Mead."

They frowned or looked blank, and George Barton asked, "Why didn't you let them in? I don't see any problem."

"One of them," said Max soberly, "is a girl. *Patricia* Mead. The girl wants to come in."

There was a long silence while the implication settled to the fear center of the women's minds. Shelia the beautiful felt it first. She cried, "No! Please don't let her in!" There was real fright in her tone and the women caught it quickly.

Elsie clung to Jerry, begging, "You don't want me to change, do you, Jerry? You like me the way I am! Tell me you do!"

*

The other girls backed away. It was illogical, but it was human. June felt terror rising in herself. She held up her hand for quiet, and presented the necessity to the group.

"Only half of us can leave Minos," she said. "The men cannot eat ship food; they've been conditioned to this planet. We women can go, but we would have to go without our men. We can't go outside without contagion, and we can't spend the rest of our lives in quarantine inside the ship. George Barton is right—there is no problem."

"But we'd be changed!" Shelia shrilled. "I don't want to become a Mead! I don't want to be somebody else!"

She ran to the inner wall of the corridor. There was a brief hesitation, and then, one by one, the women fled to that side, until there were only Bess, June and four others left.

"See!" cried Shelia. "A vote! We can't let the girl in!"

No one spoke. To change, to be someone else—the idea was strange and horrifying. The men stood uneasily glancing at each other, as if looking into mirrors, and against the wall of the corridor the women watched in fear and huddled together, staring at the men. One man in forty-seven poses. One of them made a beseeching move toward Elsie and she shrank away.

"No, Jerry! I won't let you change me!"

Max stirred restlessly, the ironic smile that made his new face his own unconsciously twisting into a grimace of pity. "We men can't leave, and you women can't stay," he said bluntly. "Why not let Patricia Mead in. Get it over with!"

June took a small mirror from her belt pouch and studied her own face, aware of Max talking forcefully, the men standing silent, the women pleading. Her face ... her own face with its dark blue eyes, small nose, long mobile lips ... the mind and the body are inseparable; the shape of a face is part of the mind. She put the mirror back.

"I'd kill myself!" Shelia was sobbing. "I'd rather die!"

"You won't die," Max was saying. "Can't you see there's only one solution—"

They were looking at Max. June stepped silently out of the tank room, and then turned and went to the airlock. She opened the valves that would let in Pat Mead's sister.

PEN PAL

By Milton Lesser

All she wanted was a mate and she had the gumption to go out and hunt one down. But that meant poaching in a strictly forbidden territory!

*

The best that could be said for Matilda Penshaws was that she was something of a paradox. She was thirty-three years old, certainly not aged when you consider the fact that the female life expectancy is now up in the sixties, but the lines were beginning to etch their permanent paths across her face and now she needed certain remedial undergarments at which she would have scoffed ten or even five years ago. Matilda was also looking for a husband.

This, in itself, was not unusual—but Matilda was so completely wrapped up in the romantic fallacy of her day that she sought a prince charming, a faithful Don Juan, a man who had been everywhere and tasted of every worldly pleasure and who now wanted to sit on a porch and talk about it all to Matilda.

The fact that in all probability such a man did not exist disturbed Matilda not in the least. She had been known to say that there are over a billion men in the world, a goodly percentage of whom are eligible bachelors, and that the right one would come along simply because she had been waiting for him.

Matilda, you see, had patience.

She also had a fetish. Matilda had received her A.B. from exclusive Ursula Johns College and Radcliff had yielded her Masters degree, yet Matilda was an avid follower of the pen pal columns. She would read them carefully and then read them again, looking for the masculine names which, through a system known only to Matilda, had an affinity to her own. To the gentlemen upon whom these names were affixed, Matilda would write, and she often told her mother, the widow Penshaws, that it was in this way she would find her husband. The widow Penshaws impatiently told her to go out and get dates.

*

That particular night, Matilda pulled her battered old sedan into the garage and walked up the walk to the porch. The widow Penshaws was rocking on the glider and Matilda said hello.

The first thing the widow Penshaws did was to take Matilda's left hand in her own and examine the next-to-the-last finger.

"I thought so," she said. "I knew this was coming when I saw that look in your eye at dinner. Where is Herman's engagement ring?"

Matilda smiled. "It wouldn't have worked out, Ma. He was too darned stuffy. I gave him his ring and said thanks anyway and he smiled politely and said he wished I had told him sooner because his fifteenth college reunion was this weekend and he had already turned down the invitation."

The widow Penshaws nodded regretfully. "That was thoughtful of Herman to hide his feelings."

"Hogwash!" said her daughter. "He has no true feelings. He's sorry that he had to miss his college reunion. That's all he has to hide. A stuffy Victorian prude and even less of a man than the others."

"But, Matilda, that's your fifth broken engagement in three years. It ain't that you ain't popular, but you just don't want to cooperate. You don't *fall* in love, Matilda—no one does. Love osmoses into you slowly, without you even knowing, and it keeps growing all the time."

Matilda admired her mother's use of the word osmosis, but she found nothing which was not objectionable about being unaware of the impact of love. She said good-night and went upstairs, climbed out of her light summer dress and took a cold shower.

She began to hum to herself. She had not yet seen the pen pal section of the current *Literary Review*, and because the subject matter of that magazine was somewhat highbrow and cosmopolitan, she could expect a gratifying selection of pen pals.

She shut off the shower, brushed her teeth, gargled, patted herself dry with a towel, and jumped into bed, careful to lock the door of her bedroom. She dared not let the widow Penshaws know that she slept in the nude; the widow Penshaws would object to a girl sleeping in the nude, even if the nearest neighbor was three hundred yards away.

Matilda switched her bed lamp on and dabbed some citronella on each ear lobe and a little droplet on her chin (how she hated insects!). Then she propped up her pillows—two pillows partially stopped her post-nasal drip; and took the latest issue of the *Literary Review* off the night table.

She flipped through the pages and came to personals. Someone in Nebraska wanted to trade match books; someone in New York needed a midwestern pen pal, but it was a woman; an elderly man interested in ornithology wanted a young chick correspondent interested in the same subject; a young, personable man wanted an editorial position because he thought he had something to offer the editorial world; and—

*

Matilda read the next one twice. Then she held it close to the light and read it again. The *Literary Review* was one of the few magazines which printed the name of the advertiser rather than a box number, and Matilda even liked the sound of the name. But mostly, she had to admit to herself, it was the flavor of the wording. This very well could be *it*. Or, that is, *him*.

Intelligent, somewhat egotistical male who's really been around, whose universal experience can make the average cosmopolite look like a provincial hick, is in need of several female correspondents: must be intelligent, have gumption, be capable of listening to male who has a lot to say and wants to say it. All others need not apply. Wonderful opportunity cultural experience... Haron Gorka, Cedar Falls, Ill.

The man was egotistical, all right; Matilda could see that. But she had never minded an egotistical man, at least not when he had something about which he had a genuine reason to be egotistical. The man sounded as though he would have reason indeed. He only wanted the best because he was the best. Like calls to like.

The name—Haron Gorka: its oddness was somehow beautiful to Matilda. Haron Gorka—the nationality could be anything. And that was it. He had no nationality for all intents and purposes; he was an international man, a figure among figures, a paragon....

Matilda sighed happily as she put out the light. The moon shone in through the window brightly, and at such times Matilda generally would get up, go to the cupboard, pull out a towel, take two hairpins from her powder drawer, pin the towel to the screen of her window, and hence keep the disturbing moonlight from her eyes. But this time it did not disturb her, and she would let it shine. Cedar Falls was a small town not fifty miles from her home, and she'd get there a hop, skip, and jump ahead of her competitors, simply by arriving in person instead of writing a letter.

Matilda was not yet that far gone in years or appearance. Dressed properly, she could hope to make a favorable impression in person, and she felt it was important to beat the influx of mail to Cedar Falls.

*

Matilda got out of bed at seven, tiptoed into the bathroom, showered with a merest wary trickle of water, tiptoed back into her bedroom, dressed in her very best cotton over the finest of uplifting and figure-moulding underthings, made sure her stocking seams were perfectly straight, brushed her suede shoes, admired herself in the mirror, read the ad again, wished for a moment she were a bit younger, and tiptoed downstairs.

The widow Penshaws met her at the bottom of the stairwell.

"Mother," gasped Matilda. Matilda always gasped when she saw something unexpected. "What on earth are you doing up?"

The widow Penshaws smiled somewhat toothlessly, having neglected to put in both her uppers and lowers this early in the morning. "I'm fixing breakfast, of course...."

Then the widow Penshaws told Matilda that she could never hope to sneak about the house without her mother knowing about it, and that even if she were going out in response to one of those foolish ads in the magazines, she would still need a good breakfast to start with like only mother could cook. Matilda moodily thanked the widow Penshaws.

*

Driving the fifty miles to Cedar Falls in a little less than an hour, Matilda hummed Mendelssohn's Wedding March all the way. It was her favorite piece of music. Once, she told herself: Matilda Penshaws, you are being premature about the whole thing. But she laughed and thought that if she was, she was, and, meanwhile, she could only get to Cedar Falls and find out.

And so she got there.

The man in the wire cage at the Cedar Falls post office was a stereotype. Matilda always liked to think in terms of stereotypes. This man was small, roundish, florid of face, with a pair of eyeglasses which hung too far down on his nose. Matilda knew he would peer over his glasses and answer questions grudgingly.

"Hello," said Matilda.

The stereotype grunted and peered at her over his glasses. Matilda asked him where she could find Haron Gorka.

"What?"

"I said, where can I find Haron Gorka?"

"Is that in the United States?"

"It's not a that; it's a he. Where can I find him? Where does he live? What's the quickest way to get there?"

The stereotype pushed up his glasses and looked at her squarely. "Now take it easy, ma'am. First place, I don't know any Haron Gorka—"

Matilda kept the alarm from creeping into her voice. She muttered an *oh* under her breath and took out the ad. This she showed to the stereotype, and he scratched his bald head. Then he told Matilda almost happily that he was sorry he couldn't help her. He grudgingly suggested that if it really were important, she might check with the police.

Matilda did, only they didn't know any Haron Gorka, either. It turned out that no one did: Matilda tried the general store, the fire department, the city hall, the high school, all three Cedar Falls gas stations, the livery stable, and half a dozen private dwellings at random. As far us the gentry of Cedar Falls was concerned, Haron Gorka did not exist.

Matilda felt bad, but she had no intention of returning home this early. If she could not find Haron Gorka, that was one thing; but she knew that she'd rather not return home and face the widow Penshaws, at least not for a while yet. The widow Penshaws meant well, but she liked to analyze other people's mistakes, especially Matilda's.

Accordingly, Matilda trudged wearily toward Cedar Falls' small and unimposing library. She could release some of her pent-up aggression by browsing through the dusty slacks.

This she did, but it was unrewarding. Cedar Falls had what might be called a microscopic library, and Matilda thought that if this small building were filled with microfilm rather than books, the library still would be lacking. Hence she retraced her steps and nodded to the old librarian as she passed.

*

Then Matilda frowned. Twenty years from now, this could be Matilda Penshaws—complete with plain gray dress, rimless spectacles, gray hair, suspicious eyes, and a broom-stick figure....

On the other hand—why not? Why couldn't the librarian help her? Why hadn't she thought of it before? Certainly a man as well-educated as Haron

Gorka would be an avid reader, and unless he had a permanent residence here in Cedar Palls, one couldn't expect that he'd have his own library with him. This being the case, a third-rate collection of books was far better than no collection at all, and perhaps the librarian would know Mr. Haron Gorka.

Matilda cleared her throat. "Pardon me," she began. "I'm looking for—"

"Haron Gorka." The librarian nodded.

"How on earth did you know?"

"That's easy. You're the sixth young woman who came here inquiring about that man today. Six of you—five others in the morning, and now you in the afternoon. I never did trust this Mr. Gorka...."

Matilda jumped as if she had been struck strategically from the rear. "You know him? You know Haron Gorka?"

"Certainly. Of course I know him. He's our steadiest reader here at the library. Not a week goes by that he doesn't take out three, four books. Scholarly gentleman, but not without charm. If I were twenty years younger—"

Matilda thought a little flattery might be effective. "Only ten," she assured the librarian. "Ten years would be more than sufficient, I'm sure."

"Are you? Well. Well, well." The librarian did something with the back of her hair, but it looked the same as before. "Maybe you're right. Maybe you're right at that." Then she sighed. "But I guess a miss is as good as a mile."

"What do you mean?"

"I mean anyone would like to correspond with Haron Gorka. Or to know him well. To be considered his friend. Haron Gorka...."

The librarian seemed about to soar off into the air someplace, and if five women had been here first, Matilda was now definitely in a hurry.

"Um, where can I find Mr. Gorka?"

"I'm not supposed to do this, you know. We're not permitted to give the addresses of any of our people. Against regulations, my dear."

"What about the other five women?"

"They convinced me that I ought to give them his address."

Matilda reached into her pocket-book and withdrew a five dollar bill. "Was this the way?" she demanded. Matilda was not very good at this sort of thing.

The librarian shook her head.

Matilda nodded shrewdly and added a twin brother to the bill in her hand.

"Then is this better?"

"That's worse. I wouldn't take your money—"

"Sorry. What then?"

"If I can't enjoy an association with Haron Gorka directly, I still could get the vicarious pleasure of your contact with him. Report to me faithfully and you'll get his address. That's what the other five will do, and with half a dozen of you, I'll get an overall picture. Each one of you will tell me about Haron Gorka, sparing no details. You each have a distinct personality, of course, and it will color each picture considerably. But with six of you reporting, I should receive my share of vicarious enjoyment. Is it—ah—a deal?"

Matilda assured her that it was, and, breathlessly, she wrote down the address. She thanked the librarian and then she went out to her car, whistling to herself.

*

Haron Gorka lived in what could have been an agrarian estate, except that the land no longer was being tilled. The house itself had fallen to ruin. This surprised Matilda, but she did not let it keep her spirits in check. Haron Gorka, the man, was what counted, and the librarian's account of him certainly had been glowing enough. Perhaps he was too busy with his cultural pursuits to pay any real attention to his dwelling. That was it, of course: the conspicuous show of wealth or personal industry meant nothing at all to Haron Gorka. Matilda liked him all the more for it.

There were five cars parked in the long driveway, and now Matilda's made the sixth. In spite of herself, she smiled. She had not been the only one with the idea to visit Haron Gorka in person. With half a dozen of them there, the laggards who resorted to posting letters would be left far behind. Matilda congratulated herself for what she thought had been her ingenuity, and which now turned out to be something which she had in common with five other women. You live and learn, thought Matilda. And then, quite annoyedly, she berated herself for not having been the first. Perhaps the other five all were satisfactory; perhaps she wouldn't be needed; perhaps she was too late....

*

As it turned out, she wasn't. Not only that, she was welcomed with open arms. Not by Haron Gorka; that she really might have liked. Instead, someone she could only regard as a menial met her, and when he asked had she come in response to the advertisement, she nodded eagerly. He told her that was fine and he ushered her straight into a room which evidently was to be her living quarters. It contained a small undersized bed, a table, and a chair, and, near a little slot in the wall, there was a button.

"You want any food or drink," the servant told her, "and you just press that button. The results will surprise you."

"What about Mr. Gorka?"

"When he wants you, he will send for you. Meanwhile, make yourself to home, lady, and I will tell him you are here."

A little doubtful now, Matilda thanked him and watched him leave. He closed the door softly behind his retreating feet, but Matilda's ears had not missed the ominous click. She ran to the door and tried to open it, but it would not budge. It was locked—from the outside.

It must be said to Matilda's favor that she sobbed only once. After that she realized that what is done is done and here, past thirty, she wasn't going to be girlishly timid about it. Besides, it was not her fault if, in his unconcern, Haron Gorka had unwittingly hired a neurotic servant.

For a time Matilda paced back and forth in her room, and of what was going on outside she could hear nothing. In that case, she would pretend that there was nothing outside the little room, and presently she lay down on the bed to take a nap. This didn't last long, however: she had a nightmare in which Haron Gorka appeared as a giant with two heads, but, upon awaking with a start, she immediately ascribed that to her overwrought nerves.

At that point she remembered what the servant had said about food and she thought at once of the supreme justice she could do to a juicy beefsteak. Well, maybe they didn't have a beefsteak. In that case, she would take what they had, and, accordingly, she walked to the little slot in the wall and pressed the button.

She heard the whir of machinery. A moment later there was a soft sliding sound. Through the slot first came a delicious aroma, followed almost instantly by a tray. On the tray were a bowl of turtle soup, mashed potatoes, green peas, bread, a strange cocktail, root-beer, a parfait—and a thick tenderloin sizzling in hot butter sauce.

Matilda gasped once and felt about to gasp again—but by then her salivary glands were working overtime, and she ate her meal. The fact that it was precisely what she would have wanted could, of course, be attributed to coincidence, and the further fact that everything was extremely palatable made her forget all about Haron Gorka's neurotic servant.

When she finished her meal a pleasant lethargy possessed her, and in a little while Matilda was asleep again. This time she did not dream at all. It was a deep sleep and a restful one, and when she awoke it was with the wonderful feeling that everything was all right.

*

The feeling did not last long. Standing over her was Haron Gorka's servant, and he said, "Mr. Gorka will see you now."

"Now?"

"Now. That's what you're here for, isn't it?"

He had a point there, but Matilda hardly even had time to fix her hair. She told the servant so.

"Miss," he replied, "I assure you it will not matter in the least to Haron Gorka. You are here and he is ready to see you and that is all that matters."

"You sure?" Matilda wanted to take no chances.

"Yes. Come."

She followed him out of the little room and across what should have been a spacious dining area, except that everything seemed covered with dust. Of the other women Matilda could see nothing, and she suddenly realized that each of them probably had a cubicle of a room like her own, and that each in her turn had already had her first visit with Haron Gorka. Well, then, she must see to it that she impressed him better than did all the rest, and, later, when she returned to tell the old librarian of her adventures, she could perhaps draw her out and compare notes.

She would not admit even to herself that she was disappointed with Haron Gorka. It was not that he was homely and unimpressive; it was just that he was so *ordinary*-looking. She almost would have preferred the monster of her dreams.

*

He wore a white linen suit and he had mousy hair, drab eyes, an almost-Roman nose, a petulant mouth with the slight arch of the egotist at each corner.

He said, "Greetings. You have come—"

"In response to your ad. How do you do, Mr. Gorka?"

She hoped she wasn't being too formal. But, then, there was no sense in assuming that he would like informality. She could only wait and see and adjust her own actions to suit him. Meanwhile, it would be best to keep on the middle of the road.

"I am fine. Are you ready?"

"Ready?"

"Certainly. You came in response to my ad. You want to hear me talk, do you not?"

"I—do." Matilda had had visions of her prince charming sitting back and relaxing with her, telling her of the many things he had done and seen. But first she certainly would have liked to get to *know* the man. Well, Haron Gorka obviously had more experience along these lines than she did. He waited, however, as if wondering what to say, and Matilda, accustomed to social chatter, gave him a gambit.

"I must admit I was surprised when I got exactly what I wanted for dinner," she told him brightly.

"Eh? What say? Oh, yes, naturally. A combination of telepathy and teleportation. The synthetic cookery is attuned to your mind when you press the buzzer, and the strength of your psychic impulses determines how closely the meal will adjust to your desires. The fact that the adjustment here was near perfect is commendable. It means either that you have a high psi-quotient, or that you were very hungry."

"Yes," said Matilda vaguely. Perhaps it might be better, after all, if Haron Gorka were to talk to her as he saw fit.

"Ready?"

"Uh—ready."

"Well?"

"Well, what, Mr. Gorka?"

"What would you like me to talk about?"

"Oh, anything."

"Please. As the ad read, my universal experience—is universal. Literally. You'll have to be more specific."

"Well, why don't you tell me about some of your far travels? Unfortunately, while I've done a lot of reading, I haven't been to all the places I would have liked—"

"Good enough. You know, of course, how frigid Deneb VII is?"

Matilda said, "Beg pardon?"

"Well, there was the time our crew—before I had retired, of course—made a crash landing there. We could survive in the vac-suits, of course, but the *thlomots* were after us almost at once. They go mad over plastic. They will eat absolutely any sort of plastic. Our vac-suits—"

"—were made of plastic," Matilda suggested. She did not understand a thing he was talking about, but she felt she had better act bright.

"No, no. Must you interrupt? The air-hose and the water feed, these were plastic. Not the rest of the suit. The point is that half of us were destroyed before the rescue ship could come, and the remainder were near death. I owe my life to the mimicry of a *flaak* from Capella III. It assumed the properties of plastic and led the *thlomots* a merry chase across the frozen surface of D VII. You travel in the Deneb system now and Interstellar Ordinance makes it mandatory to carry*flaaks* with you. Excellent idea, really excellent."

*

Almost at once, Matilda's educational background should have told her that Haron Gorka was mouthing gibberish. But on the other hand she *wanted* to believe in him and the result was that it took until now for her to realize it.

"Stop making fun of me," she said.

"So, naturally, you'll see *flaaks* all over that system—"

"Stop!"

"What's that? Making fun of you?" Haron Gorka's voice had been so eager as he spoke, high-pitched, almost like a child's, and now he seemed disappointed. He smiled, but it was a sad smile, a smile of resignation, and he said, "Very well. I'm wrong again. You are the sixth, and you're no better than the other five. Perhaps you are even more outspoken. When you see my wife, tell her to come back. Again she is right and I am wrong...."

Haron Gorka turned his back.

Matilda could do nothing but leave the room, walk back through the house, go outside and get into her car. She noticed not without surprise that the other five cars were now gone. She was the last of Haron Gorka's guests to depart.

As she shifted into reverse and pulled out of the driveway, she saw the servant leaving, too. Far down the road, he was walking slowly. Then Haron Gorka had severed that relationship, too, and now he was all alone.

As she drove back to town, the disappointment melted slowly away. There were, of course, two alternatives. Either Haron Gorka was an eccentric who enjoyed this sort of outlandish tomfoolery, or else he was plainly insane. She could still picture him ranting on aimlessly to no one in particular about places which had no existence outside of his mind, his voice high-pitched and eager.

*

It was not until she had passed the small library building that she remembered what she had promised the librarian. In her own way, the aging woman would be as disappointed as Matilda, but a promise was a promise, and Matilda turned the car in a wide U-turn and parked it outside the library.

The woman sat at her desk as Matilda had remembered her, gray, broomstick figure, rigid. But now when she saw Matilda she perked up visibly.

"Hello, my dear," she said.

"Hi."

"You're back a bit sooner than I expected. But, then, the other five have returned, too, and I imagine your story will be similar."

"I don't know what they told you," Matilda said. "But this is what happened to me."

She quickly then related everything which had happened, completely and in detail. She did this first because it was a promise, and second because she knew it would make her feel better.

"So," she finished, "Haron Gorka is either extremely eccentric or insane. I'm sorry."

"He's neither," the librarian contradicted. "Perhaps he is slightly eccentric by your standards, but really, my dear, he is neither."

"What do you mean?"

"Did he leave a message for his wife?"

"Why, yes. Yes, he did. But how did you know? Oh, I suppose he told the five."

"No. He didn't. But you were the last and I thought he would give you a message for his wife—"

Matilda didn't understand. She didn't understand at all, but she told the little librarian what the message was. "He wanted her to return," she said.

The librarian nodded, a happy smile on her lips. "You wouldn't believe me if I told you something."

"What's that?"

"I am Mrs. Gorka."

The librarian stood up and came around the desk. She opened a drawer and took out her hat and perched it jauntily atop her gray hair. "You see, my dear, Haron expects too much. He expects entirely too much."

Matilda did not say a word. One madman a day would be quite enough for anybody, but here she found herself confronted with two.

"We've been tripping for centuries, visiting every habitable star system from our home near Canopus. But Haron is too demanding. He says I am a finicky traveler, that he could do much better alone, the accommodations have to be just right for me, and so forth. When he loses his temper, he tries to convince me that any number of females of the particular planet would be more than thrilled if they were given the opportunity just to listen to him.

"But he's wrong. It's a hard life for a woman. Someday—five thousand, ten thousand years from now—I will convince him. And then we will settle down on Canopus XIV and cultivate *torgas*. That would be so nice—"

"I'm sure."

"Well, if Haron wants me back, then I have to go. Have a care, my dear. If you marry, choose a home-body. I've had the experience and you've seen my Haron for yourself."

And then the woman was gone. Numbly, Matilda walked to the doorway and watched her angular figure disappear down the road. Of all the crazy things....

Deneb and Capella and Canopus, these were stars. Add a number and you might have a planet revolving about each star. Of all the insane—

They were mad, all right, and now Matilda wondered if, actually, they were husband and wife. It could readily be; maybe the madness was catching. Maybe if you thought too much about such things, such travels, you could get that way. Of course, Herman represented the other extreme, and Herman was even worse in his own way—but hereafter Matilda would seek the happy medium.

And, above all else, she had had enough of her pen pal columns. They were, she realized, for kids.

*

She ate dinner in Cedar Falls and then she went out to her car again, preparing for the journey back home. The sun had set and it was a clear night, and overhead the great broad sweep of the Milky Way was a pale rainbow bridge in the sky.

Matilda paused. Off in the distance there was a glow on the horizon, and that was the direction of Haron Gorka's place.

The glow increased; soon it was a bright red pulse pounding on the horizon. It flickered. It flickered again, and finally it was gone.

The stars were white and brilliant in the clear country air. That was why Matilda liked the country better than the city, particularly on a clear summer night when you could see the span of the Milky Way.

But abruptly the stars and the Milky Way were paled by the brightest shooting star Matilda had ever seen. It flashed suddenly and it remained in view for a full second, searing a bright orange path across the night sky.

Matilda gasped and ran into her car. She started the gears and pressed the accelerator to the floor, keeping it there all the way home.

It was the first time she had ever seen a shooting star going *up*.

DELAYED ACTION

By Charles Vincent De Vet

This planet gave him the perfect chance to commit the perfect crime—only he couldn't remember just what it was he had committed.

*

It was just a hunch. Johnson knew that, but his hunches had often paid off in the past, and now he waited with a big man's patience. For five hours he sat in the wooden stands, under the rumpled canvas the concessionaires had put up to protect the tourists from Marlock's yellow sun.

The sun was hot and soon Johnson's clothing was marked with large soiled patches of sweat. Now and then a light breeze blew across the stands from the native section and at each breath his nostrils crinkled in protest at the acrid smell.

Marlock wasn't much of a planet. Its one claim to fame was its widely advertised Nature's Moebius Strip. For eighteen months of the year—nine months of sub-zero cold, and nine months of sultry, sand-driven summer—the only outsiders to visit the planet came to buy its one export, the fur of the desert ox. But during the two months of fall and two months of spring the tourists poured in to gape at the Strip.

Idly, for the hundredth time, Johnson let his gaze run over the tourists lining up for their "thrill" journey out onto the Strip. Most of them wouldn't go far; they only wanted to be able to say they'd been on it. They would build up some pretty exciting stories about it by the time they returned home.

There was no sign of Johnson's man.

*

The party started out onto the Strip. At the first sensation of giddiness women squealed and most of them turned back. Their men came with them, secretly relieved at the excuse.

Johnson watched disinterestedly until only two remained: the young couple he had designated in his mind as honeymooners. The girl had grit. Perhaps more than the young fellow with her. He was affecting bored bravado, laughing loudly as the girl hesitated, but white streaks had appeared along his jawline and across his temples as he waited his turn.

The young couple had gone far enough out now so that they were in the first bend of the Strip's twisting dip. Already their bodies were leaning sharply, as the mysterious gravity of the Strip held them perpendicular with their pathway. From where he sat Johnson could read nausea on their faces.

When they had followed the Strip around until they were leaning at a 35-degree angle, the girl seemed to lose her nerve. She stopped and stood gripping the guide rope with both hands. The boy said something to her, but she shook her head. He'd have to show his superiority now by going on, but it wouldn't be for much farther, Johnson was willing to wager.

The boy took three more steps and paused. Then his body bent in the middle and he was sick. He'd had enough.

Both turned and hurried back. The crowd of tourists, watching or waiting their turn, cheered. In a few minutes, Johnson knew, the kid would be thinking of himself as a hero.

Suddenly Johnson straightened up, having spotted a new arrival, who gripped a tan brief-case tightly under one arm, buying a ticket. He had bulky shoulders and a black beard. Johnson's man had come.

When he saw the bearded man go out with the next bunch to brave the Strip, Johnson rose and walked rapidly to the entrance. Elbowing his way through, with a murmured apology, he joined the waiting group.

A thin-faced odd-job man opened the rope gate and they shuffled through. The group must have walked fifty paces, with the bearded man well up in front and Johnson somewhere in the middle, before Johnson's stomach sent him its first warning of unrest. Most of those ahead had stopped and Johnson threaded his way carefully past them.

Another twenty-five steps and he left the others behind. All except the bearded man. He neither paused nor looked back.

Johnson's stomach had drawn up into a tight knot now, and his head was beginning to feel light. There was a faint ringing in his ears.

By the time he reached the end of the guide rope, nausea was creeping up from his stomach and into his throat. This was as far as it was supposed to be safe to go; the advertising literature had it that here was the point of no return. Up ahead his quarry was walking half doubled over, weaving back and forth, as though he were intoxicated. But he did not pause.

Johnson turned to look back, and felt his breakfast fighting to come up. From his perspective, the ground and the spectators watching him had swung to a position almost perpendicular to him. He felt that he was about to slide off into space. A wave of vertigo swept over him, his legs folded and he fell to the ground—sicker than he had ever been before in his life. Now he knew why the man ahead never looked back.

For a moment Johnson wondered whether he should give up. But, even as he debated, tenacity pulled him to his feet and forced him on.

And now something new was added to his vast discomfort. Tiny twinges of pain, like small electric shocks, began shooting up his legs, increasing in intensity with each step he took. The pain built up until the rusty taste of blood in his mouth told him that he had bitten into the flesh of his lower lip.

Johnson's only consolation now was the thought that the man ahead of him must be suffering worse than he. At each step the pain increased its tempo, and the sound within his head grew to a battering roar. Although he felt himself at the last frayed ends of his vitality, he managed to stagger on.

Abruptly he realized that he had very nearly overtaken the man ahead. Through eyes glazed with pain, he saw the other, still standing, but swaying with agony and sickness. The man seemed to be gathering his resources for some supreme effort.

He tottered ahead two more steps, threw himself forward—and disappeared!

If he paused now, Johnson knew he would never be able to move again. Only will power and momentum carried him on. He stumbled and pitched forward. A searing pain traced a path through his head and he felt himself falling.

*

He was certain that he had never lost consciousness. The ground came up to meet him, and, with a last effort, he twisted his right shoulder inward. His cheek slid along the dirt and he lay on his side without strength. His legs pushed forward in a steady jerking movement as he fought to quiet his quivering muscles.

Gradually a soothing lethargy bathed Johnson's body. His pains vanished, and the sickness left his stomach.

But something was wrong—terribly wrong!

Slowly he climbed to his feet and stood looking about him. He was still on the narrow arm of the Strip. On either side of him banks of white clouds, with the consistency of thick smoke, billowed and curled about the Strip—but somehow they left its pathway clear.

Johnson shook his head. The wrongness, he guessed, was in his own mind. But he was unable to determine what it was. Desperately he marshalled his scattered thoughts. Nothing. He took one groping step in the direction from which he had come—and staggered back from a wall of pain as tangible as a concrete structure.

He had no choice except to go forward. There was something he must do, he realized, but what was it? With the question came the answer to what was troubling him.

His memory was gone!

Or, at least, a great gap had been torn through it as though carved out by a giant blade. Briefly, despair threatened to overwhelm him.

"Hold it!" Johnson spoke aloud, and the words sobered him.

All fears became worse when not looked at. He had to bring this disaster out into the open where he could face it; where he could assay the damage. He had always taken pride in having a logical mind, with thought processes as clear and orderly as a bookkeeper's ledger. Closing his eyes, he went swiftly over his recollections, placing each in its appropriate column.

When he finished he found the balance extremely unfavorable, but not hopeless. On the asset side he remembered: His name. Donald Johnson. Right now he was on Nature's Moebius Strip, on the planet, Marlock. There was some man he had been following.... The rest was on the liability side of his balance sheet.

*

His name remained: All other memory of his own identity was gone. There was no recollection of his reason for being on Marlock, or whom he had been following or why. That left him little with which to work.

On the other hand, he mused, he might never be able to get off the Strip, so that didn't matter much. He doubted his ability to stand the stress of penetrating that electric curtain again. His body had been able to take the punishment the first time because the force had built up gradually. Going back would be something else again.

Still he planned his next actions methodically—only in that way could he retain his sanity. He would go forward for one hour, he decided—he checked his wrist watch and discovered it had run down—and, if he found nothing, he would return and take his chances on getting through the curtain.

At the end of ten minutes he sighted land ahead of him. When he stepped off the Strip, he stopped in amazement!

Somehow the Strip had doubled back on itself, and he had returned to his starting place!

To his right was the rough wooden viewing platform, with its green umbrella gone. The stands were empty, and not a person—tourist or concessionaire—was in sight.

As Johnson stood, perplexed, he became aware of numbness spreading over his body. He brought up his hands and watched them slowly turn blue with cold. He realized then, in a burst of wonder, that winter had come to Marlock. Yet it had been spring when he had gone out on the Strip!

*

"Good God, man!" the clerk exclaimed. "Have you been out in that cold without a coat and hat? It must be thirty below."

Johnson was unable to answer. He had run from the Strip—luckily he remembered its location in relation to the town—but it must have been over a mile to the hotel. Now, as he stamped his feet and beat at his sides with numbed hands, he breathed heavily, gasping great gulps of air into his tortured lungs.

"Come and warm yourself," the clerk said, leading him over to a hot water radiator.

Johnson made no protest. He let the heat penetrate until it scorched the skin on his back. Only after the coldness left his body and was replaced by a drowsy inertia did his attention return to the clerk.

"Did you ever see me before?" Johnson asked.

The clerk shook his head. "Not that I know of."

Any further investigation would have to wait until the next day, Johnson decided. He was dead tired, and he had to have some sleep. "Sign me up for a room, will you?" he asked.

Once up in his room, Johnson counted his money. One hundred and fifty-four credits. Enough to buy winter clothing and pay his room and board for a week. Maybe two. What would he do if he could learn nothing about himself before then?

The next day Johnson left the hotel to buy warm clothes. The town's only store was a half-block down the street—as he remembered it, one of the big Interplanet Company stores.

Johnson waited until the storekeeper finished with two of the hairy-eared natives before giving his order. As he paid for the purchase, he asked: "Have you ever seen me before?"

The storekeeper glanced at him uneasily, and shifted his feet before answering. "Am I supposed to have?"

Johnson ignored the question. "Where can I find the manager?" he asked, slipping into the heavy coat the clerk held for him.

"Go up that stairway by the door," the clerk said. "You'll find him in his office."

*

The manager was an old man. Old and black, with the deep blackness only an Earth-born Negro possesses. But his eyes retained their youthful alertness.

"Come in and sit down," he told Johnson as he looked up and saw him standing in the doorway.

Johnson walked over and took the chair at the manager's left. "I've had an accident," he said, without preliminary, "and I seem to have lost my memory. Do you, by any chance, know who I am?"

"Never saw you before in my life," the manager answered. "What's your name?"

"Don Johnson."

"Well, at least you remember something," the old man said shrewdly. "You didn't come during the last six months, if that'll help any. There've been only two ships in that time. Both the Company's. I meet all Company ships. If you came in during the tourist season I wouldn't know."

"Where else could I make inquiries?"

"Son," the old man said kindly, "there's three Earthmen on Marlock, that I know of—besides yourself, of course—the clerk at the hotel, my storekeeper, and myself. If you started asking questions at the hotel, you're at the end of the line now."

Something in Johnson's expression caused the old man to go on. "How you fixed for money, son?"

Johnson drew a deep breath. "I've got enough to last me about two weeks."

The manager hesitated, and carefully surveyed the ceiling with his eyes before he spoke again. "I've always felt we Earthmen should stick together," he said. "If you want a job, I'll find something for you to do and put you on the payroll."

Twenty minutes later Johnson took the job—and twenty years later he was still working for the Company. He worked for them until....

*

Johnson was glad when the first twinge of fear came that it brought no panic. Instead it washed through his body, sharpening his reflexes and alerting his muscles for action.

He never ceased to wonder about this faculty he had acquired for sensing the presence of danger. There was no doubt in his mind that it had come into active function through the influence of his environment. But it must have been an intrinsic part of him even before that, waiting to be activated.

A moment before he had localized the source of his uneasiness—an Earthman, following perhaps fifty paces behind him. The one quick glance Johnson had allowed himself told him his follower was above average in height, and lean—with the wiry, muscular command of himself that marked him as a man capable of well-coordinated action.

He fought the rising force of the next "sand-blaster" boiling in from the desert, until he was unable to take a step against it. Then he moved behind a mud-packed arm projecting from the native dwelling at his right. Every building had one of these protecting arms added on; even the concrete buildings in the newer, Earth-built section of the city conformed to the custom. The sandstorms raged intermittently on Marlock through the entire nine month summer season, and could not be ignored, either by visitors or natives.

Johnson huddled against the projection, but the sand whipped around the corner and pounded at his back. Fine grains sifted through his clothing and mingled with the clammy sweat of his body. He resisted the frantic urge to scratch his itching, tormented skin, for he knew the flesh would be rubbed raw in a minute and increase the irritation to maddening proportions.

As the "sand-blaster" lost its intensity, he came out from his shelter and walked away as rapidly as the diminishing force of the wind would permit. If he could reach his office before his stalker closed in, he would be safe.

Suddenly a second Earthman, a short length of pipe in his right hand, came out of a doorway across the street and ran toward him.

Johnson realized that here was the source of the warning his intuition had sent—not the man behind him.

*

For a brief instant, he weighed the situation. The man was equipped for assault, but the chances were he was interested only in robbery. Johnson could probably save himself a beating by surrendering his money without resistance. He rejected the thought. A man had to live with his pride, and his self-respect; they were more necessary than physical well-being. Setting his shoulders firmly against the wall, he waited.

The man slowed to a walk when he saw his intended victim on guard. Johnson had the chance to observe him closely. He was a short and dark man, heavy of bone, with the lower half of his face thickly bearded, and sweat making a thin glistening film on his high cheekbones.

Abruptly a voice said, "I wouldn't touch him if I were you."

Johnson followed the gaze of his near-attacker to his left where the lean man he had noted before stood with a flat blue pistol pointed in their direction. He held the pistol like a man who knew how to use it.

"A gun!" the man in the street gasped. "Are you crazy?"

"Better put it away—fast," Johnson warned his ally. "If the native police catch you with that gun, you're in bad trouble."

The lean man hesitated a moment, then shrugged and pocketed the gun. But he kept his hand in the pocket. "I can still use it," he said, to no one in particular.

"Look, chum," the bearded thug grated. "You're evidently a stranger here. Let me give you a tip. If you get caught using a gun, or even having one on you, the police'll slap you in jail with an automatic sentence of ten years. An Earthman couldn't stay alive in one of their so-called jails for a year.

"Now I've got a little business to attend to with Mr. Johnson, and I don't want any interference. So be smart and run along."

The smile never left the stranger's face. "Right now," he said, "I am interested in seeing that Mr. Johnson remains in good health. If you take another step toward him, I'll shoot. And, if I'm not successful in evading the police afterwards, you won't be alive to know it."

"You're bluffing," the bearded man said. "I...."

"Let me point out something," Johnson interrupted. "Suppose he is bluffing and doesn't use the gun: The odds are still two to one against you. Are you sure you could handle both of us—even with the help of that pipe?"

The man wasn't sure. He stood undecided, then his face showed black frustration. He mouthed a few choice phrases through his beard, turned and walked away.

The lean man extended his hand. "My name's Alton Hawkes."

The rising whine of the next "sand-blaster" drowned out Johnson's answer. He drew his new acquaintance into the shelter of a sand-arm.

As they hugged the corner, they felt a third body press against them. The musky odor, mingled with the taint of old leather, told Johnson that their companion was a native.

The storm eased its force and the two Earthmen raised their heads to regard the corner's other occupant. He was a mahogany brown, almost the exact color of the ankle-length leather skirt he wore. "Man, he stinks!" Hawkes said.

Their visitor spread his hairy, wide-nostriled nose into the native equivalent of a smile. His hairy ears twitched with pleasure and he swelled his chest. "Blee strong all over," he said. "Want him guard?"

"Why not?" Johnson answered, glancing inquiringly at Hawkes. He slipped a coin into the extended brown palm. "Guard us until we get to the big-house section."

"Pale-smells be very safe," the native said.

They left their shelter as the wind died down and started toward the taller buildings of the foreign section. "I must have said the right thing when I said he stinks," Hawkes remarked.

"Telling a native that is the same thing, to him, as calling him strong and virile," Johnson answered. "They admit, reluctantly, that we foreigners have some good fighting qualities, but we're still regarded as unmanly because of our weak odor. Their females wouldn't look twice at either of us."

When they reached one of the few three-story structures in the city, Johnson dismissed their guard. They entered the building and walked down a short corridor and through a door lettered:

DONALD H. JOHNSON
District Manager
Interplanets Trade Company

"To be frank with you," Hawkes said, as he eased his lank body into the chair Johnson offered, "I had planned to learn more about your local activities before I introduced myself. However, I've found in the past that my first judgment of a man is usually right, so I think I'll get down to business immediately." He drew a set of papers from an inside pocket and tossed them on the desk in front of Johnson. "I'm a Company Secret Service man," he said.

*

Johnson raised his eyebrows, but looked at the papers without comment. He glanced up at Hawkes.

"Do you recognize either of the men in the pictures?" Hawkes asked, when he saw that Johnson had no intention of speaking.

Unhurriedly Johnson picked up the papers and removed a rubber binder. He pulled out two photos and laid them on the desk in front of him. "The bearded one is the man who waylaid me," he said. "Of course."

"Look at both a little closer," Hawkes suggested, "and see if you don't notice something else."

Johnson studied the pictures. "There's no doubt about the first," he murmured. "Evidently I'm supposed to recognize the other also." Abruptly he sat erect. "They're both the same man," he exclaimed. "Only in the second picture he's clean-shaven."

Hawkes nodded. "There's a story about those two pictures," he said. "But first, let me fill you in on some background. You know that Interplanets has branches on more than a thousand worlds. Because of this widespread operation it's particularly vulnerable to robbery. But it would cost more than the Company's earnings to post adequate guards on every station. And it would be impractical to depend on the protection of the local governments, many of which are extremely primitive. On the other hand, allowing themselves to be robbed with impunity would be financial suicide."

Johnson nodded. "Of course."

"That," Hawkes continued, "is where the Company's Secret Service comes in. It never lets up on the effort it will make to solve a robbery and bring the perpetrators to justice. And it never quits, once it begins an investigation. That policy has proven very effective in discouraging thievery. During the Company's entire tenure there have been less than a dozen unsolved thefts—and two of them occurred right here on Marlock."

"I was a clerk with the Company at the time of the second," Johnson said reminiscently. "Been with them about three years then. That must have been over twenty years ago. I...." He paused and looked down. "I remember," he said. "The picture without the beard.... That's the thief. The photograph was taken by one of the automatic cameras set up for just that purpose; we still use them. But they never found the man."

"That's right," Hawkes agreed. "That robbery occurred a little over twenty years ago. And the other picture you have was taken at the time of the first robbery—approximately twenty-five years before that."

"But it isn't possible," Johnson protested. "These pictures are of the same man. And there's obviously no twenty-five year spread in age between them. Unless...."

"Unless one is the other's father, or a relative that resembles him very closely?" Hawkes finished. "Look at the pictures again. There's the same scar on both foreheads, the same pock-mark on the right cheek; our special section has even made measurements of the comparative sizes of the nose, ears and other features. There's no possible doubt that the pictures are of the same man."

*

How do you explain it?" Johnson asked.

"I don't," Hawkes replied quietly. "That's one of the things I'm here to learn. But did you notice this? The man we encountered this afternoon was not only the same as the one on those pictures: he still looks the same. We might, for the sake of argument, grant that a man's appearance would change only slightly in twenty-five years. But when you add another twenty-three on top of that—and he's still unchanged...?"

"If you're certain that he's the man, why don't you arrest him?" Johnson asked.

"Can we arrest a man apparently about thirty years old and accuse him of a crime committed forty-eight years ago—or even twenty-three years ago?"

"I suppose not," Johnson agreed. "What do you intend to do?"

"I haven't decided yet. First I'll have to learn more about the situation here. You can help me with that. Right now I'd like to know something about the native customs—especially in regard to legal matters."

"Their laws are fairly simple," Johnson began. "There's no law against stealing or taking by force anything you can get away with. That sounds absurd by Earth standards, it prevents the amassing of more goods than an individual needs, and makes for fairly equitable distribution. If a native somehow acquires a sudden amount of wealth—goods, in their case—he must hire guards to protect it. Guarding is a major occupation. They do an especially big business during the tourist seasons. In time the pay of the guards will eat up any native's surplus. Either way—by loss or guard pay—the wealth is soon redistributed."

"Can they even kill one another with impunity?"

"No. Their laws are rigid in that respect. In the process of—relieving another of his property, they must neither break a major bone, nor inflict permanent damage. If they disobey, they are tortured to death in the public square."

Hawkes asked, "Who enforces their law?"

"One of the clans. Its members are supported in their duties by all the others. And there's a permanent open season on murderers. Anyone, police or civilian may revenge a victim."

"How about the law against carrying firearms?"

"With them, intent is tantamount to commission," Johnson replied. "Only foreigners are ever foolish enough to be caught armed. However, all native laws apply to them also. The only concession the Company has been able to force is that a foreign offender isn't tortured: He's put in jail for ten years. None ever live to come out."

"I see," Hawkes said. "Interesting. However, the immediate situation is this. I've been sent here because the Service received reports that our bearded friend had made another appearance. And we believe it's safe to assume that he's here to attempt a third robbery. Right now we'll have to pass over his trick of longevity. Our problem is to catch him in the act. When do you think he'll make his play?"

"It'll have to be some time before tomorrow noon," Johnson answered. "Under our setup we accept furs from the natives whenever they're brought in. But we pay off only once a year. That way I'm not burdened with guarding money the whole year around. I have well over fifty thousand credits in the safe now. And tomorrow I begin paying off."

"Then we'll have to be ready for him," Hawkes said, "though I don't expect him until tonight. Probably just about the time you're ready to close. He'll need you to open the safe. I can count on your help?"

Johnson nodded.

*

That night as they waited in his office, Johnson turned to Hawkes. "I've been giving some thought to what you told me this afternoon about the robberies. I have a theory that might account for some of the things we don't understand."

"Yes?" Hawkes looked closely at Johnson.

"You've probably heard of our tourist attraction called Nature's Moebius Strip? As far as we know, no one has ever gone beyond a certain point—and returned. Suppose there's a time flaw at that point—and the bearded man has somehow learned about it. Suppose anyone completing the Moebius circle, and returning, finds—say, twenty years have elapsed, while to him only a few minutes have passed?"

"Go on." Hawkes leaned forward intently.

"He makes his first holdup," Johnson continued, "and goes around the Strip. When he comes out twenty years later they're no longer looking for him. He leaves Marlock, and during the next five years he goes through the money he stole. He returns and repeats the process. This time the money lasts only three years. Now he's back to try it again. Do you see how that would tie everything up in a neat little package?"

Hawkes smiled, as he relaxed and sat back. "A bit too neat," he said. "Also, you don't have an ounce of concrete evidence to back up your theory."

"That's right. I don't," Johnson agreed.

Outside the door a board creaked. Johnson glanced quickly across the room to where Hawkes sat with a pistol on his lap. Hawkes' eyebrows raised, but he made no sound.

*

Suddenly the door was kicked open and the black-bearded stranger stood framed in the doorway. "Raise 'em!" he barked. The gun in his hand was aimed at Johnson.

The man took two steps into the room. Hawkes shifted slightly in his chair and the gunman's head swiveled in his direction. The slug from Hawkes' pistol made a small blue hole in the upper left corner of his forehead.

The thug's face tipped up, shocked and unbelieving. He swayed slowly before he fell backward, his body rigid. His fur cap flew from his head as he struck the floor.

"I thought we'd better play it safe," Hawkes said as he rose and walked over to the fallen man. He slipped his gun into his pocket before he bent and picked up the cap at his feet. He dropped it over the upturned face.

For a long moment the silence held thin as the two men looked at each other. Hawkes stood, wiping his right hand on his trouser leg. Johnson toyed idly with the gun he had picked up from the desk in front of him.

Finally Hawkes let his body sag into a chair at Johnson's right. "This is always a dirty business," he said sourly.

Johnson sat down also. "Did you notice the look on his face when he saw you, and you shot him?" he asked, abstractedly turning the pistol in his hand. "Funny thing. In that half-second before he fell an article I read somewhere flashed into my mind. It seems that during the French Revolution a certain doctor got to wondering just how long a man's brain remained active after his head had been cut off. He persuaded some of his friends who were due to be guillotined to cooperate in a series of tests. Each man was to keep blinking his eyes as long as possible after his head left his body, as a sign that he was still conscious. The doctor counted as high as six winks."

"Very interesting, I'm sure," Hawkes said guardedly. "But a bit morbid, isn't it?"

"I was wondering," Johnson went on as though he had not heard the other, "whether he was still conscious for that instant after you shot him. And if that brought the look of surprise to his face."

*

Hawkes turned in his chair to face Johnson fully. "You're driving at something," he said sharply. "Get to the point."

"Personally I've wondered at a few things about you myself," Johnson said. He held the gun steadily in his hand now, no longer pretending to play with it. "I told you that our second robbery occurred while I was a clerk with the Company," he went on. "They jerked me in to the Home Office, and for a while I had a pretty rough time.... You know, when I joined the Company, I was an amnesiac. I remembered my name, but that's about all...."

"No, I didn't know," Hawkes muttered, growing slightly paler.

"I learned then from the Home Office that I had been a member of their Secret Service some twenty years earlier. I'd been sent here to investigate the first robbery. And I had disappeared. Naturally, they had suspected me.

"However, they had no evidence, and when I reappeared twenty years later they played it smart by just waiting, instead of arresting me. When the second robbery occurred, they closed in.

"The only thing that saved me was the fact that tests proved my memory was really gone, and that I had told the truth—as I knew it. From the few scraps of information I retained—about being out on the Moebius Strip—they and I arrived at the theory I mentioned a short time ago. I was sent back here to wait. The Company never gives up. Remember?"

"Are you insinuating that I was in cahoots with this fellow here?" Hawkes asked harshly.

"I'd say it was more than an insinuation," Johnson replied. "You made several other slips. In the first place, Secret Service men are usually better informed about a situation they're investigating than you seemed to be. Also, those identification papers you showed me were faked."

*

The skin along the bridge of Hawkes' nose had drawn tight, and now his lips grew narrower. "In that case, why did I save you from that man this afternoon?" he asked. "And why would I shoot him now?"

"Your saving me was an act, to get into my confidence. You shot him so you wouldn't have to split the loot. I figure you were in with him on the second robbery also. There had to be someone because his memory would be gone, when he came off the Strip. But you weren't satisfied. Together you decided to pull off another robbery while you were here and double the spoils. Then you decided you wanted it all for yourself and you shot him."

"There's one big flaw in your reasoning," Hawkes pointed out. "How did I plan to get away? The only ships leaving here for several months belong to the Company. Do you think I'd be foolish enough to expect them to let me slip out on one of their ships?"

"No. I think you intended to go out on the Strip yourself."

"All right then," Hawkes countered. "You admitted that this was a two-man job. How could I protect myself when I returned, if I knew in advance that I wouldn't know who I was, let alone what I had done?"

"I'll come back to that in a minute," Johnson said. "But now I'd advise you to drop your gun on the floor and give yourself up. You've got nothing to gain by carrying on the bluff. You know I'll never let you get to the Strip. And, once I put you on the ship, the Company will take over."

*

Hawkes' shoulders drooped. Finally he smiled raggedly. "There's no use my arguing any longer," he said. "But you've made the mistake of underestimating me, my friend. I've lost my gamble. That's all. You have nothing on me. I'm not as ignorant of native law as I may have pretended. Granted, I am carrying a lethal weapon. But I'm on private property. That's legal. I shot a man. But only in defense of my own life. His gun on the floor will prove he came in armed. So I'm clean as far as the natives are concerned. Right?"

Johnson nodded.

"And, as for the Company, what will they hold me for? They can't prove any connection between me and him." Hawkes indicated the man on the floor. "And this robbery—it never actually came off. Earth laws don't allow prosecution for intent. Now, where does that leave you?"

Johnson stood up. "You're right—as far as you went," he said. "But, returning to your earlier question about one man pulling this job, I asked myself how I would do it, if it had to be done alone. And I found a way. You'd probably figure the same one. Now I'll take that paper in your pocket. It will serve very well as a confession."

Suddenly Hawkes' right hand streaked toward a side pocket. Johnson leaned forward and brought the flat of his gun across the other's temple.

As Hawkes sagged, Johnson ripped open his coat and took out a sealed envelope. He removed a sheet of paper and read:

This has been written for my own information. My name is Alton Hawkes. I have robbed the Interplanets Company and gone out on the Strip with the money. When I read this my memory will be gone and twenty years will have elapsed.

... AND IT COMES OUT HERE

By Lester del Rey

There is one fact no sane man can quarrel with ... everything has a beginning and an end. But some men aren't sane; thus it isn't always so!

*

No, you're wrong. I'm not your father's ghost, even if I do look a bit like him. But it's a longish story, and you might as well let me in. You will, you know, so why quibble about it? At least, you always have ... or do ... or will. I don't know, verbs get all mixed up. We don't have the right attitude toward tenses for a situation like this.

Anyhow, you'll let me in. I did, so you will.

Thanks. You think you're crazy, of course, but you'll find out you aren't. It's just that things are a bit confused. And don't look at the machine out there too long—until you get used to it, you'll find it's hard on the eyes, trying to follow where the vanes go. You'll get used to it, of course, but it will take about thirty years.

You're wondering whether to give me a drink, as I remember it. Why not? And naturally, since we have the same tastes, you can make the same for me as you're having. Of course we have the same tastes—we're the same person. I'm you thirty years from now, or you're me. I remember just how you feel; I felt the same way when he—that is, of course, I or we—came back to tell me about it, thirty years ago.

Here, have one of these. You'll get to like them in a couple more years. And you can look at the revenue stamp date, if you still doubt my story. You'll believe it eventually, though, so it doesn't matter.

Right now, you're shocked. It's a real wrench when a man meets himself for the first time. Some kind of telepathy seems to work between two of the same people. You*sense* things. So I'll simply go ahead talking for half an hour or so, until you get over it. After that you'll come along with me. You know, I could try to change things around by telling what happened to me; but he—I—told me what I was going to do, so I might as well do the same. I probably couldn't help telling you the same thing in the same words, even if I tried—and I don't intend to try. I've gotten past that stage in worrying about all this.

So let's begin when you get up in half an hour and come out with me. You'll take a closer look at the machine, then. Yes, it'll be pretty obvious it must be a time machine. You'll sense that, too. You've seen it, just a small little cage with two seats, a luggage compartment, and a few buttons on a dash. You'll be puzzling over what I'll tell you, and you'll be getting used to the idea that you are the man who makes atomic power practical. Jerome Boell, just a plain engineer, the man who put atomic power in every home. You won't exactly believe it, but you'll want to go along.

*

I'll be tired of talking by then, and in a hurry to get going. So I cut off your questions, and get you inside. I snap on a green button, and everything seems to cut off around us. You can see a sort of foggy nothing surrounding the cockpit; it is probably the field that prevents passage through time from affecting us. The luggage section isn't protected, though.

You start to say something, but by then I'm pressing a black button, and everything outside will disappear. You look for your house, but it isn't there. There is exactly nothing there—in fact, there is no *there*. You are completely outside of time and space, as best you can guess how things are.

You can't feel any motion, of course. You try to reach a hand out through the field into the nothing around you and your hand goes out, all right, but nothing happens. Where the screen ends, your hand just turns over and pokes back at you. Doesn't hurt, and when you pull your arm back, you're still sound and uninjured. But it looks frightening and you don't try it again.

Then it comes to you slowly that you're actually traveling in time. You turn to me, getting used to the idea. "So this is the fourth dimension?" you ask.

Then you feel silly, because you'll remember that I said you'd ask that. Well, I asked it after I was told, then I came back and told it to you, and I still can't help answering when you speak.

"Not exactly," I try to explain. "Maybe it's no dimension—or it might be the fifth; if you're going to skip over the so-called fourth without traveling along it, you'd need a fifth. Don't ask me. I didn't invent the machine and I don't understand it."

"But...."

I let it go, and so do you. If you don't, it's a good way of going crazy. You'll see later why I couldn't have invented the machine. Of course, there may have been a start for all this once. There may have been a time when you did invent the machine—the atomic motor first, then the time-machine. And when you closed the loop by going back and saving yourself the trouble, it got all tangled up. I figured out once that such a universe would need some seven or eight time and space dimensions. It's simpler just to figure that this is the way time got bent back on itself. Maybe there is no machine, and it's just easier for us to imagine it. When you spend thirty years thinking about it, as I did—and you will—you get further and further from an answer.

Anyhow, you sit there, watching nothing all around you, and no time, apparently, though there is a time effect back in the luggage space. You look at your watch and it's still running. That means you either carry a small time field with you, or you are catching a small increment of time from the main field. I don't know, and you won't think about that then, either.

*

I'm smoking, and so are you, and the air in the machine is getting a bit stale. You suddenly realize that everything in the machine is wide open, yet you haven't seen any effects of air loss.

"Where are we getting our air?" you ask. "Or why don't we lose it?"

"No place for it to go," I explain. There isn't. Out there is neither time nor space, apparently. How could the air leak out? You still feel gravity, but I can't explain that, either. Maybe the machine has a gravity field built in, or maybe the time that makes your watch run is responsible for gravity. In spite of Einstein, you have always had the idea that time is an effect of gravity, and I sort of agree, still.

Then the machine stops—at least, the field around us cuts off. You feel a dankish sort of air replace the stale air, and you breathe easier, though we're in complete darkness, except for the weak light in the machine, which always burns, and a few feet of rough dirty cement floor around. You take another cigaret from me and you get out of the machine, just as I do.

I've got a bundle of clothes and I start changing. It's a sort of simple, short-limbed, one-piece affair I put on, but it feels comfortable.

"I'm staying here," I tell you. "This is like the things they wear in this century, as near as I can remember it, and I should be able to pass fairly well. I've had all my fortune—the one you make on that atomic generator—invested in such a way I can get it on using some identification I've got with me, so I'll do all right. I know they still use some kind of money, you'll see evidence of that. And it's a pretty easygoing civilization, from what I could see. We'll go up and I'll leave you. I like the looks of things here, so I won't be coming back with you."

You nod, remembering I've told you about it. "What century is this, anyway?"

I'd told you that, too, but you've forgotten. "As near as I can guess, it's about 2150. He told me, just as I'm telling you, that it's an interstellar civilization."

You take another cigaret from me, and follow me. I've got a small flashlight and we grope through a pile of rubbish, out into a corridor. This is a sub-sub-sub-basement. We have to walk up a flight of stairs, and there is an elevator waiting, fortunately with the door open.

"What about the time machine?" you ask.

"Since nobody ever stole it, it's safe."

*

We get in the elevator, and I say "first" to it. It gives out a coughing noise and the basement openings begin to click by us. There's no feeling of acceleration—some kind of false gravity they use in the future. Then the door opens, and the elevator says "first" back at us.

It's obviously a service elevator and we're in a dim corridor, with nobody around. I grab your hand and shake it. "You go that way. Don't worry about getting lost; you never did, so you can't. Find the museum, grab the motor, and get out. And good luck to you."

You act as if you're dreaming, though you can't believe it's a dream. You nod at me and I move out into the main corridor. A second later, you see me going by, mixed into a crowd that is loafing along toward a restaurant, or something like it, that is just opening. I'm asking questions of a man, who points, and I turn and move off.

You come out of the side corridor and go down a hall, away from the restaurant. There are quiet little signs along the hall. You look at them, realizing for the first time that things have changed.

Steij:neri, Faunten, Z:rgat Dispenseri. The signs are very quiet and dignified. Some of them can be decoded to stationery shops, fountains, and the like. What a zergot is, you don't know. You stop at a sign that announces: *Trav:l Biwrou—F:rst-Clas Twrz—Marz, Viin*s, and x: Trouj:n Planets. Spej:l reits tu aol s*nz wixin 60 lyt iirz!* But there is only a single picture of a dull-looking metal sphere, with passengers moving up a ramp, and the office is closed. You begin to get the hang of the spelling they use, though.

Now there are people around you, but nobody pays much attention to you. Why should they? You wouldn't care if you saw a man in a leopard-skin suit; you'd figure it was some part in a play and let it go. Well, people don't change much.

You get up your courage and go up to a boy selling something that might be papers on tapes.

"Where can I find the Museum of Science?"

"Downayer rien turn lefa the sign. Stoo bloss," he tells you. Around you, you hear some pretty normal English, but there are others using stuff as garbled as his. The educated and uneducated? I don't know.

You go right until you find a big sign built into the rubbery surface of the walk: *Miuzi:m *v Syens*. There's an arrow pointing and you turn left. Ahead of you, two blocks on, you can see a pink building, with faint aqua trimming, bigger than most of the others. They are building lower than they used to, apparently. Twenty floors up seems about the maximum. You head for it, and find the sidewalk is marked with the information that it is the museum.

*

You go up the steps, but you see that it seems to be closed. You hesitate for a moment, then. You're beginning to think the whole affair is complete nonsense, and you should get back to the time machine and go home. But then a guard comes to the gate. Except for the short legs in his suit and the friendly grin on his face, he looks like any other guard.

What's more, he speaks pretty clearly. Everyone says things in a sort of drawl, with softer vowels and slurred consonants, but it's rather pleasant.

"Help you, sir? Oh, of course. You must be playing in 'Atoms and Axioms.' The museum's closed, but I'll be glad to let you study whatever you need for realism in your role. Nice show. I saw it twice."

"Thanks," you mutter, wondering what kind of civilization can produce guards as polite as that. "I—I'm told I should investigate your display of atomic generators."

He beams at that. "Of course." The gate is swung to behind you, but obviously he isn't locking it. In fact, there doesn't seem to be a lock. "Must be a new part. You go down that corridor, up one flight of stairs and left. Finest display in all the known worlds. We've got the original of the first thirteen models. Professor Jonas was using them to check his latest theory of how they work. Too bad he could not explain the principle, either. Someone will, some day, though. Lord, the genius of that twentieth century inventor! It's quite a hobby with me, sir. I've read everything I could get on the period. Oh—congratulations on your pronunciation. Sounds just like some of our oldest tapes."

You get away from him, finally, after some polite thanks. The building seems deserted and you wander up the stairs. There's a room on your right filled with something that proclaims itself the first truly plastic diamond former, and you go up to it. As you come near, it goes through a crazy wiggle inside, stops turning out a continual row of what seem to be bearings, and slips something the size of a penny toward you.

"Souvenir," it announces in a well-modulated voice. "This is a typical gem of the twentieth century, properly cut to 58 facets, known technically as a Jaegger diamond, and approximately twenty carats in size. You can have it made into a ring on the third floor during morning hours for one-tenth credit. If you have more than one child, press the red button for the number of stones you desire."

You put it in your pocket, gulping a little, and get back to the corridor. You turn left and go past a big room in which models of spaceships—from the original thing that looks like a V-2, and is labeled first Lunar rocket, to a ten-foot globe, complete with miniature manikins—are sailing about in some kind of orbits. Then there is one labeled*Wep:nz*, filled with everything from a crossbow to a tiny rod four inches long and half the thickness of a pencil, marked *Fynal Hand Arm*. Beyond is the end of the corridor, and a big place that bears a sign, *Mad:lz *v Atamic Pau:r Sorsez*.

*

By that time, you're almost convinced. And you've been doing a lot of thinking about what you can do. The story I'm telling has been sinking in, but you aren't completely willing to accept it.

You notice that the models are all mounted on tables and that they're a lot smaller than you thought. They seem to be in chronological order, and the latest one, marked*2147—Rincs Dyn*pat:*, is about the size of a desk telephone. The earlier ones are larger, of course, clumsier, but with variations, probably depending on the power output. A big sign on the ceiling gives a lot of dope on atomic generators, explaining that this is the first invention which leaped full blown into basically final form.

You study it, but it mentions casually the inventor, without giving his name. Either they don't know it, or they take it for granted that everyone does, which seems more probable. They call attention to the fact that they have the original model of the first atomic generator built, complete with design drawings, original manuscript on operation, and full patent application.

They state that it has all major refinements, operating on any fuel, producing electricity at any desired voltage up to five million, any chosen cyclic rate from direct current to one thousand megacycles, and any amperage up to one thousand, its maximum power output being fifty kilowatts, limited by the current-carrying capacity of the outputs. They also mention that the operating principle is still being investigated, and that only such refinements as better alloys and the addition of magnetric and nucleatric current outlets have been added since the original.

So you go to the end and look over the thing. It's simply a square box with a huge plug on each side, and a set of vernier controls on top, plus a little hole marked, in old-style spelling, *Drop BBs or wire here*. Apparently that's the way it's fueled. It's about one foot on each side.

"Nice," the guard says over your shoulder. "It finally wore out one of the cathogrids and we had to replace that, but otherwise it's exactly as the great inventor made it. And it still operates as well as ever. Like to have me tell you about it?"

"Not particularly," you begin, and then realize bad manners might be conspicuous here. While you're searching for an answer, the guard pulls something out of his pocket and stares at it.

"Fine, fine. The mayor of Altasecarba—Centaurian, you know—is arriving, but I'll be back in about ten minutes. He wants to examine some of the weapons for a monograph on Centaurian primitives compared to nineteenth century man. You'll pardon me?"

You pardon him pretty eagerly and he wanders off happily. You go up to the head of the line, to that Rinks Dynapattuh, or whatever it transliterates to. That's small and you can carry it. But the darned thing is absolutely fixed. You can't see any bolts, but you can't budge it, either.

*

You work down the line. It'd be foolish to take the early model if you can get one with built-in magnetic current terminals—Ehrenhaft or some other principle?—and nuclear binding-force energy terminals. But they're all held down by the same whatchamaycallem effect.

And, finally, you're right back beside the original first model. It's probably bolted down, too, but you try it tentatively and you find it moves. There's a little sign under it, indicating you shouldn't touch it, since the gravostatic plate is being renewed.

Well, you won't be able to change the time cycle by doing anything I haven't told you, but a working model such as that is a handy thing. You lift it; it only weighs about fifty pounds! Naturally, it can be carried.

You expect a warning bell, but nothing happens. As a matter of fact, if you'd stop drinking so much of that scotch and staring at the time machine out there now, you'd hear what I'm saying and know what will happen to you. But of course, just as I did, you're going to miss a lot of what I say from now on, and have to find out for yourself. But maybe some of it helps. I've tried to remember how much I remembered, after he told me, but I can't be sure. So I'll keep on talking. I probably can't help it, anyhow. Pre-set, you might say.

Well, you stagger down the corridor, looking out for the guard, but all seems clear. Then you hear his voice from the weapons room. You bend down and try to scurry past, but you know you're in full view. Nothing happens, though.

You stumble down the stairs, feeling all the futuristic rays in the world on your back, and still nothing happens. Ahead of you, the gate is closed. You reach it and it opens obligingly by itself. You breathe a quick sigh of relief and start out onto the street.

Then there's a yell behind you. You don't wait. You put one leg in front of the other and you begin racing down the walk, ducking past people, who stare at you with expressions you haven't time to see. There's another yell behind you.

Something goes over your head and drops on the sidewalk just in front of your feet, with a sudden ringing sound. You don't wait to find out about that, either. Somebody reaches out a hand to catch you and you dart past.

The street is pretty clear now and you jolt along, with your arms seeming to come out of the sockets, and that atomic generator getting heavier at every step.

Out of nowhere, something in a blue uniform about six feet tall and on the beefy side appears—and the badge hasn't changed much. The cop catches your arm and you know you're not going to get away, so you stop.

"You can't exert yourself that hard in this heat, fellow," the cop says. "There are laws against that, without a yellow sticker. Here, let me grab you a taxi."

*

Reaction sets in a bit and your knees begin to buckle, but you shake your head and come up for air.

"I—I left my money home," you begin.

The cop nods. "Oh, that explains it. Fine, I won't have to give you an appearance schedule. But you should have come to me." He reaches out and taps a pedestrian lightly on the shoulder. "Sir, an emergency request. Would you help this gentleman?"

The pedestrian grins, looks at his watch, and nods. "How far?"

You did notice the name of the building from which you came and you mutter it. The stranger nods again, reaches out and picks up the other side of the generator, blowing a little whistle the cop hands him. Pedestrians begin to move aside, and you and the stranger jog down the street at a trot, with a nice clear path, while the cop stands beaming at you both.

That way, it isn't so bad. And you begin to see why I decided I might like to stay in the future. But all the same, the organized cooperation here doesn't look too good. The guard can get the same and be there before you.

And he is. He stands just inside the door of the building as you reach it. The stranger lifts an eyebrow and goes off at once when you nod at him, not waiting for thanks. And the guard comes up, holding some dinkus in his hand, about the size of a big folding camera and not too dissimilar in other ways. He snaps it open and you get set to duck.

"You forgot the prints, monograph, and patent applications," he says. "They go with the generator—we don't like to have them separated. A good thing I knew the production office of 'Atoms and Axioms' was in this building. Just let us know when you're finished with the model and we'll pick it up."

You swallow several sets of tonsils you had removed years before, and take the bundle of papers he hands you out of the little case. He pumps you for some more information, which you give him at random. It seems to satisfy your amiable guard friend. He finally smiles in satisfaction and heads back to the museum.

You still don't believe it, but you pick up the atomic generator and the information sheets, and you head down toward the service elevator. There is no button on it. In fact, there's no door there.

You start looking for other doors or corridors, but you know this is right. The signs along the halls are the same as they were.

*

Then there's a sort of cough and something dilates in the wall. It forms a perfect door and the elevator stands there waiting. You get in, gulping out something about going all the way down, and then wonder how a machine geared for voice operation can make anything of that. What the deuce would that lowest basement be called? But the elevator has closed and is moving downward in a hurry. It coughs again and you're at the original level. You get out—and realize you don't have a light.

You'll never know what you stumbled over, but, somehow, you move back in the direction of the time machine, bumping against boxes, staggering here and there, and trying to find the right place by sheer feel. Then a shred of dim light appears; it's the weak light in the time machine.

You've located it.

You put the atomic generator in the luggage space, throw the papers down beside it, and climb into the cockpit, sweating and mumbling. You reach forward toward the green button and hesitate. There's a red one beside it and you finally decide on that.

Suddenly, there's a confused yell from the direction of the elevator and a beam of light strikes against your eyes, with a shout punctuating it. Your finger touches the red button.

You'll never know what the shouting was about—whether they finally doped out the fact that they'd been robbed, or whether they were trying to help you. You don't care which it is. The field springs up around you and the next button you touch—the one on the board that hasn't been used so far—sends you off into nothingness. There is no beam of light, you can't hear a thing, and you're safe.

It isn't much of a trip back. You sit there smoking and letting your nerves settle back to normal. You notice a third set of buttons, with some pencil marks over them—" Press these to return to yourself 30 years"—and you begin waiting for the air to get stale. It doesn't because there is only one of you this time.

Instead, everything flashes off and you're sitting in the machine in your own back yard.

You'll figure out the cycle in more details later. You get into the machine in front of your house, go to the future in the sub-basement, land in your back yard, and then hop back thirty years to pick up yourself, landing in front of your house. Just that. But right then, you don't care. You jump out and start pulling out that atomic generator and taking it inside.

*

It isn't hard to disassemble, but you don't learn a thing; just some plates of metal, some spiral coils, and a few odds and ends—all things that can be made easily enough, all obviously of common metals. But when you put it together again, about an hour later, you notice something.

Everything in it is brand-new and there's one set of copper wires missing! It won't work. You put some #12 house wire in, exactly like the set on the other side, drop in some iron filings, and try it again.

And with the controls set at 120 volts, 60 cycles and 15 amperes, you get just that. You don't need the power company any more. And you feel a little happier when you realize that the luggage space wasn't insulated from time effects by a field, so the motor has moved backward in time, somehow, and is back to its original youth—minus the replaced wires the guard mentioned—which probably wore out because of the makeshift job you've just done.

But you begin getting more of a jolt when you find that the papers are all in your own writing, that your name is down as the inventor, and that the date of the patent application is 1951.

It will begin to soak in, then. You pick up an atomic generator in the future and bring it back to the past—your present—so that it can be put in the museum with you as the inventor so you can steal it to be the inventor. And you do it in a time machine which you bring back to yourself to take yourself into the future to return to take back to yourself....

Who invented what? And who built which?

Before long, your riches from the generator are piling in. Little kids from school are coming around to stare at the man who changed history and made atomic power so common that no nation could hope to be anything but a democracy and a peaceful one—after some of the worst times in history for a few years. Your name eventually becomes as common as Ampere, or Faraday, or any other spelled without a capital letter.

But you're thinking of the puzzle. You can't find any answer.

One day you come across an old poem—something about some folks calling it evolution and others calling it God. You go out, make a few provisions for the future, and come back to climb into the time machine that's waiting in the building you had put around it. Then you'll be knocking on your own door, thirty years back—or right now, from your view—and telling your younger self all these things I'm telling you.

But now....

Well, the drinks are finished. You're woozy enough to go along with me without protest, and I want to find out just why those people up there came looking for you and shouting, before the time machine left.

Let's go.

THE OLD DIE RICH

By H. L. Gold

It is the kind of news item you read at least a dozen times a year, wonder about briefly, and then promptly forget—but the real story is the one that the reporters are unable to cover!

*

You again, Weldon," the Medical Examiner said wearily.

I nodded pleasantly and looked around the shabby room with a feeling of hopeful eagerness. Maybe *this* time, I thought, I'd get the answer. I had the same sensation I always had in these places—the quavery senile despair at being closed in a room with the single shaky chair, tottering bureau, dim bulb hanging from the ceiling, the flaking metal bed.

There was a woman on the bed, an old woman with white hair thin enough to show the tight-drawn scalp, her face and body so emaciated that the flesh between the bones formed parchment pockets. The M.E. was going over her as if she were a side of beef that he had to put a federal grade stamp on, grumbling meanwhile about me and Sergeant Lou Pape, who had brought me here.

"When are you going to stop taking Weldon around to these cases, Sergeant?" the M.E. demanded in annoyance. "Damned actor and his morbid curiosity!"

For the first time, Lou was stung into defending me. "Mr. Weldon is a friend of mine—I used to be an actor, too, before I joined the force—and he's a follower of Stanislavsky."

The beat cop who'd reported the D.O.A. whipped around at the door. "A Red?"

*

I let Lou Pape explain what the Stanislavsky method of acting was, while I sat down on the one chair and tried to apply it. Stanislavsky was the great pre-Revolution Russian stage director whose idea was that actors had to think and feel like the characters they portrayed so they could *be* them. A Stanislavskian works out everything about a character right up to the point where a play starts—where he was born, when, his relationship with his parents, education, childhood, adolescence, maturity, attitudes toward men, women, sex, money, success, including incidents. The play itself is just an extension of the life history created by the actor.

How does that tie in with the old woman who had died? Well, I'd had the cockeyed kind of luck to go bald at 25 and I'd been playing old men ever since. I had them down pretty well—it's not just a matter of shuffling around all hunched over and talking in a high cracked voice, which is cornball acting, but learning what old people are like inside—and these cases I talked Lou Pape into taking me on were studies in senility. I wanted to understand them, know what made them do what they did, *feel* the compulsion that drove them to it.

The old woman on the bed, for instance, had $32,000 in five bank accounts ... and she'd died of starvation.

You've come across such cases in the news, at least a dozen a year, and wondered who they were and why they did it. But you read the items, thought about them for a little while, and then forgot them. My interest was professional; I made my living playing old people and I had to know as much about them as I could.

That's how it started off, at any rate. But the more cases I investigated, the less sense they made to me, until finally they were practically an obsession.

Look, they almost always have around $30,000 pinned to their underwear, hidden in mattresses, or parked in the bank, yet they starve themselves to death. If I could understand them, I could write a play or have one written; I might really make a name for myself, even get a Hollywood contract, maybe, if I could act them as they should be acted.

So I sat there in the lone chair, trying to reconstruct the character of the old woman who had died rather than spend a single cent of her $32,000 for food.

*

Malnutrition induced by senile psychosis," the M.E. said, writing out the death certificate. He turned to me. "There's no mystery to it, Weldon. They starve because they're less afraid of death than digging into their savings."

I'd been imagining myself growing weak from hunger and trying to decide that I ought to eat even if it cost me something. I came out of it and said, "That's what you keep telling me."

"I keep hoping it'll convince you so you won't come around any more. What are the chances, Weldon?"

"Depends. I will when I'm sure you're right. I'm not."

He shrugged disgustedly, ordered the wicker basket from the meat wagon and had the old woman carried out. He and the beat cop left with the basket team. He could at least have said good-by. He never did, though.

A fat lot I cared about his attitude or dogmatic medical opinion. Getting inside this character was more important. The setting should have helped; it was depressing, rank with the feel of solitary desperation and needless death.

Lou Pape stood looking out the one dirty window, waiting patiently for me. I let my joints stiffen as if they were thirty years older and more worn out than they were, and empathized myself into a dilemma between getting still weaker from hunger and drawing a little money out of the bank.

I worked at it for half an hour or so with the deep concentration you acquire when you use the Stanislavsky method. Then I gave up.

"The M.E. is wrong, Lou," I said. "It doesn't feel right."

Lou turned around from the window. He'd stood there all that time without once coughing or scratching or doing anything else that might have distracted me. "He knows his business, Mark."

"But he doesn't know old people."

"What is it you don't get?" he prompted, helping me dig my way through a characterization like the trained Stanislavskian he was—and still would have been if he hadn't gotten so sick of the insecurity of acting that he'd become a cop. "Can't money be more important to a psychotic than eating?"

"Sure," I agreed. "Up to a point. Undereating, yes. Actual starvation, no."

"Why not?"

"You and the M.E. think it's easy to starve to death. It isn't. Not when you can buy day-old bread at the bakeries, soup bones for about a nickel a pound, wilted vegetables that groceries are glad to get rid of. Anybody who's willing to eat that stuff can stay alive on nearly nothing a day. Nearly nothing, Lou, and hunger is a damned potent instinct. I can understand hating to spend even those few cents. I can't see going without food altogether."

*

He took out a cigarette; he hadn't until then because he didn't want to interrupt my concentration. "Maybe they get too weak to go out after old bread and meat bones and wilted vegetables."

"It still doesn't figure." I got up off the shaky chair, my joints now really stiff from sitting in it. "Do you know how long it takes to die of starvation?"

"That depends on age, health, amount of activity—"

"Nuts!" I said. "It would take weeks!"

"So it takes weeks. Where's the problem—if there is one?"

I lit the pipe I'd learned to smoke instead of cigarettes—old men seem to use pipes more than anything else, though maybe it'll be different in the next generation. More cigarette smokers now, you see, and they'd stick to the habit unless the doctor ordered them to cut it out.

"Did you ever try starving for weeks, Lou?" I asked.

"No. Did you?"

"In a way. All these cases you've been taking me on for the last couple of years—I've tried to be them. But let's say it's possible to die of starvation when you have thousands of dollars put away. Let's say you don't think of scrounging off food stores or working out a way of freeloading or hitting soup lines. Let's say you stay in your room and slowly starve to death."

He slowly picked a fleck of tobacco off his lip and flicked it away, his sharp black eyes poking holes in the situation I'd built up for him. But he wasn't ready to say anything yet.

"There's charity," I went on, "relief—except for those who have their dough in banks, where it can be checked on—old age pension, panhandling, cadging off neighbors."

He said, "We know these cases are hermits. They don't make contact with anybody."

"Even when they're starting to get real hungry?"

"You've got something, Mark, but that's the wrong tack," he said thoughtfully. "The point is that *they* don't have to make contact; other people know them or about them. Somebody would check after a few days or a week—the janitor, the landlord, someone in the house or the neighborhood."

"So they'd be found before they died."

"You'd think so, wouldn't you?" he agreed reluctantly. "They don't generally have friends, and the relatives are usually so distant, they hardly know these old people and whether they're alive or not. Maybe that's what threw us off. But you don't need friends and relatives to start wondering, and investigate when you haven't shown up for a while." He lifted his head and looked at me. "What does that prove, Mark?"

"That there's something wrong with these cases. I want to find out what."

*

I got Lou to take me down to Headquarters, where he let me see the bankbooks the old woman had left.

"She took damned good care of them," I said. "They look almost new."

"Wouldn't you take damned good care of the most important thing in the world to you?" he asked. "You've seen the hoards of money the others leave. Same thing."

I peered closely at the earliest entry, April 23, 1907, $150. My eyes aren't that bad; I was peering at the ink. It was dark, unfaded. I pointed it out to Lou.

"From not being exposed to daylight much," he said. "They don't haul out the bankbooks or money very often, I guess."

"And that adds up for you? I can see them being psychotics all their lives ... but not *senile* psychotics."

"They hoarded, Mark. That adds up for me."

"Funny," I said, watching him maneuver his cigarette as if he loved the feel of it, drawing the smoke down and letting it out in plumes of different shapes, from rings to slender streams. What a living he could make doing cigarette commercials on TV! "I can see *you* turn into one of these cases, Lou."

He looked startled for a second, but then crushed out the butt carefully so he could watch it instead of me. "Yeah? How so?"

"You've been too scared by poverty to take a chance. You know you could do all right acting, but you don't dare giving up this crummy job. Carry that far enough and you try to stop spending money, then cut out eating, and finally wind up dead of starvation in a cheap room."

"Me? I'd never get that scared of being broke!"

"At the age of 70 or 80?"

"Especially then! I'd probably tear loose for a while and then buy into a home for the aged."

I wanted to grin, but I didn't. He'd proved my point. He'd also shown that he was as bothered by these old people as I was.

"Tell me, Lou. If somebody kept you from dying, would you give him any dough for it, even if you were a senile psychotic?"

I could see him using the Stanislavsky method to feel his way to the answer. He shook his head. "Not while I was alive. Will it, maybe, not give it."

"How would that be as a motive?"

*

He leaned against a metal filing cabinet. "No good, Mark. You know what a hell of a time we have tracking down relatives to give the money to, because these people don't leave wills. The few relatives we find are always surprised when they get their inheritance—most of them hardly remember dear old who-ever-it-was that died and left it to them. All the other estates eventually go to the State treasury, unclaimed."

"Well, it was an idea." I opened the oldest bankbook again. "Anybody ever think of testing the ink, Lou?"

"What for? The banks' records always check. These aren't forgeries, if that's what you're thinking."

"I don't know what I'm thinking," I admitted. "But I'd like to turn a chemist loose on this for a little while."

"Look, Mark, there's a lot I'm willing to do for you, and I think I've done plenty, but there's a limit—"

I let him explain why he couldn't let me borrow the book and then waited while he figured out how it could be done and did it. He was still grumbling when he helped me pick a chemist out of the telephone directory and went along to the lab with me.

"But don't get any wrong notions," he said on the way. "I have to protect State property, that's all, because I signed for it and I'm responsible."

"Sure, sure," I agreed, to humor him. "If you're not curious, why not just wait outside for me?"

He gave me one of those white-tooth grins that he had no right to deprive women audiences of. "I could do that, but I'd rather see you make a sap of yourself."

I turned the bankbook over to the chemist and we waited for the report. When it came, it had to be translated.

*

The ink was typical of those used 50 years ago. Lou Pape gave me a jab in the ribs at that. But then the chemist said that, according to the amount of oxidation, it seemed fresh enough to be only a few months or years old, and it was Lou's turn to get jabbed. Lou pushed him about the aging, asking if it couldn't be the result of unusually good care. The chemist couldn't say—that depended on the kind of care; an airtight compartment, perhaps, filled with one of the inert gases, or a vacuum. They hadn't been kept that way, of course, so Lou looked as baffled as I felt.

He took the bankbook and we went out to the street.

"See what I mean?" I asked quietly, not wanting to rub it in.

"I see something, but I don't know what. Do you?"

"I wish I could say yes. It doesn't make any more sense than anything else about these cases."

"What do you do next?"

"Damned if I know. There are thousands of old people in the city. Only a few of them take this way out. I have to try to find them before they do."

"If they're loaded, they won't say so, Mark, and there's no way of telling them from those who are down and out."

I rubbed my pipe disgruntledly against the side of my nose to oil it. "Ain't this a beaut of a problem? I wish I liked problems. I hate them."

Lou had to get back on duty. I had nowhere to go and nothing to do except worry my way through this tangle. He headed back to Headquarters and I went over to the park and sat in the sun, warming myself and trying to think like a senile psychotic who would rather die of starvation than spend a few cents for food.

I didn't get anywhere, naturally. There are too many ways of beating starvation, too many chances of being found before it's too late.

And the fresh ink, over half a century old....

*

I took to hanging around banks, hoping I'd see someone come in with an old bankbook that had fresh ink from 50 years before. Lou was some help there—he convinced the guards and tellers that I wasn't an old-looking guy casing the place for a gang, and even got the tellers to watch out for particularly dark ink in ancient bankbooks.

I stuck at it for a month, although there were a few stage calls that didn't turn out right, and one radio and two TV parts, which did and kept me going. I was almost glad the stage parts hadn't been given to me; they'd have interrupted my outside work.

After a month without a thing turning up at the banks, though, I went back to my two rooms in the theatrical hotel one night, tired and discouraged, and I found Lou there. I expected him to give me another talk on dropping the whole thing; he'd been doing that for a couple of weeks now, every time we got together. I felt too low to put up an argument. But Lou was holding back his excitement—acting like a cop, you know, instead of projecting his feelings—and he couldn't haul me out to his car as fast as he probably wanted me to go.

"Been trying to get in touch with you all day, Mark. Some old guy was found wandering around, dazed and suffering from malnutrition, with $17,000 in cash inside the lining of his jacket."

"*Alive?*" I asked, shocked right into eagerness again.

"Just barely. They're trying intravenous feeding to pull him through. I don't think he'll make it."

"For God's sake, let's get there before he conks out!"

Lou raced me to the City Hospital and up to the ward. There was a scrawny old man in a bed, nothing but a papery skin stretched thin over a face like a skull and a body like a Halloween skeleton, shivering as if he was cold. I knew it wasn't the cold. The medics were injecting a heart stimulant into him and he was vibrating like a rattletrap car racing over a gravel road.

"Who are you?" I practically yelled, grabbing his skinny arm. "What happened to you?"

He went on shaking with his eyes closed and his mouth open.

"Ah, hell!" I said, disgusted. "He's in a coma."

"He might start talking," Lou told me. "I fixed it up so you can sit here and listen in case he does."

"So I can listen to delirious ravings, you mean."

Lou got me a chair and put it next to the bed. "What are you kicking about? This is the first live one you've seen, isn't it? That ought to be good enough for you." He looked as annoyed as a director. "Besides, you can get biographical data out of delirium that you'd never get if he was conscious."

*

He was right, of course. Not only data, but attitudes, wishes, resentments that would normally be repressed. I wasn't thinking of acting at the moment, though. Here was somebody who could tell me what I wanted to know ... only he couldn't talk.

Lou went to the door. "Good luck," he said, and went out.

I sat down and stared at the old man, *willing* him to talk. I don't have to ask if you've ever done that; everybody has. You keep thinking over and over, getting more and more tense, "Talk, damn you, *talk*!" until you find that every muscle in your body is a fist and your jaws are aching because you've been clenching your teeth so hard. You might just as well not bother, but once in a while a coincidence makes you think you've done it. Like now.

The old man sort of came to. That is, he opened his eyes and looked around without seeing anything, or it was so far away and long ago that nobody else could see what he saw.

I hunched forward on the chair and willed harder than ever. Nothing happened. He stared at the ceiling and through and beyond me. Then he closed his eyes again and I slumped back, defeated and bitter—but that was when he began talking.

There were a couple of women, though they might have been little girls in his childhood, and he had his troubles with them. He was praying for a toy train, a roadster, to pass his tests, to keep from being fired, to be less lonely, and back to toys again. He hated his father, and his mother was too busy with church bazaars and such to pay much attention to him. There was a sister: she died when he was a kid. He was glad she died, hoping maybe now his mother would notice him, but he was also filled with guilt because he was glad. Then somebody, he felt, was trying to shove him out of his job.

The intravenous feeding kept dripping into his vein and he went on rambling. After ten or fifteen minutes of it, he fell asleep. I felt so disappointed that I could have slapped him awake, only it wouldn't have done any good. Smoking would have helped me relax, but it wasn't allowed, and I didn't dare go outside for one, for fear he might revive again and this time come up to the present.

*

Broke!" he suddenly shrieked, trying to sit up.

I pushed him down gently, and he went on in frightful terror, "Old and poor, nowhere to go, nobody wants me, can't make a living, read the ads every day, no jobs for old men."

He blurted through weeks, months, years—I don't know—of fear and despair. And finally he came to something that made his face glow like a radium dial.

"An ad. No experience needed. Good salary." His face got dark and awful.

All he added was, "El Greco," or something that sounded like it, and then he went into terminal breathing.

I rang for the nurse and she went for the doctor. I couldn't stand the long moments when the old man's chest stopped moving, the abrupt frantic gulps of air followed by no breath at all. I wanted to get away from it, but I had to wait for whatever more he might say.

It didn't come. His eyes fogged and rolled up and he stopped taking those spasmodic strangling breaths. The nurse came back with the doctor, who felt his pulse and shook his head. She pulled the blanket over the old man's face.

I left, feeling sick. I'd learned things I already knew about hate and love and fear and hope and frustration. There was an ad in it somewhere, but I had no way of telling if it had been years ago or recently. And a name that sounded like "El Greco." That was a Spanish painter of four-five hundred years ago. Had the old guy been remembering a picture he'd seen?

No, he'd come up at least close to the present. The ad seemed to solve his problem about being broke. But what about the $17,000 that had been found in the lining of his jacket? He hadn't mentioned that. Of course, being a senile psychotic, he could have considered himself broke even with that amount of money. None coming in, you see.

That didn't add up, either. His was the terror of being old and jobless. If he'd had money, he would have figured how to make it last, and that would have come through in one way or another.

There was the ad, there was his hope, and there was this El Greco. A Greek restaurant, maybe, where he might have been bumming his meals.

But where did the $17,000 fit in?

*

Lou Pape was too fed up with the whole thing to discuss it with me. He just gave me the weary eye and said, "You're riding this too hard, Mark. The guy was talking from fever. How do I know what figures and what doesn't when I'm dealing with insanity or delirium?"

"But you admit there's plenty about these cases that doesn't figure?"

"Sure. Did you take a look at the condition the world is in lately? Why should these old people be any exception?"

I couldn't blame him. He'd pulled me in on the cases with plenty of trouble to himself, just to do me a favor. Now he was fed up. I guess it wasn't even that—he thought I was ruining myself, at least financially and maybe worse, by trying to run down the problem. He said he'd be glad to see me any time and gas about anything or help me with whatever might be bothering me, if he could, but not these cases any more. He told me to lay off them, and then he left me on my own.

I don't know what he could have done, actually. I didn't need him to go through the want ads with me, which I was doing every day, figuring there might be something in the ravings about an ad. I spent more time than I liked checking those slanted at old people, only to find they were supposed to become messengers and such.

One brought me to an old brownstone five-story house in the East 80s. I got on line with the rest of the applicants—there were men and women, all decrepit, all looking badly in need of money—and waited my turn. My face was lined with collodion wrinkles and I wore an antique shiny suit and rundown shoes. I didn't look more prosperous or any younger than they did.

I finally came up to the woman who was doing the interviewing. She sat behind a plain office desk down in the main floor hall, with a pile of application cards in front of her and a ballpoint pen in one strong, slender hand. She had red hair with gold lights in it and eyes so pale blue that they would have seemed the same color as the whites if she'd been on the stage. Her face would have been beautiful except for her rigid control of expression; she smiled abruptly, shut it off just like that, looked me over with all the impersonality and penetration of an X-ray from the soles to the bald head, exactly as she'd done with the others. But that skin! If it was as perfect as that all over her slim, stiffly erect, proudly shaped body, she had no business off the stage!

"Name, address, previous occupation, social security number?" she asked in a voice with good clarity, resonance and diction. She wrote it all down while I gave the information to her. Then she asked me for references, and I mentioned Sergeant Lou Pape. "Fine," she said. "We'll get in touch with you if anything comes up. Don't call us—we'll call you."

I hung around to see who'd be picked. There was only one, an old man, two ahead of me in the line, who had no social security number, no references, not even any relatives or friends she could have checked up on him with.

Damn! *Of course* that was what she wanted! Hadn't all the starvation cases been people without social security, references, either no friends and relatives or those they'd lost track of?

I'd pulled a blooper, but how was I to know until too late?

Well, there was a way of making it right.

*

When it was good and dark that evening, I stood on the corner and watched the lights in the brownstone house. The ones on the first two floors went out, leaving only those on the third and fourth. Closed for the day ... or open for business?

I got into a building a few doors down by pushing a button and waiting until the buzzer answered, then racing up to the roof while some man yelled down the stairs to find out who was there. I crossed the tops of the two houses between and went down the fire escape.

It wasn't easy, though not as tough as you might imagine. The fact is that I'm a whole year younger than Lou Pape, even if I could play his grandpa professionally. I still have muscles left and I used them to get down the fire escape at the rear of the house.

The fourth floor room I looked into had some kind of wire mesh cage and some hooded machinery. Nobody there.

The third floor room was the redhead's. She was coming out of the bathroom with a terrycloth bathrobe and a towel turban on when I looked in. She slid the robe off and began dusting herself with powder. That skin *did* cover her.

She turned and moved toward a vanity against the wall that I was on the other side of. The next thing I knew, the window was flung up and she had a gun on me.

"Come right in—Mr. Weldon, isn't it?" she said in that completely controlled voice of hers. One day her control would crack, I thought irrelevantly, and the pieces would be found from Dallas to North Carolina. "I had an idea you seemed more curious than was justified by a help-wanted ad."

"A man my age doesn't get to see many pretty girls," I told her, making my own voice crack pathetically in a senile whinny.

She motioned me into the room. When I was inside, I saw a light over the window blinking red. It stopped the moment I was in the room. A silent burglar alarm.

She let her pale blue eyes wash insolently over me. "A man your age can see all the pretty girls he wants to. You're not old."

"And you use a rinse," I retorted.

She ignored it. "I specifically advertised for old people. Why did you apply?"

It had happened so abruptly that I hadn't had a chance to use the Stanislavsky method to *feel* old in the presence of a beautiful nude woman. I don't even know if it would have worked. Nothing's perfect.

"I needed a job awful bad," I answered sullenly, knowing it sounded like an ad lib.

*

She smiled with more contempt than humor. "You had a job, Mr. Weldon. You were very busy trying to find out why senile psychotics starve themselves to death."

"How did you know that?" I asked, startled.

"A little investigation of my own. I also happen to know you didn't tell your friend Sergeant Pape that you were going to be here tonight."

That was a fact, too. I hadn't felt sure enough that I'd found the answer to call him about it. Looking at the gun in her steady hand, I was sorry I hadn't.

"But you did find out I own this building, that my name is May Roberts, and that I'm the daughter of the late Dr. Anthony Roberts, the physicist," she continued. "Is there anything else you want me to tell you about yourself?"

"I know enough already. I'm more interested in you and the starvation cases. If you weren't connected with them, you wouldn't have known I was investigating them."

"That's obvious, isn't it?" She reached for a cigarette on the vanity and used a lighter with her free hand. The big mirror gave me another view of her lovely body, but that was beginning to interest me less than the gun. I thought of making a grab for it. There was too much distance between us, though, and she knew better than to take her eyes off me while she was lighting up. "I'm not afraid of professional detectives, Mr. Weldon. They deal only with facts and every one of them will draw the same conclusions from a given set of circumstances. I don't like amateurs. They guess too much. They don't stick to reality. The result—" her pale eyes chilled and her shapely mouth went hard—"is that they are likely to get too close to the truth."

I wanted a smoke myself, but I wasn't willing to make a move toward the pipe in my jacket. "I may be close to the truth, Miss Roberts, but I don't know what the devil it is. I still don't know how you're tied in with the senile psychotics or why they starve with all that money. You could let me go and I wouldn't have a thing on you."

She glanced down at herself and laughed for real for the first time. "You wouldn't, would you? On the other hand, you know where I'm working from and could nag Sergeant Pape into getting a search warrant. It wouldn't incriminate me, but it would be inconvenient. I don't care to be inconvenienced."

"Which means what?"

"You want to find out my connection with senile psychotics. I intend to show you."

"How?"

She gestured dangerously with the gun. "Turn your face to the wall and stay that way while I get dressed. Make one attempt to turn around before I tell you to and I'll shoot you. You're guilty of housebreaking, you know. It would be a little inconvenient for me to have an investigation ... but not as inconvenient as for you."

*

I faced the wall, feeling my stomach braid itself into a tight, painful knot of fear. Of what, I didn't know yet, only that old people who had something to do with her died of starvation. I wasn't old, but that didn't seem very comforting. She was the most frigid, calculating, *deadly* woman I'd ever met. That alone was enough to scare hell out of me. And there was the problem of what she was capable of.

Hearing the sounds of her dressing behind me, I wanted to lunge around and rush her, taking a chance that she might be too busy pulling on a girdle or reaching back to fasten a bra to have the gun in her hand. It was a suicidal impulse and I gave it up instantly. Other women might compulsively finish concealing themselves before snatching up the gun. Not her.

"All right," she said at last.

I faced her. She was wearing coveralls that, if anything, emphasized the curves of her figure. She had a sort of babushka that covered her red hair and kept it in place—the kind of thing women workers used to wear in factories during the war. She had looked lethal with nothing on but a gun and a hard expression. She looked like a sentence of execution now.

"Open that door, turn to the right and go upstairs," she told me, indicating directions with the gun.

I went. It was the longest, most anxious short walk I've ever taken. She ordered me to open a door on the fourth floor, and we were inside the room I'd seen from the fire escape. The mesh cage seemed like a torture chamber to me, the hooded motors designed to shoot an agonizing current through my emaciating body.

"You're going to do to me what you did to the old man you hired today?" I probed, hoping for an answer that would really answer.

She flipped on the switch that started the motors and there was a shrill, menacing whine. The wire mesh of the cage began blurring oddly, as if vibrating like the tines of a tuning fork.

"You've been an unexpected nuisance, Weldon," she said above the motors. "I never thought you'd get this far. But as long as you have, we might as well both benefit by it."

"Benefit?" I repeated. "*Both* of us?"

She opened the drawer of a work table and pulled out a stack of envelopes held with a rubber band. She put the stack at the other edge of the table.

"Would you rather have all cash or bank accounts or both?"

My heart began to beat. *She was where the money came from!*

*

You trying to tell me you're a philanthropist?" I demanded.

"Business is philanthropy, in a way," she answered calmly. "You need money and I need your services. To that extent, we're doing each other a favor. I think you'll find that the favor I'm going to do for you is a pretty considerable one. Would you mind picking up the envelopes on the table?"

I took the stack and stared at the top envelope. "May 15, 1931," I read aloud, and looked suspiciously at her. "What's this for?"

"I don't think it's something that can be explained. At least it's never been possible before and I doubt if it would be now. I'm assuming you want both cash and bank accounts. Is that right?"

"Well, yes. Only—"

"We'll discuss it later." She looked along a row of shelves against one wall, searching the labels on the stacks of bundles there. She drew one out and pushed it toward me. "Please open that and put on the things you'll find inside."

I tore open the bundle. It contained a very plain business suit, black shoes, shirt, tie and a hat with a narrow brim.

"Are these supposed to be my burial clothes?"

"I asked you to put them on," she said. "If you want me to make that a command, I'll do it."

I looked at the gun and I looked at the clothes and then for some shelter I could change behind. There wasn't any.

She smiled. "You didn't seem concerned about my modesty. I don't see why your own should bother you. Get dressed!"

I obeyed, my mind anxiously chasing one possibility after another, all of them ending up with my death. I got into the other things and felt even more uncomfortable. They were all only an approximate fit: the shoes a little too tight and pointed, the collar of the shirt too stiffly starched and too high under my chin, the gray suit too narrow at the shoulders and the ankles. I wished I had a mirror to see myself in. I felt like an ultra-conservative Wall Street broker and I was sure I resembled one.

"All right," she said. "Put the envelopes in your inside pocket. You'll find instructions on each. Follow them carefully."

"I don't get it!" I protested.

"You will. Now step into the mesh cage. Use the envelopes in the order they're arranged in."

"But what's this all about?"

"I can tell you just one thing, Mr. Weldon—don't try to escape. It can't be done. Your other questions will answer themselves if you follow the instructions on the envelopes."

She had the gun in her hand. I went into the mesh cage, not knowing what to expect and yet too afraid of her to refuse. I didn't want to wind up dead of starvation, no matter how much money she might have given me—but I didn't want to get shot, either.

She closed the mesh gate and pushed the switch as far as it would go. The motors screamed as they picked up speed; the mesh cage vibrated more swiftly; I could see her through it as if there were nothing between us.

And then I couldn't see her at all.

I was outside a bank on a sunny day in spring.

*

My fear evaporated instantly—I'd escaped somehow!

But then a couple of realizations slapped me from each side. It was day instead of night. I was out on the street and not in her brownstone house.

Even the season had changed!

Dazed, I stared at the people passing by. They looked like characters in a TV movie, the women wearing long dresses and flowerpot hats, their faces made up with petulant rosebud mouths and bright blotches of rouge; the men in hard straw hats, suits with narrow shoulders, plain black or brown shoes—the same kind of clothes I was wearing.

The rumble of traffic in the street caught me next. Cars with square bodies, tubular radiators....

For a moment, I let terror soak through me. Then I remembered the mesh cage and the motors. May Roberts could have given me electro-shock, kept me under long enough for the season to change, or taken me South and left me on a street in daylight.

But this was a street in New York. I recognized it, though some of the buildings seemed changed, the people dressed more shabbily.

Shrewd stagesetting? Hypnosis?

That was it, of course! She'd hypnotized me....

Except that a subject under hypnosis doesn't know he's been hypnotized.

Completely confused, I took out the stack of envelopes I'd put in my pocket. I was supposed to have both cash and a bank account, and I was outside a bank. She obviously wanted me to go in, so I did. I handed the top envelope to the teller.

He hauled $150 out of it and looked at me as if that was enough to buy and sell the bank. He asked me if I had an account there. I didn't. He took me over to an officer of the bank, a fellow with a Hoover collar and a John Gilbert mustache, who signed me up more cordially than I'd been treated in years.

I walked out to the street, gaping at the entry in the bankbook he'd handed me. My pulse was jumping lumpily, my lungs refusing to work right, my head doing a Hopi rain dance.

The date he'd stamped was May 15, 1931.

*

I didn't know which I was more afraid of—being stranded, middle-aged, in the worst of the depression, or being yanked back to that brownstone house. I had only an instant to realize that I was a kid in high school uptown right at that moment. Then the whole scene vanished as fast as blinking and I was outside another bank somewhere else in the city.

The date on the envelope was May 29th and it was still 1931. I made a $75 deposit there, then $100 in another place a few days later, and so forth, spending only a few minutes each time and going forward anywhere from a couple of days to almost a month.

Every now and then, I had a stamped, addressed envelope to mail at a corner box. They were addressed to different stock brokers and when I got one open before mailing it and took a look inside, it turned out to be an order to buy a few hundred shares of stock in a soft drink company in the name of Dr. Anthony Roberts. I hadn't remembered the price of the shares being that low. The last time I'd seen the quotation, it was more than five times as much as it was then. I was making dough myself, but I was doing even better for May Roberts.

A few times I had to stay around for an hour or so. There was the night I found myself in a flashy speakeasy with two envelopes that I was to bet the contents of, according to the instructions on the outside. It was June 21, 1932, and I had to bet on Jack Sharkey to take the heavyweight title away from Max Schmeling.

The place was serious and quiet—no more than three women, a couple of bartenders, and the rest male customers, including two cops, huddling up close to the radio. An affable character was taking bets. He gave me a wise little smile when I put the money down on Sharkey.

"Well, it's a pleasure to do business with a man who wants an American to win," he said, "and the hell with the smart dough, eh?"

"Yeah," I said, and tried to smile back, but so much of the smart money was going on Schmeling that I wondered if May Roberts hadn't made a mistake. I couldn't remember who had won. "You know what J. P. Morgan said—don't sell America short."

"I'll take a buck for my share," said a sour guy who barely managed to stand. "Lousy grass growing in the lousy streets, nobody working, no future, nothing!"

"We'll come out of it okay," I told him confidently.

He snorted into his gin. "Not in our lifetime, Mac. It'd take a miracle to put this country on its feet again. I don't believe in miracles." He put his scowling face up close to mine and breathed blearily and belligerently at me. "Do you?"

"Shut up, Gus," one of the bartenders said. "The fight's starting."

*

I had some tough moments and a lot of bad Scotch, listening. It went the whole 15 rounds, Sharkey won, and I was in almost as bad shape as Gus, who'd passed out halfway through the battle. All I can recall is the affable character handing over a big roll and saying, "Lucky for me more guys don't sell America short," and trying to separate the money into the right amounts and put them into the right envelopes, while stumbling out the door, when everything changed and I was outside a bank again.

I thought, "My God, what a hangover cure!" I was as sober as if I hadn't had a drink, when I made that deposit.

There were more envelopes to mail and more deposits to make and bets to put down on Singing Wood in 1933 at Belmont Park and Max Baer over Primo Carnera, and then Cavalcade at Churchill Downs in 1934, and James Braddock over Baer in 1935, and a big daily double payoff, Wanoah-Arakay at Tropical Park, and so on, skipping through the years like a flat stone over water, touching here and there for a few minutes to an hour at a time. I kept the envelopes for May Roberts and myself in different pockets and the bankbooks in another. The envelopes were beginning to bulge and the deposits and accrued interest were something to watch grow.

The whole thing, in fact, was so exciting that it was early October of 1938—a total of maybe four or five hours subjectively—before I realized what she had me doing. I wasn't thinking much about the fact that I was time traveling or how she did it; I accepted that, though the sensation in some ways was creepy, like raising the dead. My father and mother, for instance, were still alive in 1938. If I could break away from whatever it was that kept pulling me jumpily through time, I could go and see them.

The thought attracted me enough to make me shake badly with intent, yet pump dread through me. I wanted so damned badly to see them again and I didn't dare. I couldn't....

Why couldn't I?

Maybe the machine covered only the area around the various banks, speakeasies, bars and horse parlors. If I could get out of the area, whatever it might be, I could avoid coming back to whatever May Roberts had lined up for me.

Because, naturally, I knew now what I was doing: I was making deposits and winning sure bets just as the "senile psychotics" had done. The ink on their bankbooks and bills was fresh because it *was* fresh; it wasn't given a chance to oxidize—at the rate I was going, I'd be back to my own time in another few hours or so, with $15,000 or better in deposits, compound interest and cash.

If I'd been around 70, you see, she could have sent me back to the beginning of the century with the same amount of money, which would have accumulated to something like $30,000.

Get it now?

I did.

And I felt sick and frightened.

The old people had died of starvation somehow with all that dough in cash or banks. I didn't give a hang if the time travel was responsible, or something else was. I wasn't going to be found dead in my hotel and have Lou Pape curse my corpse because I'd been borrowing from him when, since 1931, I'd had a little fortune put away. He'd call me a premature senile psychotic and he'd be right, from his point of view, not knowing the truth.

*

Rather than make the deposit in October, 1938, I grabbed a battered old cab and told the driver to step on it. When I showed him the $10 bill that was in it for him, he squashed down the gas pedal. In 1938, $10 was real money.

We got a mile away from the bank and the driver looked at me in the rear-view mirror.

"How far you want to go, mister?"

My teeth were together so hard that I had to unclench them before I could answer, "As far away as we can get."

"Cops after you?"

"No, but somebody is. Don't be surprised at anything that happens, no matter what it is."

"You mean like getting shot at?" he asked worriedly, slowing down.

"You're not in any danger, friend. I am. Relax and step on it again."

I wondered if she could still reach me, this far from the bank, and handed the guy the bill. No justice sticking him for the ride in case she should. He pushed the pedal down even harder than he had been doing before.

We must have been close to three miles away when I blinked and was standing outside the first bank I'd seen in 1931.

I don't know what the cab driver thought when I vanished out of his hack. He probably figured I'd opened the door and jumped while he wasn't looking. Maybe he even went back and searched for a body splashed all over the street.

Well, it would have been a hopeless hunt. I was a week ahead.

I gave up and drearily made my deposit. The one from early October that I'd missed I put in with this one.

There was no way to escape the babe with the beautiful hard face, gorgeous warm body and plans for me that all seemed to add up to death. I didn't try any more. I went on making deposits, mailing orders to her stock brokers, and putting down bets that couldn't miss because they were all past history.

I don't even remember what the last one was, a fight or a race. I hung around the bar that had long ago replaced the speakeasy, until the inevitable payoff, got myself a hamburger and headed out the door. All the envelopes I was supposed to use were gone and I felt shaky, knowing that the next place I'd see was the room with the wire mesh cage and the hooded motors.

It was.

*

She was on the other side of the cage, and I had five bankbooks and envelopes filled with cash amounting to more than $15,000, but all I could think of was that I was hungry and something had happened to the hamburger while I was traveling through time. I must have fallen and dropped it, because my hand was covered with dust or dirt. I brushed it off and quickly felt my face and pulled up my sleeves to look at my arms.

"Very smart," I said, "but I'm nowhere near emaciation."

"What made you think you would be?" she asked.

"Because the others always were."

She cut the motors to idling speed and the vibrating mesh slowed down. I glared at her through it. God, she was lovely—as lovely as an ice sculpture! The kind of face you'd love to kiss and slap, kiss and slap....

"You came here with a preconceived notion, Mr. Weldon. I'm a businesswoman, not a monster. I like to think there's even a good deal of the altruist in me. I could hire only young people, but the old ones have more trouble finding work. And you've seen for yourself how I provide nest eggs for them they'd otherwise never have."

"And take care of yourself at the same time."

"That's the businesswoman in me. I need money to operate."

"So do the old people. Only they die and you don't."

She opened the gate and invited me out. "I make mistakes occasionally. I sometimes pick men and women who prove to be too old to stand the strain. I try not to let it happen, but they need money and work so badly that they don't always tell the truth about their age and state of health."

"You could take those who have social security cards and references."

"But those who don't have any are in worse need!" She paused. "You probably think I want only the money you and they bring back, that it's merely some sort of profit-making scheme. It isn't."

"You mean the idea is not just to build up a fortune for you with a cut for whoever helps you do it?"

"I said I need money to operate, Mr. Weldon, and this method serves. But there are other purposes, much more important. What you have gone through is—basic training, you might say. You know now that it's possible to travel through time, and what it's like. The initial shock, in other words, is gone and you're better equipped to do something for me in another era."

"Something else?" I stared at her puzzledly. "What else could you want?"

"Let's have dinner first. You must be hungry."

*

I was, and that reminded me: "I bought a hamburger just before you brought me back. I don't know what happened to it. My hand was dirty and the hamburger was gone, as if I'd fallen somehow and dropped it and got dirt on my hand."

She looked worriedly at the hand, probably afraid I'd cut it and disqualified myself. I could understand that; you never know what kind of diseases can be picked up in different times, because I remember reading somewhere that germs keep changing according to conditions. Right now, for instance, strains of bacteria are becoming resistant to antibiotics. I knew her concern wasn't really for me, but it was pleasant all the same.

"That could be the explanation, I suppose," she said. "The truth is that

I've never taken a time voyage—somebody has to operate the controls in the present—so I can't say it's possible or impossible to fall. It must be, since you did. Perhaps the wrench back from the past was too violent and you slipped just before you returned."

She led me down to an ornate dining room, where the table had been set for two. The food was waiting on the table, steaming and smelling tasty. Nobody was around to serve us. She pointed out a chair to me and we sat down and began eating. I was a little nervous at first, afraid there might be something in the food, but it tasted fine and nothing happened after I swallowed a little and waited for some effect.

"You did try to escape the time tractor beam, didn't you, Mr. Weldon?" she asked. I didn't have to answer; she knew. "That's a mistaken notion of how it functions. The control beam doesn't cover *area*; it covers *era*. You could have flown to any part of the world and the beam would still have brought you back. Do I make myself clear?"

She did. Too bloody clear. I waited for the rest.

"I assume you've already formed an opinion of me," she went on. "A rather unflattering one, I imagine."

"'Bitch' is the cleanest word I can find. But a clever one. Anybody who can invent a time machine would have to be a genius."

"I didn't invent it. My father did—Dr. Anthony Roberts—using the funds you and others helped me provide him with." Her face grew soft and tender. "My father was a wonderful man, a great man, but he was called a crackpot. He was kept from teaching or working anywhere. It was just as well, I suppose, though he was too hurt to think so; he had more leisure to develop the time machine. He could have used it to extort repayment from mankind for his humiliation, but he didn't. He used it to help mankind."

"Like how?" I goaded.

"It doesn't matter, Mr. Weldon. You're determined to hate me and consider me a liar. Nothing I tell you can change that."

*

She was right about the first part—I hadn't dared let myself do anything except hate and fear her—but she was wrong about the second. I remembered thinking how Lou Pape would have felt if I had died of starvation with over $15,000, after borrowing from him all the time between jobs. Not knowing how I got it, he'd have been sore, thinking I'd played him for a patsy. What

I'm trying to say is that Lou wouldn't have had enough information to judge me. I didn't have enough information yet, either, to judge her.

"What do you want me to do?" I asked warily.

"Everybody but one person was sent into the past on specific errands—to save art treasures and relics that would otherwise have been lost to humanity."

"Not because the things might be worth a lot of dough?" I said nastily.

"You've already seen that I can get all the money I want. There were upheavals in the past—great fires, wars, revolutions, vandalism—and I had my associates save things that would have been destroyed. Oh, beautiful things, Mr. Weldon! The world would have been so much poorer without them!"

"El Greco, for instance?" I asked, remembering the raving old man who had been found wandering with $17,000 in his coat lining.

"El Greco, too. Several paintings that had been lost for centuries." She became more brisk and efficient-seeming. "Except for the one man I mentioned, I concentrated on the past—the future is too completely unknown to us. And there's an additional reason why I tentatively explored it only once. But the one person who went there discovered something that would be of immense value to the world."

"What happened to *him*?"

She looked regretful. "He was too old. He survived just long enough to tell me that the future has something we need. It's a metal box, small enough to carry, that could supply this whole city with power to run its industries and light its homes and streets!"

"Sounds good. Who'd you say benefits if I get it?"

"We share the profits equally, of course. But it must be understood that we sell the power so cheaply that everybody can afford it."

"I'm not arguing. What's the other reason you didn't bother with the future?"

"You can't bring anything from the future to the present that doesn't exist right now. I won't go into the theory, but it should be obvious that nothing can exist before it exists. You can't bring the box I want, only the technical data to build one."

"Technical data? I'm an actor, not a scientist."

"You'll have pens and weatherproof notebooks to copy it down in."

*

I couldn't make up my mind about her. I've already said she was beautiful, which always prejudices a man in a woman's favor, but I couldn't forget the starvation cases. They hadn't shared anything but malnutrition, useless money and death. Then again, maybe her explanation was a good one, that she wanted to help those who needed help most and some of them lied about their age and physical condition because they wanted the jobs so badly. All I knew about were those who had died. How did I know there weren't others—a lot more of them than the fatal cases, perhaps—who came through all right and were able to enjoy their little fortunes?

And there was her story about saving the treasures of the past and wanting to provide power at really low cost. She was right about one thing: she didn't need any of that to make money with; her method was plenty good enough, using the actual records of the past to invest in stocks, bet on sports—all sure gambles.

But those starvation cases....

"Do I get any guarantees?" I demanded.

She looked annoyed. "I'll need you for the data. You'll need me to turn it into manufacture. Is that enough of a guarantee?"

"No. Do I come out of this alive?"

"Mr. Weldon, please use some logic. I'm the one who's taking the risk. I've already given you more money than you've ever had at one time in your life. Part of my motive was to pay for services about to be rendered. Mostly, it was to give you experience in traveling through time."

"And to prove to me that I can't run out," I added.

"That happens to be a necessary attribute of the machine. I couldn't very well move you about through time unless it worked that way. If you'd look at my point of view, you'd see that I lose my investment if you don't bring back the data. I can't withdraw your money, you realize."

"I don't know what to think," I said, dissatisfied with myself because I couldn't find out what, if anything, was wrong with the deal. "I'll get you the data for the power box if it's at all possible and then we'll see what happens."

Finished eating, we went upstairs and I got into the cage.

She closed the circuit. The motors screamed. The mesh blurred.

And I was in a world I never knew.

*

You'd call it a city, I suppose; there were enough buildings to make it one. But no city ever had so much greenery. It wasn't just tree-lined streets, like Unter den Linden in Berlin, or islands covered with shrubbery, like Park Avenue in New York. The grass and trees and shrubs grew around every building, separating them from each other by wide lawns. The buildings were more glass—or what looked like glass—than anything else. A few of the windows were opaque against the sun, but I couldn't see any shades or blinds. Some kind of polarizing glass or plastic?

I felt uneasy being there, but it was a thrill just the same, to be alive in the future when I and everybody who lived in my day was supposed to be dead.

The air smelled like the country. There was no foul gas boiling from the teardrop cars on the glass-level road. They were made of transparent plastic clear around and from top to bottom, and they moved along at a fair clip, but more smoothly than swiftly. If I hadn't seen the airship overhead, I wouldn't have known it was there. It flew silently, a graceful ball without wings, seeming to be borne by the wind from one horizon to the other, except that no wind ever moved that fast.

One car stopped nearby and someone shouted, "Here we are!" Several people leaped out and headed for me.

I didn't think. I ran. I crossed the lawn and ducked into the nearest building and dodged through long, smoothly walled, shadowlessly lit corridors until I found a door that would open. I slammed it shut and locked it. Then, panting, I fell into a soft chair that seemed to form itself around my body, and felt like kicking myself for the bloody idiot I was.

What in hell had I run for? They couldn't have known who I was. If I'd arrived in a time when people wore togas or bathing suits, there would have been some reason for singling me out, but they had all had clothes just like ours—suits and shirts and ties for the men, a dress and high heels for the one woman with them. I felt somewhat disappointed that clothes hadn't changed any, but it worked out to my advantage; I wouldn't be so conspicuous.

Yet why should anyone have yelled "Here we are!" unless.... No, they must have thought I was somebody else. It didn't figure any other way. I had run because it was my first startled reaction and probably because I knew I was there on what might be considered illegal business; if I succeeded, some poor inventor would be done out of his royalties.

I wished I hadn't run. Besides making me feel like a scared fool, I was sweaty and out of breath. Playing old men doesn't make climbing down fire escapes much tougher than it should be, but it doesn't exactly make a sprinter out of you—not by several lungfuls.

*

I sat there, breathing hard and trying to guess what next. I had no more idea of where to go for what I wanted than an ancient Egyptian set down in the middle of Times Square with instructions to sneak a mummy out of the Metropolitan Museum. I didn't even have that much information. I didn't know any part of the city, how it was laid out, or where to get the data that May Roberts had sent me for.

I opened the door quietly and looked both ways before going out. After losing myself in the cross-connecting corridors a few times, I finally came to an outside door. I stopped, tense, trying to get my courage. My inclination was to slip, sneak or dart out, but I made myself walk away like a decent, innocent citizen. That was one disguise they'd never be able to crack. All I had to do was act as if I belonged to that time and place and who would know the difference?

There were other people walking as if they were in no hurry to get anywhere. I slowed down to their speed, but I wished wistfully that there was a crowd to dive into and get lost.

A man dropped into step and said politely, "I beg your pardon. Are you a stranger in town?"

I almost halted in alarm, but that might have been a giveaway. "What makes you think so?" I asked, forcing myself to keep at the same easy pace.

"I—didn't recognize your face and I thought—"

"It's a big city," I said coldly. "You can't know everyone."

"If there's anything I can do to help—"

I told him there wasn't and left him standing there. It was plain common sense, I had decided quickly while he was talking to me, not to take any risks by admitting anything. I might have been dumped into a police state or the country could have been at war without my knowing it, or maybe they were suspicious of strangers. For one reason or another, ranging from vagrancy to espionage, I could be pulled in, tortured, executed, God knows what. The place looked peaceful enough, but that didn't prove a thing.

I went on walking, looking for something I couldn't be sure existed, in a city I was completely unfamiliar with, in a time when I had no right to be alive. It wasn't just a matter of getting the information she wanted. I'd have been satisfied to hang around until she pulled me back without the data....

But then what would happen? Maybe the starvation cases were people who had failed her! For that matter, she could shoot me and send the remains anywhere in time to get rid of the evidence.

Damn it, I didn't know if she was better or worse than I'd supposed, but I wasn't going to take any chances. I had to bring her what she wanted.

*

There was a sign up ahead. It read: TO SHOPPING CENTER. The arrow pointed along the road. When I came to a fork and wondered which way to go, there was another sign, then another pointing to still more farther on.

I followed them to the middle of the city, a big square with a park in the center and shops of all kinds rimming it. The only shop I was interested in said: ELECTRICAL APPLIANCES.

I went in.

A neat young salesman came up and politely asked me if he could do anything for me. I sounded stupid even to myself, but I said, "No, thanks, I'd just like to do a little browsing," and gave a silly nervous laugh. Me, an actor, behaving like a frightened yokel! I felt ashamed of myself.

He tried not to look surprised, but he didn't really succeed. Somebody else came in, though, for which I was grateful, and he left me alone to look around.

I don't know if I can get my feelings across to you. It's a situation that nobody would ever expect to find himself in, so it isn't easy to tell what it's like. But I've got to try.

Let's stick with the ancient Egyptian I mentioned a while back, the one ordered to sneak a mummy out of the Metropolitan Museum. Maybe that'll make it clearer.

The poor guy has no money he can use, naturally, and no idea of what New York's transportation system is like, where the museum is, how to get there, what visitors to a museum do and say, the regulations he might unwittingly break, how much an ordinary citizen is supposed to know about which customs and such. Now add the possible danger that he might be slapped into jail or an insane asylum if he makes a mistake and you've got a rough notion of the spot I felt I was in. Being able to speak English doesn't make much difference; not knowing what's regarded as right and wrong, and the unknown consequences, are enough to panic anybody.

That doesn't make it clear enough.

Well, look, take the electrical appliances in that store; that might give you an idea of the situation and the way it affected me.

The appliances must have been as familiar to the people of that time as toasters and TV sets and lamps are to us. But the things didn't make a bit of sense to me ... any more than our appliances would to the ancient Egyptian. Can you imagine him trying to figure out what those items are for and how they work?

*

Here are some gadgets you can puzzle over:

There was a light fixture that you put against any part of a wall—no screws, no cement, no wires, even—and it held there and lit up, and it stayed lit no matter where you moved it on the wall. Talk about pin-up lamps ... this was really it!

Then I came across something that looked like an ashtray with a blue electric shimmer obscuring the bottom of the bowl. I lit my pipe—others I'd passed had been smoking, so I knew it was safe to do the same—and flicked in the match. It disappeared. I don't mean it was swirled into some hidden compartment. *It vanished.* I emptied the pipe into the ashtray and that went, too. Looking around to make sure nobody was watching, I dredged some coins out of my pocket and let them drop into the tray. They were gone. Not a particle of them was left. A disintegrator? I haven't got the slightest idea.

There were little mirror boxes with three tiny dials on the front of each. I turned the dials on one—it was like using three dial telephones at the same time—and a pretty girl's face popped onto the mirror surface and looked expectantly at me.

"Yes?" she said, and waited for me to answer.

"I—uh—wrong number, I guess," I answered, putting the box down in a hurry and going to the other side of the shop because I didn't have even a dim notion how to turn it off.

The thing I was looking for was on a counter—a tinted metal box no bigger than a suitcase, with a lipped hole on top and small undisguised verniers in front. I didn't know I'd found it, actually, until I twisted a vernier and every light in the store suddenly glared and the salesman came rushing over and politely moved me aside to shut it off.

"We don't want to burn out every appliance in the place, do we?" he asked quietly.

"I just wanted to see if it worked all right," I said, still shaking slightly. It could have blown up or electrocuted me, for all I knew.

"But they always work," he said.

"Ah—always?"

"Of course. The principle is simple and there are no parts to get worn out, so they last indefinitely." He suddenly smiled as if he'd just caught the gist. "Oh, you were joking! Naturally—everybody learns about the Dynapack in primary education. You were interested in acquiring one?"

"No, no. The—the old one is good enough. I was just—well, you know, interested in knowing if the new models are much different or better than the old ones."

"But there haven't been any new models since 2073," he said. "Can you think of any reason why there should be?"

"I—guess not," I stammered. "But you never can tell."

"You can with Dynapacks," he said, and he would have gone on if I hadn't lost my nerve and mumbled my way out of the store as fast as I could.

*

You want to know why? He'd asked me if I wanted to "acquire" a Dynapack, not *buy* one. I didn't know what "acquire" meant in that society. It could be anything from saving up coupons to winning whatever you wanted at some kind of lottery, or maybe working up the right number of labor units on the job—in which case he'd want to know where I was employed and the equivalent of social security and similar information, which I naturally didn't have—or it could just be fancy sales talk for buying.

I couldn't guess, and I didn't care to expose myself any more than I had already. And my blunder about the Dynapack working and the new models was nothing to make me feel at all easier.

Lord, the uncertainties and hazards of being in a world you don't know anything about! Daydreaming about visiting another age may be pleasant, but the reality is something else again.

"Wait a minute, friend!" I heard the salesman call out behind me.

*

I looked back as casually, I hoped, as the pedestrians who heard him. He was walking quickly toward me with a very worried expression on his face. I stepped up my own pace as unobtrusively as possible, trying to keep a lot of people between us, meanwhile praying that they'd think I was just somebody who was late for an appointment. The salesman didn't break into a run or yell for the cops, but I couldn't be sure he wouldn't.

As soon as I came to a corner, I turned it and ran like hell. There was a sort of alley down the block. I jumped into it, found a basement door and stayed inside, pressed against the wall, quivering with tension and sucking air like a swimmer who'd stayed underwater too long.

Even after I got my wind back, I wasn't anxious to go out. The place could have been cordoned off, with the police, the army and the navy all cooperating to nab me.

What made me think so? Not a thing except remembering how puzzled our ancient Egyptian would have been if he got arrested in the subway for something everybody did casually and without punishment in his own time—spitting! I could have done something just as innocent, as far as you and I are concerned, that this era would consider a misdemeanor or a major crime. And in what age was ignorance of the law ever an excuse?

Instead of going back out, I prowled carefully into the building. It was strangely silent and deserted. I couldn't understand why until I came to a lavatory. There were little commodes and wash basins that came up to barely above my knees. The place was a school. Naturally it was deserted—the kids were through for the day.

I could feel the tension dissolve in me like a ramrod of ice melting, no longer keeping my back and neck stiff and taut. There probably wasn't a better place in the city for me to hide.

A *primary school!*

The salesman had said to me, "Everybody learns about the Dynapack in primary education."

*

Going through the school was eerie, like visiting a familiar childhood scene that had been distorted by time into something almost totally unrecognizable.

There were no blackboards, teacher's big desk, children's little desks, inkwells, pointers, globes or books. Yet it was a school. The small fixtures in the lavatory downstairs had told me that, and so did the miniature chairs drawn neatly under the low, vividly painted tables in the various schoolrooms. A large comfortable chair was evidently where the teacher sat when not wandering around among the pupils.

In front of each chair, firmly attached to the table, was a box with a screen, and both sides of the box held spools of wire on blunt little spindles. The spools had large, clear numbers on them. Near the teacher's chair was a compact case with more spools on spindles, and there was a large screen on the inside wall, opposite the enormous windows.

I went into one of the rooms and sat down in the teacher's chair, wondering how I was going to find out about the Dynapack. I felt like an archaeologist guessing at the functions of strange relics he'd found in a dead city.

Sitting in the chair was like sitting on a column of air that let me sit upright or slump as I chose. One of the arms had a row of buttons. I pressed one and waited nervously to find out if I'd done something that would get me into trouble.

Concealed lights in the ceiling and walls began glowing, getting brighter, while the room gradually turned dark. I glanced around bewilderedly to see why, because it was still daylight.

The windows seemed to be sliding slightly, very slowly, and as they slid, the sunlight was damped out. I grinned, thinking of what my ancient Egyptian would make of that. I knew there were two sheets of polarizing glass, probably with a vacuum between to keep out the cold and the heat, and the lights in the room were beautifully synchronized with the polarized sliding glass.

I wasn't doing so badly. The rest of the objects might not be too hard to figure out.

The spools in the case alongside the teacher's chair could be wire recordings. I looked for something to play them with, but there was no sign of a playback machine. I tried to lift a spool off a spindle. It wouldn't come off.

Hah! The wire led down the spindle to the base of the box, holding the spool in place. That meant the spools could be played right in that position. But what started them playing?

*

I hunted over the box minutely. Every part of it was featureless—no dials, switches or any unfamiliar counterparts. I even tried moving my hands over it, figuring it might be like a theramin, and spoke to it in different shades of command, because it could have been built to respond to vocal orders. Nothing happened.

Remember the Poe story that shows the best place to hide something is right out in the open, which is the last place anyone would look? Well, these things weren't manufactured to baffle people, any more than our devices generally are. But it's only by trying everything that somebody who didn't know what a switch is would start up a vacuum cleaner, say, or light a big chandelier from a wall clear across the room.

I'd pressed every inch of the box, hoping some part of it might act as a switch, and I finally touched one of the spindles. The spool immediately began spinning at a very low speed and the screen on the wall opposite the window glowed into life.

"The history of the exploration of the Solar System," said an announcer's deep voice, "is one of the most adventuresome in mankind's long list of achievements. Beginning with the crude rockets developed during World War II...."

There were newsreel shots of V-1 and V-2 being blasted from their takeoff ramps and a montage of later experimental models. I wished I could see how it all turned out, but I was afraid to waste the time watching. At any moment, I might hear the footsteps of a guard or janitor or whoever tended buildings then.

I pushed the spindle again. It checked the spool, which rewound swiftly and silently, and stopped itself when the rewinding was finished. I tried another. A nightmare underwater scene appeared.

"With the aid of energy screens," said another voice, "the oceans of the world were completely charted by the year 2027...."

I turned it off, then another on developments in medicine, one on architecture, one on history, the geography of such places as the interior of South America and Africa that were—or are—unknown today, and I was getting frantic, starting the wonderful wire films that held full-frequency sound and pictures in absolutely faithful color, and shutting them off hastily when I discovered they didn't have what I was looking for.

They were courses for children, but they all contained information that our scientists are still groping for … and I couldn't chance watching one all the way through!

I was frustratedly switching off a film on psychology when a female voice said from the door, "May I help you?"

*

I snapped around to face her in sudden fright. She was young and slim and slight, but she could scream loud enough to get help. Judging by the way she was looking at me, outwardly polite and yet visibly nervous, that scream would be coming at any second.

"I must have wandered in here by mistake," I said, and pushed past her to the corridor, where I began running back the way I had come.

"But you don't understand!" she cried after me. "I really want to help—"

Yeah, help, I thought, pounding toward the street door. A gag right out of that psychology film, probably—get the patient to hold still, humor him, until you can get somebody to put him where he belongs. That's what one of our teachers would do, provided she wasn't too scared to think straight, if she found an old-looking guy thumbing frenziedly through the textbooks in a grammar school classroom.

When I came to the outside door, I stopped. I had no way of knowing whether she'd given out an alarm, or how she might have done it, but the obvious place to find me would be out on the street, dodging for cover somewhere.

I pushed the door open and let it slam shut, hoping she'd hear it upstairs. Then I found a door, sneaked it open and went silently down the steps.

In the basement, I looked for a furnace or a coal bin or a fuel tank to hide behind, but there weren't any. I don't know how they got their heat in the winter or cooled the building in the summer. Probably some central atomic plant that took care of the whole city, piping in the heat or coolant in underground conduits that were led up through the walls, because there weren't even any pipes visible.

I hunched into the darkest corner I could find and hoped they wouldn't look for me there.

*

By the time night came, hunger drove me out of the school, but I did it warily, making sure nobody was in sight.

The streets of the shopping center were more or less deserted. There was no sign of a restaurant. I was so empty that I felt dizzy as I hunted for one. But then a shocking realization made me halt on the sidewalk and sweat with horror.

Even if there had been a restaurant, what would I have used for money?

Now I got the whole foul picture. She had sent old people back through time on errands like mine ... and they'd starved to death because they couldn't buy food!

No, that wasn't right. I remembered what I had told Lou Pape: anybody who gets hungry enough can always find a truck garden or a food store to rob.

Only ... I hadn't seen a truck garden or food store anywhere in this city.

And ... I thought about people in the past having their hands cut off for stealing a loaf of bread.

This civilization didn't look as if it went in for such drastic punishments, assuming I could find a loaf of bread to steal. But neither did most of the civilizations that practiced those barbarisms.

I was more tired, hungry and scared than I'd ever believed a human being could get. Lost, completely lost in a totally alien world, but one in which I could still be killed or starve to death ... and God knew what was waiting for me in my own time in case I came back without the information she wanted.

Or maybe even if I came back with it!

That suspicion made up my mind for me. Whatever happened to me now couldn't be worse than what she might do. At least I didn't have to starve.

I stopped a man in the street. I let several others go by before picking him deliberately because he was middle-aged, had a kindly face, and was smaller than me, so I could slug him and run if he raised a row.

"Look, friend," I told him, "I'm just passing through town—"

"Ah?" he said pleasantly.

"—And I seem to have mislaid—" No, that was dangerous. I'd been about to say I'd mislaid my wallet, but I still didn't know whether they used money in this era. He waited with a patient, friendly smile while I decided just how to put it. "The fact is that I haven't eaten all day and I wonder if you could help me get a meal."

He said in the most neighborly voice imaginable, "I'll be glad to do anything I can, Mr. Weldon."

*

My entire face seemed to drop open. "You—you called me—"

"Mr. Weldon," he repeated, still looking up at me with that neighborly smile. "Mark Weldon, isn't it? From the 20th Century?"

I tried to answer, but my throat had tightened up worse than on any opening night I'd ever had to live through. I nodded, wondering terrifiedly what was going on.

"Please relax," he said persuasively. "You're not in any danger whatever. We offer you our utmost hospitality. Our time, you might say, is your time."

"You know who I am," I managed to get out through my constricted glottis. "I've been doing all this running and ducking and hiding for nothing."

He shrugged sympathetically. "Everyone in the city was instructed to help you, but you were so nervous that we were afraid to alarm you with a direct approach. Every time we tried to, as a matter of fact, you vanished into one place or another. We didn't follow for fear of the effect on you. We had to wait until you came voluntarily to us."

My brain was racing again and getting nowhere. Part of it was dizziness from hunger, but only part. The rest was plain frightened confusion.

They knew who I was. They'd been expecting me. They probably even knew what I was after.

And they wanted to help!

"Let's not go into explanations now," he said, "although I'd like to smooth away the bewilderment and fear on your face. But you need to be fed first. Then we'll call in the others and—"

I pulled back. "What others? How do I know you're not setting up something for me that I'll wish I hadn't gotten into?"

"Before you approached me, Mr. Weldon, you first had to decide that we represented no greater menace than May Roberts. Please believe me, we don't."

So he knew about that, too!

"All right, I'll take my chances," I gave in resignedly. "Where does a guy find a place to eat in this city?"

*

It was a handsome restaurant with soft light coming from three-dimensional, full-color nature murals that I might mistakenly have walked into if I'd been alone, they looked so much like gardens and forests and plains. It was no wonder I couldn't find a restaurant or food store or truck garden anywhere—food came up through pneumatic chutes in each building, I'd been told on the way over, grown in hydroponic tanks in cities that specialized in agriculture, and those who wanted to eat "out" could drop into the restaurant each building had. Every city had its own function. This one was for people in the arts. I liked that.

There was a glowing menu on the table with buttons alongside the various selections. I looked starvingly at the items, trying to decide which I wanted most. I picked oysters, onion soup, breast of guinea hen under Plexiglas and was hunting for the tastiest and most recognizable dessert when the pleasant little guy shook his head regretfully and emphatically.

"I'm afraid you can't eat any of those foods, Mr. Weldon," he said in a sad voice. "We'll explain why in a moment."

A waiter and the manager came over. They obviously didn't want to stare at me, but they couldn't help it. I couldn't blame them, I'd have stared at somebody from George Washington's time, which is about what I must have represented to them.

"Will you please arrange to have the special food for Mr. Weldon delivered here immediately?" the little guy asked.

"Every restaurant has been standing by for this, Mr. Carr," said the manager. "It's on its way. Prepared, of course—it's been ready since he first arrived."

"Fine," said the little guy, Carr. "It can't be too soon. He's very hungry."

I glanced around and noticed for the first time that there was nobody else in the restaurant. It was past the dinner hour, but, even so, there are always late diners. We had the place all to ourselves and it bothered me. They could have ganged up on me....

But they didn't. A light gong sounded, and the waiter and manager hurried over to a slot of a door and brought out a couple of trays loaded with covered dishes.

"Your dinner, Mr. Weldon," the manager said, putting the plates in front of me and removing the lids.

I stared down at the food.

"This," I told them angrily, "is a hell of a trick to play on a starving man!"

*

They all looked unhappy.

"Mashed dehydrated potatoes, canned meat and canned vegetables," Carr replied. "Not very appetizing. I know, but I'm afraid it's all we can allow you to eat."

I took the cover off the dessert dish.

"Dried fruits!" I said in disgust.

"Rather excessively dried, I'm sorry to say," the manager agreed mournfully.

I sipped the blue stuff in a glass and almost spat it out. "Powdered milk! Are these things what you people have to live on?"

"No, our diet is quite varied," Carr said in embarrassment. "But we unfortunately can't give you any of the foods we normally eat ourselves."

"And why in blazes not?"

"Please eat, Mr. Weldon," Carr begged with frantic earnestness. "There's so much to explain—this is part of it, of course—and it would be best if you heard it on a full stomach."

I was famished enough to get the stuff down, which wasn't easy; uninviting as it looked, it tasted still worse.

When I was through, Carr pushed several buttons on the glowing menu. Dishes came up from an opening in the center of the table and he showed me the luscious foods they contained.

"Given your choice," he said, "you'd have preferred them to what you have eaten. Isn't that so, Mr. Weldon?"

"You bet I would!" I answered, sore because I hadn't been given that choice.

"And you would have died like the pathetic old people you were investigating," said a voice behind me.

I turned around, startled. Several men and women had come in while I'd been eating, their footsteps as silent as cats on a rug. I looked blankly from them to Carr and back again.

"These are the clothes we ordinarily wear," Carr said. "An 18th Century motif, as you can see—updated knee breeches and shirt waists, a modified stock for the men, the daring low bodices of that era, the full skirts treated in a modern way by using sheer materials for the women, bright colors and sheens, buckled shoes of spun synthetics. Very gay, very ornamental, very comfortable, and thoroughly suitable to our time."

"But everybody I saw was dressed like me!" I protested.

"Only to keep you from feeling more conspicuous and anxious than you already were. It was quite a project, I can tell you—your styles varied so greatly from decade to decade, especially those for women—and the materials were a genuine problem; they'd gone out of existence long ago. We had the textile and tailoring cities working a full six months to clothe the inhabitants of this city, including, of course, the children. Everybody had to be clad as your contemporaries were, because we knew only that you would arrive in this vicinity, not where you might wander through the city."

"There was one small difference you didn't notice," added a handsome mature woman. "You were the only man in a gray suit. We had a full description of what you were wearing, you see, and we made sure nobody else was dressed that way. Naturally, everyone knew who you were, and so we were kept informed of your movements."

"What for?" I demanded in alarm. "What's this all about?"

*

Pulling up chairs, they sat down, looking to me like a witchcraft jury from some old painting.

"I'm Leo Blundell," said a tall man in plum-and-gold clothes. "As chairman of—of the Mark Weldon Committee, it's my responsibility to handle this project correctly."

"Project?"

"To make certain that history is fulfilled, I have to tell you as much as you must know."

"I wish *somebody* would!"

"Very well, let me begin by telling you much of what you undoubtedly know already. In a sense, you are more a victim of Dr. Anthony Roberts than his daughter. Roberts was a brilliant physicist, but because of his eccentric behavior, he was ridiculed for his theories and hated for his arrogance. He was an almost perfect example of self-defeat, the way in which a man will hamper his career and wreck his happiness, and then blame the world for his failure and misery. To get back to his connection with you, however, he invented a time machine—unfortunately, its secret has since been lost and never re-discovered—and used it for anti-social purposes. When he died, his daughter May carried on his work. It was she who sent you to this time to learn the principle by which the Dynapack operates. She was a thoroughly ruthless woman."

"Are you sure?" I asked uneasily.

"Quite sure."

"I know a number of old people died after she sent them on errands through time, but she said they'd lied about their age and health."

"One would expect her to say that," a woman put in cuttingly.

Blundell turned to her and shook his head. "Let Mr. Weldon clarify his feelings about her, Rhoda. They are obviously very mixed."

"They are," I admitted. "She seemed hard, the first time I saw her, when I answered her ad, but she could have been just acting businesslike. I mean she had a lot of people to pick from and she had to be impersonal and make certain she had the right one. The next time—I hope you don't know about that—it was really my fault for breaking into her room. I really had a lot of admiration for the way she handled the situation."

"Go on," Carr encouraged me.

"And I can't complain about the deal she gave me. Sure, she came out ahead on the money I bet and invested for her. But I did all right myself—I was richer than I'd ever been in my life—and she gave that money to me before I even did anything to earn it!"

"Besides which," somebody else said, "she offered you half of the profits on the Dynapack."

*

I looked around at the faces for signs of hostility. I saw none. That was surprising. I'd come from the past to steal something from them and they weren't at all angry. Well, no, it wasn't really stealing. I wouldn't be depriving them of the Dynapack. It just would have been invented before it was supposed to be.

"She did," I said. "Though I wouldn't call that part of it philanthropy. She needed me for the data and I needed her to manufacture the things."

"And she was a very beautiful woman," Blundell added.

I squirmed a bit. "Yes."

"Mr. Weldon, we know a good deal about her from notes that have come down to us among her private papers. She had a safety deposit box under a false name. I won't tell you the name; it was not discovered until many years later, and we will not voluntarily meddle with the past."

I sat up and listened sharply. "So that's how you knew who I was and what I'd be wearing and what I came for! You even knew when and where I'd arrive!"

"Correct," Blundell said.

"What else do you know?"

"That you suspected her of being responsible for the deaths of many old people by starvation. Your suspicion was justified, except that her father had caused all those that occurred before 1947, when she took over after his own death. All but two people were sent into the past. Roberts was curious about the future, of course, but he did not want to waste a victim on a trip that would probably be fruitless. In the past, you understand, he knew precisely what he was after. The future was completely unknown territory."

"But she took the chance," I said.

"If you can call deliberate murder taking a chance, yes. One man arrived in 2094, over fifty years ago. The other was yourself. The first one, as you know, died of malnutrition when he was brought back to your era."

"And what happened to me?" I asked, jittering.

"You will not die. We intend to make sure of that. All the other victims—I presume you're interested in their errands?"

"I think I know, but I'd like to find out just the same."

"They were sent to the past to buy or steal treasures of various sorts—art, sculpture, jewelry, fabulously valuable manuscripts and books, anything that had great scarcity value."

"That's not possible," I objected. "She had all the money she wanted. Any time she needed more, all she had to do was send somebody back to put down bets and buy stocks that she knew were winners. She had the records, didn't she? There was no way she or her father could lose!"

*

He moved his shoulders in a plum-and-gold shrug. "Most of the treasures they accumulated were for acquisition's sake—and for the sake of vengeance for the way they believed Dr. Roberts had been treated. When there were unusual expenses, such as replacing the very costly parts of the time machine, that required more than they could produce in ready cash, both Roberts and his daughter 'discovered' these treasures."

He waited while I digested the miserable meal and the disturbing information he had given me. I thought I'd found a loophole in his explanation: "You said people were sent back to the past to *buy* treasures, besides stealing them."

"I did," he agreed. "They were provided with currency of whatever era they were to visit."

I felt my forehead wrinkle up as my theory fell apart. "Then they could buy food. Why should they have died of malnutrition?"

"Because, as May Roberts herself told you, nothing can exist before it exists. Neither can anything exist after it is out of existence. If you returned with a Dynapack, for example, it would revert to a lump of various metals, because that was what it was in your period. But let me give you a more personal instance. Do you remember coming back from your first trip with dust on your hand?"

"Yes. I must have fallen."

"On one hand? No, Mr. Weldon. May Roberts was greatly upset by the incident; she was afraid you would realize why the hamburger had turned to dust—and why the old people died of starvation. *All* of them, not just a few."

He paused, giving me a chance to understand what he had just said. I did, with a sick shock.

"If I ate your food," I said shakily, "I'd feel satisfied until I was returned to my own time. *But the food wouldn't go along with me!*"

*

Blundell nodded gravely. "And so you, too, would die of malnutrition. The foods we have given you existed in your era. We were very careful of that, so careful that many of them probably were stored years before you left your time. We regret that they are not very palatable, but at least we are positive they will go back with you. You will be as healthy when you arrive in the past as when you left.

"Incidentally, she made you change your clothes for the same reason—they had been made in 1930. She had clothing from every era she wanted visited and chose old people who would fit them best. Otherwise, you see, they'd have arrived naked."

I began to shake as if I were as old as I'd pretended to be on the stage. "She's going to pull me back! If I don't bring her the information about the Dynapack, she'll shoot me!"

"That, Mr. Weldon, is our problem," Blundell said, putting his hand comfortingly on my arm to calm me.

"Your problem? I'm the one who'll get shot, not you!"

"But we know in complete detail what will happen when you are returned to the 20th Century."

I pulled my arm away and grabbed his. "You know that? Tell me!"

"I'm sorry, Mr. Weldon. If we tell you what you did, you might think of some alternate action, and there is no knowing what the result would be."

"But I didn't get shot or die of malnutrition?"

"That much we can tell you. Neither."

They all stood up, so bright and attractive in their colorful clothes that I felt like a shirt-sleeved stage hand who'd wandered in on a costume play.

"You will be returned in a month, according to the notes May Roberts left. She gave you plenty of time to get the data, you see. We propose to make that month an enjoyable one for you. The resources of our city—and any others you care to visit—are at your disposal. We wish you to take full advantage of them."

"And the Dynapack?"

"Let us worry about that. We want you to have a good time while you are our guest."

I did.

It was the most wonderful month of my life.

*

The mesh cage blurred around me. I could see May Roberts through it, her hand just leaving the switch. She was as beautiful as ever, but I saw beneath her beauty the vengeful, vicious creature her father's bitterness had turned her into; Blundell and Carr had let me read some of her notes, and I knew. I wished I could have spent the rest of my years in the future, instead of having to come back to this.

She came over and opened the gate, smiling like an angel welcoming a bright new soul. Then her eyes traveled startledly over me and her smile almost dropped off. But she held it firmly in place.

She had to, while she asked, "Do you have the notes I sent you for?"

"Right here," I said.

I reached into my breast pocket and brought out a stubby automatic and shot her through the right arm. Her closed hand opened and a little derringer clanked on the floor. She gaped at me with an expression of horrified surprise that should have been recorded permanently; it would have served as a model for generations of actors and actresses.

"You—brought back a weapon!" she gasped. "You shot me!" She stared vacantly at her bleeding arm and then at my automatic. "But you can't—bring anything back from the future. And you aren't—dying of malnutrition."

She said it all in a voice shocked into toneless wonder.

"The food I ate and this gun are from the present," I said. "The people of the future knew I was coming. They gave me food that wouldn't vanish from my cells when I returned. They also gave me the gun instead of the plans for the Dynapack."

"And you took it?" she screamed at me. "You idiot! I'd have shared the profits honestly with you. You'd have been worth millions!"

"With acute malnutrition," I amended. "I like it better this way, thanks—poor, but alive. Or relatively poor, I should say, because you've been very generous and I appreciate it."

"By shooting me!"

"I hated to puncture that lovely arm, but it wasn't as painful as starving or getting shot myself. Now if you don't mind—or even if you do—it's your turn to get into the cage, Miss Roberts."

She tried to grab for the derringer on the floor with her left hand.

"Don't bother," I said quietly. "You can't reach it before a bullet reaches you."

*

She straightened up, staring at me for the first time with terror in her eyes.

"What are you going to do to me?" she whispered.

"I could kill you as easily as you could have killed me. Kill you and send your body into some other era. How many dozens of deaths were you responsible for? The law couldn't convict you of them, but I can. And I couldn't be convicted, either."

She put her hand on the wound. Blood seeped through her fingers as she lifted her chin at me.

"I won't beg for my life, Weldon, if that's what you want. I could offer you a partnership, but I'm not really in a position to offer it, am I?"

She was magnificent, terrifyingly intelligent, brave clear through ... and deadlier than a plague. I had to remember that.

"Into the cage," I said. "I have some friends in the future who have plans for you. I won't tell you what they are, of course; you didn't tell me what I'd go through, did you? Give my friends my fondest regards. If I can manage it, I'll visit them—and you."

She backed warily into the cage. It would have been pleasant to kiss those wonderful lips good-by. I'd thought about them for a whole month, wanting them and loathing them at the same time.

It would have been like kissing a coral snake. I knew it and I concentrated on shutting the gate on her.

"You'd like to be rich, wouldn't you, Weldon?" she asked through the mesh.

"I can be," I said. "I have the machine. I can send people into the past or future and make myself a pile of dough. Only I'd give them food to take along. I wouldn't kill them off to keep the secret to myself. Anything else on your mind?"

"You want me," she stated.

I didn't argue.

"You could have me."

"Just long enough to get my throat slit or brains blown out. I don't want anything that much."

I rammed the switch closed.

The mesh cage blurred and she was gone. Her blood was on the floor, but she was gone into the future I had just come from.

That was when the reaction hit me. I'd escaped starvation and her gun, but I wasn't a hero and the release of tension flipped my stomach over and unhinged my knees.

Shaking badly, I stumbled through the big, empty house until I found a phone.

*

Lou Pape got there so quickly that I still hadn't gotten over the tremors, in spite of a bottle of brandy I dug out of a credenza, maybe because the date on the label, 1763, gave me a new case of the shivers.

I could see the worry on Lou's face vanish when he assured himself that I was all right. It came back again, though, when I told him what had happened. He didn't believe any of it, naturally. I guess I hadn't really expected him to.

"If I didn't know you, Mark," he said, shaking his big, dark head unhappily, "I'd send you over to Bellevue for observation. Even knowing you, maybe that's what I ought to do."

"All right, let's see if there's any proof," I suggested tiredly. "From what I was told, there ought to be plenty."

We searched the house clear down to the basement, where he stood with his face slack.

"Christ!" he breathed. "The annex to the Metropolitan Museum!"

The basement ran the length and breadth of the house and was twice as high as an average room, and the whole glittering place was crammed with paintings in rich, heavy frames, statuettes, books, manuscripts, goblets and ewers and jewelry made of gold and huge gems, and tapestries in brilliant color ... and everything was as bright and sparkling and new as the day it was made, which was almost true of a lot of it.

"The dame was loaded and she was an art collector, that's all," Lou said. "You can't sell me that screwy story of yours. She was a collector and she knew where to find things."

"She certainly did," I agreed.

"What did you do with her?"

"I told you. I shot her through the arm before she could shoot me and I sent her into the future."

He took me by the front of the jacket. "You killed her, Mark. You wanted all this stuff for yourself, so you knocked her off and got rid of her body somehow."

"Why don't you go back to acting, where you belong, Lou, and leave sleuthing to people who know how?" I asked, too worn to pull his hands loose. "Would I kill her and call you up to get right over here? Wouldn't I have sneaked these things out first? Or more likely I'd have sneaked them out, hidden them and nobody—including you—would know I'd ever been here. Come on, use your head."

"That's easy. You lost your nerve."

"I'm not even losing my patience."

*

He pushed me away savagely. "If you killed her for this stuff or because of that crazy yarn you gave me, I'm a cop and you're no friend. You're just a plain killer I happened to have known once, and I'll make sure you fry."

"You always did have a taste for that kind of dialogue. Go ahead and wrap me up in an airtight case, have them throw the book at me, send me up the river, put me in the hot squat. But you'll have to do the proving, not me."

He headed for the stairs. "I will. And don't try to make a break or I'll plug you as if I never saw you before."

He put in a call at the phone upstairs. I didn't give a particular damn who it was he'd called. I was too relieved that I hadn't killed May Roberts; destroying anything that beautiful, however evil, would have stayed with me the rest of my life. There was another reason for my relief—if I'd killed her and left the evidence for Lou to find, he'd never help me. No, that's not quite so; he'd probably have tried to get me to plead insanity on the basis of my unbelievable explanation.

But most of all, I couldn't get rid of the look on her face when I'd shot her through the arm, the arm that was so wonderful to look at and that had held a murderous little gun to greet me with.

She was in the future now. She wouldn't be executed by them; they regarded crime as an illness, and they'd treat her with their marvelously advanced therapy and she'd become a useful, contented citizen, living out her existence in an era that had given me more happiness than I'd ever had.

I sat and tried to stupefy myself with brandy that should long ago have dried to brick-hardness, while Lou Pape stood at the door with his hand near his holster and glared at me. He didn't take his eyes off me until somebody named Prof. Jeremiah Aaronson came in and was introduced briefly and flatly to me. Then Lou took him upstairs.

It was minutes before I realized what they were going to do. I ran up after them.

I was just in time to see Aaronson carefully take the housing off the hooded motors, and leap back suddenly from the fury of lightning sparks.

*

The whole machine fused while we watched helplessly—motors, switches, panel and mesh cage. They flashed blindingly and blew apart and melted together in a charred and molten pile.

"Rigged," Aaronson said in the tone of a bitter curse. "Set to short if it was tampered with. I wouldn't be surprised if there were incendiaries placed at strategic spots. Nothing else could have made a mess like this."

He finally glanced down at his hand and saw it was scorched. He hissed with the realization of pain, blew on the burn, shook it in the air to cool it, and pulled a handkerchief out of his back pocket by reaching all the way around the rear for it with his left hand.

Lou looked helplessly at the heap of cooling slag. "Can you make any sense of it, Prof?" he asked.

"Can you?" Aaronson retorted. "Melt down a microtome or any other piece of machinery you're unfamiliar with, and see if you can identify it when it looks like this."

He went out, wrapping his hand in the handkerchief.

Lou kicked glumly at a piece of twisted tubing. "Aaronson is a top physicist, Mark. I was hoping he'd make enough out of the machine to—ah, hell, I wanted to believe you! I couldn't. I still can't. Now we'll have to dig through the house to find her body."

"You won't find it or the secret of the machine," I answered miserably. "I told you they said the secret would be lost. This is how. Now I'll never be able to visit the future again. I'll never see them or May Roberts. They'll straighten her out, get rid of her hate and vindictiveness, and it won't do me a damned bit of good because the machine is gone and she's generations ahead of me."

He turned to me puzzledly. "You're not afraid to have us dig for her body, Mark?"

"Tear the place apart if you want."

"We'll have to," he said. "I'm calling Homicide."

"Call in the Marines. Call in anybody you like."

"You'll have to stay in my custody until we're through."

I shrugged. "As long as you leave me alone while you're doing your digging, I don't give a hang if I'm under arrest for suspicion of murder. I've got to do some straightening out. I wish the people in the future could take on the job—they could do it faster and better than I can—but some nice, peaceful quiet would help."

*

He didn't touch me or say a word to me as we waited for the squad to arrive. I sat in the chair and shut out first him and then the men with their sounding hammers and crowbars and all the rest.

She'd been ruthless and callous, and she'd murdered old people with no more pity than a wolf among a herd of helpless sheep.

But Blundell and Carr had told me that she was as much a victim as the oldsters who'd died of starvation with the riches she'd given them still untouched, on deposit in the banks or stuffed into hiding places or pinned to their shabby clothes. She needed treatment for the illness her father had inflicted on her. But even he, they'd said, had been suffering from a severe emotional disturbance and proper care could have made a great and honored scientist out of him.

They'd told me the truth and made me hate her, and they'd told me their viewpoint and made that hatred impossible.

I was here, in the present, without her. The machine was gone. Yearning over something I couldn't change would destroy me. I had no right to destroy myself. Nobody did, they'd told me, and nobody who reconciles himself to the fact that some situations just are impossible to work out ever could.

I'd realized that when the squad packed up and left and Lou Pape came over to where I was sitting.

"You knew we wouldn't find her," he said.

"That's what I kept telling you."

"Where is she?"

"In Port Said, exotic hellhole of the world, where she's dancing in veils for the depraved—"

"Cut out the kidding! Where is she?"

"What's the difference, Lou? She's not here, is she?"

"That doesn't mean she can't be somewhere else, dead."

"She's not dead. You don't have to believe me about anything else, just that."

He hauled me out of the chair and stared hard at my face. "You aren't lying," he said. "I know you well enough to know you're not."

"All right, then."

"But you're a damned fool to think a dish like that would have any part of you. I don't mean you're nothing a woman would go for, but she's more fang than female. You'd have to be richer and better-looking than her, for one thing—"

"Not after my friends get through with her. She'll know a good man when she sees one and I'd be what she wants." I slid my hand over my naked scalp. "With a head of hair, I'd look my real age, which happens to be a year younger than you, if you remember. She'd go for me—they checked our emotional quotients and we'd be a natural together. The only thing was that I was bald. They could have grown hair on my head, which would have taken care of that, and then we'd have gotten together like gin and tonic."

*

Lou arched his black eyebrows at me. "They really could grow hair on you?"

"Sure. Now you want to know why I didn't let them." I glanced out the window at the smoky city. "That's why. They couldn't tell me if I'd ever get back to the future. I wasn't taking any chances. As long as there was a possibility that I'd be stranded in my own time, I wasn't going to lose my livelihood. Which reminds me, you have anything else to do here?"

"There'll be a guard stationed around the house and all her holdings and art will be taken over until she comes back—"

"She won't."

"—or is declared legally dead."

"And me?" I broke in.

"We can't hold you without proof of murder."

"Good enough. Then let's get out of here."

"I have to go back on duty," he objected.

"Not any more. I've got over $15,000 in cash and deposits—enough to finance you and me."

"Enough to kill her for."

"Enough to finance you and me," I repeated doggedly. "I told you I had the money before she sent me into the future—"

"All right, all right," he interrupted. "Let's not go into that again. We couldn't find a body, so you're free. Now what's this about financing the two of us?"

I put my fingers around his arm and steered him out to the street.

"This city has never had a worse cop than you," I said. "Why? Because you're an actor, not a cop. You're going back to acting, Lou. This money will keep us both going until we get a break."

He gave me the slit-eyed look he'd picked up in line of duty. "That wouldn't be a bribe, would it?"

"Call it a kind of memorial to a lot of poor, innocent old people and a sick, tormented woman."

We walked along in silence out in the clean sunshine. It was our silence; the sleek cars and burly trucks made their noise and the pedestrians added their gabble, but a good Stanislavsky actor like Lou wouldn't notice that. Neither would I, ordinarily, but I was giving him a chance to work his way through this situation.

"I won't hand you a lie, Mark," he said finally. "I never stopped wanting to act. I'll take your deal on two considerations."

"All right, what are they?"

"That whatever I take off you is strictly a loan."

"No argument. What's the other?"

He had an unlit cigarette almost to his lips. He held it there while he said: "That any time you come across a case of an old person who died of starvation with $30,000 stashed away somewhere, you turn fast to the theatrical page and not tell me or even think about it."

"I don't have to agree to that."

*

He lowered the cigarette, stopped and turned to me. "You mean it's no deal?"

"Not that," I said. "I mean there won't be any more of those cases. Between knowing that and both of us back acting again, I'm satisfied. You don't have to believe me. Nobody does."

He lit up and blew out a pretty plume, fine and slow and straight, which would have televised like a million in the bank. Then he grinned. "You wouldn't want to bet on that, would you?"

"Not with a friend. I do all my sure-thing betting with bookies."

"Then make it a token bet," he said. "One buck that somebody dies of starvation with a big poke within a year."

I took the bet.

I took the dollar a year later.

Lightning Source UK Ltd.
Milton Keynes UK
UKHW011905300520
364134UK00008B/369

9 781515 421085